G000123617

A Flag on the Abbey

A FLAG ON THE ABBEY

A Novel

Rod Brammer

Elliott & Thompson
London

To my family who understood and supported
my compulsion to write

Part I

One Tear for Childhood

Chapter One

•

June 1950

The tiny black engine came to a squealing stop. Gouttes of steam jetted across the platform and the doors of the dirty plum-coloured carriages began to swing open. 'Southampton Central! Southampton Central! Portsmouth 'Arbour train. Ain't going any further... All change! All change!' A small, slight porter marched the length of the carriages repeating his message, looking into each individual compartment.

'Hell's bells!' Kathleen Finlay said, rising to her feet, at the same time grabbing a single small suitcase. 'We shall have to find a phone. Kee, come along, jump down.' She opened the door and ushered Keith Finlay through it and on to the platform. As she turned to close the door a thickset man approached her.

'Miss Kathy?' he asked.

Kathleen Finlay almost started, and without turning said simply, 'Brockett?' The two adults faced each other.

'Yes Miss, it's Brockett.' They shook hands and laughed, relief and recognition in Kathleen Finlay's voice.

'How did you know... to be at Southampton I mean?'

'The bridge is blocked at Red Bridge, so the old man sent me here, and Woods to Romsey. Just to make sure.'

'And where is the old man now, Brockett? Twelve years away and he can't come to meet his daughter.' Kathleen Finlay was still smiling. 'It's so good to see you, so very good to be home.'

With something almost approaching formality, the two adults held each other for a moment. Keith Finlay was perplexed. Why should his mother hug this unkempt character? Brockett was dressed in heavy corduroy trousers held up with string, wearing a grimy striped shirt, with no collar.

Suddenly they noticed him. Kathleen Finlay pushed him forward. 'This is Keith. Kee, this is Mr Brockett, your grandfather's driver.'

Brockett smiled down at Finlay. 'Master Keith.' He paused. 'You're very like your grandfather.' Finlay shook his hand, which was warm and dry and enfolded his own into nothing, so large was the hand grasping his.

'You're not my grandfather, then?' Finlay asked.

'Love you, no, young chap. Your grandfather is back home, trying to get the knotter going on the new baler.'

'That puts everything into perspective, Brockett. The hay before his daughter, not seen for twelve years!' Kathleen Finlay sighed.

'Let's get you and the boy home, Miss Kathy,' Brockett suggested, picking up the suitcase, and leading them to the station exit.

As he walked away, Finlay noticed that Brockett was so enormously bowlegged as to be almost deformed. 'Do you ride horses, Mr Brockett?' he asked.

'Not now, Master Keith. Did do though, when I were younger…'

Before he could finish Finlay fired more questions. 'Were you a soldier then? Did you fight in the war?'

'Not in the last lot, youngster. Did in the one previous. Should have finished the buggers properly that time, then we wouldn't be stuck with this mess!' They had reached the outside of the station and before them lay a vista of destruction, parts of houses sticking up and the shell of a destroyed church.

'Is that St Michael's, Brockett?' asked Kathleen Finlay, aghast at what she saw. 'Have they done any repair work?' Her hand flew to her mouth. 'Oh, my God,' she breathed.

'The east side of the town was pretty well flattened. We've got to go out Baddesley way to get back, so you'll be able to see. None of it's very pretty.' Brockett put the suitcase in the boot of a large black Armstrong.

'And the people?' Kathleen Finlay asked.

'Them as wasn't killed moved away. Lots of them are up at Stoney Cross, living in the huts of the airmen, now they're gone back to Canada…' He didn't finish.

'There's an aerodrome at Stoney Cross?'

'Yes Miss. They built lots of them on the Forest. Call the people living there now squatters. Pretty rough lot by all accounts. Pinch anything that ain't nailed down,' Brockett said, a little venomously.

'Don't judge them for that, Brockett. They had to survive. They've lost their homes don't forget, over something they probably didn't understand.'

Finlay could see by the look on Brockett's face he didn't entirely agree with his mother's sentiments. With an obvious change of subject, he asked, 'How was France then, Miss?'

'Brockett, if I never see a Frog again, it will be too soon. A nation of backsliding, obsequious, dirty, spineless jackanapes. *Entente Cordiale* indeed! We should have left them to the Germans. They certainly weren't worth the bother!' Finlay had often heard this speech. In fact, he could never remember a time when his mother had not expressed such views about the French. The car reached the Kingsland area of Southampton, where some houses were still standing, though the area mostly seemed to consist of cleared bomb-sites.

'Stop the car a moment please, Brockett,' Kathleen Finlay ordered. She turned to her son. 'Mark this well Kee. This is what the Germans did. Never forget it. They claimed to be civilized.'

As the car pulled away, Finlay looked at the acres of devastation. 'Were many people killed, Mr Brockett?' he asked.

''Undreds! 'Undreds, and many more maimed for life,' Brockett answered.

They drove on in silence. Finlay watched his mother's face and saw it had no colour, her jaws set firm. She suddenly brightened. 'Never mind Kee, we can have tea on the lawn.' Brockett's cough was seemingly non-committal. 'What's wrong, Brockett?' asked Kathleen.

'There's been some changes, Ma'am,' he said softly.

'Brockett, when you start calling me "Ma'am", I know something is very wrong.'

'Far too much to tell between now and home, Miss Kathy. And it wouldn't be for young ears, anyway,' Brockett said, with a degree of formality. The car began to slow and presently turned into a gravel-covered drive, flanked by high hedges.

'Are we there?' asked Finlay.

'Yes, home at last,' his mother answered, patting him gently on the shoulder. As the flanking hedges finished, Kathleen Finlay shrieked, 'Stop!' On both sides of the driveway were parked seemingly hundreds of tanks, bren-gun carriers and army lorries, all in various states of dilapidation, sat in a sea of mud, which in turn was liberally covered with thousands of potatoes.

'What on earth...' began Kathleen Finlay, getting out of the car.

'There are still some controls on the land, Miss Kathy. The old War Ag lot insisted on early potatoes on some of the lower ground. The river came up and washed the main of them down Southampton Water...' Brockett began to explain.

'The tanks, Brockett! Why are there tanks on the lawn?'

'Is there going to be another war, Ma?' asked Finlay, looking at the rows of armour.

'Shortly Kee, very shortly,' his mother said, getting back into the car and slamming the door hard.

'I'll send someone to find the old man, Miss Kathy,' Brockett ventured.

As they pulled up to the house, without waiting for Brockett to open the car door, Kathleen Finlay was out and up the steps to the front door. Finlay made to follow, but was gently checked by Brockett.

'I've known your ma longer than you, youngster, I think we should bide 'ere awhile.' They waited. 'Brockett!' Kathleen Finlay's voice sounded sharp and hollow.

'Oh dear, Mr Brockett. Ma sounds cross,' said Finlay.

'Not as cross as she's goin' to sound, when she knows everything, young Keith.' They moved into the house together.

'This slattern tells me she's the cook, Brockett.' Standing in front of Kathleen Finlay was a large woman, dressed in a greasy wrap-around pinafore, her lank dark hair hung awry to her shoulders, a smouldering cigarette hung on her bottom lip. 'Where does my father keep the cash now, Brockett?'

'I'll get it, Miss,' Brockett answered, with a joyful anticipation in his voice. He was back in seconds with a Gladstone bag, locked with a tiny padlock.

'Knife, Brockett,' she ordered, and was handed a small lambsfoot. She cut the leather clasp through. 'What is this creature paid per week, Brockett?'

'Four pounds, ten shillings,' the cook snapped.

Kathleen Finlay produced two large five-pound notes.

'Have you any possessions here?' Kathleen Finlay demanded.

'Only me 'andbag.' She was surly now.

'And where do you live?'

'Romsey.' A little more obsequious, the erstwhile cook could read the writing on the wall.

'Get it,' Kathleen Finlay ordered sharply. As the woman returned with her handbag, Kathleen Finlay thrust the money at her. 'Take this and get out. Don't ever come near this house again.'

The woman snatched the money. 'How do I get to Romsey? Somebody gen'ly takes me back,' she wailed.

'Walk!' barked Kathleen Finlay. 'That's what God gave you legs for.'

There was a look of happy satisfaction on Brockett's face. Kathleen Finlay sailed forward into the house, with Brockett and Finlay trailing in her wake.

'All the carpets and furniture are in the attics, Miss,' volunteered Brockett, as they entered what seemed to be a football-pitch-sized room.

She didn't answer, but went to the door on the left, tried the handle and found it locked against her. 'Why is the music room locked, Brockett? Where is my piano?' she asked.

'I keep it locked, Miss. Didn't want anybody messin'.' He produced a key, unlocked the door and allowed Kathleen Finlay to enter in front of him. The room smelt of floor polish and seemed to glow softly in its magnificence. Standing in the middle of the room was the largest piano Finlay had ever seen, its beautiful wood shown to perfection in the light streaming through the huge windows.

'I've kept it clean and dry in here, Miss. And it was tuned last week. The wife keeps the room polished...'

Kathleen Finlay didn't let him finish. She turned to Brockett and, taking both his hands in her own, said, 'Brockett, you're my Saint. You have my given thanks and love.' Finlay looked puzzled, Brockett very sheepish. She walked to the piano, lifted the lid and, standing, played a short strand of Chopin. The air was vibrant with the liquid sound. Closing the lid, she ran her hand over the polished wood. 'Oh Brockett, thank you.' She took Brockett's arm to leave the room. 'I'll go and look upstairs. Perhaps you could put the kettle on for some tea.'

Brockett seemed unwilling to release her arm. 'Perhaps we should have the tea, Miss?'

She eyed him curiously. 'Brockett?' she said, stringing out the word. 'What other horrors are waiting?'

'Tea, Miss. Please...' he begged.

Kathleen Finlay started on the stairs, Brockett took Finlay's hand in his own. Kathleen Finlay's progress could be heard going through the house, by the slamming doors and exclamations of horror: 'Oh, my Lord!' Slam. 'Hell's bells!' Slam. 'Oh no... not really!' Slam. Then: 'Jesus Christ Almighty! And who the hell are you?' Kathleen Finlay appeared across the top landing holding a naked young lady by the hair. She was propelled down the stairs, missing the last five altogether, to land in an unseemly heap outside the music-room door.

'And who is this, Brockett, may I know?'

'That's Jenny, Ma'am. She's bin staying for a bit.' Brockett walked to the fireplace, laid his arm along the mantel and rested his head.

'So you're my father's bed warmer, Jenny. Do you have a home? How old are you?' she said, standing over the naked girl.

'Only here, Miss, and I'm twenty-two,' Jenny said meekly.

'So I can't turn you out, just yet...'

At this moment, another person joined them. Kathleen Finlay flew towards him, as the old man opened his arms to receive the expected hug of welcome. The slap across the face sounded like a horse's hoof stamping on concrete. The homecoming surprise was complete. 'You disgusting old goat! You loathsome lecher!' she began, then whirled on the girl. 'Get upstairs and make yourself decent, hussy.' She turned back to her father. 'I've found tanks on the lawn, brambles growing into the kitchen, a cook who exudes the smell from Hell and a whore in your bed. Are there any more surprises?'

Her father smiled. 'Kathy, my darling, darling daughter. Welcome home, you've grown so like your mother.'

Brockett guided Finlay away from the hall, and into the kitchen.

'Don't worry about it, youngster. The old man will make her laugh in a bit, and it'll all be over. Terrible like her mother, your Ma. I'll put the kettle on. By the time it's boiled they'll be friends ag'in.' Listening to the raised voices, Finlay couldn't share this confidence.

'Did the Germans drop any bombs here, Mr Brockett?' he asked.

'Only when they missed what they was aiming at. They had several goes at the Spitfire factory in Eastleigh. Whole lot of bombs fell on the bottom water meadows and a parachute bomb blew the Post Office to bits at Ower. Killed all the family, poor buggers.' Brockett thought for a moment, lost in the memory of it all. 'No, we was lucky, till it was time for the invasion. Then we was under curfew.'

'What's curfew, Mr Brockett?'

'Well, we had to sign in and out if we wanted to go anywhere and we 'ad to be home by nine at night. Bloody nuisance that was.'

'Why?' asked Finlay.

'My, but you're all questions,' Brockett laughed. 'How old are you, and where are you going for your schooling?'

'I'm nearly ten, and I don't expect to be going to school.' Finlay paused and thought; as he'd never been to school, he didn't think he'd like it anyway.

'Not go to school! Can you read and write?' Brockett seemed shocked.

'Of course I can read and write. Anybody can do that!' Finlay said, with all the scorn he could muster.

'Can you do your sums, then?'

'Of course, Mr Brockett. You do ask some silly questions!'

'Seven times eight, then, what's that?'

'Fifty-six, for goodness' sake.'

They heard laughter from the hall and Brockett said 'Good, that's done, I'll make the tea.'

'Good!' Finlay said with some alacrity. 'I haven't eaten since we were half-way across the Channel. It's exciting on a real destroyer. Some of the sailors taught me a poem. Would you like to hear it, Mr Brockett?' Brockett looked doubtful.

'It goes like this, but I can only remember a little: Roll on the *Nelson*, *Rodney* and *Renown*, this one-funnelled bastard is getting me down.' Brockett looked more doubtful. 'I don't think you should tell your mother that one, young man.'

Brockett's forecast was slightly adrift. By the time Finlay's mother and grandfather joined them in the kitchen, Finlay was sound asleep, resting his head on folded arms, on the kitchen table. As he struggled into wakefulness, he rested his chin on his hands and was suddenly aware of his grandfather doing exactly the same thing opposite him.

'Hello Kee, I'm your grandfather.' Finlay gazed back into the blue eyes staring at him.

'Your face must sting a bit,' Finlay ventured. 'I've had two clouts like that. Makes your ears ring, doesn't it?'

The old man uttered a throaty chuckle. 'What did you do? Not the same thing as me, I hope?' Finlay's eyelids felt very heavy. He and his mother had left Paris some fourteen hours previously.

'Is there anything to eat?' he enquired sleepily. 'Then I'd like to go to bed.'

Over the following years Finlay would learn never to be surprised by his grandfather's surprises, though this first surprise he would never forget. From somewhere – Finlay was not sure from where – a large flat wicker-basket was placed on the kitchen table, opened to show within types of food Finlay had never seen before. 'Mrs Drew, the butcher's wife, put this lot up for us. You've never had proper food before, poor chap, so I'll start you off.' With ceremony, he rose and came around the table to Finlay, placing before him a plate. On it was a round pastry, a long black cylinder and some pink meat. 'A pork pie, a sausage, burnt black, and proper ham. This is what you do with it.'

He hacked the pie in four, covered part of it with a greeny-brown concoction and bade Finlay, 'Open wide.' With rough, filthy fingers, which stank of oil, he gently pushed the piece of pie into his grandson's mouth. 'That,' he announced, 'will put hairs on your chest.' Finlay was not certain he wanted hairs on his chest. What he was certain of, was that he had never tasted anything so good in his life. He took the next portion and crammed it in his mouth.

'That's one of Mrs Drew's pies, my boy. Travel the world as you may, you'll not find better, and the chutney is Mrs Fortune's.' The old man waited until Finlay swallowed. 'Well, what do you think?'

'Good!' said Finlay. 'What's this?' He looked doubtfully at the burnt sausage.

'Watch,' his grandfather ordered. He dipped it in the chutney and bit into it. Finlay did the same and again, he was astonished by the wonderful taste.

'Don't eat too much,' his mother advised, smiling her approval. 'He's not used to heavy food, Papa,' she added.

The girl, Jenny, joined them, hanging back, looking timidly at Kathleen Finlay. 'Come and eat, Jenny,' Kathleen ordered. 'We'll decide what to do about you later.'

Finlay's grandfather handed him a small glass of pale brown liquid.

'You can't give him that, Papa!' a shocked Kathleen said sharply.

Her father ignored her. 'Take a couple of swallows, Keith, see what you think.' Finlay did as bidden. The light pale ale was bitter and sharp, but cut his thirsty mouth to cleanness. 'Make him sleep sound, Kath. A drop of beer won't hurt him.'

Later, as Finlay was led to the hall, his head rocked a little. A small bed had been made up on the floor and he was sound asleep in seconds. Even later, in his sleep, he heard his mother softly playing Chopin. He felt warm and secure. He knew, at last, he was home.

Chapter Two

•

The early June dawn woke Finlay and for a moment he wondered where he was. The memories of the previous day flooded back. He lay watching the airborne dust dancing in a shaft of sunlight as the daylight washed into the room. The high ceiling remained in darkness, until the sun eventually rose above the nearest horizon. He needed to go to the lavatory, but he could not remember where it was. He got up and slipped on his shoes, before he realised he was still wearing his shirt. Things were definitely odd. In this new home, you were allowed to sleep on the floor, go to bed without washing, in your daytime clothes, and the home itself had no furniture. He gave up trying to find the lavatory, went outside, and peed in an overgrown flower bed.

From somewhere in the far distance he heard a human voice calling, cajoling, but apart from this, the world seemed empty. He became aware of a thrumming, whistling beat which he had never heard before and was startled when two swans passed over his head. Till that moment, swans had been mucky creatures on a pond in a Paris park. These were white, cream-coloured under their wings, and could fly. He walked back indoors and was surprised to find his grandfather in the kitchen. He beckoned Finlay and the old man kissed his forehead. 'Having a look around, then? See where you've washed up, Keith?' he asked. 'Must be very strange. Like some tea?'

'Yes please, Sir,' Finlay replied. 'Where is everybody?'

'Still asleep. It's only five o'clock. If you're coming with me, you'd better get dressed.'

'Yes, Sir!' Finlay replied, both to the tea and the order.

'Keith,' the old man said softly, 'I'm not "Sir", I'm your grandfather. I know you don't understand what's happening, but this is your home, it's yours. I am yours, as much as your mother is. You are mine as much as your mother is. I'm Grandad, Gramps, even James, if that suits you, but not "Sir".'

'Will I be able to live here always then, Grandad?' Finlay asked.

'As long as you want to. I hope you do. You think you'll like it here?'

Finlay sipped his tea. 'I love it here...' He thought for a moment, unable to express what he wanted to say. 'This house holds you warm, doesn't it?'

'I know what you're trying to say, my boy.' There was a catch in the old man's voice. He drew Finlay to him and hugged him tightly. 'Christ knows! These past ten years have been hard. I've tried to keep it as much together for you as I could, but the bloody war changed so much. I couldn't do everything with half the men gone. The house and gardens have gone to ruin I know, but the rest is up together. The problem is, there isn't the money to put it back to rights at the moment. Do you understand?'

'Not really, Grandad, but I shouldn't worry. Everything will get mended.'

The old man laughed. 'Of course it will.' He looked at the clock on the wall. 'Come. We must see the cows are being milked.'

Finlay dressed quickly and followed his grandfather outside. The old man glanced at him and said, 'We'll find you some proper clothes. Can't have you looking like some sort of townie!' He led Finlay into an open-fronted barn and bade him get into a vehicle, the type of which Finlay had never seen before.

'What kind of car's this, Grandad?' he asked curiously. 'Why has it not got a proper roof?'

'It's a Land-Rover, a sort of go-anywhere workhorse. The roof's canvas. I need to be able to take it off. Brockett'll teach you to drive it.' He started the vehicle. 'I use it for everything now. Up the pub, into town, shooting, fishing. Can't really be bothered with anything else.'

The next two hours were a whirl of new things and sights. Cows being milked, the dairy working, crops, and most fascinating for the boy, a veritable swarm of grey tractors – 'Fergies'.

While not really understanding what his grandfather was speaking to his men about, none the less he found it interesting. The men looked at him curiously and spoke to him in a different accent than his grandfather. They had about them, Finlay thought, a warm kindness.

As they began to head back for breakfast, Finlay's grandfather said, 'Best till last Keith! I want to show you something, I'll not say anything more. I want to see what you think.'

The Land-Rover seemed to fly along the gravelled road, throwing up an occasional stone under its body, making a loud smacking noise which, initially, made Finlay start. Eventually they pulled over a river bridge and stopped. In front of them, the river cascaded over and under a barrier which Finlay's grandfather called 'sluices'. They approached, the noise of the water getting ever louder, till it seemed to Finlay to be a crystal roar. The old man took his hand and they both gazed at the water, dark green in the deeper parts but crystal clear in the shallows. 'What do you think?' the old man shouted above the noise. Finlay didn't answer for some minutes, so taken by this new and wonderful spectacle. When he did, he just said, 'Wow!'

A small, rotund figure approached them, smiling. He stopped in front of them, hands on hips, and looked at Finlay. 'Well you'm Keith I suppose? I'm pleased to meet you at last. Ten whole bliddy years… And now you're here.' He grabbed Finlay by the hand. 'Come on, there's somebody more impatient than me.' He marched Finlay towards a small house further up the river bank. Finlay looked back towards his grandfather, who waved him to go on. As they got nearer, the front door opened and an extremely tall, middle-aged woman ran towards them, shouting Finlay's name. As she reached him, she went down on her knees and hugged him so tightly, Finlay could hardly breathe.

'Kee, Kee, my darling boy,' she began. She pushed him away to arm's length. 'Let me look at you!' She hugged him again. 'You don't remember me, do you?' By now, her tears had wetted Finlay's face. 'I'm Auntie Niney, Kee!' She paused, looking at Finlay, willing him to remember. From somewhere in Finlay's mind, a memory stirred. There was something familiar about the form of her face, the smell of her breath and deep-set beautiful eyes.

'I was with you in Australia. After we ran away from the Japs.' She was begging him to remember. 'And in Washington, afterwards.'

'He was only four, Niney. He can't remember,' a voice behind Finlay said.

'I do remember you, but I don't know where,' said Finlay.

'There, there darling, doesn't matter now. Poor little chap,' she cooed. She looked at her husband sharply. 'Why didn't you tell me they were home? I should have been there. To welcome them.'

'It was a surprise…' began the husband.

Finlay's grandfather joined them. 'Why don't you both come home and join us for breakfast?'

'Of course we will, James,' said the tall woman. 'Come on Jack, get those infernal Wellingtons off your feet. Put some shoes on.' She began pushing him towards the house. 'Get on! Get on, man! Don't just stand there with your mouth hung open, like one of your bloody salmon. Move yourself!'

Jack soon reappeared, trying to do up shoe laces on the move.

'Now, you can sit on my lap, Kee,' she said, getting into the Land-Rover. 'Jack, you get in the back.'

Finlay thought this new-found auntie bossy and, in the event, his grandfather sat in the back and Jack, the small, rotund man Finlay had met five minutes before, took his grandfather's place and drove the Land-Rover back towards the house. It was all very perplexing. His mother and new auntie hugged and kissed each other, alternately laughing and crying. They danced around in circles, hugging each other. Finlay was hungry and not a little tired of not understanding what all the fuss was about. 'Oh, Niney, he was only four. He'll soon get it all in place.' Both women looked fondly at Finlay.

'Come along, all of you. Let's get some breakfast. The hay'll be making soon and no one there to look after it,' Finlay's grandfather ordered.

They sat down to yesterday's ham, but this time, fried with potatoes. 'Is Auntie Niney your sister then, Ma?' asked Finlay, when a break came, at last, in the conversation.

'Like my sister, Kee,' replied his mother. 'Niney's father looked after the river for your grandad. When he died, Niney married Jack and now Jack looks after the river. Just before you were born, Niney came out to the East, to help me look after you and to help get us home. But the war started and we got stuck there. When we went to Washington and got stranded there, there was room for one on a plane coming home, so Niney went and we had to stay. Then we went to France, and then we came home. I don't know why your grandfather didn't explain this to you.' She glanced sharply at her father.

'Can I have that chutney stuff with this, Grandad?' Finlay asked, now bored with grown-ups.

'He likes your chutney, Niney!' his grandfather laughed. 'You'll need our sugar ration to make some more.'

Niney leant across and ruffled Finlay's hair. 'Of course he likes my chutney. You would, wouldn't you, darling boy?'

'Don't embarrass him, Niney!' her husband said, almost as a sigh, and got up. 'Got to go now. People fishing today.' He looked at his wife expectantly.

Without looking at him, she waved him away. 'You go on, Jack. Kathy and I are going to start getting this place back to rights. How many men do we need, Kath?' she asked, looking at Finlay's grandfather.

'I'm off!' Jack said, moving quickly to the door. 'This is not going to be the place to be today, Boss. See you later.'

'Take the Land-Rover, Jack, rather than be late for your rods. I can pick it up later.' Finlay's grandfather turned back to the two women. 'I can't spare any men. You girls…'

'Nonsense James, we need two. Some of the wives are coming, but we want to get some of the furniture down from the roof. Kee has to have a bed.' Niney looked pleadingly at her husband's employer.

'Just two today, Papa. But four tomorrow…'

'How many women have you arranged, for goodness' sake? How much is this going to cost?' His grandfather sounded cross to Finlay.

'Twelve to clean. Two to cook lunch for everyone and Jenny can keep her eye on Kee. I suppose she's capable of that. She must be worth more than… How did you put it so prettily, Papa? A bloody good bang!' Both women exploded with laughter.

'What are you going to do about her, Kathy? I mean, it's all round Romsey, what's happening,' Niney said, between shrieks of laughter. 'I told you weeks ago, James. It would not do, but you wouldn't listen. Bobby North asked Jack about it last month.'

'Who's Bobby North?' asked Finlay's mother.

'Lordie's new land agent. If Bobby North knows, so does Southby.'

Kathleen Finlay made tutting noises but before she could say anything, her father said, 'Southby wouldn't mind her in his bed, I know. Anyway, Keith is coming with me.' He turned to Finlay. 'Come on lad. Let's get out of here before these two harridans drive me mad.'

Both women started laughing again. 'And what do I do with Jenny, Papa?' Kathleen Finlay shouted to her retreating father.

'Let her help with lunch. She's quite a good cook,' was the bellowed answer.

'She's got all the talents then, has she?' Finlay heard his aunt shriek with laughter, though he didn't really understand why.

'I want to go to the pig unit, Keith,' his grandfather announced, once they had got clear of the house. 'Do you like pigs?'

'Only ever seen them in books, Grandad. Never been anywhere where I could see one.'

'Well, pigs are different than other animals. They're extremely clever and extremely clean, given the opportunity that is. Our pigs used to win prizes at the local shows, when there were such things. No doubt when things come back to normal, it'll all come back.' They were walking down the main drive, between the rows of military vehicles.

'Whose tanks are these, Grandad?' Finlay asked, fascinated by the various types. 'And why are they here? Ma was pretty cross.'

'We're all cross about them, Keith. They belong to the government, brought back from France after the invasion. They don't seem to be in any hurry to get them moved. Perhaps after hay-making I'll have the time to get something done.' They had reached the front gate and Finlay's grandfather stopped to fill his pipe. 'Ron the pig man will be along shortly. He'll give us a lift.' They waited in the lane for five minutes before Finlay's grandfather said, 'Ah, here he comes,' and tapped out his pipe on the heel of his boot. Finlay couldn't see anything and it was some two minutes before a small, dark blue vehicle came chugging into view. His grandfather noticed Finlay's perplexity. 'I heard his truck change gear down the bottom of the hill. All cars have their own special sound.'

A pick-up truck pulled up beside them. 'Morning, Ron! Mind if we join you? This is Keith, I'll put him in the back.' Finlay felt himself being lifted and swung over the tailboard of the pick-up. 'Sit down, and don't hang over the back, else you'll fall out,' his grandfather ordered.

Finlay was bucketed about among a set of galvanized bins, full to the brim with mixed-up food scraps. He was sitting in a large smear of yellow custard, spreading slowly across the wooden floor. They left the made-up road with a rapid left turn, shooting the bins to one side of the truck. Finlay began to wonder about his own safety. The plume of dust spiralling from beneath the vehicle hung heavy in the air. It came to a sudden stop. The bins shot forward, then in reverse towards a raised concrete platform, stopping an inch short of it. The driver got out, ran to the back of the pick-up, grabbed Finlay under his arms and swung him over the tailboard. 'Stand there,' the man ordered and ran into the building. Finlay's grandfather ignored the proceedings, seeming more concerned with something on the horizon. The man returned, still running. 'Does he know about things?' he asked Finlay's grandfather, grabbing Finlay's arm.

'Soon enough will, Ron. Got to know sometime. Today's good a day as any,' his grandfather laughed.

'Come with me boy. Stay quiet, and I'll show you how the world turns.'

They proceeded through one shed and into another. 'Now hush, 'cause she don't know you, and she might get upset.' They came to a low wall, where, as far as Finlay was concerned, the man began talking gibberish. 'Cush, cush, my beautiful lady. Now, now pretty girl, it's only me.' He gently pushed Finlay forward so he could see over. In front of him, Finlay saw his first pig up close. It seemed enormous, a large black and white slab, lying on her side panting. The man climbed the wall, talking to the pig all the time, kicking the golden straw away from her hindquarters. He bent down gently to examine what looked to Finlay like a large red balloon. The man gently rubbed the long rows of teats before scratching the pig between the ears. The pig raised its head and seeing who it was, relaxed back on to the straw. 'Salrightmybeautifulady.' The word came out as one long cooing sound.

'Won't be long,' the man announced to Finlay as he stepped back. 'She'll have some babes soon.' They rejoined Finlay's grandfather. 'So you're Keith,' the man said. 'I'm Ron. I do the pigs.' He shook hands with Finlay in a very formal manner. 'Were you in the Navy, Ron?' asked Finlay, noticing the square-necked shirt he was wearing.

'You're sharp! You see my old shirt then?' He seemed amused, his face burnt red with sunburn, crinkled with amusement. 'Yes, I was in the Navy. Only for the duration though. Couldn't get out quick enough.'

'My father's in the Navy.' Finlay volunteered.

'Ah, there's some as likes it boy.' There was a finality in the statement that precluded further questions.

'Let's go and see how Edwina's getting on, shall we?' He heard a faint chuckle from his grandfather. Ron climbed back in with Edwina, making his cooing sounds. The large balloon that had been attached under her tail lay in the straw, deflated.

'Any minute now boy,' Ron said quietly. To Finlay's astonishment, from beneath Edwina's tail, a tiny pig, enclosed in a silky sheath, fell out on to the straw. Finlay was dumbstruck. Ron picked up the small parcel and placed it by Edwina's nose. She half rose and stripped the sheath from the tiny pig and swallowed it. Ron held his finger to his lips to make certain of Finlay's continued silence. The tiny pig, a replica of its mother, lay gasping in the life-giving air, on the straw. By the time Finlay tore his eyes away from the tiny scrap of life, another had arrived and the pig man again gave the little animal to Edwina. Finlay was transfixed. He watched the birth of twelve identical, tiny pigs. 'She's done now, boy,' announced Ron. 'Let's leave her to it, and get the truck unloaded.' Finlay's grandfather had disappeared. In truth, Finlay had quite forgotten him. As Ron began to unload the bins on the truck, Finlay asked, 'What are you going to do with all this?'

'Gets steamed. I'll show you in a minute or two.'

This he did, and steam from the pipes was injected into the bins. They stayed and watched until the air was filled with a strong vegetable aroma. 'I've got to get you back boy,' announced Ron. 'Christ! You're covered with shit and dirt. Your mother'll 'ang me.'

Finlay looked at his clothes – the same ones he had left Paris in – to see that Ron was right. 'They'll wash, Ron. I shan't let her blame you. Isn't your fault I've not got any more clothes, and I've only just met you.'

'You'm something of a philosopher chap, young Keith,' Ron replied.

He put Finlay into the cab of the truck and they tore back, the way they'd come. As they passed the rows of military vehicles in the driveway, Ron suddenly started waving at them. 'This lot's nothing short of a fucking disgrace. They've had their fucking war, the bastards, and leave us all the shit to clear up!' They came to a skidding halt outside the front door.

'Thanks Ron, for showing me your pigs. Can I see the baby ones again?'

'Come over after tea, boy. They'll be feeding well by then. Cheerio.' He drove the truck away sharply, kicking up gravel which bounced off the step, leading to the door.

Finlay walked into the house and seeming mayhem. The place was filled with women, swooping, squawking and screaming like crazed seagulls following a ship. In the kitchen, he saw Jenny among the three women present. One brushed past him and called towards the hall, 'Niney, you'd better come!' Jenny came towards him. 'Look at the state of you! God! You stink of pigs!'

Niney arrived. 'Where's your grandfather, Kee? Christ you smell! Bath for you I think.'

'Where's Ma?' asked Finlay.

'I'll kill that Ron! I'll swing for the bugger! Where did you leave your grandfather?'

Finlay had had enough. 'I didn't leave him anywhere!' he snapped. 'He went off somewhere to do the hay. I watched some baby pigs being born. The clothes will wash, and it's not Ron's fault!'

'Don't you get hoity-toity with me, young man!' Aunt Niney said sharply. 'Upstairs and have a bath, at once!'

'I'd go upstairs and have a bath, if anyone could be bothered to show me where the bloody bathroom is, or even show me where upstairs is,' Finlay shouted back.

Some time later, a chastened Finlay joined the rest of the household for lunch. He was wrapped in an oversized dressing gown, smouldering inside with an oversized resentment.

Lunch was frugal because, he was told, 'Everything's on ration.' There were plenty of potatoes and other vegetables, but very little meat. The conversation around the table did not include him. Boys that swore, he was told, 'didn't deserve to be spoken to'. He caught his grandfather's eye, who winked at him and smiled slightly. 'Enough of that, Father,' Kathleen Finlay said sharply. 'He's in disgrace.'

There was the sound of a car pulling up outside. Niney rose and went to the window. 'Oh God,' she said to the room. 'It's the bloody vicar. What's he on the scrounge for?' Nobody seemed shocked by Auntie Niney's swearing, thought Finlay.

'He's brought some second-hand clothes for Keith,' Finlay's grandfather said. 'Clothes *are* on ration, as well.'

The vicar shook hands with Kathleen and beamed down at Finlay. He was given tea, a ham sandwich and joined gently in the conversation. When there was a short lull Finlay said, 'Ron told me he called the mother pig Lady Edwina, because she had kind eyes. Like Lady Edwina.' There were some quiet chuckles around the table and uncomfortable coughs. Finlay continued, his bright high treble cutting clearly through the muted hum. 'He also said that the people who left the tanks on the lawn were a fucking disgrace and were bastards.'

The vicar gazed into his tea cup, his mother's face went white. There was dead silence.

His grandfather poured some beer into a small glass and walked around the table to Finlay. 'There you go, my son. If you are going to cuss like a man, you'd better drink like one.' He put his hand on Finlay's shoulder. 'Not one word Kathleen. Not one word from you.'

Chapter Three

•

The transition from chaos to normality had been very sudden. So much so, the normality was a shock in itself. The house now had furniture, carpets and clocks that chimed through the night. The whole house was clean, aired and permeated with the smell of polish or Dettol, depending which part you were in. Finlay had his own room, his own bed and, for the first time in his short life, he felt he belonged somewhere.

The day had started in what was to become his routine for many years. Out early just after first light, then home for breakfast at around eight-thirty. The conversation, that particular morning, was centred on getting rid of the old Armstrong car and replacing it with something, in Kathleen Finlay's words, 'smaller and handier'. There was the question of what was available. Most cars were going for export, foreign cars were of necessity 'rubbish' and so the conversation flowed back and forth.

'Here's the postman,' announced Finlay's grandfather, hearing the rattle of a bicycle outside the kitchen window. 'Hop to it, Kee.' There was a crash of a bicycle being thrown against a wall and an almost strangled yell of 'Post!'

Finlay ran into the passageway and stopped dead. Approaching him was a tall, thin man in uniform, cap askew, arms outstretched waving, his legs seemingly not belonging, moving along almost in time. The postman threw back his head and uttered another strangled cry. Finlay backed away rapidly and yelled, 'Grandad!'

His grandfather and mother ran into the passage, 'It's OK, Kee. It's only Joe,' his grandfather said softly.

His mother, to Finlay's horror, approached the man and took the proffered letters. 'Joseph?' she said softly. 'Joseph Long?' 'Don't you remember me, Joseph? It's Kathy. You grew my freesias and sweet peas.' She took him by the shoulders. 'Joseph, for God's sake what's the matter with you?'

Finlay's grandfather gently eased her away, guiding the postman to the door. 'Thanks Joe. See you tomorrow.'

The man uttered another strangled cry as Finlay watched him go, arms and legs waving. He turned to his mother and saw her wracked with sobs.

Her father guided her gently back into the kitchen and sat her down. 'There my love, don't get upset,' he murmured. Finlay had never seen his mother cry. He didn't know what he was meant to do. He approached her but was driven back by the force of her emotion.

'Hush my sweet,' her father said. 'You'll upset the boy.'

When eventually she could speak, she got up and walked to the kitchen sink. She splashed her face with cold water. 'What's happened to him? Isn't anybody looking out for him? What made him like this? He was an innocent, but he was basically all right.'

'He was captured in Singapore. Three days after he landed, he spent the rest of the war in a Jap camp. The bastards tormented and beat him into the state he's in now. But he's better now than when he first came home.' Finlay had witnessed his mother's explosive temper many times, but never before like this.

'You let them take Joseph? An innocent!' she screamed. Her face blanched and in one swift movement, she swept an earthenware pot of marmalade from the table, at her father's head. The old man ducked fractionally too late, and the pot bounced off the top of his head and smashed against the Aga, spreading sticky jam, with a loud hiss, across the hotplate. 'For Christ's sake, Kath!' her father barked, dabbing his bleeding head with a table napkin. 'There was nothing I could do.'

'Of course there was! Didn't you tell them poor Joe never had both oars in the water? Did you even try?'

'Look, Kathy…' began the old man.

'Don't you bloody "look Kathy" me! He wouldn't have gone if I'd been here. I'd have shot him myself first. How could you let this happen?' She was still beside herself with rage.

'Sit down, you bad-tempered little bitch!' the old man roared.

Kathleen Finlay looked for something else to throw. Finlay had seen the look before. 'Sit down!' roared the old man, again. She sat, her breathing coming in long blasts.

'Don't you dare call me a bitch!' she snapped, calmer now.

'Now listen! And you won't want to hear this. When Joe was called up, we… I… put him down as a farm worker. We made him practise what to say, but he told the army he grew flowers in the greenhouse. He half wanted to go, of course, but he didn't understand. I went to see some Major chap in Aldershot but they wouldn't move. For Christ's sake Kath! I did what I could. I even wrote to Southby, when he was with the Home Fleet. He didn't even respond.'

'Southby!' Kathleen Finlay spat. 'Like an overgrown schoolboy, dashing about in *Kelly* trying to make a name for himself. Bloody show-off!'

'When Joe's ship docked in Southampton, he was given a travel warrant and that's all. He walked home, went to his parents' old home, broke in and stayed there. The first we knew was when Jack Terry saw the door open. He thought it was squatters, and found Joe curled up on the kitchen floor. Wouldn't leave the place and couldn't understand that his parents were dead. Every time anybody went near, he threw a screaming fit. We had to put food in the front door everyday.'

'Didn't you get the doctor to him?' she asked.

'And have him committed by some do-gooder? No! Jack used to talk to him and gradually he got a little better. I eventually got Doctor McQuitty to look at him, on the proviso that he wouldn't commit him. He's a good man…' The old man paused for breath and dabbed his head. 'We couldn't leave him there on his own, so I tried to get him working in the garden again, but as you can see, the garden as such is not there any more. So I got him a job delivering letters.'

'Where's he living now? Who's looking after him?' Kathleen Finlay asked, a little mollified.

'We gave him his parents' old place. Maybe in time he'll get better. Well enough to want to come back to the garden. Mrs Fortune makes certain he's OK. He's improving all the time.'

'We let him down, Papa.' There were tears coursing down her cheeks again. She blew her nose. 'Poor Joseph. Years in the hands of those bastards. Can you imagine what that was like for him? I saw some of the prisoners come back to Australia, poor sods. Driven insane by their cruelty!' She thought for a moment and Finlay saw her jaw tighten. 'I'm glad they atom-bombed the malignant little scum. Pity they didn't wipe the lot of them out!' She blew her nose again. 'They want us to feel guilty about the radiation sickness now. Well! Let the bastards all die. Pity they didn't drop fifty atom bombs on them!' She got up and left them. Presently they heard Chopin from the music room.

'Let's leave her to it, Kee,' Finlay's grandfather said. 'We have all got to adjust.'

Finlay looked at the smoking hotplate, the marmalade bubbling, scorching and putting out wisps of blue smoke.

His grandfather slammed the cover down. 'Bugger it all! The bloody war's a long time finishing.'

Later, when Finlay came in for tea, his mother took him to the music room. 'Kee, I'm sorry about this morning. Joseph was one of my favourites. He worked in the garden and his greatest joy was growing sweet peas for me. He used to creep under that window and listen to me playing the piano. I pretended I didn't know he was there. He was a simple soul, but he had a kindness ordinary people don't ever have. He could have lived his life out here, with no harm and no hurt. It was this family's duty to protect him, and we failed. You must never let it happen to you.'

'What could I do, Ma?' asked Finlay. 'I wasn't even here.' He looked at his mother seriously. 'I was a bit afraid of him.'

'It's OK to be afraid of things you don't understand, Kee, and God knows, unless I'm careful, you're going to be very confused with what we've come home to. Understand this Kee. People in our position are very privileged. We have land, stock and I don't know yet, some money at least. But… we have a duty to the people who depend on us for work and a home.'

'Is that why you didn't send Jenny away, Ma?'

'In part, Kee. We couldn't just turn her out, could we?' Kathleen Finlay saw her son was beginning to grow up.

'Well, you did the other woman,' Finlay said.

'There was a difference. That creature deserves no better than I served her. She was dirty, and even in these times, soap and water costs nothing. People like Ron, all the dairymen and the tractor drivers are our responsibility. So are the people in the village, even if they don't work on the estate. Privilege does not come without strings attached.' Finlay made to speak but his mother held up her finger for him to remain silent. 'Since we came here you must be wondering what I've brought you into. Things will soon settle into place. I am going to be very busy doing my bit and sometimes your needs must be left to your own devices. I would just say this to you. Remember who you are. Remember your manners and never forget this place is only as good as the good people who work it. Don't ever, not ever, even in jest, talk down to them. The mark of a real man is that he can talk to a tramp and the King in the same manner. This applies to people in this country. Be always wary of foreigners. They are, in the main, shiftless, feckless people. Be polite to them, but never let them get close to you. Do you understand, Kee?'

'I think so, Ma,' answered Finlay.

'Never forget what the Japanese did. What they would have done to us, if they'd caught us. What they did to poor Joseph and thousands like him. I will never forgive them. They are an intrinsically evil people and they richly deserved what they got.'

'Did the atom bomb kill many of them?' asked Finlay, with a boy's curiosity of war and death.

'Not nearly enough, Kee. Not nearly enough.'

Finlay felt somehow more 'grown up' after this talk, but he couldn't help wondering whether foreigners knew they were shiftless and feckless and if they did know, why didn't they do something about it. He decided he would ask Ron about this. Another incident, however, confused Finlay even more.

Mealtimes, except dinner in the evening, always seemed to be the time when the telephone rang more frequently and outside problems were brought to Finlay's grandfather's attention. One such time, there was a light tap on the door and a thin, middle-aged man appeared at the kitchen door, cap clasped to his middle.

'Yes Carl,' said Finlay's grandfather, getting up. 'Have you got a problem?'

'Yes Sir. I need you to order a bearing for one of the turbines. Here's the size.' He handed Finlay's grandfather a small shred of paper. His accent was entirely strange to Finlay, but not his mother.

'What might your surname be, Carl? Doenitz?' Kathleen Finlay snapped. 'Is this a bloody German, Papa?'

Finlay grabbed the carving knife, thinking to protect his mother, but Niney grabbed him before he could struggle up from his seat. 'Give me the knife, Kee!' she shrieked, trying to hold him back.

'Get one for yourself,' Finlay answered, struggling like a boy possessed. 'I'll kill him if he comes near Ma!'

'Keith!' his grandfather barked. 'Sit down and put down the knife. At once!'

The German looked on, bewildered seemingly by the child's determination.

'Enough!' his grandfather roared and when Finlay ignored him, he threw a glass of water in the boy's face. 'Jesus Christ, Kath! What have you been telling him?' He eventually got the knife out of Finlay's hand.

'I didn't need to tell him anything! His first view of England was Portsmouth and Southampton bombed flat. What is the child meant to think?'

Finlay's grandfather cleared a space on the table in front of Finlay and ordered the hapless German to sit down. He leant over the table to his grandson. 'Now listen to me, Keith. Carl is a German. He was captured during the fighting in France and brought to England as a prisoner. He had to come and work here. When the war was over, he wanted to stay. He looks after all the tractors, my Land-Rover and every machine on the place. He's the best mechanic and engineer I've ever had work for me. Before he was a soldier, he built pianos.' He turned to his daughter. 'It was Carl who tuned your piano.'

Kathleen Finlay looked at the German coldly. 'Well Carl, I thank you for that. It sounds beautiful.'

The German ventured, 'I sank you Madam.'

'Touch it again,' Kathleen Finlay said, 'and I'll shoot you dead.'

Niney whispered, 'Kathy, Kathy.'

'Your piano was made in Germany, for Christ's sake Kath…' began her father.

'Before the Germans decided to let the middle class run the country. Before they decided they wanted to rule the world!' She eyed the German with evident distaste. 'Will you want me to welcome a bloody Jap into my home next?'

'I sink I should go perhaps,' ventured Carl.

'Sit there, Carl! I want this sorting out now. These two had a very bad war.'

'Don't you apologize for me, Father!' exploded Kathleen Finlay.

'Kath, the war is over.'

'Tell that to the people living on Stoney Cross Aerodrome. Tell it to the widows of the sailors lying at the bottom of the Atlantic. Their war isn't over. It's only just beginning. I'll tell you this. Either he leaves this estate, or we do!'

'Now Kath, be reasonable…'

'Reasonable!' Kathleen Finlay shouted. 'You ask me to be reasonable? I finished being reasonable when the Japs killed my sister, your daughter. Reason went out of the port-hole when the Japs bombed Hell out of the ship we were on. I never knew from one month's end to the next whether my husband was alive or dead and then, and then, I come home, home to England, expecting so much and I find people living in huts and starving, because there's no food for them, and you ask me, my father, to be reasonable.' She turned to the German. 'I thank Christ for what happened to Dresden. I was glad when our bombers burnt Hamburg. I'm glad now that the Russians occupy part of Berlin and I'm glad for every rotten thing. If ever a nation deserved – richly deserved – retribution, it was yours!'

'Churchill said we should be magnanimous in victory, Kathy,' Niney said quietly.

'Churchill is a drunken buffoon!'

'Perhaps I should say something, Madam,' the German volunteered. Finlay, at that moment, almost admired him but this German had a lot to learn about his mother.

'If perhaps I could be permitted to say something,' Carl quietly insisted.

'You wouldn't be permitted to breathe if I had my way,' Kathleen Finlay snapped.

'Enough of this, Kath!' Niney said. 'Carl's a good man. I won't have him treated this way. Listen to what he has to say. Then judge if you must!'

'Let him speak, Ma,' Finlay said. 'I've never heard the enemy.'

'I am not your enemy, Master Keith. I am no one's enemy, I hope. Before the war, I worked where your mother's piano was made. I had a grandfather. I can see his work. I was proud to make such things.' He spoke directly to Kathleen Finlay. 'I understand your hatred, Madam, but I knew right from wrong. They made me become an engineer. As Jesus is my witness, I never fired my rifle at anyone. When the invasion came I was glad because the war would soon be over and I could go home. I am ashamed of what my country has done. I was ashamed in the thirties. Many Germans wanted the English to come then, and stop Hitler. Now my country is destroyed and I am sorry. I am sorry that you will not allow me to look after the piano that my grandfather built. It is the only thing of my family left. I will go now, Sir, if you permit.' He got up to leave.

'Stay Carl,' Finlay's grandfather said. He looked at his daughter, 'Well, Kathy?'

'Do you expect me to feel sorry for him? Do you expect me to say sorry to him… because I don't and I shan't,' she answered. But even Finlay could tell she was going to let him stay.

Chapter Four

•

Three things happened on the twenty-fifth of June that year, which changed Finlay's life for ever. He caught his first salmon, North Korea invaded South Korea and his mother decided to leave him in England, while she travelled to the Far East to be near his father.

Jack had arrived at breakfast and announced there to be, 'A good big fish in the bottom pool. Just right for the youngster to get blooded on.' Within ten minutes of the announcement, they were at the pool's side, spinning rod set up and ready to go.

'Cast over by the old rock there Kee,' Jack ordered. 'Let it come round gently in the current, down deep, and if he takes, bang the hooks into him hard.'

Finlay cast across the river. The large vibro spoon bounced once on the surface then sank into the green water, fluttering its way across the current. A silver fish exploded out of the water with a suddenness that made Finlay start and take a step back. His knees began to tremble. As he brought the spoon back to hand, he looked at Jack enquiringly. The keeper grabbed the spoon and with fingers, Finlay noticed, that were trembling almost in time with his knees, attached a large lob worm to the spoon's hooks.

'Same place, deep down, a little quicker,' the keeper ordered.

Again the spoon bounced on the surface, before sinking into the water and fluttering across the current. It had reached the mid-point of the river when the salmon grabbed it. Finlay struck against the tug on the line, and the fish was hooked. 'Let him run Kee. If he wants to, make him fight the top of the rod. Don't hold him too tightly. Let him run, let him run!'

The string of instructions meant nothing to Finlay as the fish took off downstream, the clutch on his reel singing merrily. 'I can't hold it Uncle Jack, I'm not strong enough.' Finlay realized he was shouting.

The keeper reached across and loosened the clutch. 'Let him run. You've enough line on that reel to reach to Southampton docks! He'll stop in a minute.' The fish had other ideas though; by now more than a hundred yards downstream, Southampton docks seemed to be where the fish wanted to go. Suddenly, the line went slack.

'He's gone, Uncle Jack.' Finlay gasped, his body shaking as though gripped with the ague.

'No he ain't. No he ain't.' He reached over and let the bale arm up. The nylon began to loop off of the spool. 'Let it go gently, get a big loop down below him,' the keeper ordered. They waited. They could see the line running down the river. Finlay looked quizzically at the keeper. 'When he feels the line pulling from behind him, he'll come back up, you watch. Don't worry. He's well hooked and there's nothing he can get snagged on.' The keeper did not sound that confident. Again they waited and the line on the spool was getting low.

'OK, here he comes, just wind in gently. Keep a big belly of line below him.' Finlay could see part of the line coming up against the current. 'Speed up a bit,' the keeper hissed. The fish, as predicted, gradually came upstream and eventually crossed the shallow lip at the bottom of the pool where they were standing. Its back showed briefly above the surface. As it drew opposite, the keeper said, 'Give him the rod again.'

Finlay applied as much pressure as his slight frame could manage. There was a tremendous thump, a pull on the line and the fish shot off downstream again. Once more, Finlay brought him back by bellying the line below him. Four times the fish ran away and by gentle cajoling, four times he was brought back to the original start place. Eventually, the fish elected to fight it out in the pool where he was first hooked. 'Just keep the pressure on him, Kee,' Jack said. 'But don't bring him to the top. If that big bugger crashes on the line, he'll snap it.'

The fish swam around and around the pool, sometimes slowly, sometimes so fast that Finlay had a job to keep track of his position. It seemed to the boy to be never ending. Once, the fish broke the surface, his great tail slapping down with an audible smack.

'Stay where you are now Kee,' Jack said. 'I'll get below him with the net.' The keeper waded out into the water, up to his waist at the pool's tail. 'Ease down to me, Kee, but keep the pressure on him.' Finlay could see what was meant to happen, and keeping the rod top up, he began to let the fish go back downstream. It drifted into the waiting net and with an exultant cry, Jack lifted it clear of the water. He half ran and half stumbled up the river bank to where Finlay was standing, shouting and cursing incoherently. 'What a bloody fish! Played him like a pro! You really are a brough of a boy.'

The fish was duly despatched, the hooks removed and it lay on the grass, a thing of such great beauty in Finlay's eyes that he felt rather sorry it was now dead.

The keeper took his hand in his and very formally shook it. 'Look around you, young Kee. Look at the river and everything about it. I promise you will remember this moment for the rest of your days!' Finlay knew he would. The keeper bent and made a small cut at the bottom of the salmon's gill. Taking some of the blood on to his fingers he dabbed it on to Finlay's cheeks. 'It's called blooding, youngster – to show your respect to the creature you have just killed. Brings you both together in a sort of bond.'

With the fish slung over his shoulder the keeper marched in front of Finlay, back towards home. Trailing behind him, Finlay wondered if his still shaking knees would allow him to effect the short journey. Home, the fish was laid out on the kitchen table and the assembled adults wanted every detail of the capture repeated again and again. Finlay was certain that Jack embellished in part. Certainly he never mentioned baiting the spoon with a worm. So Finlay didn't mention it either. The fish was weighed, photographed and weighed again. 'Twenty eight and a half, Kee,' his grandfather announced. 'I was twenty-five before I caught one over twenty pounds. Well done.' Throughout the rest of the morning, it seemed to Finlay, everyone on the estate came to admire the fish. Jack recounted the capture over and over again to each new visitor, and with every telling Finlay's battle became ever more epic.

Lunch that day began as a noisy affair, with even Jenny joining in the conversation. Finlay was glad she had. He somehow felt rather sorry for her plight, although his mother's attitude to her was still rather brittle. 'Shush!' his mother suddenly ordered, and went to the wireless to increase the volume. '…heavy fighting is continuing along the border, with South Korean and American units falling back to prepared positions,' the newsreader announced solemnly.

'Oh, for Christ's sake,' began his grandfather.

Kathleen Finlay ignored him, remaining close to the wireless. Finlay heard, 'Royal Navy units in Hong Kong and Trincomalee are leaving for the area.'

Kathleen Finlay switched off the wireless. 'Bugger, bugger, bugger,' she said softly. 'Another bloody war.'

That afternoon, Finlay wandered down to the river and lay gazing down into the pool, where the morning's drama had taken place. As he watched the dace darting about in the clear water, he wondered why his mother had been so concerned about a new war on the other side of the world. 'This war thing's a bloody nuisance,' he told himself. He resolved to go and see his friend Ron the pig man and find out what it was all about.

When he got back to the house, there was a strange car parked by the front door with a sailor, in uniform, sitting smoking in the driving seat. He waved to the sailor who, in turn, gave him a wink. Kicking off his shoes, Finlay made to go along the passage to the hall, where he could hear people talking.

'What will you do with the boy, Kath?' a male voice asked. 'Put him in a boarding school?'

'My father wouldn't hear of that,' he heard his mother answer. It was obvious they were talking about him. He went to move quietly down towards the hall, to listen more closely, but was intercepted by Jenny.

She gently guided him into the kitchen. 'Listeners never hear good of themselves young man,' she chided him softly.

'Who's that with Ma?' he asked.

'Some big-wig from the Navy,' Jenny answered. 'Would you like something to eat?'

'Has my father been killed already then?' asked Finlay, guilelessly.

'No of course not, Kee, whatever makes you think that? No, I expect he's come to tell your mama what your father is doing.'

'He was saying to Ma she should put me in a boarding school, Jenny,' Finlay said, accepting a sandwich from her. The girl gently explained about boarding schools.

'Humph!' said Finlay. 'I'm not going to one of those. No, bugger that for a game of soldiers.'

'Where do you get these expressions from, Kee?' Jenny said, somewhat sadly. 'It's that pig man chap, I'll be bound.'

'Are you going to marry Grandfather, Jenny?' asked Finlay, changing the subject to protect his friend from any criticism.

'That's not very likely, is it?' Jenny said quite sharply. 'It's not something you need concern yourself with.'

He heard his mother call. 'If he doesn't, Jenny, I'll marry you, so you can stay here always,' Finlay said, getting up to go.

As he entered the hall, a tall man in uniform got up to shake hands. 'I hear you caught something of a fish this morning, Keith. I'm Captain Agnew, a friend of your father.'

Finlay gazed up and saw a row of medal ribbons. 'What did you get your DSO for, Captain Agnew?'

'You're a bright boy, knowing that straight off. Do you know all the others?' he asked.

'Nearly, except that bottom one. I've never seen that one before. What is it, Sir?' he asked.

'One from China. Tell me Keith, are you going in the Navy, do you think?'

'Oh yes,' Finlay answered, in a very matter-of-fact way. 'It's expected of me.' He paused. 'Do you know my father well, Captain Agnew? You see, I've never met him.'

'I have to go to Trincomalee, Kee,' Finlay's mother announced at breakfast the next day. 'To be with your father. Do you want to come with me or stay here?'

'I'm staying here,' Finlay answered emphatically.

'Your father may want you…' she didn't finish.

'I'm staying here,' Finlay said, more emphatically.

'But Kee, your father hasn't seen you since you were a baby. Perhaps you should come with me.' Kathleen Finlay wasn't going to leave her son without some show of resistance.

'I'm staying here!' Finlay said, an edge of truculence now creeping into his voice. 'I'm staying here, and I'm not going to any rotten boarding school. You go to Trincomalee if you want. I'm staying here.'

His grandfather shook his newspaper and coughed.

'Yes Father?' queried Kathleen Finlay.

'Nothing my dear, nothing at all,' came an exultant reply from behind that day's *Daily Telegraph*. Breakfast continued in silence for a short while.

'You will have to go to school of some sort or another. There's no escaping that, Kee,' his mother said, almost firmly.

Before he could answer, his grandfather said, 'Peter Simmonds in Winchester, Barton Peverill in Eastleigh or Bransgore County. Any one of those will do, I should think.'

'You've looked into this then, Father, have you?' asked Kathleen Finlay, an edge of sharpness in the question.

The newspaper was lowered, a sure sign that Finlay's grandfather was about to make a pronouncement. 'Indeed yes! Peter Simmonds is on a par with Bransgore, but they have school on a Saturday, which I shouldn't think would suit. Barton Peverill is in the middle of Eastleigh. That wouldn't suit even though they have a good record. On balance, Bransgore wins hands down. The school train leaves Totton at ten past eight in the morning. He would get back at about quarter to five in the evening. Kee can go over in the morning in the milk lorry and he can either walk or cycle back in the evening. Yes, I think Bransgore would suit admirably. The headmaster there is Dr Forest. Seems a very nice chap.'

'Have you fixed a time for him to start, Father?' Kathleen Finlay asked; the edge of sharpness, coupled with a little ice, was more than apparent.

'First week of September,' Finlay's grandfather answered, returning the newspaper to its original place, a sure sign that the pronouncement had been made, the subject closed, as far as he was concerned.

'You didn't actually feel the need to ask me about this?' The edge in Kathleen Finlay's voice had gone, to be replaced by pure ice.

Finlay's grandfather lowered the newspaper sharply. 'Indeed I did not, Madam! He needs a stable home and a decent education, which he will not get trailing around the world with you. He goes to Bransgore in September. The matter is settled.'

As Kathleen Finlay rose from the table and left the room, Finlay thought if ever a person needed somebody to go up and bat for him, one couldn't do a lot better than his grandfather. And so it was that soon after Kathleen Finlay left, Keith Finlay started school.

It was certainly not what he had been led to believe it would be like. He was lucky. A prefect, Janey Grieves, was the daughter of one of his grandfather's tenant farmers. At least he had a guide as to what he was meant to do. She was a large girl with two huge school bags and a hockey stick. She seemed to Finlay to be confident and superior, and when she spoke the others listened.

'Do you know what form you're to go to Finlay?' she asked.

'No Miss. I've to see a Dr Forest when I get to the school. Beyond that, nothing.'

She had freckles and green eyes and wore sensible black brogue shoes. 'You don't call me Miss. You call me Grieves. I'll take you to Dr Forest myself. I wonder which house you'll be in?'

'I'm not staying. I'm going home tonight,' Finlay explained firmly.

Janey gently explained the house system. 'You see, I'm in Peel House. All your marks for work and sport are added to the house's total. It gives you something to have pride in, something to channel your effort toward.'

'Yes Miss,' Finlay answered, but he wasn't sure what she was talking about.

She could see he didn't. 'I'll take you in hand, I think, young Finlay, for your own good and make quite certain that at least one of your family gets dragged into the twentieth century. Where is your mother currently?' She looked sadly at Finlay.

'Trincomalee. She's gone out there to be with my father. He's fighting in Korea and it isn't going terribly well at the moment.'

'Well, Finlay, I shall help you all I can. Who is looking after you at home?'

'Auntie Niney, most of the time. Jenny is there as well.'

'Yes,' said Grieves. The word dwelt on her tongue and her look clouded.

'Jenny's all right, Miss,' Finlay countered quickly. He couldn't understand seemingly all the women he knew having a down on Jenny. 'She's always there, and she doesn't ever shout or lose her temper.'

'Yes,' said Grieves and again the word dwelt on her tongue.

The train pulled up at Bransgore station. Janey Grieves shepherded the new pupils into line. 'Right! First formers, follow me. Finlay, join the line!' Finlay decided Janey Grieves was a little formidable, someone to be reckoned with. The rest of his day was ordered. A whirl of instructions, new books, new names, more instructions and a list of required equipment to present to his grandfather. At the end of the day he found Janey Grieves waiting for him. 'Do buck up Finlay, the train leaves in ten minutes. If you miss the school train, the next one is not until five-thirty. What form are you in? What house are you in? Come along, walk faster!' They scrambled on to the train with seconds to spare. Barely had the door slammed shut when the train began to pull out of the station.

'There Finlay,' said Janey Grieves breathlessly, 'the train doesn't wait because Finlay isn't aboard.'

They moved to find a seat. 'You know absolutely nothing about the world, Finlay. I think perhaps you'd better learn quickly. How are you getting to your home from the station?'

'Walk, I suppose Grieves,' said Finlay. He hadn't given it much thought.

'Do your people have any consideration? It's four miles. What about when the dark nights are here? They thrust you out in an alien world and let you get on with it. It's the upper classes' way of toughening you up. I'll speak to your grandfather.' Finlay thought such a conversation might be interesting. When the train reached Totton, she took his satchel from him and said she would deliver it to his home, climbed on board an ancient black bicycle and was gone.

Finlay started to walk over the estuary bridge and turned left for Nursling. The road was bordered on one side by the river. He thought tomorrow he would bring some binoculars. He could see Jack Terry on the bottom beat of the fishing, with one of the paying rods. It didn't occur to him to think that he had three more miles to walk and the road he was on was a border to his grandfather's land. He was at the bottom end of the estate. Distance meant nothing. He had gone another mile when, to his delight, he saw Ron's pick-up truck approaching. It stopped and backed into a gateway.

Ron got out and waited. 'You ain't making very good time youngster. Jack Grieves's daughter has been up to the house, gave the old man a proper dressing down about the treatment of children.' He laughed.

'Is she still at the house then, Ron? She's a very confident young lady.' Finlay paused. 'Very kind though.'

'No. Your grandad put her bike in the back of the Land-Rover and took her on home. He felt a bit sorry for himself after she had finished with him. Anyway, how did your first day go? What was the grub like?'

The pick-up smelt of rotten food and pigs, better than the blackboard chalk and massed humanity he had to suffer that day. 'Both all right, I suppose. Do this, do that, sit down, sit up, don't answer back. Be here when this bell goes, be there at this time, don't dawdle. Christ you can't even go to the lavatory without you have to ask! I don't really think it's for me Ron.'

Ron laughed. 'Wondered how you'd cope with rules and regulations. Up till now you've only had yourself to please. Talk about being chucked in at the deep end. School was hard enough to cope with when you started as a toddler. You're set in your ways already.'

'I can understand the discipline side of it, but what I can't understand is not being able to say what you think yourself, even if you know you're right and they're wrong!'

'Thought that might be a problem for you. How did you get on with the other kids?' he asked.

'They think I'm funny. When I told one of the teachers he was wrong to blame Mountbatten for the partition of India, it was the fault of Attlee and Jinna, the teacher got upset and sent me out of the room. He was quite rude about it, so I told him to mind his manners. All the other children laughed.'

'I think you might be in for a stormy passage, young Kee. How was he rude then?' Ron enquired.

'He said I was an uppity toff who shouldn't be at his school at all, and that my class had had its day,' Finlay answered frankly.

'I should tell your grandfather about that Kee. See what he has to say. I'll come over to pick you up from the school if you like. Point the bugger out to me and I'll give him a cuff if you like. Commie bastard!' The rest of the journey passed in silence. Ron seemed angry and Finlay thought it best not to enquire.

Jenny, whose status had become somewhat elevated since his mother's departure, gave Finlay a cup of tea and a sandwich when he got home. He had become very fond of her and now that his mother had gone, she spent more time chattering with him. When his grandfather eventually came in, he questioned Finlay closely about his first day at school.

'That Grieves girl is a good sort, Kee,' he announced. 'Gave me a proper telling-off. I had to explain to her why I had put you to school.'

'I wish, perhaps, you'd tell me.' Finlay could talk easily with the old man and began to recount his spat with the history teacher.

'Kee, I could have put you to Eton or Winchester, but that would have done you no good at all. Your teacher, well, in part he was right. Our class has had its day. Two wars and taxes have knocked us about a bit. We're going to have to mix with the middle class and they'll run the show, so it's best you learn to deal with them. Today was your first lesson. We have about another week of harvest, then I'll have more time for you. I'll send Brockett to pick you up from the train in the evening. Meantime, take heed of what young Janey tells you. She's got her heart in the right place.'

A comfortable routine was soon in place. Brockett, who lived on the north end of the estate, picked up Grieves in the morning on his way to pick up Finlay and dropped them both off at the station, and likewise picked them up in the evening. Over the passing weeks of the autumn, they became firm friends. During school time the formalities were always observed. She was Grieves, he was Finlay. Out of school, it became Janey and Kee. By October, they spent time together on Sunday afternoons doing their homework, Janey staying to tea before being driven home. Finlay was quite proud to be able to help her with her French. She, in turn, helped him to structure his work and guide him through the etiquette of school life.

It was something of a surprise for Finlay, to be called to the headmaster's office during the back end of November, to find himself confronted by his grandfather, as well as Dr Forest. With a sinking feeling he asked, 'Has my father been killed?'

His grandfather put his hand on Finlay's shoulder. 'No Kee. Dr Forest asked me to come in and see him. Seems you're a bit of a star with your school work and Dr Forest wants to put you up a year.'

Forest coughed to get their attention. 'Finlay, it seems to be that you are a long way in front of your contemporaries. What I'm suggesting is that you are moved up to 2A after Christmas. How do you feel about that?'

Finlay looked at his grandfather, who said, 'It's up to you, Kee.'

'Do I get the same history teacher in 2A, Sir?' Finlay asked.

'No, you would...' Forest began to answer.

'OK. I'll go to 2A then,' Finlay interrupted quickly.

'I'm aware of your antipathy to Mr Finch, Finlay...'

Again Finlay interrupted. 'I wouldn't grace the bastard with my antipathy.'

Forest sighed. 'From that you can see the problem, Sir James. Having spent his life in adult company, he does rather react to a situation in an adult way and some of his language tends to be adult. What with that and his, shall we say, command of English, he is inclined to bring a lesson to a halt in seconds.' Finlay's grandfather said nothing.

'Finlay, I note you have not joined any activity. No societies within the school. Perhaps if you mixed more freely it would help.' Forest peered at Finlay over his glasses.

'I go and fence at lunch times,' Finlay said defensively.

'But you don't seem willing to join the team. I'm told you're the best swordsman in the school. Why won't you join the team?'

'Because,' said Finlay, 'they fence after school and I want to go home then. School is school. It starts at nine and finishes at quarter to four. When I get home I do my homework. I shall always give my best and work hard at that, but I don't really want to be here. So, at quarter to four, I shall always go home. As for Saturdays... Saturdays are mine for fishing and shooting.'

'You don't really see yourself as a team player then, Finlay?' asked the headmaster.

'Not really, Sir,' said Finlay.

Chapter Five

•

The Christmas holiday came and went. Finlay had spent his time fishing for grayling and shooting duck with his grandfather. Janey Grieves had come over once or twice to the house, but had largely been tied up with revision. Her father had come to the Boxing Day shoot, congratulated Finlay on his shooting and for being top of the class at school. Finlay had liked him immediately. A short, thickset man whose shooting clothes smelt of moth balls and whose shoes were polished with ox-blood. Back at school, Finlay settled easily with his new classmates and was introduced to the works of Shakespeare. He was surprised to find himself enjoying some school work and regarded the English teacher, Mr Robinson, as a friend.

On the sixth of February, once again, Finlay fell foul of the system. During a maths lesson, a teacher came into the room and whispered something in the ear of the maths teacher and quickly left again. She tapped her desk. 'Children! I have to tell you that The King has died.' She quickly left the room, obviously upset.

Finlay packed what books he needed and got up to leave. 'I'm off home, Jim,' he told the boy sitting next to him. 'I expect my grandfather could do with my company right now.'

Jim Flux smiled. 'You'll be in trouble, Fin, if you do, but don't let that stop you.'

Two hours later, Finlay walked into the kitchen, much to the surprise of everyone present.

'What are you doing home, Kee?' his aunt asked. 'You're not ill are you?'

'No, of course not. When we were told The King had died, I thought Grandad would be upset, so I came on home. Where is he?' he asked.

'Probably down the hatch pool. He always goes there when bad news comes to him. Go and find him.'

His grandfather was staring morosely into the river, yet he looked up and saw Finlay approaching. The old man put his arm around Finlay's shoulders. 'Sad day this for the country, Kee. He's done a good job, The King. Got the monarchy back on track after what his shitty brother did.'

Later that afternoon there was a telephone message enquiring whether Finlay had arrived back home, from an irate headmaster.

Next day, Dr Forest had Finlay into his office. 'What if everyone else decided just to go home? What then Finlay?'

'I do what I do, Sir. What everyone else does is up to them.'

'Get out boy!' Dr Forest snapped. 'Before I entirely lose patience with you.'

The spring term saw Finlay moved up another year into 3A. He was being pushed academically, which he found interesting. At the same time, at home, his grandfather had purchased a horse for him, a blue roan mare, an Arab thoroughbred cross.

'What are you going to call her, Kee?' his grandfather asked, pleased to see it was love at first sight.

'Blue Mist,' Finlay said immediately. 'After Lawrence's armoured car. She's beautiful, Grandfather, like a small racehorse. Thank you.'

'I'll get Brockett to teach you how to ride like an Englishman. I know you had a fair bit of tuition in France, but that isn't the same. Perhaps you can go hunting on her next season. She's going to be a bit of a handful. Bring her on slowly in your own way, but don't spoil her just because she's got a pretty face.'

Finlay laughed. 'You make her sound just like a lady, Grandad.'

'Kee, the differences between a well-bred lady and a well-bred mare are very small indeed. Treat them quietly and gently but with a degree of firmness. Let them have their little petulances sometimes, but not too often and play with their tits sometimes.' He leant down and rubbed the mare's udder. 'It's as I said Kee, women and mares. Much of a muchness.'

'What if they're not well-bred then, Grandad?' asked Finlay, amused by his grandfather's philosophy.

'I should restrict your titty rubbing to the well-bred one's Kee. They're a lot more predictable.'

Though, at the beginning of the summer term, things seemed to be progressing well for Finlay, the beginning of the end was occasioned by that summer's rain causing the Lymington river to flood. Normally a quiet stream which ran beside the Balmer Lawn Hotel, that summer, it became a raging torrent of dark peaty water. The temporary geography teacher decided it was cause for studying the effects of flooding and Finlay's whole class were ordered there. The girls of the class, somewhat bored, began swinging on the road bridge's hand rail, using it as a piece of gymnastic equipment. The inevitable happened. Finlay heard the scream from downstream and looking up, saw a child in the water being swept towards him. He ran downstream some fifty yards, shedding his jacket and shoes as he went, and then dived into the river. He swam to the middle and tried to hold his place by swimming hard against the current, but he was being swept downstream. Taking a breath, he could see an arm in a white sleeve bearing down quickly to him. He swam hard forward again, then stopped. The girl in the water cannoned into him. He grabbed her, got her head above the water, then lay on his back and let the current take them. Finlay knew downstream was a small footbridge which, with luck, would check their progress to the Solent. The girl was limp and weighed heavily. He was having some difficulty holding her up. They hit the footbridge with enough force to wind Finlay. He grabbed a support and waited for help. The current, determined not to lose its prize, pulled heavily on him. It seemed an age before willing hands dragged the girl from Finlay and on to the river's bank. He pulled himself on to the bridge, pretty well exhausted. She lay inert on the bank, with no one seeming to know what to do. He pushed them away and began to give her artificial respiration as he had seen in diagrams in a book. She spewed peaty water from her mouth and nose and eventually began to breath.

'Has anyone called an ambulance?' he snapped, annoyed now at the inactivity around him. 'Go to the hotel, you dopey cow,' he ordered the teacher. 'For Christ's sake! Don't just stand there!' The people in the hotel had witnessed the drama and an ambulance was already en route. The girl was sitting up by now, her long hair festooned with debris from the river. She began to shiver with shock.

The ambulance arrived and the girl was swept up into it. 'You'd better come as well. You've got a bad cut on your head,' the driver said.

'No,' said Finlay, with finality and turned to the teacher. 'You go with her. I'm going to get cleaned up.'

Someone handed him his jacket and shoes. He noticed that he had lost both socks. He began the walk back towards the school. His legs felt like jelly and he was cold. 'What a stupid bitch!' he kept muttering. Those about him couldn't understand his anger. They offered congratulations and patted him on the back. Finlay had had enough. 'Don't,' he snapped, looking about him.

At the school Finlay broke away from the others and went to the changing rooms. He stripped off his clothes and showered. Towelling himself dry, he changed into his sports kit.

'Finlay, are you in here?' he heard a voice call. He recognized it as Mr Robinson, his English teacher.

'I'm in here, Sir,' he called back. 'I'm changing into something dry.'

The teacher found him lacing up his shoes. 'All right, old chap?' he asked. 'You've a pretty bad cut on your head. Why didn't you go in the ambulance? Looks as though it needs stitches.' He took Finlay by the shoulders and made him stand still long enough to examine the wound.

'Are you in shock?'

'No Sir, I'm perfectly all right. Let it bleed for a while to clean any muck out. I didn't go in the ambulance because I couldn't stand the thought of being on my own with Miss Tucker.'

'Well! If you're not the most uncompromising young bugger I've ever met in my entire life, Finlay.' He smiled and began to light a cigarette.

'Can you let me have one?' asked Finlay.

'I didn't know you did.' He gave Finlay a cigarette and lit it for him.

'I don't,' Finlay said simply. They sat in the damp room, smoking together.

'Why don't you like it here, Keith?' Robinson asked. 'You're very popular with the other pupils. You find the work easy. What do you find so difficult about school?'

'I'm marked out as some sort of freak all the time. Most of the teachers dislike me, which I return in good measure. Sometimes I just wonder what I have to do to be accepted. I just hate being here, and I'm only here because my grandfather says I must be. To learn to live in the new world order.'

'I don't think they dislike you, Keith,' Robinson said. 'They're wary of you. No adult likes to be corrected by a twelve-year-old. You've found a lot of them wanting and quite frankly, it disturbs them. Anyway, old chap, everyone is looking for you. You're quite a hero now, so we had better go and make an entrance.' They walked to the door. 'Perhaps you had better put out that cigarette, else we'll both be in trouble.'

'You're a good chap you know, Robbie,' Finlay said. 'I hope you don't mind me calling you that. That's how you are always referred to.'

'Not in school time. But outside that, not at all. I think we're friends.'

'Thanks, Sir,' said Finlay.

———

He was taken to the headmaster's office where Finlay was confronted by other members of staff as well as the headmaster. Their compliments and congratulations were so effusive as to be embarrassing to the boy. 'I just pulled her out of the water. I don't think you need to make more of it,' said Finlay, ungraciously.

'You should have an award for bravery, Finlay,' the headmaster said.

'I would not want that, Sir. I should find it awkward to accept. I did what needed doing, not to win some kind of award. I couldn't see her drown, so can we leave it at that please?' Finlay was getting cross.

'I think someone should take you home after I have your statement on how this happened. We have to look at the legal consequences, insurance and things like that. Could you get Finlay's side of it perhaps Mr Robinson? I think Finlay's still in shock. Doesn't want a bravery award indeed!' The meeting was over.

Later, Finlay recounted, 'She fell off the bridge, the teacher had the vapours. About as much use as tits on a boar, so I went in and got her out. That's it Robbie. Don't make more of it.'

Robinson laughed. 'Get your wet kit, and I'll take you home.'

'This is your home?' Robinson said, in some awe.

'Yes Sir, come on in. I expect there'll be some food about.'

Finlay led him into the kitchen, where Auntie Niney was baking. The air was full with the smell of pastry cooking. She looked aghast at Finlay. 'What have you been up to now?' she shrieked, looking at his cut forehead. She came to him and studied the gash, completely ignoring Finlay's companion.

'This is Mr Robinson, Auntie, my English teacher,' he began.

She studied the cut. 'Oh it's nothing much, probably should have been stitched. Hold still. I'll clean it up.' She looked at the teacher. 'Did you let this happen to him?' she asked sharply.

'No Auntie,' Finlay interrupted, wriggling with pain. 'Wasn't anything to do with him.' The iodine swab hit the cut like a branding iron. 'Jesus Christ!' Finlay swore, gasping with the pain of it. 'Have you finished now?'

Robinson began to protest. 'You be quiet young man, I know what's best for my Kee.' She kissed Finlay heavily on the cheek. 'There, that won't scar as much as stitches. Can't have my beautiful boy marked.'

Finlay looked at Robinson. 'Please don't tell anyone, Sir,' he begged.

'I'm beginning to understand what makes you what you are. Iodine, by God! Does it hurt?'

'Nothing he can't stand, Mr Robinson. No sense making them into softies.'

The teacher began to explain what had happened and how they came to be there.

'Fancy taking children near a flooded river. Silly cow! She should be sent packing!'

Before Robinson could comment, the telephone rang. Mr Robinson and Finlay listened in amused amazement at the one-sided conversation. 'And who are you?' Niney asked.

'Yes, they are both here... No, you can't... Don't tell me what I can and cannot do...! Is that so? Well, the best thing you can do is pee down your leg and play with the steam!' Robinson and Finlay looked at each other. 'That was your headmaster, Kee,' Niney said, putting down the phone. 'Sounds an uppity little squit. He's demanding you go to the South Hants for a check-up. Never mind, would you like something to eat Mr Robinson?' It wasn't a question, more an order. 'Cheese and chutney sandwich?'

Outside Robinson laughed, 'That is one very forthright lady, Finlay. Does she give you a hard time?'

'Not at all, she's a real softie. Watch.' Finlay shouted up to the kitchen window, 'Auntie Niney.' The window flew open and Niney's head appeared.

'Yes, my love?'

'Do I have to go to school tomorrow?' Finlay asked.

'Do you want to, Kee?'

'No, not really.'

'Then you don't have to.' The window closed.

'Auntie Niney would spoil me rotten if I let her Mr Robinson,' Finlay said, in a matter-of-fact way.

'Is that a fact?' Robinson laughed.

Later that day, bored with his own company, Finlay wandered down to the river and spent the afternoon fish watching in the hatch pool. A large slob trout, up from the estuary, was harrying the fry. Finlay had just decided to go for a rod when he heard someone calling his name. He had been lying on his stomach on one of the pool's wooden fishing stations. He rose to show himself above the bankside summer growth.

'I'm over here,' he shouted. Jenny appeared barefoot, carrying her shoes. The bottom of her dress, sodden from the long wet grass, clung to her bare legs. She jumped on to the wooden boards, smiling.

'Someone from your school has come to speak to you. Do you want to be found?' She sat down and let her bare feet hang in the water.

'No, not really. Who is it?' asked Finlay, watching her feet moving backwards and forwards in the clear water. 'Where is Grandfather today, Jen?'

'Gone to a meeting in Winchester about cows getting TT.' She began splashing her feet.

'Are you always going to live with us Jen?' Finlay asked.

'I don't know, Kee. I haven't thought about it. Life just sort of drifts on here, doesn't it? We'll have to see what turns up,' she sighed.

'What happened to your parents? Have you no one of your own now?' Finlay asked, with a child's candour.

'Don't you want me to stay…?' she began.

'Of course I do, for always. Mama likes you now. You have to stay.' Finlay was emphatic. 'Where did you come from anyway?'

'Southampton. My parents were killed in the air raids. I was trying to find somewhere to live when your grandfather found me on the road. He took me in, fed me and things just went on from there.'

'Ron says you're clever and should do something with your life.' Finlay paused. 'He also says you've got amazing tits.'

Jenny giggled. 'You're not so innocent as you make out, are you? And that Ron Drew is teaching you too much, too early!' She ran her hands down over her breasts. 'They are pretty good, even if I say so myself.' She thought for a moment. 'Can you keep a secret, Kee?'

'Of course,' Finlay answered, surprised that anyone should ask.

'I'm going to be a solicitor. I've decided, and beautiful tits or not, that's what I intend.' She got up. 'I think we should make some effort to go home now.'

They got back to find the driveway almost blocked with cars. 'That's the doctor's car,' pronounced Jenny, motioning to the large black Rover. 'Somebody must be ill.'

There was a general hubbub in the kitchen. 'Where on earth have you two been?' Niney demanded. 'You've been gone for well over an hour, Jen.'

'She couldn't find me,' said Finlay. 'What's all the fuss about?'

Sitting in the corner was Mr Halliday, the school's deputy head. And above all the commotion was the almost majestic presence of Dr McQuitty. 'I've come to examine you, Keith,' the doctor said. 'Just to see you're all right. The school asked me to do so.'

Janey Grieves's father pushed forward. 'I've come to shake your hand young man. You're a brave lad.' He grabbed Finlay's hand and began pumping it up and down.

'You're a hero, Keith,' Janey exclaimed, standing beside her father. 'Everybody at school thinks you're wonderful.'

Finlay's hand was again seized, this time by a huge burly man. 'I want to thank you for my daughter's life. I'm her father. How can I ever thank you?'

A large woman embraced him strongly, crying, 'Thank you, thank you...' Finlay shook himself free. 'Is she all right?'

'Broken arm,' the father answered. 'She's staying in hospital overnight. I had to come and thank you.'

The doctor rescued him. 'Come into the hall, Keith. I need to examine you,' and guided him towards the door.

Finlay tugged at Jenny's dress, mutely requesting her to come with them. Once outside, he said, 'For Christ's sake! Get rid of them Jenny, I don't want all this...'

'Head back Keith. Look at the ceiling,' the doctor said; a bright light shone in each eye in turn.

'Jenny,' pleaded Finlay.

'Concussion,' announced the doctor, with a smile playing around his lips. 'You require bed-rest young man. I shall tell your gathered fan club that you will not be giving interviews.'

'Thank you Doctor,' Finlay began.

'There is some slight concussion, Miss Vaughne. Nothing to worry about,' the doctor explained. He turned to Finlay. 'I'll get rid of them. I think you're a little tired.'

Once in his room, the day finally caught up with Finlay and he went straight to sleep. Habit, the early-morning light and rain driving against the windows eventually woke him. Finlay lay listening to the house; the clock in the hall rang the quarter hour. He rose, dressed and went down to the kitchen. His grandfather, already up, was surprised to see him.

'Thought you might have liked to sleep on this morning, Kee. Would you like some tea?' the old man said. 'How's the head?'

Finlay gingerly touched the wound. 'Fine Grandad, I'll do some toast, I'm hungry.' He quickly cut some bread and pinned it between the old-fashioned toaster rested on the Aga's hot side. 'Want some toast Grandad?' he asked sleepily.

'No thanks, Kee,' the old man said. 'Too early for me. You want to tell me about yesterday?'

'Not much to tell Grandad. She fell in, I fished her out. They want to make me some kind of hero, which is not for me.'

'I understand. Let's leave it at that then.'

'Are we going to go TT then Grandad?' Finlay asked. 'How much will it cost?'

'Quite a bit. Might even cost us some of the older cows, but we've got to show the way and get the herds up to scratch. If it helps to cut down TB in humans, it's got to be done. Farming will be forced into it eventually. We'll probably be among the first in the county and we must start more improvement by going AI at the same time. We'll go right into it this week and look at the costings.' They discussed the upgrading of the dairy herds as Finlay munched his toast.

'You thinking about school today?' his grandfather asked, almost absently.

'I think not,' Finlay answered, languidly. 'Heard how the war is going?'

'Not too well. We'll catch up with that at breakfast. You ready?' Finlay's grandfather dismissed the subject with some impatience. There was, after all, a farm to run. By breakfast time, however, Korea was forgotten. The river was about to flood and stock had to be moved.

By the following day the river was in full flood and most of the lower part of the estate was under water. There seemed very little work to do and his grandfather was going to be away at another meeting, so Finlay elected to go to school. Janey Grieves was pleased to see him when Brockett arrived to pick him up. 'Are you better now?' she asked, peering intently at the long scab on his head.

'Thank you, yes. Sorry about the other evening, but I was very tired.' Finlay wanted desperately to talk about the normal things of life. 'Did your father have all of his hay in before the river came over?'

'Yes. But my mother's chicken house is probably somewhere off the

Needles by now. It's the highest I've ever known it. Are the sluices wide open?'

'Yes of course. But the water is going around them, over them, as well as through them.'

They chattered on until they reached the station. Brockett bade them farewell, warning that he may have to come and pick them up direct from the school that evening if it continued to rain. The trains would be cancelled.

As they made their way over the bridge to the downside platform, Janey said, 'Please let people be nice to you, Keith. Don't be surly. They're happy you saved her.' As though on cue, there was an outburst of cheering and clapping from the pupils already waiting on the station.

'I'll try Janey, I'll really try, but it's just so bloody embarrassing.'

'My reluctant hero,' she said. The train journey was punctuated variously, by congratulations and questions.

'I'm going to cut assembly,' Finlay said. Janey understood.

Halfway through the morning Finlay was ordered to the headmaster's office. He was confronted by two of the senior staff. Finlay was sure the headmaster was still smarting from his aunt's insult. 'You come from a very strange household, boy,' Dr Forest began. 'Perhaps that's what makes you the strange boy you are.' He waited for an answer. 'Nothing to say?' the headmaster asked caustically.

Finlay forced his mind to go elsewhere. He wondered what Ron was doing at that moment. 'What I've done, Finlay, is submit you for an award for your obvious bravery. It's a national thing, so you'll...'

Finlay didn't let him finish. 'What is it about you people? What is it about "no" that you don't understand? I pulled her out because she was going to drown. Not for some award. I was never in any danger, so bravery doesn't come into it. An award would be wrong. No! I don't want it and I'll never accept it.'

'Well!' exploded the headmaster. 'What an ungrateful wretch you are! Any boy in this school would love...'

'I'm not any boy, Sir!' Again Finlay interrupted the headmaster, angry now.

'Take your principles and get out, Finlay!' he exploded. 'Just who the devil do you think you are?' The headmaster's face was white with rage. There were little runnels of spittle on his chin.

Finlay looked at him calmly and said, 'I'm me, no one else, just me.'

Outside, he found he was shaking. He held his hand out and noted the tremble.

'I hope that's not fear, Finlay,' he said to himself. He leant against the wall, wondering what his next step should be. Going home, would, he thought, seem weak, so he decided to spend the rest of the morning in the library. Over lunch, he was informed by the deputy head that he was to be sent down for a week, 'until he came to his senses'. There was, he felt, some sadness in the voice of the teacher who brought the message. 'The head will be writing to your parents.'

'If you weren't quite such a rebel, Keith, these things wouldn't happen,' the friend sitting next to him observed. Finlay thought the primary decision had been made for him.

'What will your parents say?' the friend asked.

'Jim, my father is in Korea, my mother is in Ceylon. What can they say? Their finding out is going to take weeks. My grandfather will not be put out by it. In fact he'll probably be amused. He has very little time for small-minded people. Certainly I shan't be put out by it.'

Jim laughed and mimicked the last sentence.

'You're so bloody old-fashioned, Keith.'

Finlay's grandfather was amused by what had happened. 'The main preoccupation of the middle classes, Keith, is self promotion. Their confidence is so lacking, they have to trumpet anything they deem successful to the world at large. They could hardly be expected to understand our principles, nor yet the principles of the working classes. They do not have the background, nor the breadth of education.' Finlay thought he understood.

The 'sent down week', as it became known, passed quickly enough. The letter to his mother from his school was not forwarded on to Ceylon. 'No need to worry your mother with such things,' his grandfather said. 'I'll leave it on the side.'

Once back at school, he found the attitude of the teachers changed. He found himself ostracized. Even when he scored a hefty run total at cricket, he wasn't deemed a fit person to speak to. Finlay felt his school career was at an end. He did, he decided, have better things to do. 'I'm not going back to school, Janey,' he announced. 'If I pack up that which I have at home belonging to the school, perhaps you could take it back?'

Grieves laughed. 'Finlay, you can't just say you've finished with school. It doesn't work like that. I know you're having trouble fitting in at the moment. It will pass though.'

'No,' Finlay said. 'I can't be bothered with them. I'll speak to Grandfather when I get home. There's an end to it. Brockett will still take you in the morning, Janey. No need for that to change is there?'

'Do you mind if I join in the discussion? I can explain to your grandfather what has been going on?'

'Of course. Stay to tea, it'll probably be bloody salmon again. Can you bear that?' he asked.

'Just,' she laughed.

Finlay's grandfather listened calmly to the two youngsters, but Finlay could see by the set of his jaw that he was annoyed by what he heard. He lit his pipe and pondered the problem. 'You're probably right, Kee. I'll see about another school, or have you taught at home. I don't think there's any point in you going back to the one you're at.'

'Do you want me to let them know?' asked Janey.

'No, my dear. We'll let them find out. I'll have Forest sacked for this.' Finlay was amazed by his grandfather's outward show of calm. The old man went to the larder and returned with a large middle-cut from a large salmon and carefully wrapped it in muslin, then newspaper. 'Take this to your parents, Janey, with my compliments and thank you for your concern and help. Kee will take you home in the Land-Rover and Brockett will pick you up in the morning as usual.'

As far as Finlay was concerned, that ended the matter. But as Grieves had said, life didn't work like that.

Some three or four weeks later, Finlay was surprised to see a small black Morris car in the stable yard and even more surprised to see a stranger leaving the tack room. Since no one outside of the family was allowed in the yard, Finlay knew this to be trouble. He pushed his mare forward sharply and drove the stranger back into the tack room. The stranger, obviously afraid of horses, remained well back from the door. Finlay shouted loudly for his grandfather. 'Who are you, poking about here? Come to steal something, you bastard?' Finlay shouted. 'Grandad! Auntie Niney!' he yelled.

'Let me out of here,' the man ordered. He came forward waving his arms, trying to frighten the mare backwards. Confused, she laid back her ears and shook her head.

'She'll bite you,' Finlay lied.

The man backed away again. 'I'm the Attendance Officer,' he said.

'That doesn't give you the right to be poking about private property.'

The mare began to paw with a front foot. 'She doesn't like you, Mister. I think she wants to get you. Grandad!' Finlay yelled again. 'Grandad! Where the hell are you?'

To his relief, he heard a vehicle approaching. 'Grandad, for Christ's sake come!' he yelled.

Carl swept into the yard in an old Willys Jeep. 'Vot is going on?' he shouted.

'That bloke in the tack room was trying to steal, Carl' said Finlay.

Carl advanced gingerly towards the tack room but, before he reached it, Ron arrived in his usual flurry of flying gravel. 'You all right boy?' He looked at Finlay. 'Heard you shouting three fields away.'

'Da boy caught a thief in de harness room,' announced Carl.

Ron strode towards the tack room. 'Out the way Carl – I'll have the bastard!'

He briefly disappeared. There was a cry of pain, then he reappeared with the hapless stranger, hauling him along by the ear. 'Well! I'll go to sea in a bucket! If it ain't Fitchy, the truant officer!' He shook him around by the ear. 'Remember me, you fucker? Remember when you hit me round the ear? Rang for a week it did. Well, I'm going to pull yours off!' Ron shook him some more and the man yelled with agony. 'I'll give you come round here thieving, you bastard.'

'I'm not thieving, I came to see about the boy,' the man gasped, obviously in a good deal of pain.

Ron stopped shaking him, the light of inspiration in his eyes. 'Carl, go and find Niney. Tell her Fitch, the truant man, has come to take the boy,' he ordered.

The German looked perplexed. 'But what will she do, Ron?'

'Carl, you want to see a tigress upset? Go and get Niney, I tell you.'

The German shrugged and gunned the Jeep out of the yard, backwards.

Ron let go of Fitch's ear. 'Move and I'll break your legs.' Over his shoulder he said to Finlay, 'Put your mare away, Kee.'

He did as bidden and was still dealing with her when Carl drove back into the yard, Auntie Niney beside him. To Finlay's surprise, she was dressed as though ready for church, which didn't stop her leaving the vehicle before it had properly stopped. 'Kee, where are you?' she shouted.

'Here, Auntie Niney. In the stable.'

'Stay there,' she ordered. She advanced on Fitch. Ron stood to one side.

Niney was six foot tall, in her bare feet, close to eleven stone and very, very strong. The blow she struck Fitch in his stomach would have stopped any good man in his tracks. Fitch sighed and sank to the ground. Finlay winced.

Auntie Niney, his lovely, warm, caring, beautiful aunt had just felled a man of her own size with one blow. Determined and silent, she grabbed a two-grained prong and but for Ron's intervention would have stabbed Fitch there and then.

'Don't stick him on the ground, Niney,' Ron said, struggling to hold her off. 'Let him get up first.'

She let go of the prong and, standing over the gasping Fitch, spat on him. 'You ratshit of a man! You evil bastard!' She spat on him again. 'The Japs didn't get him, so I'm certain sure you won't! This, Carl, is our version of a Nazi.' She spat on him again. 'What did you do in the war, Fitch? I'll tell you what you did. You stayed at home and preyed on women whose husbands were away. I know what you did to Rosie Young.' She kicked him. 'And Pam Munday. Harried their children till you got your own way.' She kicked him again.

'Don't forget Ivy Gandy, Niney,' said Ron helpfully.

She glanced at Ron sharply. 'Ivy Gandy?' she asked. 'That lovely girl? You bastard, you scum!' She kicked Fitch again. 'Give me that prong, Ron Drew,' she spat. 'I'll spill his guts on the yard!'

'You're one lovely woman, Niney Fortune, but I can't let you stick him,' Ron said seriously. 'But how the Hell Jack ever manages you in bed, I'll never know.'

She hung on his arm, trying to recover her breath. 'You big blokes are all the same, Ron Drew. All talk and no do. My little Jack is no talk and all do! I'd be too much woman for you. You'd be worn out in a week. Get this creature up and into the kitchen. The police will be here soon. I got Jack to call them.'

'Police?' queried Ron.

'Yes, police. That's the people you get to deal with thieves.'

He handed Niney the prong and helped the hapless Fitch up. As he rose, to almost upright, she rammed the handle of the fork between his buttocks. 'There you bastard! How do you like having something poked up you that you don't want?'

Finlay and Carl watched Ron and Auntie Niney lead Fitch away. 'I swear the women in this family are all from Wagner,' Carl said.

When the police arrived, Finlay escaped from the house to look at their car. It was large, black with lots of chrome and very, very clean. He was called indoors. 'This is Sergeant Beech, Kee,' his aunt said. 'He wants to ask you what happened today.'

'How fast will your car go, Sergeant?' Finlay asked.

'About a hundred miles an hour,' the sergeant replied.

'Sergeant Beech served on the *Ark Royal* with Ron, so they know each other,' Auntie Niney said evenly, even sweetly.

'What happened this afternoon, Keith?' the sergeant asked.

'I came into the yard and saw this man coming out of the tack-room, so I thought he was a thief. So I held him there until somebody came. He tried to frighten Misty by waving his arms at her. He was afraid really though.' He could see Auntie Niney nodding slightly behind the policeman's back. 'He kept shouting at me... and that's all.'

'No, what happened when Ron went into the tack room?' the sergeant asked gently.

'He wanted to fight with Ron, but Ron just held him.' Niney smiled sweetly at him and sat down.

'He says your auntie punched him in the stomach.'

Finlay went over to his aunt's side. 'Don't be silly! Auntie Niney is a lady. Ladies don't punch people.'

She was sitting demurely in the chair, her white-gloved hands in her lap. Finlay put his arm around her and kissed her cheek.

'Take him out to the car, Fred. We'll sort this out down the station. Mr Fitch, all I can remember when I was a nipper is you twisting my arm till it cracked. This family here fed mine and dozens like it during the war, out of kindness. You're nothing but a bully.' He turned to Niney. 'I'll smooth it over, Madam. You won't be hearing any more about it.'

'Thank you, Sergeant' she answered sweetly. 'You, Mr Fitch, seem to have burnt lots of bridges on your passage through life. Do unto others should always be your maxim.'

The police car was half-way down the drive before they all burst out laughing. Finlay looked at Niney and said, 'Why are you all dressed up Auntie Niney?'

'I had, just this minute, come back from Winchester. Your grandfather asked me to go and see the Education Department.'

'Oh,' replied Finlay glumly. 'Does that mean I'm going back to school?'

'We'll see young man. We'll see.' She turned and went into the house.

Chapter Six

•

On the whole of the estate at Nursling there were but four children. Janey Grieves, if child she still was, two little girls belonging to the head dairyman and Finlay. In truth, he found children of his own age rather irksome. It came as no hardship to Finlay therefore to be taught at home, by a series of teachers drafted in by his grandfather. For company Finlay had Misty, his grandfather's gundogs and Jenny; their company he esteemed in roughly that same order. He hunted, fished and shot in due season, learnt to do most of the practical tasks of agriculture and unconsciously became an accomplished countryman.

A new employee arrived that year on the estate as head gardener. He came with glowing testimonials as to his abilities, but turned out to be an inveterate poacher. His name was Charles Hedges, known to all as 'Charlie'. It wasn't that his gardening skills were lacking, it was just that nothing that flew, ran or swam was safe from him. He caught small finches in nets and sold them to a London dealer. He took salmon from the pools that hitherto had been pronounced barren and practically cleansed the next-door estate of its roe deer population. His only defence – was that: 'I just can't help myself. If I see it, I gotta catch it.'

The matter came to a head one day early in that shooting season. Finlay's grandfather found a brace of pheasants hanging on the back door handle. He assumed them to be a gift. The next-door estate could 'dog off' their pheasants from the Nursling estate. Finlay's grandfather telephoned the next-door's head keeper to thank him and the head keeper told Finlay's grandfather that no such gift had been forthcoming. 'I wonder where they came from?' he innocently enquired from the keeper. Only to be told, that they had undoubtedly come from that estate. 'Poached by that bloody gardener of yours, Hedges!'

Finlay was in the kitchen where the conversation on the telephone had taken place.

'Keith,' his grandfather asked quietly. 'Have you heard anything to the effect that Hedges is a poacher?'

'Oh yes,' Finlay replied artlessly. 'He's really good. Can catch anything.'

'You didn't think to tell me about this? Is he taking fish from the river?'

'Only after they've gone through our stretch. He never takes any from our stretch of the river. Only from Broadlands and above, at the Island.'

Finlay's grandfather smiled. 'So Hedges is a good gardener and a man of principle, is he?' He went to the telephone. 'Niney, is Jack around? Could you ask him to come over then please. Yes… straight away.' He moved the kettle over to the hotplate on the Aga and sighed heavily. 'Go and find Hedges, Keith. Don't tell him what it's about. Just say I need him here at once.'

Finlay went out knowing that finding the gardener was easier said than done. He wandered around the garden calling for him until he eventually forgot his purpose in the garden, distracted by a bird he had not seen before. As he tried to creep up closer, hoping to identify it, he was suddenly aware he was being watched. 'That's a waxwing, Master Keith,' Charlie whispered in his ear. 'Means there's some bad weather on the way.'

'I've never seen one before Charlie… I've been looking for you. Grandad wants you… Didn't you hear me calling?' Finlay found himself irritated that he had not noticed the gardener's approach.

'OK, Master Keith. We can walk back through the walled garden. There's something there I wanted to show you.'

'I think Grandad is going out. We should go straight back, Charlie,' Finlay insisted. He turned on his heel and took the more direct route to the house, annoyed that Hedges had seemingly upset his grandfather. 'You had better take your boots off Charlie, and go in,' Finlay said, kicking off his own footwear. 'A waxwing, you say?'

In the kitchen, his grandfather bade Hedges to sit and join him in a cup of tea.

'Did you leave those pheasants on the door, Charlie?' he asked, handing him a steaming mug of tea.

'Yes Sir, caught them in some rabbit wires I had down in the garden.'

'Are you quite sure about that?' Finlay could see his grandfather was getting annoyed. 'You see, though technically the pheasants on my land belong to me, they came from next door. From our neighbours, and good manners dictate that we do not kill them. Where were the snares laid?'

'In the big shrubbery, Sir,' Hedges answered. '

Take me there, and show me,' Finlay's grandfather ordered. There was an edge to his voice.

'Well Sir, I would Sir…' Hedges was quickly formulating an excuse of why there were no snares in the big shrubbery.

'They were never there, were they Charlie? Only a fool would set snares where his employer's dogs may fall foul of them. You may be many things Charlie Hedges, but I do not believe you to be a fool.'

Jack Terry arrived. 'You wanted me, Boss?' he enquired, taking in a fairly tense situation with a glance.

Finlay's grandfather walked to the larder and picked up the two pheasants. 'Take Charlie and these up to Grass, next door. You, Charlie, will apologize for the pheasants and hand them back, and tell Grass it will not happen again. Because, if it does, Charlie, you'll be looking for another job. Got that? Jack, you come back here, when you've done it, and instruct my grandson on the subject of why poaching is wrong. I should have thought he would have known this naturally, but it seems he doesn't.'

Finlay wished the kitchen floor would open up and swallow him. As Finlay's grandfather left the room, Jack said, 'In the Land-Rover, both of you. Now!'

The journey across the estate passed in silence. Finlay could not understand what he had done that was so very wrong. It seemed a lot of fuss over a couple of pheasants. They found Harry Grass feeding his gundogs. He smiled a welcome to Finlay, but treated Jack with cold formality. 'This bugger has brought your birds back, Harry, and is going to say sorry.'

He shoved Hedges forward and threw the pheasants at him, hard. There was a mumbled apology from Hedges as he proffered the two pheasants.

Grass took two steps forward and waved his huge fist in the gardener's face. 'If I ever catch you on this ground, you'll be sorry. I'll give you a bloody good hiding, before I drag you off to the cop-shop! There's been more than enough trouble between the two families, without you starting it up again.

'Harry,' Jack said, 'Give the boy five minutes of your time and get him to understand why poaching is wrong. Do that for me… and we can shake hands and forget what's gone before.'

Grass smiled, and taking Jack's hand, shook it warmly. 'You go on back Jack, and take this bugger with you, else he'll surely find the difference between the quick and the dead. I'll bring the boy back later. Just let me finish the dogs and I'll take him indoors and get Connie to feed him. I'll put him wise about poachers and gypsies.'

Two hours later, Finlay arrived back. He thanked Harry Grass, knowing he had made a friend.

'Thank your grandfather for me young man, and I shall want to see you shoot before too much longer. I'll fix something for you.' As Finlay walked into the house, he reflected that the day had been quite instructive. But as Charlie Hedges had said himself, he just could not help it.

His mother arrived home two days before Finlay's birthday, on the fifteenth of December. Preparations for the holiday were well under way, courtesy of his aunt and Jenny. There was a large spruce tree in the hall and a party organized for everyone on the estate to come and feast. Coming home to breakfast on his birthday, Finlay was in a state of subdued excitement. He was fairly certain he was going to own his very first gun. His measurements had been taken back in the summer. As his grandfather pulled into the drive, they saw the police car parked outside the front door. 'Probably come to sign the cattle movement book, and have a Christmas drink,' his grandfather said, with failing conviction.

Sergeant Beech met them at the front door. 'Trouble I'm afraid Sir James. We have your gardener in the cells at Totton. He was caught night poaching next door.'

Finlay's grandfather sighed heavily. 'You'd better come in Beech, so as to sort out what has to happen.' Finlay's birthday seemed to be forgotten.

'You'd better have breakfast in the hall, Kee. Jenny will bring it through,' his mother said.

'Let him stay,' his grandfather said, in such a way that nobody was going to argue.

'As you know Sir James, poaching at night is a criminal offence which can carry a term in Winchester, and Hedges is sure to get put away. He occasioned violence to one of the keepers. Gave him a black eye,' Sergeant Beech announced. 'He will come up at the next sitting of the bench in Romsey, but at the moment it's whether or not you wish to bail him out.'

'Of course we'll bail him out!' Kathleen Finlay said. 'He can't stay in the cells over Christmas. What about his wife and children?'

'Kath, will you leave this to me please?' Finlay's grandfather said.

Undeterred by her father's request, Kathleen ploughed on. 'There's no need for any court. You could and should sort it out with next door.'

'I do not feel so inclined. So now, will you please leave this to me?' This time more firmly, and turning to Beech, Finlay's grandfather enquired, 'How much security do you want?'

'In view of the seriousness of the crime, bail has been set at one hundred pounds I'm afraid, Sir James,' Beech said.

'I'll send Jack down with it…' Finlay's grandfather began.

'You'll have to bring it yourself, Sir. You have to sign the bail forms,' Beech said almost as an apology.

'Bugger and damn the man!' Finlay's grandfather exploded. 'It's my grandson's birthday today. I could well do without this. Get the car out Kathleen! You've got the social conscience. Take the money and bring him back here. I want my breakfast.'

Finlay was glad his birthday was not entirely forgotten. Breakfast was eaten in silence, Jenny almost tiptoeing around the kitchen. She touched Finlay's shoulder and kissed him on the cheek. 'Happy birthday, Kee,' she whispered. Not more than an hour had passed, when there was the sound of a car on the gravel outside. Finlay watched his grandfather, to see what he was thinking. Finlay thought he suddenly looked older.

As his mother and Hedges came into the kitchen, Jenny quietly tried to almost scoop up Finlay and move him out of the room. 'Leave him, Jenny,' Finlay's grandfather ordered quietly, and looking at his daughter said, 'Both of you into the hall.' Kathleen Finlay began to protest. 'The hall, Kathleen.' He almost pushed the two women out, and closed the kitchen door after them. 'Hedges, I am sad and disappointed, because you know I'm going to have to give you notice. Not once have I had to do this, since I took on from my father. You're a wonderful gardener. You have a gift which a lot of people would treasure. Why did you have to poach? Surely you were paid enough?'

Hedges looked unhappy. 'Sir, I can't help myself. I don't need the money. You've been more than fair. When do you want that I should go, Sir? Can I stay here over Christmas, please?'

'Of course, but if you are caught poaching again, you'll stay inside. You have until the end of January to find yourself another job. I'll give you a reference, but it will be a truthful one. I cannot, and would not, fault your skills in the garden, but any future employer must be told of your other activities.'

There was the sound of another car approaching.

'Go and see who that is, Kee, and tell them I'm busy. Tell them to come back later,' Finlay's grandfather said, a little impatiently. Glad to be gone, Finlay ran to the front door and jerked it open. Standing in front of him was a tall, slender woman, dressed in a dark-skirted suit. A vision so wonderfully elegant that Finlay was shocked into confusion. She bent over, offering her hand, smiling, drenching him with her sweet-smelling breath and hair. 'Good morning, young man,' she said, as Finlay automatically took the offered hand gently. It was cool. The long slender fingers gently gripped his hand, and the smell of her perfume made his head spin. He found he was staring, his mouth slack.

'I'm sorry, Ma'am,' Finlay said, his throat dry and his knees suddenly weak. 'Grandfather said he's busy, and you've to come back later... I don't think he was...' He couldn't finish.

'I've come to see your Mama. I don't expect Kathleen is too busy, do you? And you have yet to tell me who you are.'

Finlay regained his composure. 'I'm sorry Ma'am. I'm Keith Finlay. You'd better come in.' He looked at the woman. 'Who are you? You aren't one of my aunties are you?'

'I can be if you wish. Will you take my other hand please and take me in.'

They walked hand in hand down the long corridor to the hall.

'You cannot be my auntie. Not without you are one of Ma's sisters, and you are far too beautiful to be one of them,' Finlay said, frankly.

She stopped and looked down at him, laughing. 'Oh yes, you've got your grandfather's charm. God help us all! My name's Edwina, and I live next door.'

Just for a fleeting moment he was going to tell her about the saddleback sow, but something in his mind said he shouldn't. 'Mama, someone to see you,' he said, pushing open the hall door. 'A lady called Edwina.'

The two women faced each other for just a few moments before Kathleen Finlay stepped forward laughing and, at the same time, close to tears.

'I've come to talk about gardeners, Kathy, before my husband and your father have him locked in the Tower, and now that we have at last met, your son and I, I would like to steal him away from you.' She turned to Jenny. 'And you must be Jennifer.' She looked her up and down, showing approval. 'You're a beauty, young woman.' She turned back to Kathleen. 'Something of a shock for you though, Kath. Who would have thought the old dog was up to it still?'

Jenny looked embarrassed and started making to leave the room.

'Don't be silly Jenny,' Edwina said. 'Stay, don't be embarrassed. We are all women. When the busybodies in Romsey told us about you, I laughed myself into tears. You must have been good for James. Christ knows he had it hard enough here through the war. There are plenty of others, with husbands I might add, who would have been keen enough to share his bed. Some of the sort who consider themselves much better than others.' She giggled at her own thoughts, then turned to Jenny and Finlay. 'Come along you two young ones, go and find something useful to do.' She began ushering them to the door. 'Kath and I have some social work to discuss.'

Jenny and Finlay found themselves suddenly in the corridor, the hall door firmly shut against them.

'Well really!' Jenny exploded, stamping her foot. 'Who does that woman think she is? Coming here with her New York clothes and expensive perfume, turning us out of our own home. Patronizing bitch!'

'Who is she then, Jen?' Finlay asked.

'Lady bloody Southby!' Jenny spat. 'Beautiful rich bitch!'

Finlay had never seen Jenny cross before. 'She isn't as beautiful as you, Jen.'

Jenny looked at herself, clad in old woman's Land Army corduroy breeches, a heavy submariner's sweater that had been white until she had tried to dye it black, which hadn't quite worked. She looked at Finlay. 'Kee, I'm a disgrace to look at. I've nothing nice to wear. I haven't had my hair done properly in years…'

'Don't let them put on you Jen! Go back in there and be part of it…' Finlay didn't know how to go on.

Jenny turned on her heel and marched back into the hall. Finlay heard her say, 'This is my home as well you know!' before the door slammed shut.

'Some bloody birthday this is!' Finlay said to himself, as he walked disconsolately through the front door, pulling on his Wellington boots as he went.

'Why so glum, young Finlay? It's your birthday, you should be happy.' A tall man was standing in front of him, smiling down and offering him an obvious present-wrapped parcel.

'You'd better come into the hall, Sir,' Finlay said. 'Grandfather is rather busy at the moment.'

'Season's greetings!' The tall man had followed Finlay in, still carrying the parcel.

Kathleen Finlay rose and went to him, smiling. 'It's been a bloody long war Dickie.'

Finlay went to Jenny sitting in one of the huge armchairs. 'Budge up Jen,' he said, jamming himself in beside her, swinging his legs over hers. She put her arm around him, squeezing him closer.

The tall man came over and gave him the parcel. 'Probably the best berth in the place, Keith. Happy birthday.'

'Thank you, Sir,' Finlay replied. 'This is our Jenny, Grandad's sort of wife.'

'Nicely put, Keith. I'm pleased to meet you Jenny. You helped hold the fort I'm told. Helped keep the place running as best was possible. Well done!' He accepted some rather lukewarm tea. 'I must see James about this poaching nonsense. Where is he?'

'We have dealt with that, darling,' Edwina said. 'In our own way, so there is no need for you to do anything, or worry about it.'

'My dear, it is a fairly serious set of circumstances. One of the keepers was assaulted...' Southby began.

'Oh pish! That's the same keeper who you got off a charge for shooting at somebody. The man's a thug. If he got biffed on the nose, then it's probably something he had coming. I will not be any part of having a man thrown in gaol over a few pheasants. If he is fined, I tell you now, I shall pay it myself.'

She rose, walked to the window and stood gazing out at the valley. One hand cupped her elbow and the other her chin, looking, thought Finlay, as elegant as a garden statue.

'I think Jenny has found the solution. We must find our poacher a job in a town or city, away from temptation.' She turned towards them thinking, her long forefinger tapping her cheek. 'Bournemouth! That awful woman Meason on the Corporation. I shall get her to give Hedges a job. Well done Jenny!'

Finlay could only marvel at the certainty and confidence of the pronouncement.

She walked back to them, passing a languid hand over Finlay's shoulders and hair. 'Do open your present, Keith. You must be dying to know what it is. I know I should be.'

Still trembling from her touch, Finlay broke the wrappings from the parcel. Inside he found a round leather pouch in which, nestled in blue velvet, was a fly reel – a small jewel of engineering by Hardy. Finlay rose from his seat and formally shook Southby's hand. 'Thank you so much, Sir. It really is a beauty.'

'I'm told angling has taken you by the throat, as it does, with most of us. This will be the first of many.' He rose to meet Finlay's grandfather. 'Ah, here is James.' They shook hands.

'Dickie, season's greetings! I'm sorry about this poaching thing.'

'It's sorted out James,' Lady Southby said. Walking towards him, she stood very close and touched the lapel of his jacket. 'We shall find Hedges a job with Bournemouth Corporation. My husband can deal with the police. But enough of this, it's our boy's birthday. You haven't forgotten have you?'

'Do you know, I had!' Finlay's grandfather said. 'I really don't know if I got him anything.' Finlay knew he was teasing. 'I believe I left something on my desk in the study. Go and see what you can find, Kee.'

Needing no second bidding Finlay fled the room, returning triumphant with an obvious gun case. He opened it in silence and sighed contentedly. He quickly snapped the gun together and put it to his shoulder. It was perfect. The oiled stock married with his cheek and smelt deliciously of linseed oil. He stared at the beautiful figuring of the grain and, putting the weapon down carefully on the table, went to his grandfather and hugged him. 'Thank you Grandfather. Thank you, my own gun... My very own gun.' He went back to the weapon and picked it up. Taking it to his mother, he handed it to her. 'Look Ma, a Grant twenty bore. Isn't it beautiful?'

Later that night, Finlay switched on the bedside lamp and looked again at the gun, leaning on the wall next to his bed. He reached out and touched it. It had been a good birthday he reflected. The best yet.

It seemed to Finlay, once his birthday was over, preparations for the Christmas holiday began. The stock were obviously the first concern. Because of the holiday, there would be no work on the massive constructions at the Fawley refinery and the new power station at Marchwood, in the estuary. As a consequence, the huge canteens would be idle and there would not be any of the usual food waste on which some of the pigs were fed. Lorries arrived at the pig unit with drivers who seemed all to shout a lot, loaded with sacks of meal, which smelt like biscuits, all packed in hessian bags. Ron would have no cooking to do. He complained bitterly that the whole thing was unnatural. Christmas would be, it seemed, like an extended Sunday. Only the essentials were done. Animals fed, the dairies milked and everyone was to muck in so the work was finished early and the men could spend time with their families.

Finlay had no idea of what his first job in the Christmas preparations was about. He was to help with 'necking the capons'. The birds had been in the yard since August and fed on a mix of best pig meal, powdered milk and skim from the dairy. They consumed wheelbarrow loads of this porridge and grew huge on it. They moved about slowly in what, Finlay thought, was a stately fashion, rather like tame bustards. Ron had told him it was because they 'had no balls'.

'Ron,' Finlay said one day, 'the cocks in the yard haven't got any balls that I can find. Even the big Light Sussex. I looked and I couldn't see any. He didn't half peck and scratch though, not like these dopey capons.'

Ron laughed until the tears came. 'Their balls are inside, when they got any. These have had a jab so their balls don't grow. That's why they don't crow or fight. They just ponce about, eating and dreaming of what might have been, like a bunch of old queens. Still, they eat well.'

On the due day, Ron produced what he called the necking machine, which reminded Finlay, a little, of a wooden saddle rack. 'Now then nipper,' Ron said, handing him what looked like a small shepherd's crook. 'You catch them gently with this. Don't bruise them. Lay them on their backs here and hold their legs. Old John, when he gets here, will take them from you and hang them up to cool.' He glanced at his watch. 'Come on John, you should have been here ten minutes ago.'

Eventually John turned up, a man crippled by arthritis, with skin wrecked by the wind and rain of too many winters spent ploughing behind horses. 'C'mon John. Old Hilda keep you in bed? You're late.' Ron joked.

'Ah, my old mare is past all that now boy. Can't even play with my pencil properly now. Her hands are torn up with the screws.' He smiled wanly.

'Better get yourself into Southampton John. There's plenty there as would do you a favour for half-a-crown, that ud straighten your back out!'

'Ah, you young 'uns be shagging mad. As ud all be better off like these buggers y'ere,' John said, waving at the capons. 'No balls, no trouble with women.'

'John, you only wants your pencil pulled. These is having their necks pulled. Lets get 'em done, us will be here all bloody day else.'

John, who up till now had ignored Finlay, looked him up and down. 'I can see you're your father's son. Young Kathy didn't go astray for you.'

'Enough of that John!' Ron said sharply. 'Boy's been a bit sheltered, he'll get there though.'

'If he's anything like his grandfather he will, certain sure,' John laughed.

'I said enough of that John! Keep on and I'll straighten your back with my toe up your arse! Now get the hooks on and your strings out.' He turned to Finlay. 'Take no notice of the daft old fucker. Spent the better part of his life looking up a horse's ass. Catch one up then, nipper, and I'll show you what to do.'

Finlay caught a capon with the crook. It didn't struggle and he was surprised how heavy it was as he placed it on the wooden machine.

'Put him so his head hangs there.' Ron adjusted the capon's neck. 'Now hold his legs, and away we go.' A lever was brought sharply down and Finlay felt the bird tremble. It flapped its wings briefly. 'Now, hand it to John and go and catch another,' Ron ordered.

John took the bird, tied its legs and hung it upside down on the gate. They soon got into the routine and it wasn't long before Finlay was catching up the last one.

'That's the bugger we been looking for,' Ron announced. He pulled the lever and the capon gave up its life with a tremble. The whole process had seemed almost medieval to Finlay. Ron lit a cigarette and looked at the rows of birds hanging head down on the gates of the yard. He walked along the rows feeling their breasts and legs. 'Bloody good birds, John,' he announced. 'Want a smoke?' The old man took the offered cigarette and lit it from Ron's. 'Bloody good birds,' Ron said again. The two adults sat smoking for a short time. 'Now then nipper, I'll show you what to do next.'

He took the first dead bird by its head. 'Now feel here and see where its neck's broke and all the blood has run. Take your knife and just nick it. Let the blood run out.' He cut a small slot and coagulated blood spilled out on to the concrete. 'Not too deep, just enough to let it run. Don't get it all over yourself mind, or I shall get in a rattle with your ma.'

By the time Finlay had slit the last throat, there was quite a lot of blood on the yard and half-way up his arms. Ron got a hose and washed it away, holding it over Finlay's hands until they were clean. 'He don't mind about blood then, the boy,' John observed.

'Well if he's going in the Navy, he'd be as well to get used to it,' Ron answered.

'What happens now, Ron?' asked Finlay.

'They have to cool properly and then everybody on the place gets a bird. The left-overs go to the butcher in Romsey.' He turned to John. 'You hang on here. Make sure nothing touches them and I'll go and get the game cart. Kee, I think the old man wanted you to bag up some logs to make sure everyone has enough, so away you go to the wood yard.' He walked to his pick-up truck. 'You'll want this.' He handed Finlay an axe. 'Tell Cyril to teach you how to use it, but if you cut yourself tell him I'll cut his head off his neck.'

It was a good mile to the wood yard, and there was no option but to walk. Finlay reflected that he did not know the people involved very well. Though nominally woodmen, they spent their time fencing, planting trees, felling trees and doing the less skilled tractor work. They seemed reclusive and only showed up once a week on pay day.

Walking along a gravel roadway to the north end of the estate, he was surprised to see a motor-cycle approaching. It stopped some twenty-five yards in front of him and the rider dismounted. He could see it was a police constable. He stood with his arms folded, waiting for Finlay's approach.

'And who are you? Are you the Christmas tree thief? Well I've got you, don't try and get away and put that axe on the ground,' he ordered.

Finlay stood his ground and kept the axe on his shoulder. 'And who are you? And what are you doing here?'

'Put down that axe and give me your name,' the policeman snapped, and made a grab for the axe.

Finlay danced out of his reach. 'It would pay you to keep a civil tongue in your head, and I ask you again what are you doing here?'

'You cheeky young sod…' he began.

Things might have got worse had Jenny not arrived in the Land-Rover.

'What exactly is going on?' she demanded to know.

'I got this feller. I think he's the one who has been taking trees from Broadlands…' He didn't finish.

'You must be Haseham,' Jenny snapped, thoroughly angry now.

'You've heard of me then?' The policeman seemed pleased.

'Certainly. Your reputation as an insufferable oik precedes you. What are you doing here?'

'I'm a police officer. I can go anywhere I like, young lady, in the execution of my duty.' He folded his arms again and planted his feet further apart.

'Under sub-section fourteen of the Trespass Act you are subject to the same laws as anyone and, by your own volition, you have volunteered that you are taking nothing more than a short cut over this land. You will go back the way you came via the public highway. I shall certainly report you to Sergeant Beech as soon as I have taken "this feller", as you chose to call him, to where he is meant to be, which is the wood yard.'

'I have to have some identification…'

Again Jenny cut him short. 'All you need to know, you stupid person, is that you are on private property and the only identification you'll be getting is the index number of this vehicle as I drive it over you, or your motor-cycle, if you do not leave our property.'

Suddenly he was deflated. 'I'm sorry Miss I did not know…'

'People like you, Haseham, know very little and please, do not refer to yourself as an officer. That you'll never be. Now, do you want me to flatten your conveyance?'

He walked quickly to his motor-cycle and started back up the lane. 'Quick Kee, in you get!' Jenny said, as she revved the engine. 'This will be fun.' She quickly caught the motor-cycle up and, keeping the Land-Rover in third gear, placed the front bumper no more than a foot behind the policeman's back wheel. As he tried to accelerate away, they stayed glued to the motor-cycle, until the policeman took a quick left turn into a gateway. They sped past in a welter of flying gravel. They were still laughing when they swept into the wood yard. Two minutes behind, the policeman passed, not looking in their direction.

Cyril was sitting on a bench having his lunch, 'Morning Miss Jenny, morning young man, come to join me for lunch?'

'Ours is in the Land-Rover. Kee, would you like to get it? And bring your axe.' She sat beside Cyril. 'Everything ready for Christmas at home, Cyril?'

'Yes Miss, thank you, good rest before we start the big fencing job.' He pointed to a huge stack of fencing piles. 'That's about a quarter of what we'll need. Is the boss going to buy some in, do you know?'

'Most certainly Cyril. We'll use your beautifully cleft ones for where they show, just to let next door know that we do things properly here.' Finlay felt suddenly very proud of Jenny.

'That new copper was poking about earlier, nasty bit of work he seems,' Cyril volunteered.

'Don't worry, I'm just on my way to Totton to report him to his sergeant.' She laughed as she recounted their altercation, then said seriously, 'I think we'll have to have him moved. We can't possibly have him as a policeman.'

'No Miss, I'm sure we cannot.' Cyril seemed rather overawed by Jenny's confidence.

She got up to leave. 'I'll come and get you Kee, as the light goes.'

As she drove away Cyril said, 'Her's a bloody nice wench that one, Keith. Like a breath of fresh air.'

For the rest of the afternoon Finlay split logs. Cyril showed him to note the way the grain of the wood ran and within the hour, he was fairly competent. Another person arrived to be introduced as Frank and, together, they split, bagged up the logs and loaded them on to a trailer, ready to take around the cottages of the estate workers.

At last it was Christmas Eve. The work was done and Finlay's grandfather was satisfied that everyone was going to be well fed and comfortable. The day had dawned damp and raw with fog that was destined to stay the whole day. Unusually there was a thin but keen easterly wind with it, which drove the cold moisture through Finlay's thick pullover, leaving it heavy and wet, hanging on his shoulders. He shuddered, willing his grandfather to hurry up with his errand of delivering whisky to the last of the tenants. The wind rattled the canvas tilt of the Land-Rover. Finlay cuddled his grandfather's labrador closer, stealing its warmth. The dog, happy with the attention, breathed breath that reaked of long dead and well-rotted rabbit, found earlier, and the smell made Finlay gag.

From behind, somewhere near the house, there was an enormous explosion, followed in quick succession by three more. There was the sound of a very large engine, screaming protest at ever increasing revolutions. A heavy pall of blue smoke made fanciful layers in the fog and was beginning to show above the tree. Finlay's grandfather appeared at the run, scrambling into the Land-Rover, swearing something about women blowing the house up and needing to be locked up for their congenital madness. Bucking violently they took off towards the house and, flying up the back drive, were confronted with a Sherman tank bearing down on them from the opposite direction. Kathleen Finlay was running beside it, shouting unheard directions to whomsoever was driving it. Seeing the Land-Rover, she made frantic arm signals for them to move out of the way. In truth, there was nowhere really to go. Finlay's grandfather crashed the Land-Rover into reverse and, without taking his eyes from the tank, shot back, the consequence of which was the Land-Rover ploughing backwards through the hedge. The tank clattered past, dry metal screaming on dry metal, a haze of hot oil smoke and sparks billowing out behind it, missing the Land-Rover by no more than inches.

Kathleen Finlay arrived, breathless, her face flushed red and spattered with mud. 'Carl. He can't stop it. What are we to do?'

'Keep out of the bloody way, I should think,' Finlay's grandfather snapped. 'Whose madcap, damnfool idea was this?'

Finlay climbed on to the bonnet of the Land-Rover to gain a better view of the receding metal monster. Jumping up and down with sheer glee he shouted, 'He'll be in the river soon... that'll stop it.'

As though to give the lie to his statement, the tank came to an abrupt halt. There was a crash of gears, the engine reached a high-pitched howl as the tank began to reverse back from the river bank. It seemed to be going considerably faster backwards than forwards.

'Oh, my good Christ!' said Finlay's grandfather. 'This cannot be happening.'

The statue of Venus on the lawn, her charms long since obscured by lichen and creeping ivy, was decapitated and crushed beneath the tracks. Travelling at some considerable speed backwards, across what was still euphemistically called 'the lawn', the tank cannoned into one of its rusting fellows, briefly trying to mount it, like a bull elephant. It fell silent; the engine had either smashed itself, or stalled. There was one more loud explosion from the exhaust, a flame flickered briefly.

'Do you suppose Carl's all right, Daddy?' Kathleen Finlay whispered, not wishing to break the sudden and crushing tranquillity.

Janey Grieves arrived on her bicycle. 'Happy Christmas everyone! I've brought you some brandy butter.' She gazed at the devastation and at Carl, who had half-climbed and half-fallen from the tank's turret. 'What *has* been happening?' Finlay began to giggle.

'Butter, not tanks,' said Finlay's grandfather to no one. 'That's what we need. Butter not tanks.'

Ron the pig man arrived. 'You all right up here? Heard the bloody racket over the wireless indoors.' Kathleen Finlay and Janey were leading a badly shaken Carl up to the house. 'Do you know Boss,' Ron remarked, 'that Janey is getting quite a nice bum on her.'

Finlay's grandfather began filling his pipe. 'A little thick in the fetlock Ron, but a man could do worse.' He sucked on his pipe. 'Yes, a man could do worse. Come on up to the house Ron, I need a drink.' He looked at his grandson. 'You'd better bring Janey's bike, Kee.' He ground the Land-Rover out of the hedge slowly. 'Do you know Ron, my daughter is completely mad. Should have had her certified years ago. Saved a lot of trouble.'

'Most probably Boss,' Ron answered. 'The moon affects them badly. Ain't their fault. Just the way they're made.'

Finlay arrived back at the house and was amazed to see his mother, Janey and Jenny fussing over Carl, feeding him whisky and sympathy. His mother was stroking his head, cooing, 'Poor chap, you must have been quite terrified.'

'I want to know what's behind all of this. What possessed you Carl to start messing about with the bloody thing?' Finlay's grandfather asked.

'It was all my idea, Daddy,' Kathleen Finlay admitted. 'I want the lawn back as it was and asked Carl to get one of the biggest machines going. After the holiday I'll have it parked on the main road to Southampton. Then the War Office will listen and move the damn things. They've been there seven years. Do they pay any rent for them? Do they ever intend to do anything about them?'

'No. They don't pay any rent for them, Kathleen. The reason being, they now belong to us. I purchased the whole lot. Matter of fact, I sold one of the pictures in the attic to be able to buy them. The asking price was three thousand pounds. I got the lot for two and a half.' Finlay's grandfather seemed very proud of this. 'I've sold the lot for eight thousand pounds and the scrap firm will begin moving them in March.'

'Can we keep the one Carl mended, Grandad? Finlay asked, excited that perhaps he could at some stage get to grips with it himself. 'Could you get the gun going Carl? That would be fun.'

Carl had drunk too much whisky. 'Vie you vant to have a bloody big gun? I can fix anything…'

'We shall keep the big tank with the bulldozer blade and two of the big lorries for grain carts. The rest are going. We have to fence nine miles of double fence and the bulldozer will make that easier. We're going TT next year,' Finlay's grandfather pronounced suddenly. He turned to his daughter. 'And if you interfere with the running of this place just once more, I'll tan your backside till it's raw!'

'Not before time,' Ron interjected. 'And by Christ! I'd like to see it!'

Kathleen Finlay looked at her father and smiled, 'No you won't

Daddy… because I'm going to have a baby.' There was complete silence.

Ron grabbed a chair. 'You'd better sit down Miss Kathy.'

'I didn't mean now…'

'When?' asked her father. 'Oh Kath, this is wonderful!'

The two other women began to cry and then laugh, alternately. Finlay remained stunned, silent, not knowing what to think. His grandfather and Ron gave some serious attention to the whisky bottle. Carl snored.

'Am I going to have a brother, Ma?' asked Finlay at last.

'Or a sister, Kee. We can't choose you know,' his mother answered. 'Wouldn't you like a sister?'

'Christ no! Not a bloody girl. They pee in their knickers and smell.' Finlay grimaced and wrinkled his nose.

'Well. Let's hope it's a boy then, Kee. We can't have your finer feelings disturbed by piddly drawers, can we?' said his mother.

'I think we shall have a good Christmas,' his grandfather said, ending the conversation. 'Things are moving on again. Ron, get Carl home. Kee, take Janey back in the Land-Rover. It's too dark for her to ride her bike. Is anyone going to church tonight?' Finlay's grandfather suddenly looked tired.

Chapter Seven

•

Finlay walked out of the front door and straight into a biting east wind, so cold it made his teeth ache. He glanced at the sky and noted the clarity of the stars. It was four-thirty in the morning on Christmas Day. He walked to what was an old, open-fronted cart shed, now made into quite a pretty garage for the family vehicles. The Land-Rover seats were icy on his backside, the starter only sluggishly turned the engine over before it caught and jumped into life. He had left his grandfather in the kitchen, finishing his morning tea, to go down to the pig unit to help Ron get finished early. 'I can't get there, without going on the road, Grandad. I'm not old enough to drive on the road.' Finlay thought his grandfather had forgotten.

'You'll be all right. No one's about. Just go steady,' his grandfather said, dismissing his objection.

As he pulled out on to the road, Finlay felt very grown up. Arriving at the pig unit, Ron did not seem outwardly surprised at his getting there alone. 'Grandad said the skimmed milk will be down about six this morning, Ron. What do you want me to do?' he asked.

'You do the sows and young 'uns' beds, nipper. I'll get the feeding in the big houses done. Burt and Joe will be about to help clean out shortly.'

Finlay felt pleased. To be trusted to go into the farrowing quarters with sows that could get quite uppity with someone unknowing was, he felt, quite a step up. He worked quickly through his task, shaking and adding to the adults' bedding before doing the piglets' sleeping areas. The heat lamps made the straw smell the same as it did coming over the walkers of the combine harvesters in the summer. It glistened warmly and smelt good. Finlay thought he liked pigs better than any animals, other than dogs. They had no side to them.

When Ron arrived, Finlay said, 'That gilt didn't eat all of her food Ron, and she was walking about with mouthfuls of straw. Is she going to pig today? Her milk isn't down yet.'

'You about got this pig job off, young 'un.' Ron walked to the pen where the gilt was. 'You're right, she'll pig sometime today. Well done boy!'

Finlay glowed with pride. 'Should we stay with her?'

'No, she'll be all right for a few hours. We'll leave her to make her nest. I'll come back down later to keep an eye on her. Here comes the skim.' He nodded towards the lights coming towards them. By six-thirty, everything was done. 'Better get back nipper, it's starting to get a bit light. You don't want to get caught driving on the road. That new copper is a proper bastard. I 'spect he and I will fall out before long. You get off nipper. I'll see you later when me and the missus come round for a drink.'

When Finlay got back to the house, Jenny was the only one up. 'Happy Christmas, Jen.' Finlay kissed her on the cheek.

She hugged him back, then wrinkled her nose. 'Pigs!' she exclaimed. 'What, do you do cuddle every one of them? Want some tea?'

'Please Jen,' he answered. 'Now Ma is going to have a baby we must be careful about hygiene. Make sure nothing from the stock can affect her. Better wash hands in the downstairs lavatory, not in the kitchen sink.'

She smiled her approval. 'How do you feel about a brother or sister?'

'OK I suppose. Would be happiest with a brother though. Don't suppose it will make much difference. Another couple of years and I'll be at Dartmouth.'

'Doesn't sound long does it?' she sighed. 'What will I do when you're gone? I'll be losing my white knight.'

'Not ever Jen, not ever. You're like my big sister.' He got up from the table and kissed her lips. She tasted of toothpaste and Finlay's skin tingled. He shook himself. 'Blimey! Somebody just walked over my grave.'

She held him at arm's length and gazed into his eyes. 'No my darling Keith. You have suddenly grown up. Come, drink your tea. I'll cook you breakfast while you get cleaned up. We'll have a house full shortly.'

He got up to leave the room, but Jenny caught his arm. She hugged him closely. 'Lots of girls will kiss you, Keith. And somebody will walk over your grave. Happy Christmas my love.' She pushed him from the room gently. 'Come and look at the hall. We've put the decorations up and it looks like something from an old picture.'

'Who did this?' Finlay exclaimed, amazed at the transformation. Every inch of the walls had been covered with spruce branches, holly and ivy. Above both huge fireplaces, the walls were covered with the bare branches of larch with long rows of cones. The room smelt of the fir woods, with the almost bitter, earthy smell of the fresh-cut holly.

'That's amazing!' Finlay exclaimed again. 'When did you do it?

Where did this bloody great table come from?' The table ran practically the whole length of the room.

'It's a surprise for your grandfather. Do you recognize it from anywhere?' Jen asked, obviously pleased with his reaction.

He thought for a moment. 'The picture on the top landing. It's the old picture on the top landing.'

'It was Niney's idea. We put it together while you were out. You've no idea the game we had hiding all of the branches. The table we think is the same one in the picture. Niney found it in the roof when first you came home. I remember her saying then that it should come down for Christmas.'

'Where is Auntie Niney now? Is she still here?' Finlay asked.

'No, she's gone home to get Jack's breakfast and change. She'll be back later before anybody arrives. You know how she likes to arrange everything.'

'Are people going to be eating? Where's the food...' Finlay began.

'Enough of your questions. Go get changed, clean and don't be long. We shall want the breakfast things cleared away in good time.'

By the time Finlay came back downstairs his grandfather was halfway through his breakfast. 'Happy Christmas Kee. Are the pigs OK?' he asked.

'Yes, Grandfather. A gilt may pig today. Have you seen the hall? It's smashing, isn't it?' He took his seat opposite his grandfather. 'Blimey Jen, that's the first time I've seen you in a dress. You look a real glamour pants.'

Jenny was dressed in a velvet dress of a dark green colour, her hair braided across her crown. She curtsied to him. 'More glamorous than Edwina Southby do you think? Her, who you were making sheep's eyes at the other day,' she asked tartly.

'Jen, you gotta be the most beautiful woman in the world...Well, next to Auntie Niney,' he said, with an artlessness.

His grandfather tried to stifle a chuckle.

'What a little charmer you are!' Jenny said, putting his breakfast down before him. 'You really know how to put somebody in their place. Get your breakfast and try not to get it down yourself.'

There was the sound of a vehicle arriving and Jenny went to the window. 'The lady in question has just arrived, you'll be very glad to hear, Prince Charming. I suppose Jack had to have the car to bring her here. Such a glamorous creature couldn't possible arrive in a Land-Rover.' They could hear Niney berating Jack about something. Snatches of conversation floated through the window. 'Stop moaning about your tie. Do get a move on.'

High heels were heard in the passageway before Niney swept into the kitchen. 'Happy Christmas everyone!' She kissed Finlay's grandfather on the forehead in passing and went to Finlay. She ruffled his hair with both hands. 'Don't slick your hair down with water like that, darling. Makes you look like the Duke of Windsor!' She kissed him heavily on both cheeks. 'Do you like my new dress, Kee?' It was dark blue, which accentuated her height, and her hair was piled up to give her even more loftiness.

'Of course he likes your new dress Niney. After all, you are the most beautiful woman in the world, according to him. I run a poor second,' Jenny said huffily.

'You do look lovely, my dear, but out of the mouths, as they say… Jack, where are you?' Niney shouted at the open door. 'I made him put a tie on and he's been fussing ever since. Jack, for Christ's sake! Get in here and wish everyone a happy Christmas.'

He came into the kitchen, sat down and helped himself to some toast. 'Happy Christmas everyone,' Jack said glumly.

'Bloody well look happy, Jack!' Niney said sharply. 'And leave your tie alone.' She moved to his side and leant over, straightening it. Jack put down his knife, placing his hand up Niney's dress and slapped obvious bare flesh, winking at Finlay's grandfather while doing so.

'Get from there Jack Terry!' she said sharply, moving away. She looked at Jenny. 'Honestly, he saw me in suspenders this morning and it's turned his head.' Finlay's grandfather started to laugh.

'What are suspenders, Auntie Niney?' Finlay asked brightly.

Niney lifted her skirt, showing her stocking tops and, with her free hand, snapped a piece of elastic. 'Those are suspenders, darling, and they'll turn your mind soon enough, mark my words,' Niney answered. For the life of him, Finlay could not see why they should.

'Where did you get those drawers, Niney?' Jenny asked. 'Very glam.'

'Marks, my dear. First time on today.' She was about to show them off again, but Finlay's grandfather was laughing so much now, he started to hiccough.

'Where's, Kath James…' Niney began.

'Upstairs being sick,' volunteered Finlay. 'She's all right though. Something to do with the baby.'

Niney looked at Finlay's grandfather. 'You'll have to give her what she fancies, now James…' She didn't finish.

'Twas 'aving that, that got her like it,' Jack said, through a mouthful of toast.

Finlay's grandfather rushed to the sink, coughing and spluttering. 'I'm out of here!' he gasped.

'Niney, you're a bugger.'

Niney smiled sweetly. 'Right you men, I want you out of the kitchen in five minutes. I'll go and see Kath.'

After she had gone, Finlay's grandfather said to Jack, 'That is one hell of a woman Jack. If I've said that once, I've said it a thousand times.'

'She would be, being the most beautiful woman in the world,' Jenny said. 'This frump had better wash the breakfast things.' She gave Finlay a playful dig in the ribs.

'I know, let's go down to the hatch pool,' Finlay said, getting up. 'We can see how many kelts are coming down.'

'That's the best words I've heard this morning, Keith. When times and things get you down, go and look at the river.'

It was ten minutes to nine when they got back from the river. There was a red van parked by the front door, with its back doors open. 'Who's that Grandad? On Christmas Day,' asked Finlay surprised.

'The food and drink, Kee,' his grandfather answered. 'Having a do like today is a bit much for our women folk to deal with. They could, but it would be an enormous job for them.' Both could hear Niney giving someone the benefit of her sharp tongue.

'She's on topform this morning, Boss, and no mistake,' Jack said quietly.

They crept into the kitchen to find Kathleen Finlay and Jenny helpless with laughter. Kathleen Finlay motioned them to be quiet. From the hall they could hear Niney letting someone know what she thought about his decorative table-laying skills. 'Not like that… that is not what I want… sit there and don't move…' There was the sound of crockery being shifted around. 'That's how I want it. Have you got that? Then get on and do it!'

They heard her approaching towards the kitchen. Jenny quickly wiped her eyes. No one said a word. 'Ah Jack. When these people have gone, go and put a match to the fires.' She went to the cupboard and pulled out a bottle of gin, poured some in a draining breakfast cup, added water from the tap and drank it in one pass. She hiccoughed once, muttered an imprecation to Heaven, smiled and said, 'I think it's ready for inspection.' She hiccoughed again, poured some more gin and swallowed it neat. Kathleen Finlay looked ready to be sick again. Niney rinsed the cup under the tap. 'Come along then. Let's see if it passes muster.'

They trooped into the hall. The men doing the setting out stood back and looked for their reaction. 'That's truly beautiful Niney. You've done us proud,' Finlay's grandfather said. He addressed the four men. 'Thank you very much. You've done a grand job. Can we offer you some refreshment?' They all said not. It was obvious they wanted to be gone, quite as quickly as possible. Finlay's grandfather handed them an envelope. 'Something for your trouble, I'm sure you earned it.' This was said through a smile. The men knew what he meant, and left. The table was laden with small snacks, biscuits, chocolates, Dundee cake, fruit and a centrepiece of a large whole cheese. The sideboard was stacked with bottles of spirit, sherry and some wines. The large window-sill was stacked with bottled beer. Jack lit both fires and watched to see that they caught properly.

'Thank you, Niney,' Finlay's grandfather said warmly. 'Just like the old days isn't it?'

Four hundred years of a traditional Christmas had been brought to a halt by the Kaiser's war. Then, the house had been requisitioned for a hospital. Despite the severe agricultural depression of the thirties, the tradition was maintained. With Hitler's war, the house was again requisitioned, as an officers' billet, and not returned to the family until 1947. When Finlay's grandfather was given back possession and he saw the state it had been left in, with no prospect of compensation, he wrote to Winston Churchill. He told him in no uncertain terms that he would burn the house to the ground before he would allow it to be requisitioned again. In due time, a reply came, with a cheque from the Ministry of Works for one hundred pounds, and a note from Churchill stating he was sure that one hundred pounds would more than cover the costs of any damage to the house. Incandescent with rage, Finlay's grandfather returned the cheque with a note stating he would as lief clean his backside with the cheque as pay it into the bank. It was an insult, a slap in the face for doing his patriotic duty. There was no reply. For seven years there had been no Christmas proper. Now, 1952 saw the tradition return.

By eleven in the morning, the hall was full of happy people enjoying a break from the government's austerity drive. Finlay's grandfather had insisted that Charlie Hedges, his wife and children attend, no doubt to inform him of what plans had been made for his future and to show that there was no animosity. Finlay saw his grandfather speaking with him, his hand on his shoulder as a mark of respect, even friendship.

When Carl arrived, there was a spontaneous cheer. His escapade with the Sherman was known around the village and Romsey, and the destruction was evident for all to see. When Auntie Niney and Jack arrived, bringing with them Joe the Postman, everyone cheered again and gently made a great fuss of him. Joe was delighted and soon settled into a chair where Niney could keep an eye on him. The biggest cheer was reserved for Ron Drew and his wife Wyn. Ron was probably the most popular man on the place, a mainstay. Always there for everyone, able to turn his hand to anything and take charge in a crisis. He and Wyn made their greetings known, then Ron abandoned his wife and attended the whisky bottle.

When it was judged that everyone who was coming had arrived, Finlay's grandfather called for quiet. Fairly unsteady and with his hair fallen over his face, he motioned his daughter and Jenny to him, one on either side. He thanked everyone for their efforts over the year. Things, he thought, had gone roughly to plan and because of this he had felt able to resurrect the traditional Christmas party. He was certainly not going to talk shop, only to announce that because of increased office work he was going to have to create a position of farm foreman. There was sudden quiet. An innovation, to be sure. The position would be taken up by Ron, who would, from thenceforward, be responsible for the day-to-day work. Nobody, it seemed, was more surprised than Ron. He was told not to worry. He would still have his beloved pigs, but such things as collecting the swill and cleaning out would be done by somebody else. Finlay's grandfather asked Ron to come to him and say something. The crowd parted to let him through, some patting him on the back by way of congratulation. In passing, he took his wife's hand and led her forward and, standing by the large open fire, he began: 'I can only say bugger me! But thank you, Boss, for this trust. I know I can make it work for all of us, and your first job after the holidays, Carl, will be to do the brakes on my old truck. If anybody else starts driving her, they may forget how long it takes to stop her when she's loaded. I wish you, Boss, a very happy Christmas and you Miss Kathy, and a special happy Christmas to your Miss Jenny, Boss. She's a proper lady, who keeps things going when you're away Kathy, and looks after the second pig man, my mate Keith.'

There was silence. He had mentioned the unmentionable. The status of Jenny Vaughne. One of the dairymen said loudly, 'Yes, we all agree with that. We're proud of Miss Jenny. You're a good lady and I'll crack the head of anyone who says differently.' The room erupted with shouts and cheers. Finlay looked at Auntie Niney, saw her smiling and nodding her head. Finlay knew that Jenny's place had become somehow official. He was pleased. When he went over to her and took her hand, he thought she was going to cry.

When the cheers died down, one of the tractor drivers shouted, 'How about a tune, Miss Kathy, and a bit of a warble from you, Niney?' Somebody else suggested, ''Ark the 'erald angels! That's a good bit of a song fer today.' The music room was unlocked and the doors flung wide. ''Ow about Jerusalem. That's a good 'un,' someone suggested. 'Nah, us don't want a be singing bliddy ol' hymns, not at Christmas for God's sake. We altar sing sommat good an' 'appy. Wos that one you sings Niney, that makes every bugger cry? Thas a song, that one!' Frank, an ancient carter, never held church and vicar in anything other than contempt.

There was a general call for Niney to sing. She pretended she didn't really want to, but was shoved forward. Finlay had never heard her sing before. As she sang, 'I Vow to Thee My Country', the ancient carter's request, Finlay was stunned by the lovely richness of her voice. When she had finished, handkerchiefs and tear-soaked cuffs were the order of the day. Jack sat watching her, beaming proudly at his beautiful wife. After the clapping had died down, Kathleen Finlay said, 'And this is specially for Joe.' She played one of Chopin's waltzes. He beamed and moved his hands in time with the music and when it ended, people went to him and shook his hand and told him he was and would get better.

There followed a toast to the new Queen and the National Anthem was sung without the piano. Niney led the singing, and sung with a conviction that showed she meant every word.

By one o'clock the last of the revellers had left, swaying down the drive in various states of inebriation. All declared it had been a good do, but now it was lunch time and the capons, slow cooking over the morning, would be ready to eat. A quiet descended on the house, disturbed only by Jack's resonant snores as he slumbered in a chair. 'Let's all sit quietly and have a cup of tea,' Kathleen Finlay suggested. All was Jenny and Finlay; his grandfather had gone off somewhere in the Land-Rover. Niney had taken Joe to the Days', where he was invited to lunch and from there she would go to her home, let the dogs out for a pee, before returning to the house while Jack slumbered on.

'It's good how it all works, isn't it?' stated Finlay.

'How what all works? What is running around your head now?' his mother answered.

'Well, how everyone looks after the other one. Like the Days taking Joe for his lunch and Cyril cutting the logs down small for Granny Fortune, because she's not very strong. He stacked them all indoors, so she didn't have to go out in the cold. Why didn't Janey and her parents come to the party, by the way, and where were the Brocketts?'

'Questions, questions, questions!' Jenny said, handing him some tea. 'The Brocketts are having their holiday now and go to Somerset to be with the rest of their family.' She thought for a moment. 'Why didn't the Grieveses come, Kathy?'

'They're Methodist, Jenny,' Kathleen Finlay answered. 'No strong drink, Hell Fire and the sins of fornication. All that sort of thing. Alice closes the curtains if a bull is put to serving a cow in the yard.'

'What's fornication, Mama?' asked Finlay. Jenny got up and busied herself at the sink.

'Not today, Kee,' his mother said, with forced gaiety. 'We've got the hall to tidy up… and Jenny, you're closer to his age. Maybe you could help out here.'

Jenny didn't turn to face them when she said, 'Let this cup pass from me…'

Finlay knew the biblical quotation. 'OK, I'll ask Ron.' Both women said, 'No!' almost together, and began to laugh. 'No, it's not something that Ron should be asked by you,' Jenny said quickly. 'You'll get entirely the wrong idea.' Finlay knew them to be hiding something, which made him even more determined to get an answer, but it could wait.

There was the sound of a bicycle being flung against the outside wall and running footsteps. 'Can I come in?' It was Janey Grieves. She arrived in the kitchen. 'Happy Christmas everyone. Hope you don't mind me just turning up, but we have some very dull company at home and I've been to two services already this morning.' She paused. 'It is so boring! I came here to cheer myself up.'

'And you're more than welcome, Janey,' Kathleen Finlay said. 'Would you like some tea and cake?'

'Mmm, please. Did your party go well? Has everyone gone? I missed all the fun. Did you enjoy it, Kee? What a lovely dress, Jenny. Could you show me how to do my hair like yours?' The words kept tumbling out of her mouth. Kathleen Finlay glanced at Jenny, alarmed. She got up, went around the table and put her arm around Janey. 'Janey. Stop my love. Whatever is the matter? Get her a little whisky, Jen,' she said quietly.

Janey started to sob. 'Everyone has fun but me. Christmas has become a nightmare. I'm sick of Hell Fire and Damnation!'

'And no fornication!' Finlay interjected, helpfully.

'Oh, shut up you!' she sobbed. 'I know the whole village laughs at us...'

Jenny reappeared with glass in hand. 'Drink this Janey. Down in one!' she ordered.

Janey swallowed a large mouthful and began to choke. She drew in a deep breath and hiccoughed loudly. Her eyes looked glassy. Unable to speak, she handed the glass to Jenny.

'Another?' Jenny enquired.

Janey nodded her head vigorously. 'Just a small one then, else you'll be drunk.'

This time, Janey swallowed the whisky slowly and didn't cough. 'Lumme, that makes you giddy. My arms have gone wobbly!'

They heard the Armstrong arrive. Niney was singing something about a lady who lived in a caravan called a gypsy. Finlay had heard it on the wireless. Niney walked into the kitchen, still dressed as she was earlier, but this time carrying her shoes and wearing Wellingtons. She kicked off the Wellingtons and put them by the Aga. 'Bloody soaked!' she announced. 'Hello Janey. What are you doing here?' She looked more closely. 'Are you puggled?'

Janey nodded slowly and seriously. 'I think I may be drunk, Mrs Terry. Do you think that's awful?'

'Never felt awful to me...' Niney began.

'What's fornication, Auntie?' Finlay asked.

'Best thing in the world, Kee darling, nothing better! When I was abroad, I couldn't wait to get back home and get down to some serious fornicating.'

'Whey!' Kathleen Finlay said, looking shocked. 'It's hardly the thing...'

'Oh nonsense Kath! When I got back, I got Jack into bed and kept him there for the day,' she sighed. 'But if you look at him today, you would never think he had a good "fornikay" in him.' She hooted with laughter at her own joke. 'What's brought this up? We must get the hall tidied and the vegetables done for tonight.' She leant elegantly around the doorway. 'Jack darling,' she called sweetly, 'time to wake up.' Getting no response, she called louder the second time. 'Jack! Get up and get out into the air, you drunken bugger. Get your head cleared or there will be no fornication for you this night!' She turned to the other women. 'Then the suspenders and new drawers will have been wasted.' Kathleen Finlay and Jenny laughed. Janey Grieves was not sure whether she should or not.

'You two young ones, take the milk churn down and hang it on the bridge.' Kathleen Finlay got up and handed them a miniature churn. 'The dairyman will take it down when he goes to milk. Don't let Janey fall in the river, she looks a bit shaky.'

Finlay took the churn and helped Janey up from her chair. She staggered slightly. 'Perhaps I'd better stay,' she slurred, and sat down heavily again.

'Yes, on second thoughts, you had better stay. I think we could have a woman's talk, the four of us,' Kathleen Finlay said, giving Niney a significant look.

Finlay went outside. The east wind was blowing harder, working itself into half a gale. He shivered and set off to deliver the milk churn. The rippling surface of the river looked cold and the ripple prevented him from seeing beneath the surface with any clarity. For just a moment the sun shone through a passing hole in the cloud, enough to let him see a small group of dace, hanging on the current. The whole world seemed to be asleep. There was such quiet, just the sound of the water lapping around the bridge's parapets. A robin sang a short snatch of song from behind him somewhere, thin and reedy. A disturbance in the shallow water at the far end of the bridge caught his eye and he moved across, crouched low. In the slack water, lying on its side, was a large kelt, dead and fungus-covered, being eaten by two huge eels. He tried to prise a stone from the frozen earth to throw on top of the eels, but it wouldn't budge. Determined now, he cut a stick from a hazel, leant down and moved the salmon into the current, sending it seaward. The despised eels were left behind as the river caught the kelt and took it spinning away. Finlay's dislike of eels was occasioned by being bitten by one, some eight pounds of writhing muscle, the previous August during eel-catching time. It had laid hold of his thumb, bitten it to the bone, and refused to let go. Uncle Jack cut off the eel's head, while Finlay had shouted long and loud with the pain. Finlay looked at the scar and remembered clearly the night it had happened. The river had yielded up almost a ton of eels, some of them huge creatures that had perhaps lingered in the old drowner streams of the water meadows for years. Others had come from the chalk waters of the river, having grown quickly huge on trout and their ova. They were despatched to London by lorry in great heaving boxes of slime which stank and shuddered from the movement within. Finlay was told the people of London considered them a great delicacy to eat. He could never imagine that he would ever be hungry enough to follow their lead. Jack had told him of two boys, refugees from the Blitz, who had spent the better part of the war catching and eating eels and they had begged some black peas from a local pigeon fancier to boil up with them. They were, according to Jack, 'rum buggers', stealing anything that was not 'nailed down bloody tight' and the village was glad to see the back of them.

Finlay wandered back towards the house, the wind now seriously blowing. He turned and walked backwards into it occasionally, giving his freezing front some respite. By the time he had reached the house, he was chilled to the bone. The Land-Rover was in the yard, so Grandfather must be back. He went through the back door of the house, unusually, not wishing to open the front and allowing the east wind the vicious joy of chilling the legs of the women in the kitchen. They were not all in the kitchen, however. As he passed the open door of the drawing room, he heard Auntie Niney talking to his mother:

'...the child is repressed, I know, but you cannot interfere, Kath. It's a great pity. I've seen it so many times before. As soon as they leave home they just run wild, and get into trouble...' That was all he heard, but he knew they were speaking of Janey.

Jenny and Janey were still in the kitchen. Janey was happier now, chattering brightly about university. 'Christ that's bloody cold!' announced Finlay. Grabbing a chair, he put his feet on it and sat on the front of the Aga. 'You all right now Janey?'

'She will be if you stay quiet!' Jenny answered for her. She came to him and slapped his leg. 'Get off. You sit there and you'll give yourself piles.'

'Well we've nine miles to double fence, so a few more piles might help,' Finlay joked. 'Where's Grandfather?'

'Well, my dear, he's spent the better part of the time he's been gone in the Three Tuns, so where do you think he is?' She sounded disappointed more than cross.

'He's a bit puggled then. Never mind, he'll soon wake up again,' Finlay said nonchalantly. 'You still a bit that way Janey?'

Janey turned and answered very seriously, 'Yes, I am a bit. I'm staying to tea so that it wears off. Jenny and I have been talking... very seriously...'

'Janey... you sound like some old judge,' Finlay laughed. '"Very seriously",' he mimicked. 'Maybe we should try Janey on something else. Give her some vodka. Perhaps if the mists and glens of Scotland make her serious, the icy blast of the steppes may cheer her up. Always makes Mama dance about.'

'Shut up you little snot!' Jenny snapped. 'You can be such an aggravating little shit. Go and do something useful.' She aimed a half-serious blow at Finlay's head. 'And I've told you before. Get off that bloody stove and get from underfoot!'

Niney arrived and summed up the situation in a second. 'Darling, the fires are getting low. Would you go and put some logs on for me?'

Finlay jumped down from his warm seat on the Aga. 'Yes. Of course, Auntie Niney.'

As he left the room he heard Niney say, 'Let that be a lesson to you girls. It's no good bossing them. Make them feel useful and men are very biddable. A bit like dogs.' He heard her laugh. 'You'll find out though, they're only of any real use in bed,' and then he was out of earshot. As he reached the hall he heard a gale of laughter coming from the kitchen. It was good, he thought. Janey was laughing loudest.

He could not see that the fires had burnt down so very low. He stacked some logs on, mixing the ash, apple and oak as he had been taught. The ash logs caught quickly and were sending bright yellow flames upwards. The oak and apple hissed happily, driving out the moisture within themselves before they caught and burnt with smaller flames of greens, reds and blues, the air redolent suddenly of the woods in summer. He stayed kneeling on the large flagstoned hearth, watching the darting blue-green flames of the apple wood until his face burnt. He went to the sofa and flopped down, his hands behind his head, thinking of the day, now losing its light to the night outside. He was asleep in seconds.

———

'Come along sleepy head, wake up.' Finlay woke slowly to his mother's voice. 'It's tea time. Go and brush your hair and wash your face. Have you had a good sleep?' she asked.

With his brain still clogged with sleep, Finlay sat up and swung his feet down on to the floor. He smiled at his mother. 'I was tired I think…' he began.

'The cold I expect. You were really calling the cows home, snoring louder than your father does.' She urged him upright. 'Come along. We're waiting to have tea, and Janey has got to go back home.'

With some reluctance he rose, stretched and headed for the stairs. 'Won't be long,' he said. Perfunctory would best describe his ablutions. The cold water on his face made him gasp and the hairbrush pulled painfully. 'Sod it,' he said, throwing the brush on his bed. 'That's enough of that.' He clattered back down the stairs into the hall.

His grandfather was standing by the fireside, whisky glass in hand. 'The gilt had nine pigs. Five boars and four gilts, one of which…' he paused for effect, 'had sixteen tits!'

'Wow!' Finlay said, delighted. 'She'll be a good one to keep. Sixteen tits. Is she marked properly? Does her white come right down?' Finlay knew the markings on pedigree pigs were very important and the white shoulders of Saddlebacks had to be perfect for shows and the herdbook.

His grandfather smiled. 'You'll be able to see her in the morning, but don't go in her pen without Ron's there. He said she was a bit possessive of her babes.'

'It's Christmas Day you two. Can we talk about something other than tits on female piglets?' Kathleen Finlay said it smiling, with mock severity.

Finlay ignored her. 'It would be good to win at the Royal Counties with a maiden gilt. She'll be seven months when the show comes around again.'

'Don't rush your fences, Kee,' his grandfather said. 'She's only hours old.'

'Now that's enough,' Finlay's mother said. 'Sit at the table, and no more pigs!'

The others arrived in the hall. Niney carried, with some ceremony, a large iced cake. 'Happy Christmas everyone! This is a joint effort. I made the cake, Kath iced it and Jenny did the artistic bit on the top.'

Finlay and his grandfather clapped the cake's arrival as it was placed on the table looking, Finlay thought, like a snowy crown. Finlay's mother cut the cake, handing his grandfather and Jack a large wedge each. For the others, the ration was somewhat smaller. Niney offered the two men a wedge of cheese with it and Finlay, not to be outdone, took some cheese as well. The mix of flavours was new to him.

Niney took a piece of cheese. 'This would have been about a week's ration, Kath.' She waved the cheese around, showing everyone. 'So now I am going to eat a week's ration. Just for the sake of doing so.'

'It was a bugger,' Jack said, taking another wedge.

Janey Grieves, who had been quiet till then, asked, 'What are you all doing tomorrow?'

'Well, we'll finish early again. Catch some grayling for breakfast, pop across to Lyndhurst to the Meet, come home, have a cold lunch and then shoot some ducks. What will you be doing Janey? You're welcome to join us, if you wish.'

'Thank you, but I expect my parents have something planned. If they haven't, perhaps I could come to the Meet. Would you mind?' She seemed a little doleful.

'Is your father shooting anywhere tomorrow? If he isn't, he could join us for the evening flight,' Finlay's grandfather suggested.

'Mother doesn't like Father shooting over Christmas. Says it's disrespectful to Jesus,' Janey answered sadly. 'I know he'd love to.'

'In that case I'll take you home and invite him myself,' Finlay's grandfather said.

'What about Jesus?' Janey began.

'Bugger Jesus!' Finlay's mother said, with some venom. 'All he ever seemed to do was make people miserable.'

'Kath!' Finlay's grandfather said sharply.

'It's OK,' Janey said. 'I like coming here because you're all happy and a bit mad.' She looked at Finlay. 'Do you believe in Jesus, Keith?'

'Never really thought too much about it, Janey,' he answered, through a mouthful of cake. 'The old vicar is a good enough sort I suppose, but to have to be so bloody well-behaved and perfect all the time and be nice to people you can't stand, that must be trying.'

'Well said Kee!' Niney interrupted. 'Who for Christ's sake would want to be pleasant to Miss Satchel, bloody scandal-mongering old maid. He sucks up to her all the time, probably hoping she'll leave her money to the church.'

'Well,' began Jack ponderously. They waited to see what he was going to say. 'Well,' he said again. They still waited. 'Well, I can tell you this, the vicar cheats at whist and tells lies and that minister from your lot, Janey, is banging somebody who ain't his wife. I found him under the willows by the boards last August, when I was coming up to set the eel traps. There they was lying down together in the grass...' He paused for effect. 'He said as how they was listening for corncrakes, but you don't have to take your knickers off for that, and hers was on the grass, longside her and afore they saw me, her frock was all up around her bum!'

Kathleen Finlay, Jenny and Janey sat with their mouths open with amazement. Niney was laughing so much that cake crumbs were flying from her mouth over the table. She leant her head back and through her laughter said, 'Jack, you bugger, you didn't tell me about this!'

'Didn't want to... 'twas one of they ladies from the Women's Institute. That one as does the White Elephant stall at the fête...' He didn't finish.

'Naomi Phillips!' Niney screamed through her laughter. She hugged Finlay's mother. 'Who would have thought that? Naomi Phillips...'

'She was at home this morning,' Janey said, looking still a little shocked. 'Telling everyone how standards have fallen. Honestly!'

'I think I should take you home, Janey,' Finlay's grandfather said. 'This conversation is not something that you should be, perhaps, listening to.' He turned to face the other three women, still giggling. 'Behave yourselves. This is no way to behave in front of these young ones!' This made them laugh even more.

Janey said, 'Please let me stay a little longer.' She could contain herself no longer and started to giggle.

'I give up!' said Finlay's grandfather. 'Join me in a drink Jack. Shall we go through into the kitchen and let these women dissect poor Mrs Phillips? Kee, you'd better come as well.' As he got to the doorway, he turned and said, 'Niney Fortune,' using Niney's maiden name, 'I'm going to speak to your mother about you. She did, I know, bring you up to behave properly!'

'Yes James. I had a very repressed childhood,' she said, with mock sadness. 'Wasn't till Jack came along I knew what life was about.'

The kitchen was filled with the smell of gently roasting meat and the large table was covered with vegetables, ready prepared in pots and dishes of water. Looking at them Finlay's grandfather said, 'Our stay here won't be lasting long, that beef smells good.' He poured some whisky into two breakfast cups. 'Try that, Jack, tastes better in china.' The wind whistled around the windows and an ivy branch tapped gently, but insistently, on one of them, as though the ivy itself was asking for board, such was the cold. Swallowing his whisky, Finlay's grandfather said, 'I think I should get young Janey home. Beginning to sound as though it may get rough tonight.' He drained the cup in his hand.

'Fancy having to live with all that pious stuff,' Jack said sadly. 'Her will run wild, for certain sure when she leaves home, always the bloody same.'

'She may not, Jack. She's a sensible girl. She must see through all that nonsense her mother spouts. We'll keep an eye on her.' He went to gather up Janey, leaving Jack and Finlay in the warm delicious-smelling kitchen.

'We are going to catch some grayling in the morning, Uncle Jack?' Finlay asked. 'Are you coming with us?'

'No youngster, got the dogs to do and Granny Fortune is with us all day. She should be with us all the time but her's a bit too independent for her own good. When she and your Auntie Niney get together, it's like two bloody fighting cocks squaring up to each other. I shall get her over and then go to the Meet, just to keep out of the way.'

'They are a bit like each other,' Finlay observed.

They heard the car returning and Finlay's grandfather came into the kitchen, stamping his feet with the cold. He made a straight line for the Aga. 'That's bloody cold Jack. Ice on the puddles, holding the weight of the car.' He paused and suddenly looked somewhat exasperated. 'That poor bloody girl! The Grieveses had a house full and the bloody lot of them were hymn singing. Poor little bugger been here all day and I don't suppose they even missed her.'

'Honest, Boss,' Jack said. 'Why these buggers have to bring all this religion into Christmas, I'm buggered if I know. 'Tweren't ever a bloody Christian thing. Was a proper thing, the turning of the year an' all that. They fuck-up Whitsun as well, the psalm-singing bastards.'

Sitting with his grandfather and Jack in the kitchen, Finlay could tell by the conversation they were anxious for the day to be over, the normal routines that governed their lives disrupted. Boxing Day was for such men the best day of Christmas, when outside they met with like-minded friends to pursue the sport of their choice.

There was just one more ritual to partake in.

The women folk of the household soon chased them from the kitchen and between them produced the Christmas dinner in short order. Finlay could not know the prior planning that allowed this. From wonderful smells to a shout of, 'Can someone come and carve', seemed no time at all. Part of the long table was set, the food brought in on oval platters, the remains of their capon and ribs of beef came in as well, to be carved by whoever wanted second helpings. Roast potatoes and parsnips, their insides fluffy white and delicious, sprouts made sweet by the prevailing frosts, wild damson jelly and herb stuffing and above this, marbled beef slow-cooked, still full of blood and the white meat of the capon. It seemed wholly right to Finlay, as he ate the breast meat, that having been part of its slaughter, he should eat it. That was the way of things.

By nine o'clock, Christmas Day for Finlay was over. He was packed off to bed. There had been no giving or receiving of presents. It was not something the family did. Individual birthdays could be lavish, but Christmas was the feast before the beginning of winter proper. Something that was remembered through the devastating, chilling cold of January, thought softly of in the rain of February when the mud was almost knee-deep. The river ran turbid green, cleansing itself of the mud washings from the riverside fields. By March, with longer days and drying winds, Christmas was forgotten and the annual rebirth of spring filled men's thoughts.

Chapter Eight

•

The peal of the small alarm clock woke Finlay. Slowly, he reached out to switch it off and the cold made the hairs on his arms spring up. He lay for a few moments listening to the funereal dirge of the wind around the house and knew it to be cold. He counted, 'One, two, three', aloud and, on 'three', sprang from the bed, out of his bedroom, down the corridor and into the airing cupboard, the warmest place in the house. His clothes, laid on a shelf, were dry and warm. He dressed quickly. A vest went over the top of something called a liberty bodice, which his mother insisted he wear. He pulled his trousers over his pyjama bottoms, knowing he would get 'in a rattle' for doing it, but he was determined to stay warm. Today was Boxing Day and there were things to do.

His grandfather was already up, drinking his first cup of tea. 'Are you sure you have enough clothes on Kee? It's damn cold outside.'

Finlay pointed to his pyjama bottoms, hanging out of his waist band. 'I'll be all right Grandad.' He poured himself some tea. The kitchen was warm, the windows running with condensation.

'I'll drop you at the pigs. Get Ron to bring you back. I need the Land-Rover.'

They drank their tea in silence.

'Did you enjoy your day yesterday, Kee?' his grandfather asked, absently.

'Yes thanks Grandad, did you? Today will be better though. I can't wait to see the new litter.'

His grandfather smiled. 'Don't go getting too fond of them. They all have to go at some time, even the best of them,' he warned.

They went out into the inky blackness of the night. The dry wind stung Finlay's ears. He kicked at the soil in a flower bed and found it hard as rock. 'The stars aren't showing Grandad,' he said, following the light of his grandfather's torch.

'There's husbandry in heaven,' his grandfather answered. 'Probably means it's going to snow.'

The Land-Rover's front end was draped in a heavy tarpaulin and two hurricane lamps had been placed underneath to keep the frost out. 'Put the lamps under the car, Kee,' his grandfather ordered. 'Make sure they are nice and stable.' The Land-Rover's doors were stiff on the hinges and complained screechingly at being opened. The engine whirred quickly into life, the sump oil warmed by the oil lamps, thinner than the previous morning. Along the driveway, the lights picked out a fox loping towards the river. It stopped briefly and watched them, its eyes glowing red in the lights, before trotting away in an unhurried canter. 'He'll be hungry, Kee,' his grandfather observed. 'Looked in good condition though.' Finlay didn't answer, his face buried deep in a woollen scarf, a draught from up under the dashboard cutting into his legs. As they drove through the village, here and there, downstairs lights were showing, testament to another very early start for the stockmen.

At the pig unit all was quiet and dark. 'Ron's not here yet,' his grandfather stated. 'Don't go into the farrowing pens till he gets here mind.'

'I'll get on and feed the Danish house first,' Finlay said, getting down and into the wind. 'Ron will be here shortly. We're just a bit early. See you for breakfast.'

If his grandfather answered at all, he didn't hear it above the rattle of the canvas tilt on the vehicle. The Land-Rover lights lit his way to the Danish house. He struggled with the door in the wind, but once inside, he heard the Land-Rover pull away. The moment he flicked on the lights the pigs began to protest their hunger as the strip lights down through the house hummed and clicked into life. The noise grew. The house, warmed by the heat from the pigs, smelled mealy and good and the noise from one hundred and sixty hungry porkers was deafening. Feeding was accomplished from a large wooden box on four rubber wheels, holding about half a tonne of meal. From this, the required number of bucketfuls was spread out along the trough at the front of the pen. The number required was a chalk figure on a slate above the pen, which varied as to the age and size of the pigs. The wooden box, at first, was about as much as Finlay's slight frame could move, but as he progressed down the centre aisle, it got lighter as the meal diminished. Quiet descended on the house as the pigs in each pen were fed. Just the occasional squeal of protest when one pig perhaps thought another was getting his share. Pulling the meal box back to its original starting place, the boy emptied a large paper sack of what looked like thick biscuits into a wheelbarrow. They smelt heavily of fish. Pushing this down through the centre aisle, he threw four or five double handfuls into each pen and the pigs, already replete with food, picked them from the concrete floor in a leisurely fashion and chewed them like epicures.

As he fed each pen, Finlay cast his eyes over the pigs moving about, looking for signs of illness, lameness or fighting. Seeing nothing amiss, he refilled the large meal box, covering himself with dust in the process. His hair was now white with floury meal. The activity of feeding had raised the temperature of the house by some five degrees, Finlay noted, on the thermometer. He switched the ventilation system up slightly, the big fans whirled faster and as he walked down the centre aisle again, a cursory check of each pen made, he was pleased to see that in some pens the pigs were already lying down in ranks like sardines, settling down to sleep. He went back and switched the fans back down to minimum, the air was soon cleaned of dust and quiet descended on the house. This routine never varied. The pigs knew what to expect and got what they expected, so they were content and grew steadily. There were, he had seen, three pens almost up to weight. Very soon they would go for slaughter. On these days, Finlay had to steel himself against what he thought and saw as the ultimate act of betrayal.

He found Ron in the farrowing house washing out a wheelbarrow over a drain, a sure sign that he too had finished his work. The house was quiet and warm, like a hospital Finlay thought.

'Thanks for doing the fatteners nipper,' Ron said. 'I know who you want to see,' he smiled. They walked together down the length of the house. 'Only us girl,' Ron said quietly to the gilt as she raised her head sharply. 'She thinks she's the only one as ever had babies at the moment, bit protective she is. No bad thing that though. She'll be a good mother.' They leaned over the rail of the creep. Under the heat lamp lay a circle of piglets, full of their mother's milk and sound asleep. Ron bent over, lifting one of them up and handed it to Finlay. 'There you are. A proper little princess, isn't she?'

The tiny pig nestled into the front of Finlay's pullover. Finlay stroked the tiny creature and studied her colouring. 'She's perfect Ron, just bloody perfect!' He pushed his nose into the piglet's side and smelt the sweet smell of her. 'Oh you little beauty,' he breathed. 'What shall we call her, Ron?'

'Well, you give her a name. Better be a good one though,' he warned. 'Can't have sommat daft going in the herd-book.'

Finlay thought for a few moments. 'I think we should call her Starwort.'

'That ud be about as good a name as any pig had, Keith!' He turned and picked up a large steel spoon from a shelf, the spoon he mixed some of his secret medicines with. Pretending it was a microphone, he said, 'And the winner of the maiden gilt class is Nutshalynge Starwort!' He took the tiny pig from Finlay and kissed its nose. 'Yes pretty one, we shall see your name in lights if we've got anything to do with it.' He placed her gently back under the heat lamp with the rest of the litter. The piglet had not woken up from the time she was picked up.

When Ron dropped him back at the house, it was a little after six-thirty. The wind had dropped a little but the cold was still biting. Finlay dropped some of his outside clothes, which reeked of pig, in the passageway and went into the kitchen. As yet there was no one up and he left his Wellingtons in the same heap and went to the gun room. He was half-way through threading a line through the rings of his fly rod when Jenny appeared still in her nightclothes, with a blanket wrapped around her shoulders. 'You are surely not going fishing in this?' she exclaimed. 'You'll get chilled to the marrow. Let me get you something to eat at least,' she added, seeing at once that her warning about the cold had fallen on deaf ears.

'That's all right Jen, you go back to bed, I shan't be long. I'll just catch one, and then come back. You should see the little pig, Jen. She's really beautiful...' He didn't finish.

'Pigs. Pigs. Pigs,' she sighed. 'I shall make you some tea. You've plenty of time, it won't be light for at least another hour.'

He finished putting his fishing tackle together and went back to the kitchen, laying the rod along the skirting of the passageway, along with his bag and landing net.

'I've switched the heating on,' Jenny said, as he went into the kitchen. 'The pipes will get frozen if we get much of this weather.' Finlay could hear water bubbling and coursing through the ancient system. There was the faintest whiff of burning diesel. 'There's your tea and some toast and dripping. That'll stop the wind cutting right through you.'

'Thanks Jen,' Finlay said and hugged her.

'Don't shower me with pig food!' she exclaimed, pushing him back. 'Your hair is thick with it. I don't know how you manage it.'

'You can't moan about Ron, Jen,' Finlay said, triumphantly. 'Not after what he said yesterday. He really likes you, you know.'

'It was sweet of him to say what he did, and I'm glad that I am appreciated. If this pig thing is going on, you will have to have some overalls.' Just for a moment Finlay thought he was going to cry.

'Is it light out there yet?' Finlay asked, as she was near the window looking out.

'No, not yet. Go and clean your mare out. By the time you've done that it will be… don't stuff her full of food though… she's doing nothing, so she won't need it. I'm going to have a wash. Don't stay fishing too long Kee. You really will get cold and make yourself ill.'

He stayed a little longer in the house and then went outside again, having re-dressed himself. The mare heard him coming and whinnied, but as he entered her box she backed away. 'What is it with you women?' he said to the mare, tartly. 'Little smell of pigs and you don't want to know me! I'll come and see you when I'm clean.'

He finished the stable and was down by the river just as it was getting light. Sliding down the bank into the shallows, he faced upstream. 'Now, if I was a fish, where would I be on such a bloody morning?' he said, aloud to himself. His first cast was snatched by the wind and carried across the river. He brought it back, waited for a lull and dropped his nymph in a deep back eddy that looked as black as tar in the half-light. The line came quickly back towards him. He cast again and got the distance he wanted. The floating line shot forward with a jerk and he tightened into what felt like a heavy fish. Unable to keep the line in any way tight, the fish shot back downstream, passing his Wellington by no more than a foot and finishing up twenty yards downstream in the pool below him. By the way it powered back and across the current, he knew he had a goodish grayling on. He tried to gain some line but the heavy thumping through the rod told him to ease off. The fish shot across the current and into the heaviest of the stream against the far bank. For a second, Finlay thought it was gone then it was in the slack water of the pool. None of this he could see because of the light. The fish kicked again and tried to reach the heavy water. Finlay guided it away, into the streamy shallows below him. It spun briefly in the current and then came easily to the net. Finlay was shaking with both cold and excitement as he saw the fish properly, for the first time.

'You gotta be more than two pounds!' he said, looking at the silver fish still kicking about in the net. On the bank he killed the fish with his priest. It felt warm almost in his hands. His feet were painfully cold though. He went straight home as quickly as he could. His feet, aching with the cold, made him limp as though crippled. The kitchen was warm but empty. He laid the fish on the draining board and studied it. The huge dorsal fin was like a piece of iridescent jewellery. The greens, blues and purples showed different depths of colour at different angles. He washed his hands under the tap and, moving to the stove, was surprised to see two large, dried field mushrooms still with the thread on them, that held them together during the drying process.

He laughed when Jenny came back downstairs. 'I might not have caught anything!' he said, pointing at the mushrooms.

'Well, there seemed no doubt in your mind, so why should there have been in mine?' She went to look at the fish. 'That's a beauty. We must weigh it and can I have some, if I cook it? I love grayling.'

'Course you can,' Finlay said. 'Do you want me to gut it for you?'

'No, no, no. Leave it for your grandfather to see. It really is in lovely condition. Where did you catch it?' she asked.

'Bottom right side of the hatch pool. Didn't half fight. If we had not need of it for breakfast, I would have put him back,' Finlay said, suddenly sorry that he had killed the fish.

'Listen!' Jenny said suddenly, her head cocked, one-sided.

Finlay listened, baffled. 'What am I listening for?' he asked.

'The wind has died,' she said, still listening.

After days of hearing the wind moaning around the eaves and roof, the sudden quiet was profound. They both went outside, as though they did not wholly believe the change. The sky was leaden and the cloud seemed too low, and despite the lack of wind the air seemed colder. The leaves on some of the shrubs were brown around their edges, burnt by the cold. The grass on the small patch in a circle on the driveway was the same colour, as though suffering from summer drought. Jenny shivered and hugged herself. 'I'm going in,' she announced. 'You'd better get cleaned up, Kee. Your grandfather will be back shortly for breakfast and you know how grumpy he can be if he's kept waiting.'

Keith Finlay loved water. He loved the river, ever moving, bright and clear here, dark and green there. The noise it made running over shallows, crashing through the hatches and, most of all, the gentle glide of it. The sea had left him awestruck. The wonderful smell of it. The waves coming from far out to smash themselves into sunlit pieces on the beach. Finlay loved water, except when it was hot, steaming and smelling of soap in a bath. It was one thing to get wet all over in summer and let the sun dry him comfortably or sink down into the water and see the dace dart away from his approaching bare feet. Or take it in his mouth, to shoot it out like a fountain tasting the earthy chalk. Bath water, not the same stuff.

The bathroom was icy cold. Drips of condensation on the window frames had formed into tiny icicles and the panes of glass were frosted with fern-like patterns. He waited fully clothed until the bath was filled, wondering whether he could get away with not bathing at all. He looked at himself in the mirror and thought probably not. He had left the door open, hoping to capture some of the warmth of the central heating in other parts of the house, but the icicles remained shining on the window frames. The steam drifted against the glass and made even more intricate patterns. He swore softly to himself and undressed quickly, shuddering with the cold, cursed again and climbed into the water. He lay down with only his face showing above the surface and let the water warm him. Fitfully, he scrubbed at himself with the soap, rubbing it briefly in his hair and working it into a lather. He ducked beneath the water again, shaking his head to rid it of the soap. With sudden determination, he pulled out the plug, jumped from the bath and fled to the airing cupboard, not quick enough to avoid the icy cold and the hairs on his arms jumped to attention. 'When I'm old enough to do as I please,' he said aloud, 'I'm not going to bathe from September till May. If it's not warm enough to swim in the river, then it's not warm enough to have a bath.'

Fish in any shape or form was not something that Finlay enjoyed eating. Salmon, which seemed to be very much part of the household's summer diet, he had had enough of. Trout, Finlay declared, was tasteless and not worth the fiddle with the bones. Grayling was acceptable sometimes. As he approached the kitchen the smell of fish frying filled the air. Suddenly he wished he was having a normal breakfast of eggs and bacon. His grandfather was very complimentary about the fish. There was two pounds, six ounces of fish, in chunks frying in butter, with mushrooms. Finlay dredged his share with pepper to give it some taste at least and when he had finished, he said, 'Thanks Jenny, that was smashing!'

Both his grandfather and Jenny burst out laughing. 'Your proper breakfast is in the oven. Be honest, you didn't enjoy that one bit,' Jenny said.

'Well, I know everyone else likes fish and I wanted Grandfather to have some.' He went to the oven and got his breakfast. 'Thanks Jenny,' he said, abashed that he had been caught out.

'Thank you for the fish, Kee.' His grandfather smiled. 'I'm very flattered that you suffered the cold to catch it for me and flattered that you sat and ate what you call pap, for my sake.'

'Where's Ma?' Finlay asked, suddenly realizing she was not present.

'Being sick again, Kee,' his grandfather said. 'It's called morning sickness. Nothing to worry about.'

'There speaks the voice of sympathy,' Jenny said, somewhat sharply. 'Nothing to worry about…'

'Well it isn't, is it?' Finlay's grandfather answered, somewhat surprised by Jenny's tone.

'Can I come in?' There was a shout from the front door. It was Janey and she walked into the kitchen. 'It was so quiet, I thought there wasn't anybody here. I'm frozen!'

'Well, Niney's not here today, so it would be quiet. I didn't hear your bicycle. Did you walk?' Finlay's grandfather asked.

'Yes. The front tyre is ripped and there's nowhere open today,' she said, struggling to undo the ties on her mittens with her teeth, but her mouth was too cold and stiff to be able to do it.

Finlay rose. 'Come here,' he ordered, and undid the ties. 'Why didn't you telephone? I'd have come up and fetched you. Are you coming with us to Lyndhurst?'

'If you don't mind.' She addressed this at Finlay's grandfather. 'Mother said I could.' She paused. 'We have another house full today you see, and it's so jolly boring.'

Finlay's grandfather snorted crossly. 'Eating your father out of house and home no doubt!'

He was about to go on, but Jenny stopped him. 'James, that's not our business,' she said softly.

'You're quite right, Jenny.' Turning to Janey, he said, 'I'm sorry I said that.'

'Well, you're quite right, Sir James. It is extravagant with money so scarce. One of our calves made just one pound in Salisbury last month. Didn't even pay the commission and transport, and now Daddy is worried about the cost of fencing. He says that if you go TT he'll have to. If we don't, our butter job will come to an end and that's all that keeps us going at the moment.'

'I'll go see him tomorrow then,' Finlay's grandfather said. 'The fencing will be our concern. Don't you say anything Janey, else he will think we have been discussing his business, and that would never do.' He reflected for a moment. 'We are all of us going to have to modernize and move forward. This TT thing is going to happen whether we like it or not. And anyway, I couldn't live with the thought that our milk, from our cows, was in any way responsible for anyone getting TB.' He looked at his watch. 'Come along Jack, you're late. We'll all be late for the Meet. There won't be any hunting, but we shall have to put in an appearance and pay up. Get dressed Kee, Jack will be here shortly. Are you sure you don't want to come my dear?' he asked Jenny.

'No James, I'll stay. Far too cold for me,' she answered.

They heard the strange whistle of the Armstrong's pre-selector gear-box, before the car swept into the yard. 'Come along you two young ones. Out you go, else we'll spend another ten minutes getting Jack out of here.' Finlay's grandfather ushered them out.

Boxing Day meets are more about the social cohesion of rural England than about hunting. Today was no exception. With the ground too hard for any serious movement across it on horseback, the hunt still met, just to show off hounds and for the mounted to show their horses. The journey to Lyndhurst was by way of Ower and Cadnam, Jack electing to go the 'forest way' rather than over the estuary and through Totton and Ashurst. The forest looked bleak, the oaks dark and som-bre in their outline against the leaden sky. What ponies they saw were picking at the sparse keep available to them, their coats long and thick against the cold.

'They'll have to bring them in or feed them surely, Jack, if this goes on. The buggers look as poor as crows,' said Finlay's grandfather. 'Bordering on cruelty else.'

'They've been here for hundreds of years like this. They always sur-vive and if you feed them, you'll weaken the process of natural selec-tion,' Janey announced emphatically from the rear of the car.

'Still looks like starvation to me. If I let our stock get down like that, the RSPCA would be around double quick time,' Finlay's grandfa-ther said, ending, as far as he was concerned, the argument.

They turned left into the High Street and threaded their way down the hill towards the Bench, a small knoll with fenced-around yew trees growing at its summit. There were several hundred people there standing around in groups, drinking and conversing happily. About forty mounted followers, their horses blanketed against the cold, moved up and down through the press, keeping their mounts moving and waiting, no doubt, for official word as to whether any actual hunt-ing was going to take place.

Not coming from a hunting family, Finlay did not know many people. The land at home was criss-crossed with streams, many too wide for a horse to jump and Nursling was not officially in any hunt's country. The New Forest beagles came twice a year by invitation and a high old time was had on both days. There was always a good hare to hunt and his grandfather pushed the boat out as far as hospitality went. Everybody seemed to go home 'part puggled' and soaked. Streams that fox hunters would not face, the beagle followers waded, sometimes chest deep.

Finlay looked around for Janey but saw her in deep conversation with a young man. He decided to leave her to it and began walking back to where the car was parked. 'I say... I say!' a voice behind him shouted. A girl clattered up on a dark bay gelding. 'It's young Finlay isn't it? I wondered if you were gong to be here. I hardly recognized you in smart clothes. You're always so scruffy.'

Finlay had no idea who she was. He thought perhaps he should have done because he had to admit she was strikingly pretty. 'I'm sorry,' he said. 'I have no idea who you are.'

'Well, I think that's almost rude of you. At least pretend, until my name comes to you.' She seemed offended.

She looked about sixteen, with light brown hair and deep brown eyes. 'Nope, sorry Miss, I'm certain we've never met. Maybe you're mixing me up with somebody else?' Inspiration came to him. 'You're not some relative I've met at a family function. You couldn't really expect me to remember.'

'My father,' she snapped, 'fishes on your river. I was introduced to you about a year and a half ago, by your water-keeper. Obviously I made no sort of impression.'

'Eighteen months ago I wasn't much interested in girls and I was probably busy with something else. Look, I don't want to be rude but perhaps if you tell me who you are it would help.'

'Well really,' she exploded. She turned her horse and trotted away.

Finlay sighed. 'Who could fathom the human female,' he thought. 'Come to that, who bloody wants to.' The last statement was aloud.

Janey had disappeared with the young man. Grandfather was nowhere in sight and Uncle Jack was holding court with about twenty other men, from which group there came raucous laughter at regular intervals. Finlay started back towards the car.

'Wait... wait Finlay!' It was the girl on the gelding again. She pulled up beside him and sprang off the horse. 'I'm sorry Finlay. Could we start again, do you think? I'm Caroline Keighley. I live in Little Testwood and I would like to get to know you better.' She shook hands formally. 'How does that sound?'

Finlay laughed. 'Now I remember you. Eighteen months ago you were like a stick insect with a mouthful of wire, helping your teeth grow straight. You've sort of plumped up a bit since then!'

'Plumped up! What am I... a pillow now?' She seemed offended again.

'Don't start getting on your high horse. You wanted this conversation. You wanted to get to know me. I can't think why. I seem to offend you every ten seconds. For Christ's sake, stop being so spiky,' he said in a matter-of-fact way, not crossly.

'Oh dear, this is going badly. I've so wanted to talk to you. Do you get lonely and bored with no one young to talk to? I do. And I see you doing interesting things, driving your Land-Rover and the tractors, fishing. I saw you last spring doing something in the field below our grounds. You were there all day, up and down, up and down. I was meant to be revising but I wanted to wave to you. You never looked my way and then a blonde lady brought you something to eat.'

'Look,' said Finlay, 'I've got to go. I expect Grandfather is looking for me. Can I box your horse for you?'

'Yes please. He can be an absolute devil sometimes,' she answered.

Finlay led the horse up the ramp and tied his head. 'Do you want his saddle off? I don't think you'll be going hunting.' Without waiting for a reply, he unsaddled the horse and rearranged its rug. 'There you are, should be all right now,' he said.

Finlay went to leave the box but she stopped him, holding his arm. 'Do you want to feel my breasts?' she asked, seeming a little breathless.

'Why? Is something wrong with them?' Finlay asked, not catching the girl's intensity. 'You should, perhaps, see the vet or a doctor.'

She looked perplexed.

'Look,' said Finlay. 'I've got to go!'

'Can I come over and see you, I'm on holiday...'

'Of course, if you wish. You had better telephone first in case I'm busy.' If it sounded ungracious, he had meant it to. She was very pretty, Finlay thought, walking away, but... He could not think what he wanted to think. The right thoughts did not seem to come. He suddenly felt disturbed.

Back at the car Finlay's grandfather and Uncle Jack were waiting.

'Well, here's one of them,' his grandfather said. 'Have you seen Janey?'

'Yes, she was with some young bloke earlier, so I left her to it. Do you want me to go and find her?' he asked. He could tell his grandfather was a little testy.

'No, we'll have you both missing again. Where did you see her last?' He started the car.

'You puggled, Uncle Jack?' Finlay asked. 'Up that way, Grandfather.' He pointed to the left.

As the car backed out they saw Janey approaching at the gallop. She dived into the car. 'Sorry. Have I kept you waiting?'

'Only a little. Keith seemed to get hung up as well,' Finlay's grandfather said. 'Who was that pretty little thing Kee? Did I see you leading her horse for her?' There was mischief in his voice.

'Somebody called Caroline Keighley. Said her pa came fishing at home, wants to get to know me because she's nobody to talk to…'

Janey didn't let him finish. 'Her for goodness' sake! She's man-mad. Goes to Young Farmers.'

'The world needs a few man-mad women, young Janey,' Jack said solemnly from the front seat. 'Helps things along a bit.'

'I really can't see why!' Janey said. 'Causes nothing but problems as far as I can see.'

Jack turned to face her. 'When you goes to that university place, Janey, perhaps you'll get to see a bit further.' Jack turned back from her and stared solidly out from the windscreen. Finlay was somewhat perplexed by all of this. He knew it was all due to this 'fornication' thing, and decided the best person to clear all this confusion in his mind was Ron. He would tell him what he needed to know. As the car sped homeward, Finlay thought about Caroline. He thought especially about her tight jodhpurs and how he could see the line of her knickers through them.

Once home, Jenny had carved some cold meat and made a huge mountain of fluffy mashed potatoes. There were pickles, chutney and salad cream in a shop-bought bottle.

'Where's Ma, Jenny?' Finlay asked. He remembered he had not seen her that day.

'Getting ready to go back East, Kee. She had a lot of packing to do,' Jenny said cautiously.

Finlay flung down his fork with real anger. 'For Christ's sake, I didn't know she wasn't staying…'

'Your mother wants to be with your father, Kee,' she said gently.

'And who the bloody hell is he, for Christ's sake! I don't even know the bugger!' He slammed out of the room.

In the kitchen they heard the Land-Rover start and leave the yard in a flurry of flying gravel.

'The sparks will fly when they do meet, Jenny. Oh yes, the sparks will properly fly,' Finlay's grandfather sighed. 'Did nobody think to tell Keith his mother was leaving him again?'

'I suppose not,' Jenny answered quietly.

'That's what I call rank stupidity.' He covered the mashed potato with salad cream and looked thoughtfully at the cupboard opposite him.

About an hour later Finlay returned, calmer now, but still burning with resentment. He walked into the kitchen and, ignoring his mother, said to his grandfather with forced brightness, 'Are we gong to shoot some ducks Grandad? I saw loads coming in to the ponds.'

'Yes. Perhaps we'd better try your new gun.' He glanced at his daughter who affected not to notice her son's slight. They put the guns in the Land-Rover and two leather bags of cartridges. Calling the dogs, his grandfather climbed into the passenger seat. The dogs were excited and leaned over them, whining.

'About your mother going Kee. You should understand...'

Finlay cut him short. 'What's the best way to come at them Grandad? I think we should walk down the feeder stream from the bridge and space ourselves under the alders there. They'll come in downwind for us.'

Realizing his grandson's mood, the old man agreed. 'We've put enough tail barley down to feed every duck in Hampshire, Kee...'

They crept from the vehicle and, staying below the bank of the river, approached the ponds where the ducks would be feeding. 'We'll drive them up and get in place, Grandad, sounds as though there are plenty there.'

When the two men showed themselves, the air was suddenly filled with flying ducks. The sound of their wings was like a train going by. 'Good God!' Finlay's grandfather said. 'There must be more than a thousand of them!' But something was wrong. These ducks were normally unapproachable. They flew around in a tight circle and, ignoring the humans, landed again. Two ducks passed within inches of Finlay's head, landing no more than ten feet in front of him.

'The poor buggers are starving, Keith. So hungry, they're not afraid of us.' It was obvious he was right.

Finlay unloaded his gun and slipped it back in its sleeve. 'Let's leave them to feed in peace Grandad. It wouldn't be right to shoot any.' Finlay bent to pick up his cartridge bag, glancing at his grandfather, who was smiling at him. 'We should make sure there's plenty of grub down here for them while the weather stays like this, don't you think?'

His grandfather put his arm around his shoulder. 'My boy, you've a new gun unfired. You've been wanting to shoot some ducks all week. I knew they'd be too hungry to fly, but I wanted you to show me that you're what I think you are. You were angry when you got here. That's gone and yes, we'll keep them fed as long as the weather stays like this. They'll be here next year.'

They made their way back to the Land-Rover. The dogs, disappointed, fell in behind disconsolately. 'Look at this lot coming Grandad,' Finlay said, pointing at skeins of ducks coming from upstream. 'Must be a couple of hundred of them!' The ducks passed over them, not ten feet above their heads, their pinions whistling in the cold air.

'They're really beautiful aren't they?' Finlay said. He laughed. 'The buggers know we ain't going to shoot them.' Another group passed between them. The ducks were flying so low, the wind of them brushing their faces.

As they got back into the Land-Rover Finlay's grandfather said, 'Don't let your mother go with bad blood between you, Kee.'

'No, of course not Grandad. I wouldn't do that. We'll be all right together.'

'I'm sure we shall, Kee,' his grandfather said.

When they came back his mother said, 'You weren't gone long. No ducks about?'

'Thousands of them Ma, but they were so hungry they just flapped about our feet almost. Didn't seem right to shoot any. When are you off then?' He had decided to make his mother comfortable.

'Tomorrow afternoon. Your Uncle Jack will drive me to the aerodrome. You will do your school work properly, won't you? I've got some photographs of you to take back and show your father. With your mare and fishing and things like that.' She seemed sad.

'I'll be perfectly all right Mama. Tell my father I shall wave in passing as our ships pass in mid-ocean. Just tell him to look for the cleanest, best-run ship in the fleet. That'll be mine. Tell him also that I do know about my duty to the country and The Queen. I shall get two DSOs and a bar to go with them.' He got up and left the room.

'Leave him Kath,' his grandfather said as she got up to follow. 'He's a young man now. Let him go. He'll be all right.'

Finlay woke suddenly in the night. He had been dreaming about the girl on the horse and there was a wet stickiness on his pyjamas. 'Now I understand,' he thought. 'I wonder if I'll get that dream back.'

Chapter Nine

•

When Finlay woke the next morning he felt tired. His head felt thick and muzzy and the air in the bedroom was icy. Dressing quickly, he crashed down the stairs. He needed to see Ron. His grandfather, as usual, was already up, drinking tea and thumbing through a farming journal. 'Morning Grandfather. Are you ready?' he said impatiently.

The old man peered at him over the journal. 'What's your rush? Starwort will still be there in ten minutes you know. Drink some tea to warm you up boy. Wake up properly.'

When Finlay was dropped at the pig unit, Ron had already fed the Danish house. 'Got here a bit early again. Have to see the boss at midday to get sworn in as foreman.' He laughed. But Finlay could see that he was proud.

They changed the beds in the farrowing house. Starwort was again cuddled and made much of. Finlay said, 'Ron, there's something I want you to do for me, something I need to ask you.'

'Let's go and look around the outside sows. You can talk there. Your ma going again?'

'No, it's a bit difficult to start.' Finlay stopped.

'Not about that little filly you met up with yesterday? I'm not sure that such things are part of my being farm foreman.'

They were outside walking towards the sow's paddock. 'Well, it is a bit. Yesterday that Caroline asked me to feel her breasts, so I asked her what was wrong with them.'

It took Ron some time to recover from laughing. 'I'm not laughing at you nipper... I know, you thought she wanted you to see if she had one of those mammary cysts. Maybe we do have a problem, but it's nothing that can't be sorted out. I'm still not sure that I'm the right one to do it, though.'

'Please Ron. Nobody will talk to me about fornication. They just keep avoiding the subject and I need to know,' Finlay pleaded.

'Poor little bugger! What a way to bring up a lad like you! Well I'll tell you all you want to know, and probably more, but don't you ever tell Niney we had this talk. Got that?'

'Course not. But I don't see why Auntie Niney should get cross about it. She talks about Jack and her a lot,' Finlay said.

Ron cleared his throat and began. 'Mothers, aunties, grandmothers.

They all try to keep boys not knowing for as long as they can. You see, they want you to stay their little angels. When you find a girl who may take their place, they get jealous and angry. My mother was a right bloody cow about it. I remember!' He continued. 'Right! Let's get down to the brass tacks of it. You know when we let old Bosun out to serve a sow. He goes to her, smells her fanny, nuzzles her ears for a bit, then he mounts her. His willy goes into her fanny and he bides up there pushing and shoving for about twenty minutes. Then he lets go the old jungle juice – that's sperm – grunts a couple of times and then gets off again...'

'Is that what...' Finlay interrupted, surprised.

'Hush, or I'll lose where I am. No. That's not exactly what humans do. Animals come in season. Bulling or hogging we call it. That's when the sow is ready to have the boar. The boar knows because she smells different. You've seen old Bosun tasting their piddle. He's just making sure she's right and ready. Animals have sex to breed. Humans have sex for pleasure and breeding. Unlike animals, women don't come on heat. Well, not technically anyway. It wouldn't be any use to rush up to one, smell her fanny, nuzzle her ear and then get on top of her. Women have something called periods, once a month. The inside of their womb sheds its lining and comes down through their fanny. Among themselves, they call it stupid names. The curse, wrong week or the painters are in. They make a mystery of it and some of them make such a bloody fuss. When that's done with, their wombs are empty, no eggs available. You remember the eggs the vet took from the sow through her side, well, halfway through the month their eggs arrive. If you want a child you have sex then. And there you are, they may have a baby. So the mechanics are the same but not the same, if you see what I mean. Young Caroline asked you to feel her tits because that would feel good to her, as well as you. Sex with a woman is a gentle sort of thing. What you, the bloke, is saying is I love you or I really fancy you. So you go slowly at it. When you gets your hands on young Caroline's tits she will go all stupid, breathe a bit heavy, like she's got asthma. Her nipples will grow up like threepenny bits, she be sort of coming into season at this stage. If, and only if, she wants more, you have to get her drawers off. But if she says no, then don't do it, else you'll end up down the cop shop. Now mind that bit. Their fannys ain't like a sow's. It's tucked up under and covered in curly hair.'

'I know that bit. I saw Jenny's fanny and that was covered in blonde hairs.'

'Well, ain't you a lucky bugger! Generally their fanny hair is same colour as that on their head. You gotta fondle them there and then they're ready. You just slip your willy in gentle and slow and leave the rest to happen.' Ron sighed, relieved to have the talk over. He started again, remembering. 'Hang on though, you have to stop the baby bit, else they'd have babies all the time. You get that equipment from the chemist. It's called a Durex or a French letter. You put that on your willy and it catches the jungle juice so your sperm and her eggs don't get together.' He stopped again, pleased he had covered so much ground. 'Anything else you need to know?'

Finlay thought for a moment. 'How old were you Ron, when you first did it?'

'Bit older than you. You sort of had lots of fumbles and feels before. A girl might give you a quick wank, but eventually one will open her legs and let you in. Then you'll find a girl who means more than a quick jump, and you'll marry her and then have kids. I don't want to talk about love. That's far too intricate. You'll know all right when that happens. Just take it gentle and slow and mind where you're putting your willy. Have a look behind their ears while you do the nuzzling, like Bosun. If that bit ain't clean, then you can depend on their fanny not being clean. And keep away from that sort!'

'How many different women have you had sex with, Ron? Is that an all right question?' Finlay asked, fascinated by what he had heard.

'Quite a few. Some were special, some not. You'll get the hang of it nipper.' He stopped and smiled. 'I tried to get into your Auntie Niney's blouse when we was about your age. Didn't she ever give me a smack in the mouth. We was both a bit drunk on some cider at the time.' He smiled at the memory. 'Always fancied Niney. When she was sixteen she'd knock your eyes out. That there Jane Russell had nothing on her, nothing at all,' he remembered again. 'Then I met Wyn and that was it. There wasn't anybody else in the world. Even when I was in the Navy I never went astray. Would have seemed like betraying her. I knows that probably Niney is more beautiful, if you had a picture. And I'd like to think that I'd had me hand in her knickers, but me and Wyn just sort of fits, if you see what I mean.'

'I think so Ron, but what about...'

'That'll be enough for one day nipper. Better get you back for breakfast and no chatter boxing about our talk, OK?'

'Shan't say a word Ron, and thank you,' Finlay said.

'You know some of what it's about nipper. We blokes is always learning and women use their power over us. That power being the place between their legs. But that's the way of it, and I don't suppose we'd have it any different,' the older man said. They climbed into the pick-up.

'So sex and fornication are the same thing, then? Sex is all right to do, but fornication isn't? Is that how it is?' Finlay asked.

'Sex is all right. It was given to us. Fornication is what the churchy buggers call it. They pretend to be all above it, but they are sometimes the worst of the lot. We have to get this pick-up to Carl. Have the brakes sorted out.' Ron badly wanted to change the subject.

'Is banging somebody the same as sex?' Finlay had a lot more questions he needed an answer to.

'Questions! Questions! Questions! Where did you hear that one then? Yes, having a bang is the same as having sex,' Ron answered. 'Now can we talk about something different?'

Unabashed, Finlay continued. 'What you said about church people was right then. Uncle Jack said that he saw the Methodist minister having a bang with Naomi Phillips, under the willows down by the boards!' The pick-up had been spinning along the gravel road at Ron's usual hell-for-leather speed.

He brought it to a skidding stop, abrupt enough to throw Finlay forward. 'Thought you said the brakes were bad!' Finlay exclaimed, rubbing his shoulder.

'Naomi Phillips! Well I'm buggered.' He was laughing again. 'Old Naomi. Still at it. Well, I'm buggered!'

'You know her then?' asked Finlay.

'Know her, why bless you boy, I should think every nipper in the town knew her, and have reason to be thankful to her. You didn't need any talks on the birds and the bees once she got a hold of you.' He started towards the house again. 'She laid hold of me down the bottom straw barn one morning, and I was just like you then. She had my trousers off and that was it. I'd gone there for your grandmother to pick up the eggs, 'our an 'alf I was gone and after that I thought I was King Kong. When I gave your granny the eggs, her said to me, "Ronnie Drew", that's what she used to call me, "Ronnie Drew, you've been gone long enough to lay these yourself." But her knew what I'd been up to. She said, "You have as many girls as you can, Ronnie Drew. The Huns will be starting again before you're a man, and you may not have the chance then."'

'You knew my grandmother, Ron? Nobody ever mentions her at home. What was she like?' Finlay asked.

'A grand lady she was. She had her funny ways. Liked everything just so, and she had the same temper as your mother. Took a horse whip to her brother for messing about with one of the dairy girls. Laid his face open to the bone she did, but if you was right with her, she'd 'ave done anything for you. When my old man fell off the binder and broke his leg, he was off work for six months. She'd be down two or three times a week with grub and went to get anything me mum needed.'

'What happened to her then? How did she die?' asked Finlay, curious why there was nothing of her in the house.

'Drowned they supposed. Her father's boat got run down in the Channel coming back from France. They found her father and mother but never her. Till Miss Jenny come along, the boss was all to buggery sometimes. Bad do that was,' Ron said. 'Then the fucking Japs killed one of his daughters. No wonder he goes on a major piss-up sometimes.'

'You don't like the Japs much as well. Mama hates them,' Finlay said.

'Look,' Ron said. 'I didn't like the war. Scared the hell out of me. I couldn't wait for it to be over and get home. When VE Day came, I thought I'd be coming back home. Then I got a draft chit for a cruiser to go out to fight the Japs, and do you know, I wanted to go. Ah yes, after what they did to your Auntie Bibby, I wanted to go. I'd ud been very 'appy to go and kill some of them, the bastards!' He spoke the last words with real hatred. Finlay thought Ron was remembering something special. 'Young Bibby was a lovely gal. Quiet and kind. More like your grandad than anybody. Headful of dark curls and the biggest blue eyes you'd ever seen.'

'Was she one of the special ones, Ron?' Finlay asked.

The older man looked at him. 'You got the same eyes as her had… and I think you catches on a bloody sight too quickly,' he said softly.

They swept into the front drive, the back end of the pick-up sliding wildly on the icy puddle by the entrance. 'Whoops!' Ron laughed. 'Nearly came unstuck that time.'

A strange Land-Rover was parked askew across the drive, so they came to a sliding halt just behind it. 'What dozy bugger left that there like that? Nobody can get round.' Ron turned to Finlay. 'Now don't forget. Not a word about what we bin talking about.'

Jenny appeared at the front door. 'Ron Drew! Stay there, I want a word with you.' She disappeared inside again.

'Now what?' Ron snorted. 'God save me from bossy women.'

She reappeared, her hair now covered with a woolly hat pulled well down over her ears. 'Now listen you…' she began fiercely, then she smiled. The smile that made her almost as beautiful as Auntie Niney, Finlay thought. She handed him a key. 'You have to leave your old pick-up here for Carl to collect and take your brand-new Land-Rover! And don't tell me Ron Drew you weren't just a little worried a second ago! Our farm foreman has to have a vehicle as befits his station!'

'Well I'm blowed. I'll go to sea in a leaky bucket. I thought I was losing the truck and going to have to go to a bike… and yes… I wondered what I'd done when you first showed. Is that really for me? You ain't pulling my leg Miss Jenny?' Finlay had never seen his friend so nonplussed.

'I think James wanted to show you that you are appreciated and it's his way of saying thank you for making my Christmas. For what you said.' She briefly touched his arm.

Finlay and Ron got down from the pick-up and went to look at the new vehicle.

'It came down from Winchester this morning,' Jenny said. 'It is rather smart isn't it?'

'It's a beauty, Ron,' Finlay said, running his hand over the wing. He jumped inside. 'It's even got a wireless! We can listen to the news while we are having something to eat,' he shouted.

'You'll be going back to your school work shortly young man. So there won't be too much riding about the place, like Lord Muck.' She smiled at his pulled face.

Ron positively glowed. 'Well, I'd better get back for breakfast…'

'Yes,' Jenny said shortly. 'You're to bring your lovely Wyn lunch time. We have to know she's happy with your new job.'

Ron went to get into his new vehicle. He looked somehow embarrassed when he got in, but he waved. 'OK! See you lunch time then.' He drove away rather more steadily than he had arrived.

'Come along then, Kee, get cleaned up and changed. When you've seen your mother off, we have to go to Southampton to get you some clothes.'

'Oh Jen, I don't want to do that!' Finlay objected. 'I hate going into Southampton.'

'Don't care a jot what you like and don't like. You, young man, will do as you are told. Indoors and get your breakfast before I give your ears a box!' She chased him up the steps laughing.

Indoors, his mother was bustling about. 'I thought you were not going until after lunch, Ma,' Finlay said, noting her two cases ready by the door.

'There's snow over the Alps and moving north my dear. The plane is going early to avoid the storm. Uncle Jack will be here shortly. I'm sorry, it can't be avoided,' his mother said. 'Maybe it won't be too long before I'm back here with your father. The truce talks are going on a bit, but at least they're all talking.'

Finlay ate his breakfast in silence. Jenny sat quietly beside him, drinking tea, waiting for an explosion of temper from Finlay.

'I don't mind you going Ma. Next time, please tell me though. That's all I ask. Don't keep things from me. I've got nothing to complain about, have I? I've plenty to do. I want to be here and not abroad, and Auntie Niney is a much better cook than you.' Finlay didn't mean to be rude, but the look on his mother's face had told him that he had been. 'Look Ma, let's face it. Your Yorkshire pudding is like unleavened bread straight out of the Bible. It's not your fault. You'd sooner spend your time on your piano, and you can make the piano sing. Nobody else can do that…' He left the speech unfinished.

'Well I'm glad I can do something to please you at least. When I'm across the other side of the world, I shall spend my time perfecting my cooking.' She laughed. 'Perhaps you could learn to play the piano?'

'No, my fingers don't work like that and I don't have time…'

They heard the car arrive in the yard. It stopped the conversation going any further. Finlay was pleased. He could see where it might lead: piano lessons.

Jack came into the kitchen rubbing his hands together vigorously. 'That gets a bloody sight colder I think! We mustn't hang about Kathy. There's snow forecast.'

'Where's Auntie Niney, Uncle Jack?' Finlay asked.

'Home boy. She don't much like goodbyes, specially between her and your ma. She'll be here later.' Jack picked up the two suitcases. 'Where's the boss?' he asked.

'Gone to Winchester,' Kathleen Finlay answered. 'He said cheerio earlier.' She paused. There was a long silence. 'Well,' she said. 'I'd better get under way.' She gave Jenny a long hug and then kissed Finlay on both cheeks, 'Look after my piano darling.'

They walked out of the front door. Jenny and Finlay remained at the top of the steps, then suddenly the car was half-way down the drive. Finlay watched it turn towards the main road, heard the engine pick up as it disappeared behind the roadside trees, and he waited for the glimpse he knew he would get as it crossed the river bridge. Then it was gone. 'That's that then,' he said, matter-of- factly. 'Shan't see her again for a couple of years.' He sighed heavily and turned to go indoors. 'Think I'll go fishing for a while Jen, if you don't mind. I'll be back lunch time.'

He went to get his rod, still set up from the day before. Jenny went to the kitchen without saying a word. On the way out, he saw she was sitting at the table sobbing. He dropped the rod and went to her. 'What's the matter, Jen? Don't cry like that. Are you upset 'cos Ma's gone too?'

She looked up at him, her eyes red from her tears. 'I'm all right Kee... just being silly.' She sobbed again and suddenly stood and banged her fists on the table. 'No! I'm not all right, not a bit all right! How can anybody treat another human being like that?' She rushed from the room.

He had been fishing for about half an hour, his mood as leaden and sombre as the winter sky. He suddenly became aware of somebody watching him. It was Jenny. 'Hiya Jen,' he called. 'Look what I've got for you.' He lifted his landing net. 'Quite the biggest grayling I've ever seen. If you put a bit of tinned salmon with it and some water cress, it would make fish cakes.' He splashed out of the river. 'I was just going to come home anyway. Did you want me for something?'

They studied the grayling together. 'If the other one was over two pounds, this one must be close to three,' Jenny said enthusiastically.

'Did you want me for something?' he repeated, worried she'd forgotten with her enthusiasm for the fish.

'No, I just came down to see you were all right. Not too upset about your mother going... that sort of thing.' She looked at him quizzically. They began walking back to the house.

'Well,' he said at last, 'well, the vicar cheats at whist and tells lies.'

'What does that mean?' Jenny asked.

'Only that nothing is what is seems. I'm not bothered now about Mama going. Might almost be better if she stayed away. Then we wouldn't have this upset every time she goes.'

'You shouldn't say such things Kee. Your ma came all the way home to see you. She wanted to be with you.'

'Not enough to stay!' Finlay said tersely.

Finlay's grandfather was home by the time they got back. He was in ebullient mood. 'We've got the go-ahead for the change to TT, Keith, finalized this morning. Did your mother get off OK?'

'Yes Grandfather, got away smoothly. Are Ron and Wyn staying for lunch?' he asked.

'Yes. I'll take them into the hall and let Ron know what's expected, then we can have lunch. How does that sound?' Finlay's grandfather was not exactly excited, more happy anticipation. 'On the way back from Winchester, I stopped off at Motisfont and saw the contractor chap. Starting tomorrow, they'll be in with their big equipment to get all the outside muck heaps spread while the ground is still hard. It'll be a longish haul but we'll spread everything over the Rownhams' side. I've a feeling that when this weather softens we'll be in for a fair bit of rain.'

They studied the grayling laid on a large floral dish on one of the draining boards, its purple and blue iridescent marking still bright. 'That's quite the biggest grayling I've ever seen come out of the river. Beats my biggest by some! Where did you catch it?' his grandfather asked.

'Down in the hatch pool, in the deep part by the right-hand fishing platform. Didn't it ever fight! Went off downstream like a rocket. When it got across the current, I thought I was going to lose it,' Finlay answered.

'They fight well this time of year,' Finlay's grandfather said. 'You went down to the hatch pool after your mother left then?' he asked nonchalantly. He gave Jenny a look and she, in turn, gave the briefest of nods. Finlay noticed.

'I know what you are saying to each other!' Finlay said impatiently. 'Yes, I went to fish because Mama had gone again and I was upset. I'm not a child you know. I understand the sort of codes that adults have and the little innuendos, whatever they are!'

His grandfather laughed, 'Innuendo Kee, well done! And I should have realized you're not a child any more. Something to do with that little bay filly you met at Lyndhurst?' he teased.

'What little filly was this then?' Jenny asked, joining in.

'Young Keighley has her eye on him. Pretty little thing too,' his grandfather said.

Jenny snorted. 'Oh, her. Yes, I know the one. Niney sent her packing twice in the summer.'

'Why?' asked Finlay. 'She seems like a nice girl. Poor thing has no one to talk to,' thinking that Ron Drew was quite the wisest person he knew.

'Niney says she's fast and too old to be hanging around for you,' Jenny said emphatically. 'Anyway you have to concentrate on your studies.'

Finlay decided to play these over-protective women at their own game. 'What? She rides her horse too fast, Jenny? I wouldn't rush Misty about. I know about horses. Poor Caroline only wants to be friendly.'

'Not that sort of fast!' Jenny began.

'Well, what sort of fast, Jenny? I don't understand what you're on about.'

His grandfather made to leave the room. 'I'm sure Jenny will explain Kee. I must get some things ready for when Ron gets here.' Finlay was sure he heard him chuckling in the passageway.

'What sort of fast, Jenny?' Finlay repeated his question, determined to press his advantage.

'Ask your Auntie Niney, Kee. I must get on and set this table,' Jenny said, making a big show of getting the cutlery from the drawer.

'Well you said it, Jen. So you must know what it means,' Finlay persisted.

'As I said. Ask your Auntie Niney. She can explain better than I. Would you like to get the side plates out for me?' Jenny was obviously uncomfortable.

'Which ones you want, Jenny?' he said getting up. 'Yes, OK, I'll ask Auntie Niney.'

'Not while there's anybody here though,' she warned. 'You have this wonderful ability to ask the most awkward questions just at the wrong time.'

As they busied themselves laying the table, they heard a vehicle arrive. 'Ah, here they are,' Jenny said. 'Niney has brought lunch I hope.'

Niney had indeed brought lunch. She came sailing into the kitchen carrying a large oval dish. 'Open the top oven Kee darling,' she ordered and pushed the dish into the oven. 'Lancashire hot pot. Go tell your grandfather that Ron and Mrs Drew are here. Jenny, is there any beer left after the party and can you take Ron and Wyn's topcoats and darling, haven't you any socks at all without holes?'

Finlay said a very polite, 'Good morning Mrs Drew,' and to Ron, 'When can I have a drive of your Land-Rover, Ron?'

Before he could answer Niney said, 'Go and get your grandfather. Never mind Land-Rovers.'

He had time to smile and raise his eyes to heaven as he passed Ron, who smiled back. Finlay returned with his grandfather. 'Come on through to the hall. This won't take long,' he said to the Drews. Finlay wandered back into the kitchen. 'Auntie Niney, can I ask you something?'

'Of course you can, darling,' Niney answered.

From behind her back Jenny made movements, but Finlay smiled sweetly at her and said, 'What does fast mean?'

'Well, what a silly question! It means going quickly I suppose.'

'No. I mean if a girl is said to be fast, what does that mean?' Finlay had his chin cupped on his hands, trying to look as innocent as he could.

'It's not something I have the time or wit to talk about today, perhaps...'

'If a girl is fast does that mean she likes having her titties rubbed?' Finlay wasn't winning the battle of not smiling.

'You little sod!' Jenny exploded, grabbing Finlay by the ear. 'You knew all along! You were just having me on this morning!'

'Well, Grandad said I should restrict my titty rubbing to only well-bred girls. I wondered whether Caroline was well-bred enough?' Finlay was laughing, even though he was being dragged around the room by his ear. 'Oh Jenny, you're hurting,' he yelled mockingly. She let him go, laughing herself and through her laughter, explained about the earlier conversation.

Niney put an arm around him and kissed him heavily on the cheek. 'So my little Adonis, you've suddenly discovered girls and found you have some lead in your pencil,' she sighed heavily. 'Well, the cat's out of the bag and will, no doubt, become the pussy in the knickers.' Jenny was giggling uncontrollably; Niney looked upwards. 'Mothers of Hampshire, lock up your daughters if you want to keep them chaste. Another generation is about to go on the rampage.'

Finlay's grandfather and the Drews joined them in the kitchen. 'What's for lunch Niney?' the old man asked. 'I'm just about ready for it!'

'Hot pot, James,' Niney answered. 'Made with your uncle's lamb Ron, so it should be good.'

'Did you get everything sorted out James?' Jenny asked. 'And are you happy Wyn, about it all? It'll mean a lot more work for Ron.'

Wyn agreed that it would and she was happy about the arrangement. She was a diffident and shy lady, it seemed. 'I'm sure if he hasn't got the swill run to do and the steaming, I'm certain he'll be able to cope,' she ventured.

'Of course he will. I'm helping with the pigs and I...' Finlay began confidently, but Jenny cut him off.

'"I may be able to help with the pigs when I've got my school work done." That's what you should be saying young man, because that's how it will happen.'

'Well, I have to go and see Starwort...'

Again Jenny interrupted. 'Starwort! Starwort! Starwort! That's all I hear from you. Honestly, the way you talk about Starwort, anybody would think she's some sort of Eastern princess, instead of just a piglet. Maybe we'd better go and look at this competitor of ours, Niney?'

Niney placed the large oval dish on the centre of the table and a wonderful smell of food stopped the conversation dead. The slightly crisped slices of potato on the top of the hot pot fizzed nicely.

Niney filled a plate and put it down in front of Finlay. 'Try that darling,' she said. 'Help yourselves everyone, there's plenty there.' Silence is the biggest compliment that good food can get.

After five minutes, Finlay's grandfather said, 'Niney, you've surpassed yourself. This is wonderful!'

Niney, aiming for something that did not sit well with her, modesty replied, 'It's very simple and a handy way to feed everyone.' Modesty fled. 'Attend to the detail, then it comes right. It is very good though, I must admit.'

'Prince Charming, here, informed his mother that her going was not a problem for him, since Niney was a much better cook and that she'd better stick to her piano,' Jenny said.

Finlay suffered embarrassment in roughly the same measure as Niney suffered modesty. Ron had started to chuckle at what Jenny had said, his grandfather was about to say something, but was stopped by an enormous blue flash, followed almost at once by a clap of thunder that rattled the windows. Something hit the windows like spent shot. A door slammed heavily shut somewhere in the house, as a sudden wind rushed around the outside. There was another vivid blue flash. This time the thunder seemed to be in the very room, then there was silence.

'Come and look!' Niney exclaimed, looking out on to the yard. It had a thin covering of what looked like shattered windscreen glass. Even in the failing light, it sparkled like diamonds. Somewhere away to the west there was another grumble of thunder.

'Must be static,' Ron said. Another vivid blue flash seemed to rush across the sky and, as one, they stepped back from the window.

'Well, Southampton is out,' Jenny said. 'I'm not going out in this.'

'Good!' said Finlay.

'Wretched boy,' Jenny answered. She was standing behind him, both arms around him, her chin resting on the top of his head. 'I honestly believe you like going about dressed like a tramp.' The telephone rang.

'Here's trouble,' Finlay's grandfather said.

Niney answered it and suddenly looked solemn. 'Yes of course,' she said, handing the earpiece to Finlay's grandfather, 'Oh James... someone's been killed.' They all listened to the one-sided conversation quietly.

Finlay's grandfather finished the call. 'We'll be there as soon as possible.'

He rattled the earpiece holder up and down. 'Put me through to Carl please, and this time stay and listen. I'll have more calls to make.' He waited until the connection was made. 'Carl, go and shut the electricity off...Yes, at once...There's been an accident by the recreation ground. Bring the safety marker to me there as soon as you've done it.' He waited for the operator. 'Now get me through to Cyril please.' Again he waited. 'Cyril, get the winch tractor down to the recreation ground. A tree has come down and the power lines, ours included. Get your crew down there, but wait until you get the all clear from the electric people. They'll be there. Now operator, stay on the line and let everyone know what's happened when they try to ring here to say their electricity is off. Thank you...Yes, that would be a help.' He put the phone down. 'A tree has snapped off and fallen across the power lines near Romsey. There looks like two people dead in a car and someone electrocuted when they went to help.'

The lights in the kitchen dimmed quickly and went out. 'I'll get a couple of the Fergies down there Boss, and a fore loader. Keith, get dressed. You'd better come with me, in case we need to get any messages home. C'mon boy, jump to it!'

'You will not!' An ashen-faced Jenny pushed Finlay back down in his chair. 'You will not!' She glared at Ron. 'Don't you think he's had enough upset for one day with his mother going? He doesn't need to be helping with dead people.'

'Sorry Miss Jenny, I didn't think...' Ron seemed taken aback by Jenny's vehemence.

'Well, it sounds like a long job for somebody and the pigs will still need feeding. I think perhaps it would be best if we three went and did that. Then we can see what we are up against with this bloody creature, Jenny,' said Niney. 'We'll have to walk over there, so shall we all get ready?'

'Thank you, Niney,' Finlay's grandfather said quietly. 'Where would we be without you?'

'In the poo! Get me some of your clothes, James. I don't want to have to walk back home for mine. Well, come along you two!' Niney said to Jenny and Finlay. 'Get changed. Can you pop into my mother, on the way by her house please, Wyn, and make sure she has some light? Tell her I'll come later.' Within ten minutes they were walking down the lane together, the cold making them hurry.

'If anybody were to see us now Jen, they'd take us for pikies out on a robbing expedition,' Niney joked. She was dressed in Finlay's grandfather's clothes. They were not long enough and far too wide.

'Damn you Niney Terry,' Jenny gasped, trying to keep up. 'You look good even in that. How do you do it?'

'Underwear my dear. Nothing but underwear. Get the most glamorous sets you can – makes you feel glamorous and makes you act glamorous.' Niney laughed, slowing down a little.

'I feel a little bad going for Ron. It broke my heart to see Kee's face watching his mother drive away this morning, poor little sod. Watching him fighting back the tears'. Jenny said. 'I was really angry,'

'Kathy will be different with the one she's carrying now. She's always known Finlay was only hers until he was old enough to be taken into the Navy. He'll be all right Jen. He's a tough little bugger. That's why I haven't put my foot down about being so close to Ron Drew. Maybe he'll change his mind, and Ron is quite a good influence on him... sometimes. He was wild once. Bloody girls used to chase him and he didn't run away, I can tell you.' She laughed at the memory.

'Did you run, Niney?' Jenny asked.

'Oh, he tried it on once, I remember. I gave him a smack in the clock for his trouble. I already had my eye on Jack. Maybe if Ron had tried earlier, things might have been different.'

'And what about this Caroline girl, Niney? What happens there? You've sent her packing twice.' Jenny was fascinated by Niney's directness.

'She's trade Jenny. Nothing will come of that, and the boy has to sow his wild oats. Don't forget, once he gets to Dartmouth his feet won't touch the ground. It's still a tough school, even in this day and age.' Niney looked a bit wistful.

'Sounds positively brutal Niney. It's so old-fashioned. Do they have to be so harsh with them?' Jenny asked.

'Yes they do. It makes for very humane men. I think the theory's what they have inflicted on them, they themselves would not inflict on anybody else.' She laughed without humour.

An hour later the two women joined Finlay in the farrowing house. They crept in silently, as they had been told to do, and Finlay motioned them to follow. He took them to the creep where Starwort was. They leaned over and saw for a moment what Finlay always saw, the joy of well-kept stock.

He bent over and picked up Starwort. 'Well, what do you think,' he whispered. 'Isn't she beautiful?'

'Can I hold her, Kee?' Jenny whispered back.

'Gently then, she's not really awake,' Finlay said, lifting the tiny scrap of life into her arms.

Niney took the piglet next. 'Yes, I suppose you do have something,' she said, putting the piglet to her face. 'Here,' she said, handing the pig back. 'Put her with others before she takes the cold.'

'I'll just check the generators have enough fuel for the night, then we'd better get back,' Finlay said.

The village was in total darkness. Under the lowering sky, there was no light at all. In the distance, they could hear the crackle of a chain saw. It was colder than ever. 'They're still at it by the sound of it,' Niney said. 'They must be frozen through.' A car passed them, giving for a few brief seconds light to see their path. When it was gone, it seemed darker than ever.

'Niney, please slow down. I can't see a thing. Where are you?' Jenny yelled.

'Here love. Just keep walking towards my voice.' She began la-la-laing a tune. 'Where are you, Kee?'

Finlay poked her backside with his forefinger. 'Right here!'

Niney giggled. 'Hold my hand, both of you. We'll never get home else.'

They set off slowly in the inky blackness. Another vehicle was coming up from behind them and Finlay heard the whine from the Armstrong's gearbox. 'It's Uncle Jack.'

'Thank God for that!' Niney said thankfully.

'What the bloody hell are you doing out here?' Jack shouted from the open window. They bundled into the warm car. 'What are you doing out in this weather?' Jack sounded exasperated. 'Has the river frozen and the turbine stopped?'

'Just drive us home Jack,' Niney ordered. 'Of course the river hasn't frozen. The lines are down and there's been an accident in Romsey.' The car was very warm. Finlay and Jenny clung together in the back seat, moaning and gasping as the various parts of them came back to life. They turned into the driveway. As the car lights swept across the front of the house Niney muttered, 'Thank Christ for that!'

Jack pulled a torch from the glove box as they stopped. 'Careful now,' he said. 'Walk behind me.' They trooped in single file. The kitchen was warm and welcoming and looked the more so when Jack lit an oil lamp.

'Turn the Aga up full, Kee, there's a good chap, and open the tops and oven. That will soon hot the place up,' Niney said.

Jack lit another oil lamp. 'I'll stoke the fire in the hall. Then you can tell me what has been going on,' he said.

Warm again, Niney said, 'Put the big stew pot on Jen. These blokes will want feeding when they come back. Put about six pints of water in and get it boiling quickly.' She went to the phone, lifted the earpiece and listened. 'Well that's handy. The bloody thing isn't working. Now nobody knows what's happening!' Abandoning her quest for contact with the outside world, Niney started searching the cupboards.

'Kee, get me a medium cabbage and three large onions from the vegetable store. Jen, put the kettle on the slow plate and eight of the big white soup plates in the bottom oven.' Niney was flying. In her element. 'One gallon of very best soup coming up!' The cabbage and onions were shredded in what seemed seconds. 'Pig bucket, Kee,' she ordered. 'Keep my work space clear. Chuck a handful of salt in the water, Jen, and tell me when it's boiling.' From the fridge came some cold cocktail sausages, three breakfast sausages and the ribs of beef from Christmas Day.

'Water's boiling Niney.' Jenny loved to see the way Niney produced meals. 'Put the cabbage and onion in and keep it stirred, else it'll stick with the stove up that high.' The carving knife made short work of the sausages, cut into small chunks, and a pound of cold beef, treated the same. She stopped and pondered. 'Not enough, not enough. Jack, come here and open a tin of corned beef please. Is that cabbage soft yet Jen?'

'Just Niney. I wish I knew what you were doing though,' Jenny answered. Niney scooped up the sausage and cold meat and dropped them in the stew pan, in one movement. Almost like a conjuring trick, the kettle was on the hotplate and the stew pan on the warm plate.

'Kee, in the bottom of that cupboard you'll find some blocks in waxed paper. Can you get me two please?'

On his hands and knees, Finlay almost disappeared into the back of the cupboard. 'These things?' he queried.

'That's it darling,' she said, taking them from him. 'This is the backbone of it Jenny. Soup blocks.'

'But they're from the war. Are they still OK?' 'Good until 1955 it says here on the label. You've had plenty of it without knowing.' She broke them up on the chopping board. 'Perfect! Good as the day they went into the wrappings.'

The powder went into one of the dairy jugs, boiling water was added and the thickening mix was poured into the stew pan. 'There you are Jen. How to feed eight people for less than ten shillings. A little sherry and a lot of cream, and when the men get back, we'll be heroes.'

'Where did you get the soup blocks?' Jenny said, amazed.

'My love, I stole them. Along with half of one year's harvest of peaches from California and about three bullocks of Texas beef. What do you think all the boxes are in the oil shed? I'm never going to let us be hungry again. There's enough tinned food to last a year,' Niney laughed. 'When the Americans were packing up to leave and in a hurry to go home as they should be, I just put a padlock on the stable door where they were storing it. They assumed it had gone as it was destined for Germany, but bugger that! They caused the problem, no sense rewarding them. All this needs now is livening up.' She put in a heaped spoon of black pepper and three of mustard and gave the whole pot a stir. 'Here you are Kee, try some.' She offered a spoonful. 'Careful, it's hot.'

Finlay thought the soup wonderful, though the mustard made his eyes water. 'I think Jack must be asleep in the other room, Niney,' Jenny volunteered.

'Leave him. All that driving on icy roads must have worn him out. We'll know when the men are coming home when the lights go on again. Till then, like women the world over, we just sit and wait.'

It was the lights coming on that woke Finlay. He had drifted off, his head on his arms on the kitchen table, listening to Auntie Niney and Jenny. The lights, dim and flickering at first, gradually got brighter as the great wheel at the mill gathered speed. Finlay imagined the noise it was making as the leet pushed and shoved it to its predetermined momentum. The world may come to a stop, the electricity may be cut, but the river always rolled its course down the valley.

Niney, glancing at the lights, knew the wheel was up to speed. 'Switch the heating on, Kee, else the whole house will freeze, and go and wake your Uncle Jack.'

Jack woke, but slowly. He got up stiffly and stretched. 'That was a bloody long way in this weather, boy. Shouldn't want to be doing it again tomorrow.' With the heating on, the house seemed to be gathering itself together, creaking and groaning into a proper welcome for the homecoming men. In the kitchen, Jack said, 'Well that's something at least. You two looking a bit more respectable. Why on earth were you wearing the boss's clothes?'

'You missed the strip show Jack. We changed in the kitchen, it's so cold in the house. Me and Jen in our lacy knickers, that would have sharpened you up, perhaps,' Niney joked.

'Or bloody killed me! Now can somebody tell me what's been happening and doesn't anybody want to know if Kathy got off OK?' Jack was tetchy with tiredness. Finlay felt guilty that he had not given his mother a single thought all day.

'Oh Jack, stop being so cranky. Come here and give me a kiss. I haven't seen you all day. I was getting worried about you.' Jack kissed her briefly and went to move away. 'Oh no you don't Jack Terry!' Niney said, grabbing him. 'You kiss me properly or I'll find some bugger to do it for you!' Finlay loved to see Niney and Jack having a cuddle. They obviously adored each other.

The yard was suddenly lit with the lights of vehicles and they could hear Ron laughing loudly. 'Can somebody tell me what's been happening?' Jack said almost plaintively.

Finlay's grandfather, Ron and Carl arrived in the kitchen, bringing with them the smell of frost, exhaust smoke and fresh-cut timber. Ron and Carl were laughing out loud. Finlay's grandfather was trying not to.

'What's the matter with you two silly buggers? People dead and all you can do is giggle like schoolgirls!' Niney said sharply.

'Haseham broke his leg, you see...' Ron could get no further before he burst out laughing again.

'Can someone tell me what's been happening?' Jack asked. 'What's this about people dead?'

Niney started serving the food as Finlay's grandfather explained about the day. How the tree was so frozen, the saws blunted trying to cut it. How the axes had just bounced off and how they had had to rip it apart, limb from limb, with the winch. When he described getting the bodies from the crushed car, Niney and Jen gasped with horror. They had had to wait while the electric cables had been repaired. All in all, a gruesome affair.

'So what are you finding so bloody funny?' Jack asked Ron and Carl, with more than some sharpness.

'You would have laughed Jack, if you had been there to see it,' Ron said defensively. 'We'd about done when Haseham decided that he would lead the few cars waiting out on to the Southampton road. Anyway, he went on his silly little bike, full of piss and importance, waving his hand for them to follow. Stupid bugger thought he was John Wayne leading the cavalry. Then he skids on some ice and pitches over the bridge railings by the lodge...' Ron became helpless with laughter again. Carl was no better.

Trying to inject some levity into the conversation, Finlay's grandfather said, 'The poor man broke his leg. He'll be laid up for weeks. You should have some sympathy!'

'It vas de boots. Dey vent like this,' Carl said, describing the perfect arc of a flying policeman.

Even Niney started to giggle at this. 'You're all thoroughly wicked, laughing at the poor man.'

'This is a wonderful meal, Niney,' Finlay's grandfather said. 'Wonderful. Must have taken you hours to prepare.'

'Absolutely James,' she said.

Chapter Ten

•

The earth seemed to shrink in the intense cold. It looked tight and uncomfortable. On this new morning, it seemed tighter still for the temperature overnight had fallen yet further. Where the frost-burnt grass had burned off, large cracks had become evident in the earth, allowing the sinking cold air to penetrate deeper. The cold seemed to squeeze and kill the earth, crush the life from it. The very air seemed turgid and heavy and it caught in Finlay's throat, making it sore. The day before's ice shower seemed to be the last wringings of moisture available to the world. The conifers were brown, wind-blasted and stiff. Below them, in the scattering of needles, dozens of small birds lay dead, their tiny bodies unable to carry enough sustenance to cope. Giving up overnight, they fell to the rock-hard earth. Daylight itself seemed to be nothing but a brief interlude around midday. The sky seemed too close to the earth. The cloud complete, almost brown and unmoving, hung like a filthy ceiling above him. Even to the south, where the sea had always imparted its special glow to the horizon, not four miles from where he was, light had seemingly lost its battle with the oppressive sky.

Finlay was on a mission to find a fox. It had been trying to get into the hen run. The fox, he felt, could have waxed fat on the small dead birds but would rather slaughter twenty hens, to take one. It had to be taught the error of its ways.

A movement caught his eye under some laurels. There were two rats feasting upon a dead blackbird. His natural abhorrence, an abhorrence in every countryman, made him forget the fox. As he moved closer, the rats eyed him almost insolently and carried on with their feasting. His shot pattern covered them both, some of the pellets ricocheting from the hard earth up through the laurel. The rats were but a red splash on the frozen earth. Finlay had a passion for blackbirds. The fox, frightened by the shot, ran from the laurels. Crossing from right to left, Finlay swung the gun and caught it behind the left ear. The fox cartwheeled over and lay still with just a small twitch in one of its back legs, a reflex of a sudden, quick death. He walked across and pushed the fox with his toe, opened his gun and two empty cartridges flew over his shoulder and rattled on the hard earth. Bending, he checked to see how much flesh the fox was carrying. Its back was full and well muscled.

'The cold didn't do you any harm then Toby. You've done all right but you should have stayed away from the hens. You were told often enough,' Finlay said. He left the animal where it lay, knowing the carcass would attract magpies and other villains. He would hide and shoot them when they came, obeying an unwritten law in the country. Never miss a chance to kill a magpie, the most blackhearted robber of songbirds' nests.

Away to the north, Finlay could hear the contractor's machinery shifting the huge muck heaps, a pall of black diesel smoke evidence of where they were tearing the huge heaps apart. When they arrived earlier they had almost to chip away the surface of the heaps, so frozen were they. Further away still, he could just make out flocks of birds, gulls, rooks and crows feeding on the softer dung from the middle of the heaps, taking the worms and slugs overwintering in the warm compost, as the spreaders flung it in a dark rich carpet over next year's hay fields. He debated whether or not to go over to where the birds were feeding, knowing that magpies would be present as well, but his hands and feet were numb with cold, so he turned for home.

Jenny was preparing some lunch when he got back. He cleaned his gun and put it into the rod room.

'Did you shoot anything?' she asked.

'Yes. I got that fox, and two rats feeding on a dead blackbird. There are dozens of dead birds under the Douglas trees, poor little things,' Finlay said, washing his hands in the kitchen sink.

'I know, Kee. I put plenty of food out for them, but they die in the night. It's so long now, if this cold goes on there won't be any of the tiny birds left. I wish the weather would change, but the forecast on the wireless was much the same for the foreseeable future. Did you see how the dung spreading was going?' Jenny asked.

'They were going at it hammer and tongs just now. The air's so still that the tractor smoke was hanging in layers. It won't stink the people out in Rownhams. Must be pretty well frozen by the time it hits the ground. I thought I might go over there and shoot some of the magpies. There were thousands of gulls.' He sat at the table.

'I'm afraid not young man. You've to go to Carl this afternoon and start learning to be a mechanic – strict instructions from your grandfather.'

'Where is Grandfather?' he asked.

'Southampton. Gone to have lunch with the vet. Big decisions to be made about the herds and starting an AI service. Just don't ask me what AI is, all innocent, because I know you know already, you little snot!' She handed him his lunch. 'Fish cakes made with tinned salmon, grayling and water cress from the mill stream, as ordered.'

'Oh Jen, you didn't traipse all the way down there for water cress, did you? You must have got frozen.' Finlay was sorry now he had asked.

'Huh! You've got a mighty big opinion of yourself thinking I'd do that for you. No, Jack got it for me. Mmmn,' she said, her mouth full. 'They are good. I've put some aside for your grandfather. See what he thinks.'

They ate in silence. 'Where's Auntie Niney? Gone with Grandfather to drive him home? Every time he and the vet get together, they always end up puggled.'

'Niney went in with him. She's going to buy the clothes we were going to get for you. She's taken a pair of your trousers and one of your shirts to get the size. I said you should go, but as usual, because you didn't want to do something, Niney said you did not have to. She'll even do any alterations needed. It's not good for you to be so spoilt you know.'

'I'm not spoilt Jen!' Finlay objected strongly. 'Auntie Niney knows what I like and don't like and she never makes me do anything I don't want to.'

'That's as good a definition of being spoilt as I've ever heard,' she laughed. '"Auntie Niney, do I have to do that?"' Jen said, mimicking Finlay. '"Oh no darling, not if you don't want to." Now you had better get going because you have to be back here at half-past four on the dot. Don't forget.'

'Why half-past four? Tea is when we get here,' Finlay said.

'Not today ducks, you have a visitor. Caroline asked if she could come over so I said yes, we'd be delighted to have her to tea.' Jenny burst out laughing.

'Oh Jen, you didn't. That's a bloody rotten trick to play!' Finlay was horrified at the thought of the embarrassment he would suffer at the hands of Ron and Uncle Jack.

'Told you I'd get you back, you bugger!' She hugged him. 'Come along, you'd better get off to the workshop, and try and stay clean. At least you won't smell of pigs.'

The workshop was Carl Bendt's citadel, a place Finlay was to find out was run with Teutonic efficiency. Housed in the main yard, it was half of a large concrete and asbestos single-span barn and totally enclosed. Walls of concrete blocks and huge sliding doors ran to the eaves and opened wide enough to allow the combine harvester inside. Let into one of these huge doors was a smaller one to allow access without opening the big doors. The doors were always locked when Carl was not actually present. There were just three keys; one for Carl, one for Ron Drew and one for Finlay's grandfather. Not to prevent pilfering – it was always thought this would not happen – but to prevent the removal of tools by people who worked on the estate. It had been the case over the years that tools removed from the workshop never ever came back. They would be found resting, rusting in obscure places, lonely creatures maybe destined to become curiosities for an archaeologist in later centuries. There was a gate post at the top end of the estate where a spanner, used to adjust the swing height of the gate, was rusted solid to the hinge nut. Distracted perhaps, the user had left it there at the start of winter. By spring, it had welded itself for ever on the adjuster nut, mute testament to old countrymen's scorn for things mechanical. Finlay's grandfather had insisted it stay, to make a point. Over the years it had become part of a rusting blob of fused metal, its hold on the nut as firm as that gripping Arthur's Excalibur in the rock.

The mainstay of the estate work was the Ferguson tractor, an innovation in machinery so profound as to affect agriculture and agricultural machinery for generations to come. Called the Ferguson System, the tractor itself was small, light and handy, twenty-odd horse-power, depending on the engine type. They flew along a metalled road at over twenty miles per hour, when other tractors could barely manage eight. The startling thing about them was their own internal hydraulic system and 'three-point linkage' where implements could be attached or detached in minutes. A whole series of implements, designed to go with them, could balance to the tractor: ploughs, mowers, buckrakes, everything a farmer could need. And the farmer's wife was not forgotten. There was even a washing machine, designed to run from the tractor, the drudgery of coppers and boilers all gone. With a self-starter, any lady could drive them like a car and it was nothing to see a farmer's wife or daughter coming into town on the Fergie, the small transport box swinging between the hydraulic arms at the rear of the tractor, ideal for carrying the weekly shop.

The little, battleship-grey tractor became a cult. Kept clean and sparkling, even waxed, whole conversations in the pubs could be centred on 'my Fergie'. No one thought such things amiss. Once, there was an outright scandal. Farmer Culley sprayed his Ferguson red, pillar-box red for goodness' sake! Fred Light, Culley's tractor driver, was mortified and deeply ashamed. He had to take not a little abuse from his fellows in the local pub. 'What you doing, delivering letters?' He became known as Red Fred, a name he took to his grave. One of the estate tractor drivers was more than affronted. 'Painting a Fergie red, fer Christ's sake, whatever be 'ee thinking about. 'Tis wus than saying shit to The Queen!' Such was its status, the Ferguson helped bring about the end of rationing and they were definitely grey – not any grey – they were Ferguson grey.

When a new Fergie was delivered to a farm it came with a basic tool kit. It came in an oil-cloth bag which should have been housed in the tractor's tool box bolted on to the back wing. The most important spanner was an open-ended one, marked along its shank like a foot ruler in inches. It doubled as a measure. More importantly, it was the spanner which adjusted the tilt on a plough, or could remove the linkage pins on any of the tractors's equipment. It was heavy and could be used to hit things. Finlay's grandfather, ploughing one springtime, had hit a wet spot in a field. His Fergie gently sank to its ankles, the plough hopelessly stuck. It would have been a simple job to have removed the linkage pins and pulled out, leaving the plough behind. Simple, if he had had the correct spanner. Finlay's grandfather trudged two miles over plough and mud back to the workshop and it was raining heavily at the time. According to Ron, 'Old man was steaming, proper bloody steaming.' He told Finlay the story: 'Wasn't the fact of getting stuck nor yet not having the spanner, 'twas the hindignity of 'aving to leave the Fergie for all the world to see. He come home, changed and was back down the yard about quarter-past four, and then he waited. Oh my word, was that good to watch. Anybody in before time had a real tongue lashing. As each tractor came in so the old man checked the tool box on it. He found lunch boxes, fags and matches but hardly any spanners. He went bloody mad. He told 'em each tractor would have a new tool kit, and a coat hook bolted on a wing for their lunch bags. If he ever found spanners missing, the driver would be very sorry, and that's what happened.'

Finlay himself fell foul of his grandfather's wrath. He had borrowed an Allen key to adjust the trigger on his air rifle from Carl's workshop, forgot to return it and found himself banned from the workshop for eighteen months. Known as the Reichstag, to the workers on the estate, Finlay was soon to find out why. Carl had welcomed him very formally, though the first thing that struck Finlay was how warm the place was. There was a constantly moving wind of warm air. It was almost painfully tidy, clean and very quiet with only the hum of a heating system in the background.

'Good. I hav to make you into a mechanic. Come viz me,' Carl ordered. He took Finlay to a steel-legged flat bench with a large metal vice clamped to it. 'Ziz is your bench vile you are here. You vill keep it tidy and very clean. You vill see three boxes. Dis one is your big spanners, ze vones vid the open ends also ze vones vid de rings. Der are three sets. Please look and be counting zem. Each vone has de K on, your letter. OK? please count now.'

'Eighteen Carl,' Finlay said, wondering whether he should have learnt to speak German before coming here.

'Ze second box has two socket sets each with zere own place in the box, OK? Each part of zees have de K, OK? In ziz box are de pliers, zee sidecutters, zee moles, zee screwdrivers, zee saws, zee chisels, zee punches and zee hammers, OK? You will count please.'

Finlay counted them out. 'Sixty-two different tools, Carl.'

'Good! Zo, at the end of each day there is always the zame numbers. They will also be clean. OK?'

'OK,' answered Finlay.

'Now put your name on this, to say you hev the tools. OK?' He handed Finlay a book. 'Also in dis same book, you vill put down vot you did each day. OK?'

He walked Finlay over to a corner of the workshop. 'Here, as you zee, is ze lavatory and here the place to wash your hands. You will note please zey are wery clean. Please keep it so. Now, zees are de rules made by de boss. If you lose ze tools, for each one, one extra day school work. If you leave things dirty, one extra day school work.'

Finlay walked over to where Ron's old pick-up stood, gleaming like new. There were two Fergusons, nose to nose about six-feet apart in the centre of the workshop, and another in two pieces supported in cradles.

'Vee service all de tractors while zey are not vorking, ready to plant the barley. Vee start vis dees two, OK?' Carl quickly went through the various parts of a tractor that needed regular maintenance and told Finlay to follow what he did on one tractor while Finlay copied him on the other. Anything that required doing was recorded on index cards.

Half-way through the afternoon, Ron came into the workshop and told Finlay to learn as much as Carl could teach him. It would, he assured Finlay, stand him in good stead for the rest of his days. As he left, he said to Carl, 'Don't forget Carl, he has to be home by half-past four. There's a young lady coming to see him and she has the prettiest new tits you'd ever wish to see.'

'At zat time he can zink about ze tits. Now he has to zink only about ze machine in the front of him, OK.' He did not smile as he spoke.

At five past four Carl said, 'Good! You have done good vork, now you put your tools away and get your hands clean. Putting oil on de brand-new tits is not good.'

'Is that a joke, Carl?' Finlay asked.

Carl peered at him over his glasses. 'Vy should you zink so? You vill be here at seven-thirty in the morning. Please take this and this.' Carl handed him two manuals. 'Tomorrow, you do zee wheel bearings in tractor number fourteen and you will have to know how. Haf-past seven! Do not be late. Good night.' He shook Finlay's hand, muttering, 'Good! Vee make something of you maybe!'

Leaving the warm workshop, into the extreme cold, made Finlay shudder. He realized there was a slight wind coming from the north east and looking he could see, at last, gaps in the cloud cover. The first stars were beginning to show. He could hear the contractors' machines still working and see the occasional sweep of headlights across the fields. Clutching the workshop manuals he hurried to the house. He was not hurrying because he was looking forward to seeing the Caroline girl, more that Jenny had asked him to be on time. Indoors, she told him his clothes for the evening were laid out on his bed and to hurry and get into them. She, meantime, would be getting the food ready.

By the time he came back downstairs he could hear voices in the kitchen. Suddenly he was apprehensive. He wondered why he was agreeing to this meeting. Jenny, and what he took to be Mrs Keighley, were chattering in the kitchen when he walked in, something about the dreadful weather. 'Ah, here he is!' Jenny said smiling at him. 'Kee, this is Caroline's mother, Mrs Keighley.' He shook hands. Caroline was sitting at the table seemingly studying the complex pattern of the grain in the table top.

'Well Jenny, what time would you like me to pick her up again? Thanks again for inviting her over. She needs to know more children of her own age,' Mrs Keighley said, smiling at Finlay.

'I'll phone when Caroline has had enough, perhaps. Everyone is out at the moment and the only vehicle here is the Land-Rover. Caroline will get frozen in that, dressed as she is,' Jenny said. Finlay glanced at the light summer clothes she was wearing, and thought Caroline looked like a mannequin he had seen in a shop window in Southampton, not exactly a country girl.

Having seen Mrs Keighley out, Jenny returned. 'Why don't you take Caroline to the hall, Kee, and get to know each other. I'll bring you something through in a moment or two. I must say your dress is very smart, don't you think so Kee?'

'Yes,' Finlay said enthusiastically. He got up, picking up the two manuals Carl had given him, and waited for Caroline to go through the door.

Jenny intercepted him. 'Leave those here darling. I'm sure Caroline doesn't want to know about the workings of farm machinery.' She wrested the manuals from him, smiling sweetly. Finlay poked his tongue out but Jenny just smiled the sweeter, and dug him in the ribs as he passed her.

Caroline stopped suddenly in the hall doorway. 'Why have you got bits of tree all over the walls?' she exclaimed.

'That's Christmas decorations. Don't you think it looks and smells super? Auntie Niney and Jenny put them up,' Finlay said proudly.

'We have balloons and coloured paper, crêpe paper all twisted together. It's pretty and happy. Don't these branches bring in lots of creepy crawlies?'

'Oh, there wouldn't be much on them, this time of year. The spruce and scots are to show the green, the ivy, constancy, the holly with the berries, abundance and the larch over the fireplace, with its cones, are to remind us that winter will come to an end. I think it looks splendid.' Finlay seemed still unaware that the girl was puzzled.

'Well I think it's strange, and a bit spooky. I mean, bits of trees on the wall!' She seemed disgusted.

Finlay had been told to behave. He very badly wanted to swear at her. How could anybody criticize anything that Auntie Niney did? 'Look! I've explained why we do this. On New Year's Eve they're taken down and burnt in the fireplace. It's the end of the year and the start of the new. That is how it should be. Why do you put up balloons and coloured paper?' he asked.

She thought for a moment, 'Well I don't know, but everybody does.'

'So if everybody goes and jumps in the river, you would too I suppose! At least there's a reason for the way we do it, and I think our way is best. And we don't have to go and buy things. We get our decorations from the woods,' Finlay said triumphantly.

'It seems a bit Pagan to me. Are your family even Christian? We never see anything of you in church, even though your workmen look after it…'

Finlay cut her short, 'Of course we look after it. It belongs to us.'

'Don't be stupid! How can the church belong to you?'

Finlay was getting cross. 'It belongs to us, because we built it, or my ancestors did. And it's on our land!'

Jenny arrived with a tray. 'Oh dear. Arguing already. Kee, you remember Caroline is a young lady. What an earth are you arguing about?'

'Well, he says the church belongs to you. I think churches belong to the Church. Don't they?' she asked.

'Not always Caroline,' Jenny said. 'This family does own the church. It's leased to the Church of England which is why Keith's grandfather has final say on who becomes the vicar. You have to understand this family has been here rather a long time. Now here's your tea and Kee, try to be more patient. Caroline comes from the town and you can't expect her to know what you know. You should help, not snap at her.'

She left and Finlay, duly admonished, handed Caroline a plate. 'Have something to eat. Janey tells me you go to Young Farmers. Do you enjoy that?'

'It's OK, I suppose, but they are so dismissive of me all the time. Janey Grieves runs it and we don't like each other. She called me a trollop.'

'I'm not sure what that is, but I'm sure she didn't mean it. She's always kind to me. Helped me a lot when I went to school. She was here over Christmas,' Finlay said, thinking not to elaborate why.

'Who looks after your mare? Are you ever going to take her hunting? She's so pretty. You might enjoy it.' She seemed more relaxed now.

Finlay explained he was having to learn so many things and then there was school work to do. There never seemed to be much time, not even time to look after his horse. 'One of our old carters looks after her when Mr Brockett isn't here. He's Grandfather's driver,' Finlay said. When Finlay told her about Starwort, she dismissed pigs as 'ghastly'. He changed the subject on to his current task of mechanics which she described as 'deadly boring' and how 'absolutely terrible for you'. She, in turn, could talk only of fashion and the latest films, and enquired whether Finlay ever went to the cinema.

'I went with Auntie Niney once to see *Gone with the Wind*. That was good,' Finlay said, remembering.

'Why do you call Mrs Terry, Auntie Niney? She isn't your real auntie is she?' Caroline asked.

'Her family has been with our family for generations. They become more important than family really. Granny Fortune is past ninety and she lived here when she was a girl. Anyway, Auntie Niney is quite the most important person there is,' Finlay said with some emphasis.

'She's very beautiful and so elegant. My mother gets really cross. Auntie Niney outshines everybody,' Caroline said suddenly, realizing a way through to Finlay. 'Could you teach me to drive your Land-Rover?'

'When the weather's better perhaps. But it's a farm vehicle and Grandfather uses it all the time.' Finlay was not going to be in any way committed. 'Maybe we could on a Sunday, when you don't have to work so hard. It would be available then.'

Caroline was not going to be put off.

'Grandfather goes to the pub on Sunday and he generally gets a little drunk. He needs the Land-Rover to get home. If he had the car he might well bash it or drive into one of the feeder streams.' Finlay tried to sound negative and convincing at the same time.

The front door bell rang. Voices sounded in the passageway and Mrs Keighley preceded Jenny into the hall. 'Oh, what a beautiful room!' she exclaimed. 'And your decorations are wonderful. A properly decorated country Christmas. How marvellous!'

Finlay gave Caroline a triumphant look.

'Did you do this, Jennifer?' she oozed.

'No, I helped Mrs Terry...' She couldn't finish.

'What a clever woman she is. We always buy her cakes at the fête. Such a competent woman, and so beautiful.'

'Yes. Makes you sick doesn't it, to be always in the shade,' Jenny said, with genuine fondness.

'We will do our main room this way, Caroline, next year. Do you think Mrs Terry would help me?' She was still oozing.

'You would have to ask her yourself, but I doubt she would have time. Christmas is pretty frantic here.' Jenny was certain she wasn't going to ask.

'Mother! No!' Caroline said firmly. 'What would my friends think, our home full of branches!'

'Better than bloody silly balloons,' Finlay muttered but only Caroline heard him.

Caroline and her mother made moves to leave. 'Would you like to come again?' Jenny asked.

'Yes please!' Caroline answered enthusiastically. 'It's been very interesting and I'd love Finlay to teach me how to fish and drive a Land-Rover.'

'I'm sure he would love to, Caroline. Wouldn't you, Kee?' Jenny said, and seemed serious about the offer.

'Yes. Of course,' Finlay answered, through gritted teeth. 'Perhaps on your next holidays.'

After they had left, Jenny said, 'There. That wasn't so bad, was it? You will have to deal with the opposite sex at some stage. I thought she was quite a nice girl. Didn't you?'

'No I didn't! I thought she was stupid! Don't ever invite her here again, not even as a joke! It was like trying to talk to a dolly. Her mind can't get further than the next pair of shoes her mother is going to buy her in London!' He snatched up the machinery manuals Carl had given him. 'I'm going to study these until dinner time. I have to know how to change some wheel bearings by morning.' He stomped away back to the hall, leaving her thinking just how much like his grandfather he was.

She left Finlay for an hour and then went to him in the hall. He was sitting in his grandfather's chair by the fire, studying the Ferguson manual. 'Budge up,' she said, and squeezed into the chair beside him. 'I'm sorry Kee. What started out as a joke became a bit serious. I just thought that, maybe, some time spent with someone of your own age would do you good. Am I forgiven?'

Finlay put his arm around her. 'Of course you are... Jennifer.' He began to giggle, knowing she hated to be called by her proper name.

She struggled, but he found he could hold her easily. 'You little sod! Let me go!' she said.

'Not until you promise never to do anything like that again.'

'I promise! I do! Let me go! God, you've got strong suddenly,' she laughed.

Finlay kissed her on the cheek. 'Is there any likelihood of some food in this establishment tonight, wench?' He let her go.

She stood up, took his hand and pulled him up from the chair. 'Our little boy has become quite the man suddenly. Your dinner is ready when you are. I wonder where James and Niney have got to?'

They ate in the kitchen. When they were alone together, they always read at the table, something Niney never allowed. Jenny read one of her law books, Finlay, on this occasion, the tractor manual. He began to wonder whether he would ever grasp the intricacies of a transfer reduction gearbox. Afterwards they went to the hall and listened to the wireless together, the fire warming them, until Finlay began to nod with tiredness. 'Think I'll go on to bed, Jen. Do you mind?'

'Of course not love.' She paused, wanting to say something. 'Kee darling, whatever happens in your life, I want you to remember, as I will, evenings like this. When it's peaceful and quiet, spending time with someone who loves you.'

He got up and kissed her. 'I will Jenny. We are mates, aren't we?'

'The very best... Night, night. See you in the morning,' she said.

In between the moment of being awake and being asleep, Finlay heard the car come up the drive. His bedroom was briefly lit by its headlights and then sleep came.

When he came down the next morning his grandfather had already gone. His cup and an open farming journal were still on the table. Finlay made some tea and toast. It was dark outside and a wind played around the ivy without malice. He picked up the manuals and left for the workshop. Walking down the back driveway, the stars, bright in the frosty sky, lighted the way. Though cold, the air was clear and fresh and the reflection of the sea glowed on the horizon. Away to the north east, he heard one of the contractors' huge machines bellow into life, lifting a flock of ducks from the river who whistled overhead in the darkness. The working day had begun.

Carl and Ron were already in the workshop when he got there. He saw Carl glance at his watch. 'How did the heavy date go, nipper?' Ron asked laughing. 'Get your hands on her new tits?'

'No I didn't!' Finlay answered. 'And I can't see myself ever wanting to. What a silly little bitch she ever is!'

Carl and Ron started laughing.

'You're not having a joke, Carl?' Finlay said, almost crossly.

The German looked at his watch once more. 'You are early. You have another just two minutes to joke. Then you change zee front wheel bearings in zat tractor.'

Finlay found the instructions in the Ferguson manual easy to follow. The old bearings came off easily and the new ones were slipped into place. 'Finished!' he announced. 'Would you like to come and check it?'

Carl walked over to where he was standing. 'If you have done it by zee book, I should not need to check, but on zis first time I vill, but not again, OK?' Carl spun the wheels of the jacked-up tractor and grasping the top of the tyre, jerked the wheel back and forth, looking for any play. 'Is good!' He glanced at his watch. 'Vun hour. Zee next vun in forty-five minutes. Now you go fer de breakfast. You have de same forty-five minutes.' He allowed himself a smile. Finlay made to leave. 'Hey! You hev not vashed de hands. You vont Mrs Niney to stick me vis de bloody prong.'

Finlay ran back to the house, arriving breathless, his face flushed with cold. 'Morning Grandfather. How did your meeting go?' He crashed down in his chair.

'More to the point, how did your meeting go?' his grandfather said, from behind the newspaper.

'I changed the front wheel bearings in one of the Fergies, without Carl telling me how to do it. "If you do it from de book, it vill be right,"' he said.

'I meant your tea-time meeting with little Caroline, as well you know!' and still from behind the newspaper, 'Pretty little thing, isn't she?'

'Pretty bloody stupid!' Finlay said. 'She thinks pigs are ghastly! She's going to this special school where she's going to learn to be a lady and learn manners. Honestly, I would think in both cases that's a waste of time. Either you are a lady and have manners or you're not. I shouldn't think it can be learnt!'

Finlay's grandfather exploded with laughter, 'That's true. Truer than you know.'

'You can be such an insufferable little prig, Keith Finlay. That's something you may think, but it's not perhaps what you need to say,' Jenny said giggling.

'Oh, sorry Jennifer, I'll remember that.' Finlay was already ducking the slap.

'Prig, spoilt sod!' Jenny said. '"I don't want to do that, Auntie Niney,"' she mimicked.

Finlay's grandfather coughed and disappeared behind his newspaper. 'I wouldn't upset her again Kee. Jenny can dream up horrible revenge.'

'Sorry Jen,' Finlay said quickly.

'How you getting on with Carl?' Jenny asked. 'He won't let you get away with anything.'

'I like the way everything's so ordered and quiet, and I didn't think I'd be very interested in the workshop, but it's good to learn something really practical.'

Finlay's grandfather was still behind the newspaper. 'Carl's the reason all our machinery works properly. Even in this cold, there was never a tractor that didn't start. And he gets along famously with Ron, so things should run smoothly when I'm tied up. I'll tell you what was discussed yesterday, this evening, Kee. You'd better be getting back. I don't want it said that because you're my grandson, farm timekeeping doesn't apply to you.'

'Let him sit for a while James,' Jenny said, putting her hand on Finlay's shoulder.

'Now who's spoiling him? Workshop, Kee, now! It's not good for you to be hanging around all these adoring women, and that includes this Caroline,' he chuckled.

Chapter Eleven

•

The old year slipped away but didn't die for many years to come. It would be for ever the Year of the Coronation. Time was somehow measured from it. 'That udd be the Coronation Year,' or 'That udd be two or three years afore the Coronation,' or 'Let me see now, Coronation wus fifty-two so 'twould 'av bin couple years after that.'

The Coronation had been a bright, colourful spectacle of pageantry; the new Queen was young and beautiful and her very being made the country happy and proud. This brightness spilled into the New Year almost as though the old year was not to be bested. The weather was bright and cold, the land still frozen hard. With the weather seemingly set, the dairy herds were let out in the daytime to make the most of the watery sun. They lay down happily on the hard dry fields, cudding contentedly, remaining clean and dry and feeding on the long lines of hay, silage and kale dropped for them from the feed trailers. Finlay worked in the workshop until the beginning of the second week of January, then had to take up his school work. Caroline had not been in contact again and had, he was told, departed again for her school.

Slowly, very slowly, the days became longer, allowing Finlay the time to go to the pig unit and watch Starwort's progress. The rest of the outside pig herd minced about on the hard earth, their feet more tender than those of the cattle and huge compounds of straw bales kept them warm and out of the wind. The river, the ever constant vein of their lives, unperturbed and lovely in the cold sun, flowed as always to the sea.

By the end of the month, everything was ready for the spring sowing. The tractors and field machinery waiting in the sheds, expectantly almost. The seed corn on trailers. 'When the weather gives, it's going to be balls to the wall time,' Ron had said. 'I've had more than enough of finding jobs for tractor drivers not able to get out on the fields.' It was only talk though. The redundant men had tidied yards, restacked sagging hay stores, mended tracks and fences so that when the weather did ease the whole place looked spick and span. Finlay's grandfather, despite the mounting pressure of the administrative needs of the estate with the impending move to TT, always went around the farm daily and liked what he saw. The gates swung properly, fences were tight and the ruts filled with hogging from the local gravel pit.

Towards the end of the month the wind veered to the west, the temperature rose above freezing for the first time in weeks and the land began to ease. At first, when the frost began to leave the soil, it became sticky and slippery on the first inch of depth. It was difficult even to walk on the land without losing your footing, but at last the frost gave up and the land work began. The little grey tractors, released at last from the bondage of their sheds, plied up and down the ploughlands, six to a field, twelve black furrows turned as they laboured line astern, the gulls and rooks wheeling above them, only stopping briefly for lunch when quiet returned for half an hour and then on till dark.

The farm yards were deserted in the hours of daylight. A quiet pervaded them and only the sparrows, those remaining after the hard weather, sang and quarrelled among themselves as they made ready for their breeding season. On the odd occasion, Carl would show himself and eat his lunch in the sun, sitting on a seat squab from a Land-Rover, his back against the wall, out of any wind. Just before dark the first of the tractors would return to re-fuel ready for the next day. Carl would replace any plough points needed and check oil levels, the tractor drivers, infected with the new foreman's enthusiasm, wondered how long the overtime would continue. By mid-March it was over. The barley and spring wheat were sown, harrowed and rolled. The grassland harrowed, rolled and fertilized, taking on the striped effect of silver and green as the sun sucked the green shoots upwards. At the end of it all, the men were given a long weekend off. From Thursday night till Tuesday morning and a few extra pounds in their pay packets.

Finlay, stuck with his studies, had missed all the frantic activity. Only on Saturdays and Sundays could he take up his rod or gun. Twice, during a two-month period, had he been called to 'feed the Danish house' when Ron had been very busy. Another time, he was delivered to the wood yard to help unload fencing stakes from lorries that had come down from the Midlands. Starwort, weaned now and living with just one barrow pig, was housed in an old-fashioned 'cottage sty' receiving the best of food and being 'handled' ready for the day when she would be put on display to the world. Already, showing the promise first seen on the day of her birth, she was turning into a beautiful young animal.

Finlay was tired. He had had to work all over the Easter holidays, watching the experiments that he had learned in theory and now had to do in practice. Physics was not his strongest suit. He knew he was tired because Shakespeare had become a chore, and when that happened he knew he needed a rest. With the evenings now getting longer with every passing day, he began to ride after tea. Just a gentle amble around the fields seeing how the crops had taken and noting how the new leys were growing. The small bird population had suffered badly, but the summer birds were arriving. The first swallows were hawking at insects on the river and the first broods of ducklings had arrived. The beech trees were showing their first leaves, dark against the misty green of the larch coming into needle and the few remaining wild daffodils nodded their acquiescence to the river. He was riding on the furthest easterly part of the estate, along a small, unused cart track. The old ridges of iron-shod wheels had left narrow ruts either side of a grassy rise in the middle. He eased his mare around an overgrown bend and was confronted by another rider coming towards him. For a moment he thought it was Caroline. Whoever it was stopped and seemed unsure whether to come on. He could see now it wasn't Caroline. She stopped about ten yards short of Finlay.

'Am I trespassing?' she asked.

'Yes you are, but you'll be all right. We've given up shooting trespassers for the summer,' Finlay smiled. 'Where are you going?'

She removed her hat and shook her hair. 'I was trying to get to Little Testwood. I have a friend who lives there…'

'Caroline Keighley. Well, I'm going back now. I'll show you the way. It's a bit round and about because of the streams, and you'll have to cross the little river. Is he all right in water? It's not very deep.' Finlay was more than a little taken with her. 'It'll be pretty well dusk by the time you get there though, and you'll be riding back in the dark.'

'You're the Finlay boy aren't you?' she said, more a statement than a question. 'I recognize your horse.'

'Yes, I'm just taking some time out from studying. It's a bit heavy going at the moment. If you still want to go to Little Testwood, we had better get a move on,' he said, turning his mare.

'Well, I don't really. Sorry. I saw you out two nights ago and thought maybe I would meet you. I wanted to ask Sir James if I could ride over his land and was going to ask you whether there was any chance before I made the approach. Your grandfather is a bit formidable.' She rode up beside him.

'Grandfather!' Finlay laughed. 'Formidable? He likes pretty girls on horses. What's your name and where do you live?'

'Rownhams, and I'm Jill. Jill MacFarlane. Do you think your grandfather will give me permission?' she asked.

'Well, if you kick on a bit you can ask him. I can hear his Land-Rover coming up from the wood yard. Come on!' He squeezed the mare with his legs and she started to trot. 'It gets wider up here and we can scat on a bit.'

Soon, both horses were cantering along one of the made-up tracks. Finlay stuck his fingers in his mouth and whistled as soon as he saw the Land-Rover. It stopped immediately; his grandfather got down and began filling his pipe. The two riders arrived together. 'Hello Grandfather. Look what I found on the old cart track,' Finlay joked.

'You two look happy. Introduce me to the young lady, Kee,' he replied, his eyes smiling.

'Grandfather. This is Jill MacFarlane, who lives at Rownhams. She was on her way to see if you would give her permission to ride over the estate. Jill, this is my grandfather, Sir James.' Finlay could see his grandfather was equally taken.

He raised his hat and shook her hand. 'I'm very pleased to meet you, Jill MacFarlane from Rownhams, and I thank you for having the manners to ask. If you come across to the house now I will give you the required permission in writing, which the insurance company insists on. Then I'm sure Kee will show you where it is safe to go. Where you must not go, because of animals and where best to cross the rivers and streams.' He got back in the Land-Rover and said, slowly, 'I'll go up the back drive… and I bet you five bob, I'm there before you!' The Land-Rover shot away.

'Come on Jill MacFarlane! Get your bum in gear. We can't let him win!' Finlay's mare knew this particular game and took off at a gallop on Finlay's bidding.

'I shall have to stay behind you, I don't know the way,' she shouted.

'You'll have to stay behind, Jill MacFarlane, because your horse can't run like this one,' Finlay shouted back.

After a few hundred yards, he reined in and waited. 'Will he jump?' he asked, as she caught up, a little breathless but laughing.

'He will, but I won't. I haven't done anything much except riding around the parks in London. You'll have to go on, if you must win.' She was calm again.

'No, we'll let him win for once. Come on, we can ride steadier. He still won't win by much,' Finlay said, impressed by the girl's pluck. 'How long have you lived in Rownhams?'

'Only a couple of years. My father's a big wheel in Ford's and he's down here to get the Southampton factory going. How well do you know Caroline?' she asked.

'Not very well. Jenny, my grandfather's sort of wife, asked her to tea last Christmas, because she thought I needed more company of my own age. But I don't think she liked coming.'

'Did you like her?' the girl asked directly.

'I don't know how well you know her and, anyway, I shouldn't talk about people in a personal way. Oh bugger it! No I didn't like her. I thought she was silly... You're all right though,' he said.

'How do you know? I've only known you for about ten minutes...' she began.

'Well, you ride about half-decent, you don't have silly affectations that I can see and you laugh a lot. And I don't think you would have to go to a special school to be taught manners.' The last part was said with as much scorn as he could muster.

She burst out laughing. 'What a prig you are! I go to the same school, Cheltenham. I do know Caroline and you're perfectly right, but be a little charitable.'

'Jenny said I was a prig, so I must be. It's not something that worries me. I'm not even sure of its exact meaning. Maybe I should look it up,' Finlay said.

'Well, you'd better look up trollop as well. Caroline said you didn't know what that meant either. You've been a bit sheltered,' she said, looking at him curiously.

'So that's what you do at Cheltenham. Discuss other people's short-comings.' He laughed. 'I don't have the luxury. I'm taught at home and just now it's bloody hard work.'

'I didn't say shortcomings. I think it's rather fun to meet somebody with your sort of upbringing. You're so lucky to travel. I've only ever been to France. Don't you miss going abroad?'

'Like I would miss having TB! My mama wanted me to go back to Ceylon with her...' He didn't finish.

'Mama! Where's that come from? You really are very quaint.' She was laughing at him and he found himself not minding.

'We can cut through the garden if you like,' he said, turning right through a hole in the hedge. 'Carl, our mechanic, made this hole with a tank. They're still on the lawn. Should have gone in March but we're still waiting,' he said, sadly. 'We do rather want the garden back.'

'What do I call you?' she asked, suddenly.

'Finlay will do. Anything you like. My real name is Keith, but most people call me Kee.'

Once at the front door, Finlay got down and led his mare up the steps and shouted. Getting no answer, he dropped the mare's reins and walked in. The mare followed him. Jill started to giggle as there came a shout from within the house. 'Will you please get that horse outside!'

Finlay and the mare bundled out of the door, with Jenny in hot pursuit. 'How many times do I have to tell you...' Jenny stopped when she saw the girl. 'Oh, I'm sorry. I didn't know you had someone with you.' She looked at Jill. 'I was sitting at the breakfast table reading. I look up and his horse is staring at me, wanting sugar knobs! I'm Jenny, and you must be the young lady who wants to ride over us.' She shook hands. 'Kee, take the young lady's horse. Then she can sign the insurance form.'

'I'm Jill MacFarlane, by the way,' Jill said getting down. She started to giggle again.

'Don't laugh. It only encourages him to be such a sod,' Jenny said, pretending to be angry.

They went into the house, leaving Finlay to sit on the steps and wait. Twenty minutes passed. It was getting quite dark, too dark to see across to the public road. He yelled for the two women to hurry up and waited again. Eventually, they both appeared, chattering amicably.

'Good Lord, it's dark,' Jenny said.

'It gets that way when the sun goes down, Jen,' Finlay said. 'Happens every day!'

'Don't be facetious Kee. How is the poor girl to get home? Why didn't you shout?' Jenny said. She seemed worried.

'I did shout. Shouted my head off.' Finlay snorted.

'Well, you didn't shout loud enough!' Jenny snapped.

'So it's my fault 'cos it gets dark now. Honestly Jen, you're impossible sometimes. What's there to worry about anyhow? Jill's horse can stay here overnight and someone can run her home. Simple!' Finlay said smugly.

'There's no one here, James went straight out again...'

'I don't want to be any trouble...' Jill said.

'Perhaps you should leave your horse here and ring your parents to come and get you. You can't ride home in the dark, especially if you're not sure of the way. That main road at Rownhams is dangerous at night with all the traffic,' Jenny suggested.

'My parents are in London, I'm afraid, so I could leave my horse and walk home or wait until somebody comes with a car,' Jill said. 'We should have seen how dark it was getting.'

'No,' Jenny said. 'Kee will put your horse away and you can stay the night. If James and Jack stop at the pub, you could be here all night anyway.'

'If it's not too much trouble. Ben will be OK, just turned out. He's out at home.'

'I'll put him in the paddock with Misty and give them a handful of hay. They seem OK with each other. You two go on in. Is your house all locked up Jill?' Finlay said, getting up but he didn't wait for an answer.

It was half an hour before he walked indoors again. Jenny was talking on the telephone and Finlay listened. 'No Gloria. Just put the calls to that number through to here… Well bend the rules. The young lady in question is staying here tonight… Thank you, Gloria,' she finished and hung the earpiece up again. To Finlay's enquiring look she said, 'Jill's parents will probably ring to see if she's OK so I asked Gloria to put it through. You'd think I was asking for the earth.'

'Grandad tells them. He doesn't ask. Where is he, anyway?' Finlay asked.

'The sluice has gone at Paulton's and the coarse fish are escaping. The River Board wanted our grills, so Jack and he have taken them to Ridge to block off there.'

'What's a sluice?' Jill asked.

'It's a gate to control the flow of water. Paulton's one is into their water wheel and drives the sawmill. The headwater is a big lake. Holds a huge amount of pike and they mustn't get into our river, or they'll spoil the fishing,' Jenny replied.

'We've lots of them,' Finlay added. 'The big ones are spectacular. The mill here makes lots of cattle food and generates electricity for us and Romsey.'

'And the grills? What are they?' Jill asked.

'They're wire racks which clip together and go across the river. They stop the fish moving up or down. The River Board will electro-fish the Blackwater if many escape. But they should have a spare gate, so perhaps it won't happen,' Jenny said, glad at least that this particular young woman asked sensible questions.

'Is there anything to eat?' Finlay asked. 'It'll be a long night if Uncle Jack and Grandad get in the pub.'

The two women made some corned beef sandwiches. Finlay thought Jill seemed quite happy to join in.

'Let's go through to the hall, shall we?' Jenny suggested. 'We shall hear the phone in there if your parents call. Where do you go to school, Jill?' she asked.

'Cheltenham, I'm afraid,' Jill responded. 'Where females who have no manners naturally, have to go to be taught them!'

'Oh Kee. Honestly! You shouldn't say things like that to people you don't know. I'm sure Jill has perfect manners.'

'I didn't say that about Jill. I said it about Caroline Keighley. And if either of you think I'm going to take out every word and look at it before I speak, you can think again,' Finlay said, a trifle more truculently than he meant it to sound.

'How does your schooling work Finlay? Being taught at home? How do you do your exams, for example?' Jill asked.

'It's just the same. I have to keep to normal school hours and follow the same subjects. I'll do the same exams as you. I'm working for some early GCEs. Get them out of the way. I take them in June, same as you,' Finlay said.

'What's your worst subject? You seem so bloody competent. There must be something, some chink in your armour,' Jill said.

'Well, I'm not that good at physics,' he admitted.

'OK, so what are you good at?' she asked.

'English. I love English literature. That's one I'm taking in June…'

She cut him off. 'How old are you then? I'm taking mine in June and I'm sixteen.' Jill seemed surprised.

Jenny interrupted. 'He's quite the clever clogs. If he'd not given up school, his life would be easier.'

'I hear you were expelled. I think that's good. Just think. I was at Cheltenham Ladies' College, but got expelled. You could dine out on that for a year,' she laughed.

'I left,' said Finlay shortly.

'What books are you doing in English? Which Shakespeare, for example?' she asked, as though she didn't really believe what he was saying.

'*Macbeth*, Joseph Conrad, Steinbeck, Gray and Blake,' Finlay said, sounding as bored as possible. 'I don't want to talk about school work, for goodness' sake.'

'Well, I'm doing the same set as you. Oxford University. Isn't that strange!' she exclaimed. 'Do you think you'll pass?'

'Of course,' he said, lightly.

'My God!' she laughed. 'You really are a cocksure bugger. How do you know?'

'I'll get a torch and go see the horses are OK together,' he said firmly.

Jenny coughed. 'I think Jill is teasing you Kee. You've maybe met your match.'

'Finlay, come back. I'm only teasing you,' Jill said, but he had gone. She looked at Jenny. 'The male ego thing is such a bore. Should I go after him?'

'If there was time I would explain, Jill, but if you want him as a friend I should go after him. Maybe we can speak later,' Jenny said.

Jill hurried after Finlay. 'Finlay come back. Don't be huffy. I was teasing you, I'm sorry.' She caught up with him and put her arm through his. 'I'm sorry Finlay, please let's be friends.'

Finlay found he could not but like this girl. He found her laughter infectious. 'It's me that should be sorry Jill. I'm a bit tired and you've thrown my equilibrium. I think I like you and that's odd, because I'm not really that keen on girls,' Finlay said.

'Good. I know I like you and if I have to destroy your awful selfpossession to get to know you, then that's what I'll do. Ho hum. I go back to school at the end of the week, so can we spend tomorrow together? We can compare notes on our English. Sorry, but you're interesting and kind. Us town girls can be a bit pushy.' They were silent for a few moments. 'Tell me about your equilibrium, Finlay.' There was compassion in her voice.

'Oh, it's just this problem I have with people my own age. It was the same at school. I think they viewed me as some kind of oddity. I know what the problem is. I've never had any friends of my own age, but don't think I'm sorry for myself.' He stopped.

'Go on Finlay. Tell me. Then it's done. I don't think you're odd, I promise.' She put her arm around his shoulder.

'When I met you tonight, I thought, "I really like this person. Or maybe I don't." Maybe I just wanted to talk to you. Just for once, I felt I didn't have to be the boss's grandson,' Finlay said. He felt relieved he had said what he had said.

'I think you're just lonely and tired,' Jill said.

'And then here you are. I've known you for all of two hours and suddenly I'm relaxed and happy with you. It's a bit scary,' Finlay said.

'Then be glad we met. I know I am. I'm able to ride over your land, I've made a new friend and there are only two things I want. Give me some of your aristocratic confidence, and I want you to show me how to have your way with animals.'

There was a shout from the house. 'Hey, you two!' It was Jenny. 'Come in can you? Your mother's been on the phone Jill.'

'OK, Jen,' Finlay shouted back.

'Finlay,' Jill said quietly. 'If it helps, I think you are going to be a bit special to me.' They walked back to the house holding hands.

'Have the horses settled together?' Jenny asked, when they were back indoors. 'Your mother telephoned. I'm sure she'd like to hear from you. There's the number. Just lift the earpiece and the operator answers. Would you like us to leave the room?'

'No, of course not,' Jill said. 'In fact, I want Finlay to listen. She'll want to know all about him and I shall have to put her mind at rest. She thinks all boys just want one thing.'

'I'll leave you to it then, and get your bed ready.' Jenny ran her hand over Finlay in passing.

'Hello Mother,' Jill said, as the connection was made. 'No, I'm perfectly all right... Yes, he's out in the field with Finlay's horse...' There was a long gap. 'No Mother. He's a pet. Very old-fashioned with beautiful manners... Oh, he's much younger than me... No, he's only a boy...' She made a face at Finlay. 'No I shan't forget. I'll see you when you get back. Bye.'

She came over to the table and put her arm around his shoulders. 'Sorry about the boy bit. Had to say that or she would have been on her way here by now!'

'Well, shows she cares at least. Let's go and find Jen and see where you're sleeping.' He got up and led the way through the hall and up the stairs.

'This is a lovely old house Finlay,' Jill said, as they got to the top landing. 'How old is it?'

'Queen Anne. The one before that got burnt down. Costs a lot to keep up to scratch and it's as cold as anything. Still, it's a homely sort of place,' he said absently. 'Where are you, Jen?' he shouted.

'In your mother's room,' came the reply.

'Homely! I shan't be able to find my way back,' Jill laughed.

They found Jenny putting the finishing touches to the bed. 'You go back down Kee. I'll sort Jill out and show her where everything is.' It was an order.

'Shall I put some milk on? Do you like cocoa Jill?' he asked, knowing Jenny wanted him gone.

'Please! I don't think I've had cocoa in years,' she replied.

In the kitchen, Finlay dutifully measured out three mugs of milk into a saucepan. The thick milk, luscious and creamy from the short-horns, would soon become a memory for people on the estate. The TT regulations would see to that. It seemed stupid to Finlay. For three hundred years they had drunk what was now called raw milk with no ill effects. Soon they would have to drink pasteurized liquid, and he wondered how the older people would like it.

The milk saver in the bottom of the saucepan began to rattle its protest that the milk was boiling, so he moved the pan over to the warm side and watched the skin develop, just how he loved it. He heard the Land-Rover arrive in the yard and glanced at the wall clock. It was only ten-fifteen. 'Not been to the pub tonight,' he said, aloud to himself. His grandfather's drinking never bothered Finlay. It had always been the case. Sometimes it worried him, when he saw how some nights his grandfather was incapable of putting the Land-Rover in the garage. Some mornings he would find it parked in a flower bed under the windows. On one memorable night, the car was half-way up the steps to the front door. Finlay's grandfather claimed he had forgotten he was in the vehicle and just went to go indoors. Carl had mended the track-rod and the doctor his grandfather's head.

'Hello my boy,' he said coming into the kitchen. 'Got the cocoa going I see. Splendid!'

'I'll have to put another mug of milk in the pan. We have a guest overnight,' Finlay said, going to the ancient refrigerator.

'Didn't know we were having company. No matter. They're very welcome,' his grandfather said, as he washed his hands in the sink.

'Did you manage to stop the lake emptying?' Finlay asked.

'Eventually. They're a pretty hopeless lot up there. No equipment at all. Never mind, it'll hold till morning. That's what counts. Jack and I were having a talk on extending the fishing, the feeder that runs from the top bridge...'

Jenny and Jill MacFarlane came into the kitchen and Finlay's grand-father stood, looking surprised. 'Hello again,' he said to Jill. 'Didn't expect to see you but you're very welcome.' He looked quizzically at Jenny.

'It was too dark for Jill to go home, so we decided she could stay. Her horse is in the paddock with Misty.'

'They're OK together I take it.' He started making a sandwich. 'Have you all eaten?'

Jenny gently took over the sandwich making. 'Sit James, you look exhausted. I honestly don't know why you had to turn out. I don't think you should be doing that sort of thing with all you've got to cope with. We should get away. It'll soon be silage time, then hay and then harvest will be on top of us. A couple of weeks away will do us good. Niney can look after Kee.'

'A week would be enough, surely...' he said.

'Two! Argue any more and I'll insist on three. You've got a farm fore-man now. Leave Ron to it,' Jenny said forcefully. 'Kee is worn out as well. All the pair of you do is work. He thinks while you're working, he has to.'

'Do I get a holiday then?' Finlay said hopefully.

'When you've done your exams,' Jenny said. 'And you can take some time off now. You should do as Mr Pearce suggested, remember? And have a day on the Forest. You could ring him in the morning. I'm sure Jill would love to do that with you.'

'Would you?' asked Finlay.

'Of course I would. Tomorrow we can ride around. I have to be back to school at the end of the week and it would be super to dream about riding every day. I want to see your O-level work as well.'

Finlay's grandfather held up his hand. 'I'd forgotten. Jen, can you and Niney interview the prospective gardeners tomorrow? Look in my diary for their names and times they're due. If you think one is suitable, take him on for September. Show him his house and intro-duce him to Ron. There's one who has applied from Motisfont. He sounds about right, but don't let me sway you. I'll leave it to you.'

'If he's confronted with Niney and myself, he'll run a mile,' Jenny said seriously.

'Pick the one that doesn't run Jen 'cause he'll be a brave man!' Finlay laughed.

'Enough of your cheek, buggerlugs! It's past time for you young ones. Off to bed,' Jenny said. 'And James, I need to speak to you about something.'

'Who is Niney, Finlay?' Jill asked as they went up the stairs.

'Auntie Niney is... well, Auntie Niney is different. You'll see in the morning. We have breakfast about half-eight.' They had reached her bedroom. 'I'm opposite. If you want anything in the night, come and wake me.'

'Night, night Finlay,' she said and kissed him on the cheek. She looked him in the eyes. 'See you in the morning.'

Chapter Twelve

•

Finlay's thoughts were tinged with sadness as he lay awake the next morning. The sun was only just above the horizon and his room was still suffused with grey-blue shadows. Outside what there was of the dawn chorus was thin and patchy. He lay there and counted just two blackbirds singing. There wasn't a wren to be heard, nor yet a robin. The winter frost had done its terrible work. Even the cheering sound of house martins, just waking beneath the eaves, failed to cheer him. Away in the far distance, a cock pheasant shouted his challenge at the spreading dawn soon answered by another, hard by the house. They were silenced by the majestic crowing of General Auckinleck, the huge, light Sussex cock, who lived in the grain store. Auckinleck crowed again, daring all to challenge his majesty. He was a bird with a singular lack of a sense of proportion, known to attack anything from Ayrshire bulls, in themselves always something of a handful, to lorries making deliveries. Only Joe the Postman would be let cross the yard unmolested.

Once, Finlay was in the yard when a gaudy cock pheasant made a half-hearted advance on one of Auckinleck's wives. There was a brief silent struggle of flying feathers and the cock pheasant lay fluttering in the dust; his temerity had cost him dear. Auckinleck treated Finlay with an uncompromising hostility, having suffered several indignities at his hands. Finlay, needing an opponent to practise his fencing, had chosen Auckinleck. Not only would he be a doughty and unforgiving opponent, but any failure on Finlay's part would mean bloody legs. They fought for several minutes before his grandfather had come apon the scene. The boy, dancing and fending off the bird with his foil, his legs streaming with blood. The bird, bruised by being whacked by the sword's edge, silent and determined.

Finlay's grandfather had laughed at the spectacle at first. Then the bird flew at Finlay's face. The fend-off was not wholly what it should have been. Blood flowed from Finlay's cheek and wrist. 'Enough!' his grandfather had shouted and threw his jacket over the bird, trapping it, a struggling ball of fury. 'The bloody bird will have your eye out. Don't you think he's bad enough already without you provoking him?' A breathless Finlay had been shepherded to the kitchen to have his battle scars swabbed with the inevitable iodine. The pain made Finlay wince and resolve to seek a return match.

With the sun now driving the shadows from the room's corners and the moorhens fussing and clucking on the stream in the garden, Finlay rose, dressed and thought about the girl sleeping in his mother's bed. She couldn't be said to be pretty. Rather, she was striking, with dark brown hair and green eyes. The eyes overarched with thick eyebrows and complemented with enormously long lashes. In shape, she was what his grandfather would have described as being 'nicely put together', having a 'touch of quality' and not 'too fine-boned'. An adage from Ron on the opposite sex brought a smile to his face. 'If you're going to buy milking cows or thinking about a wife, you wanna see 'em fust thing in the morning. If either don't look right then, they ain't worth your time.'

He went outside, thinking to look at the horses. The sky's blue was speckled with small puffs of cloud, very high, their undersides glowing gold with the sun climbing higher. Old John was in the tack room ferreting about. 'Morning John,' Finlay said. 'What are you about so early for?'

'Morning Master Keith.' John always used this address. 'I been told to get these 'osses ready for out by Miss Jenny and I can't find 'ead collar for the big 'un. Who's he belong to? Nice sort, ain't he? Bin shod bad though, 'is feet want cutting back a fair whack.'

'Belongs to a girl who we've got staying the night. How are your joints today, John?' Finlay asked.

John seemed to be moving better than when Finlay last saw him. Ignoring the question, John said, ''Er as lives over the back of Rinhams. Nice-looking little wench. Always says a nice thank you when you goes by with the tractor.'

'If you knew, why did you ask?' Finlay laughed.

'I was just sayin'… there'll be plenty more like 'er 'anging around now as you growed up a bit. When their little fannies start to itch, they'll all be round wanting you to scratch 'un.' He started walking away chuckling, heading for the paddock. He came back leading both horses. Handing Misty to him, he said, 'I'll do 'er. I'll make a better job of it than you. Don't want that Miss Jenny thinkin' as 'ow I skimped the job.'

'How long you worked here, John?' Finlay asked. 'I hope you don't mind me asking.'

John began grooming the gelding. 'I wos born here. That ud be 1873. My mother 'ad me up top end. 'Er was 'oeing and got took a bit short so she 'ad me under the hedge that runs along by the top feeder.'

He smiled at the thought of it. 'Her wrapped me in a summer fly blanket from one of the 'osses after she washed me in the stream, cleansed herself, had a bit of a splash in the river, then went on 'oeing. When the boss come, one of the other wimmen told 'un wot 'ad 'appened. 'Ee went bloody daft. Put my mother and me in the gig, took back to the 'ouse and kept 'er there a fortnight. The best room, best grub and people waitin' on 'er. Old boss, your grandad's father, said nuthin' like that must 'appen again. 'Ee was to be told when anybody was 'aving a baby. Said as 'ow he was so ashamed that one of his own people, that's what 'ee called 'em, 'is own people, had 'ad to suffer that. Then, they planted an oak tree up there, an' the woodman was told if it died, so wud 'ee. That tree was there to show every bugger how ashamed the old boss was. Well then, Cyril come from Embley and your grandfather tells 'un to look after the tree. When they ol' Jerries starts their bloody bombing lark, Cyril goes to see the vicar and says could they pray for the tree. Well, old vicar says they would, if he ud come and do 'is garden in 'is spare time. Well, one Saturday afternoon boss wants 'un. Cyril's missus tells where 'ee was and, bugger my boots, boss goes, gets him and gives the vicar a bloody good earful. Being the dopey bugger 'ee was 'ee do answer back an the Old Man sacks 'un on the spot. On the bloody spot! Your grandfather said as 'ow 'ee 'ad bugger-all to do all week, 'cept on a Sunday and the fat bastard should do 'is own bliddy garden. The vicar said 'as 'ow your grandfather couldn't sack 'un. "Us'll see about that," says your grandfather. Well, that week we wus all put to moving straw and we must have put the better part of four hundred tons in the church. We moved all the pews and bits of carpet and just filled the bugger up. "Lease is cancelled now vicar, so you got no bloody church," and your grandfather locked the door and that was that. Now come 'ere and feel these 'osses. That's done proper now.'

Finlay had to admit he had never achieved such perfection. He pushed his face into the mare's shoulder. 'They smell lovely, John, don't they?' he said.

'Ah, best smell in the world. A groomed horse on a warm mornin', better smell than any woman.' He fondled the mare's ears. 'You're a little witch, ain't you my beauty.'

'Thank you for doing that,' Finlay said.

''Tis my pleasure Master Keith, specially now I got to go and wash some machine or other fer Carl. No good talking to them bloody things,' he said grumpily.

A townsman in the country is often amazed at the accuracy of a countryman's awareness of the time of day. If asked, the countryman will look at the sun, perhaps chew his lip for a few seconds and say something along the lines of, 'Be about half-past eleven.' The townsman, amazed at the accuracy, more so if the sun happened to be obscured by clouds, will wonder how it was done. Finlay, walking away from the stable yard, knew it to be about a quarter to eight, not because of the sun's position but because he could hear the dairyman's collies barking, shepherding the cows to pasture. Milking was finished. He registered the rattle of the milk lorry crossing the bridge on the main road, a good mile away. He decided to see Carl. He needed some advice on a job his grandfather had briefly mentioned the evening before, extending the fishing.

Getting to the workshop he smiled and gingerly opened the door. 'Carl, I've got Queen Elizabeth here, wants you to have a look at her Land-Rover.'

'Tell her to come back in vone hour, maybe I look then,' he said from beneath the Armstrong. 'Miss Jenny say dis machine has to be ready by nine, so ze Queen vill hav to vait!'

On his hands and knees Finlay peered under the car. 'Could you have a look to see what I would have to do to make the sluice on the big feeder work? But only when you have the time.'

'Ya dis I vill do, I nearly finish here, so tell ze Queen to vash her own Land-Rover, zen I look at it,' he said.

'You ain't making jokes Carl, are you?' Finlay asked.

'Today vee can make ze jokes. I hav found my brudder who I vas thinking vas dead, he thinking I vas dead. So ve can make jokes.' Even with Carl's strangled English, Finlay could see the man was near to tears.

'Carl, that's bloody wonderful! Are you going over to see him? Have you told Grandfather? He'll be so pleased for you.'

'Go and hev your food. Tell Miss Jenny I vill bring ze car... now go.' Carl could barely speak.

Finlay ran to the house and rushed into the kitchen. Only Jenny was there. 'Jen, Carl has found his brother who he thought was dead. Isn't that amazing? We have to do something to get him to Germany...'

'That's what I wanted to speak to James about last night. Somebody telephoned to check that Carl was the right chap. Brockett is going to drive him to Harwich this afternoon. His brother's coming over on a ship and we'll tell Carl when he brings back the car,' Jenny said.

'That's wonderful Jen! Why didn't you say last night?' Finlay asked.

'We needed to think of the best thing to do. If you remember, we had a visitor last night, or had you forgotten?'

Finlay realized. 'Oh yes, I had forgotten. Is she up yet?'

'You really are bloody hopeless, Kee! The poor girl spends the entire evening giving you adoring looks and come the morning, she's forgotten. Jill is up. I heard the bath water running. Which reminds me, how long since you had a bath young man?'

'Oh, two or three days,' Finlay answered lightly.

'Much more like seven or eight! After breakfast you can go and have one and no bloody arguments about it!' Jenny ordered. The way it was said told Finlay it was pointless to argue.

'When are you having a holiday Jen?' he asked, quickly changing the subject.

'Don't try that one. You're having a bath. Why this much fuss I'll never know,' she sighed.

Finlay's grandfather's Land-Rover arrived in the yard, followed by Ron's and a saloon car that Finlay didn't recognize. They could hear Niney directing operations. The saloon's driver turned out to be the owner of the tractor firm the estate dealt with. Niney was first to arrive in the kitchen. 'Good morning both of you.' She kissed Finlay. 'You need a bath!' she said to him, wrinkling her nose. 'After breakfast!'

Jenny glowed with triumph. 'Told you so!'

Everybody arrived at once, talking about Carl's good news. Finlay's grandfather kissed Jenny and asked if all was prepared. From somewhere, Finlay heard his name being called.

'Go and get her Kee. Poor girl is probably shy,' Jenny ordered.

Jill was hanging back by the hall doorway. 'What's happening?' she asked.

'Bit of a celebration. Come along and meet everyone. I'll explain in a minute.' He took her hand and led her forward. As they entered the kitchen, conversation stopped.

'Ah yes,' his grandfather began. 'This is Jill MacFarlane from Rownhams, everyone. Kee captured her last night and brought the prisoner back here for interrogation.'

The girl began to blush and, much to Finlay's surprise, Niney took her arm and guided her to a chair. 'Take not a bit of notice my dear. Come and sit here. I'm Niney by the way.'

Finlay glanced at Ron. 'Any more like that about, nipper?' he asked. 'I found one like it down by the boards, but she was a gurt tall gangly thing. Her name was Annona.'

Uncle Jack laughed with the others.

'Must be something about the place. I found this one at Toothill,' Finlay's grandfather said, putting his arm around Jenny.

'Enough!' snapped Niney. 'As far as you're concerned Jack Terry, you couldn't find the thing in your trousers till I came along!'

'Now you've met my Auntie, Jill,' Finlay said. He got up and put his arms around Niney. 'Told you she was different.'

Niney hugged him tightly. 'Here's the man of the moment,' Niney said.

As the Armstrong pulled into the yard she abandoned Finlay, took Jill's arm and led her out, explaining what news Carl had had. The mechanic seemed confused by the group clapping his arrival. 'Vy are you clapping?' he asked.

Jenny stepped forward. 'Because we're pleased for you Carl. Your brother is arriving in Harwich late this afternoon and Mr Brockett is taking you to meet him.'

They took it in turn to shake his hand and there were tears in his eyes. 'I don't know vat to say.'

Brockett arrived in his highly polished Morris and Finlay saw his grandfather pass something to Brockett. Money for petrol he thought, most probably.

'Can I zay zank you…' Carl began.

'Another time Carl, it's a long drive,' Finlay's grandfather said.

They all waved as the car went away down the driveway.

'Now my dear,' Niney said to Jill, taking her arm. 'Come and have some breakfast and you can tell me about yourself.'

Finlay made to follow, but Jenny held his arm. 'Give them a couple of minutes to get sorted, Kee. This has come as a bit of a shock to Niney.'

'What?' asked Finlay.

'Far too subtle for a man to comprehend,' she replied softly.

'Sorted what?' asked Finlay.

'Whether Jill's likely to be the one who displaces her. You're the child Niney never had. She's possessive of you, even more than a mother. Her instinct, women's instinct, will tell her,' Jenny said seriously.

'You're not serious are you?' Finlay said.

'Never more so. You must be specially loving to Niney. Now come along, time for breakfast,' Jenny said, guiding him towards the door.

'You're not put out by it, Jen, are you?' Finlay said.

'Of course not! You and I are different. Nothing will ever come between us, not even Niney. Not even bloody Starwort!' She guided him indoors.

Niney and Jill were laying the table for breakfast. To Finlay, they seemed amiable enough, chatting about horses. He thought women were far too complex to understand as he ran his hand over Niney's back. She, in turn, affected not to notice but Jenny saw her smile.

'Shout James his breakfast is ready, darling,' Niney said. 'Where are you going to ride today?'

'All over I suppose. I'll show Jill where she can go and where to cross the river. Then we can compare our school work,' he said.

'Ah, here we are,' Finlay's grandfather said, walking into the room. Looking at Jill he asked, 'Did you sleep well young lady?'

'Yes, thank you,' she replied. 'Do you always get up so early?'

Jenny placed a large flat earthenware dish in the middle of the table. It had been in the bottom oven, the bacon and sausages in it beautifully married to the tomatoes. 'Help yourself Jill,' Jenny ordered. 'Before the men get there and wolf the lot.'

'We have to get up early because of the dairies. If we didn't the people in Southampton wouldn't have any milk,' Finlay's grandfather explained.

'But our milk comes in bottles. Is that the same milk?' Jill said.

Finlay's grandfather explained how the distribution system worked and added, 'Our bacon is from our own pigs, a pig that didn't grade properly. We have it back and the butcher cuts it for us.'

'Bacon is from pigs?' Jill seemed incredulous.

'Of course. Where did you think it came from?' Finlay's grandfather smiled.

'From the grocer. I'd never really thought about it.'

'This is going to be a big problem in the future, Jill. Town people are getting too far away from the land. Their food neatly packaged and completely divorced from its origins.'

'James, don't downbeat the girl so,' Niney said.

'Wherever it comes from, it's wonderful,' Jill said, which was just about the best thing she could have said.

'From what you're saying Jill, you've yet to meet Starwort?' Jenny said, looking at Finlay.

'Oh Jen, don't go on about her. You exaggerate so,' Finlay objected.

'Let me tell you Jill. Starwort, according to Kee, is the most beautiful female ever to tread the earth. The prettiest face, the most beautiful legs and the shapeliest bottom any female could have.'

Finlay tried to stop Jenny talking, but she held him off, laughing. 'I've known him walk four miles in the freezing cold just to see her... And this female's a pig.'

'A pig!' Jill exclaimed. 'A pig!'

'I'll show her to you tonight,' Finlay said, resuming his seat. 'We're putting her in the maiden gilt class at the Royal Counties. Then you'll be eating your words!'

'I'm a little lost,' Jill said. 'I haven't the faintest clue about Royal Counties.'

Finlay's grandfather explained how it all worked, how important such things were to farmers and finished by saying, 'It's our equivalent of a fashion show, I suppose.'

'I've already got my new hat, Jen,' Niney said. 'Very wide and very glam. I got it in Winchester.'

'If you're on to hats, I'm off. Don't forget to do a proper job on these gardeners. You both know what to look for,' Finlay's grandfather said.

'What do we look for first in a new gardener, Niney?' Jenny asked, looking a little impish.

'A nice pert bum I should think, Jen. We don't want to be cruising around the garden and suddenly come across some slack old bugger do we,' Niney said. 'Something a bit easy on the eye.'

Finlay's grandfather grunted. 'As long as this one's not a blasted poacher!'

'You picked him!' Niney and Jenny said, almost together.

'Now,' Niney said, getting up. 'You have something to do upstairs Kee I believe, so get gone. Is there anything you need, Jill?'

'No, Jenny has dealt with that. I'd better get my horse in and get him ready,' she said.

'That's done. Old John has groomed them and done their feet,' Jenny said. 'Let's get the breakfast things away. Niney, did James speak to you about he and I going away for a couple of weeks?'

Later, as Jill and Finlay were saddling up, Jill said, 'Jenny's so kind. She gave me a toothbrush and a clean pair of pants. I thought that was so thoughtful.'

'What did you think of Auntie Niney?' he asked.

'Completely wacky! She gave me a good once over before she was satisfied. You didn't tell me she'd been to Cheltenham. God, she's so beautiful. Fancy having to live in her shadow.'

'Which way do you want to go?' he asked. 'Everybody lives in Auntie's shadow, even Grandfather, even my mother. I don't know how the place would function without her.'

'Can we ride over to Caroline's house? I haven't seen her this holiday,' Jill asked.

'Surely. Is your horse OK in water? We'll have to cross a little river.'

'How deep's the water?' she asked.

'About up to his belly. What's his name by the way?' Finlay said, leading out his mare.

'Laddie. He might cross it. We'll have to see. Give me a leg up, Finlay.' She proffered her leg and Finlay obliged. They rode down through the main yard and John, washing down a trailer, stopped to allow them to pass.

'Mornin' agin, Master Keith. Mornin' Missy,' he said, touching his forehead.

'Thanks for grooming my horse, John. He looks super,' Jill said.

'Ah, he be a nice sort, but I told Master Keith he do want his feet cut back fairish. You 'ave a good day mind.' John was anxious to get his job done.

Around the corner of the barn, Jill started to giggle. 'Master Keith! That's a bit feudal. And he touched his forelock!'

'Don't laugh at what you don't understand,' Finlay said, perhaps a touch more curtly than he meant to.

'Sorry I'm sure!' she answered tartly. 'Did Master Keith get out of the wrong side of the bed this morning?' She touched her hat. 'Should I ride behind you Master Keith? You really are a bloody scream Master Keith.'

She rode up beside him. 'You're cross aren't you? Well, I'm not going to let you be.' She leant over, grabbed his rein, moved across and kissed him. 'Open your bloody mouth, Finlay,' she said laughing. 'I'm not going to eat you!'

The kiss lasted some time. They parted a little breathless. 'That's what's known as a French kiss, Finlay. Could you possibly get the hang of it? You might know lots about lots, but you know nothing about girls. Now let's try that again.' They did. Finlay was more enthusiastic, amazed how sweet she tasted. His hand strayed gently to her right breast. It felt firm but pliant. Jill mumbled what he took to be approval. Her nipple was trying, it seemed, to burst through her shirt.

She suddenly pulled back from him. 'That's what I call quick learning,' she gasped. 'Let's go somewhere where we can get down.'

Finlay led her to a small point where a stream joined the river by a sluice spillway, shielded by hazel and alders. The horses were abandoned to crop the turf and she pulled him down beside him. They began to kiss again. It was just as Ron had told him. She undid her shirt and got the now expected asthma attack, as Finlay touched her naked breasts. 'I've never done this Jill. Have you?' Finlay's head was spinning. He tried to undo the waistband of her trousers. Her hand came down and stopped him.

'You can't really go in there today. I'm having my period, and it's a bit heavy. But let me try this.' She undid his trousers and released Finlay. He had never felt such sensation and as he came to a climax, he desperately wanted to kiss her.

'Oh wow!' she gasped, looking at the sticky liquid shining on the grass. 'We did that! I did it for you. Isn't that great?'

She lay back on the grass. 'The sun feels lovely on my boobs. Next time I'm home, can we do it properly? Your nose has little beads of sweat on it.'

They lay side by side for some minutes. 'I've never done sex with a boy before. We do sort of experiment at school. We have to find out, don't we? Grown-ups are so stupid. After all, what harm can a finger do?'

Her matter-of-factness made Finlay laugh. 'I don't see why I should be shocked. Heifers are always riding each other.'

She yelled with laughter. 'Honestly Finlay, you're such a card. Going to bed with another girl doesn't mean I'm a lezzie, but it's nice all the same. Some of the older girls are really stuck on it, so I thought the sooner I can find a chap I really fancy, the sooner I can do it, and get this whole virginity bit out of the way. When I met you I thought yes, that's him. Shocking, but you see my point, don't you?'

Finlay said he did and began playing with one of her nipples. 'You've got a man's hands, Finlay. Is that all the work you do?'

'Probably,' he answered. The small pink nipple swelled and became hard, just like a threepenny bit.

She reached for him again. 'Will it work again, do you think? I've read that you have to rest in between times.'

Again there were the consuming sensations. A spinning head, the sudden awareness of the brightness of the light, the greenness of the grass and the tumbling of the water. 'I think it's truly wonderful. Absolutely fascinating, you see. That's life.' She put her finger in the opaque liquid and studied it closely. Almost trance-like, she ran her finger around her nipple, shuddered slightly.

Finlay was perplexed. 'Perhaps I should read some books?' he suggested.

'No, no!' she exclaimed emphatically. 'I don't know why I just did what I did. My mind said do it and it was right. It's instinct and books would spoil that! I want to explore. You see, I'm going to be a doctor and a doctor has to know about instincts.'

'Am I an experiment then?' Finlay asked, not quite knowing what to feel.

'Don't be silly. Of course not. Let me explain. Would you have done what we have just done with Caroline? Truly now.' She was studied with intensity.

'Of course not. She's such a dopey bugger and, well, I don't know, I wouldn't want to. I don't know why.'

'The difference is you like me, fancy me if you will. There's something when you first meet somebody that tells you that. Another instinct. I think that's quite astounding. I must write it down.' Jill appeared intense. 'Think about something you do Finlay, something you know is going to happen and you don't know why. Help me Finlay!'

He teased his brain to think properly. It took several minutes to find what he thought she was looking for. 'I know! I know!' he said. 'When you're fishing, suddenly you know you are going to catch one. You just know when your fly goes out that it's that cast. That's the one. So you're ready and bang! You get him.'

She began to dress again. 'That's exactly the sort of thing. You don't know why but you are absolutely certain. Finlay, I'm sixteen and a bit, but one thing I am certain of is that instincts are vital. You and fishing, that must be part of your hunter instinct, the one that fed the family in man's early days. Let's have a pact Finlay,' she said. 'That you and I will always say what we really think to each other.'

'OK,' he replied easily.

They rode on towards the river, side by side.

'What kind of doctor do you want to be?' Finlay asked.

'A surgeon I think. That's what I'm aiming at anyway, but it's difficult enough to be a female doctor, leave alone a surgeon. I'll probably have to go to America. What do you want to do? Stay here I suppose.

Be the local squire, and have your way with all the local girls!' She laughed.

'I'm going in the Navy. I'm away to the college in eigteeen months. That's why I'm taking exams early.'

'I shall have to make the most of you, then. Is that your father's photograph in your mother's room? You look like him,' she said.

'So I'm told. He's in Korea at the moment, fighting, and my mother is in Ceylon. She went out directly after Christmas to be near him.' Saying it, he realized that he had not given her a thought in days.

'Do you miss them? I mean, being away from you?' she asked.

'Not really. You reach a stage when you don't even think about them. They just become someone in your life,' he said.

'That's a terrible thing to say...' she began. '

We are always going to say what we think. That's the pact,' he said.

She stopped suddenly. 'I want to go back to where we were just now.'

'OK. We shan't get very far round at this rate.' He turned his horse.

When they reached the spot on the small point, Jill dropped down and started searching for something on the ground. 'What have you lost?' Finlay asked.

'Nothing. Here it is!' She picked up a small pebble from off the grass and put it in her shirt pocket. 'It was sticking into my bottom when we were lying here. I suddenly wanted it for a keepsake. Get down and give me a leg up, will you?'

Finlay dropped to the ground. They kissed briefly. He loved the taste of her tongue.

'Come, we have to go back to the house,' she said.

'But...'

'Not want to Finlay... woman's stuff,' she said urgently.

He lifted her on to her horse.

'It's days like these when I wish women still rode side-saddle!' She laughed.

'Do you want to scat on a bit?' he asked, concerned only because he was not sure of what was happening.

'A brisk walk please. Look Finlay, I won't go into details. It could be very embarrassing,' she said, seeing he was puzzled. 'You really should know more about women, you know.'

They rode into the stable yard. The girl got down and threw Finlay her reins. 'Deal with him for me, I've got to go.' She marched off solidly for the house.

'Lot of fuss about having a pee,' he thought. Still, it had been a good morning and he felt protective of this girl. He dealt with the horses, turned them out and watched them roll in the grass. 'Very uncomplicated creatures, horses,' he said aloud.

Indoors, Jenny was in the kitchen writing. 'Hello Kee. Had a good day?' she asked, absently. 'Want some lunch?'

'Not really, thanks, Jen. What's the matter with Jill? We had to come back. Where is she?' he asked, concernedly.

'Oh, she's OK. Just having a quick bath.'

'Odd, she only had one this morning. How were the gardeners?'

'Well, the one from Motisfont didn't seem to have much imagination, the second one was very churchy and Niney has just gone to get the last one. He's arriving at the Royal Pier. He comes from the Island.' She pushed him the paper she had been writing on. 'There you are. What they were like, ready for James. Just in case none of them suit.'

'Has Jill got a tummy upset Jen?' Finlay asked. 'She did act strangely.'

Jenny sighed. 'Not exactly Kee. You'd better come with me, since no one else seems disposed to educate you. The way things are, you'll be turned out into the world knowing nothing, except about sport and farming. Come with me.' She led the way upstairs and into her dressing room. 'Sit down and listen,' she said softly. 'This should have come from your father or grandfather. It makes me angry they just let you drift on, with only adults for company. I hope Jill sticks around for a while, just to let you have someone to talk to. She's perfectly all right. Jill's having a period and at her age, they can be a problem. Let me show you.' She went to the drawer and pulled out some packages. 'This is a sanitary towel and this is a tampon. Get hold of them, they won't bite!' she laughed.

Twenty minutes later, they left the dressing room. They walked down the stairs, arm in arm. Two people, very close to each other.

'Now do you really not want anything to eat?' Jenny asked. 'Ham sandwich?'

'Yes please, Jen,' he said. 'And thanks.'

Jill joined them in the kitchen, 'Sorry about that Jenny,' she said.

'Nonsense Jill. Oh, by the way, Mr Pearce is away tomorrow, so the Forest ride will have to wait. Here's Niney with number three. You two get a tea tray made up and bring it in when you judge everyone is sitting down. You do the honours, Jill, if you wouldn't mind. What impression this would give, I dread to think!' She gave Finlay an imaginary slap, left the kitchen and shut the door behind her.

'She's a love, Finlay,' Jill said.

'Yes I know. We had a talk while you were in the bath. Jen explained things to me, so now I know.'

'Well, I'm glad somebody has.'

'What about Auntie. What do you think about her?' Finlay asked.

'A little wary of each other at the moment. I've only known any of you for a short time, but it's lovely that you just accept me. You're unconventional, but I don't think there's anything nasty in the wood shed,' she said. 'Help me with the tea. I don't know where anything is.'

When she returned, having taken the tea tray in, Finlay asked, 'What was he like?'

'Fortyish, comes from "oop narth" and seems very intense. I don't know really. Chap who does our garden only comes once a week. He gets drunk at lunch time and breaks wind very loudly.' Her apparent dislike turned to giggles. 'We had some big-wigs down from Ford and my mother insisted on tea in the garden. Suddenly there's this enormous report. I had to go indoors, I was laughing so much. My mother told me off...' She started laughing again. 'Grown-ups are so stuffy. What my mother doesn't know is that when she farts in the bath, you can hear it through the ceiling.' They became helpless with laughter.

Finlay took both her hands and held them from across the table. 'Thank you for coming to be with us.'

It was an animated Niney who came into the kitchen. 'That's the one!' she announced. 'Seems like a really good chap. Jen will take them to see the cottage and then Ron will take them back to the ferry. His wife's a hairdresser, so we win all round.'

'Where did he work on the Island, Auntie Niney?' Finlay asked.

'Carrisbrook, constructing the new gardens. Before that at Heron Court. He likes starting from scratch, getting a garden back to where it should be. This one will tax his ingenuity!' She continued, 'Now, you've had a good day, the both of you? I must say, Jill, you look flushed, but content. You haven't been rolling in the grass together?' It was said as a joke.

'Yes, actually we have!' Jill said brightly.

For once Niney had no quick response. 'Well you're a straightfor-ward young lady. I like that. I hope you both enjoyed it!' She thought for a moment. 'I was fourteen when I got my first roll in the summer grass and I took no harm from it.'

'Was that with Ron, Auntie?' Finlay asked.

'No it was not!' she said sharply. 'I never rolled in the grass with that bugger, much as he might have wanted to. No, Kee. It was a friend of your father, a young midshipman. I got him down to where the stream joins the Blackwater by the sluice. Spent a very pleasant couple of hours with him there. Poor little bugger was killed in the war, like so many of them,' she said.

'That's where we were,' Finlay said, catching her sadness.

'That's as it should be then,' Niney said. 'Please God there's no war for you two.'

Finlay and Jill were in the music room going over his English course. They never heard Jenny open the door. 'Hey, you two, this was not meant to be swatting time!' she said. 'Your mother's on the telephone Jill. I did happen to mention you might be revising.'

'Thanks Jenny. That would have impressed her.' She got up quickly. 'Don't lose the place, Finlay, and wait till I come back before going on please.'

They had been studying Walter de la Mare's poetry and at one point had argued quite sharply about a passage in one of them. Finlay liked the way she wouldn't give ground. She, in turn, had teased him unmercifully over his pedantry, her green eyes taunting him. 'Alack, there lies more peril in thine eyes,' he had said.

'Fourteen and a bit and quoting Shakespeare. Precocious prig!' she had rejoined.

When Jill returned, she seemed a little subdued. 'They're back around midday tomorrow, so I'll have to go in the morning. I was rather hoping they would be delayed. Then back to school the following morning. I shan't see you again until after the exams. We could write to each other though, just sometimes. Ten whole weeks! You will write Finlay, won't you? If you don't, I'll not forgive you.'

'Of course. And ten weeks will pass quickly enough, and then it'll be summer. Swimming and fishing in the evenings, beautiful bright mornings with the river so clear, you can almost see the bottom of the hatch pool.' He stopped. 'Bloody exams before that though.'

She came and sat beside him. 'I am going to be so sad tomorrow.'

'But not today! There's no sense in having tomorrow's toothache today.' Finlay said, emphatically.

'One day, when I'm a famous surgeon, I'll read about you. A daring and gallant sea captain wins a wonderful victory and I'll say to my friends, I knew him when we were young. He was a precocious prig even then!' Finlay grabbed at her but she was far too quick and she ran from the room laughing, out on to the landing and jumped the bottom stairs into the hall, with a crash.

'Prig! Prig! Prig!' she yelled. She allowed Finlay to catch her. She struggled, but not much, giggling.

In the kitchen, Niney and Jenny smiled at the racket from the hall. 'All seems to be going rather well, Jen,' Niney said.

'They seem rather taken with each other,' Jenny said. 'I had a quick listen through the door earlier. I think she has the measure of him. A bright girl that one.'

Not long after six that evening, Finlay's grandfather arrived home from his day-long meeting. It seemed a long time ago since they had bid Carl the good wishes and goodbyes that were his due.

'Can I have the Land-Rover, Grandad?' Finlay asked. 'I'd like to show Jill Starwort.'

'Yes, but not on the road, and don't be late for dinner.' To Jill, he said, 'That'll be your responsibility, Jill MacFarlane from Rownhams, and it's gratifying to see someone so young and obviously sensible, spending more than twenty-four hours in this mad-house.'

'C'mon Jill! Let's go, see Starwort and you'll see what I mean.' He didn't wait for her to follow him out of the door.

'I shall see he's back for dinner,' she said.

After they had left, the old man said, 'That's a pleasant young lady, so bright. How did the gardeners go, ladies? Have we employed one?'

Niney and Jenny recounted their day and confirmed there was a new gardener whose main attribute seemed, to Finlay's grandfather, to be that his wife was a hairdresser.

Jenny announced that they were due in Stavanger the following Wednesday for 'at least' a two-week fishing holiday and the invigilator for Finlay's examinations had been chosen and booked. Niney and Jack would stay in the house while they were away, to look after Finlay and be generally on hand.

'I should have more all-day meetings it seems,' Finlay's grandfather said. 'You're right Jenny, I need a holiday and Norway's an inspired choice. Thank you.'

'Between now and Wednesday, I want you to run down, James. Do less, so that you can relax when we get there. Ron's checking the dairies from tomorrow morning. For the first time in years, you can lay abed.'

He wanted to argue but never got the chance.

'You can take me into Southampton. I want some new clothes.' 'I think I may enjoy that.' He smiled. 'What's happening about this young lady?'

'Home tomorrow and back to school the next day. I don't want Kee distracted before his exams. No doubt she'll be back in the summer. It's a fairly bad case of puppy love, I'm afraid,' Jenny said.

'Oh well. It had to happen. Do you want me to have a talk with him?' Finlay's grandfather asked.

'What about?' Niney and Jenny said together.

'James, you're bloody hopeless! If it was left to you it would never happen. Reading between the lines, I think Kee asked Ron about what he needed to know and Jenny gave him a talk this morning on the workings of the female form. You should be ashamed James. When you come back from Norway, you'll have to spend more time with him. He gets a bit lost you know,' Niney said.

'I hadn't realized he had reached that particular phase of his life,' Finlay's grandfather said. 'He seems so very young to be facing that sort of thing. He never complains about the working tasks I set him.'

'Only because he worships you. If you're up he feels he has to be. He does his school work and then goes and helps unload lorries or feeds the pigs. He never stops,' Niney countered.

'Right! As soon as we get back and his exams are over, I'll spend more time with him. In between hay and harvest perhaps we can get him away somewhere, all of us together.'

The subject of the conversation was changed as they heard Finlay and Jill coming back. 'I must say it's good to hear him laughing. He'll learn to cope, I'm sure,' he said.

'Well?' said Niney, as Jill came into the room. 'What do you think of Starwort?'

'Extraordinary! I have never witnessed anything like that!' She sat down next to Finlay's grandfather. 'I must ask you Sir James,' putting her hand on his arm, a gesture as charming as it was intense, 'can pigs reason? If they can that would put them up with dolphins. Winston Churchill said, "Pigs treat us as equals". I never knew what he meant, but I do now.'

'That observation would indicate you have a good brain, Jill,' he said, taking her hand. 'Yes. Pigs reason. They are super clever. Tell me what you saw.'

Niney and Jenny looked at each other, somewhat nonplussed by what they were seeing. 'Leave aside the circus tricks, extraordinary in themselves. The pig hid from Finlay and then they played tag. The pig took its turn to be it.'

Finlay walked into the room, drying his hands on his clothes. 'Starwort is a show-off, especially if she has an audience.'

'No Finlay, the pig worked out how to hide from you. When she tipped you over, she waited until you were half up, at a disadvantage, and tipped you up again. It was thought out. I can't believe what I saw.' She turned to Finlay's grandfather. 'What I saw was constructive play, I think. Can you tell me if I'm right?'

'To a degree Jill. You'll make a fine doctor I'm sure, but such a brain would be wasted. You'd make a wonderful vet! What you saw was Kee imitating the pig's behaviour and the pig responds in kind. A good stock man observes and notes in his mind. Pigs do play very constructive games among themselves. Starwort is allowing Kee to join in.'

'I'm not at all certain you're correct, Sir James,' she said, which made him smile. 'A chimp at that age runs on pure instinct. The pig was reasoning, I'm certain of it. Can I come and study them in my summer holidays?'

'My dear girl, of course you can, and I'll introduce you to our vets. They're extremely clever people. I must say I've never been put in my place so beautifully.' He laughed.

'I'm sorry, I didn't mean to be rude…'

'You weren't. You're just discovering things, my dear,' Finlay's grandfather said.

'What is that wonderful smell?' she asked.

'Roast beef for dinner, and could we have you two smelling a little less like piglets, please,' Niney said. 'Kee get cleaned up.' She turned and opened one of the drawers. 'Write it down Jill, before it goes from your mind,' she said, handing her a pad and pencil.

'How did you know that's what I wanted?' Jill asked.

'Because, young lady, I was sixteen once and very earnest like you.'

They were silent for her while she was writing then Jenny said, 'Good God! I do believe Kee's having a bath! I think that's maybe something to do with you, Jill.'

Jill got up and went to the sink. 'Could I borrow this, please?' she asked, picking up a large enamel jug and filling it with water from the cold tap. 'Finlay has been so pompous today, I'd like to take him down a peg or two. Where does he bathe?'

'Next door to his bedroom. Are you quite certain you want to do this though?' said Niney.

Jill left the room. The adults waited.

'What an extraordinary child,' Finlay's grandfather said quietly. 'Very clever... and so confident.'

'So, we're having a mad scientist and a priggish poet for the summer,' Jenny said, sighing. 'Won't that be fun!'

There were shouts and screams from upstairs and the sound of an enamelled jug crashing to the floor.

'They have few inhibitions the young, these days. I'm not certain that a young lady should go into a young man's bathroom,' Finlay's grandfather observed solemnly.

'Don't be so stuffy, James,' Jenny said. 'We had a war... this generation has the atom bomb.'

'Yes, I suppose so,' he said simply.

'And who was it who used to swim in the river at night with naked girls, when they were younger?' Niney said brightly. 'My mother told me all about it, James.'

Jill arrived back. 'I'm not certain he saw the funny side of that!' She laughed.

The conversation in the kitchen centred on what Carl's brother would be like, and the forthcoming holiday in Norway. 'You don't think he's having a sulk do you?' Jill asked. 'He's taking a long time to come down. Perhaps I should go and look.'

She left the room and made for the hall. There was a scream, giggling and then silence.

'As I said, James, a very bad case of puppy love. And she'll learn that Kee wouldn't know how to sulk. Sulk indeed!' Jenny observed.

'I'm sure she didn't mean it as a criticism, Jen,' Niney said, glancing at Finlay's grandfather significantly.

Dinner time that evening was noisy. Jack came in at about seven and dinner itself got under way half an hour later. They were, as usual, eating in the kitchen. The long pine table had been set in the semi-formal manner of farm houses, fresh crusty bread left overlong in the oven, with the top burnt almost black, huge jugs of beer and the beef joint resting on the Aga, dribbling fat and blood.

The telephone rang. Finlay's grandfather went to answer it. 'We are just about to sit down for dinner,' he said into the mouthpiece. 'Can you call us for the hour please?'

Jill started to giggle. 'Does your grandfather always treat the exchange as his own?'

'Generally,' said Finlay. 'What he is going to do when everything is like town telephones, I don't know. Probably shout at the operator when a call comes through at the wrong time.'

'Don't whisper you two!' Niney said severely.

'Sorry Auntie Niney,' Finlay said. 'We were just laughing at Grandfather and the way he treats the telephone exchange.'

Finlay loved the way meals happened. One moment the table was a large blank space, the next there were plates and dishes, all trying to make spaces for each other.

'There was about forty fish on the last tide James,' Jack said. 'So I telephoned some people on the waiting list. We should have a good day tomorrow. Some of them were gone thirty pounds.'

'What's the biggest salmon that's ever been caught here, Mr Terry?' Jill asked.

'I'm Jack young lady, but thank you for the courtesy. The biggest one ever was fifty-four pounds but that was more than one hundred years ago. The biggest one lately was forty-two pounds and that was last year. Do you fish, Jill?'

'No, but I'd love to have a go sometime. The way Finlay talks about it, you would honestly think there was nothing better in the world.'

'Well, in your summer holidays we shall have to get you out there. See if you can't beat the boy. His first one was twenty-eight pounds and a bit, but it was on a spinner, so I think if you can do a twenty on a fly that would equal it.'

'I think you can tell their age by scale markings can't you?' she asked. The men were impressed.

Jack said, 'Do you know about salmon? Is it something you are taught about in school?'

'Hardly! I know that Caroline's father comes here to fish for salmon, so I looked into the subject.' She paused. 'It always seems such a waste when the fish die after spawning, or the bulk of them. Is there perhaps a way to get the kelts back to the sea?'

'It's been tried, but if you think about it we're only a couple of miles off the salt from where we're sitting, and quite a few must make it back. I'm more inclined to think they are just smolts that hang in the sea an extra year.'

'Thanks, Jack,' she said. 'One can read about things in books, but you sometimes get the impression that the writers of such books have just gleaned it from other books.'

Finlay's grandfather was smiling. Jenny and Niney, who had been talking about holidays, suddenly became transfixed by the girl's conversation. Finlay was amazed by knowing a girl who was interested in pigs and knew something about fish. Jill either did not notice or affected not to, but all conversation had stopped.

'I wonder what Carl's brother will be like,' Niney said, trying to steer the conversation away from aquatic science.

'I'm sorry,' Jill said.

'Not at all Jill,' Niney responded.

'Does your father ever fish, Jill?' Finlay's grandfather asked.

'No, not at all. It seems their whole lives are geared around the Ford company. It's meetings, seminars on all manner of things. Even at weekends they all have to go to each other's homes and talk Ford. It gives us, my family that is, a very secure financial foundation but no real life at all. Not for ourselves, to be together. I know I get my horse, good school and all of that, but we never sit and eat together like this, not without there is somebody else there.'

'Come along, come along!' Niney suddenly said. 'This is all getting a bit dreary. I'm sorry I said what I said Jill. Now let me ask you a question...' She pretended to think for a moment or two. 'Does Cheltenham still insist on everyone wearing those awful grey knickers, and do they still itch as badly?'

'They are awful!' Jill giggled. 'And we still have to wear skirted swimming costumes. We all do our best to look glamorous when we go into the town, but the boys there just laugh at us, and there is even one who regularly throws stones at us!'

'In my day they used to whistle Dixie,' Niney said.

'Why'd they do that?' Jack asked.

'Grey Jack, Confederate grey!' Niney said, exasperated.

'Well that just shows that some of them had seen the girls' knickers. Else they wouldn't know, would they? They couldn't have all been stone throwers!'

It was Jill who came to Niney's rescue. 'Which school did you go to Jenny?' she asked.

'A convent school in Surrey and before anybody asks it was not Roman and we had to wear dark blue bloomers with elastic around the legs and special bras that didn't allow your boobs to move. "I can see your chest moving, Jennifer, do something about it," that's what Sister Basil used to say. They were vicious, cruel bitches. A coven of frustrated lesbians. I couldn't wait to leave. Now when I see nuns in Southampton, I want to stop the car and beat them to death with the starting handle.'

'Were they physically vicious, Jenny?' asked Jill.

'Oh yes. One of them deliberately broke my little finger. When I told my parents they just would not believe it. I hated them. Now I live here in this wonderfully godless place.'

'The problem is if the human female is deprived of her natural function...' Jill began.

'Jill,' Niney said. 'Shut up.'

Everyone burst out laughing, even the girl herself. Niney put her arm around her and said, 'We're only teasing Jill. Our way of defending ourselves against a formidable intellect. Just be the lovely young lady you are. So much more fun.'

'You will come and see us in the summer holidays young lady won't you?' Finlay's grandfather said to her. 'You'll be good for us all.'

'Of course I will James,' she said. Jill used his Christian name quite easily. 'I shall be here as soon as the exams are over. We can have some sort of celebration, Finlay and myself, when we get our results.'

The evening over, Niney and Jack made ready to leave. She kissed Finlay and then took Jill's hand. 'You won't see me in the morning. I've to go to Andover first thing, so I shan't see you till the summer. Do well in your exams Jill. I know you will.' She kissed her on the cheek. 'You are a real delight Jill MacFarlane.' Then they were gone.

'Off to bed then you two, and don't forget tomorrow. If you're up early don't make a lot of noise in the yard. Good night then, off you go,' Jenny ordered.

Upstairs, Jill seemed unhappy. 'I don't want to go back yet, Finlay. I want to stay with you for longer.'

'We have all summer...'

'It seems so far away.'

'Come on Jill, don't be sad. You've got work to do if you want to be Dr MacFarlane.'

They kissed and went their separate ways.

Finlay was aware that somebody was standing by his bed. In the darkness all he could see was a white form that suddenly bent over him. He could smell it was Jill, it lashed his senses.

'Finlay,' she breathed. 'Wake up.'

'I am awake,' he said sleepily. 'What's the matter?'

'Get up. I can't do this waiting thing. Take me outside somewhere. I want to be with you,' she said urgently.

Finlay rose. 'What time is it?'

'One-ish. For goodness' sake be quiet. Do you always sleep like that?' she asked.

He was naked. He dragged his trousers on, sleep still clogging his brain. 'Why do you want to go outside?'

'I just do. I want it like today again, so hurry up, please.' She moved to the door ahead of him.

Outside there was a distinct chill in the air, the mist from the river smoked in layers across the lawn. His throat was so dry he could barely speak. 'Stay here, the ground will be wet with this dew.' He went quickly towards the stable and grabbed a summer rug. Misty, hearing him, whinnied and came towards the fence. 'Hush poppet,' he said, touching her face. The mare nuzzled his chest.

He led the girl down through the garden towards the hatch pool. As they got closer the smell of the rushing water and the noise made the girl hesitate. 'What's that noise?' she asked.

'The hatch pool. I'd forgotten, you haven't seen it yet. My favourite place on this earth.' They crept past the cottage where Granny Fortune lived and down through a small orchard, towards the sound of the rushing water. 'There,' he said. 'I know it's quite dark, but you can see how beautiful it is.'

Through the spring night the water looked dark, the turbulence at the gates showed white and a fine mist of spray drifted away on the slight breeze. 'What a fantastic place. It's a bit scary, the water going so fast.' She held Finlay's arm, trembling or shivering, Finlay couldn't tell which. They moved further down the pool, where Finlay spread the horse blanket among the longer grass. 'Thank you Finlay, for picking your favourite place.' She knelt down on the blanket and removed the dressing gown Finlay had given her. There was enough light for Finlay to see she was wearing a small pair of white knickers and nothing else.

Finlay tried to force his mind back to what Ron had told him. He could almost hear him saying, 'You just got to go steady at it.' He tried to swallow but couldn't. He shucked off his few clothes and knelt beside her. 'Are you a bit nervous?' he asked.

'A little,' she murmured. 'I want you to do everything Finlay. Everything.' She slipped her knickers off. At the bottom of her stomach, Finlay saw a dark upside-down triangle. 'Lay down with me,' she said.

He was stunned by the smoothness of her skin and even in the chill it was softly warm. They touched, kissed and explored each other, sometimes lying there, then standing as their excitement flowed between them. Finlay did not know exactly what to do next. Then thought was abandoned. They struggled together trying to adjust, then he was inside of her. She gasped at once, then groaned and clung to him. The noise of the rushing water was drowned by the noise of rushing blood inside Finlay's head. The feelings they had explored earlier in the day rushed upon them tenfold. She shouted something in Finlay's ear and then went limp, her breath coming in short gasps. They lay there until their breathing became more normal. She kept repeating, 'Finlay, Finlay,' as he kissed her throat. He went to move away from her. 'No, stay there. Stay still!' she said. They lay together not speaking. A thin moon showed briefly between the clouds. 'Finlay, thank you. I was really scared, you made it wonderful.' She put her hand on his cheek. 'I didn't want to go back… now we both know.' She moved slightly and the movement reawakened Finlay. As he began to grow again inside her, she groaned and pushed against him. In seconds the world exploded around them once again. She lay beneath him, exhausted, it seemed. He went to move again. Her eyes opened and she stard at him. 'Finlay at this moment I truly adore you.'

He touched her face with his lips and found it wet. 'Are you crying?' he murmured. 'Are those tears on your face?'

She laughed quietly. 'Just one tear for childhood.'

The eastern horizon began showing pink before they left the hatch pool.

Part II

Milk and Honey

Chapter One

•

Had it not been Thursday, the story would have been like a summer spring, bubbling from the ground slowly, trickling this way and that. A gentle thing of not much consequence. But it was Thursday, when old women went to collect their pension at the Post Office, and younger women, their child allowance. So, the story was like a summer flood, rushing down the river, hitting the sluices and spreading across the estate in an hour. Jack had intended to be on the river bank at first light, and would have been but for Niney's insistence that he stay in bed for a little longer, the morning sun having stirred her blood. He was the first to note the flattened grass.

'Bloody poachers!' But it didn't really look like it had been them. The little tricks Jack left about – small sticks, a cotton line across a path – were still intact. He walked downstream, but could see no other signs of disturbance. He scratched his head, perplexed, walked back to Granny Fortune's cottage and opened the door. 'You up Granny?' he shouted.

'It's light ain't it!' she answered tersely. 'What d'you want?' She didn't really approve of Jack. He hadn't given Niney what she most wanted, a child, and as the years passed, her disapproval became more rampant. She had said to Niney on one occasion that if the hens had no chicks, you had to change the cock.

'You hear anything last night, Granny? See anybody about?' he asked.

'Ah,' she answered.

'Well, did you or didn't you?' Jack had never liked her much, either. She had the cottage he wanted and Granny had refused to move.

'Just said I did, didn't I? Gone deaf or something?' She walked to the door, bent now with age and rheumatism.

'Did you see who it was?' Jack was trying to be patient.

'Two little river spirits, beautiful they was, like little fairies.' She chuckled. 'They hid out there in the grass, mother naked and beautiful, trying to make babies.'

It was almost an accusation. 'Who was it?' Jack snapped.

'Thas not fer you to know. I should never say. They was like two little fox cubs playing. Proper beautiful it were. My own bearing been dry this forty year, but watching they made her perk up a bit.' She chuckled again. 'Less there's anything else you wants, you'd better bugger off Jack before I gets you in 'ere to find out what you ain't doing right!' She slammed the door in his face and he could hear her laughing all the way back to her kitchen.

'Crazy old bastard!' Jack muttered and stomped away.

The same light that had kept Jack in bed woke Finlay. He had slept barely half an hour. He wondered whether it had been a dream, the past night, but a certain slight soreness told him that it had not been. He turned over and slept for another hour. When he eventually got to the kitchen Jenny was already there. 'Morning Jen,' he said, giving her an absent-minded peck on the cheek.

'Hello you. Had a good sleep?' she enquired.

There was just an inflection in her question that made Finlay wary. 'Yes thanks, Jenny. Any tea in the pot?' He dismissed the thought she might have known.

She handed him some tea. 'How many corncrakes, then?'

'Sorry,' he said. 'What did you say?'

'I said, how many corncrakes did you hear last night? If that's what it's called these days?' She wasn't facing him, so he could not see whether she was joking or not.

'Oh,' was the only reply he could make.

'I saw you going out. Misty shouted, so I got up to see that she hadn't fallen out with Jill's horse, and what did I see? You and Jill headed off towards the hatch pool. So would you like to explain what you were doing for two hours?' She was still busying herself in the cupboard, not looking at him.

'Oh,' Finlay said again. 'I don't think I can.'

She came and sat beside him. 'Well my darling heart, I don't really want to know. Judging by the look on your face I can guess... and so what. I could see she wanted you. She would be rather silly not to... but do take care. Let's hope nobody else saw you. I don't want the world and his wife tittle-tattling about it.' She kissed him gently. 'I'm not shocked and I won't let Jill know. Maybe it's a good thing she is going today. It'll give you the chance to sort things out in your head.' She kissed him again. 'You'd better have a proper breakfast. Nights like that can be taxing!' she giggled.

'I love you, Jenny,' Finlay said.

'I'm as certain of that as knowing the tide will go out today,' she answered. 'Here, eat your breakfast.'

But a secret it was not to be. Frank, the head dairyman, out early to see one of his charges due to calve, had seen the two youngsters and reported it to his wife. She went to the Post Office that morning. By nine-thirty there was a gaggle of women outside the old tin building, looking for all the world like geese, honking and cackling with nodding heads. 'You wouldn't believe it! The young these days!' Naomi Phillips, most vociferous in her condemnation, clucked her spiteful disapproval for all to hear. 'The minister would have something to say on Sunday.' Miss Satchel, the post mistress, joined them outside. An embittered old maid, whom Ron once described as being much like one of her lost parcels: 'To be returned unopened', was vitriolic. She spat fire and damnation on the whole family.

Niney swept past them in the Armstrong, smiling, giving them a happy wave. Miss Satchel had just reached the height of her indignation. 'There's another. When she was younger she was never any better than she had to be. No wonder she doesn't mind a hussy under her roof. Her blood ain't so pure. When she was born there were talk of her not being her father's daughter. No need to look too far as to who was her father, swanning about in his car like Lady bloody Muck!'

When Jill came downstairs, bubbly and bright, she ate a good breakfast, chatting happily to Jenny, while Finlay went to saddle the horses. 'I'll miss you all,' she said. 'It's been such fun.'

'The term will pass quickly, I'm sure. We'll still be here when you come back. Kee will miss you, but do your best. Then you can relax properly in the summer,' Jenny said.

'Finlay will pass his exams easily, won't he? He's so clever and, if you don't mind me saying so, he is rather special.'

'Well, I certainly think so,' Jenny said almost nonchalantly. 'He has his grandfather's kindness.'

'I don't really want to go, Jenny,' Jill said suddenly. 'I really don't.'

For a moment Jenny thought she was going to cry. She went to her quickly. 'Now come along. All this will calm down soon. It's all been a bit sudden for you. Once you're apart for a while, you'll settle down again. He'll be here when you get back, and I'll make certain he writes to you.'

'Thanks Jenny. I suppose I'd better go before I make a complete fool of myself. Will you say thank you to everybody?'

'Where is everyone?' Niney said, as she arrived back in the house. She glanced at herself in the mirror. 'We should go and have a hair-do before you go on holiday Jen. Mine needs cutting. Poor Jack thought he'd had a visit from poachers last night.'

'Niney,' Jenny interrupted, but she ploughed on.

'He said he would have caught whoever it was had I not kept him, but Granny said it was a couple of youngsters down there cavorting in the grass. She wouldn't say who it was though.'

'Niney,' Jenny said.

'Granny seemed to think they were river spirits or something. Couldn't get any sense out of her at all.'

Niney started sorting some of the shopping she had brought back.

'Niney!' Jenny said sharply. 'Sit down and listen, will you!'

'OK, I'm listening.' She swept her hair off her face.

'The river spirits were Kee and Jill,' Jenny said.

'Oh Lord,' Niney said. 'Oh Lord... Little bugger! He doesn't let the grass grow under his feet. I hope to God he hasn't put her in pup!'

'Not very likely. Jill had only just finished her period...'

'How do you know that?' Niney asked.

'Because I had to give her some pads and some clean drawers, and before you get on your high horse, she refused tampons because she said she was still a virgin.'

'Are you sure they actually got down to it?' Niney said.

'Nothing more certain I'd say, by the look on Kee's face. Jill came down this morning looking like the cat that had stolen the cream, which I suppose, in a manner of speaking, she had.'

'Well, there'll not be any stopping them now. He'll have to have a serious talk on babies and the like. I'll skin the little bugger alive when I get hold of him!' Niney exclaimed.

'No!' Jenny said. 'Leave it Niney. You said yourself it had to happen and now it has. Just leave it alone and don't embarrass him. You could do enormous damage.'

'Where are they now?' Niney asked.

'He's taken her back home.'

'Tears?' Niney asked.

'Nearly, but she has her head on right. She'll calm down once she's back at school.'

'Well somebody will have to talk to him. I'm his guardian so I suppose it'll have to be me,' Niney said.

'You have a word with Ron quietly, Niney. That would be the best way. Men together and all that,' Jenny suggested.

'Does James know?' Niney asked.

'No, so don't say anything. I'll tell him when we're in Norway. Then if he flips, he'll have calmed down by the time we get home.'

Niney sighed. 'Bloody men! They're all the same. Soon as they get some sap rising, it has to be scattered over the county!'

'It's not at all like that Niney!' Jenny snapped. 'It's rather beautiful. A Romeo and Juliet sort of thing.' She paused. 'Here he is now coming across the yard. Not one word Niney, mind.'

Finlay wandered in. 'Hello Auntie Niney. How was Andover?' he asked. He kissed her and ruffled her curls.

'Get out of my hair you bugger! Come and give me a proper kiss. Bloody men! Just a kiss in passing.' They hugged each other. 'That was a nice surprise for you. Young Jill out of the blue like that. She seems a thoroughly nice girl.'

There was a loud knocking on the front door. 'Who the hell is that?' Niney exclaimed.

'Hey, are you in there? Come out and help me up this step,' a querulous voice demanded.

'Good Lord, it's Granny,' Niney said, jumping up and running towards the front door. She led Granny Fortune into the room, bent and leaning wearily on a stick. She smiled at Finlay and ignored Jenny. 'Now my beautiful little cock bird, I wants to have a little chat with you, so give me your arm and take me into the hall,' she said. As Niney and Jenny got up, she snapped, 'You two stay there and mind your own selves. This ain't got anything to do with you. Now come on my darling, I needs to sit.'

Finlay led her into the hall and closed the door. Jenny and Niney looked at each other. 'What do you think this is about? She hasn't been up here for years.' They waited, straining their ears to perhaps hear what was being said. Twenty minutes later, Granny Fortune and Kee reappeared, laughing together, and came into the kitchen.

'You sit next to me young Keith.' She shot a look at Niney, challenging her to say something. She put her hand on Finlay's thigh and squeezed it. 'You puts me in mind of your great grandad. He looked just like you. He used to come riding round on his mare. "Morning Miss Brake," he used to say, looking at me with they same eyes as you got. He didn't know what he was looking at any more than you did when that pretty little wench come looking for you couple of nights ago. I was pretty and proud in them days. Prettier than 'er!' She jerked her thumb at Niney. ''Er who's taking a bloody long time to get me a cup of coffee with some brandy in. Well, he were a bit younger than me and I 'adn't ever laid with a man before so I thinks to myself, he'll be my first and he was. I trapped 'un by the hatch pool first time and any time after that I could.' She chuckled deep in her old throat at the memory. 'When he were dying of the flu, I was sent for to go up to the house. James, that's your great-grandad, sends everybody out of the room and he were terrible sick. He says to me, "Charity I'm dying and I want you to know that I always loved you best. There's something left for you in my will so you never need want for anything"…and he died that afternoon. Last night you made two women happy, that little wench and me. You made me remember how lucky I was to have had one just like you, and I love you for it.'

By the time she had finished, tears were coursing down Jenny's face and Niney was strangely quiet.

'Where's that coffee, girl?' Granny snapped at Niney.

'I didn't know of this, Granny,' Niney said quietly.

'There's a lot you don't know madam, and a lot you don't ever need to know. But don't think I haven't had my moments, so if there's any row about the boy, I'll start telling the whole story. Now get my coffee and then take me back home.'

Before she left, she said to Finlay, 'Give me a kiss, my beautiful, and let me hold you for a little moment.'

After Niney and Granny Fortune had left, Jenny said, 'I was really quite proud of you for a few moments just now. Sometimes you can be quite charming.'

'Granny's always been all right with me. She knows so much,' Finlay said. 'If you think she was born just before the American Civil War started and has lived long enough to see her world turned on its head several times, it's no wonder she's fascinating.'

'I've never heard her described as fascinating. Acidic, foul-mouthed and lots of other things, but never fascinating!' She laughed.

'Well, my great-grandfather obviously found her to be!' He smiled. 'If you close your eyes, the picture of Granny swimming in the hatch pool without any clothes on, it really doesn't come does it? What's she mean by the whole story? Do you know?'

'No, I don't and moreover I really don't want to. You got Jill back OK, I take it?' Jenny asked.

'Yes of course. She was a bit sad, but she'll be all right.'

'What are you going to do for the rest of the day, darling? Anything planned?' Jenny asked.

'Think I'll get on with some school work,' he said.

Late April that year was a spring of wonder. The air seemed to shine and the sun warmed the earth into life, drawing up the grass into stands of almost impossible green. The ley grass fields were filled with sterile walls of such green, which blew in the breeze to change to almost smoky blue, as the first seed heads appeared on the grass. It was deemed fit to harvest. The swallows and martins chased and snatched the hawthorn flies from the river's gliding surface, competing without need with the trout and grayling. The world was suddenly luxurious.

Indoors, studying, Finlay heard the moaning hum of the grass chopper as it shredded the fresh-mown grass and blew it into the silage clamps. Thursday and Friday saw frantic activity far into the night, and then silence. The grass in the clamps, now about four feet deep, was allowed to heat over the weekend, then silage-making began in earnest. There would be no stopping now until it was finished. The fields that had recently been so wonderfully green, now became shorn of their crop and showed yellow, the yellow stubble of the ryegrass, sick-looking and sad, but soon covered with birds gathering the now homeless insects.

As each field was cleared, it was spread with ground chalk from the local quarry or basic slag from the steel works of the north, sweetening the next crop of grass, which would make the hay. In eight days the harvest was finished, the moaning grass choppers silent for another year.

The water meadows, a system from the last century, were seldom cut. Grazed by cattle over the centuries and flooded regularly by the river, the sward was sweet and full of flowers, making summer milk of the purest and sweetest taste. The meadows, home for countless peewits, curlews and a myriad of ducks. So the year wandered into May. The urgency of spring giving way gently to the blowsiness of summer. The yellow flags lined the river banks and the starwort swayed and belly-danced its long tresses in the summer river's current.

Finlay's exams drew nearer. He was working with some intensity, quietly in the music room, hour after hour. There were letters from Jill to relieve the tedium, asking questions and perhaps querying a point made in a previous one from him. He had barely missed his grandfather and Jenny when they went to Norway. He was even surprised when they came home. The time they were away passed so quickly.

Niney had fussed over him, feeding him his favourite meals and quietly bringing drinks at regular intervals and insisting that he stop for breaks. At dinner, Jack would entertain them with the day's happenings and Finlay thirsted for the day when exams would be over and he could spend all his time fishing and just being with the river. The image of the girl, naked in the grass, which had been in sharp relief in his mind's eye for a couple of weeks, had faded and could be recalled only with effort. The image now was misty, like the meadows at dawn.

Finlay, in his mind, knew that only the very best results would vindicate the inordinate sums of money his grandfather had spent on his education. His grandfather had dismissed the subject, saying, 'You will, I know, do your best.'

The day of Finlay's final exam, his grandfather came in at tea time, leaving the hay field to find out what he needed to know. 'Well, now that's all over, how do you think you've done?' he asked. He had made no mention over the past two weeks about what his grandson had thought.

'Well Grandfather, I've got four for certain. Scraped the Maths and failed the Art and Latin is anybody's guess.' He said it matter-of-factly, because that is what he believed.

'Good. Shall we go fishing?' Finlay's grandfather smiled. 'The hay is in good hands.'

With a couple of rods, the relevant bags and a net loaded in the Land-Rover Finlay's grandfather asked, 'Where to?'

'Hatch pool, I would think,' Finlay said.

'Not a case of returning to the scene of the crime, perhaps?' his grandfather said seriously.

'Oh, have we to talk about that?' Finlay said.

''Fraid so young man. It has to be spoken about, but not in any critical sense. I just want you to be a little more discreet… for the sake of the girl.'

'Yes I see. I really thought we had been discreet. Who told you?' Finlay wasn't exactly embarrassed, just a little uncomfortable.

'Jenny. When we were in Norway, and then I got it from Ron, and innuendos from all over. So let discretion be your watch-word.'

They pulled up by Granny Fortune's cottage, who was on her hands and knees, digging at a flower bed. 'Hey!' she called. 'Come and give me a hand up off my knees.'

Finlay opened the gate and helped her up. She put both arms around him cackling. 'See how easy it is? I trapped you the same as I trapped your great-granddaddy. You watch they women my beauty, us all be out to trap men.' She hugged him fiercely, then shoved him away. 'Get on with your fishing.' She began to cackle again, dropping to her knees, like a woman forty years younger.

Finlay was laughing when he joined his grandfather. 'Granny says I look like your father, Grandfather.'

'We don't want to go too deeply into that one, Kee.' He smiled. 'She really is a crafty old baggage. She was showing you, and warning me I think.'

'What's the whole story she was talking about, Grandad?' Finlay asked.

He waited a long time for an answer and then said, 'It doesn't matter really. I could not possibly love Auntie Niney more than I do already.'

What would have been another perfectly executed cast by his grandfather, landed in coils in front of him. 'Bugger!' he said. 'How did that happen?'

Finlay wasn't fishing. He was lying face down on a fishing platform gazing into the depths. The river was about eight feet deep below and he could just make out the bottom. He was watching grayling, rising and falling on the current. A smoky blue shadow passed underneath him. 'Jesus Christ Grandad! There's a monster down here. It has to be thirty-odd pounds! Go over by the fish pass and cast across from there. I can still see his tail. He's standing still.' Finlay heard the swish of the line. He was watching the fish. 'He saw it Grandad. He was going to have a go. Take it across him slower.' Finlay again heard the fly line whistling in the air. The great fish seemed to tremble. There was a flash from his huge silver side and he was hooked.

Finlay grabbed the net and ran fifty yards downstream, splashed into the water, wading to the middle. The water swirled about his waist. 'Don't try to hold him in the pool!' Finlay yelled. 'He's too big for that. For Christ's sake give him line!... Grandad let him run, let him run...'

The fish cartwheeled over in the air and bored towards Finlay. He hit the surface of the water with the net, turning the fish back into the main pool. 'Let him swim about the pool, Grandad. Don't put too much pressure on him. I saw the fly, he's well hooked...'

The fish circled the pool, at first at high speed and then slower. It tried once more for the sea, but again turned back into the pool. 'Make him swim in the flow, Grandad!' Finlay shouted.

Granny Fortune, hearing Finlay, came to join in the fun. 'Jamie! Jamie! Get him under your bank.'

Finlay moved across the river into the current which threatened to pull him over. He could see by the line that the fish was coming down towards him. He moved further into the current, barely able to stand now. The fish was suddenly in front of him. He pushed the net down horizontally and the fish hit it at speed. As Finlay lost his footing, he bagged the top of the net with both hands, dropping the long handle. They saw him disappear beneath the surface, then briefly twenty yards down surface again. Arthritis forgotten, Granny Fortune paced Finlay's grandfather down the river. Finlay came to an abrupt stop on the lip of the next pool, sitting with the water foaming around his chest. He tried to stand but couldn't for a moment. He was shaking so much. He was laughing and yelling his excitement. 'We got him Grandad. He's a big bugger. Can you come in and take him?'

His grandfather splashed in and took the net, the fish still kicking and struggling. Finlay crawled to the bank and sat shaking with cold. 'What about that one, Granny?' he gasped.

'I thought you were going to drown, Kee,' his grandfather said, almost crossly.

'No chance of that Grandad. She might drown some people... but she wouldn't me.' He was now shuddering with the cold. 'Come back home and get dry, boy,' Granny ordered. 'You can go and get him some dry clothes, Jamie.'

They walked back slowly, Granny now acknowledging her infirmity. Once in her cottage, Finlay removed his wet clothes and clung to the rail of the Rayburn, trying to find warmth that wouldn't come. Granny reappeared from somewhere with a harsh, dry towel and began rubbing him down. 'You're a bit shocked with the cold my boy,' she said gasping, the effort of her scrubbing costing her dearly. 'Get they wet drawers off,' she ordered. 'You won't get warm with those clinging to your arse.' Finlay was standing there naked, his limbs almost palsied, his head spinning. 'Ah, you're like two peas in a pod, you and your great grandaddy. Same pert little dimples.' She rubbed his back more vigorously.

When Finlay's grandfather returned, with Niney accompanying him, they found him sitting on top of the Rayburn wrapped in a blanket, warmer and smiling at them.

'You silly little sod, you might have drowned,' Niney said. She seemed unsure whether to give him a clout or hug him.

'Auntie Niney,' Finlay said, in an over patient, patronizing manner. 'There was never any danger of me drowning...'

'I've seen dogs drown in that stretch! What on earth possessed you?' She was angry at his manner. 'Get these dry clothes on! Why didn't you let go of the fish?' Finlay's grandfather seemed very quiet. Finlay thought he had maybe already caught the rough edge of Niney's tongue. The fish turned out to weigh thirty-six pounds, and the serious talk his grandfather had said they needed to have, never happened.

Chapter Two

•

Finlay felt a little lost after the exams were finished. The hay harvest was just about done with, and men not engaged on this were fencing. Finlay wondered whether they felt lost with the frantic activity of silage and haymaking over. He decided he would go and help Carl.

He welcomed Finlay with something approaching enthusiasm, 'Zo exams are over… vot now?' he asked.

'Don't really know, Carl,' Finlay said. 'Perhaps I'll go and look at that sluice.'

'Good. Is not good for you to be idle. Take your big sockets, and a tub of ze cheap grease… let me know vot you do.' Carl went back to what he had been doing, a sure sign of being dismissed.

'Could I borrow your Jeep, Carl?' Finlay asked.

'No,' was the only reply.

The June sun was warm, even hot as he walked the good mile to the sluice. He was sweating freely by the time he got there. Carl had been as good as his word and had liberally soaked the winding gear and ratchets in oil. Finlay stripped off his shirt and began taking the gear on the first gate to pieces. Some years of rust gave way eventually to the heavy spanners and the winding gear began, under squealing protest, to work at last. The heavy wooden gate began to move. Pleased that his persistence had paid off, Finlay decided to tackle the other gate. Ron pulled into the field, bouncing over the hard ground towards him.

'Hello nipper,' he said, smiling. 'Haven't seen you for a while. I've had to come looking for you. Nobody knew where you were.'

'Carl did. Sorry I never thought to leave any word. What time is it?' Finlay asked.

'Well gone five. Didn't you see the cows go out?' Ron said.

'I suppose I got so involved with this I forgot the time.' Finlay gathered and counted his tools.

'You've been here some time, judging by the way the sun has caught you. Anyway, hop in. I've just got to pop into Romsey. I've run out of fags.'

On the way to the town, they chatted about the hay, the not far distant harvest and the ongoing fencing job. Ron thought the winter frost had done in most of the injurious bugs that made a nuisance of themselves in the grain crops. Stopping outside the newsagents, Ron handed Finlay a couple of half-crowns. 'Pop in and get me a packet of Players nipper, while I turn around.'

The inside of the shop was cool and smelt of freshly printed paper. 'Can I have a packet of Players, please,' Finlay said absently, trying to read the headlines on the *Echo*. He proffered the two half-crowns. The newspaper was proclaiming that rationing would finally be coming to an end.

'Your Players?' the girl behind the counter was saying to him.

'Sorry,' he said, leaving the newspaper. He looked up into the most beautiful green eyes he had ever seen and an exquisitely formed face, covered with freckles, the whole surrounded by copper-coloured curls.

'Um, yes,' Finlay said. 'Sorry, I was miles away.'

'Obviously!' She laughed. She handed him the Players and dropped the change into his hand. Only then did Finlay realise how filthy he was.

'You're the boy from the big farm up the road, aren't you? You have a grey horse?' When she smiled it was with her eyes and mouth.

'Yes, I'm Finlay.' He went to shake hands, but then withdrew. Her hands were milky white against the grease and rust stains on his. 'Just done a dirty job,' he said awkwardly.

'I'm Janet. I've sometimes seen you in town...'

Finlay heard the squeal of the Land-Rover brakes. 'I'd better go. It's nice to meet you, Janet.'

'Come and see me tomorrow...' She came from behind the counter and walked to the door with him. 'You won't forget... will you?'

'No, of course I won't,' he said, and ran to the Land-Rover.

'Gracious me, Ron!' Finlay exclaimed, handing him the Players. 'Did you see her? What an absolute stunner!'

Ron pulled into the traffic. 'I did.' He sounded not the least bit impressed.

'Well, don't you think she's a looker?' Finlay asked. 'Her name is Janet something. I wonder where she lives?'

'Apart from her red hair, I suppose she's not bad. But they redheads is a bit too high-octane for my taste. She's one of the Ward girls from over Lopperwood. There's three of them and a mother, all bloody redheads! I don't know where the father is. Out of it if he's got any sense, four bloody redheads in the house. We sold them some hay and straw last winter. Got some good horses, they have though.' By the look on his face Finlay could tell he disliked them.

'What's wrong with redheads, Ron?' Finlay asked. Ron was, after all, the fount of all knowledge, as far as Finlay was concerned.

'They're like chestnut mares. They all got a worm in their brain. One minute they're OK, next minute – Bang! they go bloody wild. I tried one once, never again. Time she finished with me, I was like a bit of chewed string.' He paused. 'You'll find out what I mean.'

'She wants me to see her tomorrow…'

'That's what I mean. She sees you and thinks ah, he's a good-looking chap. They always got to be the centre of attention. I'd steer well clear if I was you. But I wouldn't any more than you are going to.' He allowed himself a chuckle. 'Anyway, the other one will be 'ome soon won't she? From what I've heard, she'll keep you busy enough. You mind what I said about getting them up the duff though. Niney asked me to do something, but I forgot. Anyway you was busy with your schooling. I'll deal with that tomorrow.'

'Sorry I'm a bit late,' Finlay said walking into the kitchen. 'Didn't realize how the time had passed.'

Jenny was sitting at the table, reading. 'No matter,' she said, not looking up. 'Do you want a sandwich or something?'

'No thanks Jen.' Finlay did not want to disturb her. 'I'll make a cup of tea and go for a quick swim. I've been mending a sluice in the old main feeder.'

'Hmmn,' she answered, again not looking up.

Finlay smiled to himself and rinsed his tea cup in the sink. Walking past Jenny he ran his hand over her shoulders. 'Thank you, darling,' she said.

'What for?' asked Finlay, surprised by her reaction.

'For acknowledging I'm here.' She smiled. 'I like the way you always touch something. Do you want something to eat?'

Finlay laughed aloud. 'Jen, you asked that already. What are you reading?'

'Manslaughter. Heavy stuff!' she sighed.

'Well, come for a swim with me… only a quick one,' he suggested.

'Too cold yet. Another couple of days like today and I will, but not in the hatch pool. I'm not a newt like you. Terrifies me when you get in there. Don't be long, else I'll worry,' she said.

Seeing the car gone Finlay assumed his grandfather was out, so he took the Land-Rover down to the cattle bridge. He had been swimming for about five minutes when he heard someone say, 'That must be very cold, and very dangerous. Hello again.'

He swam back to the bridge. Janet was sitting on a bicycle, leaning on the hand rails.

'Yes, it is a bit cold,' Finlay said looking up. 'What are you doing here?'

'Just out for a ride. Thought I'd come this way for a change. Aren't you afraid of polio?' she asked.

'No, not in this river. Probably too cold for polio bugs to live in,' he said.

'You've been in the sun a lot. You're as brown as a berry,' she remarked.

He swam to the bank, climbed out and walked up on to the bridge, getting his towel from the Land-Rover in passing, and began drying himself vigorously. 'I'll just get dressed,' Finlay said, getting the Land-Rover between himself and the girl.

'I've seen you go past our house lots of times on your horse. She's very pretty isn't she? What do you call her?' she asked.

Finlay thought he had heard this conversation before. 'Misty or you bastard, depending on how she is behaving.'

She laughed. 'My elder sister said the other day, "I bet he's got a nice bum." Now I'll be able to tell her first hand!' She began to giggle.

'I beg your pardon!' Finlay said coming from behind the vehicle, putting on his shirt.

'If you come here a moment,' she laughed, pointing at the large wing mirror. 'You should be careful about mirrors!'

Finlay smiled ruefully. 'A lady would have looked away,' he said.

'A lady would have done. Do you swim here often? I would like to, if I may,' she said confidently.

'Most people swim at Testwood or Redbridge, when the tide comes in. It can be pretty dangerous at other times, because of the current,' he said seriously, and with a touch of patronage.

'I don't want to swim where the ordinary people swim. They're loud and their children are awful. Anyway, I expect I can swim better than you. I swim in the school team,' she said proudly.

Finlay laughed. 'What are ordinary people then?'

'You know what I mean!' she answered with at least the good grace to seem embarrassed by what she had said. 'Can my sisters come and swim here?'

'I'm the only one allowed to swim here after the anglers have gone home. If the keeper finds you here in the daytime, he'll hook you out of it in short order,' Finlay said seriously.

'I know. He's a devil he is. He found us up there one day,' she said, pointing upstream, 'where the river comes through those gate things. He was cross and very rude to us. I was pretty frightened by it.'

'School team or not, if you fell in there you would drown. I expect he was just as frightened. We had a bullock go in once and it tossed him about as though he were a leaf,' Finlay said. 'Now the weather is warmer, you could meet me here perhaps to swim. So that I can keep an eye on you.'

'You really are a patronizing bugger aren't you?' she said archly. 'Keep an eye on us! Who do you think you are?'

'I'm meant to be here, and not let you do anything stupid, but if that doesn't suit, you'll have to swim with the ordinary people.' Finlay was trying hard to get the conversation back to where he wanted it to be.

'Can we see you here around this time tomorrow then?' she asked. 'If the weather is warm again, we could bring some tea and have a picnic.'

'I have to go,' Finlay said. He suddenly did not feel comfortable with what was happening. He watched her cycle away. She waved as she passed out of sight, and Finlay couldn't help but think how beautiful she was.

Jenny was still reading in the kitchen when he got back. 'Had a good swim? You look all freshened up.' She closed her book with a snap. 'That's quite enough of that! I'd better think about some dinner.'

'What have we got?' he asked.

'Salmon, new spuds, fresh peas and salad,' Jenny said, knowing what his response would be.

'Bloody salmon again. It's no wonder I can swim so well. I've more salmon blood in my veins than my own!'

'I've made yours into fish cakes. Spoilt sod! There are plenty of people who would love to have fresh salmon.'

'I know. They're starving in India…' He suddenly realized he was being thoughtless. 'But thanks for the fish cakes, Jen.'

'Your grandfather loves salmon. Now get out from underfoot and shell the peas,' she ordered.

'Jen,' he said. 'Can I ask you something?'

'As long as you get on with the peas,' she returned.

'Well, there's this girl you see…' He got no further.

'Another one!' she laughed.

'I met her when I went to get Ron's fags,' he began.

'The very pretty redhead?'

'Yes, that's the one…'

'Well go on. I'm all ears.'

'She came along while I was swimming earlier and the upshot is, I've agreed to have a picnic with her and her sisters and go swimming with them tomorrow night.'

'And the problem is?' she asked.

'Well it doesn't feel quite right. Jill'll be home soon.'

'Jill will be home next Wednesday. She telephoned earlier.' She turned to him. 'I'm pleased you feel a loyalty to Jill. You have some moral sensibilities, but you don't understand the female mind. You meet a girl in a shop and suddenly she turns up where you've never seen her before. She didn't, I can assure you, arrive there by chance, despite anything she said. Any more than Jill did. It's up to you to judge them. If you don't feel right about having a picnic with the Ward sisters, then don't do it.'

'So how do I backtrack on this? I really don't want to do it,' Finlay said.

'Right Kee, on this occasion I'll help you. I'll come to the picnic. That'll put them off. Honestly! You're not fifteen yet and you've already got woman trouble. Just this once. Got it?' She was smiling.

'Thanks Jen,' he said getting up, giving her a kiss.

'Learn to say that little word No and don't get beguiled by every pretty female.' She began stripping a lettuce to pieces.

The ringing of the telephone made them both start. Wiping her hands on a tea towel, Jenny answered it and Finlay got up to leave. 'Kee,' Jenny said sharply, motioning him to stay. She was nodding to the unknown caller and then said, 'Yes Jack, we'll go now.' Putting the phone down, she turned to Finlay. 'The river is out at Longparish. They've had immense storms up there and the water's over the bridges at Stockbridge. Jack says to get both the boats out into the lane and start getting the gates right up.' She paused. 'A child has been swept away and they can't find him.' She went to the phone again and got through to the police at Totton. 'There's a big flood coming down Sergeant Beech… Good, you know then… Make certain there's nobody bathing at Redbridge. We're having to let the river go. Good… See you later then. Come along Kee, we must see Granny's OK.'

Arriving at the mill, they could see Granny Fortune in the garden. 'Don't you worry young Jenny,' she shouted. 'I'm ready to go should I need to.' Carl was already there, making preparations to lift the wheel away from the leat should the flood be a bad one. Jenny and Finlay dragged the boats out of the sheds on their trailers and tied them to Granny Fortune's fence. 'We must wait for the police to tell us there are no bathers down at Redbridge, Kee,' Jenny said. 'One child in a day is enough. I wonder how long it's going to take to get here?'

Granny came to join them. 'It'll be here within the hour my dear, and the tide is just coming in. I shan't be sleeping here tonight.'

The air-raid sirens started to sound in Romsey. The up and down tone came down to them on the breeze. Jenny started to shake and held Finlay closely. 'It's all right Jen. It's only telling people there's going to be a flood.'

She was clinging to him tightly and he could feel her whole body shaking.

Granny Fortune began stroking her hair. 'It's all right my lovely. 'Tain't them bloody old Jerries coming. 'Tis only a drop of water.'

The police arrived at the same time as Ron, who had with him three of the younger tractor drivers. 'The bathers are out of the way,' Sergeant Beech announced. 'I'll get off up the valley.' The black Wolseley left in a cloud of dust.

'Get the bigger of those boats into the mill stream,' Ron ordered. 'Tie it tight on this long rope and lay the oars in the bottom. Get the little one tied to Granny's fence.' He looked at Jenny. 'Sirens upset her?' he asked. Not waiting for an answer, he said, 'Fuck the bastards! Come on nipper, let's get the gates open.' Jenny made to come with them. 'No Miss,' Ron said. 'You get the Land-Rovers turned around and up the lane a bit and put Granny in mine. We don't know how much is coming.'

The river was clear and bright running at a normal summer level. The sun hot on their backs, the men turned the handles that lifted the heavy gates and the sound of water increased, crashing through into the hatch pool. It seemed like a beautiful June day. Only a steep and heavy bank of cloud to the northeast betrayed the fact that all was not well. The river behind the gates began to drop very slowly, despite the fact that at the outfalls, the water was moving so quickly it stood in troughs. The fish in the next pool down were beginning to show, revelling in the sudden flush of heavily oxygenated water.

Jack arrived, looking worried. 'Blackwater's out already Ron. Coming down as black as a cow's guts. This is going to be a bad bugger!' The gantry walkway began to shudder gently as the pent-up water crashed through.

The sun was still shining on the clear water and to Finlay, the whole thing seemed surreal. 'I'm going to see that Jenny's all right, Ron,' he said. He found her in the lane, sitting on the Land-Rover tailboard. 'You OK Jen?' he asked, sitting down and putting his arm around her.

'Hello, white knight,' she said. 'Sorry about that. Brings it all back to me.' They sat on the tailboard together. 'There won't be any picnic now,' Jenny said. 'Bloody little harlots coming around sniffing after my white knight. Who do they think they are?'

'You don't mind really Jen, do you?' Finlay asked seriously.

She looked at him quizzically. 'Of course I mind. I mind like Hell. Saucy little baggages with their pert little tits. If I was your granny I'd mind. We are a jealous and possessive lot, we women. You wait until those Ward girls come up against Niney. She doesn't think they're any good.' She laughed. 'What has to be, has to be, and there'll be a lot more young ladies coming to call, I've no doubt about that.'

It began to rain. 'You don't mind if I go back, Jen?' Finlay said.

'Go and look at your precious river,' she laughed.

The men had moved off the gantry. It was humming with the press of the water. Behind the gates it had only fallen by about a foot, but the current was considerably faster. At last the clearness gave way to an opaque-looking green.

'Here it comes,' Jack muttered.

'Look at they bloody salmon going over the sills!' one of the tractor drivers said.

'They'll be back soon,' Jack answered. 'Look at this lot coming.'

The first indication of the flood was rafts of unbaled hay, swept from the fields further upstream. They were coming down the middle of the river in long lines.

Carl emerged from the mill. 'Zee veel is up and locked. No bloody lights for anyone tonight.'

The first of the hay washed through the hatchway and disappeared around the next bend.

'We better keep our eyes open for the little lad in a couple of hours, poor little sod,' Ron said.

Jack looked at his watch. 'Not from here Ron. Tide'll be full in three-quarters of an hour, and this place will be feet under water. I think you should get the boy up to the top lane now.' To Finlay, this didn't seem feasible. He had seen the river come out before and flow around the hatches, but his Uncle Jack was obviously talking about a different sort of flood.

'OK, Jack,' Ron said. 'I'll take your word for it.' He turned to Finlay. 'Away you go nipper. Get up to the top lane with the Land-Rovers.'

Finlay wanted to argue the case, but Ron was adamant. 'Up the top now!' he ordered.

Finlay found Jenny in Ron's Land-Rover, chatting to Granny Fortune. 'We've got to get the Landies up on the top now Jack says. The tide's coming in.'

'He ain't a lot of good for much, but he knows what the river does. Us 'ad better get up there,' Granny Fortune said glumly. 'Didn't get chance to get my bits upstairs. Bugger and damn it! Another wet carpet.'

By the time they got up on to the top lane, a matter of two or three minutes, it was obvious it would not be long before the river came out.

'Have a look through these, Kee,' Jenny said, handing him his grandfather's field glasses, always kept in the Land-Rover. 'I think there are some dead sheep coming down.'

Through the glasses, the water looked a milky green, chalk from the quarries further upstream. 'Yes, sheep. About twenty of them.' He trained the glasses to the left. 'It's going around the hatches already. I hope Ron is out of the way, and Uncle Jack. Look, the Blackwater is coming over the fields!' He handed the glasses to Jenny. Like a dark stain, the fields on the far side of the valley became quickly engulfed from what was normally a small river, barely bigger than a main feeder stream.

'I hope to God they've seen it,' Jenny gasped. 'Oh my God, look at this lot!'

It was like a moving lake, coming down the valley bottom, hundreds of yards wide flowing slowly, filling the valley bottom as it came, and joining up with the flow from the little Blackwater. In five minutes, the valley floor was full. Jenny and Finlay watched, with some horror, at what was happening.

'I'd better go and see where they are,' Finlay said.

'You just stay where you are!' Jenny snapped. 'Don't you dare leave me.'

Finlay was startled by the way she had spoken. He could see she was frightened.

'You stay here boy,' Granny Fortune ordered. 'I've seen her come up like this before and she's a long way from done yet. They got the boats and young Ronnie Drew knows what 'e's about. If them'm in the river, there's bugger-all you can do.'

'But Jenny... Uncle Jack... what will Auntie Niney do...' Finlay shouted.

'They will be all right... You'll see... Don't you leave me Kee... I'm frightened. Come here.'

Finlay went to her quickly.

They waited, both soaked through by the rain. The river rose higher very quickly. Held back by the tide, the water had nowhere to go except outwards. Through the glasses Finlay could see that Granny's cottage had water up to the second-floor windows. He decided to keep this to himself. Then he saw them, two boats cutting across the current. 'There they are!' Finlay shouted and gave the glasses to Jenny. 'Down below where the island is.'

'Go and get them, Kee,' Jenny said. The relief in her voice was profound.

He turned the Land-Rover around and went back up the lane to pick the rowers up. When he got to them, they were animated. Glad they had done their job and cheated the water.

'Bloody Hell, Uncle Jack!' Finlay said. 'Why did you wait so long? We thought you were washed away.'

'We couldn't get the boats out until the water was deeper than the fences. It was a good job Ron had the big one in the mill stream. We wouldn't have got out else. Is Granny OK?' he asked.

'Yes, she's in the other Land-Rover. Her house was pretty much under water,' Finlay said.

'Let's get the boats tied up and get back home. I've had enough of water for one day,' Ron remarked. He seemed very calm. 'There wasn't any sign of the child, but he could be anywhere by now. You taking Granny back home Jack?'

'Ah,' Jack said, without a shred of enthusiasm.

The driveway was under about a foot of water as Jenny turned in the gateway. 'At least we shall be dry again shortly. I'd better find out if the Grieveses are all right.'

'I'll do that Jen. You go and have first bath. You'd better leave your water in because there won't be much hot water with the electric off.'

The kitchen was as they had left it. A meal half-prepared, half-cups of cold tea, but the air was warm and smelt of that day's butter making.

'Put the spuds on, Kee,' Jenny said. 'I wish I knew where James and Niney are.'

'Where did they go?' Finlay, suddenly realizing that he had not missed them, went to the telephone and lifted the earpiece. 'That's not working, so wherever they are, they can't get in touch.'

'They went to Winchester. I don't suppose they can get back. Put the spuds over when they are boiling, darling. I'll have a quick bath… I'll shout when I've done.'

'Bring the portable wireless down Jen. Might be something on the news…' but she was gone.

Sitting in the kitchen alone, Finlay listened to the rain against the windows and wondered how everyone was coping. Over the centuries houses that had been subject to flooding had been replaced on to higher ground. Only the mill cottages and the church were still vulnerable. Finlay looked out of the front door at the lawn. The feeder was still spewing water in a stream across the garden and the crushed Venus statue looked more forlorn than ever. He moved the potatoes on to the warm side and tried the telephone again. It remained silent.

'I'm out of the bath, Kee,' he heard Jenny shout. 'There's not much hot water, so hurry up… Are the spuds boiling yet?'

Finlay walked into the hall and shouted up the stairs, 'Yes, they're on the warm side. The phone ain't working still.' He ran up the stairs and headed for the bathroom, meeting Jenny in just her bra and pants. 'Christ Jen, you look great!'

She cocked her bottom at him. 'Ward sisters, who do they think they are?' She disappeared into her bedroom. 'Not bad for a step-grandmother!' she called, laughing.

Downstairs, Jenny was finishing the cooking. 'You smell gorgeous Kee,' Jenny laughed. 'So much better than pig or TVO.'

'Hang on… I can hear a vehicle!' Finlay said, getting up and going to the front door. 'Jen, there's a fire engine coming up the drive.'

Joining him, Jenny said, 'Maybe they think we need pumping out.'

As it pulled level with the door, they could see Niney sitting in the cab. One of the fireman got down. 'Got somebody here for you,' he said to them, and to Niney, 'Would you like me to lift you over, Mrs Terry?'

'My dear boy, the whole reason for going in your wonderful fire engine, was so that you would lift me out!' She started to slide out of the high vehicle, her skirt hanging up on something so that she showed her stocking tops. 'If you look away young man, I shall be very offended,' she said smiling.

The fireman lifted her bodily on to the front steps, blushing furiously.

'You are a lovely fireman,' Niney said, kissing him on the cheek.

As they waved the engine goodbye Jenny said, 'You really are impossible Niney. That poor chap didn't know where to look!'

'He'd have had a bigger shock if my skirt had gone higher. I haven't any drawers on. I took them off in the National Provincial Bank, and there's not many who can say that! Lend me a pair of yours Jen. I always feel a little vulnerable without knickers!'

Finlay was shaking with laughter. 'Auntie Niney, why haven't you any on? An angry polar bear would feel vulnerable, coming up against you!'

'Come on, let's go in,' Niney said. 'I took them off because they got soaked and kept hooking up around my bum, darling. What an exciting time. Is Granny OK?'

'Jack has taken her back to your house Niney. Did they find the little boy?' Jenny asked.

'Yes darling, and alive! He clung on to a straw bale and they fished him out at Motisfont. Cold and shocked, but alive.'

'Where's Grandfather?' Finlay asked.

'Helping in Romsey. The water's coming down the Hundred like you would not believe and they're moving the old people to the school. It's going to be a hell of a mess when it goes down, shit and mud everywhere,' Niney said.

'Do you want to change into something dry before we eat?' Jenny asked.

'No, let's eat. I'll stay here tonight. Can you light some lamps, Kee? I don't expect we'll have electricity for a few days. The cows and pigs have generators. We do without,' Niney said.

Over their meal, they discussed the day's events. 'So you got out of your little problem, without my help,' Jenny laughed.

'Ah yes, but you said "just this once", so if it happens again, that's still on the books surely?' Finlay wheedled.

'What problem?' Niney asked, looking at the smile on Jenny's face and seeing mischief there.

'One of the Ward girls, Niney,' Jenny said. 'Just happened to run into him!'

'I suppose it's the middle one from the paper shop. She just happened along did she? Likely story!' Niney snorted. 'Did you meet her, Jen? Saucy little bitch. Her mother's the one you see about the town with a chiffon scarf tied around her head. I don't know what she thinks she looks like!'

Both Jenny and Finlay were laughing. 'You wear a chiffon scarf around your head, Auntie Niney...' Finlay said.

'The difference, my dear, is that I can carry it off. She most certainly can't!'

'How dare she...' Finlay couldn't get the words out, as he was laughing so. 'How dare she try and look as glam as you, Auntie Niney.'

'That'll be the day! If she was the woman she makes herself out to be, her husband would have stayed home and not run off with his secretary!' Niney scoffed. 'Your mad scientist will be home shortly Kee. Much more suitable than some flibbertigibbet redhead!'

'I want to ask something seriously, both of you please. What do people have against redheads? Even Ron said they were nothing but trouble. He said they were too high-octane,' Finlay said earnestly.

'They're a bit like chestnut mares, Kee. A bit scatty, temperamental and always have to be the centre of attention,' Jenny said.

'That's almost word for word what Ron said. He really doesn't like them,' Finlay exclaimed.

Niney gave another 'Huh! He would say that. Got his fingers badly burnt by a redhead. Little Irish girl, she was. Went after him like a stoat after a rabbit. Ron didn't have the sense to run. It was lucky the war came when it did. She went back home quick and left Wyn the field, but I think he was cut up about it.'

'So there you are, Kee,' Jenny said triumphantly. 'But that'll make her all the more fascinating, so I won't say a word.'

'Oh Jen,' Niney said. 'You're wasting your breath. All men want to know the answer to the eternal question, and it's bold buggers like this one who have to find out first hand.'

'What question?' Jenny asked.

'Whether the collars and cuffs match, of course!'

'What does that mean?' Finlay asked.

'Darling, you must work that out for yourself. I'm going for a bath. Can you find me some drawers Jen, please?' Niney asked.

The next dawn was bright and sunny as June mornings should be. The sun was already hot. The flood water had dropped back considerably and where it had, the earth began to throw off spirals of steam. The house was very quiet as Finlay walked along the top passage. He walked into the kitchen to find Niney up and making tea. 'Is Grandad back?' Finlay asked. 'I can't see the car.'

'Shouldn't think so. Expect he took a bed in the Three Tuns. He'll be back, don't worry,' she said.

'The water has gone down quite a bit. I should think you could get a car through now,' Finlay said.

'Only because the tide has run back out. I'm going back up. Now Kee, promise. If you go outside you won't go down to the water,' she demanded seriously.

'No, I promise,' he replied.

'I'll come down later and cook you breakfast,' and she was gone.

Outside, the water was no longer running across the lawn. Its previous course was plainly marked by the grass flattened in one direction, with strands of river weed spread down its length. The fence was clogged, heaped with weed and twigs and leant at an angle, testament to the force of water. The drive itself did not seem to have suffered. The once fairly clean gravel was now sticky with sediment with any surface water, full of freshwater shrimps. Further up the lawn, a group of half a dozen black-headed gulls were squabbling over something in the mud. Interested, Finlay went to look and found the remains of a sea lamprey, half-eaten now and beginning to smell slightly.

Finlay was more than pleased to see Ron approaching along the top lane. As he splashed into the driveway the Land-Rover slid to a stop. 'Here, stick these in your pocket.' He handed Finlay a small package. As Finlay went to undo it, Ron stopped him. 'Not here for Christ's sake!' he said quietly. 'They're baby stoppers, rabbit welly boots. Niney told me to get them. Put 'em in your pocket.'

'Thanks Ron. You coming in to see if Grandad's about?'

'Hello Ronnie Drew,' Niney said, as they walked into the kitchen. 'Hero of the hour again, I hear. Is there much damage?' Niney asked.

'Difficult to say till it goes right back. Granny's house is still up to the bottom windows. I think we should give that one up.'

'Can't see Granny agreeing to that!' Niney said shortly, in a way that showed she didn't agree with the suggestion either. They heard the Armstrong arriving.

'Here's the boss!' Ron said. 'We'll know what's happening outside now.'

Finlay's grandfather came in smiling. 'Hello everyone... what a night! Got to bed at three this morning, but all the vulnerable people are up at the school.'

'Have you eaten, James? You look all in,' Niney said.

'Yes, thanks my dear. I'll go have a bath I think. Come over for lunch, Ron, and you can fill me in on damage here. Where's Jenny by the way?'

'Out on Misty, looking to see what damage there has been. You'll have two reports,' Niney said. 'Now go and have your bath and a bit of a snooze. There's nothing to be done outside,' Niney ordered.

The weekend passed and the river dropped back within its banks. The breeze was full of the smell of decaying fish and rotting vegetable matter and, in the air, the gulls wheeled and screamed over the bounty on the soaked earth. The hedges and fences were festooned with debris from the river and the branches of the apple trees by the mill leat, snapped off and gone.

Granny Fortune made no objection to moving further up the valley. Her own home would never be a place to live again. Her new home was one of the dairy cottages, modern and warmer. Her old cottage would become a fishing lodge, but it was still a great sadness. She had gone there as a bride at seventeen, had been delivered from the church to the cottage in the carriage with her husband, on the same day that Custer fought the Sioux at the Little Big Horn.

Chapter Three

•

On the Tuesday before Jill came home, Finlay spent the morning freeing up the sluice gate he had left unfinished before the flood came down. The stream, now unfettered, rushed with a joy of its own towards the main river half a mile away. Finlay walked down with the new flow, watching the behaviour of the water, already mapping in his head where the trout would lay. As it joined the main river it created a large eddy, small whorls of water spinning away downstream. He walked back to the sluices and closed them down again till the flow was what he judged it had been. More than satisfied with his efforts, he watched a pair of moorhens who had seemed perplexed by the sudden drop in the water, their nest suddenly floating again.

He was glad to see both the Armstrong and the Land-Rover in the yard. His grandfather was indoors and Finlay badly wanted to tell him about the sluices. There was also a Morris Minor pick-up parked in the yard which he didn't recognize. It was green with a buff tilt. 'Sorry I'm late Jen,' he said coming into the kitchen, and to his grandfather, 'I've got both sluices going Grandfather. It's going to make a lovely little stream. Whose is the little pick-up in the yard?'

His grandfather smiled at him. 'Well, it's a farm vehicle, for the under-pig man, the under-mechanic and the new drowner. Yours in short.'

'Really! Mine to use all the time?' said a delighted Finlay.

'Spoilt brat!' Jenny said, equally delighted. 'Whoa! Have some lunch,' she added. 'Before we do a protracted inspection and test drive!'

'It won't use much petrol, but it's not going to be a reason for giving up walking anywhere.' His grandfather was trying to be severe. 'It's obviously not new, but it's been looked after. You'll have to service it. Give you a good idea of looking after a vehicle.'

'I quite like mechanical things now Grandfather. I like the order,' Finlay said. 'And it's good to have the knowledge.'

The wireless suddenly began to crackle. 'Good! Carl must have the turbine going again,' Finlay's grandfather said. 'That'll make everyone happy.'

'Didn't we ought to have a generator for the house, Grandfather?' Finlay asked.

'Not really, Kee,' he replied. 'I don't really see the need, and it's good to know how to cope without electricity. They always used to, and if we had a gennie for here, surely we would in truth have to fix everyone with one. Otherwise it wouldn't be very fair, would it?'

'I hadn't thought about it like that,' Finlay said. 'Anyway, I love the smell of the oil lamps.'

'Will you let your meat stop your blathering, Kee,' Jenny said. 'And if you are out in the sun you keep a hat on your head. You'll be getting sunstroke. You can wear that blue cotton sun-hat,' she suggested.

'Oh Jen! I look like a child in that!' he objected.

'You'll wear that hat young man!' Jenny insisted. 'If you don't there will be a row, I can assure you.'

'Perhaps we should look at the new pick-up Kee...' Finlay's grandfather said, trying to avert a clash of wills.

'Not without a hat he doesn't,' Jenny said very quietly.

'I'll go and get it Jen,' Finlay said.

After he had left the room his grandfather said, 'Perhaps I should get him a more grown-up sort of hat.'

'I think he'll do as he's told! A little discipline over a footling thing like this will do him good. He's far too spoilt James. He twists Niney around his little finger the whole time, and it's certainly not good for him, and neither would sunstroke be. He'll do as he's told, and there's an end to it. I love him very much, James, and I don't want him ill.'

They went outside to inspect the pick-up, Finlay wearing a blue cotton sun-hat.

'Get in then, and have a go,' his grandfather ordered. Finlay drove to the end of the drive and back, finding it strange and sharp. Not so forgiving as the Land-Rover, it was certainly a lot quicker off the mark. 'It's splendid Grandfather,' he exclaimed.

'Will I be able to borrow it Kee?' asked Jenny, 'I can cut into Southampton to do the shopping.'

'Of course you can Jen,' Finlay said, glad of her enthusiasm. 'I'll make certain it is always clean for you.'

'Well, there's work waiting,' his grandfather said. 'First job you can do Kee, is go to the wood yard and pick up some bags of sawdust and take them up to the Grieveses' place. I believe Janey is home, so we will see you at tea time.'

It was a very proud Finlay who drove away down the back drive. He wondered if Ron knew about the little Morris. The wood yard was deserted. Cyril and his men were out fencing and the sawdust bags were already filled and waiting. He loaded them on the pick-up and headed off towards the Grieves farm. The little Morris pulled along happily, the extra weight not seeming to make any difference. Janey was sitting under a huge umbrella on the lawn, reading. She looked annoyed at first by the intrusion until she realized who it was. 'Hello Finlay,' she said happily, jumping up and coming towards him. 'How lovely to see you. What are you doing up here?'

'I've brought some sawdust for your ma. Where should I put it?' Finlay said. She helped him put the bags of sawdust in the cart shed.

'Have you been playing tennis, Janey?' Finlay asked, noting how she was dressed.

'No, it's just so hot, so I put this on to stay cool. It's a bit revealing but my mother is away for the day…' She let it go at that. 'Come along in and I'll get some lemonade. We can sit in the shade and have a long chat.'

'The afternoon's mine. Grandfather said you might be at home, so I hoped I'd see you.'

They went into the kitchen, which smelt of buttermilk and was cool. 'Grab the rug and we'll go down under the chestnut tree in the cool. Come and sit and tell me what you've been doing. You've finished exams? You must have been outside a lot. You're really tanned, and you've grown so much. Not a bit like the little chap who I shepherded on his first day at school, and what about this scandal you caused?' She was smiling.

'Oh, you heard about that then?' Finlay said, a little embarrassed, but not overly so.

She laughed at him. 'You don't have to tell me Finlay, but my mother was so shocked by it, and not only that. Everybody heard about it!'

'Oh dear,' Finlay said. 'Well. It just happened!'

'It hasn't just happened to me yet! I shall die virginal and bitter like that awful Satchel woman,' Janey sighed.

'But I thought you had a boyfriend, the chap at the Meet.'

'Did have, but he was so conventional and so proper, I just thought I'm not getting into this. Life's so boring at home, I certainly don't want any more of it, so we went our separate ways. Anyway, my mother thought he was wonderful, so that put the kibosh on it.' She laughed, but not with any conviction.

'I'm sorry about that,' Finlay said. He really didn't know what to say. This was Janey, the prefect, the bossy one, the one who rode a bicycle just like an old maid.

'Well come on then… who was she?' Janey said, suddenly intense.

'A girl from Rownhams, Jill MacFarlane.' Finlay suddenly realized where this was going.

'I don't know her. Is she very pretty, this Jill?' Janey asked.

'Not really. Beautiful in an unconventional way. Very clever though. I mean it's difficult to quantify isn't it?' Finlay wanted to go.

Janey became thoughtful. 'Yes, I suppose it is. It's just that all my friends from school seem to have boys one after the other. Am I so very repulsive?'

'Don't be so bloody silly Janey! Of course you aren't. It's just that you are, well…' He stopped. He did not know how to say it.

'What?' she almost wailed.

'Well, a bit like a school prefect,' Finlay said.

'Oh God,' she said and started to cry.

'I think I'd better go,' he said. 'I'm always saying the wrong thing.'

'See, even you won't tell me the truth.'

He went to comfort her, putting his hand on her shoulder. 'C'mon Janey, you don't have to cry about it.' He gently pulled her face around. 'You're not the least bit repulsive.'

She laid over on her back, her arm over her face, sobbing. Finlay put his hand on her breast.

'What are you doing?' she said, but she didn't remove his hand. 'We shouldn't be doing this!'

The kiss, when it came, was maidenly and rather chaste, until Finlay gently forced his tongue into her mouth. The result was spectacular. Janey came alive. As he found the warm, silky stickiness in her knickers, Finlay heard the throb of a heavy diesel engine. A horn began to blow. Finlay turned and saw the obvious roof of a cattle lorry turning into the farm entrance. 'There's someone coming, Janey!' Finlay said urgently.

'Oh lumme! It's Mr Pearce. Do you think he saw us?' She was dishevelled and heavily flushed. Jumping up, she adjusted her clothes and they started towards the yard where the lorry was heading.

'Hello you two,' Ernie Pearce said. 'Got a couple of heifers here from Salisbury. Put them in this yard your father said. Been playing tennis, the pair of you?'

Janey was flustered. 'No, studying,' she said.

'Well! Must have been hot work by the look of your faces.' He dropped the back of the lorry and ran the animals into the yard. There was just a ghost of a smile playing around his lips. 'Yer dad ain't far

behind me and I shall see you in the morning nipper. Got some bacon-
ers to pick up.' With the back of the lorry up again, he climbed back
into the cab. 'Mind what you're up to then.'

'He guessed what we were doing. You'd better go before my father
gets back. If he finds you here and me looking as I must, he'll shoot
the pair of us,' Janey said, almost pushing him towards the little pick-
up. She aimed an awkward kiss at his mouth, missed, and fled towards
the house.

He was just at the farm entrance as he met Janey's father. 'Afternoon
Mr Grieves. How are you?'

'And good afternoon to you young man. It's good to see you. Seen
Janey?' he asked.

'Brought some sawdust up for your hen house. Excuse to use this.'
Finlay patted the door of the vehicle. 'Mr Pearce came by. Two nice-
looking heifers.' Finlay wanted to keep him talking.

'Yes, I'm rather pleased with them. Must get on though. Nice to see
you.' He pulled away past Finlay and headed for the house. Finlay did
not stop until he was halfway home, and doing so he reflected on the
past hour and breathed a sigh of relief at his avoiding what might have
been. He glanced at his right arm. It ached and he saw a blue and yellow bruise on his bicep, an obvious bite mark. He was curious that he
had not felt it when it happened. 'That's it!' he said, aloud to himself.
'I'm giving up the opposite sex. Far too complex for me to understand.'

From where he was sitting he could just make out the Ayrshire collecting yard. It was half full with cows still waiting to be milked, so he
judged it to be about half-past three. Revelling in his new mobility, he
decided to study the proposed new fishing stream, where he had mended the sluices. The stream had cleared down beautifully, the height
was as it was, and the moorhens seemed very settled, busying themselves feeding on passing scraps of floating weed. Finlay liked
moorhens. They always seemed busy and happy. Uncle Jack did not
and but for Finlay's affection for the birds, he would have made sure
there were fewer.

He began walking down the stream quietly, trying not to startle any
fish that might have been there. There were fish there, pike. He spotted four, one at least in double figures. 'Must have come from the
Blackwater,' he mused. Something would have to be done about them.
If there were four here there would surely be many more in the main
river. 'Finlay!' He heard someone calling his name. Emerging from

the trees, by the stream, he saw a rider standing by the pick-up. Even from the distance between them he could see the copper-coloured curls shining in the sun and the resolution so recently made was forgotten. He waved and watched as she turned her horse and came trotting towards him.

'Hello Finlay,' she said happily. 'I've come to see you. The lady in the house said you were out somewhere.'

'Lovely to see you, Janet,' Finlay said. 'Have you come about swimming?'

'No, I've come to see you…'

'Well, give me a pull,' he said, taking hold of a stirrup leather. Looking up at her he said, 'You've had your hair cut. Lost some of your curls.'

'I'm flattered you noticed,' she said. They had got back to the pick-up. 'If I get down, will you get me back up please? He's my sister's horse and a little big for me.'

'Of course.' He went to take the horse's head.

'No, you'll have to come here and get me down,' she said.

She slid down from the horse and Finlay caught her. She was light and slim. He held her fractionally longer and perhaps closer than was absolutely necessary.

'That was nice,' she said lightly, pushing him away. 'Where can we sit?'

They sat side by side on the tailboard of the pick-up truck. 'The flood was terrible wasn't it? I was in town. It was such a shambles until your grandfather and Mrs Terry got things organized. He really is quite something isn't he? Now Finlay, I've been hearing things about you. The lady who comes and cleans told my mother. Is it true?' she asked.

'Is what true?' Finlay asked innocently.

'What you and Jill got up to. You know what I mean, so don't look so bloody innocent.' There was a certain mocking tone in her voice.

'Do you know Jill?' Finlay asked.

'Of course I do stupid! We did Pony Club together and she comes and rides with us sometimes. I had a letter from her. She said she had met you and stayed over at your house, had a wonderful time with you and your family and intimated that the special thing had happened. I can't wait to see her. Isn't she home tomorrow?'

'It's like some kind of conspiracy!' Finlay said. 'I don't know I like that very much.'

'Don't start going all pi about it. Of course we all talk to each other about such things, the Pony Club Mafia and all that. If it's any sort of fillip for you, she's mad about you, and I might add, warned me to keep off the grass.' She laughed.

'So what are you doing here?' Finlay asked. He didn't know whether to be angry or not.

'All's fair in love and war. I can tell you fancy me. You do don't you?' she asked in a matter-of-fact way.

'Well you seem fairly certain about it!' Finlay said.

'I am. You were really pleased to see me just now and I wasn't sure that you would be after our first meeting. And you were pretty rude about Caroline, so you must be quite sensible.'

Finlay laughed aloud. 'You really do fancy yourself, Janet Ward, and that is as it should be. Auntie Niney has style because she knows she's beautiful and can make men do as she wants. Even me. So carry on being as you are and you'll achieve your aim.'

'You do fancy me then?' she asked.

'Of course,' Finlay laughed. 'You are and will be a great beauty...'

Ron drove past in his Land-Rover and blew its horn. He was smiling broadly. 'That's the bugger who pinched my mother's bottom, when some hay and straw was delivered. She was really shocked,' Janet said. She sounded scandalized, but Finlay doubted her mother was. 'When can we go swimming?' she asked.

'When the water has the all clear. We don't know yet what was washed into it by the flood. Should know tomorrow.' He got up. 'Let me get you on board again Janet. I really ought to go and do some work.'

'OK. So when do we meet again?' she asked.

'Anytime at all Janet. Just come on over and get the official permission to ride over the place. Just turn up, somebody will know where I am.' He was not that worried any more about Jill and Janet meeting up, now he knew the truth of it.

She stood ready to have a leg up. 'Finlay,' she said. 'Why do you wear that child's hat?'

He bent to take her leg and hoisted her on to the horse. 'Finlay, we are going to be friends aren't we?'

'Nothing more certain Janet.'

She bent and kissed him, just as friends should. Finlay watched her ride away.

She stopped about fifty-odd yards away. 'Finlay,' she shouted. 'You've got a nice bum!'

He heard her laugh as she moved off again. He watched her until she reached a bend. She turned and waved, he waved back and said aloud to himself, 'That really is a tidy filly Finlay. How do you think you're going to keep them both?'

At home tea was under way and Finlay was pleased to see Jack in attendance. He washed his hands and went to the Aga to get a towel. In passing, he pushed his face into Niney's hair. 'Hello my beautiful Auntie. How are you?'

'Oh yes, and what have you been up to? You only do that when you want something or you've been up to no good.' She grabbed his arm and put her face up to be kissed. Finlay obliged.

'You bugger,' she said fondly.

He took a plate and went to sit in his usual place, beside Jenny. He pushed his chair up tight to hers so they would be touching, something they always did. 'Well, I take it Miss Ward found you, by how late you are?' Jenny said. She pushed her knee against his. '"Please Miss Jenny, is Finlay in?"' she said, mimicking Janet.

'Silly little thing!' Niney snorted.

'She said some nice things about you and Grandfather organizing things in the town the other night,' said Finlay.

'Well, it's a wise daughter that spots her own mother's failings,' Niney said. 'I suppose she might have some sense about her.'

His grandfather, who had been buried behind the *Telegraph*, suddenly looked up and said, 'Niney you are more than impossible. Did you get the sawdust up to Janey's father, Kee?'

'Yes. It was great seeing her again,' Finlay said.

'Her father telephoned. Said nice things about your manners, darling, and would you like to bat on Sunday. They're playing Landford. He wants you in at four or five,' Niney said.

'I'll give him a call later. I wonder if he'll let me have a turn at bowling.' Finlay was pleased with the invitation.

'Well, I expect your ladies will turn out and clap for you. The Ward girl does the scoring, I'm told,' Jenny said, with a touch of acid.

'They're a coven of witches. Jill and Janet know each other well, even to the point of correspondence. Neither one said anything about it to me,' Finlay said, affronted.

'Why should they?' Jenny said. 'Stops you playing them off against each other, as you probably have plans to do...'

'I saw some pike in the main feeder today, Uncle Jack. Do you want me to have them out?' Finlay thought he had adroitly changed the subject.

'Don't cut across my bows like that, you ill-mannered boy,' Jenny snapped, and slapped his arm.

'Ow!' Finlay shouted. 'That hurt Jen!'

She looked at him. 'What's that bruise on your arm?' She took his arm and studied it. 'That looks like a bite.'

'It is. It's a little love bite. It's nothing. I didn't even notice when it happened.'

'Who gave it to you? Love bite indeed!' Niney said, annoyed.

'Misty of course! Who do you think gave it me?' Finlay said tersely.

'Could be one of any number, I'd have thought,' Uncle Jack said laughing. 'Yes, I wouldn't bother trying to catch them Kee, I'd just shoot them. The water's shallow enough.'

'Did you clean that bite?' Niney asked. 'I'd better put some iodine on it.'

'I wonder you don't spend more time with Janey,' Finlay's grandfather remarked, from behind his newspaper. 'Still something of the school prefect about her. Keep you on the straight and narrow perhaps.'

'I know she has fined down a bit, but as you say Grandad…' Finlay was skating on fairly thin ice.

'I wasn't thinking about her as a potential conquest. Just somebody as a friend.' His grandfather went back to his newspaper.

Chapter Four

•

It was a little before six the next morning. Finlay crept very slowly by the feeder stream, hoping the biggest of the pike he had seen would still be in the same place. The water was crystal clear which would allow him to see it easily, but it would also allow the pike to see him. He had walked to where the stream joined the main river and was gradually working his way back upstream. The pike was still in place, hovering in the stream. To study it would have been folly, giving it maybe a chance to escape. He shot at it with the choke; the water erupted with the force of the shot. The pike was in two pieces, dead. The noise of the shot sent a cloud of peewits into the air on the other side of the river. He was sad to see so few young ones among them, for many had drowned in the flood. From behind the black poplars a female sparrowhawk dashed among them, snatching one from the air. Its impetus carried it towards Finlay who fired, bringing it down between the feeder stream and the main river. He walked across and picked up the peewit, stroking its beautiful, iridescent crested head. There was a lump in his throat. He looked at the sparrowhawk, only wounded, sitting back on its fantail, its talons ready to strike at him as he got closer. He flicked it into the river with his Wellington. It arched over, fluttering, and splashed on to the surface struggling. 'Black-hearted bastard!' he said. 'The river'll take care of you.' He watched its struggles until it passed around the next bend, knowing there was nothing to save it from the bottom hatches at Testwood. He looked at the broken beauty in his hand, warm and soft, its crest sunk back flat now. Very gently he buried it in the bankside mud.

Finlay heard tractors starting back in the main yard so he knew it to be about seven. The sun was already hot and the air still smelt foul from the rotting corpses of fish and birds. He knew it would be gone soon as the various carrion was eaten or rotted. He went back to the house to drop his gun off and change into something suitable for the pig unit, where he was to help load the bacon pigs. The kitchen was cool and smelt of milk and butter. Nobody was there, so he left a note to say where he was. This was a new rule from Niney, who suddenly needed to know exactly where he was.

He went to the farrowing house to see all was well there. It was quiet and smelt sweet and clean with the smell of warm straw over everything. The sows and piglets, back to sleep after the disturbance of feeding. He heard the lorry arrive and back up to the ramp of the bacon house. Finlay hated sending pigs off to the bacon factory. It always seemed to him like the ultimate act of betrayal. He knew the pigs were fully aware of where they were going.

Ron was with Mr Pearce. He saw them begin to laugh together. Finlay wondered whether Mr Pearce was regaling him with finding him with Janey. With the pigs stamped and loaded and going on their final journey, Ron said, 'Where's your pick-up, nipper? I was relying on a lift.'

'Back by the dairy crossing. Grandad says I shouldn't even cross the road with it, now that Haseham is back on the beat,' Finlay answered. It did seem a little foolish to him. Had the local council not insisted that the road should become public, there would have been no problem.

'Now, I'm glad of the time to have a quick chat,' Ron began. 'Who do you think you are for Christ's sake, General Auckinleck with his hens! You ain't really supposed to go around all the little pullets and tread them. Ernie said you was up the top farm with Janey yesterday afternoon, and then I sees you with that little redhead long before milking was finished. Bugger, you'll wear it out!'

Finlay tried to explain what happened with Janey.

Ron laughed. 'I suppose she comes hossing like the rest of them, poor little mare. But seriously, I should leave well alone there. Her old man would probably shoot you or give notice to quit and your grandad wouldn't want that. The little redhead, mind, is a different job altogether. She be after you proper and despite my warnings, you still go ahead. Knew you would. Fascinating buggers they are and 'er more than most. Just take care. Get one in foal and it'll cost you a fortune.'

'Well Ron, I just want to ask you something…' Finlay began.

'No bloody questions this morning. I'm too busy,' Ron said.

'What I want to know is,' Finlay said firmly, 'if you are so dead set against redheads, why were you pinching Mrs Ward's bum?'

Ron was silent for a moment. 'Well, I thought if I upset her, she wouldn't want us back again. It's a bugger of a place to turn a trailer in.'

Finlay dropped Ron off at the workshop and went towards home for breakfast. He was trying to think of a project he could take on. Waiting for exam results was proving irksome. He drove the pick-up into the stable yard and started undressing. He wanted to see Misty, but she would object mightily to the smell of pigs on him. 'Morning John,' he called, pulling on his shorts. He heard him answer from the cool of the stables, as he splashed about in the water trough. 'How's the witch today John?' he asked, pulling on his Aertex shirt. 'Might take her out this evening, when it's cooler. Chuck me a dandy brush please.' John obliged and Finlay began brushing the dust from the piggery out of his hair.

Indoors, Jenny asked the man sitting at the table, 'Can I get you anything else to eat, Mr MacFarlane?'

'No thank you Jenny. It's a long time since I've eaten a breakfast like that. Delicious!' he remarked.

They heard Finlay slam the front door. 'Hello Jen,' they heard him call. 'Oh,' Finlay said as he walked in. '…Hello Jill. How are you? How did your exams go and where's your horse?'

She smiled at him but seemed flustered.

'Kee, this is Jill's father,' Jenny said. 'He brought her over today.'

'Pleased to meet you, Mr MacFarlane,' Finlay said, and shook hands.

Jill's father was tall, thin and balding. His suit was certainly not one that would normally be available to buy in Romsey.

'I just wanted to thank you, young man, for being so wonderfully kind to Jill. She has talked about nothing else since and insisted I bring her over here as soon as we got home. Being her father, I had to see she was in safe hands, which I have assured myself she undoubtedly is. What do I call you?' Mr MacFarlane seemed happy with the situation.

'You bastard,' Finlay thought. 'If you knew what had happened to your daughter.' But said, 'Most people outside the family just call me Finlay.'

'Or Master Keith!' Jill said quietly, and began to giggle. She seemed more relaxed after her father's pronouncement.

The front door slammed. Niney swept into the kitchen, because Niney swept everywhere, leaving people trembling or adoring in her wake. 'Jill! How lovely to see you! How are you?' Niney seemed pleased to see her. 'And this must be your father.'

Mr MacFarlane was standing and Finlay could see already that Niney had cast her spell on him. They shook hands.

'Mr MacFarlane, you've raised a charming and clever young lady. You must be proud of her. I'm Niney by the by.'

MacFarlane was obviously smitten. 'Thank you. Yes I am proud of her.' He couldn't take his eyes from her face.

Niney seemed quite taken with him and gave the poor MacFarlane her very best smile. She turned to Jill. 'Now then young lady, stand up and let me look at you.' Jill did as she was ordered. 'Yes, lost a little weight. Exams I expect, but no matter. We can put that back on you easy enough. Can't have you getting down poor. Nothing to fall back on if you get ill.'

Jill looked a little embarrassed. 'They did rather take it out of me, I must admit, but Finlay's letters kept me going. Made me feel I was part of what was happening here.' She allowed herself a fond smile at him in front of her father. 'How do you think you did, Finlay? I thought English was a pig!'

'I'm not thinking about it. We'll have the results next week. I'm not giving it a single thought. Am I getting any breakfast by the way?' he said, suddenly remembering he was hungry.

'No, I gave it to Jill's father. Serve you right for being late,' Jenny said severely.

'Not really!' MacFarlane said, somewhat aghast.

'Daddy, Finlay is the most spoilt person I've ever met or am ever likely to. Jenny's joking. She'd drive into Southampton and get something for him rather than see him go without,' Jill said.

'Well, I'm glad you spotted that, Jill!' Jenny said, going to the Aga. 'There's your breakfast, spoilt brat. Two days Jill has spent with you and she already recognizes your failings.'

'Sounds to me as though you have the ladies in your life sown up, young Finlay,' MacFarlane said. 'You must let me in on the secret.'

'They treat me abominably, Mr MacFarlane,' Finlay said laughing. 'You don't mind if I carry on eating.' He waved his hand at the thought.

'Are you staying today, Jill?' Finlay asked. 'I mean, can Jill stay Mr MacFarlane?'

'Of course I'm staying! Why do you think I'm here?' Jill answered. 'If that's OK with Niney and Jenny.'

Niney smiled. 'We've been looking forward to it Jill. Kee has been wondering what to do with himself and we just assumed you'd be staying.'

'Where is Laddie Ben? I mean where is he liveried?' Finlay asked

'Moneyhills Stables. We can't get him back until late Friday, because you seem to have every available lorry booked,' Jill said almost as an accusation.

'We're clearing out the stores, Jill,' Niney said. 'It's a big job getting them all to market, and there's two loads of pigs to the Wall's factory.'

'Sounds like a big operation you've got going here. I know nothing of farming but even from Rownhams we see and hear what looks like an efficient operation,' MacFarlane said.

'We're going TT,' Finlay said. 'Which means lots of changes. After August, we'll be a closed herd, so we're clearing the decks now.'

'One day you can explain all of this. Meantime my masters at Ford require me. I can pick Jill up this evening Niney, if you're sure she's not going to be in the way.'

'Of course not. Let me see you to the door,' Niney said.

After her father had gone, Jill seemed to relax. 'I'm here Finlay! I'm actually here! My mother was going to drive me mad at home. That's why my father brought me round. He'll have to give her a report when he gets home tonight. She has become so middle-class! She's even talking about joining the WI.'

'Has she met Mrs Phillips yet, Jill?' Jenny asked, with a warning look at Finlay.

'Oh yes. She thinks Mrs Phillips is wonderful,' Jill said simply.

Finlay burst out laughing. 'She has a tongue like an adder and is a pretentious hypocrite!'

'Enough Kee!' Jenny said sharply. 'Don't speak about people like that! Think it by all means, but keep it to yourself.'

'Sorry Jen,' the admonished boy answered.

'What a lovely chap,' Niney said coming back in. 'And seems happy for you to be here, Jill. Has Kee told you yet he's playing cricket on Sunday? We've to get all glammed up, make ourselves look beautiful to squash Landford's ladies. They're doing the teas. Must keep our end up. Do you have a suitable hat, my dear?'

'I don't know anything about cricket, Niney, and I've never worn a hat, not a proper one at least,' Jill said.

'Oh, it's not about cricket, my dear. It's showing these town ladies how dowdy they are. One year we made it to the final in Bournemouth. We didn't win, but all the photographs in the *Echo* were of the wives and girlfriends. I expect all the Ward women will be there,' Niney said with a studied indifference.

'Doesn't the young one do the scoring, Kee?' Jenny said.

'If Janet Ward's going, I'll certainly be there,' Jill said.

Finlay didn't think that Janet Ward was going to be put off by anything these three hatched. He certainly hoped not. He liked her.

'I'll sort out a hat for you, Jill. I've got just the one to suit and I'll fetch it after lunch. We had better get our jobs done, so you two hop off and find something to do. I expect Kee will get you driving his pick-up, Jill. Don't be late for lunch.'

Once outside she took Finlay's arm. 'I'm so pleased to be with you, Finlay, Master Keith I mean. Let's go somewhere quiet.'

'Let's just check on Misty first,' he said. 'The flies have been bothering her.'

They went into the stable and studied the mare. She came and nuzzled his chest and took Finlay's breath through her nostrils. He spoke to her softly, playing with her ears, then he scrubbed her face with a damp towel, something she loved.

'There you are, darling girl,' he murmured to her, kissing her nose.

'She really loves you… doesn't she?' Jill said.

'Of course she does… She's my darling girl,' he said to the mare again.

'I was hoping I was that too, Finlay,' Jill said quietly, snuggling up close to him and putting her hand under his shirt.

'You are, Jill,' Finlay said, looking at her.

'But you might have told me about Janet.'

'You've seen her then?'

She didn't seem embarrassed. 'Saw her yesterday. She said you'd written to her…' he said.

'Oh… but it wasn't really like that. I wasn't boasting. I was just so glad to not be a virgin any more. It sorted the girls together thing out at school. When I saw two of them together snogging I thought you poor souls, what you need is a Finlay. There! Now you know.' She laughed again, the moment of seriousness had gone.

'Come on then, I'll teach you to drive. You haven't seen my pick-up yet.' They went outside to the little Morris.

'Is this really yours?' she asked. 'If it is, Jen's right, you are a spoilt brat. But Finlay, I just adore spoilt brats.'

'Right,' he said. 'I'll take it out to the woodyard track and we can start there.'

On the way there, she rested her hand on his bare thigh, which made him shudder. 'If you do that we won't get there,' he choked, but she didn't remove it. He stopped at the top of the track and made to get out.

'No, sit a minute Finlay. I want to say something serious to you. If you teach Janet to drive, please don't do it in this little car. Likewise, please not at the hatch pool. If you teach her fishing, not in the same place as me, and teach me first. That's all.'

'But…' Finlay began.

'No buts, my darling. We're too young for any commitment. In twenty years we'll just be a lovely memory to each other. A special memory and I don't want her to spoil it. She's after you I know, and you won't resist because you're a man, and I shan't miss a slice from a cut loaf anyway. This next six weeks I'm going to have you as often as possible. She can have what's left!'

'Blimey,' Finlay said, and swallowed hard.

'Yes, blimey! Don't be too blatant about it or I'll kill her… very slowly. And I want you to kiss me and get in my shirt. Later, you can get in my shorts, but only after I've driven this.' She bent for a kiss and he touched her breast. 'After you've shown me how to drive,' she mumbled through their kiss.

It was more than an hour before Jill began to master the basics of driving. She had lost her temper twice, cried once and attacked Finlay for being patronizing. 'Whoever heard of a doctor who was too stupid to drive!' she raged at herself. Suddenly she found the required co-ordination. She turned the pick-up in a gateway and took off back towards the wood yard. 'Whee!' she shouted happily. 'Finlay, I can drive!' She stopped for a moment. 'Can I drive it back to the house? Just to show Jen I can?'

'Of course, and when your pa comes, you can show him,' Finlay said.

She wasn't really listening. Concentrating, she now had to make it perfect.

Towards the fairly sharp turn into the back drive, Jill changed into second gear, approaching with great caution. Suddenly a car came round at very high speed. There was a flurry of flying gravel and the car lay straddled across the track in front of them. 'Don't drive so bloody fast, you stupid woman!' the driver roared.

Finlay, seeing who it was, ducked behind the dashboard as Jill got out and marched towards the other car. 'How dare you speak to me like that, you stupid, idiotic man! You oaf, you inconsiderate nin-compoop, you're… you are… fat!' Jill yelled.

The driver started to roar with uncontrolled laughter. Jill got back into the pick-up and slammed the door, shaking with temper. The other car pulled alongside and the driver, still laughing, said, 'And you're lovely!'

'Bastard!' Jill spat, which made the driver laugh the louder.

They heard him say, 'Absolutely lovely!' again, as he pulled away.

'Finlay, why are you down there hiding?' she said crossly. Finlay was on his knees with his head on the seat, his head and shoulders covered with Misty's blanket. She dragged the blanket from him. 'What are you laughing at? That man was a fat fool.' Jill couldn't help but start laughing herself, seeing him in such a state.

'You told him though, Jill. Fat fool…what was it? Nincompoop? He's Grandfather's best friend, the head vet, Sir George Goulding.' Finlay was crying with laughter again.

Jill started slapping him. Finlay's head finished up in her lap and he kissed the inside of her bare thigh.

She stiffened and groaned, pulling his head in closer. 'No, not here. I'm all wet and it will show through my shorts!' She pushed him away, her eyes shining. 'I adore you Finlay, you're such a sod!'

When they pulled into the yard Jill sat still, getting her breathing under control again, like a pilot landing solo for the first time. 'What will your grandfather say, Finlay?' she asked. 'I was pretty rude to him.'

'Dine out on it for weeks. Don't worry about it. Sir George will see the funny side of it. He always drives far too fast and he's always crashing.' Finlay started to laugh again.

Once inside the house, Jill recounted what had happened, very seriously. When she had finished Niney said, 'Wonderful! He's a real love Jill, but gets a bit pompous sometimes. I bet he makes an excuse to come in and find out who you are. He certainly won't leave it at that. Where were you when this was happening Kee? I hope you stood up for her?'

'He was hiding under a horse blanket, laughing his head off!' Jill said, affecting complete disgust.

'I didn't want to offend him by laughing. Anyway Jill seemed well able to deal with him,' Finlay said.

'Deal with who?' Jenny said, coming into the room. 'What have you been up to now?'

The story was retold but Jenny was not amused. This was the man that Finlay's grandfather spent evenings with at the Yacht Club in Southampton, and very often they could not get home un-aided. 'What do you want for lunch, you two?' she asked. 'Shall I make you some sandwiches?' She really didn't think much to the vet.

'Oh come on Jen,' Finlay said. 'It was funny.'

'Hmmn. What do you want, meat or cheese?'

Finlay went and put his arm around her. She softened immediately and put her face up to be kissed. The telephone rang and made Niney, Jenny and Finlay start. This time of day it meant trouble usually. Niney answered it, visible relief spreading over her face. They all listened to the one-sided conversation.

'George my dear! How are you? Her name is Jill and she is Kee's friend... Yes, I know, absolutely delightful and very clever... Well, somebody has to put you in your place...My dear George... you are fat... Yes, I'm sure she would love your apology. I'll just get her. She's in the hall...' She put her hand over the mouthpiece. 'Now Jill, he's on the back foot. Make him grovel and he'll love you for ever. Don't forget! Cheltenham! Cheltenham!' She handed the phone to Jill.

'Yes... hello... Jill MacFarlane, I live in Rownhams... Yes that's it... I believe one of your sons looks after my horse... though he must get his beautiful manners and charm from his mother...'

'Ouch!' Niney whispered.

'Your apology is accepted, thank you. In turn I will say sorry for calling you fat. That was unforgivable. The rest however must stand...'

'Well done! Well done!' Niney whispered.

'Thank you yes, I look forward to meeting you, perhaps... Thank you... goodbye.' She put the telephone down, blushing furiously.

The others clapped her performance. 'Well done Jill,' Niney said. 'He'll respect you for ever and I bet next time your horse needs a visit he comes out.'

They ate lunch and chatted, laughing and joking about the soonto-be cricket match. Niney produced a wide-brimmed hat with ribbons for Jill to wear. 'Oh yes!' Niney cooed. 'Just the thing. Makes you look so sophisticated, what do you think Jen?'

'I look stupid in a hat, and I'm as jealous as Hell!' She didn't mean a word of it.

'Jenny, I want you to do your hair like a Viking princess and you can carry my bat. No hat doesn't mean you ain't just as glam as these two. Just do your hair the way I like it and you'll steal the show,' Finlay said earnestly.

'Well,' Niney said. 'That's us put in our place Jill. What a fickle bugger he is.'

'My white knight rides to the rescue again,' Jenny said, smugly.

A vehicle arrived, sliding to a stop. 'Good Lord! It's Alan. What's he doing here?' Niney and Jenny almost fought for possession of the mirror, adjusting hair and clothing.

Jill looked perplexed, Finlay disgusted. 'Who's fickle now?' he said.

'Anybody home?' they heard him call. Alan, Sir George's son, walked in carrying flowers. 'Hello everyone. I've been ordered by Father to deliver these.' He made a show of reading the label. 'To Jill. Sorry!' He sat down at the table. 'May I?' he said, picking up a sandwich. 'How's the beautiful Starwort, Finlay? You've got Burgate worried. I'll bring you a special wash a couple of days before the Show. Bring out her saddle marking properly.'

Finlay liked Alan enormously. He had always treated him as an adult from when they first met. 'Thanks Alan. Are you going to be there?'

'Certainly, but not in an official capacity. Father will be at the AI stand with your grandfather, so with any sort of luck, I can escort the beautiful ladies from Nursling. Are you going to be there, Miss MacFarlane?' he asked.

Jill seemed tongue-tied. 'Yes, I expect so,' she gulped.

'Good, I'll introduce you to my father properly. We must see if we can't all work on you to become a vet.'

'I don't really think my exam results will let me qualify for that. I'll have to settle for being a doctor.'

'Can I quote you on that one? My father would love to hear you say that in a crowded room.' He laughed.

The telephone rang. 'You're nearest Jill,' Niney said.

It was Sir George again. 'Your father Mr Goulding,' she said, handing the instrument to him. Everyone could hear the irascible tone.

Alan smiled. 'He's impossible! I was on my way to Netley Marsh when he radioed me to come here. Now he's asking why I'm not there. I'd better fly. Goodbye ladies, goodbye Finlay. See you Sunday at the match.'

As he left, the telephone rang again. Jenny was nearest. She just said, 'Yes, thank you. Yes thank you very much.' Sitting down again, she said, 'The river's pretty clean again, but probably best to leave it a couple of days. 'What about going to the beach tomorrow Niney?' she suggested.

'Now that's a good idea,' Niney answered enthusiastically. 'Would you like to go to the beach tomorrow Jill?'

'Yes please! Where do you go? Bournemouth?' she asked.

'No. Hengistbury. We can ask your father this evening, and we can come back Sunday morning early, in time for a little batting practice before the match.'

'Do you stay in a hotel?' Jill asked.

'No, we've a beach hut down there, on the spit. This year, we've been too busy with the land and Kee's exams, to go. Jenny, you're inspirational! We get bogged down here. The men can eat at the pub. I know I need a change! Whether they like it or not, that's what we'll do.' Niney's mind was made up.

'Pity the cricket's this Sunday. We could stay till our results come,' Finlay said. 'It's splendid there Jill. You can swim I take it?'

'Of course I can! Probably better than you! I hope Daddy lets me go. Well, Daddy will. I'm not sure about my mother though,' Jill said.

'Would you like me to speak to her, Jill?' Niney asked.

'Would you… please Niney?'

'I suppose we'd better look to see what James is doing, so we know which vehicle we can have. Go and have a look in his diary Kee,' Jenny suggested.

'I'm going to look so old-fashioned in my school swimsuit,' Jill said. 'If I ask my mother to buy me a more modern one, it'll only give her more reason to object.'

'Nonsense my dear! We can get you one in Christchurch and you can leave it down there. Jen, you start getting our stuff together and Kee's… I'll cook something up to take with us. We won't need much. Kee lives on ice cream and ham sandwiches and we live on the plaice he catches. Now you two go and find something to do. I'll put your flowers in water, Jill, and don't be late for tea,' Niney seemed very happy there was something to organize.

'Winchester tomorrow, Leatherhead Friday, so we can have the Land-Rover and get right up to the beach hut,' Finlay said, coming back in.

'Well, I think I might buy myself a new swimsuit,' Jenny remarked. 'Can't have this little minx outshining me. How about you Niney? Nothing's on ration now.'

'I'll go without. Outshine everybody on the beach,' Niney said.

'That should make the front page of the papers,' Finlay laughed.

Finlay suggested they do some fishing. It would be pretty hopeless because of the sun, but it was a way of being on their own. They went to the little Blackwater river, cleared down now and running fairly well up on its normal summer level. The only place suitable was where an old sluice system had once been. Now there was just a concrete sill spilling into a small pool. There were always a few trout and grayling in the pool, but the approach to it had to be very careful because they spooked easily.

Finlay explained the principles of what he was doing to Jill. His first cast, as so often is the case, produced a fish. A brown trout of about a pound and a half. He got her to net it for him, so that she was involved, and once netted, he asked her if she wanted it. She wasn't sure, so he gently released it. 'Why did you catch it if you were never going to take it home to eat?' she asked perplexed.

'Just to see if I could,' was the only way he could explain it. 'Now just over there...' He pointed to the edge of the concrete sill. 'There's a monster living there. He's about four pounds, but I could never get him interested. Let's just give him a try.'

'I thought fishing was just an excuse to be alone, so that you could pay me some attention,' she said, quietly.

'I will in a minute or two. Just let me have a few more chucks at him,' Finlay said, softly executing quite a difficult cast into the wind. He carried on for a few more but just could not drop the fly on the right spot. He had forgotten about the girl.

'I'll catch it with my hands,' he heard her say. She was swimming towards the spot that he was casting to, naked and beautiful. 'Put that rod down and get in here, boring man. It's very cold but the current isn't too strong.'

Finlay dropped his rod on the gravel bank he was standing on and in no time was swimming beside her.

'How deep is it here?' she said breathlessly.

'About five or six feet. You can probably touch the bottom.' He tried but couldn't, so took her hand and coasted back to where they could. Standing, they kissed and shivered. Her breasts, covered in small drops of water, felt very cold until the hot sun on their backs warmed them again. Grabbing their clothes, they went to the far bank and lay down under the alder branches, and for the second time in their young lives made love. It was delicious and easier for them this time. Afterwards, as she lay beneath Finlay, breathing easily into his shoulder, she whispered, 'I love you Finlay.'

They swam again briefly, cooling and fresh the water around them. She took his hand, led him to the bank and lay in the sun to dry, just touching down the length of their bodies. 'If we go to the beach, will we be able to do this? If we can't maybe it would be better if Mother says I can't go,' she said, touching his face.

'Of course! Niney and Jen always go into Bournemouth to listen to the orchestra, or go to the cinema,' Finlay said.

'Good,' Jill said as though she was wondering how it all happened.

Finlay went and picked up his rod and net, then dressed again and wandered back towards the house.

'Doesn't time go quickly, Finlay? We've been gone two hours. And you don't have to bother about getting any more of the thingummyjigs you used. I've dozens of them. A girl at school gets boxes of them from somewhere and she sells them at an enormous profit. If we go to the beach I'll bring lots and when I said that about love, don't trouble any about it. A man is not programmed at your age for that. Female brains are programmed early for home and babies. The hunting instinct is stronger in the male, but I don't expect to have to be naked to get your attention always.'

'I sometimes feel like a medical experiment!' He laughed at her. 'Tell me this then, why does the sight of your bare bottom do it for me?'

'It's the breast syndrome again. Round orb-like structures...' She screamed as Finlay grabbed her and wrestled her to the ground, kissing her. They started walking again. 'Seriously. This is why the male will always risk his life for a baby, anybody's baby. The round orb-like face triggers some instinct...'

'I love your bum, OK?' He laughed. 'Furthermore it looks nothing like a baby's face. More like a white peach.'

They walked across the field, towards the big bridge. 'I wonder if Niney got any sense from my mother. She can be so difficult.'

'She's only worried about you. You know, falling in with the wrong company,' Finlay said, trying to be wise. 'It's about quarter to five. What time does your father finish work?'

'How do you know it's about quarter to five?' she scoffed.

'Well, look where the sun is and how far up the skylarks are, and if you look very, very carefully, you can see the hawthorn leaves tippin' around.' He sounded very knowledgeable.

'I wish I had a watch on. It's some trick. Nobody can tell the time just by the sun!' She laughed.

'Not just the sun. Look how high that skylark is,' Finlay said, pointing into the sky. 'I can hear it, but I can't see it,' she said, gazing upwards.

They stopped on the bridge. No angler can pass a bridge without looking into the water.

'Hey Finlay,' Jill called. 'There's a huge fish down here. It's a brown trout. Come and look.'

Finlay looked where she was pointing, 'How heavy is it?' she asked.

'About six pounds. Shall we try to catch it?' Finlay answered.

'OK! If you can catch it, I'll believe you about the time!'

'Stay here and watch what he does and where my fly goes. If I hook him, you come down and net him.'

Finlay climbed the gate by the bridge and got below the fish. Jill was lying on her stomach hanging over the edge of the bridge watching the fish. It was this sight that arrested Mr MacFarlane as he and Niney came around the corner. 'Good Lord! Is that my fastidious daughter lying in the dust? What on earth is she doing?' he asked, seemingly quite amused.

'Probably looking at or for a fish. Kee must be in the river. Let's stay very quiet. You'll be quite amused at the way they speak to each other. It's so good for him to have someone who gives as good as he dishes out.' They were about fifteen yards from the upturned Jill by now, and so they stopped.

'To the left... about a yard to the left... No stupid! To the left... that's it... He's going for it... no he's not... Now, stay to the left... that's it... that's it... He's going for it... Finlay, he's got it!' Finlay had already seen the line check and had tightened, the fish turned and shot downstream past Finlay.

Jill jumped up and started for the gate, but seeing her father, stopped. 'Oh, hello Daddy... um. Got to go!' She scrambled over the gate and ran down the bank and picked up the net.

Finlay was up to his shorts in the water, trying to control the fish which was walking across the surface on its tail. 'Get in up to your knees just down from me a bit, Jill. Lay the net just under the surface. Don't jab at it... I'll pull him over it.'

'I know what to do!' she yelled. 'Just do your bit!'

The fish was going from one side of the river to the other, using the current to best advantage. It leaped clear of the water again and started upstream towards them.

'We've got him now!' Finlay gasped. 'Christ, he's strong!'

The fish fought for another five minutes before coming into the slack water, just below where Jill was waiting.

'Now hold still. He's coming. Hold still,' Finlay said.

'I am holding still. Damn it, Finlay! Just shut up and concentrate!' she yelled back at him.

At last, Finlay got the fish over the net and the girl lifted it up and splashed to the bank. Finlay joined her quickly, killed the trout with a small rock and removed the fly from its mouth.

'We got it Finlay! We got it!' she said.

'Yes Jill, we got it. Thank you for the we,' he said.

There was the sound of clapping. Finlay had not seen the adults approach and was surprised. Jill walked back into the river and washed the mud from her legs. She looked at Finlay, smiling. 'You're the most exciting person in the world to be with.' She said it quietly, so her father didn't hear.

'Niney,' MacFarlane said. 'That was a wonderful thing I've just witnessed, almost primeval. They are... they are... well I don't know.'

'They are beautiful together. Is that what you are trying to say Tom?' Niney said, looking at him.

'I never thought to see my daughter covered in mud and not even notice. She used to fuss over a speck of dirt on her hands. Now look at her... and so happy,' MacFarlane said. 'He's a very good angler, your young man.'

'It wouldn't do to say so. He's brilliant with a rod, better than James or Jack. It comes so easily to him. I hope he never becomes bored with it,' Niney said, softly.

Jill and Finlay joined them on the bridge. 'We've been fishing,' she laughed, showing him the fish. 'He's very clever is Finlay. He catches fish all the time and oh, what's the time exactly?'

'Three minutes to five. Why exactly?' her father asked curiously.

'Well, Finlay can tell the exact time by the sun and the skylarks. He really can,' she said. 'Just now he said it was a quarter to five. Isn't that amazing?'

'No my dear, it isn't. He's having you on. He saw the cows almost ready to go out. That's how he knew the exact time,' Niney said lightly.

'You pig Finlay! You absolute sod! You really had me believing you. Hold this Daddy. I'm going to kill him.' She almost threw the net at her father. Finlay started running, with Jill chasing him.

MacFarlane was holding the net away from his beautifully cut suit.

'Let me take that, Tom,' Niney said. 'I think they'll be back to the house before us.'

'Wouldn't it be wonderful to be that age again, Niney? God, I hope they never have a war to cope with. That's why I spoil her. They must have everything they want. We've brought them into a very precarious world,' MacFarlane said seriously.

'I prefer to think that sanity will prevail. Atom bombs won't be used. Nobody would win. Is that the precarious you mean, Tom?' Niney asked.

'Yes, but this is a little maudlin, perhaps. What should Jill pack for this beach trip? It's very good of you to let her tag along. Waiting for these blasted exam results. I think we put them under a lot of pressure, don't you?'

'Not really. Life's about pressure, ambition, keeping up with your peers and that sort of thing. Give them their head and let them fly, but above everything, let them be happy,' Niney said thoughtfully. 'Don't ever inflict them with our worries.'

They were nearly back at the house. 'It must be wonderful to know where you came from and where you're going, Niney,' he said, looking at the house. 'This place is like an island. You don't really need my world do you?'

'Not really. We only take from it what we have to,' Niney said, understanding him.

Indoors again, they found Finlay's grandfather and Jenny having tea. The introductions were made.

'Look at this James,' Niney said, showing him the trout. 'They caught it together by the big bridge.' She put it on the scales. 'Six pounds and a bit,' she said proudly, as the scales thumped down.

'Best this year!' Finlay's grandfather remarked. 'We're all going to have to look to our laurels.'

'Where are the two young ones?' MacFarlane asked. 'I ought to get Jill back home.'

'Down in the stables. They've made arrangements for Laddie Ben to come here Friday. John'll look after him,' Jenny said. 'They're just getting a stable ready for him.' She went to the window and called for them to hurry up.

MacFarlane watched them coming back towards the house, deep in conversation. 'I've never seen Jill look so healthy. Just one day out with young Finlay and she is absolutely glowing.'

'Fresh air and sunshine Tom,' Niney said emphatically, but in her mind she had an inkling of where the glow came from.

Chapter Five

•

After they left, arrangements having been made for the morning, Finlay made ready for net practice. His bat felt unfamiliar and, perhaps now, a little lighter than a year ago.

Mr Grieves was already on the ground with Janey, helping with the guy ropes, tightening down the nets. 'Hello Keith,' Grieves greeted him.

Janey just smiled, pretending to be busy.

'I've put you in at number five on Sunday, and I've never seen you bowl. Are you any good?' he asked Finlay, sizing him up.

'Off break, which can be good if the batting area is a bit roughed up, but if it's not, they'll score runs. I'll have a go tonight, if you wish,' Finlay said.

'OK. Here comes Ron and some of the others. We can get started,' Mr Grieves said. He went to meet the others and started what looked like a serious conversation with Ron.

Janey walked nonchalantly towards him. She had a heavy woollen skirt on, despite the warmth of the evening, white blouse and grey cardigan, the finishing touch being grey ankle socks and lady's black brogues. It was as though her mother wished her to remain a school prefect for ever.

'Hello Finlay.' She smiled. 'That was a close call the other day. Has anybody said anything?'

'No Janey. Don't worry about it. Had you changed out of your tennis clothes?' Finlay asked, remembering the difference in Janey when she at least tried, or was allowed, to look more like the beauty she could be.

'Look at me now for goodness' sake. Mother is worried men might look at me.' She laughed shortly. 'If I'd been wearing this the other day you doubtless wouldn't have looked twice.'

'Well I'm looking now. I know what's underneath as well.' Finlay hoped he was saying the right thing.

'You're the only one who ever took the trouble to find out!' She started to giggle.

'Janey!' they heard her father shout. 'Your mother will be here in a moment.' He was obviously trying to think of something to say. 'Can you unlock the pavilion?'

Practice started and there was the usual banter and fun. Mr Grieves was anxious to see more of Finlay's bowling. 'Yes,' he said, after Finlay had found his line. 'I'll try you on Sunday if the pitch is right.'

Mrs Grieves arrived on their Ferguson, bringing refreshments. She did say a fairly curt, 'Good evening!' to Finlay, but he could tell she would rather have not had to, and she made quite sure that Janey kept away from him. He was angry at the stupidity of it. Ron, in deference to Alice Grieves's disapproval of smoking, moved away from the group and lit a cigarette, though Finlay could not see why anybody should defer to someone quite so stupid. He walked away with him to chat.

'Her don't trust you with her daughter, nipper. She thinks perhaps you'll have her away like the other one, but Christ knows, it would do her a favour.' He glanced away to the other side of the recreation ground. 'Here comes trouble. It's the two youngest Ward girls by the look of it. They'll get cursed at if they ride over the square. Can't see Chilly Alice enjoying their stay.'

'Would be hard to choose between that pair, Ron. Doesn't the youngest have an interest in cricket?' Finlay said, shielding his eyes from the evening sun.

As they approached closer, there was a murmur of appreciation from some of the younger cricketers. The girls' long bare legs, hanging loose from their stirrups, looked milk white against the bay of their mounts. 'Hello everyone,' Jo, the youngest, said. 'Getting ready for the match on Sunday?' She was bright and bubbly, aged about fifteen and promised to be as beautiful as her sisters.

Seeing the look on his wife's face, Mr Grieves said, 'Keep out the way with those horses. Haven't you got any other place to ride?' Janet walked her horse over to where Ron and Finlay were standing.

'Hello Janet,' Finlay said, smiling up at her. 'Bit of a frosty welcome on such a warm evening.'

'Hello Finlay. Hello Mr Drew. He really is a miserable old sod isn't he, that Grieves man? I think we'll watch for a while just to make him crosser.'

'Well, don't go distracting nipper here. He's meant to be practising,' Ron said, without any hint of meaning what he said. 'You shouldn't ride about bare-footed Janet. You'll hurt your feet if you brush up against anything.'

'Can you help me down, Finlay, please?' Janet said, swinging her leg over the saddle. 'Don't make such a meal of it as you did the other day. You'll have people gossiping about us.'

'And that would worry you?' Ron laughed.

'Only trying to save what little is left of his reputation, Mr Drew,' she said.

Finlay caught her as she slid down.

She kept him at arm's length this time, but smiled into his face. 'I'll walk over here and watch for just a little while.'

'Are we here for practice, or what?' Mr Grieves said testily.

Finlay picked up his bat and walked to the wicket. Passing Mrs Grieves, she said, 'The Lord has ways of dealing with people who consort with harlots.' It wasn't said to him, but generally into the air.

'I'm sure he has, Mrs Grieves,' Finlay said, generally into the air.

'If you have all finished eating and drinking, we'll be getting off home. Come along Janey,' she ordered, and started her walk to the Ferguson.

As Janey passed him she said quietly, 'I'll phone you.'

Finlay took his guard. 'OK,' he said.

Jo Ward was sitting on the grass, supporting herself on her elbows, her legs wide apart. She smiled at him sweetly. The first ball had just left the bowler's hand when she said, 'I think my sister would like you to roger her.' The ball swept past Finlay's bat. There was a clatter of wickets. 'Sorry,' he shouted to the bowler. 'Bugger off Jo,' he said shortly to her.

'Try and keep your eye on the ball, Keith,' Grieves said crossly.

As the second was coming down, she asked, 'Do you think you will roger her?'

There was a second clatter of wickets. Grieves said something to Janet and took her horse. Janet came running up and grabbed her sister's arm. 'Leave him alone you bloody little tart. He has to bat and he can't do that with you flashing your hairy-mary at him!' She dragged her away. Finlay could see Ron's back shaking with laughter.

'You want to get your breath back a bit, nipper?' the bowler shouted. The others in the group were laughing, except Grieves, who looked very cross indeed. Finlay batted for three overs. Of the eighteen balls, there may have been one which might have made a difficult catch for a slip fielder.

'OK Keith!' Grieves said. 'Come out and bowl some up to me.'

'Don't get him out, for fuck's sake nipper!' one of the others said. 'He'll hold a grudge for the rest of the season.'

Finlay's first two balls strayed a bit. 'You'll have to do better than that!' Grieves shouted sarcastically. The next ball beat him easily. It slid off the side of his bat, an easy catch for a slip. 'Owzat?' someone shouted. 'Oh, I don't think so!' Grieves shouted back.

'Well, watch this one!' Finlay said, thinking about the way Janey was treated. The next ball sent the stumps over.

'Do you think that was out?' someone shouted.

'Try me again with that one, Keith,' Grieves ordered. 'The light isn't so good.'

Finlay's next ball left his hand, spinning like a child's top. Grieves saw the spin and tried to block it. The ball climbed up his bat, gripped his shirt sleeve and spun over his head, hitting the top of the net.

'That's out. Caught behind!' Ron said. 'Where did you learn to bowl like that nipper?'

'Mr Barry at Bransgore showed me,' Finlay said, quite amazed that he could still do it.

'About the only good thing they did teach you, I would think. You gonna let him have a go Sunday, Captain?' Ron asked.

'We might let him have a couple of overs, Ron. He's easily distracted and we have to beat them. We'll see,' Grieves said, rather grandly.

Jo Ward came over. 'That was good bowling Finlay. Your batting's crap. I'm scoring Sunday. It should be a good game.'

'Would you please moderate your language, Miss Ward. A little less profanity would be nice,' Grieves said.

Janet joined them, leading both horses. 'Chuck me back up Finlay. Can we ride home over your place, it's getting a bit dark for going back along the road?'

'Of course Janet,' Finlay said. 'Cut in by the lodge gate, I've got a key to open the boundary gate. I'm sure they won't mind next door. You don't want to be crossing the main road in the dark.'

'Where did you leave your pick-up, nipper? Down by the lodge?' Ron asked.

'Yes, gonna give me a lift?' Finlay asked, knowing that he obviously would.

'Well, thank you all for turning out,' Grieves said. 'Meet here at eleven on Sunday?' They all agreed, and the practice broke up.

It was only a mile that Ron had to drive Finlay. 'You bowl like that Sunday, nipper, and you could make the team permanently. We just got to keep those Ward girls away from you when you're batting!' He laughed. 'Ain't they got some bloody lovely legs on them?' he said, with a lot of enthusiasm.

'Thought you didn't like redheads!' Finlay said accusingly.

'Only some redheads. I'm warming to those saucy little madams, I must admit!' Ron said.

'Do you know, Ron, I think I am as well. Janet looks at you direct, sort of challenging. And she's a bloody stunner!'

'I'll see you in the morning, nipper,' Ron said, dropping him off at the lodge. 'Don't you go interfering with they girlies, mind!'

Finlay caught the two Ward girls up, passed them and went on ahead to open the gate that joined the two estates. They clattered up to him. 'Thank you, Finlay,' Janet said in passing. 'Can you see us across the road, if it's too dark when we get there?'

'Don't be bloody silly, Jan. We'll be there in ten minutes going this way,' her sister scoffed, trotting away.

'Wait by the big bridge, Finlay,' she said urgently. 'You will won't you?'

'Yes,' Finlay said easily. 'I'll see you across the road.'

He drove past them, parked by the bridge and waited for about twenty minutes. He heard them come off the tarmac and on to gravel near the cottage where Granny Fortune had lived. They pulled up beside him. 'You go on Jo,' Janet ordered. 'Wait the other side of the Blackwater bridge, and don't look round.'

She slid off her horse, landing easily. 'Now Finlay, was there something you wanted to say?' Finlay only had to look at her and his senses jangled. Now here she was, challenging again with her green eyes. He was kissing her gently at first, but as she thrust herself against him they became more urgent. She tasted different than Jill. She wasn't sweet-tasting. It was more feral somehow. She pulled away a little and smiled at him, her nose touching his. 'I have you now,' she said, pushing her hips into him.

'No, Janet,' Finlay said, gasping. 'I think you and I deserve each other. We're both a bit wild.' He nuzzled her small breasts through her blouse, and felt her pushing hard against him.

'Finlay, you really are a bastard! I knew you wanted me the first time you saw me in the paper shop. Fickle as the wind.'

'Don't go on about it. I just can't help myself with you.' He did feel guilty, but she was here with her milky white skin and freckles, and in truth, she was wriggling like that trout he had caught earlier, exactly on this spot.

'I must go, it's getting dark,' she said. 'Will I see you tomorrow?'

'No, we're going to the beach for a couple of days,' he said. 'I'll see you Sunday at the match.'

'Chuck me up again. Jo may go on, just to be awkward and get home before me.'

He lifted her back into the saddle again. She smelt very female.

'See you Sunday, Finlay,' she said happily. She knew, whatever else, Finlay was besotted with her.

Eight o'clock the next morning saw them passing the race course at Lyndhurst. Everything was packed in the back, with Jill and Finlay sitting on cushions among the baggage. They had rolled up the sides of the canvas tilt and the wind filled their clothes and kept them cool, for it was already hot. The New Forest was parched, but the ponies and cattle looked well on what they were getting to eat. So different from the last time Finlay had passed this way. Lyndhurst was its usual sleepy self. There was very little traffic, mainly lorries which the Land-Rover flew past. The speedometer was waving about between forty and eighty as Land-Rover speedometers were prone to do.

'Slow down, you mad mare,' Niney yelled, excited by Jenny's wild driving. 'You'll get us gonged. Don't forget, we want to get Jill new swimming gear.'

'I won't forget,' Jenny said, and gunned on through Hinton Admiral.

'I can smell the sea!' Finlay yelled.

'Are we here already?' Jill exclaimed. 'You know you're all wacky. I thought we might be there by coffee time.' She laughed aloud. They were all excited. They were going to the sea.

A police car, coming the other way, flashed its lights and rung its bell as she entered Christchurch, objecting to Jenny not giving way.

'We must get Carl to put a bell on here,' Niney shrieked.

'That would be fun,' Jenny said, taking the Land-Rover through a gap between cars that made Niney draw her breath in sharply, and Finlay wince.

'Stop fussing you two,' Jenny laughed. 'There was acres of room.'

'Slow down over the bridges, Jen,' Finlay said. 'I want to see the rivers.'

Jenny slowed and drove sedately over the first bridge. 'That's the Stour,' Finlay said to Jill, who was looking just a little pale. Further on, they crossed the Avon bridge and saw the Priory. 'We can row up here,' Finlay said to her. 'Those chaps in the boat are fishing for sea trout.'

Jenny drove slowly into the town and parked. 'There's a good shop just here,' she said. 'You stay with the Land-Rover, Kee. Is there anything you think you may need?'

'No thanks. Don't be long though,' Finlay answered.

'And don't leave the Land-Rover,' Niney ordered firmly. 'Not even for a second.'

'I shan't Auntie Niney. My spinning rod is here,' Finlay answered, amazed to think that anyone would imagine he would ever leave a rod unguarded.

They were gone the better part of an hour. Finlay was getting impatient, annoyed by the passing shoppers looking at him curiously. Niney and the other two were laughing, coming towards the Land-Rover, loaded with carrier bags and brown paper parcels. 'Sorry we've been so long, darling,' Niney said. 'But you know what it's like when you have the chance to shop somewhere different.'

Jill clambered into the back. 'These two should not be let out alone, Finlay,' she said seriously. 'They had male shop assistants jumping through hoops for them.'

'Well, I hope you were watching and learning, Jill,' Niney said. 'If you want a man to do what you want him to do, just act helpless!'

Out of the town they took the tiny lane for Tuckton and then left again on to a sandy track. The sea lay beneath them now, the Needles and Alum just visible through the early haze. Jenny stopped, dropping the Land-Rover into low box and crept it down the steep drop on to the beach. The wind was filled with the smell of sea. There were some gannets diving just out from the breakers, falling like white shining arrows into the green water. On their left, as they drove along the tide line, was Christchurch harbour, almost empty now of the shipping that had been there during the war. Just a few moth-balled minesweepers, tethered like tired horses swinging on their buoys. There were seven beach huts on the spit and about twenty people on the entire beach. 'What a magical place,' Jill said, awed by it all.

'Yes my dear,' Niney said. 'There used to be just two beach huts here. We must make the most of it before it gets developed. We weren't allowed to come down after the war, not until all the barbed wire and mines were removed. In a few years this will be covered with people.'

The beach hut was, in fact, a summer house purchased at an agricultural show. Set on heavy piles sunk into the spit, it was looked after by a fisherman and his wife. In return, they had the use of it for their visiting relatives. A telephone call to the pub on the harbour made sure that the hut was vacant and cleaned. Finlay was determined to spend at least one whole summer down here. He loved the place almost as much as his home.

When they had finished unloading, Jenny parked the Land-Rover beside the hut. Niney called Finlay and Jill back from the waves where they were splashing about in the water, paddling.

'Now sit down there and listen, both of you,' she said seriously. 'These are the ground rules, and if you break them it's straight back home. Got it? You will not, under any circumstances, swim or take the boat near the Run. You keep the boat in the harbour or up the river. You can go down and watch them netting the salmon, but even then you'll not even get your feet wet. If you disobey me on this Kee, I will never forgive you. Do you understand?'

'Of course Auntie Niney,' Finlay said. 'I absolutely promise.'

'Good! Now Jill, you can see how friendly we are going to have to be in such a small space, so don't be embarrassed about what you have to do. The loo is down the beach towards the Run, as is the only tap. If you need a pee in the night go and squat in the dunes. Don't go into the water at night unless one of us is with you.' Rules over, Niney went to see about the boat.

'What's the Run?' Jill asked.

'The harbour entrance. Even I wouldn't swim there. People who fall in invariably drown. When the tide's running out it's ferocious, I promise,' Finlay said. 'The only reason to go down there is to watch the salmon being netted. It's a bit sad, but you'll have to see it, because of the way they do it.'

They heard Jenny calling them. 'Come and watch.' Terns, as elegant as swallows, were plunging into the sea after small fish, dainty feathered beauties, too small seemingly to withstand the swell now running.

'Come on then, Jill,' Jenny said. 'Let's do the changing thing and start the fashion parade. Watch the terns Kee, much more healthy for you.'

He walked along the tide line, relishing the feel of the wet sand under his feet, studying anything that caught his eye. He said good morning to another family in passing; the beach made friends of everyone. He heard Jenny calling and turned to go back. Jenny and Jill were standing together, posing on the small verandah. Finlay realized just how beautiful Jenny was. Here she seemed so happy, relaxed and girlish. Finlay wondered if she needed more time away from home. Jill, standing beside her, looked troubled by the way he looked at Jenny. 'Hello, I'm here!' she said.

'You're both stunning,' he said, putting his arms around the two of them. 'And your new swimsuits are perfect, barely covering the bits they should. In fact, they're not quite doing that!' Finlay changed into the small shorts he always wore and they all swam together. Jill was as good as her word and was an excellent swimmer. Jenny was like a dolphin, and could easily outpace them both. Exhausted, they collapsed on to the hot sand, letting the sun dry them and burning them almost uncomfortably.

'Where is Niney all this time?' Jenny remarked.

'Let's walk down and see if she's by the lifeboat. I'll grab some money in case the ice cream chap is about. It must be about midday,' Finlay suggested.

There was no sign of her on the beach. They reached the old Customs House on the harbour mouth and assumed Niney must have got the ferry to the other side of the Run. 'Need any help?' the man who rowed people over the Run shouted.

'Has a very tall lady gone across in the last hour? You'd remember. She's very beautiful.' The words might have sounded artless to any listener, but to Finlay it just described Niney in the simplest way.

'She's over here in the pub trying to make a phone call. I'll come over and get you. I think she's going to be a long time.' The ferryman was also the youngest of the fishermen who netted the salmon in the Run.

'Thank you, but no thank you. I don't like crossing that place. No disrespect but it terrifies me. We'll wait and she may come out,' Jenny shouted. 'I'm not going in a rowing boat over that,' she said to Finlay and Jill. 'And you two certainly aren't!'

The ferryman marched to the pub and was gone for about five minutes. He reappeared, pretending badly to be the soul of patience. 'Kath has had a boy. Everything OK. Go back and get something to eat,' the ferryman yelled. 'That's the message. I'll bring her back over in your boat.' The fisherman walked back towards the pub.

'Well Kee, you have a brother. James must have left a message at the pub and Rollo came to find her. I expect Niney's trying to phone your mother. Well! What do you think Kee, a brother?' Jenny asked.

'Better than a sister I suppose,' Finlay said.

'Aren't you pleased?' Jill asked, surprised at his seeming lack of response.

'I don't know what I am,' Finlay said lightly, feigning nonchalance. 'Well, she won't come back for me, so there's nothing I can do. I don't even think about them now.'

They started walking back to the beach hut. Jill remained silent, not really knowing what was happening. Jenny took hold of Finlay's arm and knew what he was feeling. They were almost back to the beach hut when Finlay stopped suddenly. 'No God damn it! I'm not going to let her spoil this time down here. She spoilt Christmas and I've not had so much as a letter from her. Tell me why Jen? Just tell me why I should mourn for her?'

'Shall I run on ahead and put some tea on or something to eat?' Jill asked.

'You really are a darling Jill MacFarlane!' Finlay said. 'No, of course not. They're on the other side of the world. They have their lives, we have ours. Let's get on, for Christ's sake!'

'Kee, I don't think you should...' Jenny began.

'No Jen. Be fair. It cuts both ways. I wouldn't leave you for them, and in truth, I haven't written to Mama either.' He shrugged. 'I'm probably as much to blame as them.'

Jenny sighed. 'You haven't got to be the white knight all the time you know.' She paused. 'But that doesn't count for me.'

The sun was now at its highest. It was intensely hot. The sand smelt wonderful because of it, like sugar under their feet. The tide had run back leaving great pools, waist-deep, where mullet flashed busily, temporarily trapped. They all swam again, the water cooling them and joined another family to play cricket on the exposed hard sand. They were breathless and happy. 'You'll have to bat better than that on Sunday, Finlay, else you'll never be invited again,' Jill said, laughing. 'What do you think, Jenny?'

'Oh, I think cricket's his game. But not when it's mixed with girls. Far too heady for such a dullard!' Jenny said. 'At the moment, his life seems taken up with women he can't cope with.'

They heard voices. It was Niney and Rollo, the fisherman who looked after the place. 'I've brought the boat back and Niney, if you want to come and watch, we'll be netting the Run about seven this evening.' He touched his forehead and was gone.

'I'm sorry. Bloody telephones don't seem to work properly down here. Well, Kath has had a baby boy. I did manage to speak to your father, Kee. Everything seems fine. Gordon's had to take a posting with the New Zealand Navy, for two years, so they'll not be home for a while yet. He hopes your exam results please you.' Niney looked at Jenny, pleading for support.

'OK,' Finlay said. 'I'm glad everything went well.'

'He'd like to know your results as soon as you get them, so that he can congratulate you.' Niney was trying to sound placatory.

'OK,' Finlay said, easily. He looked at Jenny who was studying the table top. Jill was being discreet, pretending to read a book.

Niney knew his indifference was his way of covering anger. 'Darling, he is interested…' she started to say.

'I don't think we should be having this conversation in front of Jill. It's making her embarrassed,' Finlay said.

'I'll go for a walk,' Jill volunteered.

'No, let's go and catch some plaice. I don't want this conversation anyway.' He got up, picking up the little spinning rod, bag and net. 'Come on Jill, I'll show you that I'm better at fishing than cricket.'

She was glad to agree. 'I'll get a hat and towel.'

After they had gone, Niney said, 'Well, that could have gone better!' Jenny said nothing. 'He'll get over it Jenny… Boys do,' Niney said.

'Right at this moment, Niney, I feel so bloody savage I've a job to think straight. He must feel so rejected. Rejected by a mother he adored. Why she wanted another child I cannot think. She doesn't want the one she has. She doesn't give a fig.' Niney wanted to say something. 'Don't stop me now, Niney! I'm going to tell you something. If she comes back to Nursling, I shall go, and what's more, I'll take Kee with me and I tell you now, I'm sure he would come. Do you realize he'll be commissioned before he sees his mother. I'll not see him treated like this. I've a bloody good mind to take him now!' She was crying.

'Jenny, don't talk silly. You can't just take him away. He loves his home and James. Anyway, when they do come home, James won't have them living at Lee. He can't stand Gordon. Personally, I think that's why Kathy goes to him. Kee'll be past sixteen by the time they're back, and he'll make up his own mind where he wants to be,' Niney said. She had always known this crisis would happen, but like the elephant in the corner, nobody spoke about it.

'He'll be staying with me, regardless. I'll see to that Niney,' Jenny said. 'Wherever we are. I'll buy a house in Dartmouth if I have to.'

'Mind you don't get hurt. Kee will bounce back in here in a bit, his mother forgotten. He'll be OK. I keep telling you. Don't do anything stupid, just to spite Kathy. He will be OK,' Niney said, not liking what she was hearing.

'There's nothing about spite in this. Just about Kee. I'll do anything that it takes to allow him to become the man I know he's growing into.' She was calm again. 'I must go for a swim to wash my face. If he sees I've been crying...'

They went out on to the sand. Niney brought the binoculars, training them on the boat Finlay and Jill were fishing from. 'And what about her Jen?' Niney said. 'Where is Jill going to fit, do you think?'

Jenny took the glasses. 'She's a sharp young lady that one, too sharp to let the childhood sweethearts thing get in the way of her ambitions. She'll drift away probably and Janet Ward will take her place, if she hasn't already. Let's hope the transition is trauma-free.' She began to laugh. 'He's waving. He can see we're watching.' She didn't remove the glasses and waved at them. Finlay waved back. He held up what she took to be a fish. She handed the glasses back. 'I'd better have a swim. They're coming back. The clever bugger has already caught enough for a meal.'

As Jenny walked to the sea Niney said, 'Take care Jen. Please don't make him choose between you and Kathy.'

'I think you'll find, Niney, the choice was made last Christmas. Without any prompting from me.'

Jill was carrying two large plaice, one in each hand. Finlay was struggling with the tackle and another smaller fish. 'Oh well done, you two!' Niney exclaimed. 'What super fish! Jill darling, your shoulders are burnt to a frazzle. I'd better put some calamine on. You gut these Kee, and go find Jen.'

'I'll save one of the heads, Auntie Niney. I can use it as bait. We may be able to catch a bass this evening.' Finlay set about his task.

'Kee, soak a towel in tap water for me. Jill's really burnt up. Her shoulders need to be cooled.' Niney handed him a hand towel. 'Be quick, there's a love.'

'Now Jill,' she said, when Finlay had gone. 'Don't worry about what you heard earlier. He'll weather it. Jen gets very angry but there's a lot more to it. Nothing is ever simple in families.'

'I thought Jenny was going to explode. She was seething,' Jill said.

'My dear, she did. She's having a swim now to wash the tears away. They are very, very close. Probably too close. It's silly really, he used to be almost my little boy. But now it's him and Jenny. Closer in age I suppose, so be very careful what you say to her about him, even joking. Say the wrong thing and she'll tear strips off you.'

'I thought it was you I had to be circumspect with, but now I know it's Jenny. I wonder she puts up with me...' Jill stopped, wondering if she had overstepped the bounds of propriety.

'Not at all. She likes you enormously, because you're good for Kee. Make him do things other than work. You can give him that which she cannot. I think you know what I mean,' Niney said.

'Yes. Of course I do. Remember, I'm the budding doctor. We're a funny species, women. Much more sensible then men. I said to him the other day, in a few years' time we'll be but a fond memory to each other. I love him dearly, but I have my ambitions and I'm not too worried when Janet Ward comes after him. I think Jenny understands what I am.'

Niney gave a small sigh of relief. 'Thanks Jill. I'm glad we've spoken. Stay as discreet as you are, and I'll pretend not to know. That's best.'

'You do know then... that. Well, you know...' Jill was embarrassed.

'Shush my love. Of course I don't know. That lovely glow you've got is the sun.' Niney kissed her cheek, smiling.

Finlay came back with the towel, now soaked.

'I think it's not too bad Kee,' Niney said absently.

Finlay laughed. 'It would have been far less effort in this heat, if you'd said you wanted me out of the way so you could speak to Jill.'

'Subtle my dear. Devious and manipulative, that's what we are. But you must have some calamine. Jill, drop your straps down and I'll pat some on.' Niney rummaged in her bags for the bottle. 'I think you should do this young man. Just dab it on with the cotton wool.' She handed the bottle to Finlay. After he had finished, Niney asked if he could spot Jenny with the binoculars.

'I've got her. She's down by the rocks looking in the pools. I'll go get her, shall I?' Finlay suggested.

'Well, somebody had better, if she wants to eat,' said Niney.

Jenny was about four hundred yards away, quite near the base of the actual headland, sitting on a rock staring out at the waves. Finlay watched her as he covered the distance between them. He could see she had undone the large plait that she usually put into her hair and it hung around her shoulders free. The dry sand under his feet made his knees ache as it gave little purchase, so he moved on to the tide line and began to trot. The air was hot but pure and he felt good.

'Penny for them Jen,' he said, climbing up beside her.

'Cost you more than that buggerlugs. Did you catch enough to feed us all?' She pulled him closer. 'Sit with me for a minute.' She looked at him. 'You've gone all bronze and your hair's getting bleached. Another day like today, and it'll be almost white.'

'You look like a mermaid.' He took some of her hair in his hand and studied it. 'Niney's getting some food ready,' he said. He put the hair in his mouth absently. Though salty, it still tasted of her. 'It's OK, you know, Jen. I don't mind about my mother.'

'Come,' she said, getting up and jumping from the rock. 'We'll go back to the deep pool and rinse the sand off.'

They walked back towards the beach hut, hand in hand, and then to a pool left by the tide. It was a hole rather than a pool, caused by an anomaly of the local tide, about six feet deep and green, like their river in summer. They swam to the middle and tried to touch the sandy bottom. Facing each other, with hands on each other's shoulders, they sank down and made faces, mouthing words to see if the other understood. Then they bounced to the surface and made guesses. Jenny swung her legs up and caught him around the waist, laughing. 'Mermaids drown sailors by taking them to the bottom like this.' They sank down to the bottom of the pool and for a moment, they clung together before bursting to the surface again.

Niney walked to the verandah and banged a tin plate with a spoon. 'Do you want to eat?' she called.

Jenny and Finlay left the tide line and walked toward the hut, laughing at something together, arms around each other's waist. 'It would be a brave or foolhardy woman who tried to come between those two,' Jill said softly.

'Yes. I certainly can't any more,' Niney said.

They ate together. 'The tide's coming in again. When we've cleared up, we can go and watch the boys net the Run. It'll be interesting to see how many salmon are coming up. They're entirely different fish Jill,' Niney said. 'A different shape. There's a school of thought that says they taste better than ours.'

'Poor Niney,' Jill suddenly said. 'You haven't even had the chance to try your new costume yet. Are you coming to swim this evening?'

'No my dear. First thing in the morning I think. I'm still winding down. It's been a lovely day. Tomorrow, I want to go into Bournemouth, eat lots of ice cream and shop for some really glamorous clothes. Do you want to come with me, Jen?'

'Yes, I will. There's some good bookshops in the old part now,' Jen said. 'You two'll be all right here won't you?'

'Remember what I told you,' Niney said sternly to Jill and Finlay.

She looked at her watch. 'Come on then, let's go and see them do the netting.'

They wandered down towards the Run, picking up some shells and interesting stones between them.

The fishermen were busy on the quay, weaving the net across the water. There were four large fish kicking in the net, as it came on to the water's edge. Finlay made to get closer, and talk to Rollo.

'Stay here,' Niney said quietly. 'You can see in a minute. They'll show you, and probably put the net around again.' They did, and this time there were a lot more fish. 'Now you can go and look,' Niney said.

Jill and Finlay ran across to where the fishermen were despatching the fish. 'Christ! Will you look at the size of that one Jill. Must be all of forty pounds, and that sea trout must be ten,' Finlay said.

One of the fishermen said, 'You know a bit about fish then boy?'

'He ought to,' Rollo said. 'That's Niney's boy.'

'You don't see them this big on your river then?' the fisherman said.

'Not often, not the salmon anyway. I think our sea trout generally run bigger though,' Finlay answered. 'Your fish seem deeper as well.'

Niney and Jenny joined them. 'You wicked bugger, Rollo!' Niney said. 'Think how that one would have gone on a rod!' she said, touching the enormous fish with her toe.

'If the silly buggers could catch them, they don't take the same on this river as yours. How many did you catch in June, Niney?' he asked.

'Two forty-eight and the biggest was thirty-six and a bit. I hear they've caught some monsters on the Frome.'

'Could I possibly have a few scales from the big one?' Jill asked. 'I'd like to see how old it is. Could I have just two or three from about there?' she said, resting her forefinger three-quarters the way back from the fish's head.

'Of course you can, pet,' Roll said, casting an appreciative eye over her. 'You keen on fish then? Want to know how they come in all shapes and sizes? Well, he's about ten years old, I'd say.'

Jill was down on her knees, opening the mouth of the fish. 'Yes, I would say so too, beautiful condition.'

Rollo cocked an eyebrow at Niney, amused at what the girl was saying. 'You want some scales, Missy?' he said to Jenny.

'No. About three inches of steak from the middle will do me.' She laughed. 'Unlike some, I've never got fed up with salmon.'

Rollo laughed. 'You'm a bit like me then, boy. Can't stand the bloody stuff. Sooner have a proper smoked kipper.'

'Are you going to put the net round again?' Finlay asked.

Rollo looked at the water, 'No, they'll be coming through now in bloody great packs. We'd catch too many and the price would go down.'

'How do you know?' Finlay asked.

'Well, how do you know when your fish run in?' Rollo asked.

'It's pretty well slack water now. Ours come in two feet off low water with the tide on the make. We know, because you can see them at Redbridge,' Finlay said.

'Well. I'll tell you. Your fish have lots of Scots blood. That old Palmerston had loads of spawn brought down years ago, and that's why they're a different shape.'

'I must find out more about this,' Jill said. 'I wonder how long ago it was and what river the eggs came from. We should look into it Finlay, and then see some fish from the Scottish river. It'll give us an insight into their genetic past… You see. Sorry, I'm off again.'

'No little maid, you do it. And I should like to know what you finds out. The more we know, the better we can look after them. Them silly buggers from the River Boards is as silly as hedgehogs and don't know diddleysquit. I 'spect they're the same on your river, ain't they, Niney?' Rollo gave another admiring glance at Jill. 'You're a bright little thing, buggered if you ain't!'

'Thanks for saying so,' Jill said. 'Next time we come down, I'll let you know what we've found out. We are coming down again aren't we, Niney?' she asked.

'In between barley and wheat harvest, if the weather's right, my dear. We'll have to see. Might even get another few days in before that,' Niney said. 'Come along then. Let's not stop these men working. I'm up early for a swim.'

'When you going home again, Niney?' Rollo asked.

'Early Sunday morning,' Niney said.

'I'll see if I can get you a lobster to take back for the old man,' he said.

'He'd love that Rollo, he really would. I can't see him getting down here himself this year.'

They walked back to the hut, Jill carefully carrying the salmon scales in the palm of her hand. 'What a nice man,' she remarked. 'He was very kind.'

'Lovely family, Jill. Been here since the year dot. Rollo was on the convoys during the war, so his wife and sister did what fishing they were allowed to. They survived, but only just,' Niney said.

'Look over there!' Finlay said, pointing out to sea. 'It's the *Elizabeth* coming in. Isn't she beautiful?'

They stopped and watched the huge liner coming up the channel between where they were standing and the Needles, looking like something from a fairy tale. All twinkling lights and bunting. He ran to the beach hut and fetched the binoculars. 'Have a look.' He gave the glasses to Jill. 'The port pilot boat is alongside her, just back from the second funnel.' They handed the glasses back and forth between each other, sharing their admiration for the great ship.

'We'd better sort out the beds,' Jenny said. The sun had gone down below the headland and the air was less full of seabirds.

Niney lit a small gas lamp in the hut. It hissed and cast its yellow light gently into the corners. 'Go and look at the sea Kee, while we get undressed. On your way back, get the torch from the Land-Rover.'

Finlay walked down to where the waves were gently lapping on to the sand. The Needles light flashed its warning. There was just the hint of a southerly breeze, smelling of salt. He wandered back to the Land-Rover and took the torch from the middle front seat. 'You all decent in there?' he called.

The three women were in bed. Jenny and Niney shared the double bed and Jill was in the bottom bunk bed. The light muslin curtains had been pulled across the doors, which were pegged back and the breeze gently swayed the curtain. The gas light flickered, a tiny moth careering around it, bent on dying. 'Put the gas light out darling, and leave the torch on the table,' Niney said. She was lying on her back with her hands clasped behind her head. Jenny was reading with a small torch.

All that was visible of Jill was her eyes and forehead above a blanket. 'Night, night Finlay,' she said. 'I've had a super day.'

He touched her face. 'Night, all of you.' He climbed into the top bunk. The cedar wood of the walls exuded a special tang, smelling like expensive shampoo. He turned and pulled the woollen blanket over his shoulders and looked down on Jenny, still reading, her hair spilling over the pillow. Her bare shoulders had broad white stripes where the sun had not reached. Outside the waves lapped lazily on the sand. This was peace.

He woke with the bright light of morning streaming in through the muslin curtain. He could see Niney standing on the verandah in her swimsuit. Without moving, he could see Jenny still asleep. He watched her eyelids flickering slightly, until he began to doze again. Her movement woke him. She climbed quietly out of her bed and crept up to the curtain and pushed her head through. The light showed her in beautiful detail. Her skin had an almost iridescent quality. She turned and walked back to the bed, but saw him looking. Her hand instinctively went to cover the golden curls below her stomach. 'Close your eyes buggerlugs,' she whispered. 'You're not supposed to see me like this.' She kissed his forehead, touched his face and turning, began to dress. He watched her unashamedly. There was no great tumult in his blood as she bent and pulled on her briefs, nor even when she slipped her breasts into the fine lace of her bra. This was Jenny. His Jenny, whom he loved deeply. She stood, saw his look and came and kissed him. 'Shall we go and look for Niney?' she whispered. 'We can let Jill sleep on.'

He climbed down from the bunk and pulled on his shorts. They crept together out on to the now cool sand. They saw Niney walking in the waves, her hair tied with a scarf, to keep it up while she was swimming. 'Hello, you two. I beat you to it. Isn't this just a heavenly place?' She walked in from the waves smiling. 'What a bugger we have to go back. I could spend forever here. I swam all the way to the headland and back, and I'm not even puffed. Farm life keeps you fit doesn't it? Where's Jill, still asleep?' she asked.

'She was. The sea air has got to her. I don't think she even stirred in the night.' Jenny looked at her watch. 'We're still on farm time, it's only just past six.' She smiled. 'Perhaps we're just not good at holidays. Nobody is stirring in the other beach huts.'

'Just as well, my love. The way you're dressed, or rather not dressed. I can see everything you've got Jenny. That old boy from Birmingham in the second hut would have a heart attack!'

They walked along the beach together, just keeping in the water, which was cold to their feet. When they reached the Run, they could look across to Mudeford Beach. It was deserted except for someone walking a dog. 'It's as though we're the only people on earth,' Jenny said wistfully. 'Incredible to think it was ten years ago exactly, the doodlebugs were coming down on us. Everything was all arse over head still, the skies were filled with aircraft morning, noon and night. Now look at it. Here you would think the war had never happened.'

'It's rather wonderful,' Niney said. 'There were times when I thought we would never get home. Now the thing most in our minds is whether Kee has passed his exams and the Armstrong will last long enough till we can have a new one.' They walked back towards the beach hut, the sun already warm upon their backs.

Jill was still seemingly asleep, 'She is all right I suppose. She did get a bit too much sun yesterday,' Niney said. 'Go and look at her Kee.'

Finlay bent over the sleeping girl and gently rested the back of his hand on her forehead. She was cool; her eyes flicked open. 'Hello Finlay,' she mumbled. 'Have I overslept or something?' She pulled his head down and they kissed. She tasted wonderfully warm.

'About bloody time too!' Niney said. 'You didn't kiss her goodnight or anything last night. Are you all right Jill darling?' she asked.

'What a wonderful sleep!' she said sitting up. 'Have you all been swimming already? Ow!' she said. 'My back is sore.'

'I'd give the sun a rest today, Jill,' Niney advised. 'Else you'll be like an orange. Have a quick walk or swim before the sun gets hot. If you need a pee, go out and squat by the Land-Rover. The world is empty of people at the moment.'

'Um... I um...' she stumbled.

'Kee, go for a walk,' Niney said, seeing the girl's embarrassment.

'We've only just come back...' Finlay began, not thinking.

'Walk!' It was an order.

'Come on... I'll come with you,' Jenny said, pushing him out of the door. Jenny and Finlay walked towards the headland. 'What was all that about?' Finlay asked, amazed to find himself out again, when all he wanted was his breakfast.

'Jill wanted to go, but she was too embarrassed to say in front of you. God, you can be solid sometimes. It meant asking for lavatory paper. She's not used to roughing it. Leave it to Niney,' Jenny said. 'We are different my love. She wants to be clean.'

'Sure... but...' Finlay said.

'She's still a bit maidenly. Which is only right. When you get a bit older it doesn't matter so much. Oh God! Why do you make things so difficult? Look, this morning you saw me with nothing on, naked, everything showing. That's OK because it's you. But it wouldn't be, if it was Rollo. Well, Jill would mind, even if it was you... in front of other people. Do you see?' Jenny said.

'Probably,' said Finlay. 'Anyway, you didn't mind me looking at you, did you?'

'It's time for breakfast I should think. And I didn't mind, but perhaps I should. I'm a bit muddled at the moment. I just want what's best for you,' she said, almost sharply.

'How did you know about Mother, before Auntie Niney said? You did know, I could tell. And why had you been crying yesterday afternoon?' Finlay asked quietly, not looking at her.

'There was a telegram to your grandfather. It came when you were all out. It said your father was going to New Zealand for two years and your mother was going with him. I knew you were going to be upset by it and I didn't want it to spoil this time down here for you, so I didn't say anything. The baby was just another knock, which I didn't know about. I was going to tell you when we got back, but Niney just blurted it out,' Jenny said.

'That's what all the wild driving was about then. Just to get here, on the spit out of contact?' he said. 'What about the crying? Did Niney have a go at you about it?'

'No, she doesn't know about the telegram. I had a real go and said some things I shouldn't have. I flew off the handle properly about the way you'd been treated...' She didn't go on.

'Oh Jenny,' Finlay sighed. 'I really don't mind any more. I really don't.'

'The point, my love, is that you should mind. When you're older, you'll understand what I'm trying to say. Let's not talk about it now. We can do that later. Let's make the most of these few days here, and the rest of the time we have together before you go to Dartmouth.'

'Jenny, you're not thinking about leaving. Are you?' Finlay said, horrified at the thought.

'Of course not! I should never leave you. I don't find white knights under every bush. Come, we must go to breakfast.'

They walked back to the beach hut together.

Chapter Six

•

Breakfast over, Niney and Jenny made ready to go to Bournemouth. 'Do you want to come Jill? You'd be quite welcome. Failing that, is there anything you need?' Niney asked, knowing that both offers would be declined.

'There must be some sort of camping shop there,' Jenny grimaced, struggling with her hair. 'We need some kind of arrangement to shower, my hair's in a terrible state. We can't go to the cricket looking like the Wreck of the *Hesperus*.'

Finlay laughed. 'The boy stood on the burning deck…'

'That's quite enough from you… thank you!' Niney said. 'We could get a big watering can.' The conversation stopped. They looked at Niney, both perplexed.

'What do you mean, a watering can?' Jenny asked.

'To wash our hair with!' Niney said crossly.

'Oh, I see,' Jenny said, not liking the idea at all.

'What a couple of softies!' Niney said scornfully. 'OK. We'll get Carl to fix something up that runs off the Land-Rover. Good grief, when we were running away from the Japs…'

'Shut up, Niney!' Finlay and Jenny said, in unison, laughing.

'Wasn't funny. Your mother and I carried you for miles and miles!' Niney said sniffily. 'If I knew then what an insufferable little shit you were going to turn out like, I'd have left you in the jungle!'

Finlay put his arms around her and held her tightly. 'Let go of me, you sod,' she laughed, struggling or pretending to. 'You wouldn't be so strong if either one of these were cooking for you. You'd soon learn which side your bread was buttered. They may have pretty arses, but neither one can boil an egg. Let me go, you little bastard!' she screamed. They wrestled for a while laughing, sending one of the chairs crashing over. 'You are a bastard!' Niney said, out of breath, and she bit his nose to make him let go.

'Oh you two!' Jenny shouted. 'It's not big enough for your horse-play,' happy to see them back to their normal behaviour.

'Are they often like this, Jen?' Jill asked, not knowing quite what to make of their rough play or Niney's language.

'Yes, 'fraid so…'

'I used to be able to hold him down and make him do as I wanted.

• 248 •

He's a bit big for that now.' Niney laughed, pulling Finlay's hair playfully.

'Don't start again. I thought we were going to Bournemouth,' Jenny said, trying to sound cross.

'Yes, we ought to go,' Niney said. 'I should keep your shirt on today Jill, and get him to put some more lotion on your shoulders.'

'You really are a wacky lot,' Jill said, as they watched the Land-Rover climb back on to the ridge. 'I can't see my mother wrestling with me. Niney's so kind and understanding. And I'm going to cook her something one day, just to show her that I can.'

'That'll be good. I suppose the time is coming when we ought to invite you all around to dinner one night. Let your ma see where you are and all that. What about asking them down here for the day?' Finlay suggested.

'I don't think so. My mother couldn't cope with this. She's not the least bit free and easy. I honestly don't think she'd know how to react when Niney screams "Bastard!" at you.' She giggled.

'Well, she does do it *à la* Cheltenham at least. Are you going to have a quick bathe before the sun gets too hot?' Finlay asked, seeing one other person walking down to the water.

'Yes, just for a little while. I'll go and change.' She looked a little coy. 'Could you stay out here please. I know we swam together in the river, but I feel a bit shy here.'

'Of course. You like it here though?' He seemed concerned that she was suddenly diffident about him.

'I love it, silly. It's just a female thing,' she said, and went into the beach hut. She reappeared in her bathing costume. 'I'm a bit over-awed by Niney and Jenny. They're so confident with what they are. I wish I could be more like them. I mean Jenny, this morning, just wandering about in her bra and pants. And yesterday, in the shops, they just took over. Bought this swimsuit for me, and had the shop assistants rushing about like slaves.'

'I can imagine.' He laughed. 'Come on, we're on our own. Just be you. You were confident enough when I first met you, on your horse.'

'That was before I met those two. Supposing I fail my exams. They're going to think I'm stupid, as well as a plain Jane,' she said.

Finlay led her into the water. 'So that's what this is about. Exams, results and what people will think. It doesn't matter what people think, and anyway you'll pass. Stop worrying. I haven't given them a thought.'

He swam away, turned and swam back quickly, grabbing her and taking her under with him.

'Finlay you bastard! I didn't want my hair wet,' she said, as she surfaced, smiling again at last.

'A little less profanity, Miss MacFarlane, please,' Finlay said, tipping her over again. As she surfaced, he was swimming away. He allowed her to catch him and they began to roll about in the swell together.

'Let's go in. The sun is getting hot,' she said. They swam back to the beach and went inside.

'Let me pat your shoulders dry,' Finlay said, turning her face away from him. 'I think you should stay out of the sun, Jill...'

'I don't intend to go outside until I hear the Land-Rover coming. And I need to get this wet costume off.' She was sounding very husky as she slipped out of her swimsuit. 'Hang it out to dry for me, please. We can swim again this evening.'

Finlay did as he was bidden and returned to find her drying herself. 'Perhaps you'd like to do this Finlay?'

He took the towel and began to dab her dry. 'My legs are wet, Finlay,' she murmured. He pushed his face into the dark triangle of curls. 'That's what I want. What you tried in the pick-up.' She began to shake and Finlay could taste the sea salt on her. She backed away on to the bed silently, pulling him after her. 'Do that, do that,' she gasped. Suddenly she went into a spasm, groaning heavily. 'Thank you. That's what I wanted.' She lay there, trembling and shaking, the body-wracking spasms becoming less. 'I read about that in a book. I wanted to see whether the author knew what she was talking about,' Jill said, her voice shaking and stilted. 'It was just as she described. God! That's so deep inside.' She opened her eyes and stared at him. 'That was a little selfish of me I know, but I needed to know what it was like. Poor you! You haven't even been allowed to get your shorts off yet.'

'I am a bloody medical experiment!' Finlay thought to himself, as he pulled his shorts off.

They lay side by side, kissing and touching each other, making love for the rest of the afternoon, until the temperature in the closed beach hut was too much to bear. Finlay got up, pulled the curtains and pegged the doors back. The light breeze dried the sweat on their bodies and refreshed them again. He drank some water and gave her the glass, which she gulped at greedily. Her hair was sticking to her forehead and she smiled at him, seemingly exhausted. 'That's an afternoon I'll remember all of my life, Finlay.' She was breathing heavily and it was hard for her to get the words out. 'Could we try it just once more?'

'Bloody Hell, Jill! You're insatiable. I'm whacked,' Finlay said.

'Well, shall I go to the door and shout for somebody?' She giggled.

'You opened the flood gates. Now you can't cope!' The light breeze had woken him up a little. It was just four o' clock, Jill lay curled up on the bed, her eyes challenging him. He took up the challenge and won through.

Niney and Jenny were back, animated and noisy. 'Hello my beautiful ladies. What have you been doing?' asked Finlay.

'Spending lots of money and eating so much ice cream we're certain to be ill, but it was worth it!' Niney said. 'Hello young lady. Had a good day?'

'Well, you look well on it, if perhaps a bit tired,' Jenny said. 'Give me a few moments and I'll show you something I've got for you, but I need some tea first.'

'When I'm an old biddy and my patients are being bloody, I'll remember today and that will get me through,' Jill said.

'That good, eh?' Niney said, looking at her closely and smiling.

Finlay had his face buried in a newspaper. 'It says here people have been burning their ration books. Isn't that great! No more bloody Food Office people coming round and sticking their noses in.' He looked up, surprised at their laughter.

'Ah, here it is. Look what I've found, Jill.' Jenny handed a large heavy book to her. 'I hope you haven't got it already.'

'Oh, wow!' she exclaimed. 'Where did you find it? I've wanted this for years and years, and could never find it. Thank you Jen.' She went into the bright daylight to scan it through. Even from where he was sitting, Finlay could smell the book's mustiness. 'Look Finlay. This is regarded as the Bible of genetic theory. Thanks again Jenny,' she said.

'Here's yours buggerlugs,' Jenny said, with pretended ungraciousness. 'Your own to take to Dartmouth.'

He saw what it was. 'Thanks Jenny,' he said simply, looking at the leather-bound book. He stood up and kissed her gently.

'Amazing isn't it Niney? Give them a couple of old books and suddenly it goes very quiet.'

Jill came in and picked up Finlay's book. *The Seven Pillars of Wisdom*, she read. 'What's that about? Learning or comprehension?'

'Comprehension, Jill,' Finlay said.

'Well, I had to deal with fripperies. Food and clothing,' Niney said, feeling left out. 'I've got you some new shorts, Kee. Yours were getting indecent and a couple of shirts, easy stuff. Jill, I've got you this. I hope you like it. It's lovely to see something pretty without a Utility label. Here, try it on.' Niney handed her a beautifully cut blouse, with its own hanger, an indulgence not seen for years. It was the palest powder blue and very feminine.

'Oh, you're so kind to me,' Jill exclaimed. 'Isn't it beautiful?'

Finlay had to admit that it was and wondered how Niney always put the right clothes on the right person.

After they had eaten and cleared away, they settled down to the evening. Outside, the sun sank below the headland without showing the wonderful red of the previous evening. The breeze died to nothing and all they heard was the lap of the waves outside and the suck of the shingle. There was silence from the world of people. Looking out to the Isle of Wight, Finlay saw the occasional car headlights, tiny from this distance, like dancing fireflies. The Needles lighthouse flashed its warning. The world seemed theirs, in the hut. Niney lay on the bed, listening to the portable wireless. The other three read. Outside, the world went quietly into night and began to sleep.

It was Niney who eventually shattered the quietude. 'Bloody plays never have proper endings these days. You're left up in the air, wondering whether they did or they didn't!'

'You're meant to make your own mind up about it, Niney,' Jen said absently, deep in her book.

'Well I think he did,' Finlay said. 'The only thing wrong was the horse he rode away on. Only had three legs. Whoever was working the sound, didn't know how horses move.'

'I thought you were reading,' Niney said.

'I was listening as well. The horse only had three legs Jill, didn't it?' He turned to where she was lying on the bunk bed, but she was sound asleep.

The wireless crackled ominously. 'Thunder about,' Niney said. 'It's been working up to it this evening.'

'Anybody want a last drink?' Jenny said, putting down her book.

'Not for me thanks, Jen,' Finlay answered. 'Should I wake her, do you think?'

'Well, she shouldn't sleep in her swimsuit. Come on, sleepy-head.' Niney shook Jill gently.

She woke, wondering where she was for a moment. 'Oh, sorry, I went to sleep.' Her voice was sleep befuddled. 'I need to go outside.'

'I think I'm going to turn in. I don't think we'll have much sleep by the look of the flashes over the back of the Island,' Niney said. She undressed quickly down to her underwear and climbed under the blankets.

Jill came back in yawning, 'Thank you for the book, Jenny.'

'Glad it's what you wanted Jill. Kee, go and look at the lightning for a moment on the verandah, so we can get undressed,' Jenny ordered.

They settled down quickly. Jill was soon asleep again and Jenny was reading with her torch. Niney's breathing showed her to be asleep as well. Finlay watched Jenny, as the night before, thinking to drift off the same way. She looked up, aware of his gaze and wrinkled her nose. 'Kee, can we change pillows? This one is too hard,' she whispered. He threw his down to her and caught hers, lobbed back to him. 'Thank you,' she said. He settled back down. The pillow smelt of her breath and sweat. He lay listening to the now very distant thunder, trying to count how long after the lightning stroke the sound came to him. He was soon asleep.

It was a scattering of raindrops hitting the roof of the beach hut that woke Finlay. He got up quickly and went outside to see that the Land-Rover windows were closed. The few raindrops falling were large and warm on his shoulders. He clipped the front doors of the beach hut, so that they were open to a bare foot wide. The wind had picked up again, and it blew the muslin curtains into gentle curves. The women were sleeping soundly. He could see the white shape of a foot at the base of the double bed and judged it to be Jenny's. The rain now drummed heavily on the shingled roof. It sounded an octave higher on the bonnet of the Land-Rover, outside. The lightning, now almost continuous, was still a long way off, looking like gunfire through the rain. There was no sound from the thunder above the sound of the rain on the roof. He sat down in the darkness watching.

'What are you doing, Kee?' Jenny said beside him, her approach hidden by the drumming on the roof.

'I was staying awake in case the thunder on its way woke you suddenly and you were afraid.'

'I'm OK. It's only sirens that make me like that. Go back to bed,' she said.

'If you're sure you're all right,' he said. 'I've shut the Landie's windows and the doors are pegged. Night, night then.'

As the rain began to ease, the lightning became more vivid. The air itself smelt burnt on the breeze and the thunder now became sharply audible from about ten miles away. He got up again to watch its approach. His movement made Jenny sit up. 'I'm going to watch it,' he whispered.

'Put your shorts on,' she whispered back.

He went to the door and looked to the south west. The storm looked enormous now, covering the whole sky. Great forks flickered down on to Bournemouth and Boscombe, the sky almost wholly purple with electricity. It began to look dangerous.

Jenny was beside him again, this time in a bathrobe. 'Bloody Hell, is that headed for us?' she said aloud.

'What's happening?' they heard Niney ask, sharply. There was another enormous flash, closer this time. 'Christ!' she swore. 'Come away from the door, you two. You'll get hit by it.' Niney was half-way across the hut, coming towards them, when an enormous fork of electricity seemed to split, one fork hitting the Island and the other the Head on their side of the Solent. The noise was immense. The ground seemed to shake through the hut's flooring.

'I'm a bit frightened, Finlay!' they heard Jill say, her voice quivering.

'Come and look,' he said. 'This is like a great big firework display.'

She got up and joined them, and watched transfixed as the lightning danced back and forth between the Head and the clouds, continuously. The sea was dead flat. Not a movement or a ripple showed when the lightning lit up the surface. To Finlay, it looked almost sinister.

'I don't like it, Finlay,' Jill quavered. 'I'm getting under the bed!' In the flickering light, he saw her dive under the bunk bed, pulling a blanket over her head as she slid deeper. The next strike seemed to dance around the beach hut. Niney screamed and hid under the blankets. The hut shook and quivered in the concussion of noise.

Jenny had been standing behind Finlay, her arms around him and her chin resting on the top of his head. They often stood like this at home, when they were watching something together. 'Are we going to die, Kee?' she asked softly, but matter-of-factly. 'I want you to hold me.'

'It'll be OK Jen,' he said, trying to reassure her, and then, as if taunting them, the lightning hit the ground in front of the verandah. This time there was no sound from it. The doors burst open and the air smelt scorched.

'Stay still Jenny,' he said. 'It'll pass us. It won't hit us.'

The storm slowly marched down the beach towards the Run. The noise was immense and shook the hut. 'I want to go home now,' Jenny said quietly and clung to him, shaking the same way she did when they heard the sirens during the flood. She seemed like a child.

'Come on. Get back into bed, Jen.' He led her to the bed and eased her on to it. Finlay realized she was shocked. He took her little torch and went to look at Jill. She seemed all right, when he found her under all of the blankets. 'Finlay, that was completely terrifying.'

He helped her out, kissed her then climbed over Jenny to Niney, 'Hello beautiful Auntie. Are you OK?'

'Christ, I thought we were gonners! You're a ballsy little sod, darling. So ballsy, that if you didn't belong to me, I'd have you in my bed now. I'm proud of you.' She grabbed him, held him tightly and kissed his mouth, hard and long.

'I'd better see if the other people are all right, I think. I'll take the big torch.' He went to get up.

Niney kissed him again. 'You'll pass muster darling. I know you will.'

Outside, he could hear children in the other huts crying. He went along the line and asked if they were fine. He couldn't see any damage in the dark, but he knew for sure there must be some. At least none of the occupied huts had been hit. He went back to their own and lit the tiny gas mantle. 'I'm going to put the kettle on and make some tea,' he announced.

Niney crawled across the double bed and sat down on one of the chairs. 'I need a piddle enough to break my neck, but I'm buggered if I'm going out there! Did the Land-Rover catch it?' she asked.

'May have blown some of the electrics. I'll see when it's light,' Finlay answered.

'I must go out for that pee, else I shall bust and it's just dark enough still...'

'I'll come too,' Jill said. 'I'm not going to that loo again... it smells!'

'Wait for me,' Jenny said.

Finlay heard them coming back, talking and laughing. Jenny sounded over her fears and they walked into the hut, three veritable beauties. They had just settled down to sleep again when there was a knock. 'Coastguard! Can somebody come to the door, please?'

Finlay heard Niney swear quietly. 'This bloody beach is getting like Bond Street!' she said, loud enough for the person knocking on the door to hear. 'Coming,' she sang out, sweetly. She opened the door to a middle-aged man in uniform. 'Oh, come in,' she cooed. She still had Finlay's shirt on over her underwear, and looked very good in it.

'Don't think I should Ma'am,' he said, looking her up and down. 'Just come to see that everything is all right, and whether we can call anybody for you. All the phones are out and the electric, and several people killed. If you'd like us to get in touch with relatives we can for you. Can I ask where you are from, please?'

'Romsey,' Niney said, shocked. 'Let me give you the phone number. It's Romsey 379 and our local police station is Totton, Sergeant Beech. My name is Niney Terry. If it's that bad they'll be frantic.'

'The two end chalets here got struck, and there's a very big hole in the front of this one. Never seen lightning on the land like it. Gets bad here because of the Island, but never like this. Ringwood had the worst of it. Lots of houses hit, and there were two people killed in a chalet on the other beach. There's another storm coming along. Might miss, but I wouldn't bank on it. I'll get on then Ma'am, I'll get a message through to Sergeant Beech for you. Thank you then, goodbye.' He began to leave.

'Thank you, you're very kind.' Niney was a bit stuck for words. 'Did you hear all of that, Jen?' Niney asked. 'Specially the bit about another one coming. See if the Land-Rover will start Kee. We need to get back in case they don't get the message through. I wouldn't be surprised if James and Jack are not on their way already.'

Jenny was out of bed and dressing quickly. 'Come on Jill MacFarlane, up and at 'em.'

It was with more than some relief that the Land-Rover jumped into life as soon as she was asked. There were no lights, wipers or heater, but she was running. As soon as it was light enough, Finlay went to look at the hole where the lightning had hit. It was around four feet wide and about three deep. The sand had fused into glass around its edges. 'That was a close one, Finlay,' he said, aloud to himself. He wandered up the beach and looked at the two huts which had been hit. Both looked like a heap of kindling wood that had been scattered in the wind.

'Kee, come on here,' he heard Jenny call. 'Come now!' She seemed distraught, so Finlay hurried.

'The tide is coming in and with all the water coming down, I think we should go now,' Niney said. The hut was almost empty of their holiday gear. 'I may be wrong, but look what happened to us the other week. It may happen here. You heard what he said about Ringwood. So get with it,' Niney ordered. They began packing the Land-Rover as the coastguard came along the beach with a loud hailer, telling everyone to evacuate the spit in twenty minutes.

'OK! That's it. Let's get gone. You drive up the slope, Kee. If it's wet after the rain, you'd be best at it. Have you locked up Jen?'

She answered that she had and clambered into the back with Jill. 'Home hero! Get me out of here.'

People were walking quickly back towards the Run, carrying their luggage as they drove the opposite way towards the headland. Finlay clawed the Land-Rover up as it slipped sideways in the wet, which made Jill yell encouragement to it, until they were on the top.

'What an absolute bugger,' Niney swore. 'That was shaping up to be a good rest. Worst thunderstorm in years and it falls on us.'

'Well, I loved it,' Jill said brightly. 'It was really exciting.'

They started to laugh, mainly with relief at what had been a close-run thing. They reached the gate which led on to the public road.

'Who's going to drive?' he asked.

'I am,' Jenny and Niney said together, but it was Jenny who climbed over from the rear, before Niney could get her long legs untangled. 'Well, not quite so bloody wild, girl, as when we came down,' Niney said, conceding defeat.

They had just got into Christchurch when Finlay remembered. 'We've forgotten the boat!' he said.

'Bugger the boat! Rollo will find it and if he doesn't, he doesn't,' Niney said emphatically.

Christchurch had no electricity and they saw several fire engines pumping out houses, as they crossed the Avon Bridge. By the priory, the river seemed tranquil enough, but there was no one fishing. The traffic lights at Purewell were not working. A policeman, doing his arm-waving duty for the few cars that were moving around, looked very bored.

'What's the time?' Finlay asked.

'Quarter-past seven,' Jill answered. 'Thought you would've known!'

The sun was already warm and the newly washed air was crystal clear and fresh, blowing their hair, still sticky with salt, into tangles. 'Keep an eye out for the car all of you. They might be on their way to find us,' Niney ordered.

Despite Niney's protestations, as soon as they reached the open forest, Jenny gave the Land-Rover its head. The speedometer needle was soon bouncing on the maximum stop and she drove in much the same way as she rode, with verve. 'Nearly home,' she announced needlessly, as they came over the top of Pauncefoot Hill. The abbey and town were bathed in early-morning sun below them, the last of the river's mist wreathed around the abbey tower. 'I can smell the river,' Finlay said, pleased. 'Slow down over the bridge, Jen, so we can look.'

The landlord of the Horse and Jockey was stacking empty bottles, ready for collection, as Jenny changed into third and went slowly over the bridge. 'It's still there,' Niney said to him fondly.

'Hello, beautiful river!' Finlay shouted. 'Have you missed us?'

'It hasn't rained here,' Jill observed. 'And that pub has electric.'

'What a perfectly sane girl you are, my dear,' Niney said. 'Unlike this mad cow!' She gave Jenny a sharp dig in the ribs.

They drove into the yard and stopped by Finlay's pick-up. As the women dashed to the house, Finlay stayed in the yard, listening and scenting his home. The birds sounded softly sweet after the raucous yelling of the sea birds. He watched the house martins swinging in the air around the roof of the house, hawking at the flies. A moorhen clucked in the feeder stream above the lawn and a pair of mallard arced down towards the water meadows, their pinions whistling as they cut the air. He breathed in deeply. The air was rich with the smell of animals, cow dung and ripe barley and he knew he was home. Through the open window, he heard the hubbub in the kitchen and decided to avoid it. He drove the pick-up to the hatch pool and walked out on to one of the fishing platforms. The water was clear and gentle. He dropped off his clothes and dived into the deep back eddy. Dace and grayling scattered in front of him and the water was cold as it passed over his body. He swam along the bottom towards the current, watching the weed swaying. It caressed his legs and feet as he swam past it. On the surface he took some of the water in his mouth and fountained it up in the air, tasting the chalk and the earth. He went down again, rubbing the salt from his hair and skin. On the surface, again he rubbed and cleaned his teeth with his forefinger. There was a greenfinch in the damaged apple tree above him, looking at him curiously, complaining at his presence. 'Shut up you,' he smiled. 'It's my place as well.' He climbed up on to the fishing platform and dragged his shorts on over his wet skin. Slipping into his shoes, he walked back to the pick-up and flung his screwed-up clothes in the back and went back to the house. Tom MacFarlane's Ford was in the yard.

Jill met him at the door. They went into the kitchen. He said his greetings to his grandfather, Uncle Jack and shook hands with Tom MacFarlane. Taking the towel, placed there for him on top of the Aga, an act he took entirely for granted, he wrapped it around his wet shoulders and dripped gently on to the floor. 'Well?' his grandfather said. 'Have you entirely wrecked my Land-Rover?'

'Electrics are buggered and she ain't charging properly, so I imagine all the fuses are blown,' he said. 'It's nothing serious. You can use my pick-up until Carl fixes it though.'

'Well, thank you very much. I'm very grateful. That's the least you can offer, I'd have thought,' he retorted.

'They didn't know anything about last night. Hadn't heard anything until Niney switched on the news!'

'Yes, bloody marvellous isn't it? There we were facing death and destruction and these two buggers were playing crib in the Three Tuns until all hours,' Niney scoffed.

'I was worried that the wheat would get flattened, but I can't see that you've had any rain at all. The river is as clear as crystal,' Finlay said. 'Is there any breakfast please Auntie Niney?'

'This is not false modesty, Tom,' Niney said to MacFarlane. 'Darling, we were telling everyone how cool you were and then went to see how everyone else was. Perfect strangers.'

'You weren't the least bit afraid, were you Finlay?' Jill said.

'I was bloody terrified!' Finlay said. 'When the doors blew in, I thought the next one was for us.'

'I am very proud of you, Kee,' his grandfather said. 'I suppose that's coolness under fire.'

'I should get the Land-Rover to Carl,' Finlay said. 'Is he very busy, Grandfather?'

'Somebody else can do that. Get something on and have your breakfast. Then go and see your mare. Jill's horse will be here later, or had you forgotten?'

'Do you know, I've lost track of the days,' Finlay said. 'I'd forgotten... We did have a lovely break though, Grandad, and certainly I'm not going to be put off the place by last night. I'll be back there in between the barley and wheat, even if I have to go on the train. You should have seen the plaice, Grandad... like that they were.' He measured them with his hands.

'Well, they were nearly that big!' Jill said quietly, laughing at his enthusiasm.

'Ask Jenny how big they were then,' Finlay said offended.

'Jenny would claim they were even bigger!' Niney said. 'Big or small, they were wonderful to eat. Now you eat this, and you'll feel better.' She put a plate of bacon and eggs before him.

'Thank you Auntie Niney,' Finlay said. 'Oh yes, Madam,' he said to Jill. 'You said you were going to cook something, just to show my wonderful auntie that you could. When can we look forward to this?'

'Now that will be something!' Tom MacFarlane said.

'Don't let them get at you, Jill!' Niney laughed. 'Tell them to cook their own food. These buggers haven't washed up since we left. They've been eating at the pub, and there still isn't a clean plate in the place.'

'Well, I'd better go. I take it you're staying, Jill?' MacFarlane asked.

'Yes, of course. Is Mother home then?' she answered.

'No, conference, WI in Winchester...'

'Good, I'll ride home tonight, when Laddie Ben comes back. Bye Daddy.' She waved at him from the other side of the table, a harmless but insolent dismissal.

'Thank you, Finlay, for keeping her safe,' he said, and left.

Jack, who had kept his head firmly stuck in the newspaper, asked, 'How big you think those plaice were, nipper?'

'One was over two pounds, Uncle Jack...'

Jill and Niney cried him down laughing. 'We ought to have some time down there, Niney. Could do with a break. The boy can look after the rods for a few days... You could, couldn't you nipper?'

'Of course, Uncle Jack!' Finlay felt he had just been paid the biggest compliment of his life.

'If you two go out for an hour, there'll be enough hot water for you to have a bath and a hair wash Jill,' Niney said. 'I'll get this place back to rights by then.'

'Do you want to have some casts in the hatch pool Jill? There were lots of fish just now. It's time you had a rod in your hand,' Finlay offered.

'Tomorrow perhaps, Finlay,' she said. 'I'm worn and ragged and we didn't get much sleep last night. I'd want to do it right for you. Do you mind if I just sit and read in the hall, Niney?'

'Of course not. I don't know what you got up to yesterday while we were in Bournemouth. Whatever it was it seems to have worn you out,' Niney said, both hands occupied in the sink and not looking at them.

Finlay and Jill made no answer, but Jill began to blush. 'I'll go and read,' she said.

'Mmm,' Niney said.

'I'll go and see Misty, then,' Finlay said, going to the door.

'Do mind she doesn't bite you again, darling.' Niney smiled. 'That other mark on your arm hasn't faded yet.' Finlay suddenly thought the problem with his auntie was that one never knew what she actually knew.

Chapter Seven

•

After seeing his horse was comfortable, Finlay decided to have a protracted walk around the estate with his gun. It had been decided by the landowners in the area, before the protection order on sparrowhawks was made law, that the birds be shot and trapped out, to save the small bird population. The shorthorns were on the bottom meadows, big red and red roan cows that had been bred pure here for more than two hundred years. They watched him idly as he moved among them, their milky breath hanging in the air and making it sweet. There were about ten actually in the river, up to their bellies in the water, grazing on the starwort fronds, pulling them out in long whisps, gazing into the distance while they chewed and swallowed. Sitting down among them on the bank, it wasn't long before some of them walked over to investigate him. They were a quiet and contented breed, blowing their breath over him, their huge wet nostrils taking his scent, and the older animals were prone to lick his skin with their huge rough tongues. Finlay stayed sitting among the animals for a good half-hour, watching the countryside. Far away to the north, he watched a wood pigeon deviate in its straight flight. The movement was sudden and quick and he thought there must have been somebody up there. As the sun rose higher, the cows slowly made their way to the willows and poplars by the bend in the river to escape the flies.

As the morning air became warmer, he decided that nothing much would be moving about. He had not glimpsed a sparrowhawk for at least two weeks and was satisfied that what few that might have been locally were keeping low. There was one last place to look, in the kitchen garden. There were lots of small birds there which might have attracted a hawk. The garden looked parched and dry, any small birds in the shade as the heat had become too oppressive for them. He wandered up the back drive towards the stables, bent on putting his gun indoors and going to the workshop to fix the Land-Rover, if Carl had not started on it. He heard female voices in the stables and recognized the voices of Jill and Janet Ward. His inclination was to stay and listen to what they were saying, but he thought better of it and walked the long way around to the workshop. He knew that Carl hated guns in any form, so he hid his in the rafters of the old cart shed and went to the workshop.

Carl was working on a Ferguson. 'Vell, you are the bloody fine vone! Already dis morning I hev had de girls looking fer you. Vere ver you? I told zem to bugger off vis their bums and tits. All zey do is ask de bloody silly questions.'

'I'm sorry about that, Carl. I've come to see if you would like me to start on this,' Finlay said, walking to the Land-Rover.

'De book is on ze shelf. Electrics is so kaput, you lucky to get home. I speak to Mrs Niney. She come and get de young frauleins out. De small vone ask if I fix her bike. I say I fix her arse with a stick if she not get from mine workshop! Now, get on vis de Land-Rover or go avay!'

The workshop descended into silence. With the book open, Finlay went through the circuits and put in new fuses and replaced the wire running to the back lights. Finding a wheel bearing gone on the front off, he replaced that. He saw Carl look across at what he was doing occasionally, but he was leaving him to it.

Finlay worked on steadily till lunch time. 'That's all done now, Carl,' he said. 'Here's her card with everything done and what spares I've used.'

Carl studied it. 'Zis is all good. You are now a good use with the tools. If you vant I have another job. You do ze engine on ze bale machine, zis before vee cut ze barley. You think yes maybe?'

'Yes please Carl, I'd love to. What needs doing to it?' This was a great step forward, Finlay thought.

'Grind in the valves and de-coke. I find ze book, you study, then com down and do.' He put his hand on Finlay's shoulder. 'You good chap, boy, learn ver quick.' He found the engine's manual and gave it to him. 'Good, now go and face ze bloody music. Vye so many girls, vot they want?' he asked.

'Five thousand acres and four miles of river, Carl, probably,' Finlay laughed.

'You not even little bit silly!' Carl said.

Finlay drove the Land-Rover back to the house, and through the open kitchen window he could hear female chatter. Jenny met him at the door. 'Hello buggerlugs. Where have you been hiding? Your little entourage is here. Their horses in the stable eating us out of best hay and Niney is giving cooking lessons to keep them out of everyone's hair.'

'Oh shit,' he said. 'Is she very cross?'

'Making out she is, but she's enjoying being Queen Bee. There'll be enough cakes to feed an army. Go in and explain yourself, then.' She was enjoying his discomfiture.

'Where have you been?' Niney asked. 'These bright young things have been all over looking for you.' Jill and the Ward sisters were variously beating eggs, rolling pastry flat or spreading jam.

'Went out with my gun and then went to the workshop to fix Grandfather's Land-Rover. Hello, you lot! What are you doing here?' The last question was aimed at the Ward sisters.

'We came to find you and see how you all were,' Jo Ward said. 'Then Mrs Terry said she would show us all how to cook, so we rather forgot about you. Anyway, the German chap very nearly chased us back up to here. He's pretty fierce isn't he?'

Finlay laughed. 'You rested now, Jill?'

'Yes, I hope you don't mind. We put two more horses in your stables. John seemed thrilled to bits to have more to look after,' she said.

'Well, if it means a little more horse muck, then I'm all for it. But I'll have to arm-wrestle the new gardener for it. There's nothing like it for growing peas,' Niney said.

'You three look good,' Finlay observed. 'Rested and bathed with the salt out of your hair.' He ruffled through Niney's curls.

'Oh, I wish you wouldn't do that!' she said. 'You've got these three to aggravate. Do it to them!' She was obviously pleased that he had.

Finlay sat down beside Jenny. 'Just like that on Sunday, Jen,' he said, looking at her hair. 'Knock their eyes out.' Her hair was a complicated array of plaits and waves cascading over her neck. It looked beautiful.

'Can we ride out together when it's cooler?' Janet said, looking at him squarely with her green eyes.

'That's up to you. If you've signed the insurance form, you don't need me with you.'

'We want you with us, stupid!' Jill said. 'Niney said that you don't really have to work quite all of the time. You just always choose to.'

'Well, he certainly wasn't a dull boy last night!' Jenny said with just a touch of sharpness. Niney shot a glance of warning. Enough to make Jill quickly add, 'You're not ever dull really, Finlay.'

'Among all this cooking, flying whisks and beautiful legs is there the slightest chance of something to eat?' Finlay joked. 'We can't go swimming until the rods have gone and we can't go fishing for the same reason. So what if we have a walk round and I'll show you which birds are which?'

'I'll stay here and do some more cooking, thank you!' Jo said. 'We have nature walks at school.'

'Sounds good to me. It'll be lovely to know what birds are what. Always good for an essay at school. Blind them with science,' Janet said enthusiastically.

'That's using your brains,' Jenny said. 'Are you sure you want to stay here, Jo?'

'Yes please. I want to learn to cook properly. Mother's hopeless,' Jo said, despairingly.

Jenny and Finlay cringed, waiting for some comment from Niney, but she just gave them both an exaggerated smile. They knew what she meant.

'Shall we go then?' Jill said, getting up.

'Well, I would like something to eat first. If nobody minds, that is.' Finlay was sitting patiently, waiting.

'Well, get it then!' Jo said. 'Why do men always think we should wait on them? When I'm grown up, I'm not going to be slave to a man. Get it yourself.' Jo was the spiky one, forthright and feisty. Her hair more red than copper.

'My dear girl,' Niney said. 'Look after them and they are biddable, like dogs. They want two things to keep them happy and food is one of them.'

'That's just disgusting… No thank you!' Jo said, getting animated.

'Shut up, you stupid tart,' Janet snapped. 'You'll finish up on the shelf. Listen to what Mrs Terry said. The reason we don't have a father any more is precisely because Mother is such an appalling cook and, well, he went off with his secretary. Am I not right Mrs Terry?'

'Why don't you call me Niney my dear,' Niney said sweetly.

Jenny covered her amusement by getting Finlay some corned beef sandwiches. 'Thanks Jen,' Finlay said brightly, giving Jo the most withering look he could muster.

She snorted her disgust. 'If you lived in our home, you'd have to shift yourself, I can tell you.'

'Ah,' Finlay said, amused. 'I don't live in your house though, do I?'

'You're just a spoilt brat, Finlay!' she said, getting cross.

'Enough, enough,' Niney said. 'Good Lord! You are a feisty little madam. Calm down and let them get gone. Then I'll teach you how to make a fruit cake.'

'When you're an old maid like Miss Satchel, you'll be able to eat. You should have better manners when you're in somebody else's house, Jo,' Janet said in a patronizing manner.

'Oh shut up, you stupid cow!' Jo said to her sister.

'Come along. Stop this!' Niney said sharply. 'You three get on out. I'm sure Jo's fine when she's left alone.' She shepherded the others towards the door. 'Now stop taunting her, Janet. I don't know how your mother copes with you.'

Outside, Janet said, 'She's so bloody tiresome. She's become nothing but a blob of hormones!'

Jill and Finlay laughed. 'Niney'll calm her down. She is a bit lost without a father figure. Remember when you were like it Janet? You had an absolute fixation with your gardener chap,' Jill said.

'I did, didn't I? Seems funny now when I look at him. What about you Finlay? Do you have fixations on women, now you don't look like having a mother?' Janet asked.

'Of course he does!' Jill answered for him. 'Look at the way he and Jenny are. You would think they were lovers.'

Finlay said nothing.

'Where are we going to go, Finlay?' Jill asked.

'Let's go to the Blackwater. Where we were the other day.' They wandered across the fields, chatting about how difficult the exams were.

'I'll get qualified and then have a riding school and livery yard,' Janet said decidedly. 'You don't own that land behind us do you, Finlay?'

'No. Belongs to the Masons. Why?' he asked.

'Well, we could easily have twenty boxed at home. If we had some of that land behind our place, I think it would work. Whatever I do, I shall dedicate my life to the horse,' Janet said dreamily. 'You should go hunting, Finlay,' Janet said. 'It's such fun and your horse would love it.'

'I think Jenny intends to. Talks about getting a box for the Land-Rover. We spend our time shooting in the winter. If I had the time, I'd take up falconry or coursing. The college has a beagle pack. I think that must be the best way to learn hound work. Down in among them.' As they approached the pool beneath the broken sluice, Finlay said, 'Now go very quietly. Don't get above the bankside grass and tread softly. Fish can feel vibrations.' They crept up to the bank.

'Can we talk?' Janet asked.

'Very quietly and no giggling,' Finlay said sternly. 'You'll hear what's happening around you.'

They waited. 'That's a kingfisher,' Finlay said listening. 'Sometimes they pitch quite close to you.' A mallard duck came into the pool, from a small side stream, with a small brood of late ducklings, jerking about the surface, catching insects. 'Don't move. If something dramatic happens, stay quiet,' he ordered.

The ducks skittered about the surface happily. 'Christ! What was that?' Janet said. 'Something just ate one of the babies.' The female duck called her babies and headed for the bank. There was another swirl, a soft splash and another duckling was gone. 'It's an otter,' he breathed. 'Look on the other bank where the buttercups are and stay quiet.'

The otter whistled softly and scrambled up to where Finlay had told them to watch. Two otter kits emerged and began eating the proffered ducklings. One of the girls moved, and the otters were gone. 'Crawl away slowly,' Finlay ordered. Well back from the river, they stopped and lay down in the sun. The fresh growth of grass, recovered from the hay harvest, was short and cool on their bare limbs.

'How did you know they were there, Finlay?' Jill asked.

'She made a home there about ten weeks ago. Even if they go into the main river they won't do much damage. Except take the Grieveses' chickens maybe.' He grinned.

'How do you know all this Finlay? How do you see it all?' Janet asked.

'Just by being aware of everything. It's no good just walking along looking for tracks like it says in the books. Everything interlocks. Be aware of your surroundings. Understand what animals do. When you see an old cock pheasant, as soon as you see him, he's aware that you are there. Once you get tuned into everything, you'll know when something's watching you. You can feel it.'

'You don't mind about the otter killing the ducklings? You kill lots of things Finlay, without a second's thought. I'm not saying you're wrong, I just don't understand,' Jill asked.

'It's about balance. If we had dozens of otters, we would shoot some. The only animals we always shoot, I suppose, are those that do most damage. Cormorants, herons, squirrels, magpies. Things like that.' He wanted them to understand. 'This part of the valley is known for its birds. That isn't an accident. We keep the predators in check and have done for a few hundred years. It's that simple.'

'The Methodist Minister told Mrs Phillips he was going to report you if you carried on killing all the sparrowhawks. She told my mother the other day,' Jill said.

'Did he tell her when he was screwing her?' Finlay laughed.

'He's shagging Mrs Phillips?' Janet squealed. 'How do you know that, Finlay? Illicit sex and rampant adultery. What fun!'

'Uncle Jack saw them down by the main river one night and she had her knickers off.'

Janet burst into hysterical laughter. 'I wonder if she takes that awful hat off. It looks like a jelly mould. Just hang on there Minister, while I get my hat off.'

Finlay was still laughing. 'How did we get to this?'

'Well, I think it's very sad,' Jill said. 'Just think how humiliated his poor wife must feel.'

'She probably thinks it was ordained by God, stupid cow! Don't be so bloody pi, Jill. It might even make the Sunday papers. "Minister was intimate with her on several occasions". That's what they'd say. Bunch of bloody hypocrites,' Janet scoffed scornfully.

'You can be so coarse sometimes, Janet,' Jill said, getting up. 'Maybe they really love each other!'

'Crap!' Janet said emphatically. 'They're bloody hypocrites. I expect he spies on his daughter in the bath. When my father fucked off with his PA, he came around and asked my mother if she needed help with anything.'

Finlay fairly yelped with laughter. 'Maybe he was just being Christian, and felt for her.' He got up and stood beside Jill, taking her hand.

'Yes, that's probably what happened, Finlay,' Jill said. 'You make it all sound tawdry and cheap Janet, and sex is not like that at all!'

'Because you're all starry-eyed over Finlay, wait until your father buggers off with someone not much older than your elder sister. You'll have a different perspective on things then,' Janet said, rolling over on to her back and staring at the sky.

Finlay bent over, took Janet's hand and hauled her to her feet. 'Come on. This ain't talk for this afternoon. Let's go and see if Laddie Ben's back yet.' They walked up the back drive. The horse hadn't arrived and the two Ward horses were contentedly eating small nets of hay, Misty, her hard food and all three, no doubt, glad to be in the shade, away from the flies.

'Any news from Mr Pearce, Auntie Niney?' Finlay asked, following the two girls into the kitchen. The air was filled with the smell of fresh baking.

'Yes, I'm sorry Jill. Your father telephoned and said I had to take you home when you got in. Something has come up and Laddie Ben will have to stay at the livery stable for the moment,' Niney said, taking off her apron. 'I don't know what it's about, but he did say as soon as possible. We had better go.'

Jill sat down, shocked. 'It probably means somebody has died or something. I'll give you a call, Finlay. Let you know what's happening.'

'Don't worry Jill. Your father would have told Niney if it was something that bad.' Finlay had the sudden thought that her parents had heard about the intensity of their relationship.

After they had left, Jo Ward showed off her afternoon's cooking. 'I have a strawberry flan to take home. I cooked it!'

'Well, we've been watching otters and talking scandal. Much more fun than cooking,' Janet crowed.

'Do you know where Jenny is, Jo?' Finlay asked.

'Gone to Southampton. Don't ask me why. Why didn't you say you were going to see some otters. I would have come with you,' she said sulkily.

'Because we didn't know they would be there.' Finlay smiled at her.

'I bet you did. You just didn't want me with you.' She pouted rather prettily.

'I did ask you to come, but you were on a man-hating mission at the time. Remember?' Finlay was trying to be pleasant.

'I don't hate you Finlay. I just said you were a lazy sod. Will you take me to see the otters?' She gave him an entirely false smile.

'Not without me! Remember, I was at the cricket nets the other evening,' Janet said firmly.

'You quite liked it Finlay, didn't you?'

'What are we going to do now?' Janet asked. 'Can we go for a ride?'

'Let's wait and see what's happening with Jill,' Finlay said.

Jo was getting irksome.

'Would you like some tea, Janet?' he asked.

Finlay heard Niney coming back first. He watched her walking across the yard looking thoughtful and troubled. He went out to meet her. 'Not good news, darling,' she said sadly. 'Jill and her family are leaving for America as soon as they can. Tom has had a hefty promotion.'

Finlay swallowed the lump in his throat. 'How long for?'

'For the foreseeable future. Some years, probably,' Niney said, putting her hand on his shoulder.

'Is she upset? I mean... Having to go?'

'Of course she is. Said she wasn't going and wanted to be here, but she knows if she wants to be that famous surgeon, there's not much chance of it in this country. Best she could hope for here would be just an ordinary doctor. Her father said he'll bring her around in the morning. Don't be too upset darling. You're both very young.'

'I'm OK Auntie Niney,' Finlay said. 'We knew it would come to an end. We spoke about it. When are they going? Any idea?'

Niney sighed. 'Tomorrow lunch time. Back to Essex to see their relatives. The house belongs to the company and they've got to pack their personal things. It's probably best they're going so quickly, for Jill anyway. I didn't like her at first, but she was old enough to love you. Be gentle tomorrow.'

'Of course! What about her horse?' Finlay asked.

'Tom wants James to find a good home. She'll be too busy getting her qualifications to think too much about horses anyway.'

'I don't think I want to ride tonight. Wouldn't seem right, really. Poor Jill. Parents really balls things up don't they?'

'Mine did. But we get over it. Want me to get the beautiful sisters gone for you?'

'No,' he laughed. 'I'll do that. How did you get on with that Jo? She's a tricky bugger ain't she?'

'Certainly is. But sharp, very intelligent and quite fun. She's suffering from being the youngest. She'll grow up into a lovely young lady one day.' Niney smiled. 'Got a good touch with pastry. That's a gift. It can't be learnt.'

Finlay thought Janet seemed genuinely sorry Jill was leaving, but Jo remarked that Jill was too intense to be anything but a bore. 'You really are an insensitive bitch, Jo,' Janet snapped at her. 'I expect you'd like us to go Finlay. You'll miss her.' She turned to her sister. 'Come on Jo, we'll leave Finlay to it.'

'What about my flan?' she said, in answer.

'We can pick it up tomorrow evening. I expect Finlay will want a shoulder, maybe.' She gave Finlay a passing kiss on the cheek as she left. He heard them give their farewell to Niney as they went.

'Do you want anything to eat, Kee?' she said, coming back into the kitchen.

'I don't think so. I'll go to the top of the old main feeder and walk down through. We'll probably have to let a fair bit of water in from the river. I'll think how we can do it.'

'Good idea! Can't see James or Jack having the time till October.

You'll have your results next week, then it'll be interviews and things. A good project like that stream will keep your feet on the ground.'

'Where's Grandfather?' he asked.

'NFU Cereal Committee. Another excuse for a booze-up. Jen has your pick-up, so dinner will be around eight. Go and look at your stream, and just be glad you knew her, darling,' Niney said quietly.

The inlet to the feeder stream was at the top of the estate on the other side of the river. He could have swum across, but instead, decided to walk the long way around. It was three-quarters of an hour later when he got there. The sun had lost some of its fiercest heat and the swallows and martins were lower than at midday, patrolling up and down the river, catching the flies as they hatched. The inlet had been badly poached by the feet of cattle over the past few years and was just a muddy pool. The grey mud, speckled with the white of chalk, sucked at his bare feet as he studied how much would have to be removed. He became aware that he was not alone and realized he was being watched. He didn't turn to look but studied the mud more intently, gradually turning to face where he thought the watcher was. He looked up suddenly and saw a movement in the hazel bushes just over the boundary.

'Hey you! What are you doing in there?' he shouted. 'Come out and show yourself or I'll come in there and wrap this stick around your head.' A youth of about his own age came from the bushes.

'Don't think you will. You haven't got a stick!'

Finlay could see that he was wearing the tweed uniform of the next door estate. His hair was bleached as white as Finlay's and he was smiling broadly.

'I'm Bill,' he said, reaching over the boundary fence to shake hands. 'Sorry. I didn't see who it was until you were up close. Thought you might have been a fucking pikie when I saw you had no shoes.'

'I'm Finlay. My shoes are over there. I was looking to see what mud we had to shift. Are you the new keeper for this end?' Finlay liked him at once.

'Keeper's boy!' he said, amused by the title. 'I'm down this end killing squirrels and hawks. Shot fifty-two today.'

'Squirrels, I take it,' Finlay said. 'I'd hate to think there were that many sparrowhawks. I've had sixteen this year.'

'Are you going to take any notice of the protection order? We're going to have to, our boss being a public figure. We can't set ride nets after the end of the month he says, so we'll have to keep them down quietly.'

'No, we'll just carry on. But watch that church minister. He's one of these bloody do-gooders. Fucking johnny-come-lately, but I'll curb his enthusiasm. I'll ban him from coming here. We don't have any public footpaths, like you. He's an evil swine. Always poking about, and might have to go in the river yet,' Finlay said, meaning every word of it.

'I find him about here with some old bird sometimes. They used to park up in Lee Lane last winter, till we let his tyres down while he was shagging. I crept up on them last month when you was silage-making and got her knickers on the end of a hazel rod. Didn't they get in a tizz! I tied them to the wing mirror of his car.' He started laughing at the thought. 'Haven't seen him since.'

'You handled her knickers?' Finlay said, with as much disgust as he could muster.

'Only on a stick! I put lots of baler twine round them so I didn't have to touch. They was they big old blue things that the girls at school used to wear. She must have got a fair old sweat-on in those.'

They chatted some more till Bill heard the head keeper's Land-Rover coming. 'I'd better go. See you again soon, perhaps,' he said, as he went back into the bushes.

Finlay washed his feet in the river and began walking back down the feeder stream. It would need a lot of clearing out. Silt and rotting vegetation from the last ten years had almost blocked the flow. Hiring a digger for a month would be astronomic. He was wondering if there was a driving course he could go on to learn to use one, when he spotted Jenny coming the other way.

'What are you doing?' she said breathlessly, after he had swung her around.

'Looking what to do with this. It's going to need a lot of work and create mountains of silt for the kitchen garden. What do you think?' he asked.

'I think you're clever, resourceful and a good chap. Who was that you were talking to earlier? I was watching you through the glasses, thinking what a gorgeous bastard you are.' They were walking with their arms around each other.

'His name is Bill. I think he's Mr Grass's new chap. We had a good laugh together,' and he recounted the tale about the minister and the underwear.

'He'll liven things up by the sound of it. I'm sorry about Jill, Kee. She's a nice girl and we'll miss her.'

'It was always going to happen, Jen,' he said. 'Probably best that it happens this quickly. No long sadness, as we wait for the day of leaving with protracted goodbyes.'

Jill's departure was swift. Almost brutal. The MacFarlane car arrived in the yard, with a pale Jill sitting in the back. 'I'm sorry this is rushed,' Tom MacFarlane said. He told how Jill seemed suddenly grown up; she had been happy to be with Finlay, and he was grateful. Mrs MacFarlane did not get out of the car and, suddenly, they were driving away. Jill waved from the rear window.

'What a sensible man,' Niney said. 'No chance for any hysterics.' She went back into the house quickly.

'Well I don't know what to think,' Finlay's grandfather said. 'There doesn't seem to be time or permanence at all these days. Everything outside of here always seems so transient.'

'Is Carl working today, Grandfather?' Finlay asked. 'I'd like to start work on that baler engine.'

'Not working, but he is about. Don't disturb him at home. Here, take my workshop key.' He removed it from his key ring. 'I won't say leave the place as you found it.'

Finlay worked through the day, thoroughly absorbed with working on the engine. Ron came in briefly, surprised to find him there. 'Hello nipper,' he said. 'Don't hurt your hands. We want to destroy Landford tomorrow. I've come for a monkey wrench. There's water pissing out of a tank up the top.' Then he was gone. Finlay worked until around four and then cleaned everything up, checking again that everything was in place. He had made a lot of progress on the engine. The house was empty and quiet when he went in, the table already set for a formal tea. The whole thing was draped in a muslin cloth.

'Where are you, Jen?' he called.

She had been washing her hair and was drying it in the rear garden, a towel draped around her neck. 'Hi buggerlugs, been busy?' she asked. 'Come and give my hair a brush for me.'

He brushed the thick dark gold hair with infinite care and shook it, the same as he would Misty's tail. 'I'm not a bloody horse!' she laughed.

When he had finished, she braided it into the long loose single plait that was her normal way. 'I'll do it how you like it tomorrow. Those Ward girls are coming to tea with their mother. James and Niney are visiting Granny, so we have to do the entertaining.'

'Why on earth?' Finlay asked. 'Is Auntie Niney going to teach them all to cook?'

'I think the mother wants to check where her daughters keep disappearing to, and to meet this wonder man they keep talking about,' Jenny said.

'Girls are pretty stupid really, don't you think, Jen?' he asked, embarrassed.

'Well, that means you think I'm pretty stupid or you don't consider me to be a girl. Which is it please?' Jenny asked, giving him a playful dig.

'Not you! You're about as female as they come, and you're not the least bit stupid. If all girls were like you I'd get into all sorts of problems.' He laughed.

'Meaning you don't already! Are you eating tea like that?' she said.

'I'll wash and put on a clean shirt, but not more,' he said emphatically.

'I rather think Niney is going to bring Granny back for tea,' Jenny said. 'She's missing seeing people in her new house.'

'That's great! I'll have a bath and put clean shorts on as well. Is the water hot?' Finlay was suddenly very enthusiastic about tea.

'You're funny. You won't bathe for me, except under protest, and you won't for a bevy of redheaded beauties. But for an acerbic old faggot like Granny you jump through hoops!' Jenny said. 'Those young ladies will be put out if you give Granny all your attention.'

'Granny knows everything Jen. She's like a living history book. She even remembers Kerensky,' Finlay said.

'Let joy be unbounded! Who the Hell's he anyway?' Jenny said.

'The leader of the Duma during the Russian revolution. He was a lawyer,' Finlay said.

'Go get your bath and be sweet-smelling for the old girl.' Jenny laughed.

'Should we put a cushion on a chair for her, do you think?' Finlay asked seriously.

'I'll get one. Just make sure you put a cushion out for me when I'm ninety-two and have a bony bum!' Jenny said.

'It's a long way from that, Jen,' Finlay said, stroking her bottom.

'Don't do that, you sod! I go all goose pimples. Go and get your bath!' she ordered.

Finlay was drying himself when he heard what to him was a strange vehicle arriving. He dressed quickly and ran downstairs, barefoot and still damp. Mrs Ward was, as Niney once described her, 'a tryer', but even Finlay could see that what she was wearing didn't seem to belong to her. She looked a little like a creation by Claris Cliff, though Finlay supposed it to be modern. The three girls, in shorts and blouses with fine, open sandals, looked beautiful. Jo wore a look that said she was here under protest. Introductions made, Jenny made small talk until they heard the Armstrong arrive. Finlay excused himself and went to meet Granny as his grandfather was helping her out of the car. She was wearing a deep blue silk dress, black satin shoes and diamonds. Finlay, for a moment, could see what his great-grandfather had seen.

'Oh Granny, you look absolutely stunning!' Finlay exclaimed. She gave him a playful whack across his bottom with a slim ebony cane.

'Thank you, my beautiful. You looks good enough to eat. Come and give me a kiss.' She came indoors, on his arm.

'This is Mrs Fortune, Auntie Niney's grandmother. If she likes you, she will, no doubt, let you call her Granny. If she doesn't, she'll probably hit you with her stick!' The Wards looked a little doubtful as he helped her to the cushioned chair.

'Where you sitting, darling?' she asked. 'Next to you Granny,' Finlay said.

'Good! I can put me hand on your leg and pretend I'm eighteen again.' She looked at the three sisters. 'Well! You're three beauties and no mistake, and you, young lady, are the best of them!' she said to Jo. 'What beautiful bones you've got my dear. Face of an angel.'

Jo wriggled with delight, and shot a triumphant glance at her sisters. 'That's a wonderful, wonderful dress Mrs Fortune. I don't think I've ever seen such sheer silk, and can I ask if those are real diamonds?'

'Fake diamonds are like fake tits my dear. Worthless when you take 'em off! My dress was made in London when I was a bit older than you. Course I was bigger then, but Niney altered it for me. This one here,' she said, lifting the diamond hanging around her wrinkled neck, 'came from Kimberley when the mine was first started. Take it off darling,' she ordered Finlay. 'Let her try it on. Pretty love like you should have men bring her diamonds.'

'You're honoured Jo. I've never been allowed to wear them,' Niney said, peeved.

'You'll have them when I'm gone, madam. Now, have I to get the brandy myself?' Granny cooed.

Jo picked up her chair and set it down next to her. 'Finlay says you remember General Custer, Mrs Fortune.'

'Yes my dear. I was married on the day he was killed. We didn't hear about it for weeks, of course. Then, he seemed too clever by half, poor bugger! But he was a nice-looking chap. Looked good on a horse.'

Janet moved her chair nearer. 'Did you like horses, Granny?'

'You had to, darling. There wasn't any other way of getting about, except walking. Yes, but I loved them, like you do now.'

The eldest Ward girl joined them. 'Did you go to school Mrs Fortune, when you were a child?'

'Not to school. We had to go up to the hall and have lessons. Keith's great-great-grandfather saw to that. He would have us learn to read and do our sums, but reading was what we had to do. We all had to read bits out of the newspaper, every day.'

Tea was forgotten about. Even Jenny came and sat on Finlay's knee, all enthralled by Granny's memories.

Finlay's grandfather, Mrs Ward and Niney remained, at the other end of the long table, deep in discussion, oblivious to Granny's holding court. They would suddenly start laughing among themselves, but it was Granny who held the fascination with the younger ones. They talked about history, transport, communications and how Romsey was when she was a child. Swimwear at the beach and lack of it in the river, travelling players. About all facets of rural life in the previous century. They even talked about sex. Granny's frankness on the subject made them giggle.

The spell was broken after about an hour with Niney saying, 'Jo, what are you doing laying on the table?' She wasn't cross. 'Shall we eat the flan you made yesterday?'

'Sorry,' Jo said, embarrassed. 'I had to hear what Granny was saying.'

'Of course you did my dear. Doesn't matter, as long as you're happy.' Niney had obviously taken a liking to Jo. The tea party was a great success. Jo handed back Granny's diamond with some sadness but felt she had learned a little about how to acquire her own. Janet was definitely going to take up fishing and Cassy had a list of words she had never heard of. The word 'ain't' would figure in her vocabulary because it was, despite Jenny's protestations, according to Granny, much more proper than 'isn't'.

When they had gone and Finlay was sitting alone with his grandfather, they discussed the probable costs of turning the main feeder into a trout stream, and the best way to do it. 'We'll get a hire price for a digger, Kee. Work out the cost of digging the length from the river to the sluice. The rest is just taking down some alders. You had better keep that workshop key. I'll have another cut for myself,' he said. Finlay knew this to be a large compliment and was grateful for it.

'Grandfather, I think we should stop that minister coming on to our land. He's going to report us to the police if we carry on killing sparrowhawks.' Finlay was unsure of his ground. Provided people stayed on the tracks, Finlay's grandfather was fairly easy about outside visitors.

His grandfather thought for a short time. 'OK. I think I agree. Might upset the Grieveses, but the minister should see it as a privilege removed. Tell him, and then back it up with a letter. Jenny can type it for you.'

Chapter Eight

•

It was Sunday. The day of the cricket match. Finlay lay in bed, listening to the birds waking and going about their daily survival. It had been a good breeding season, lots of species having two or even three broods. He listened to a blackbird singing, the song not so intense and vibrant as the early urgency of spring. Finlay smiled. He thought the blackbird may have decided that singing no longer brought females, so he wouldn't bother that much. Last to rise were the house martins, usual with them, their mud nests crammed with youngsters as big as their parents. They seemed like children complaining about having to get up. The swallows rose earlier and, from his bed, Finlay could see them feeding on invisible insects flying over the ash trees at the top of the kitchen garden.

He got up, pulled on his shorts and shirt and went downstairs. It was just after five and he had to check on the young stock scattered in various groups around the farm. The house was quiet and still cool. The kitchen smelt of baking, butter and the sweet tang of milk. He drank some, cold from the refrigerator, poured another glass and cut some brown bread to soak in it.

Outside, the air was cool, but it needed rain to clean it. The earth was already looking dry, despite the flood. He checked his horse was comfortable and gave her some hay. He knew Old John would deal with her before he got back for breakfast. He thought about Jill and wondered whether she was awake yet, and whether she was excited about America. He reflected sadly on how she would have enjoyed the previous evening's tea time. Stables were a natural place of trysting somehow and he walked the length of them thinking that perhaps his great-grandfather had met Miss Charity Brake here one early morning before the world was awake. And whether he had felt the empty sadness of losing her, forced apart by the rigidity of what were then society's rules. Maybe Ron Drew had met his mother's sister, Bibby, here and come back to the stables alone, to mourn her death. He walked outside and splashed his face in the horse trough. There was work to do. In the distance he could hear one of the dairymen calling the cows in for milking. The day had begun. He stopped the pick-up on the big bridge, got out and looked at the river. This time of the morning, the river was crystal clear because of the light. In the bed of the river, clearly defined in eight feet of water, he watched the grayling watching him, ready to flee should he make a sudden movement.

The skittish Ayrshire youngsters capered around him, flinging their hind legs in the air, making mock charges at him. Beautiful agile animals, they were highly strung and temperamental. The Shorthorns he found still lying down in a break of oak trees. They eyed him softly but didn't rise and lay chewing their cud, burping softly. He walked in among them speaking softly, their huge eyes following him as he inspected each in turn. This particular bunch would have their first calf in September and would have to be watched closely from now on. The day was still cool and he began to wish he had come on Misty, rather than driven. There were not too many flies about and she would have enjoyed the ride. He drove to the north end of the estate to view the last bunch of the morning, another contented group of Shorthorns. With no oak trees to shade them, their red coats shone healthily in the sun. They were picking what little grass was available and paid him no heed. From where he was standing he could hear the milking pump of the Grieveses' farm. He could imagine Mr Grieves filling his thoughts with today's match. Janey, he thought, would be up already, feeding the calves and the few pigs they kept. He knew she would be at the match today, her mother keeping her on as tight a leash as ever. She knew she would be outshone by the Ward sisters and feel uncomfortable. He thought he disliked Mrs Grieves.

Back at the house Jenny was getting breakfast. She said a sleepy good morning to him and handed him a cup of tea. 'Where's Grandfather, Jen?' he asked. 'His Land-Rover was gone before I went out.'

'He was out all night. They netted the bottom pool for some mullet. Jack said there were some huge shoals, so they took the opportunity to catch a load for the market tomorrow,' Jenny said, still half asleep.

'Bugger! I would like to have done that.' He was disappointed he had not been asked.

'You weren't told because James didn't want you up all night. You work plenty hard enough already. How many eggs do you want?' she asked.

'You could have told me, Jen. I could have gone with them for a while at least.' He felt cross, suddenly.

'By the time I knew, you were asleep anyway. I came in to look at you and you were dead to the world. If you look at your tum, you'll see I tried to wake you.'

Finlay lifted his shirt and saw crosses drawn in lipstick over his stomach. 'Jenny, you bugger! I didn't feel a thing.'

'As I said, you were very tired. Better go and get that off, else your young ladies will wonder what you've been up to. See buggerlugs, you're not the great white hunter, ever alert. I caught you out,' she said. 'You didn't take me to see the otters!'

Finlay gave her a look that told her everything.

She smiled back at him and said, 'I know… I know.' She paused. 'Go get cleaned up and get Misty ready. I'll ride down and watch the practice before getting dressed up.'

'Will you do your hair how I like it?' Finlay asked, gazing at her.

'Of course I will. I'll put those Ward girls' noses out this afternoon. Just let them know you're just on loan.' She went to the mirror. 'Oh yes! I can see those little madams off any time I choose to.'

They had been at cricket practice for about half an hour when Jenny arrived, on Misty. She had obviously swum the horse over the river as her shoes, with laces knotted together, hung over the saddle. She was wearing a riding skirt and had let her hair down from the constraints of plaiting. 'Morning everyone,' she said, brightly. 'Are we going to win?'

'Touch and go Miss Jenny, as far as the cricket is concerned. But you girls will win the beauty contest!' Ron answered.

'Can you hold Misty for me, Jo?' she said sweetly, 'so I can see Kee bowl from behind.'

'Sure Jenny,' Jo Ward said keenly. 'Can I get up on her and take her around the ground?'

'You can try, but I doubt she'll let you. She's very much Kee's girl,' Jenny said, handing her the reins. She walked away and left Jo to it.

'Can we get on!' Mr Grieves said, impatiently.

The bowling commenced as Jo tried to get up on Misty, but she spun away from her. 'Can you hold her head please, Mr Drew?' determined to prove Jenny wrong, but the horse broke away from both of them and went to Jenny.

'Sorry Jo,' Jenny said. 'She's a bit possessive.' Jenny remounted and sat watching, making the right comments and offering encouragement to Finlay. She stayed for about three-quarters of an hour, then made her goodbyes. She trotted down the side of the ground and pushed Misty into a canter. They saw her go over the river bank into the water.

'Do all your family have to be so bloody superior, Finlay?' Jo asked smiling. 'Honestly! Even your bloody horses are stand-offish.'

When everybody had had a bat and the bowlers had flung a few up each, Mr Grieves gave them the batting order. Finlay was in at six. 'You can have a couple at the tail enders, Keith.' Finlay was happy enough at that. He knew he had to prove himself. 'Back here at one-thirty sharp, and for those of you not going home for lunch, it would be good if you didn't turn up smelling of strong drink. It's not pleasant for the ladies,' Grieves said, dismissing them as though they were in the army.

Ron dropped him at the lodge gate. 'I was sorry to hear about that Jill, but it looks as though you'll be busy with at least one of the Ward girls, if Jenny doesn't crab the deal. She put little Jo in her place this morning properly. Remember no strong drink lunch time. The ladies don't like it, which means old Chilly don't.' He drove away chuckling.

What lunch was available was on the table. Niney had said there would be plenty to eat later. George Goulding and Finlay's grandfather were in a rumbustious mood. Uncle Jack was reading the newspaper.

'How many mullet did you get, Grandfather?' Finlay asked, after shaking hands with the vet. He did not want to sound peeved that he had not been invited, but he must have done, for his grandfather answered that he thought he had needed sleep. It was not a night for getting wet and cold.

'About half a ton in the first haul and more than that in the second. Enough to get ourselves and Jack's cars replaced, anyway. I've never seen so many mullet come in on one tide. If we do it again, we'll have to get Ron on it as well. Some of them went nearly four pounds each.'

'Where's Alan, Sir George? I thought he was coming,' Finlay said.

'Coming to the ground. He has a surprise. He's bringing his new fiancée. A lovely girl, also in practice. We're all very pleased,' he said, beaming.

'Can't think all the ladies will be. You should see ours. They go all to buggery when he arrives. All stupid and girlie. It's going to break a lot of hearts in this neck of the woods,' Finlay said emphatically.

'Well, perhaps he'll get around the farms quicker. Not so much tea, cake and idle gossip,' Sir George said.

'We're going to the ground in Sir George's car, Kee,' his grandfather said. 'Perhaps you'd better get changed.'

It was as Finlay expected it to be, the short ride to the ground, very fast and a little hair-raising. They swept along the top lane at close to seventy miles an hour, leaving a vortex of flying dust behind them, the draught from the vehicle almost capsizing Miss Satchel on her bicycle, doubtless on her way back from some Chapel function. 'Do you think she was ever tupped, James?' Sir George said, conversationally.

'Not hardly! She used to have a very close lady friend, but she went off with a society lady from London. Made her more vicious-mouthed than ever,' Finlay's grandfather said.

'Was she a lesbian then, Grandfather?' Finlay asked, excited by the possibility.

'Well, she certainly didn't like men,' his grandfather answered.

Sir George parked the car carefully, looking at the wickets already in place. 'A five-pound note young man, if you can smash my windscreen.'

'Even Uncle Jack couldn't do that!' Finlay said, excited now.

Ron came walking over to greet them. 'Afternoon George, Boss. Looks like a good afternoon for it. Ready for the fight nipper?'

'Yes,' Finlay said, not quite as confident as he watched one of the Landford bowlers practising.

'Mr Grieves seems to be on his usual form, James!' George said, watching Grieves wagging his finger at one of the Romsey team. 'Young Janey seems to be shaping up into a nicely put together filly. What do you think, Ron?'

'Better ask the boy about that one George, so I'm told,' Ron answered, with mischief in his voice.

'Ah good. You've decided to take my advice then, Kee. Much better company than a plump of redheads,' Finlay's grandfather said.

'Wise words James. My mother was a redhead. Do you know we never had a complete dinner service in the house? It was nothing to be drinking out of a cup painted with roses, coupled with a saucer with bluebells. Two words out of place and you'd find the Wedgwood bouncing off your head.'

Cars were arriving, parking well back from the boundary. The lady supporters had obviously put enormous effort into their outfits, as the men watched them make their way to the seating in front of the pavilion. Niney and Jenny arrived in the Armstrong and walked elegantly to their seats in the front row, affecting not to notice the admiring looks. It was all very much a fashion show, which Niney stole easily. 'My God, James!' George said softly. 'Your Niney's a rare beauty. What an absolute vision.'

'Modest as well,' Finlay's grandfather said. 'She's probably told them the game can start now.'

Landford won the toss and elected to bat. Finlay was sent to field on the off-side boundary and two hours later had touched the ball twice. They batted well and rapidly passed one hundred and fifty. There was a small collapse of their middle order and suddenly, Finlay was called to bowl. His first ball was sent for four, his second, he thought, touched the bat. The wicket keeper caught it, slips shouted for a dismissal and the umpire agreed. The tall spare batsman walked past Finlay, back to the pavilion. 'It wasn't out! Ball never touched the bat. I bloody well wasn't out!' he hissed.

Finlay said nothing, but Ron said, 'You look in tomorrow night's *Echo* and you'll see you was out!'

They waited for the number nine bat to appear. There were some ironic cheers and clapping from his own side. He bowed and grinned. Even his own team mates didn't expect him to survive long. Finlay's ball beat him easily and the batsman gave him a nod of appreciation. The next ball came around his legs and he was out, bowled. The batsman walked past him smiling. 'Should have put you on earlier boy. You're nearly as good as me!' The last man came in and flailed his bat at the ball ineffectively, but didn't hit it. Neither did Finlay connect with the wickets. Uncle Jack came in from the other end. There was a clatter of wickets and Landford were out for two hundred and ten.

Finlay was sitting down next to Jenny eating egg sandwiches, when Janet and Jo joined them, bubbly and excited. 'Are we going to win, Finlay?' Jo said. 'You're a wizard bowler. That stupid old Grieves should have put you on earlier. Look at the stupid old sod now. He thinks he's Montgomery!' This brought laughter from Finlay's grandfather and Sir George and a sharp reminder from Niney not to criticize quite so loudly.

'Has anyone seen Janey?' Finlay asked, looking around at the spectators.

'Not here. She's having to do the milking. Pity that, having to leave. But that's the way of it. She might get back before it's over,' Finlay's grandfather said.

'I expect she's so disappointed. She should be allowed to mix more. Look at her mother sucking up to the minister. Frosty-arsed old stick,' Niney said disgustedly.

Both Ward girls started to giggle.

'You don't know that Niney,' Jenny said. 'Maybe old Grieves is miserable because she won't let him sleep at night and he's tired all the time.'

'If that was the case, he'd have a contented look like Jack, instead of eyeing up all the girls' legs!' Niney said in a dismissive way.

The game got under way again with Ron and Mr Grieves opening. Landford put on their spin bowler. Ron came down the wicket at him and put the first ball out of the ground, on to the main road. There was clapping and laughter. The first over cost Landford fourteen runs. Grieves played well against their pace bowler and the score went to sixty-four in a very short time. Grieves was out on forty-eight, with the score at one hundred and eleven. Ron was batting solidly. Pace or spin, it made no difference. Anything loose went to the boundary. It was a good start that was not to continue. Finlay was told to pad up and found himself walking out with the score at one hundred and thirty-two. Ron was still in place and came to speak to him. 'Just whack the loose ones nipper,' he said. 'Else the buggers will have us beat.'

There was a change of bowler and Finlay faced the chap who argued about being out. He came walking down the wicket, pretending to examine its surface and looked at Finlay, tossing the ball idly up and down. The message was clear: he had vengeance on his mind. The first ball lifted sharply and hit Finlay on the point of his left shoulder, making his arm feel numb and useless. It was very painful and the second, longer pitched, struck him in the ribs with a sharp crack. Finlay had the breath knocked out of him. 'OK?' the umpire asked. It had been a heavy blow. Finlay nodded and blocked the expected yorker, but the next ball hit him in the ribs and he went down on all fours, gasping. The umpire came running in. 'Can you continue boy?' he asked. Finlay couldn't answer. Ron joined them.

'You want to go off, nipper? Vicious bastard! I'll have him after the match.'

Finlay was helped to his feet. 'No. I got the measure of him, Ron,' he gasped.

'Well, it don't look like it from where I'm standing!' he said.

There was a ripple of applause when Finlay stood up, leaning on his bat. 'Come on then,' he said. 'Let's get the game won.'

The bowler sent another bouncer down which Finlay lifted over the keeper's head for four; the next, a lower skiddy ball, he edged between the slips for another four.

'It's OK, Ron,' he shouted. 'He's all Hell and no bloody notion! I've seen better bowlers at the primary school.' The bowler, passing him to go to his fielding position, said, 'All right clever bugger, I've seen better bats in a bloody cave!'

Finlay started to laugh but his ribs hurt too much to continue. He coughed and noticed there was blood in his sputum.

Ron and Finlay batted on steadily. The fast bowler had Finlay on the ground again with a ball which skidded off his face, making it bleed badly.

'I think you should go off, young man,' the umpire said. 'I'm going to put a stop to this!'

'And have him beat me?' Finlay answered. 'Not on your bloody life! He won't get me.'

Finlay was out on fifty-two. The spin bowler sent one down, there was the mearest touch on his bat and the keeper caught it. The umpire looked doubtful, but Finlay began to walk. 'It was out, Umpire,' he called. 'I did edge it.'

'Thank you then,' the umpire replied, relieved the decision had been made for him.

'You all right, nipper?' Ron asked as Finlay passed him. 'You look a bit pale around the gills.'

'Yes,' Finlay said lightly. 'Wasn't going to let him beat me.'

A little way from the boundary, Niney and Jenny came to meet him. 'Look at the state of you! Why didn't you come off? Are you all right? You look terrible.'

'Don't go on please, Auntie Niney. I think I'm hurt, I'm coughing blood up,' he said.

'Alan,' Jenny yelled. 'We need you. Kee's coughing up blood. Come quickly.'

Alan Goulding came at the run, grabbed Finlay's arm and led him to the pavilion. He helped him off with his shirt. The bruising was extensive and he felt around it, making Finlay grunt with the pain. Niney and Jenny were hovering, pale and anxious. 'Is he all right Alan?' Jenny asked.

'No, not at all right. Get my stethoscope from the boot darling,' he said to a rather gorgeous lady at his side.

Finlay's grandfather and Sir George arrived. 'Problem?' Sir George asked. 'Apart from the contusions.'

Janet Ward came creeping in quietly. 'You were bloody good, Finlay!' she said. Finlay coughed and gasped a great mouthful of blood.

'Hospital, I think!' Alan said.

Janet Ward was out cold on the pavilion floor. 'Pick her up, Jenny!' Niney said impatiently. 'All this over a game of cricket!'

Alan's young lady came back with the stethoscope and he listened briefly to Finlay's breathing. 'Punctured lung, I think. Let's get him to the car.'

The minister arrived, full of professional concern. 'You didn't have to walk you know, young man. The umpire didn't think you were out.'

'I knew I was out,' Finlay said, now very breathless. 'That's what counted.'

He was close to fainting by the time they arrived at the small hospital. He was laid out on a trolley and knew very little of what happened thereafter.

Through his half-closed eyes he could see Niney reading a book, beside the bed which was hard and strange to him. He knew he was still in hospital.

'Hello beautiful Auntie,' he said. 'What's for dinner? We didn't have much lunch remember?'

'Hello you bugger. If you weren't so battered about already, I'd give you the hiding of your life!' She bent over and kissed him. 'Does it ever occur to you to give in gracefully?'

'Did we win?' he asked.

'By two runs. And that's all I'm saying about the bloody cricket match, thank you.' She was smiling at him.

'How many did Uncle Jack score?' he asked, trying to move without hurting badly.

'I'm not speaking about it. Three sixes, first three balls and then he was clean bowled,' Niney said. 'It was enough though.'

'Good, I'm glad. Makes it worth it.' He tried to laugh, but it hurt.

'Grieves has banned Jo Ward from the matches. She emptied a milking bucket of Mrs Grieves's special lemonade over the chap who did this to you. Walked up behind him while he was sitting down eating and just emptied it over his head. It was bloody funny.' She started to laugh. 'I think that bugger Ron put her up to it. So that if he tried anything with her, Ron would've had an excuse to biff him one.'

'Not too much excitement then! She's a stroppy little thing. When am I getting out? What's exactly wrong with me?'

'Cracked ribs and some internal bleeding. You've got a drain in your chest. Probably be home in the morning. You should know that you've been offered a place in the team, but if you take it, Jenny will put you back in here.' It was a matter-of-fact statement.

'What time is it Auntie Niney? It must be late as it's dark outside?' he said, trying to shift to a more comfortable position.

'About one I think,' she said absently. 'I'll go and see about getting you something to eat.'

'One in the morning! No, you must go and get some sleep Auntie Niney. I'll be home in the morning. I can last till then.'

'If you're sure darling. I have to be able to go back and tell everyone you're awake. I'll come back in the morning to get you. Try and go back to sleep and don't give the nurses any flannel.'

'Thank you for being here, when I woke up,' Finlay said.

Niney walked to the door, looked back and blew him a kiss. 'Behave yourself, right!'

When he woke the next morning Finlay felt better. He could hear voices somewhere outside and was desperate for a pee and a cup of tea. He was dressed in a garment open all the way down behind him, so he found a towel, wrapped it around himself and walked out of the small ward.

A group of nurses were chatting together in what looked like a small kitchen. 'Any tea about ladies? And could somebody point me towards a lavatory?'

'You're not meant to be out of bed!' one of them said. 'Go back there at once! Somebody will bring you a bottle.'

He wandered out of the room and eventually found a lavatory. He wondered where his clothes were. He wanted to go home. A clock in the corridor showed eight-thirty and he knew his grandfather would be just coming in for breakfast. A nurse, sent to find him, could not have been much older than him, but she was sharp and bossy.

'You are supposed to be in bed until the doctor comes. Would you mind going back there now, please. At once if you don't mind!' She was surprisingly slim and quite pretty.

'What time does the doctor come round? Could you tell me please?' Finlay said, ignoring her sharpness.

He wandered back towards the room where his bed was. 'When he gets here!' she answered. 'We cannot have patients walking about, just pleasing themselves. Get into bed and stay there!'

He found a book in the locker beside his bed. He read for about an hour and got bored with it. He was pleased when he heard Niney's footsteps coming down the corridor outside.

'Hello you,' she said, sweeping into the room. 'Has the doctor chap been yet?'

'No Auntie. Did you bring any food?' Finlay asked.

The same sharp nurse arrived, obviously upset. 'No visitors until two this afternoon!' she said.

'That hardly applies to me, my dear. We gave the hospital to the town, now cut along to fetch the doctor,' she ordered. The nurse didn't move. 'Now!' Niney said.

'I've got your clothes with me. When I phoned they said you would be ready. Getting these people to shift their arses is bloody near impossible. Sitting about drinking tea and chattering,'

When the nurse returned, she began to apologize. 'I'm sorry Madam. I didn't realize you were one of the trustees.'

'That should be of no consequence!' Niney snapped. 'This hospital was put here for the good of the town, not so you and others could sit around drinking tea and chattering. Has this patient had any breakfast or even a drink? If I had more time I would go around the patients and check what's been happening.'

The doctor arrived, flustered. 'I'm sorry, Mrs Terry, you've been kept waiting. We're very busy.'

'Rubbish! There are more medical staff than patients here. I shall come in one day next week. This room is filthy! Now get on with the job you came to do. Which you said would be done by nine, and you, young lady, go and tell the chauffeur to bring the car to the front door.'

It was ten minutes later and Finlay was sitting in the Armstrong with Niney beside him.

'Take me home please Mr Brockett. Then you can bring me straight back. If those people are not off their bums, there'll be some sackings here today!' Finlay noticed her nostrils flared just like his mother's when she was really angry.

'Yes Miss Niney,' Mr Brockett said. 'Things not as they should be in the hospital?'

'A long way short Mr Brockett, a long way short,' she said.

As he got out in the yard, Niney said, 'I'm going back to the hospital now Kee. You're going to have to sort something out with Jenny. She's not best pleased over this.'

Chapter Nine

•

Finlay walked into the kitchen. Jenny was sitting at the table reading. She got up, gave him a very careful hug and the merest sort of kiss.

'Hello Jen,' he said, realizing at once that she was angry.

'I'll cook you some breakfast,' she said shortly.

'What's the matter?' he asked.

She put the frying pan on the Aga. 'How many eggs do you want?'

'Two please. What's the matter, Jen?' he asked again.

'How can you ask that? How can you be so completely stupid?' She wasn't shouting in the usual way when she was angry.

'I'm sorry. I don't know what you're on about,' he said.

'I'm on about the state you're in, and quite honestly, I cannot think what you think you gain by being so bone-headed obstinate. I'd like to put it down to stupid male ego, but it's deeper than that with you. It's almost a fetish, a need to be... well, I don't know what you think you need to be. The only one with massive principles I suppose. May be it's something to do with being virtually abandoned by your parents. You have to prove you're always right.'

'I still don't follow Jen,' he answered. 'Is this because I got a bit roughed up at a cricket match?'

'It's about getting thrown out of school because of your need to have things your way. Nearly drowning yourself in the river rather than lose your grandfather's fish. And getting yourself injured so badly over a game, you finish up in hospital. If you approach the Navy in the same way, you'll finish up a hero. A dead one and I will not be hanging around to watch! What on earth do you think it does to me? A performance like yesterday's. I wanted to die when you were on the ground. The whole thing was totally selfish... selfish towards me.'

'I don't know what to say, Jen.' It was all he could answer.

'Eat your breakfast!' Jenny said, handing him his plate. She picked up her book and left the room.

He was used to having Niney giving him a tongue lashing, but never Jenny. Upset by it, he wolfed down his breakfast and went to find her. She was sitting in the hall reading. He went and sat beside her.

'Look Jen, I don't even understand why I'm like I am,' he began.

'Jill telephoned earlier to say goodbye. She was upset that you weren't here. Have you given her a single thought since she went?' she asked.

'Of course I have. I am upset about it, of course I am. But there's nothing I can do. I wanted to blub about it yesterday but couldn't let myself. What do you want me to do?' Finlay said, exasperated now.

'I want you to realize that what you do has consequences with and to other people. Especially me, so please think before you do things. That's all I have to say on the subject. Now take your shirt off and let me see how badly you're hurt,' she ordered.

He was going to argue but thought better of it and began to undress. Jenny studied the bruising closely, finally looking at the cuts on his face.

'I want to be so bloody angry with you,' she said quietly. 'But I can't and it wouldn't be any use.' She sighed deeply. 'Why do we turn each other inside out?'

'I would never knowingly hurt you, Jen,' Finlay said. 'I'm sorry I'm a bit thoughtless sometimes.'

He sat in the big old armchair, the one they always used to share. He didn't need to ask. Jenny came and sat with him. 'It used to be the other way when you were smaller. You sitting on me,' she said.

Finlay could feel her breath on the side of his face and he buried his face in her hair. He thought he would remember this moment for ever.

'Will you be all right Jen? When I go to Dartmouth?' he asked. 'You know what I mean.'

'Of course I will, silly. Don't forget, I get your horse and pick-up and I'll steal all your shirts. What did you think I'd do? Pine away?' She laughed.

'No... seriously?' he asked.

'My love, if it gets too bad, I'll buy a house in Dartmouth. It would probably be a wise move anyway, buy a biggish place and convert it to holiday flats when you have finished there. But that's just a thought for the future. Right now I just want to cherish the moment.' She buried her face into his shoulder. 'I love your smell. Even when you were small you smelt gorgeous.' He felt her tongue on the side of his neck and shuddered. 'Sorry,' she said. 'I forgot you were a chap now.'

They stayed silently sitting together, their faces almost touching. The spell was broken by the sound of voices and bicycles crashing against the wall. 'Here's the coven, love,' she said smiling. 'They can't keep away, can they?'

'You don't mind?' he asked.

'I'd only mind if I thought for one moment one of them would replace me. Bed them all you bugger, if that's what they want. If I was their age that's what I would want.' She kissed his mouth. 'It's me you'll always love.'

As Jenny went to let them in she was shouting to them, 'I'm coming... ten seconds' wait won't hurt you!'

He heard voices. Janet and Jo, and Jenny telling them that he was tired and pretty knocked about, so there was no question of going outside and doing anything too energetic.

They came almost tumbling into the hall looking happy.

'Hello Finlay,' Janet said, looking at him. 'I've brought you these.' She handed him some books. They were what he would have described as not really his style, but he thanked her with enthusiasm.

'Jo, what on earth made you tip a bucket of lemonade over that bloke? He was a good bowler, doing what he was meant to do,' Finlay said.

'Mr Drew gave me ten shillings to do it. You should have seen the mess. Ham sandwiches floating on a tide of lemonade. Really spoilt their tea. Anyway, I'm sacked. I was fed up with scoring anyhow, and ten shillings is ten shillings,' she said philosophically.

'There'll not be much about the game in the paper. It'll be about you Jo! I was so embarrassed. I'm sure the *Echo* photographer took some pictures. Mother is incensed,' Janet said, sniffily.

'There's someone coming in on a pop-pop bike,' Jo said, ignoring her sister's condemnation and looking out of the window. 'He's quite something too. I wonder who he is?'

'God, you're such a bloody tart Jo Ward!' her sister said. 'Anything in trousers with you, isn't it?'

'You can talk! Finlay, she has your photo on her bedside table and says goodnight to it. Honestly! How stupid is that!' The scorn in her voice was enormous.

'You little pig-faced bitch!' Janet said, moving towards her with some intent. 'I'll bloody kill you for telling him that.'

Before they would have come to blows, Jenny arrived with the new visitor. 'Hey you two, behave yourselves at once! Kee darling, someone else to see you.'

It was the young keeper from next door. 'I just came in to see how you were, Keith. I didn't know you had visitors, so I won't stay.' He seemed a little shy.

'That's OK Bill. Stay and sit for a bit. This is Janet and this is Jo. Good job you came along. Janet was just about to do for her sister.' Finlay laughed.

'Good morning Miss,' he said, very correctly, to Janet. 'I already know this one,' he said, with evident distaste. 'She keeps setting off my traps. Nearly caught her the other day.'

'You shouldn't go round killing everything!' Jo said. 'I found a poor little animal the other day.'

'If I catch you Miss, I'll have to report you to the head keeper. You shouldn't be in our woods anyway,' Bill said, looking awkward.

'And you shouldn't be so bloody cruel!' she said, loud enough for Jenny to hear, who came quickly into the hall.

'Jo! You'll be sent home shortly if you keep this up. Come into the kitchen all of you. You can have some tea and biscuits and just calm down a bit. Honestly Jo, what has got you going now?' Jenny was clearly cross.

'He sets all the traps to kill things, and I think he's horrible,' Jo said, sulkily.

'Jo has been springing Bill's vermin traps next door,' Finlay explained.

'And throwing ride nets into the river,' Bill added.

'Oh dear! Jo, what are you thinking? You're going to make yourself very unpopular and get into trouble,' Jenny said.

'Well I don't care. It isn't right!' she said.

Nobody had heard Niney arrive. 'Hello everyone,' she said brightly and, seeing the mood, added, 'What's been happening? Good morning young Bill. Settling in up there?'

'Yes, thank you Madam,' Bill said, seeming ever more awkward.

'Jo has been springing Bill's vermin traps next door, and interfering with his work in his coverts,' Jenny said.

'Jo my dear, that's very naughty and you must stop it at once. It isn't you that has been kicking fox snares out here, is it?' she asked.

'Yes,' she answered.

Niney sighed. 'Jo my dear, how dare you interfere with what we do here? When my husband finds out it was you, he'll have you barred from coming on to the place. We've a project here to save a rare bird species. It's my project and you're undermining it. I really don't think you'll be welcome here again.'

Jo started to cry. 'I didn't know,' she snivelled.

'You stupid little tart!' Janet snapped at her. 'Now look what you've done. When I get you home I'm going to give you what for!' Janet was close to tears herself.

'Listen to me,' Niney ordered. 'Bill, could you bring yourself to have Jo with you? Explain about your job, if I can fix it with your boss? Just two or three days, perhaps?'

'I'll do it for you Mrs Terry, but I'd just as soon see her drown in the river myself. I hate redheaded girls. They smell bad,' Bill said, disgustedly.

'I don't want to spend time with him,' Jo said, sulking.

'Well. You'd better pack up now and go home Jo,' Niney said quietly. 'We cannot have people who, out of ignorance, interfere with what we do here. Perhaps you can explain to your mother, Janet. I'm very sorry but that's the way it's got to be.'

'I'll do it,' Jo said quietly.

'Good. Then come with me Jo and we'll find Jack and you can explain yourself to him,' Niney said firmly. 'I shan't be too long, Jen,' Niney said, as she left.

'Lumme,' Janet said quietly. 'Niney was pretty cross. Jo's not so bad really, Bill. Just a bit headstrong and she's quite clever. Do you really think that redheads smell?'

Bill gave her a broad grin. 'Only thing I could think of at the time.'

'I don't think Uncle Jack will wear it though,' Finlay said. 'He hates anti's with a passion.'

'Niney will work her magic on him, you'll see,' Jen said. 'She must like Jo an awful lot. Normally, over something like this, it would have been a case of "out and stay out!" Where do these silly girls get their ideas from?'

'I'm glad really. Three days with her out of my hair. Make her work hard Bill, but don't be too horrible to her,' Janet said.

'I have to go and do some work. Thanks for the tea. I hope Mrs Terry can sort Jo out. Would be a shame to see her in trouble.'

After he had gone Jenny said, 'He's a nice-looking chap, don't you think, Janet?'

'Yes, he has a nice smile as well. Who knows? Jo might even take to him,' Janet said, relieved the drama was over.

'Shall I get you both a sandwich or something else?' Finlay offered.

'Don't worry Janet. He's not having a mental breakdown. It's boredom. Yes please darling. You could make up some cucumber sandwiches for me.'

They sat around the kitchen table chattering and eating sandwiches.

'You get your results tomorrow Finlay, don't you? Poor Jill'll not have hers for another week. Mine, by the end of the week. It's hard waiting when everything so depends on them,' Janet said.

'What will you do, Janet?' Jenny asked. 'Stay on and do A levels?'

'No, I'm not that academic Jen. If I get the passes I shall go and do a horsey course somewhere, then come home and set up my own yard. Whatever I do, it'll be with horses,' Janet said. 'If you get your exams Finlay, what happens to you? You're surely too young to go in the Navy at the moment?'

'Work for some more passes over the next year, and then go, a year this September if they accept me. I might have to spend some time down there before that so they can assess me, see if I'm what they want,' Finlay said. For the first time, he wondered what he would do if he proved unacceptable.

'What would you do if they said they didn't want you?' Janet asked.

'Be a doctor or an engineer, I've not really thought about it. Going in the Navy now means they educate me up to a degree. I think enough's been spent on me already,' he said.

'Well, you two,' Jenny said. 'I haven't done a thing all day, so I'd better get on and pay some bills. You can go as far as the stables Kee and no further. No exertions or coughing.'

'Come on then Finlay. Let's go and talk to Misty. You look pretty tired already and it'll be lovely to speak to you without my bloody sister.' Janet helped him to his feet. He felt a little sore and sorry for himself.

When they were halfway across the yard, Finlay asked her about the photograph. 'Where did you get it from?'

'I took it from an upstairs window, when you were going past our house one day. Now you'll think I'm a bit silly about you. It's just there's no one else around of our age.'

'Well thanks for that!' Finlay laughed.

'I'll show you what I think in the stables,' she said, looking at him, challenging again with her green eyes. 'Oh shit! Here comes Janey Grieves... no chance to hide now.'

'I wouldn't anyway. I like Janey. She's been very good to me and has an awful lot to put up with. You be nice to her,' Finlay ordered.

'You haven't been shagging her as well, Finlay?' Janet whispered.

'Shush, she'll hear you! And no I haven't.' He smiled his most innocent smile.

'Hello, you two. Are you all right Finlay? Heard you took a bit of a pasting,' Janey called.

'Just a bit sore,' he said.

'Hello, Janey,' Janet said, without any enthusiasm.

Finlay could see there was something very wrong. Janey had been crying and she looked very pale.

'What's happened?' he asked.

'Finlay, I'm trying to stay very calm. I've left home and I need to speak to your Auntie Niney. Can we go indoors please?' Her voice was shaky.

'Do you want me to make myself scarce, Finlay?' Janet asked.

'No Janet!' Janey said. 'I've done nothing to be ashamed of and I don't mind who knows!'

'Niney isn't here, but Jenny is. She won't be long. Come in Janey. Go and find Jenny,' Finlay asked Janet and, as she went on ahead, Finlay asked Janey what the matter was.

'I can't go back there, Finlay. Not ever!' She began to cry.

'You won't have to Janey, not if you don't want to. If somebody's hurt you, I'll bloody do for them.'

Jenny met them at the door. 'Come in Janey,' she said quietly, seeing the state of her. 'Come in the kitchen. Kee, go and get the brandy.'

They sat Janey down in the kitchen and Finlay gave her a small brandy, remembering what happened last time.

'I'm trying to stay very calm about this Jenny. I don't want to be anything but strong,' Janey said firmly. She began to remove her blouse and showed them some heavy weals across her back.

'Who did this to you, Janey?' Jenny asked, shocked.

'My father. The minister tried to touch me and when I told my parents they said I must have led him on. Finlay, they said I was a whore.' Her composure left her and she began to weep.

In a silent rage, Finlay went to the telephone and asked for the local surgery. 'I'd like a doctor to come as soon as possible please. It's too difficult to explain. No, it's Miss Janey Grieves. She's at our house... no, she's not ill... she has been assaulted... thank you.'

Jenny and Janet were trying to comfort Janey. 'Do you want to make this formal, Janey? I can telephone for Sergeant Beech if you like.'

'I don't know what to do Finlay, I really don't,' she sobbed.

'What did the minister actually do to you? I'm sorry to keep on but I must know what to do. Where the bloody Hell is Niney?' he said, exasperated and angry.

'He shoved me down on the calf-shed floor, put his hand up my dress and tried to get my underclothes off. He put his fingers inside of my...' She began to weep. 'It made me feel dirty.'

'I'll bury the bastard!' Finlay said. 'I'll see him in gaol for this.'

He went to the telephone, rang the police station and eventually spoke to Sergeant Beech.

'Sergeant Beech, it's Keith Finlay. I have Miss Grieves with me. She's been assaulted. Can you come please? …yes, the Methodist Minister, and her father has beaten her with a stick… yes the doctor is on his way. No, we'll keep her here… thank you.'

'Do you want anything, Janet? Tea or something? I could make it for you?' Finlay asked.

'No, not yet anyway. Some brandy would be good though,' Janet said, looking distinctly pale.

'Not too much Kee. The police may need to speak to her. This is terrible! What if Janey's father comes to take her home?' Jenny said, worried.

'I'll knock his head off his shoulders, if he tries!' Finlay said sharply.

The doctor arrived first and calmly took control. 'Can you go into the hall please and wait there, Keith? Take Janet with you. It is Janet isn't it? You all look so alike.' He smiled.

In the hall Janet took his arm. 'Christ Finlay, this is terrible. I feel like Cassandra. Remember? I said something like this would happen? Bloody Hell, I feel almost guilty!'

'Don't be daft Janet. Here, have that brandy to steady you a little.' Finlay handed her the glass.

'Lumme, Finlay, you really are a calm sort of person. Must be great to be so assured. This may not be the most appropriate time to say this Finlay, but I really fancy you!' She even managed a slight smile.

'I know. You say goodnight to my photograph,' he said.

'Bastard! This brandy's good. Can I have some more?' she said. Her face was getting flushed.

'When this is settled. You have to stay coherent. Then you can have what you will. Here's the police now,' Finlay said, going to intercept them.

He explained briefly to Sergeant Beech and a policewoman who was with him what had happened and told them that the doctor was with Jenny in the kitchen. Beech knocked on the closed door and waited. Jenny's face appeared through a tiny opening. 'Let the doctor know I'm here please Miss Jenny.' He then went with Finlay into the hall and began to question them, the policewoman taking notes.

'Well, you've done well young man. What happened to you?' he asked.

'Cricket,' Finlay said.

Some half an hour later the doctor came through with Jenny and Janey. 'I've given her a sedative, Sergeant. We'll put her to bed here.'

'Can I just ask one question, Doctor?' said the sergeant. 'I need it from her you see.'

'Just one then, no more,' the doctor answered.

'Who did this to you Janey?' Sergeant Beech asked quietly.

'The minister and my father. They called me a whore,' she answered, seeming dazed.

'Come along Janey. Let's get you in bed for a sleep.' Jenny and the doctor led her away upstairs.

'Get on the wireless, Constable. Tell them to pick them up now,' Sergeant Beech ordered. 'When you telephoned, Keith, we sent a car to the Grieves' farm. They'll have them in a minute or two.'

'Good!' Finlay said. 'Can you arrange for that psalm-singing bastard to have a good kicking at the same time?'

The sergeant made no answer.

The doctor reappeared. 'Sorry you two, I need to speak to the sergeant. You'll have to go outside please,' he said.

'Is Janey OK, Doctor?' Finlay asked.

'Yes. She's sleeping by now and Jenny is with her. Come along then, outside please.' He ushered Finlay and Janet out of the hall.

'We'll sit on the front steps Janet, else Niney is going to go barging in. Not that she won't anyway, but at least we can stay her a little,' Finlay said.

Outside was getting cooler but it was still uncomfortably hot. The martins and swallows drifted almost lazily across the yards, replete after a day's obviously good feeding.

'I can never make up my mind whether I like blackbirds or house martins best,' Finlay said, sitting on the steps by the front door.

'Those are swallows with the house martins, not blackbirds,' Janet said scornfully.

Finlay laughed. 'I know that dopey. I was watching the martins. Do you know the difference between the swallows and martins?'

'I'm sure you're going to tell me,' she said. 'Clever bollocks!'

'Well I was going to. But since you choose to be so bloody rude you can go on in ignorance.' He shuffled up closer to her and put his arm around her shoulders. 'What a bloody day.'

'It could get better if we went to see your horse,' she said.

'I know it would, but I must intercept Niney. Can you get out of your house at night?' he asked.

'Yes! Of course I can.' Her eyes became bright.

'Meet me by the big bridge at about one o'clock. If we go to the stables now, it would be quick and rushed. Not what I want for you. Anyway, Niney may come back at any moment,' Finlay said, hoping she would agree.

'Come and meet me by the end of the footpath. I'm a bit scared about walking all that way in the dark on my own. You really mean it, you will come?' she breathed.

'Of course I will. Bring a towel with you and we can have that swim together at last!'

Finlay heard the whine of the Armstrong on the top lane. 'Thank Christ for that! Niney's sorted out the hospital and your darling sister, and now she can sort this lot out!'

'What do you mean? What's it to do with her?' Janet asked.

'Well, the Grieveses are tenants of ours. If he goes to gaol, the tenancy will end. There's also the question of where to put Janey. And if he doesn't go to gaol, do we want him as a tenant?'

'You can't throw him off if he doesn't go to gaol, surely. If he is innocent,' Janet objected.

'He hit Janey with a stick. I want him gone and so will Niney,' Finlay said angrily.

The Armstrong swept into the yard. 'What the bloody Hell's gone wrong now?' Niney said, before leaving the car.

'Come and sit for a minute Auntie. We're all right. Come over here. I don't want to be shouting it out for the whole world to hear. Where's Jo anyway?'

Finlay didn't know how or where to start. Whatever way he approached it, Niney was going to want somebody's head or even balls in this case.

'What have you done?' she asked.

'The Methodist Minister tried to get in Janey's knickers. She got the blame and she's now upstairs under sedation. Her father beat her and said she was a whore. The doctor is speaking to the police and Jenny, last seen, was making sure Janey is OK. That's about what's happened, and whatever happens, I want the Grieveses off this estate.'

Finlay had rushed it out and before Niney could interrupt, asked, 'Where's Jo?'

As Finlay spoke, Niney went white. 'Jo is with Bill, happily feeding the pheasant pens. He'll bring her back here.' She paused. 'Go through that again darling, slowly.'

Finlay did as he was asked.

'Where are Grieves and the minister now?' she asked.

'In the police station, I think,' Finlay said.

'Are their cows milked? Do you know?' Niney asked.

'I don't know. Does she ever milk, I mean Mrs Grieves?'

'She may not be in any fit state to. You may have to go and do it. I'm sorry, but whatever happens, they'll have to be done. Stay here and I'll find out what's happening. Jesus Christ! As if there isn't enough to do already.' She went indoors.

'Why do you have to milk the bloody cows, Finlay?' Janet asked, scandalized by the idea.

'Not their fault, is it? They can't be left to suffer and there are calves to be fed,' Finlay said absently, thinking of dealing with Mrs Grieves under the circumstances.

'Come in here you two.' They heard Niney call.

Everyone was sitting in the kitchen. 'Sergeant Beech is going to see what's happening at the Grieveses. He's a little concerned she might have become unstable, so he doesn't want any of us up there,' Niney said.

'Do they even know where Janey is?' Finlay asked. 'Mrs Grieves was already certifiable before this. Christ knows what she'll be like now. Is Janey OK?'

Doctor McQuitty chuckled. 'I know my job Keith. You don't have to worry about Janey.'

'We may be able to bail Grieves, if he was only hitting Janey. Then he can go and milk his own cows,' Sergeant Beech suggested.

'You make it sound as though hitting Janey was nothing. Did you see her? She looks as though he hit her with a drain-rod!' Finlay objected.

'What's a drain-rod Keith?' Doctor McQuitty asked.

'A thick bamboo cane with brass ends. I could see the shape of it, Doctor,' Finlay answered.

'If you have one, can I look at it please?' McQuitty asked.

'I'll get one now, there's a set in the stables.' Finlay left the kitchen.

He was very angry as he walked across the yard. Determined in his own mind that Grieves was going to pay for his actions, as for the minister, if the law didn't deal with him, he would.

Finlay returned to the kitchen and put the drain-rod on the table

'I see what you mean Keith. Maybe you should look for one up on the Grieveses' place, Sergeant,' McQuitty suggested.

'I'll go up there and see what's happening,' Beech said. 'You'd better stay Constable, you never know with these religious buggers. I wont be long.'

'Well Keith, thanks for being so level-headed. If you need anything more Niney, just call me. She should sleep at least until eight, just keep her calm. I'd better get back to the surgery.' McQuitty was shown out by Niney, and Finlay heard them talking for some time before he heard the doctor's car leave.

Both alone, Janet said, 'I suppose our one o'clock date has gone by the board?'

'No, I'll be there.' He smiled. 'I'll say I'm going to fish for some sea trout.'

'Good Finlay. I need to have a long talk with you over something,' Janet said looking him square in the eyes.

Niney came back, looking tired. 'This is an almighty balls-up! We'll just have to wait and see. You're meant to be resting all day Kee. Get to bed early.'

'Tell us about Jo, Auntie. How did you swing that one?' Finlay said. It all seemed a long time ago.

'Jack was OK. He was a little cross but glad to know the culprit. He explained gently where she was wrong. Harry was a bit more cross, but he sent Bill and Jo off together, last seen getting on famously. She's only guilty of caring in her own way. I've a meeting tomorrow and I'll see some nurses and that bloody idle doctor gone; Doctor McQuitty's in full agreement. I'll just go and see what Jen is doing. I think you'll have to eat fish and chips together darling. Somebody can pop into Romsey.' Niney always had everything organized.

'I'll go and put Misty out. The flies have pretty well packed in for the day,' Finlay said, getting up.

'I'll set the table Finlay,' Janet volunteered. 'I take it I'm staying for fish and chips, as my sister has made off with the gamekeeper. She really is a trollop, that girl!'

The mare welcomed him noisily. 'OK, OK you wicked witch. Just another demanding female, that's what you are,' he said to the mare softly. 'John's been spoiling you. Come on, you can have a pick about in your paddock.'

He turned the mare into the field and watched her rolling, shaking herself. She came trotting back to him. 'I know. You're getting bored. I'll take you out tomorrow darling.' The mare pushed her face close to him and took his breath, snuffling into his chest, giving him a lick with her tongue and tasting the salt of his sweat. He was half-way back to the house when Ron came into the yard.

'Sent for! Niney! In no uncertain terms.' He smiled. 'What's happening?'

Finlay briefly explained. 'Poor little wench. Bastards! Who's looking after the cattle?'

'I expect we might have to. Sergeant Beech is up there now, seeing what the crazy old bitch is doing,' Finlay sighed.

'She's madder than a cut rat. Doesn't deserve a gal like Janey! Better see what Niney wants,' Ron said, walking beside him to the house.

She asked Ron whom he could spare should the need arise to look after the Grieveses' animals. 'Old John can milk and turn his hand to most things, Cyril and Malcolm are the same. They could go up there and I'll arrange what has to be done. What time's the old man get back tonight?'

'Ten o'clock train. Mr Brockett's going to pick him up,' Niney said.

'Stand him down, Niney. I'll get the old man. Give me time to tell him what's happened,' Ron volunteered.

'Thanks, Ron. That would be better, perhaps,' Niney said.

'Where's Janey, Jen?' Finlay asked.

'Having a bath. I've sorted out some of your mother's clothes for her to wear. She wants to burn hers. She's OK now. Just very angry,' Jenny said, sadly.

The telephone rang. Niney was first to it. 'Yes Sergeant…

Well yes… I suppose so…

I don't think she'll want to anyway…

She is past eighteen. She can make up her own mind…

That'll give him time to get his story straight for his wife…

Thank you Sergeant. I'll call you if he comes here.'

Niney replaced the telephone.

'They're both out on bail at the moment. The minister is insisting that Janey encouraged him. It's her word against his and he's walking home. Grieves has been taken back to look after his animals and been told not to come here after Janey on pain of being locked up. So the cows are settled. What a bloody mess this is! How are we going to tell Janey, I wonder?' Niney gave an exasperated sigh.

'I'll do that bit Niney,' Jenny offered. 'It'll be her word against his and it's up to Janey if she wants to bring an action against her father.'

'If the minister is walking home, maybe he'll have a fit of conscience and jump off the bridge. The tide'll be running back,' Finlay said

'You mustn't say things like that, Kee,' Niney said severely. 'You'd feel terrible if he actually did go in the river.'

'I would not! Best thing he could do!' Finlay said. 'Janey will have to go all through it again if she has to go to court.'

'She'll cope. She's pretty angry and very, very hurt,' Jenny said.

'The good thing is she is still a virgin, the doctor said, which shows she never had the experience to encourage him. The bastard bruised the Hell out of her though. He should be done for attempted rape. We must stop talking about it. Janey might be down in a minute. Who wants something to eat?' Ever practical, Niney took command.

'What would you like Janet?' Finlay asked. 'We seem to have lost your sister.'

'I'll go and see if Janey wants anything,' Jenny said.

'That's a good sign,' Niney said when Jenny came back to report that Janey wanted some food.

Jenny took the pick-up and tore away up the drive.

'God, that girl is a bloody mad cap,' Niney said. 'Kee, get a couple of bottles of that white wine the Americans left. I'll ring Jack. Let's have a party to cheer this place up. Janet, put the big willow pattern dish you'll find in that cupboard on the Aga-top to warm. We must cheer Janey up. Then telephone your mother and say you're eating here and somebody will run you back home and find out if your sister is back yet. Ron, you can open the wine,' Janet and Finlay started to giggle.

'You get it organized Auntie Niney,' Finlay laughed.

'Less of your cheek, you. You're not too big for a good clout around your ear!' she said. 'Go get a couple of cans of peaches and sing "God Bless America" while you're doing it!'

Janey walked into a happy roomful when she arrived with them. She was wearing a green dress that Finlay recognized as one of his mother's posh frocks and thought it certainly looked better on Janey.

'I don't want anyone to say anything, if that's OK,' she said. 'I'll just say thanks to all of you.'

'That's the way Janey. You can stay here for as long as it suits you, love. Jen will be back at any moment with the food,' Niney said.

Uncle Jack arrived, bringing Jo Ward and Bill in with him. Already briefed on the phone about Janey, he was bonhomie and full of fun.

'What sort of day have you had, Jo?' Niney asked.

'Fantastic. Bill's so clever. He knows more than you, Finlay, about wild things.'

'Well get yourselves washed up and sitting down,' Niney ordered.

'Is it all right if I stay, Madam?' Bill asked.

'Only if you stop calling me that. Makes me sound as though I'm running a house of ill repute, instead of a mad-house. In here I'm Niney. Outside, in front of anybody, I'm Miss Niney. Now get your hands washed and sit down.'

'Bill shot so many squirrels today, I lost count. He cut their tails off to send away for making fishing flies. He's such a good shot. Never ever misses,' Jo piped up.

Bill looked embarrassed by this sudden adoration and shuffled uncomfortably on his chair.

'I bet you miss lots of times, Finlay,' she continued.

'Oh shut up Jo!' Janet said impatiently. 'Only this morning Bill was a slavering beast who killed anything that moved. Just be quiet. You make yourself look stupid!'

'You're the stupid one. Fancy saying goodnight to Finlay's photograph every night! Mother says Janet has to keep her hands above the bedclothes as well!' Her sister squealed with delight.

'You little bitch!' Janet cried, but Uncle Jack and Ron could not help laughing loudly. Even Janey had difficulty covering her amusement and Finlay pretended to take no notice whatsoever.

'Jo! Be quiet! Janet sit down and take no notice. How your mother copes with you I do not know. Stop laughing you two. It only makes her worse,' Niney snapped.

'She spits in the fire when Mother isn't watching and when the loos were frozen she peed in the hand basin,' Janet said.

Ron and Uncle Jack were now almost crying with laughter. 'Told you about redheads nipper,' Ron said. 'But you wouldn't listen!'

'Well I just don't know!' Niney sighed. 'Thank Christ you're not a girl, Kee!'

'She's thankful anyway!' Jo got in. '"Goodnight Finlay, you're so lovely,"' she mocked again.

Verbally trounced and without the opportunity to inflict physical violence on her sister, Janet sat down quietly seething. 'Fucking little bitch,' she muttered.

Jenny came in with a large newspaper parcel. 'Sorry I've been so long. There was a queue,' she said. 'Hello, have the girls been fighting again?' she said. 'It's like living with a couple of cats. Spend your time keeping them apart.' Jenny found them fun and amusing.

'I'll drown the pair of them before long,' Niney sighed. Jo made to say something. 'Shut up you little sod!' Niney snapped at her and then to show she really wasn't that cross, adjusted the collar of Jo's shirt. 'Shall we eat?' she sighed.

'Having trouble with the bitch pack, Kee?' Jenny asked him brightly. 'They do get a bit scratchy this time of year. Boredom probably.'

The meal progressed to its finish, everybody chattering happily. Even Janey joined in laughing, talking about the cricket match.

Afterwards Niney gathered up the Ward sisters and Bill to take them home. Friends again, their volatility forgotten. 'I think you should get on to bed Kee. Where you should have been all day, truth to tell.'

'Yes, it seems to have been a long day. Goodnight then everyone.' He gave Janet a questioning look.

'See you later, Finlay,' she said. 'You get your results tomorrow. See you then.'

As he left the room, Ron and Uncle Jack settled down to finish the wine, and Jenny eased Janey into the hall to talk. She would have to give a statement to the police in the morning about the day's events.

Finlay, in the quiet of his bedroom, knew he was very tired. His ribs hurt and he wondered if he would wake for his meeting with Janet. The evening had been fun, amusing and informal, which was probably just the thing Janey needed, he reflected.

Chapter Ten

•

'Wake up buggerlugs.' Finlay was vaguely aware of Jenny shaking him. 'You've almost slept the clock around. It's breakfast time.'

'What time is it?' he mumbled.

'Gone eight long since. The post has been and it looks as though your results have arrived. Are you going to get up?' Jenny asked.

'Is Janey all right?' he asked, getting up and pulling on his clothes.

'Yes, she's downstairs eating breakfast and talking to Niney. Come on. We're all waiting to see how you have done,' she harried him.

'I'd better wash, Jen,' he mumbled.

'Well, that'll be a first!' she answered. 'Do I get a kiss?'

'Of course!' He kissed her already smiling lips.

'"Goodnight Finlay, you're so lovely,"' she mocked. 'Come, hurry up.'

'I suppose this is the first day of the rest of my life,' Finlay said. 'Bugger the wash! I'll have a swim later. Let's go and see what I've got.'

They walked into the kitchen together. 'Come on for goodness' sake! We've been waiting to know!' Niney said, very impatiently.

Finlay picked up the small cardboard tube, sitting ominously on his breakfast place mat, prised off the top and withdrew the green paper certificate inside.

'Well bugger me! I've got them all. Even art!' he exclaimed, handing it to his grandfather.

'Well done, well done my boy! Fantastic stuff,' he said. 'These are the marks out of... down the side?'

'I suppose so,' Finlay said, now enveloped by Niney and Jenny.

Janey was looking over his grandfather's shoulder. 'You've done brilliantly, Finlay! I'm so pleased for you. That'll be a smack in the teeth for the school.'

Jenny wrested him from Niney. 'Oh you clever sod!' Her tears fell over his face.

'Well you deserve it Kee, darling,' Niney said. 'You worked very, very hard. You didn't pick up a fishing rod for more than two months and I know how hard that must have been.'

'I think we'll have a celebration,' Finlay's grandfather said. 'What would you like to do, Kee?'

'Go down to the beach hut when the barley is finished?' he asked.

'Nothing more than that?' He smiled.

The telephone rang. 'Good morning Mr Robinson,' Niney said into the machine. 'Yes, with some style. I'll get him.' She handed the telephone to a hovering Finlay. 'It's your old teacher,' she said.

'Morning Sir,' he said. 'Yes Sir, thank you Sir, it's yours as well as mine... ninety-three per cent Sir... if you would like to come for lunch that would be great... thank you Sir for all of it.'

'How are you this morning, Janey?' Finlay asked. 'I'm sorry, I should have done that first. Asked how you were I mean.'

'Can we talk about that later, do you think?' she replied. 'Let me get the police bit done first.'

'Well you look better in my mother's clothes than she does,' Finlay smiled.

'Thank you kind sir!' she said.

'We must wait until we know what's happening with Janey. Before we make any decisions about another stay at the beach hut, though in truth there is no reason why she shouldn't go down there with whoever goes. We shall have to see,' Finlay's grandfather said.

'I don't want you to be put out in any way by what has happened. It would make me feel terrible,' Janey objected quietly.

'Whatever the outcome Janey, we'll support you. You were very supportive of Kee, when he went to school. I certainly haven't forgotten that,' he said.

It was another hour before the police eventually arrived. There was the usual black Wolseley and another unmarked pre-war Rover.

'Come with me into the hall, Janey,' Jen said. 'I'll stay with you while they talk to you.'

Sergeant Beech arrived and introduced a detective inspector from Southampton. The inspector spoke to the woman constable in a patronizing manner. He reminded Finlay of the headmaster he had known.

'There's been a development overnight that you should know about. The Reverend Martin Jenks jumped from the bridge at Totton last night, on his way home,' he said solemnly.

For a few seconds Finlay tried hard to go along with what the inspector obviously thought was a serious moment, but he couldn't stop himself from laughing out loud.

'Keith!' his grandfather said, shocked at Finlay's amusement.

'Where did they pull him out? Calshot Spit?' he said, trying to control his mirth.

'He was not drowned. Apparently he waited for some time before jumping. There wasn't much water under the bridge and he landed on the concrete below.' The inspector was glaring at Finlay.

This pronouncement only added to Finlay's mirth. 'You mean the tide had gone out by then?' He was now choking with laughter. 'So he's a fraud or a bigger bloody idiot than even I first thought.'

'I find your laughter inappropriate,' the inspector said. 'The minister has very serious injuries.'

'Stop this, Kee!' Niney said sharply. 'Good God, whatever are you thinking about?'

'I'm thinking about the state Janey arrived here in yesterday Auntie, and the way the bloody so-called reverend buggers up people's lives. I hope the bastard rots in Hell!' Finlay said, raising his voice.

Hearing the anger in Finlay's voice, Jenny came running in. 'What's going on?' she demanded, standing next to Finlay and gripping his arm tightly.

'The bastard who tried to rape Janey jumped off the causeway bridge last night, and this pompous twat thinks I shouldn't find that funny!' Finlay said.

'Well it isn't necessarily funny Kee. But it's good news. Where did they fish him out, off the Needles?' she asked in a matter-of-fact way.

'Go and look after your horse Kee. And you're supposed to be looking after Janey, Jennifer,' Finlay's grandfather said quietly and sternly.

Finlay was half-way to the stables when Ron's Land-Rover came into the yard. 'Hello nipper. Is Janey all right? Thought a reaction may have set in by now.'

'She seems OK Ron. Ate a good breakfast and has her colour back. Have you heard about the minister?'

'It's all over everywhere. Couldn't even kill himself properly. It'll prolong the agony for that little wench though. Expect everyone'll be feeling sorry for him now. Some poacher was under the bridge waiting for a salmon to come through. Pulled him up on to the bank and telephoned for an ambulance. Needs his arse kicking. Should've left the bastard to drown,' Ron said angrily.

'I've just been flung out. I laughed like buggery when that copper came in and told everyone. Niney went for me,' Finlay sighed. 'She'll give me a good roasting when the coppers have gone.'

'That'll be the day!' Ron laughed. 'Go and have a look around the young stock on your mare. She'll be over it by then. I'll let them know where you are.'

'Thanks Ron,' Finlay answered. 'How long before the barley's ready?'

'Another three weeks I shouldn't wonder. Be a good crop if the weather holds.' He climbed back into his Land-Rover and left.

Finlay went to the bottom end of the estate first, which meant riding out through the village and over the railway. A train being due just after twelve made him push the mare on. She'd a horror of trains and he wanted to be there and back quickly. Coming towards the Post Office he saw the usual gaggle of women gathered outside talking. He said a polite, 'Good morning,' as he reached them.

'I suppose you're happy now the minister is seriously injured?' he heard one of them say.

He reined in the mare. 'No I'm not,' he said. 'I'd be happy if he was dead!'

'He be crippled for life, you know.' Miss Satchel said.

'Then you'll be able to commiserate with him, you being one of life's cripples.' He turned the mare to go and began to move away.

'That Niney Fortune don't mind how many harlots she has under her roof, it seems,' Naomi Phillips said loudly. 'The redeemer sees all you know!'

'Well, I hope he saw just how funny it was when Jenks jumped off the bridge when the tide was out. I know I did.' Finlay laughed aloud and trotted away as a large pebble hummed past his ear.

He was out for nearly two hours before the flies became a problem for the mare. He turned for home and began to hurry the horse on.

As he was coming to the big bridge he saw Janet coming the other way on her bicycle. She waved as she saw him.

'Are you very cross with me for not turning up? Didn't wake up, I'm so sorry. Did you wait for very long?' She looked contrite.

'Two hours! I got very cold,' he lied.

'Please say you're not angry with me. I'll make it up to you.' She looked at him from under her lashes.

'Where are you going now?' he said.

'Home. Your place is filled with police. I just grabbed my bike and came this way hoping to see you. To say sorry,' she said.

They stopped on the bridge and Finlay got down.

'Finlay, I'm so sorry I didn't turn out. It wasn't that I didn't want to. I just didn't wake up.'

Finlay put his hand around her. 'Do you know, I didn't either!'

'Oh you sod!' she shouted. 'All the time you were laughing at me, let me go.'

'I could have stayed quiet for longer.' He laughed. 'If I let you go, no biting.'

'I don't bite. Only when I mean it.'

'I'll chuck you up,' he offered. 'She'll let you, if I'm here.'

They walked back towards the house, Finlay pushing the bicycle. 'Heard about the minister?' he asked.

'Yes, the postman told us. I just burst out laughing. Cassy went all pi and Mother said I was wicked. I don't care, he deserved it,' Janet said.

'Same with me. Niney is going to give me Hell,' Finlay sighed. 'I don't know what the outcome will be though I expect Janey will stay with us for a bit.'

'Oh Finlay, I forgot! Your results?' she said suddenly.

'Yes, got them all, even art for Christ's sake!'

'That's wonderful Finlay! Will you celebrate? Last night was great. Even Janey enjoyed it. Jo is a cow, but I love her, even though she says awful things.'

'Like keeping your hands on top of the covers?' he said.

'Shut up!' she answered, blushing heavily. 'If you hadn't gone to sleep last night you could have done it for me.'

Finlay suddenly felt sad. 'I'd really like to have some idea what Janey may be feeling.'

Janet shuddered. 'I'd feel dirty, like Janey said. To have somebody force themselves on you like that. I want you, because it would be natural, and nobody else. Jill said it was like a huge balloon inside you and then it goes bang. You sort of lose control. She said the feelings were exquisite. I can't imagine that what happened to Janey was anything but awful.'

'I hope it doesn't put her off men,' he said.

'It might. Jill was affected by going to bed with another girl. Had some idea she was a lesbian. Like catching a disease. At school, they get so intense. All that suppressed sexuality coming out. Having a big argument if one them so much as speaks to another girl. Couldn't really be bothered with it,' she said scornfully.

'So you don't go in for two girls together then?' Finlay asked, amused.

'Much too normal for that, and anyway I've always found if you want something doing properly, you'd much best do it yourself.' She laughed at him with the almost inevitable challenge of her green eyes. 'Maybe you could prove otherwise?'

The Grieveses' car was in the yard.

'I think we should stay out of it,' Janet said. 'Especially you Finlay. Any delicate negotiations going on, you'd probably wreck them.'

'Well! Thanks for the vote of confidence!'

'You'd only want to bash him and that isn't what's needed at the moment,' she said, seriously.

'Clever little thing, ain't you,' he said fondly.

He put the mare in her stall, sponging her off with cooling water and was putting her fly rug on when Niney arrived. 'Can you two find something to do? James is trying to sort out what's to happen about Janey.'

Janet gave Finlay a knowing look. 'I said we should stay out of it. Is he thinking of taking Janey back?'

'No and I have to go. You'll find out later what we've decided.' She turned and went back towards the house.

Janet was sitting on a hay bale. 'What shall we do Finlay, and don't say the obvious.'

Finlay gave it some thought. 'Let's go down to the main feeder and walk to the river. I've never really studied its bottom. Will it matter if your shoes get wet?' he asked.

'What about the creepy crawlies in there and how deep is it?' She didn't seem enthusiastic.

'I'll make it interesting, I promise,' he said.

'I don't know anything about fishing rivers, Finlay,' she said.

'You don't have to know anything. Probably best if you don't. Sometimes people like me, who think they know everything, miss the obvious. I'd value what you think.'

'Wow! You only think you know everything, Finlay!' She pretended amazement. She walked across to where he was tidying up his mare's stall, and put her arms around him. 'You're a super bloke sometimes, Finlay,' she said.

They drove out to the big bridge in the pick-up and walked to the top of the main feeder. The sun was hot on their backs and they were sweating freely by the time they reached the muddy area that had once been the feeder's inlet. He explained to her how he intended to control the flow in and she nodded, saying nothing. He wondered if she was bored already. As they walked downstream he pointed out the level of silt to be removed and again she said nothing. By the time they reached the newly repaired sluice, Finlay decided she was bored and he'd best find something else to do. They sat on the top of the sluice, their feet dangling above the stream bursting under the gates.

'How much are you going to spend on this?' she asked suddenly.

'What it costs I suppose,' he answered.

'It will need to be pretty. The part we've just covered is nothing more than a canal,' she said. 'I want to draw you something. When we go back I'll show you. Can I be involved Finlay?' she asked, very seriously.

'I'd love you to be, Jan,' he said, just glad that she wasn't bored.

'That talk I wanted with you, we can do that now. That's the second time you've called me Jan. I want us to be friends, as well as everything else Finlay.'

'You see Jan, you see things that I take for granted, I'm glad you're interested.'

He lowered himself down into the stream water. 'Slide down and I'll catch you,' he said, holding up his arms to her.

'How deep is that?' she said, alarmed.

'It's only just above my knees. Come on, trust me, I won't drop you.' He laughed.

'I trust you Finlay, but you can be a bit of a bugger.' She let herself go and was suddenly down in front of him.

'Jesus! That's bloody icy!' she gasped. 'Finlay, we're going to have to be careful. About getting me pregnant.'

'Why are you saying that now?' he said.

She looked at him quizzically. 'I can feel that you want me. Even though we're frozen.' She felt him growing against her. 'What can't speak can't lie,' he said and they began to kiss. She pushed herself into him, working herself from side to side the better to feel his passion.

'God Finlay! Don't get me pregnant. Can't we go up in the grass somewhere?' She could hardly speak. Her breathing was so violent.

'Let me get up again and I'll pull you up,' Finlay said, his senses battered by her need.

'Finlay, Janet! Where are you?' They heard someone calling above the rush of water, swirling around their bare legs.

'It's Jo. What on earth is she doing here?' Janet said, still trembling and twisting her hips against him. 'Stay quiet. She might go away.'

But she was coming closer. 'Here,' Finlay called, stepping into deeper water which swirled up to his waist.

'That's put an end to that!' Janet said, angry but smiling as well.

'Where are you?' They heard Jo calling impatiently. 'Don't play about. I know you're hiding.'

'Over by the sluice,' Finlay shouted, all thoughts of passion gone.

Jo appeared above them. 'What are you doing down there?' she asked.

'Studying the bottom of this stream,' Janet said, her voice as cold as the water around them.

'Good, help me down Finlay,' she said, sliding into the water. It swept her feet from under her and she gasped with the sudden shock of cold water. She slipped off the concrete sill on her bottom and went under the surface. Finlay grabbed her and made her stand.

'Bloody Hell, I'm soaked now!' she said, pushing Finlay away, her curly hair suddenly straightened and wet with water. 'You might have said how strong the current was!'

'Oh shut up Jo! What are you doing here anyway? Why aren't you with Bill?' Janet snapped.

'Why? What were you two doing? Trying for Love in a Cold Climate? Bill told me to bugger off. I told him off for shooting a sparrowhawk. He's a pig anyway!' She began to shiver.

'Last night he was wonderful! Go and do something on your own!' Janet snapped.

'Come on. She'll only take a chill. Let's get to your house,' Finlay said.

'I'm not going home!' Janet said firmly. 'She was stupid enough to fall in!'

'Oh sod it!' Finlay was impatient with them both. 'Get back to the truck and you can get dry in the stables.'

As he lifted them both up to the top of the sluice sides, his ribs suddenly gave him enormous pain, 'Shit! Something's gone again,' he groaned. He staggered back to the pick-up. 'Hurry up!' he ordered. The girls began to argue who was going where. 'I am not riding in the back,' Jo sulked.

Finlay started the engine as Jo sat on the grass. 'Get in Jan! I've had it up to there with her,' he ordered.

'You've gone a funny colour Finlay,' said Jan.

He didn't answer. Finlay had lost patience with both of them. Driving into the yard he went indoors quickly, bent almost double, and went upstairs. There seemed to be nobody in the house. He wished he knew what was happening with Janey. Lying on his bed, the pain in his ribs began to subside and he breathed easier. He lay there listening to the sounds of the house. He remembered the first time he had listened, when he awoke after the first night he had slept in his own room, the night he realized that this was his haven.

A group of noisy sparrows argued and fought high up in the bed-room chimney, sending small particles of grit into the fireplace. They had somehow breached the defence of the wire mesh that was meant to keep them out. He suddenly became aware that the constant back-ground twittering of the house martins was not there. Neither could he see them from where he was lying. Gingerly, he got up and went to the open window to see where they were. He smiled to see them sweeping low around the stable yard, inches from the ground. Groups of them swept in and out of the buildings, swinging around corners and low over the fly-ridden muck heap. It was going to rain. When they flew so low it always presaged rain and Finlay hoped for a gentle rain that would plump up the barley and freshen the wheat. He stripped off his damp clothes and got under the blankets, his ribs still painful but bearable. The sparrows had called a truce and the only sounds now were the distant hum of a tractor and far away the rush of the hatch pool.

He recognized the sound of the back door closing and the mumble of voices. It was too far away to recognize who it was. He was almost asleep when he heard Jenny's footsteps on the passageway.

'What's the matter Kee? Why are you up here?' She came to his bed-side and sat on the edge of his bed.

'I hurt my ribs, so I came to lie down. I was tired as well. It's been a funny two or three days,' he said, stroking her arm.

'Janet's down in the kitchen, sitting alone and looking lost. If you're feeling better perhaps you should come down. I sent Jo to find you. Where did you leave her?' she asked.

Finlay explained what had happened, and how finally his patience had run out. He just wanted to be away from them.

'They are lovely, but very wearing. Better kept apart I think. Come on darling, get up and send her home or have the good manners to be with her,' she said, and left him to dress again.

Finlay got up and went downstairs again. He felt vexed. Though good manners dictated what he felt he had to do, he thought back to the time not long ago, before this sudden influx of women in his life, when the only person he had to please was himself. He felt a little resentful of their intrusion.

'Where is everyone, Jen?' he asked, when he entered the kichen. 'What's happening about Janey?'

'Her father came to take her back, but she wouldn't go. For the moment she's going to keep Granny company and stay there. James and Niney have taken her to get some clothes as her father refused to send any. As far as the minister's concerned, he's made a statement to the police. Janey was a willing participant in what happened. So it's as I said. His word against hers. It would mean a court case. She has to decide which way she wants to go. It's a bloody mess!' Jenny said.

'Is Grandfather going to give him notice? We don't want him here surely?' Finlay said. It was stated more than a question.

'Difficult one. He could appeal and that would bring more problems. Giving his daughter a beating is not sufficient grounds for getting him out,' she sighed.

'Jesus Christ!' Finlay snapped. 'That bastard pays three pounds an acre rent, which doesn't even go partway to the upkeep and we can't get him out? That house should go to Ron Drew, and the buildings would be useful for our youngstock in the winter.'

'That's not your grandfather's way and you know it. Much best to let the problem sort itself, galling as it may be to you. Tenants are still our responsibility, good or bad,' Jenny said firmly.

'Jenny's right,' Janet said. 'You're very angry at the moment. You mustn't set yourself up as some kind of robber baron. Don't sacrifice your kindness for people like that. Now, if you'll get me paper and a pencil, I could show you what I've thought about your muddy stream.'

Jenny gave her an approving look. 'Well said Janet! Look in the roof Kee. You'll find your mother's paper, paints and everything with it. I've got to get this bed linen up to Granny's. Can I take your pick-up?'

'Yes, of course. I didn't know my mother had inclinations towards art,' he said, surprised.

'Well, that's all it was really, an inclination,' she said. Janet giggled.

Jenny gathered up a large parcel in her arms. 'Tell Niney, I'll be back as soon as I've done. There's trifle in the fridge and you, Kee, stop being such a crosspatch!'

'She doesn't like your mother,' Janet said smiling, after Jenny had left.

'What makes you say that?' asked Finlay.

'Oh come on! Niney said something about your mother the other day to Jenny, and she didn't even answer her. Anyway she's so possessive about you, she thinks you're hers. If anyone says anything the slightest bit critical about you she bites their head off!'

'That's your imagination working overtime,' he said, getting up.

'Don't get me wrong Finlay. She's lovely, kind... Jenny's just a bit tricky about you. That's all.' She followed Finlay out of the room.

They made their way to the top of the house, up the barely used staircase and into the roofspace.

'Wow!' she exclaimed. 'What a place!'

The roof on the south side had huge reinforced glass panels allowing the light to flood the whole area. The air was dry and hot and smelt of dust and age.

'What a studio this would make,' Janet exclaimed. 'What's all this old furniture about?' she asked, removing a dust sheet from a small Pembroke table and stroking its mahogany top.

'It's from the rooms we don't use I suppose. Now there's no such thing as servants it has to stay up here. This is where they used to live, up here. I suppose, now they're gone, the furniture they looked after lives here.'

'It's a wonderful place. Look! I can see our house from here and lots of the river,' she exclaimed, excited. 'Finlay, I can see your muddy stream. I can really see what to do with it now!' She turned and looked at him, smiling. 'If I ever married you this is where we'd live and have our bed under this window. It would be like having the stars for a blanket.' She moved around the dormer windows, excitedly telling him what she could see. She squeezed between the packed-up furniture. 'Come and look Finlay. I can see ships in Southampton docks.'

He eased his way past packing cases and furniture covered with heavy linen cloth and, next to her, looked into the distance. 'We'll get a telescope up here, Jan,' he said, infected by her enthusiasm.

'Have you ever been up here before?' she asked, almost scornfully.

'Only a couple of times Jan. I don't see things the same as you. You look and see a picture. I look and see the barley nearly ready,' he said.

'Don't be so bloody stupid!' she snapped. 'You who look at otters for hours. Who can tell what bird is what just by the way it flies. You must be able to see what I see. It's not being soft to see things as an artist does.'

'Blimey Jan! That's a bit profound. Don't be impatient. Show me what you see,' he said, aware that she was serious.

'Sorry Finlay,' she said quietly. 'I got a little carried away. It just amazes me you've only been up here a couple of times. Honestly, you mustn't take all this for granted.'

She sighed and shook her head. 'You really don't see, do you? I'll have to marry you one day to save you from yourself, you silly bugger.'

Finlay didn't know what to say, as they walked back to the large roof window.

'Just here, Finlay,' she said and put her arms around him.

They kissed and touched easily. 'Get something to lie on,' she said, her voice sounding dry. Finlay led her to the stored carpets on the floor. 'No! Under the window, Finlay. Find something.'

He flung a heavy drugget on the floor and she lay, pushing her shorts down and stripping off her shirt. She struggled momentarily with her bra, and then she was naked, pulling him down with her. Her small breasts were firm, almost turgid in his hands and mouth. She was urgent in her demands and when he kissed and touched her copper curls between her thighs, she suddenly began to moan. She tasted as sweet as fresh milk as he struggled to remove his own shorts. At last they came loose and he was free and tasted again the milky sweetness of her. She trembled then lay still, 'Now, now,' she gasped.

From somewhere in the house a door slammed and they heard voices. 'God! Not again!' Janet said. She pulled on her shorts and blouse, searched for her bra and stuffed it quickly into the drawer of the Pembroke table.

'For goodness' sake Finlay! Make that go down again,' she giggled.

'Is that you up there, Kee?' They heard Niney shout through the ceiling of the room below.

'Yes! We're looking for some paper and paints that Jen said were up here,' Finlay shouted back.

'By the wall at the back side of the house. You'll see them by an easel leant against the wall. Come down when you've got them and spend some time with Janey. She's a bit fragile,' Niney called. They heard a lavatory flush beneath them.

'OK!' he shouted back.

Janet was giggling quietly. 'Well! It was good for me. How was it for you?' She started to giggle louder.

'Bloody frustrating and uncomfortable,' he muttered, finding, at last, an obvious artist's case.

'One day you'll actually get to have my virginity. When we go down, if you'll pardon the pun, I'll have to stay still so no one sees a large wet patch on my shorts.' She clung to him again. 'Do you know Finlay, I actually think I love you.' She was laughing at him again.

'You, Madam, are saying that just so that you get this place.'

'Not at all! I just want your body, but we are going to have a problem,' she said, as they went towards the staircase. 'A question of accommodation I think.'

Finlay burst out laughing. 'Would be good to find out maybe. Given enough time that is!'

They kissed again, a deep long moist kiss. 'You taste of me Finlay,' Janet said, her green eyes holding his. 'Much better than a do-it-on-your-own session.'

The kitchen door was closed against them, a sure sign that discretion was called for. Finlay tapped on the door. 'Can we come in?' he asked.

'Not yet! Janey is changing. Shan't be too long,' Niney cried.

'We'll go outside,' he said.

Janet and Finlay went into the yard. 'It's going to rain. Look at the martins.'

'You don't get me on that one again, Finlay,' Janet laughed.

'Seriously. Look how low they're flying. The air pressure has fallen so the insects are low down. I promise I'm not pulling your leg,' he said.

The martins and swallows were dashing past, lower than waist high.

'Never mind the bloody birds. I want to speak about just now,' Janet said. 'What you did was great, it really sent me. I know I have a big bum, but the other bits are very small and I don't think it'll work. I'll have to speak to my cousin.' She stopped him interrupting. 'We must never get in that situation again without the means to stop me getting pregnant. I don't want that, but I wanted you like I've never wanted anything else. My whole instinct demanded it, and that sort of thing means unwanted pregnancies. There must be other ways of stopping babies, but nobody speaks about it. It's just too stupid.'

Finlay knew she was right. 'I had to find out about it from Ron,' he said. 'Nobody would speak to me. Why do they find it so hard?'

'I'm glad I've an older sister, I really am. My stupid mother didn't even tell me about periods. There was a girl at school and because nobody told her what was going to happen, she was in a terrible state.' Janet sounded disgusted.

They wandered down towards the stables, an instinctive love of horses pulling them there. They sat together on the dung-heap wall. The air was cooler and grey clouds were moving up from the west.

'Do you believe in God, Finlay?' she asked seriously. 'Caroline Keighley said your family were Pagan. Are you?' 'I don't think about it. I know what I see around me is special. But people like Jenks spoil it. I think the whole thing's bollocks!' she said emphatically. 'It does more harm than good. Look at the state Janey's in. My life is going to be horses and the ridicule of organized religion!' She jumped down from the wall and walked a few paces away from him. 'I really wanted that bastard Jenks to have drowned. I hope he never comes out of hospital, but that's thought terrible by adults.'

'I find the whole thing confusing…' he began.

'You Finlay? Confused? I don't believe that!' She laughed.

'Honestly. When that copper told us, I burst out laughing. He was shocked by that, and Auntie Niney went for me. I still think it's funny. A bit rough on his wife perhaps, but that's all.'

The first drops of rain began to fall. They seemed to hit the dusty yard and bounce, forming tiny dust-covered balls. Janet's white blouse became spotted and streaked with warm raindrops. She remained standing, kicking at a loose stone in the yard's surface and watching him.

'Do you think you and I will come to anything Finlay? I mean together?' she asked.

'I'm comfortable with you Jan. We can talk about anything and we're friends as well as… well, sex as well,' he said, smiling at her.

The warm rain became slightly heavier. 'Let's go in the stables, Finlay. My boobs will be showing if my blouse gets any wetter.'

Finlay could see the pink of her nipples through the wet fabric. They leant on the half-door watching the rain and smelling the earth dampened now. 'That's such a wonderful smell,' he said, taking in lungfuls. 'If it just rains like this for a while it'll fill the barley beautifully, without making it go down.'

'Why are you going in the Navy, when you love this place so much? I don't want you to go away. I know I'll go on to somewhere, but I need to know you're here.'

He put his hand down the back of her shorts and caressed her firm bottom, running his fingers down the crease. It was almost an absent-minded touch.

'I don't know. I just want to. It's something I have to do. The thought of leaving here tears my guts out, but we have to grow up,' he said. He started to remove his hand.

'No!' she said. 'Leave it. I like the warmth. I love to feel your hands on me. It feels reassuring.'

They watched, amused at a group of house martins on the dung-heap wall, washing themselves in the warm rain and chittering excitedly, able at last to clean their feathers.

'Do you want something to eat?' Niney called, from the kitchen window.

'OK!' Finlay yelled back. 'Come on, Jan, we'll have to run,' he said.

'Can't. My tits'll fly all over the place. Remember?'

'I could harden them up a bit,' he offered, laughing.

'I'll hold them!' she answered shortly. 'Else we won't make it to the house!'

They arrived breathless and spattered with rain.

'Hi Janey! Been shopping?' Finlay said, asking the obvious. He had never seen her dressed in anything feminine before.

'Morale booster, Finlay,' she answered. She looked drawn, her eyes had lost the light that had always been within them.

Niney was busy preparing food. 'Janet! Can you get the table laid please? Lay it for eight. Jack may be early now that it's raining.'

'Would you like to help me with a little job of making a new fishing river Janey? After tea?' Janet asked.

'Yes of course. But I need to speak to you Finlay. I think you can answer some of my worries. How I came to this. You and I know each other well enough for you to be frank with me.' Janey's voice had a sudden catch in it.

'Now?' Finlay asked.

'Yes. There's something I have to know about men. I couldn't ask your grandfather.' She seemed very serious.

'Provided you don't give me lines if I get it wrong,' Finlay said, trying to lighten her mood.

It made her smile. 'I was hard on you at school Finlay, for your own good. You were an ill-disciplined sod and I had to show you. No special treatment, just because we were chums.'

'Well thanks Janey. I knew it was for my own good. Funny it didn't feel like it at the time.' He laughed. 'Come along to the music room. We can talk there.'

Niney was looking concerned. 'Are you sure that Kee's the right person to ask?'

'Absolutely Niney. He's probably the only one,' Janey said.

In the music room, alone, Janey relaxed. 'Everyone is saying that I led him on, and that it was my fault...'

'That's balls...' Finlay started to say.

'Listen. I need to know. About the other day. Did I lead you on? Did I somehow initiate what happened? If I did, it was unintentional and it's making me wonder whether I did do something the minister misconstrued. I'm beginning to wonder whether the whole thing was my fault.'

'It was me, Janey. Wholly me. Think about it. The first time I'd ever seen you in anything that didn't conceal what was underneath! Suddenly, there you were with little left to the imagination. It just made you so different. You weren't that severe, bossy girl. You were just like other girls...' He paused, not knowing how to continue.

'I wanted you. It was my fault, if there was fault. It may have left you a bit confused. It didn't me. It was me who started it. It was me who tried to get your clothes off,' he said, taking her hand in his.

'I didn't try to stop you though, when perhaps I should... but it made me feel happy... not dirty.'

'Of course! That's what it's meant to do... and at that moment I was the right person. That minister would never be that. Now, I look at you. Dressed sensibly and looking great, I would do it again. You're beautiful Janey. You look great in slacks!' Finlay said, hoping he had explained properly.

'Trousers are the first step to perdition. That's what I was always taught. They might show a girl's shape,' Janey said, with a touch of bitterness.

'Well bring on perdition for Christ's sake! Your bum looks great!' he said.

He led her to the door but she made him stop to give him a hug. 'Thanks Finlay. You're a good bloke. Don't ever change. The world needs sinners like you, if sinner you are.' They kissed briefly, and more for devilment than anything else he ran his hand over her bottom.

'You bugger Finlay! And thank you,' she said, her voice suddenly shaky again.

'Being a sinner is much more fun.' He laughed.

'Well, I'm here for the rest of the summer, and feeling your hands on me, I intend to be a bit sinful myself. I think we should think about that.' She let him go and they walked back to the kitchen.

'Well! I don't know what you two were talking about, but it seems to have worked. He can be a charming little sod Janey. All blue eyes and innocence, but he can talk sense,' Niney said, touching his shoulder in passing.

'We spoke about sin, Auntie Niney,' Finlay said, making it a joke. His aunt looked aghast at him until she saw Janey blushing.

'Could you take me into the music room Finlay? Talk to me about sinning, now you're the expert? Might be rather fun,' Janet said.

'Not in the music room, my dear,' Auntie Niney said, affecting nonchalance. 'The floor needs sanding. You might get splinters in your bum.'

'I love being with you all,' Janey said.

'We love having you. Two or three days' quiet with Granny will see you back to your normal self. I'm quite certain your mum and dad will come to their senses and see the wrongness in what they think. You can have your university correspondence left here by the postman. Jenny and James will help you with that side of things. You'll have nothing to worry about. We'll see to that.' Niney was emphatic.

'What are you going to study Janey?' Janet asked.

'Journalism, I think. I've been offered a place with the *Echo* in Southampton, so I think I'll be all right. What about you?' she asked.

'Horses! And with respect to your feelings Janey, I'm going to become a crusader against organized religion. Become an eccentric horsey bird with strong opinions about everything. I might even become a firebrand politician and fight the evils of Socialism,' she said, half joking.

'Keep the ordinary people in their place!' Finlay said.

'Exactly! Save the stupid buggers from themselves!' Janet said.

'Here's Jenny back,' Niney said, wiping some of the mist from the window. 'Good girl, she's got Granny with her.'

'Great!' Finlay said. 'I'll get a cushion. Unlike you two, she's a bony bum!'

'Hello my little cock-bird. Give me a kiss please,' Granny said to Finlay.

She sat down at the head of the table. 'Well Niney. Where's the brandy bottle?'

Brandy was produced. 'So you're coming to live with me young Janey? Most welcome! What's happened has put you away from they bloody church people. Bastards! Look on the bright side my pretty one. Probably saved you from a boring life and a cold marriage. Get out now and find yourself a proper man. You needs to be put away a few times wet and well ridden, my dear.'

'Granny!' Niney said. 'I expect Janey would like to avoid that sort of subject.'

'Not really, Niney,' Janey said. 'I know Granny's right. My life so far has been more than stilted.'

'You get your book learning done, Janey. Then you can make your own life. And as for you young Ward, you do the same. Now. Are we waiting for anybody? I could do with something to eat, that brandy has gone to my head,' Granny said, pouring another large helping into her glass.

Halfway through tea, Finlay's grandfather and Uncle Jack arrived. They smelt of the rain and the wet earth. 'Everything settled then Niney?' Finlay's grandfather asked.

'Yes James, of course. We'll have to get her a driving licence so Janey's mobile. Shouldn't be a problem. She's used to driving a Fergie.'

'Were the fish excited by the rain Uncle Jack?' Finlay asked. 'How many today?'

'Twenty-one Kee. First of the grilse coming in. You should go out first light and try with a dry fly. The rain will have cleared by dawn, and all I've got tomorrow is people from London, so you can have the river until eight,' he said.

'I'll go to Nutsey pool I think. They hang in there beautifully. Any orders for fish?' Finlay asked. 'If not, I'll only take two or three.'

'The confidence of the man!' Jenny laughed.

'Can I come with you?' Janet asked. 'Jill said you were a wizard with a rod.'

'I'd like to come as well,' Janey announced. 'I want to see what the lure of fishing is.'

'Well I don't think...' Finlay began, sounding doubtful.

'Of course you can girls!' Niney said. 'He'd love to show off how wonderful he is. Wouldn't you darling?' It was said in a way that indicated he had to agree.

'Yes of course,' Finlay said. 'I'll leave it at a couple then, Uncle Jack.'

'Girls or fish?' he answered back.

'You take them both, my beauty,' Granny said, smiling at him. 'Then when they're older and working away, they'll have something to remember. I'll pack Janey off early. There's nowhere better than the river at daybreak.'

'What time Finlay?' Janet asked.

'Half-four I think. Do you want me to meet you?' Finlay said.

'No, I'll wait on the big bridge, and you'd better not forget this time!' she said.

'This time?' Jenny said. 'We didn't hear about the first time, did we Niney?'

'I don't think we were meant to Jen. Not looking at Janet's face. You've been caught out young lady. Little midnight swim arranged was there?' she said mischievously.

'He didn't wake up!' Janet said, embarrassed.

'Alone on the river bank at midnight! I wouldn't give him a second chance, Janet.' Niney laughed.

'Well! Come along you girls,' Jenny said, around nine-thirty. 'Time to get to your beds I think. And you Granny, you're half-way puggled. You'll let the side down in the morning.'

'I'll be up before light, Madam,' Granny slurred. 'I'm never late.'

That night, in bed, Finlay thought about Janey. It would be good to have her settled again and happy. He marvelled at her seeming composure about being thrown out by her parents. Then Janet claimed his thoughts, the milky whiteness of her skin where the sun hadn't touched and where it had, the explosions of freckles. With this in his mind he drifted off to sleep. Somewhere in the chimney there were the last arguments of the sparrows.

Chapter Eleven

•

Janey came quietly into the kitchen at around quarter past four the next morning. She was dressed in khaki shorts and a white blouse. The shorts, which normally were made to stop short of her knees, were folded upwards.

'Hello Janey. Now that's an improvement on your trousers even.' He kissed her cheek.

'Thank you,' she said softly. 'What do you think from the rear?' She turned, looking over her shoulder for his reaction, and was pleased to catch his admiring look.

'Very good, Janey,' he laughed. 'Do you want anything?'

'No thanks. Granny fed me tea and toast. She remembers everything.'

'I just love her. She's a cunning old bugger and twists Grandfather around her little finger. I bet she was autocratic when she was younger. You can see where Niney gets it from,' Finlay said.

'She thinks you're lovely. You look like your great-grandfather,' Janey said, innocently.

'They were lovers for a long time. From when they were about our age. He left her lots of money. Caused a bit of a stir.' Finlay laughed.

'Really! The way people talk, you might think that sex was something that didn't happen, but I suppose it must have done else we wouldn't be here.'

'Come on, we mustn't be late,' Finlay said. 'The gear is in the pick-up already.'

They drove down to the big bridge and waited. Through the half-light they saw Janet approaching along the path towards them. When she got closer, they could see she was carrying her shoes and walking in the longer grass.

'Washing my feet!' she said noting their puzzled look. She sat on the bonnet of the pick-up trying to pull her shoes on to her wet feet. 'Sod it!' she said happily. 'Shan't bother.'

They walked downstream together, watching the light coming from the east as the first birds awake started to sing to it.

The sky in the east showed golden and clear. The dust of the past few weeks washed from the air and, coming from that direction, a flock of birds were silhouetted in sharp contrast.

'What are those birds, Finlay?' Janet asked.

'Curlews. Going down to the estuary to feed on the mud. They follow the tide back. Beautiful aren't they? Now stay low, below the bank. We need to see if any fish are moving.' They reached Nutsey pool, which looked dark and almost forbidding in the poor light. They crouched down on their haunches watching the water swirling from the back end of the pool. Along the far bank were elm boards supporting the bank on its long bend. Wild gunera hung drooping towards the water, dripping the last of the evening's rain from their huge leaves, the drops making surface bubbles which swept towards them.

As the light reached the pool, the water showed green and deep along the boards but the shallows on their bank showed so clear that individual stones showed clearly their shapes and the huge shoals of fry that moved among them.

'I feel like we're the only people left in the world,' Janet said softly. Another skein of waders flew overhead towards the salt estuary, calling and piping to each other, their pinions audible even from their great height. A fish showed briefly at the end of the boards, rising to a small leaf in the eddy at the end of the bend. Finlay cast at it and watched the fish come to the fly, turn away and sink out of sight again.

'He nearly took it!' Janet whispered.

Finlay cast again, only for the fish to show again and touch the fly with its nose and sink away, interested in the offering.

'Clever sod!' Finlay said to himself. He changed the fly as quickly as his trembling hands would allow. This time his offering was a large buzzer which he smacked down on the surface hard.

'That wasn't very delicate Finlay. Christ!' Janey yelled. The fish had taken the fly with an enormous jump, and in turning down, had hooked itself well and had dived deeply, bending the rod in an arc, the line now cutting through the water. As the fish passed them going downstream, they saw its silver side flash in the water, turning it across the current. The fish came clear of the water again and landed with a heavy smack on its side. It powered around the pool below them and then slowly came upstream again. Finlay eased his line towards himself and netted it fairly easily.

'Well done, Finlay!' Janey exclaimed. 'That was a wonderful show of reverse psychology, beautifully done!'

Janet was silent. 'How did you know?' she said at last. Finlay killed the fish and washed his hands in the river. It was six or seven pounds of firm muscle, its flanks covered in sea lice, and it smelt of the sea.

'That's a grilse. Been in the sea for a year,' Finlay said, his voice shaking.

'Why are you trembling, Finlay?' Janet asked.

'Still do every time I catch one. Never ever got over the wonder of it I suppose.'

He bit the cast, tied the original fly back on and greased the line again. 'If I catch another, would either of you like to land it? You know, let me hook it and give you the rod, then you'll know why I love it so much?' Janet looked doubtful. 'You Janey, you have a go.'

They crept upstream slowly, keeping below the bank and watched the main pool for some time before Finlay saw a fish on the far side, moving against the boards.

'Look there.' He pointed. 'You can see his tail come above the surface. He's a bit bigger so if I hook him let him go. Don't try to hold him back. He'll probably go tearing back downstream.'

Finlay's first cast missed by some distance. 'Come on Finlay, concentrate!' Janet said. His second cast was too strong and the fly went sailing into the boards, the line collapsed in coils and the fish turned downstream, took the fly and sped away upstream.

'See! You don't know everything,' Janet yelled triumphantly.

Finlay handed the rod to Janey. 'Try to hold him in this pool. You'll have to walk up in the water to see where he is.' The fish was out of sight around the bend. Janey waded along the underside of the bank well above her knees. 'Lift the rod up Janey. Let him fight that for a little while,' Finlay said, trying to remain calm, but wishing he had the rod in his hands.

'Lumme, do they always pull like this? I'm barely strong enough to hold it,' Janey gasped. The fish made to run upstream but turned again to the power of the rod and circled the pool, flashing its side and once, leaping clear of the surface. Grim-faced, Janey guided the fish away from the flow, only to have it charge towards her, almost colliding with her legs. She screamed with either fear or excitement and jumped out of its way.

A few more circles of the main pool saw it on the surface. 'Gently Janey. Bring it down to the net. Keep as still as you can doing it.' The fish netted, they came back around the pool to get out of the river. Finlay killed the fish and looked at Janey. She was shaking violently but smiling broadly, unable to speak.

'Well done, Janey!' Janet shouted. 'See. Girls can do it as well. Clever sod Finlay!'

'Some girls can. You flunked it when offered!' Finlay laughed. 'I suppose you want one now?'

Janey walked a few steps away from them and was sick. 'Bloody Hell! That was the most exciting thing ever. I cannot believe how strong they are.'

'Do you want me to hook you one, Jan?' Finlay asked again.

'No, that would be stealing Janey's thunder. I'll start with something smaller. How big is that one, do you think?'

'About nine pounds. You have to be blooded Janey!' he said, pulling out his knife and nicking the fish's gill. He gently dabbed a spot of blood on each of her cheeks. 'There, a confirmed lady angler!'

'You really are such fun, Finlay,' she said. 'You may be all sorts of bugger, but you're fun! Thank you for that.'

There was a heavy splash in the main pool. 'Oh Christ! She's fallen in!' Finlay said, jumping to his feet.

'I rather think not!' said Janey, laughing loudly. 'There are her clothes.'

'Oh no! She'll drown in there,' he said, running up the bank.

'Hiya Finlay!' Janet shouted from the middle of the main pool. 'You thought I'd fallen in didn't you?' She swam back to him against the current. 'Told you I could swim better than you, didn't I?' She sounded triumphant.

'I think you can, I can't swim against that. How do you do it?' He was amazed at the way she seemed to glide through the water. She turned and ducked below the surface and swam to the bottom. Janey joined him, laughing loudly, as they watched her pull her way across the river bed with her hands. 'She didn't want to steal my thunder! She's like a porpoise and with nothing on she would steal anybody's thunder!'

Janet surfaced at the end of the pool. She wasn't even breathing heavily. 'Come on you two, it's beautiful in here!' she called.

'Do you want to go in Janey?' Finlay asked.

'Yes, but not with you here. Inhibitions won't go overnight. Can you clear off for me?' she asked.

'Sure. I'll go home and take the fish back. You come on when you're ready.'

'No, you'll have to hang around, in case somebody comes. Go up by the island and wait,' she said shyly.

He picked up his fishing gear and the fish and walked the hundred yards up to the island. From where he stood he could see them just, swimming in the pool and heard their laughter. He watched the river gliding past, the starwort swaying in the current, and listened to the sounds around him. Two swans, intent on landing in Nutsey pool, flew down past him but seeing it already occupied twisted upwards and flew on down towards Testwood.

As they climbed up the bank, Janey waved at him. They began to dress and caught him up as he walked back to the pick-up, just wearing their shirts and pants and letting their legs dry in the now emerging sun. 'Finlay, the water made me feel as though I was swathed in the sheerest silk. What a way to start the day,' Janey said, ecstatic. They both knew that a large measure of the enforced inhibitions of her life were gone down the river, along with the passing swans.

Finlay laid the two fish on the bass square he had put in the back of the pick-up and folded the horse blanket which was always in the front across the seats. 'Last time there was an argument. You get in the middle Jan, then we can all be in the front.'

'Very diplomatic Finlay, but I don't really want the handbrake handle up my bum now, do I?' Janet said.

'Get in, you pair of witches, before I leave you both to walk.' He smiled at them, pleased they seemed to like each other.

When they got back to the house Finlay was surprised to see the Armstrong already out, with Mr Brockett wiping some imaginary dust from its long bonnet.

'Good morning,' Finlay said. 'This all looks very formal. Where are you off to today?'

'London. With your grandfather and Sir George,' Brockett answered.

'Well. The old girl looks very smart,' Finlay said, admiring the black coachwork. 'I think we're having a new one shortly, aren't we?'

'I hope not Master Keith. Modern cars are trashy things,' Brockett said with much formality.

'Would Master Keith please dismiss his handmaidens, get them indoors and sat on the Aga. Their bums are cold and their knickers are damp,' Janet said. Brockett's face collapsed in laughter.

Indoors, his grandfather and Sir George Goulding were drinking tea, discussing an obviously very weighty matter.

'Morning Sir James. Morning Sir George. We've been fishing and swimming. Can Janey and I sit on the Aga please? We're a little damp?' Janet asked, and grabbing a chair, rested herself on the cooker's top.

Still a little diffident, Janey said her greeting and leant against the front of the cooker. When Finlay came in with the fish, he was surprised to see Sir George there.

'Where's your car Sir George?' he asked. 'Have you crashed again?'

'In for service, and why is it that you always catch fish and then assault our senses with beautiful females?' He was in an ebullient mood.

'How come you're not damp, Kee?' his grandfather asked. 'Sent away while the girls bathed? Two nice fish. Many down there?'

'He's very clever, Sir James, but his casting's a bit wayward. I think he needs some lessons.' Janet was flirting.

'The pool was full of fish and would have taken my shoe if I had chucked it at them. Uncle Jack should have a good day. Why are you going to London, Grandfather?' he asked.

'Money matters. The AI service is having to move out on to the Brockenhurst road and expand. We're going to London to get the funding,' Finlay's grandfather answered. 'Niney and Jenny are coming with us to do some shopping. You'll have to shift for yourself today, but I'm sure you'll be looked after. Don't burn the house down and write down the phone messages.'

'Of course! Have you told the exchange you're going to be out?' he asked. That his grandfather treated the local exchange as his own was not strange to Finlay.

'I don't want you being idle,' Finlay's grandfather said, quite firmly. 'You're the oldest Janey. You're responsible. In between times, get Kee to start you driving my Land-Rover.'

Niney and Jenny arrived, high heels clicking on the hard floors. 'Now you three,' Niney began. 'Ground rules for today. Don't alter the Aga. There's plenty of food about so, for once, you can get your own. If it rains you can start rearranging the attic to suit yourselves. Janet's right about the place. Make it your own. If it doesn't rain, I want both girls driving by the time we get back. I don't want you being idle, that will only lead to trouble.'

Jenny glanced at Finlay and smiled. 'There now, darling. You've had your orders. Don't forget. No swimming until the rods go home tonight, and for goodness' sake, clean your pick-up.'

'For goodness' sake! All of you! Do this, do that...' Finlay began.

'Don't answer back, Kee,' Niney said. 'It's not what I expect of you. You can go to the beach hut next week but there's lots of things to do before that. Oh, we're finding out about your uniforms today as well.'

Finlay wished they would all go off to London and be gone, and then, at last, they were.

'This is the first time I've had this place to myself. I bet Auntie Niney was tempted to say, "And don't get into any mischief while I'm gone."'

'Poor Finlay! Suddenly you've got to start doing as you are told. It's their way of giving you responsibility. At least you don't have a set of rules written down as I have. Never mind, I'll gut the fish. You clean the pick-up and Janet get on with your drawing. We can have an early lunch and then go swimming in the Blackwater. Driving can wait,' Janey announced to them.

You sound like Niney mark two!' Janet laughed. 'But you're right. Go and wash the pick-up Finlay.'

Finlay left, shaking his head and muttering about organizing females. He was back within the hour, though, and found the two girls sitting on a large sofa, in the roof, studying a photograph album. 'Finlay, it's fascinating and a bit scary really. Come and look,' Janet said.

'Who are these other two?' she asked. It was a picture of three teenage girls. Finlay looked and recognized his mother at once. 'I'm not certain really. That's my mother and that must be my auntie. The one the Japs killed. Who this is, I've no idea.'

'Look! There's one of Niney when she was our age.' Janet flicked back a few pages.

Even Finlay caught his breath. Niney was beautiful. Underneath was written: ANNONA. 18TH BIRTHDAY.

'I don't think we should be looking at this,' Finlay said doubtfully. He was looking at Niney's eyes and saw his own.

'Well just look at this one, Finlay,' Janet said. She turned the pages back to almost the start of the album. The photographs were brown and white and there was a portrait of what might have been himself.

'That must be my great-grandfather,' Finlay said, almost to himself.

'It's no wonder that Granny Fortune likes you so much,' Janey said. 'She told me all about him. It's sad, but so lovely a story.'

'Wouldn't it be amazing if he and Granny Fortune had done it on exactly the same spot as you and Jill, Finlay?' Janet said almost wistfully.

Finlay shut the album quickly. 'I don't really want to talk about this!' he said awkwardly.

'We do! Janey and I have been,' Janet said gleefully.

'Well, we should do some driving, don't you think?' Finlay said, getting up. 'Can you put this back where you found it perhaps?'

'Don't get all huffy Finlay. You can't help being what you are, any more than Janet and I can help being just a tiny bit curious.' Janey was teasing.

They heard the telephone ringing. 'Bugger! I'll bet that's them ringing to check we're not being idle,' Finlay swore.

'Don't be silly. They can't possibly be in London yet,' Janey said.

'I'll go shall I?' Janet said, getting up and clattering down the back stairs. 'I'll say there's nobody at home.'

'I'm glad you're getting along together, Janey,' Finlay said. 'Janet's a bit mad, but good to be with.'

She came clattering back up. 'It's a bloody nuisance. I'd forgotten I have a dental appointment in Southampton. I have to go home. Bugger it! Mother will bring me back again in a couple of hours.'

'Do you want me to drive you over to the big bridge, Jan?' Finlay asked, getting up.

'No, my sister's bicycle's still here and she wants it back. I'm late, so I'm going. Please don't go swimming without me.' She clattered away again.

'That's a pity,' Finlay said. 'Still it's early yet. We seem to have been up for ages. Shall we go and do some driving?'

'I'd rather stay and talk for a little while, if you don't mind,' she answered. 'This house is always so busy and crowded. What I wanted to say was… well, I don't know how to start.'

'Just out with it, Janey.' Finlay laughed. 'Do you want to talk more about what happened?'

'No. I did feel as though I'd rejected you when I saw you standing up, waiting for us. That's why I waved to you.'

'It made a beautiful picture. If I could, I would paint that. The sun on you both, not close enough for any detail. It wasn't erotic, just beautiful, if you see what I mean,' he said.

'Well I wasn't standing where you were, was I?' She giggled.

'I didn't think you'd go in. You know? Without anything on…'

'Because you thought I was Janey, the prefect, the old maid…' she said.

'Hey, I didn't think of it that way,' he said, getting up and offering his hand. She took it and pulled him back down with her.

'Whether this is right or wrong Finlay, it doesn't matter. Finish what you started the other day. Please.'

'Sure…'

'More than,' she said quietly.

'Let's go to my bedroom,' he gulped.

He led her downstairs. 'Look. Get undressed and into bed, then you won't be embarrassed. I'll wait out here.'

'Thanks Finlay. I wanted you to say that.' She went into the room and closed the door.

Waiting outside, he thought about Niney and not getting into mischief. He wondered if he was going to be sorry.

She was deep under the blankets with only her eyes showing and shaking like a trapped bird. He dropped his clothes on the floor and slipped in beside her.

'You will take care, Finlay.' She croaked almost.

'Come here and let me hold you for a minute,' he said, gently.

She was soft, warm and damp with sweat. 'I'm a bit scared...' she mumbled into his chest.

He started kissing her shoulders, arms and touching her flanks and hips. When he kissed her mouth, she opened it easily to allow him to push his tongue in. She was enjoying the sensations and holding him tightly, kissing him back and suddenly laughing quietly.

'You are a bugger you know. That little boy on the train... such a sweet little chap... who'd have thought...'

She took his hand from her breast and placed it firmly between her open legs. It was all going too quickly. He wanted to somehow savour the moment, but she didn't. As he pushed gently inside her, she was gripping him so hard he could barely get his breath. He tried to move but she was insistent, her hips suddenly banging violently against him. She sighed deeply and relaxed, her breathing long and even. She opened her eyes and stared into his and started a long slow kiss. This time it was her tongue exploring his mouth. She was laughing aloud between kisses. She pushed him off and propped herself on an elbow looking down at him. 'I know you don't believe in saving souls, but you've just saved mine. Having unlawful sex with a minor, Janey Grieves, how could you?' She glanced at her watch. 'If you haven't recovered in ten minutes, I'm giving you five hundred lines!' She cocked her head back. She was laughing.

'Finlay, I'm a real honest-to-God woman now. I don't think you need any more time.' She threw the bedclothes off. 'Look at me Finlay!' she demanded. 'Look at Janey, the old maid! Eat your heart out Miss bloody Satchel!' She snatched the sheath from his hand. 'Do it without Finlay, I want to feel you, not some piece of rubber!'

Finlay remembered what Ron had told him. 'Don't stay on the train all the way to Bournemouth. Get off at Boscombe.' But Ron had never explained what to do if the train didn't stop.

She dismissed his worries. 'I'm a dairy farmer's daughter. I know about conception. Let me go to the bathroom. It's no problem this time of the month.' She bounced out of the room, turned at the door and said, 'Stay there!'

Coming back, she sat on the bed next to him. 'Oh, Finlay!' She leant over and bit his stomach. 'I thought nobody would ever want me. I was always such a frump.'

'Even when you gave me lines, even got me caned, I never ever thought you were anything but my dear, dear Janey.'

'Smooth-tongued toad!' She laughed.

He grabbed her down and began to bite quite hard on her breasts. It made her squeal and they came together again, quickly.

'Bathroom again, I think! Get dressed again now, and I'll get you something to eat.' This time, she fairly danced out of the room.

He rolled off the bed. He felt as though he had faced the Landford bowler again and rather the worse for wear. Janey came back. 'Don't forget to deal with the evidence Finlay, and put that bed back as it was.'

When he got to the kitchen she had made some sandwiches and put out some pickles. 'There you are Finlay. Eat something, you look washed out. Got up too early I expect.'

'Wasn't that. I didn't expect a couple of hours with you. I'll never be able to look at you without seeing your lovely bum.'

'Good! Now eat some food. You've got to get me driving,' she said.

'You won't tell Janet, will you? Everybody knew about Jill. She happily told her friends.'

'Of course not. I think she was rather hoping for your services today, though,' Janey laughed.

'You don't mind?' he asked, surprised.

'If a bull's shut in a yard with two bulling heifers, he's going to serve them both, if he's any use at all. I was getting in first and if that makes me a sinful woman, so be it. I don't mind now the ice is broken. I shan't want to know, but I'm sure she'll tell me. I'll look surprised and a little shocked. By the time I go off to university I'll be able to drive and get men to do my bidding. Just like Niney does. But until you go, I indeed keep it solely for you. That's my promise.'

'Blimey!' he said. 'Thanks for being so broad-minded.'

'Comes from being narrow-minded in the past. Now I can swear, drink, smoke and have you. Do as I wish. I'm so happy, Finlay, you cannot believe.' She came around his side of the table and they kissed again. 'I'm a bigger girl than Jill or Janet. They're tiny little things against me. I've seen horses serving mares and you wonder where it all goes. Anyway, I wanted you inside me. Almost as though you were going to wipe away the horror of Jenks, and you have. I know I'm normal now.'

Finlay looked at her. The honey-coloured hair and deep blue eyes, the smattering of freckles across her nose, the wide mouth with strong white teeth. This surely was a descendant from the Norse invader.

'Have those lines ready by the morning Finlay or I'll have you in detention.'

They left a note on the door for Janet, and Finlay drove the Land-Rover out towards the wood yard. Letting Janey drive, he explained how the gears were in the same position as the Fergie. Janey was soon flying about the estate lanes, revelling in her new-found freedom.

'Let's go and see Granny, Finlay,' Janey suggested. 'I'm sure she'd love to see you.'

'She'll see that you are different. She says she always knows when a rose has been plucked.' Finlay sounded a little doubtful.

'Good, let's see if she does.' She laughed.

They found her drinking gin and water in the garden. 'Hello you pretty ones. Learning to drive young Janey? That'll get you out from here and into the world. What about you, cocker?' She gave Finlay a hug and looked at him fondly.

'We found some pictures in the roof Granny,' Finlay said.

'Leave them there darling till you'm older. When you can properly understand,' she answered, her look clouding. 'Promise me that.'

'If that's what you want... You've started work on the garden I see.'

'You ain't up here to look at my garden, darling. Has Janey come to tell me you made her happy?'

The two youngsters looked amazed. 'Don't look like that. I spect it was you Janey, wanting to tell me. Could see the minute you got out of the car. You looks ten times more beautiful than when you left. Mind what yer about though. They'd blame you for having him, being older. They'd say you led him on and then people would believe that bastard Jenks.'

Janey was blushing. 'Is it so obvious, Granny?'

'To me it is, darling. You watch a horse with his mares. He'll go round them all. But the one he stands with in the shade is the one he loves. You go and stand in the shade with him Janey and leave me with my gin. I'm glad you came and told me. You look after her darling. You'll go around the other mares I know, but this 'un is yourn.'

They drove away in silence towards the wood yard lane. Janey turned in the yard and headed back towards the house. They found Janet. Finlay got out and let her sit in the middle seat. She was angry.

'What's the matter, Jan?' he asked, getting in beside her.

'I've been fitted with a bloody chastity belt,' she exclaimed.

'What on earth do you mean?' Janey laughed.

She showed them both the metal brace in her mouth. 'What man is ever going to kiss me now. It has to stay for at least six months, for Christ's sake!'

'Finlay, will you just kiss her, else she's never going to learn to drive this day. Give me a chance to go solo,' Janey said. 'A short five minutes. Just convince her that she's still a love, else the day will be spoilt.' She gave Finlay a flashing smile and left.

'Come here you,' Finlay said, taking her into the sawmill shed.

'Finlay, the brace is in my mouth, not down there!' she squealed, delighted. They heard the Land-Rover coming. 'Why do we never have time, Finlay?' She giggled.

'You're a good friend, Janey,' Janet said, getting into the Land-Rover.

'Better than you know, Janet,' she said. 'Well, convinced you're not some kind of monster?'

'Yes, but it was a very short five minutes,' Janet said tersely.

'Not by my watch it wasn't.' She laughed. 'Finlay, you look all in. I'll teach Janet, much better girl on girl.'

He didn't argue. Once back at the house Finlay checked his bedroom. He was tempted to go back to the photograph album and find out what Granny was so adamant he shouldn't see. But his promise given, stayed him.

He lay on his bed, which still smelled of Janey, pondered on what Granny had said, and drifted into sleep.

'Come on Finlay, it's past five. We want to go swimming. Mr Terry says we can have the hatch pool.' Janet was shaking him violently.

'How did the driving go Jan?' he asked, trying to shake the sleep from his head.

'Oh it's easy with Janey. I can drive you down to the river, but hurry up!' she said impatiently.

'I'm not swimming with a monster with a wired-up jaw!' he said, pulling her on to the bed.

'Stop it!' she whispered. 'They'll hear us downstairs.'

Finlay kissed her and played with the wire in her mouth with his tongue. 'Sod,' she breathed and kissed him back.

He followed her down the stairs and into the kitchen, 'Hello Uncle Jack, had a good day?'

'Some and some. I wish these people would learn to fish properly before they come; they hooked plenty and then lost half of them. How did your day go, nipper? Asleep at tea time says something. One of these girls would be enough for most people.'

'Have you seen the drawing of the new stream yet Jack? Shall I go and get it?' Janet asked, already leaving the room, her bare feet slapping on the cold floor.

She returned and laid it out on the table. 'What do you think?'

'Did you do this, Janet?' Jack asked seriously.

'Well Janey helped this afternoon. Do you think it will work?' she asked.

'I'm amazed. How do you know about the way the water flows?' Jack asked.

'But do you like it?' she asked enthusiastically.

'I think it's bloody brilliant! Better than mine or James's idea. Tell me, which is the prettiest pool, do you think?' he asked.

'This one. Just before the little brick bridge. Just like a miniature hatch pool if we put a big rock or something here. Will it work?' she asked, pleased by Jack's reaction.

'We'll make it work, and that pool will be called Janet's Pool. In a hundred years' time people will want to know why and look in the records. You're a clever girl Janet Ward.' He kissed her cheek.

Janet was delighted. 'Can we get it going, before we all go our different ways?'

'Probably,' Jack said. 'Depends on how soon the harvest comes and we don't know what's happening with young Kee yet. By the way, you're to get the girls home by nine Niney said. Did you answer her back this morning?'

'Yes, I'm afraid I did. If the vet hadn't been here I'd have got a wipe around the clock for it.'

'You won't learn. She still thinks you're her little boy. The good thing about that is when she's wild with you, she ain't with me,' he said.

'Are we going swimming?' Janet asked, impatiently.

'Take care what you are about by the hatches,' said Jack. 'Leave the key in the Land-Rover Kee. I'll pick it up in the morning, and don't forget to leave the door unlocked when you've gone to bed.'

They met Cassy on her horse on the bottom lane going to the hatch pool. Janet was pleased. 'Hello Cassy,' Janet said, stopping, pretending that driving a Land-Rover was nothing new to her.

'Your results have arrived, sister dear, special delivery. Would you like to come home and let us know whether Father's money was entirely wasted?' Cassy felt her position as the eldest very strongly.

'Oh blimey! Will you two please come with me?' Janet said, confidence suddenly gone.

The Ward house was modern by Finlay's standards, clean, tidy and ordered. Mrs Ward welcomed them happily, tense as well, wanting to know what her middle daughter had achieved. There was a large buff envelope in the middle of the table. Janet picked it up and looked at her mother. 'If it's bad news, please don't be cross. I did try very hard.'

'Don't be silly Janet. Now come along and open it. We're dying of suspense,' Mrs Ward said quietly. Finlay liked her. She was kind and patient with her girls, who must have been quite a trial to bring up alone.

'Well, here goes,' Janet said, breaking the seals on the envelope. She read the contents, sat down hard on a chair and burst into tears. Mrs Ward grabbed the certificate from her hand and read, her face softening with pleasure.

'Well done darling, you've passed them all.' She went and put her arms around her daughter. 'Why the tears? You've got what you wanted.'

Janey hugged Janet. 'Come on Jan, you can do what you want now.'

The certificate was handed to Finlay. 'Jan, you're a real old clever clogs.' He went and held her. 'Hey, come on copper-nob, you're meant to be happy, not blubbing your eyes out. You'll make your face uglier than it is already!'

'Shut up you horrible sod!' she said. 'It's such a relief, such a relief.'

Jo came in, smelling of horses and molasses. 'Suppose you've done well, by all the noise. What are you blubbing about you silly tart?' she said ungraciously.

'Oh dear Keith, you do have a way of stirring up my daughters,' said Mrs Ward.

The three girls shouted with laughter. 'Keith!' Jo scoffed. 'Who is Keith for goodness' sake? He's called Finlay!'

'Don't let them tease you Keith, I mean Finlay. You've done great things for my daughters, ungrateful wretches,' Mrs Ward said to him smiling.

'Let's do that swim,' said Finlay, suddenly and went to turn the Land-Rover around. He watched the girls approaching in the mirror. They seemed thin and waif-like against Janey, all of them a head shorter than her.

They arrived at the mill intact and excited. The hatch pool was sparkling in the evening sun, the water smelled of chalk and wild celery as lines of the current from under the gates foamed, bubbled and pressed over the end of the pool like broken crystal. They plunged in together, but the light was just beginning to go and the first bats of the evening flitted from somewhere within the mill roof.

Afterwards, as they drove back, Janet and Janey made arrangements for their trip to Southampton the following day and Jo was talking to Finlay about air-guns.

'There we are. That's as far as we can go,' Janey said, stopping in the gateway. 'We won't come in. I have to get back to Granny's place. Finlay was told to have you home by nine as well as me, and he always does as he's told!'

They were quiet together as Janey drove back to the house. In the kitchen she spread her underwear, wet from their swim, on top of the Aga. 'They'll be dry in an hour,' she said quietly. 'Come. Granny won't mind if I'm late.'

They went to Finlay's bedroom, now cool and shadowy in the evening light. The sun had gone down behind the trees surrounding Little Testwood. What breeze there was carried the smell of ripening barley into the room, filling it with a biscuit scent, mingled with the smell of the stables. Janey dropped her shirt and shorts on to the floor and remained dreamily looking out of the large window. The failing light caught her whiteness and seemed to make her glow. Finlay went and stood with her, his arm around her waist. 'Look at the lights coming on already. Summer has turned the corner,' she said sadly. Across the fields single-lighted windows showed from the cottages. There was a hum from a tractor working somewhere off the estate. The sound of someone far away calling a dog drifted in on the barley-scented breeze.

'Beautiful isn't it?' she breathed.

'Yes it is. The quiet and the light,' he answered. Just above their heads the house martins complained about being kept awake by their voices. They had long since gone to snuggle together in their little mud nests.

Finlay shed his clothes. They lay in a heap with hers below the window. Her hair smelt of the river. She felt cool and firm as they pressed together. The bed was still in a tangle as they lay together above the covers, their faces together, taking each other's breath. Finlay touched and studied every inch of her.

'Turn over on your front,' he said.

'No. My bum is too big for detailed study,' she answered, but turned over anyway. When he kissed, she started to pull at him. There was no urgency in her demands this time. Her breathing quickened when he began to kiss and taste the sweet stickiness between her legs. The soft caressing of her thighs against him felt like the caress of the water in the river.

Afterwards, Janey was the first to wake. She eased herself out from beneath Finlay and shook him gently. He stirred and put his arms around her.

'Whoa Finlay. It's gone ten and I must go. Get my underwear, just in case there's anybody down there.'

The kitchen was warm and inviting, silent apart from the refrigerator making its own strange noises.

Janey was in the bathroom when he went back up to the bedroom. He flopped on to the bed and waited, listening to the velvet silence of the night. Janey dressed again quickly with Finlay watching her movements, marvelling at her litheness.

'Do you want a drink of anything?' he asked.

'No, run me back to Granny's and I'll see you after we've been to Southampton. Come on Finlay, move yourself,' she ordered.

They could see Granny was still up, reading a book through the undrawn curtains. They saw her look up when the vehicle lights briefly strayed across the front of the cottage.

'Hope we haven't kept her up,' Janey said. 'Come on, kiss me goodnight and go.' Driving back across the farm, an owl was sitting on a gate post and only lifted off when Finlay was right by it, its wing-beats slow and deliberate. In the vehicle's lights, myriads of moths and insects stretched away in the twin tunnels of light in front of him. There were no rabbits now as there used to be, so the delight of seeing a skulking fox was gone.

Back indoors, he made himself some tea. He was tired and confused by the deep feelings he had for Janey. He washed his cup and refilled the kettle with cold water. It would be the first thing Niney went to, giving her the knowledge of when he went to bed. It took a lot of effort to fool Niney. Better not to give her the clues she looked for.

In his bedroom he checked there was nothing that would tell anybody of Janey's presence. Dragging the bed back roughly together, he collapsed into it gratefully. There was still the dampness of their sweat and his pillow smelt softly of Janey. He pushed his face into it, remembering the taste of her breath.

Chapter Twelve

•

The light streaming into the room woke Finlay early the next morning. It was just before six and the house was silent, save for the tap of the ivy on the window and the gentle squabbling of the sparrows in the bedroom chimney.

Downstairs, the debris of the returning travellers was spread across the large kitchen table. He made himself some tea and left the large kettle on the warm side of the Aga. Though hungry, he was too idle to get himself anything.

Outside, the breeze there the evening before had picked up a little, enough to whip the dust on the yard to small spirals. The clarity of the air meant that rain was on the way and he went to the workshop to work on the baler engine.

Carl was surprised to see him. 'Maybe vee start it up. Vill be good to see how you hav done, I zink you hev done a vere good job,' Carl said. 'Today I have to fix the bicycle of the little Jo.' He allowed himself a smile. 'I say no. Miss Niney say yes. I check with the boss. Miss Niney find out. Carl has a boat load of shit up the creek, no paddle.'

By half-past eight Finlay was very hungry. Five minutes later, he walked into the kitchen where the smell of frying bacon filled the room. 'Hello everyone. Where's Jenny?'

'Thank you darling,' Niney said. 'Jenny is out on Misty and I'm cooking your breakfast! Go out and come in again. Try: Hello Auntie Niney, thank you for cooking my breakfast. Hello Grandfather, hello Sir George and then after a suitable pause, and only then, you ask where Jenny is.'

Finlay walked across to the Aga and put his arm around her. 'Hello my beautiful Auntie. My breakfast smells wonderful. May I give you a morning kiss, please?'

'That's much better!' she said severely, bending for the kiss. 'I hope you haven't got dirty. There are lots of new clothes to try on, ready for any interviews. Busy day yesterday? I can see you cleaned your pick-up properly.'

'Yes thank you. I'm very hungry Auntie Niney.' He let his hand wander down to her backside and pinched it gently.

Niney dropped the spoon and grabbed him roughly. 'Get your hand off you sod, and give me a proper kiss,' she said.

'Has my Land-Rover still got a gearbox, Kee?' his grandfather asked. 'You might have taught them in your pick-up.'

'I did think about it, but they can't do any harm to the Land-Rover or themselves. They were quick to catch on, especially Janey, but she's used to driving a tractor.'

'Is she all right now, Kee?' his grandfather asked, concerned.

'Yes, seems to be. She gets on well with Janet. They're going shopping in Southampton today, so I can finish the baler engine,' Finlay said.

'Not this morning, darling,' Niney interrupted. 'Lots of clothes to try on. I may have to alter some and you have to get your application forms posted.'

'I should telephone Carl and let him know that I won't be back until after lunch.' Finlay was trying to please.

'I have to see if he's finished Jo's bike. I'll let him know then,' Niney said, then added almost nonchalantly, 'What time did you get those girls home last night, darling?'

'Oh plenty early. We had a good swim in the hatch pool and then I took them all home.'

'I'm glad you've taken up with Janey, Kee,' Finlay's grandfather said. 'She's going to need a lot of support before she goes off to Oxford.'

'I shouldn't mind giving her support!' Sir George said.

'Enough of that, George!' Niney said a little sharply. 'What Janey wants is the friendship she has with Kee, with no pressure attached. They've always adored each other, ever since she took him to school.'

'She used to give me lines and put me in detention,' Finlay said, wishing Jenny would come back and the subject could be changed.

'You know you think the world of her. You would've killed that bloody minister if he wasn't in hospital.'

'I still might!' said Finlay

'Well said young Kee!' Sir George said. 'If I get the chance I'll run the bugger down, wheelchair or not!'

'George! He looks like being crippled for the rest of his life!' Niney said, shocked.

'Niney, the man is a complete charlatan. If he'd meant to kill himself he would have jumped sooner,' Sir George said.

'I still don't think you should say things like that, George,' Niney insisted.

'Enough you two,' Finlay's grandfather said. 'Keep calm about it please, and Kee, mind what you are saying. Being rude about Mrs

Phillips and insulting her and her friends, it doesn't do in this day and age you know.'

Finlay exploded with rage. 'How can you talk like that Grandfather? She said something about Auntie Niney and that I won't have from anybody!' He jumped up and pointed his finger at his grandfather. 'I'll tell you this, and by Christ I mean it! Next time I see that bloody woman, I'll ride right over her!' He slammed out of the room and out of the front door.

'For God's sake James! You've no idea how to deal with him, have you? Why didn't you ask him why he spoke that way to the bloody woman? Then, if you thought he was wrong, lay into him?'

'I'm sorry. You'd better go after him.'

'No. Leave him to cool off. I'll get Jenny to get him back,' Niney sighed.

'Christ! He's like his mother. I didn't know he had a paddy like that, James,' Sir George said.

Finlay's grandfather shook his head sadly. 'I'm afraid there's a lot of his mother, and his grandmother. I'd hoped he'd grown out of it.'

'You've a champion there Niney! Riding down the peasants for speaking ill of you,' Sir George said, trying to lighten the moment.

'I still don't think it proper Kee should be riding people into the hedge like some latterday Lord of the Manor. We have to live with these people,' Finlay's grandfather said.

'No James. They have to live with us! Right at this moment, I'm making plans to get people like the Phillipses gone!' Niney said firmly.

'What do you mean? How do you propose to do that, Madam?' Finlay's grandfather did not appear very pleased with the idea.

'For a start, they can pay for the water they use. And their electricity from our mill. Let them have the Electricity Board. They won't be able to afford the new line and poles, which we won't allow over our land. They'll have to move and we buy the house. Simple, James.'

'Anybody else you think needs their lives totally disrupted?' Finlay's grandfather was getting cross.

'Oh, I've only just started,' Niney came back, just as crossly. 'The Satchel woman can go. Even by GPO rules, she's too old to run the Post Office. And the top lane will be closed off. It's a privilege granted by us which everyone takes as their right. The Council don't maintain the lane, we do. It comes back to us, forthwith. Do you want me to go on?'

'I can't agree with this, Niney...' Finlay's grandfather started to say.

'You don't have to. If anything happened to you, half of this place would be mine immediately. As it is, I've some say in its running. As for the church, James, I want it shut again.'

'Why Niney? It wouldn't be right. What's brought this on?' Finlay's grandfather asked. He knew Niney was serious.

'The cost. Keeping it open, maintaining the lane. Keeping the bridges up to scratch. It costs thousands, and when the bloody vicar demands we cut the trees back in the churchyard, at our expense, then for me, that's the end. Either pay a proper rent and help maintain the lane, or it closes. It was a privilege granted by us. It's time these people learnt which side their bread's buttered.'

'I think I'll go and see if my car is finished,' Sir George said, getting up.

'Sit down and shut up!' Niney snapped, now angry with everyone. 'Not one penny more to that bloody church! I have had my say, and now I need to get Kee something to eat. You can take it down to him George. Where the bloody Hell has Jenny got to? Swanning about with her head in the clouds again I suppose.'

Niney wrapped a bacon sandwich in greaseproof paper. 'Right! Get these down to the boy George. You, James, can stay here. We'll sort out what's to happen with these bloody people.'

The promised rain arrived. Finlay watched amused as the house sparrows joyously marched about the concrete yard with their wings spread, allowing the large drops to cleanse them. As it came on heavier he ducked into the stables to shelter. His mare was back in her stall but she very pointedly ignored him, miffed no doubt because he had paid her scant attention for a couple of days. The swallows, not liking the rain, came swooping through the open doors and pitched chattering in the rafters. As suddenly as it had started the rain stopped, leaving the roofs he could see from the stable door dripping and smoking with steam, as the sun burst out again hot, across the valley. A line of shadow raced across the fields changing the ripening barley in the distance back to gold.

He went into the house knowing he had an apology to make, not for what he said, but for how he had said it.

'Hello Auntie Niney,' he said to her back, as she busied herself. 'Sorry about losing my temper earlier.'

'No matter my love. Try this,' she said, turning from her task and offering a lump of yellow butter on her fingernail.

He sucked it clean, savouring the texture.

'Not too salty is it?' she asked, drying her hands on her pinny.

'No. Lovely stuff. How much have you made?'

'Three pounds. Help me pat it up. Then we'll finish that form and try on your new outfit.'

'Did you enjoy London?' he asked, holding the great lump of butter in both hands while Niney emptied the large china bowl of salty water.

'London's so samey. Everybody rushing and tearassing about and it stinks to high heaven.' Finlay dropped the wet butter into the bowl. Niney squeezed the water from the butter in handfuls and dropped it into another bowl. They sat together patting the butter at the kitchen table, the air sweet with the smell.

'Where's Jenny? I haven't seen her yet today,' he said.

'In the office. We're taking the top lane back and probably closing the church.' She explained what had happened that morning, her eyes searching for something in his.

'Did my grandfather agree?' Finlay asked, surprised.

Niney got up, came around the table and sat down next to him. 'Darling. There's something you should perhaps know. It's gone on long enough. Darling... I'm your mother's half-sister. Your proper auntie, if you see what I mean. I have a say in what happens here. You're old enough to know the truth of it.'

'Yes, I know. I've known for ages. I just wanted you to tell me yourself. You see, Auntie, if you told me, that would mean you weren't ashamed of me. Like my mother is.'

Huge tears started in her eyes. 'My love! She's not ashamed of you. Oh Jesus! What have we done to you?' He had never seen her cry like this. He put his arms around her. 'I'm sorry. What a bloody shambles this all is.'

'Stay there Auntie. I want to show you something.' He ran up into the roof and found the photograph album. He showed her the portrait with both hands covering her face, except for the eyes.

'The man at Hengistbury thought you were my mother. You can see why. It makes no difference Auntie Niney. I couldn't love you more than I do anyway.' He turned the pages to another photograph. 'Is this one Bibby? And who's this?'

Niney dried her eyes. 'Where did you find this old thing?' She looked at the photographs. 'That's Bibby and this is my younger sister. My mother had two daughters with James. Her name's Ella and she lives in Scotland. I stayed here to be with my father.'

Finlay turned the page back to the beginning. 'Let me try and get this straight. This is my great-grandfather, the one whom I look like. He had a fling with Granny Fortune when he was about my age. She goes off and marries somebody else and has a daughter. This daughter has two daughters with my grandfather, you and Ella. He also has two daughters with my grandmother, my mother and Bibby. It's all a bit complicated, isn't it?' Finlay could not help but smile.

'Yes,' Niney sighed. 'It's a bloody shambles!'

It was something of a milestone, Finlay felt, when he handed the registered envelope back to the post mistress in Romsey. It contained his application to the Admiralty. The post mistress handed him back the receipt. 'You'll be off then soon?' She smiled.

'Maybe,' Finlay answered.

Niney had given him several errands to do in the town. He walked to the bank and the smell of the brewery pervaded the air. The pavements seemed to sparkle after the morning's rain. In the draper's shop he gave the assistant the list that Niney had given him and waited while she bustled about. She packed everything in a box and handed it to him. 'Are you all right now?' she asked.

'I'm sorry?' Finlay replied.

'The cricket match. It was my husband. When he heard you'd gone to hospital, he felt terrible.'

'I'm OK. Thanks for asking.' He laughed. 'It was a good game. Tell your husband though I'll have him out again next time we meet.'

Walking through the town, he thought how infrequently he ever left the estate and how few people he knew, though they knew him. Passing the saddlers, he was stopped by a woman asking about his mother. She seemed a little put out by the vagueness of his answers.

Walking home, he heard what was obviously a Land-Rover coming up behind him. He turned to see if it was his grandfather's or Ron's. It stopped beside him. 'Hang on a minute, youngster,' the driver ordered. He got out and came towards him. 'It's Niney's boy, isn't it?' he asked. He was dressed immaculately in tweeds, polished boots and gaiters.

'Yes, but I'm sorry. Should I know who you are?' Finlay asked.

'I'm Bob Hodinott,' he said, shaking hands. 'I just wanted you to give Niney a message. Say we're all grateful to her for sorting out the hospital. She's quite a girl!'

'Yes,' Finlay said. 'Niney keeps us all in order.'

'I bet she does! Give my best to your family and tell your grandfather I shall expect to see you shooting with me this season. Don't forget to give your auntie my thank-you.'

Finlay said he wouldn't. As Hodinott drove away, he said, suddenly, aloud to himself, 'My auntie, my honest-to-God auntie.'

He began to hurry. He wanted more than anything else in the world to be with her.

Part III

Big Boy's Games

Chapter One

•

There was an almost instant response from the Admiralty. Finlay was instructed to present himself at the Navy Hospital in Gosport for a medical examination. On the day Niney drove him there it never occurred to him he was anything else but fit and healthy. He was surprised to find himself blowing up a large rubber bladder, lifting some heavy weights and sitting in total darkness watching tiny pin-pricks of red, green or white light at the far end of a large room. He was prodded, poked, weighed, photographed and asked pointedly about his sexual orientation. Finally he was sitting in front of a surgeon commander, being offered tea and biscuits.

'I served in the same escort group as your father,' the surgeon began. 'In fact, took his appendix out in Londonderry. Still got yours?'

'Yes Sir. Which ship were you on, Sir?' Finlay asked.

'The *Taff*. Your father was on the *Spey*. How is he?'

'He must be OK, Sir. Actually, I've never met him. He's in New Zealand at the moment. Another couple of years before he's home.' Finlay wanted to sound as matter-of-fact as possible.

'Mind not having met him?' the surgeon asked, lightly.

'I'd like to put a face to a name but, as I can't do anything, there's no point in thinking about it,' Finlay answered.

The surgeon made some notes. 'Right, Finlay. The first hurdle done with. I'm happy with your health and you've passed. You'll have to do some rigorous fitness tests, so keep up with the swimming and start walking long distances. Ten or fifteen miles, at least twice a week, gradually trying to cut down the time.' He stood and shook hands. 'Give my regards to your father next time you speak,' he ordered.

The next examination was with a civilian, a Dr Williams. Finlay entered the waiting room where a young man he judged to be a couple of years older than himself was sitting down, looking glum. Finlay's greeting was returned with nothing more than a mumble. 'Something wrong?' Finlay asked.

'You'll find out. He's a shrink and I've just wrecked any chance of going into the service. He's a real slimy sod. My name's Andy Bretton.' They shook hands and he seemed to cheer up a little.

'Well, you can never tell... Don't give up,' Finlay commiserated.

'You're a bit young aren't you?' Bretton said.

'My father's a serving officer. Dartmouth is more like school for me, or that's what I'm told. I've passed the exams. Besides, I'm a lot older than Nelson when he got in.'

A nurse called his name and Finlay followed her out, giving Andy a friendly gesture in passing.

Doctor Williams was sitting at a large desk, head down, writing quickly. He did not look up. The top of his bald head was peeling and his shirt collar was dirty. Finlay waited for a few minutes, then walked to the side of the room, picked up a chair, walked it back to the desk and sat down. Without looking up, Williams asked, 'Did you wipe your feet when you came in?'

'There was nothing to wipe them on,' Finlay answered.

'Did I ask you to sit?'

'No,' Finlay said. He was beginning to dislike this man.

'I'm going to show you some cards with shapes on. Say the first thing that comes into your head, please.'

He held up a card. 'An oak tree,' Finlay said.

'How did you get here today?'

'In a car,' Finlay answered.

'Why not a train? It's an easy journey from Romsey.'

'Convenience,' Finlay answered.

'Your mother brought you. Are you a mummy's boy?'

'My aunt brought me,' Finlay said.

Another card was shown. 'A hare,' Finlay said, noting the doctor's dirty fingernails.

'You're a shooting man I see. How do you justify that?'

'I've never had to.'

'Try then,' Williams said.

'You wouldn't understand.'

Another card. 'A gannet,' Finlay said.

'I want to understand why you shoot, Finlay,' Williams said. 'I'm a doctor, I might understand.'

'You aren't a proper doctor, so I doubt you would,' Finlay said.

'Do you have any pets, Finlay?'

'A pig and a horse,' Finlay answered. He had him beaten.

'A pig?' Williams said, looking to see if Finlay was serious.

'A pig,' Finlay said.

Another card. 'A bluebell,' Finlay said.

'What kind of pig?'

'A Wessex Saddleback gilt.'

'And what's this pig called?' Williams asked.

'Starwort. After the yellow flowers in the river.'

'I know what Starwort is, Finlay,' Williams said.

'I wouldn't have thought you would have,' Finlay answered.

'What's the best book you've ever read, Finlay?' Williams asked.
It seemed, this time, his manner was conciliatory.

'*Seven Pillars of Wisdom*. T. E. Lawrence,' Finlay answered.

'A wonderful book. Did you understand it?'

'Yes I did. Did you?'

'I think that'll do, Finlay. Thank you.' Williams got up and shook
his hand. Finlay picked up the chair and put it back against the wall.

'Finlay,' Williams said, holding up another card.

'A daffodil.'

Outside, Finlay walked back to the Armstrong. There was a note under
the wiper blade. 'Come and find me in the canteen. I've been picked
up by a sailor.' Smiling, he followed the signs to the canteen. Niney
was working her fascination on three young navy-medics.

'Hello darling,' she said, seeing him. 'Couldn't resist these jolly
jacks. Have some cake. It's terrible, but these chaps tell me the food's
better on the ships.'

He shook hands with them. 'Well, I passed the medical bit Auntie.
Don't know about the psycho chap. An odd sort of bugger.'

'Who did you see?' one of the medics asked.

'A scruffy chap called Williams. Seemed perplexed about me having
a pig for a pet,' Finlay answered.

'He's meant to be one of the best!' the medic said.

'Didn't seem very bright to me.' Finlay laughed.

'How old are you?'

'Nearly fifteen. It's not how old I am, it's how much a person understands,' Finlay said. He was fed up with people asking his age.

'Well said sprog! You've probably made yourself a good report from
Williams. Most people just wilt.'

'Finlay was raised to know who he is, and keep the peasantry in
order,' Niney said, emphatically.

'And how do the peasants feel about that?' another medic asked.

'My dear boy! They absolutely love it! Just as your matelots drip
about bloody officers, so peasants drip about the bloody gentry. Gives
them something to complain about. Then, when they want some-

thing, they come snivelling around. Most of them are hopeless at running their own lives.'

'That's spot on,' the first medic said. 'I had a rough time at medical school because I'd been to Eton. But they were quick enough to come on the cadge. I think you'll fit!'

'We really must go home. It's been lovely. You give me hope. The country has not gone completely to the dogs,' Niney said, getting up.

'No chance of a date, I suppose?' one of them asked wistfully.

She gave him her best smile. 'One sailor in my life is more than enough. But thank you, anyway.'

Half-way home, Niney dropped the bombshell. 'Kee. Be very careful about Janey. Darling, I know she's been to your bed. She could get into awful trouble.'

'You know then?' Finlay said, quietly.

'Of course I do! I make your bed and wash your clothes. I know the signs. I can see why it happened, but please, please be discreet.'

'It wasn't Janey's fault,' Finlay said. He told her of the afternoon when he had delivered the sawdust. 'I get mixed up. I like being with Janey and I like being with Janet. Should it be that way?'

'I don't know, my dear. Janet throws herself at you. I did find her brassiere in the roof!' This time, there was a degree of approbation in her voice.

Finlay laughed. 'You came home too early, Auntie! That was my fault.'

'Plain lust, my dear. I can understand that. Wiggling her bum, challenging you to do something about it. Avoid being alone with her, or only being with her when Janey's there. Just be careful, especially with Janey. Her feelings must be a little bruised.'

'I never mean to get into these scrapes. I think to myself I'm going to keep away. Simply be friends. Then suddenly, there you are helping them off with their clothes.'

Niney laughed. 'It's called growing up. Society says "no", but your instinct says "yes", and that bit's always stronger. You're surrounded by females all the time. It can't be good. They're all of an age and there you are. All blue eyes and blonde curls. It's a heady mix.'

'What's going to happen? Are we going to take their farm back?' Finlay asked.

'When you're not sure what to do, it's best to do nothing. Her father's ruled by his wife. She'll have nothing said against Jenks, and blames Janey. Granny's no long-term solution. She'll probably make her base with us while she's at university. Can't let Janey down, can we?'

As they passed through Southampton, the town seemed to have struggled out of the past, determined to grow again. 'Oh look!' Niney exclaimed, delighted. 'The *Queen Mary*'s in dock!' She slowed the car. The liner seemed close enough to touch, as they drove along the Millbrook road. She looked majestic. Solid, with her bow almost hanging over the railway line. Figures of men, the size of ants, were working on her, bringing the great ship back to her magnificence.

Finlay said, 'Can you imagine the gloom? If the Jerries had sunk her?'

'Unimaginable. She *is* Southampton! Losing her to those barbarians would have been worse than the *Titanic*.'

Then, at last, they were home. As they swung into the driveway, they could see that work had begun on what had been the lawn. Three tractors were ploughing up and down the slight slope. The smell of the TVO hung in the air and gulls wheeled in a cloud behind the ploughs. The military vehicles had been removed and the tortured scrubbed-up area was going back to grass again. Finlay's grandfather had said they could not afford pretty. It would be run into the field next to it and, eventually, be brought back into production.

Their sadness was tempered somewhat. The huge specimen trees which had been planted by Finlay's forebears would be left standing. The limes, chestnuts and oaks had always been the visible clock of the seasons. Two huge wellingtonias were almost his own. He had always clambered up into their tops, nearly two hundred feet, and, with his grandfather's binoculars, seen the Isle of Wight and the busy waterway of the Solent.

Niney seemed subdued when they went indoors. 'Something amiss, beautiful Auntie?' Finlay asked.

'Only this Navy thing. My little chap is grown up. By the time there's grass on the lawn, you'll be getting ready to leave.'

'They haven't said they want me yet. I'm not much of a team player and the Navy put great store by that.'

'I don't remember Nelson being a team player. They'll want you all right. You've got brains, balls and charm and you certainly aren't any kind of beefer!' Niney laughed.

'What's that?'

'Someone who prefers sex with another bloke. You must have heard the expression before!'

'For goodness' sake, Auntie Niney! That's disgusting. The doctor asked me if I was one like that.'

'You didn't mention Janey?' Niney asked, urgently.

'Of course not! I told him I preferred girls' bums, especially yours!' They sat, sharing an early tea of boiled eggs and toast. Nobody came back to the house.

'I'll go and see if Carl is about. He'll know where everybody is.' Finlay said, getting up.

Carl was locking up, making ready to leave. Finlay asked his question.

'Ya, Miss Jenny is up at the Grieveses' farm. Zey're going. De boss is up at the dryer,' Carl said. 'Is good zey bastards go!'

'I'd better go. Give Niney the news.'

By the time he got back to the house Jenny had come back harassed, with reams of paper. With her, sitting at the kitchen table, was the auctioneer. She explained what had happened. Grieves had given notice. He wanted to leave the farm as soon as possible. It meant that the estate had to work out his outgoings and balance them with what value the crops he was leaving would make. It was a complicated job when normal notice was given but under these circumstances, right before harvest, it was a nuisance.

'How's Janey taking it? I bet those psalm-singing bastards haven't given her a thought,' Finlay said.

Mr Lunn smiled. 'They'll not even talk about her, young man.'

'Where is she anyway?' Finlay asked Jenny.

'When she found out what was happening, she said she wanted to go for a walk... She'll be OK, Kee,' Jenny said.

'Change your clothes before you go looking,' Niney ordered. Finlay glanced at his aunt. She jerked her head in an action to tell him to hurry.

Finlay found her under the ash trees, by the sawmill. 'Come to find your mare in the shade?' she asked sadly. She was sitting on the bole of a tree cut down the previous year.

He went and sat beside her, taking her hand. 'Something like that. I thought you might be needing me,' he said.

She looked at him quizzically. 'I'm abandoned. My parents don't want me and I don't belong any more.'

'Don't be silly. You belong here, with us. If they put that bastard Jenks before you, then sod them! Niney says you're to make your base here, if you want to. Anyway, I'd like you here.' He said the last statement quite fiercely.

'If my parents believe it's my fault, other people must think the same,' Janey said.

'People who matter don't think that!' he snapped. 'What does it matter what those bastard Christians think?'

'You've been brought up to think that way, Finlay. You never put restrictions on yourself and none of your family do, either.'

'That's because we're right. Your parents were going to be left to make up their own minds, as were you. We'll get the Phillips woman out of the village, get the Post Office shut down and if we owned the chapel, we'd close that too.'

Janey laughed. 'Honestly Finlay, you're so arrogant!'

'Assured, surely?' Finlay said, smiling. He kissed her hand. 'Come on Miss, let's take you back to your new home. You're going to be OK.'

She got up and intertwined her fingers through his. 'How do you always make things right, Finlay?'

'It's the truth we dare not speak perhaps. Come on, we've a pig to prepare for the show,' he said.

Finlay's grandfather was back indoors when they got back. 'Hello you two,' he said. 'I hope he's looking after you.'

'I couldn't wish for anybody better,' Janey answered.

Finlay glanced at Niney. She wrinkled her nose at him in approval.

'Keep him on the straight and narrow, Janey. None of the waywardness of some of the young ladies swarming about,' the old man observed.

'I've had too much of that in my life to want to inflict it on Finlay. I like the free spirit he is. Some of it might rub off on me,' Janey said, easily.

'Well, yes. Maybe that could have been put better,' Finlay's grandfather said.

The telephone rang and Niney answered. 'That was the County Council, James. Complaining about the gate across the top lane,' Niney said.

'I rather thought we were going to talk about this,' Finlay's grandfather answered, shortly.

'We did,' Niney said.

'Oh great! Now I can go straight to the pig unit and there won't be any more parking across the road at the church. Good on you, Auntie Niney! Time the buggers knew their place!' Finlay said, delighted.

'I'm not very happy about the church, Niney. Lots of good people go there. We should give them time to come to an agreement over access.' Finlay's grandfather knew he was losing the argument.

'If they'd consider paying something to its upkeep. There were fifteen cars there last Sunday morning. The lane was blocked yet again. When the bloody vicar arrives, I'll deal with him, James!'

'I want to be there to see that!' Finlay announced. 'Get the buggers gone, Auntie Niney!'

'Well,' Finlay's grandfather said, 'it's not going to make us popular.'

'It's costing us four thousand every year. That's in a context you can grasp, James, the barley crop from all the fields along the main road.' Niney had the winning punch waiting. 'Look at the bank statements, James. We're down to the last five million and things are not set to get any better!'

'I can't pretend I'm happy about it,' Finlay's grandfather said.

On the way to the pig unit, Janey asked if Niney was serious. 'Our wages bill's over thirty thousand and the cost of TT is going up and up. Grandfather doesn't really understand money. Unless we buck up a bit, this place will start losing. The fact is, Janey, we'd be better off selling and putting the money on deposit, at Hoare's.'

'You'd never sell, would you?' Janey asked, suddenly.

'No. You and I will always live here.'

'What do you mean by that, Finlay?' She was suddenly serious.

'I've made some decisions and I want you to listen. I'll not stay in the Navy long. I'll come back here and be with you. I'd like there to be this understanding between us. If you'd like that.'

'You're a deep bugger and no mistake! When did all this come into your head?' she asked, not knowing quite what to say.

'At the cricket match and when I came to look for you this afternoon. I just wanted you to know...' he said.

'Finlay! I'd love to have an understanding.' She was trying not to cry. 'But it's nothing more than that. I can't ask you to commit yourself to me, even though I did to you.' She suddenly giggled. 'Would it help if I dyed my hair red?'

'Janet's lovely, but she ain't a country girl and she ain't you,' Finlay said. There was from that moment a sudden, profound change in what was between them. It was light, happy and easy. They were confident in each other and spent the next hour scrubbing, brushing and covering Starwort with raw linseed oil, as Ron had instructed. The pig gloried in the attention.

—

'How's the beautiful Starwort?' Niney asked, as he walked into the kitchen.

'She kept laying down and wouldn't get up again,' Finlay said.

'What do you expect!' Jenny laughed. 'Bathe and rub oil. Any female would lay down.'

'Shout for Janey to hurry up, darling,' Niney said. 'I'm hungry and I need to speak to you both.'

Finlay went through to the hall and yelled. When Niney wanted to speak to you, it only meant trouble.

They began eating silently. 'There's no easy way to start this,' Niney began. 'You'll have to live here, Janey my love. Granny's finding it a bit much. I've made up a room opposite Kee's for you and I've also made an appointment at the birth control clinic. I'll come with you of course.' Janey drew in a sharp breath. 'Now darling girl, please don't hang your head. There's no hypocrisy in this household. You've done nothing you need be ashamed of. What I don't want is unwanted pregnancies. I hope you love him as much as you look as though you do. And as for you Kee, no more of this studding around with the Ward girls. If I catch you, I'll geld you, for sure! There's as much point keeping you apart as trying to stop the tide coming in.'

'I don't know what to say,' Janey said softly.

'Best not to say anything then, love,' said Niney.

Finlay was sitting alone in the pig lines at the Royal Counties Show with Starwort, asleep in the small pen allocated to her, snoring loudly. Poole, close to Sandbanks and Bournemouth, was full of holiday makers, thousands of whom had decided to come to the agricultural show. Finlay felt strange. He was dressed in the traditional show manner. Polished brown boots from Hoggs, polished brown leather gaiters borrowed from Old John and whipcord breeches borrowed from Jenny, a country check shirt and Country Landowners' tie and over all this was a brilliant white laboratory coat, borrowed from the vet. Finlay was peevish. Niney insisted on recombing his hair and removing some dirt from his face with her handkerchief. It had brought laughter from the other stock men, waiting for their turn in the main ring.

At last the gilt class was called and Finlay, his pocket full of cod-liver-oil biscuits, called Starwort awake. He instructed the pig to be on her best behaviour and then they were out in the sunshine, parading around the main ring in front of hundreds of people. 'Stay close Starry,' Finlay said. The pig, sensing the biscuits, followed him like a dog. They were placed second and walked together back to where Niney, Jenny and Janey were waiting for them. Finlay saw his grandfather deep in conversation with an elderly gentleman.

'Kee, this is Lord Keith. He'd dearly love to buy Starwort.'

'I'm sorry, Lord Keith, but we're keeping her. We'll sell you a gilt from her second litter if you like, but you can't have her,' Finlay said, very firmly.

'How about a thousand guineas and a rod on my water, the Spey, for five years,' Lord Keith offered, smiling.

Finlay snorted dismissively. 'Our river would knock that one into a cocked hat! The Spey!' he scoffed. 'Huh!'

His grandfather and Lord Keith burst out laughing. 'Well said, darling!' Niney interrupted. 'Bloody awful place Scotland. All midges and no water! Hello, Angus,' she said. 'Lovely to see you again. Like a day on a good river, while you're down here?'

'Love to, Niney. Perhaps look over the rest of the pig herd as well.'

'How many sows do you run, Lord Keith?' Finlay asked.

'Around one hundred and fifty,' he replied. 'There are thousands who would give their eye-teeth for a rod on my river. What do you say about that?' He was still testing, mocking Finlay.

'Well Sir! I might well give my eye-teeth, but I wouldn't give you Starwort,' Finlay smiled.

'I'll give you two thousand, five hundred pounds for her. That's my final offer,' Lord Keith said.

'Well Sir, I'm glad that's your final offer,' Finlay said.

'Nicely put. I'll enjoy fishing with you, young man. Will you ghillie for me, please?' he said. 'Do you have a place tomorrow, Niney?'

'I'm sure we can fit you in.' Niney smiled her best smile.

'Will I catch anything, Finlay? That's what I must know,' he asked.

'If you listen to me, I'm sure we will,' Finlay said.

Angus Keith glanced briefly at Finlay's grandfather with just a hint of a smile.

Above the noise and hubbub of the end of the show, Finlay heard their own Land-Rover arriving with the stock trailer. Starwort was loaded. Ron, Finlay and the pig started the journey home. It was some two hours later they unloaded Starwort into her sty and fed her. It had been a long and very successful day.

'Seems a bloody long time since the day she was born, Ron,' Finlay said.

'It must seem that way to you. We'll get her served next time she comes hogging, and she'll join the others.' He scratched Starwort between the ears. 'The easy days are over little lady,' he said. 'And I suppose yours are too, nipper. You're going to join the others.'

Promptly at nine, next morning, a large black Lagonda arrived in the yard, driven by a liveried chauffeur. Niney went to the front door and brought Lord Keith into the kitchen.

'Thought we'd look over the pigs before we started, young Finlay. What do you think?' he asked.

The boy looked at the clock. 'Do you want me to show you around?'

'No, I've some other things to discuss with your grandfather. I can go around with him and meet you back here some time around eleven. I'm going to need convincing this stream is all it's cracked up to be!'

'Sir, I checked in the records last night. You were here regularly from 1943 to 1947. Were you based hereabouts?' Finlay smiled at him.

'You've been checking up on me.' Keith laughed.

'Of course. You called Auntie by her first name. I knew you knew her. I just wondered how,' Finlay jousted with him.

'Caught out properly, Niney! Sharp little bugger, ain't he?' Lord Keith remarked.

'Too clever by half and too cheeky by a long chalk,' Niney said, ruffling Finlay's hair.

'What were you then? Something to do with the SOE? I know you were at *Safeguard*.' Finlay said.

'How'd you know?' Lord Keith said, with consternation, but still amused.

'A groundsman where I play football told me. There was a corrugated-iron fence around the place and he said that spies were trained there during the war. When it was part of HMS *Safeguard*. I just put two and two together.' Finlay tried to be nonchalant, even innocent.

'Well I'm blessed! You don't miss a trick!' Keith said.

'Try not to Sir,' said Finlay.

'It's not something that needs talking about. Even now, darling,' Niney said quietly.

Finlay continued, 'Way things are shaping up in the world, it'll probably need to be used again. Somebody should have a word, or sack the groundsman.'

'How old are you?' Lord Keith asked.

'Old enough to see and wonder about things, Sir,' Finlay smiled. 'I'll get the fishing gear ready.'

Some two hours later Lord Keith came back with his grandfather. 'I've bought some of your pigs. Even the sister of your Starwort. What do you think about that?'

'I hope you paid enough for them!' Finlay said.

'And some. Your grandfather drives a hard bargain. Well! Are we going fishing?' Finlay felt he was still being tested.

They started at the top pool, against the boundary. It was a large, slow and deep eddy which required a silent approach. 'Cast across, almost upstream Sir. Then let your fly come around the bottom of the eddy. Walk back a pace and do the same, and don't forget to bring it back along the bank in jerks,' Finlay ordered.

'I've never fished this one before. I'm in your hands, Finlay,' Keith said, casting across the river.

'Just trust me, Sir,' Finlay said.

'Can I trust you, Finlay?' he answered.

'Of course.'

'Then I do.' Lord Keith made his second cast. A fish flashed in the deep and the rod bent in a violent arc.

'Sea trout,' Finlay said. 'Don't try to hold him. Let him go downstream.' The fish fought hard and long, making several rushes downstream and then powering back against what current there was. The fish showed twice, tail walking upstream and flipping over, rushing away downstream again. Then it was ready for the net. 'Good start, Sir!' Finlay cried, striking the fish on the head. 'About eight pounds, I'd say. If we just hang about quietly for a few minutes, we might catch another from here. This one just shot out of the pool, so it won't be too badly disturbed,' Finlay suggested. They waited and watched. The water was far too deep to see anything clearly.

'There are some more down there. I can sense that much. Try coming across a little quicker, just so that it looks different to them.'

Keith cast again. Before the fly had got properly into the main pool, it was snatched again. This time, by a big fish. 'Salmon, Sir,' Finlay said, excitedly. 'And he's a big one. Give him plenty of time.' The fish fought hard for a good half-hour. The rod was a little light, but Keith was good and patient. Even when the reel was down to the last of the backing, he was gently composed and won the line back gradually. When it was over, and the large salmon lay dwarfing the sea trout, Finlay said, 'Hell of a river! Best in the world, I shouldn't wonder!'

'Touché! You're making me feel wholly inadequate. He shook Finlay's hand. 'Thank you for your expertise, young man.'

They were walking over the big bridge when Niney found them, bringing food and drink. They sat together looking at the river. 'Finlay, this was one huge camp of Allied soldiers. Just a small part of the biggest enterprise of the war. Now look. It's gone back to its gentle beauty. I wonder how many remember swimming in this wonderful river, hearing the birds at dawn and watching the sun come up,' Lord Keith said. 'This really is a little part of Heaven.'

'He knows that, Angus. That's why he's here and his parents are on the far side of the world,' Niney said. 'But he still insists on going into the forces.'

'Because of this place, Auntie. We must be always ready to defend what we love. When I was born, we were on the brink of losing it. That must not happen again. You do see that, don't you?' Finlay sighed.

'He must do his duty, Niney. There are precious few who want to these days and I fear the idiot politicians. They hate our class because they're afraid of us. Land and privilege go together. They'll see it gone in the awful name of equality before the end of this century. James always said, when the middle class get hold of power there'll be no place for the aristocracy.'

'Ain't that the truth!' Niney sighed.

Chapter Two

•

Next morning, Finlay rose quickly and dressed. He drank half a cup of tea and scratched a quick note on the pad telling anyone that he had gone out, on his mare. The air outside was cool and full of the smell of ripening cereals. A song thrush dashed off a quick song from the wellingtonia, before dropping to the newly sown lawn to search for food. The mare welcomed him noisily, stamping her feet, impatient to be off. When he placed the saddle on her back, she rubbed at him with her head, urging him to hurry.

He circled her gently around and aimed her at the rails. There were the heart-stopping moments as the mare sailed over the rails and, collecting herself, cantered along the hedgerow of the long narrow field that ran around the back of the parkland. By the time they had reached the park gates, the mare had run off her excess energy and was ready to be reasoned with. 'What was that about, madam?' he said. She waggled her ears, listening to him. 'Oh, I know. You can smell Janey on me. Well, it's still me, so don't take on so.'

They turned left out of the gate on to the main road, crossed the bridge by the Horse and Jockey and turned right on to Whiteparish Road. The long slow hill before them was the beginning of the chalk escarpment, the chalk that made the river what it was. He pushed the mare into a fast trot. There was no traffic on a Sunday and the sun had barely lifted above the trees on the eastern horizon. The world seemed to be theirs alone. At the summit he turned the mare into the wood on his right and, keeping her at a fast trot, was soon through it and looking down into the valley below. He dropped from the mare and removed her bridle, allowing her to crop the short grass at the woodland edge. Confident she would not leave him, he stood gazing at the town and the river below. The abbey looked almost pink in the morning light and the river was a silver ribbon, winding its way through the flat meadowlands that bounded it. 'This is what it's about!' he said to himself, aloud.

He watched in the far distance a herd of yellow-coloured cows being brought in for morning milking. Further away still, blue-looking, were the chalk hills of King Somborne, running up to the Downs. This was his England. A home so nearly lost in his lifetime to just another vile bunch of barbarians from Europe. The Germans now lay quiet. The French, another horde of malcontents, having previously tried the same thing, were now trying to cover their shame with lies about their magnificent resistance against the very Germans who had wanted his England. He had lived with wars all of his life. They didn't seem to end, bloodshed and conflict. Korea had ended unresolved, the French had been ejected from Indo-china and the Russians, so lately allies, were now seemingly the new enemy. Would they come and try to take these islands? The Union flag, hanging limply on the Abbey, might easily have been a Swastika. He knew then which road he had to take.

Another combine harvester, and a letter from the Admiralty arrived on the same day. He had passed the medical requirement and was therefore to present himself at Greenwich the following week. The large red combine told everyone that summer was nearly over. By the time it left the estate, autumn would have arrived. The combines began their trek across the estate. They looked like slow merchantmen being shepherded by the little grey Fergies with their trailers, for all the world like escort vessels. The malting barley was the first crop to get their attention and as each machine trekked across, a sweep of over thirty feet lay shorn behind them. The chaff and dust flew up around them and ducks began to fly in to pick up the gleanings.

The malting barley had to be bagged off from the dryer and cleaner into big sacks. When the morning sun had dried the dew from the barley, it required no drying and the cascade was speeded up. The four men, working with the sacks, were hard pressed to keep up. For hours they carried the heavy sacks to the edges of the barn and stacked them two deep. By lunch time it seemed that every muscle and bone in Finlay's body ached and he was more than pleased when they were relieved by the next four men. The others went to lunch, but Finlay had to take a tractor and trailer and help bring the barley from the fields. Niney had objected fiercely to this but his grandfather said Finlay had to earn the respect of the men by doing what they did, and more. The combines continued cutting until around ten at night. He worked sixteen hours a day. In five days the malting barley was finished. Finlay was very fit.

He had intended to go to Greenwich alone on the train. The idea was quickly overruled by Niney. They were to go up in the car with Mr Brockett. The pristine cleanliness which Niney had insisted on was not to be compromised by the railways. On the morning of the interview Finlay looked at himself in a full-length mirror. He was an almost stranger to himself.

Finlay had seen photographs of the Naval College, but it did not really prepare him for the grandeur of the actuality. 'Hell of a place for a school!' he remarked.

As the car stopped in the car park, Niney handed him two five-pound notes. 'Take this. Mr Brockett will take me to Bond Street. When we're back here, if the car is empty, we'll be in the museum.'

A large Chief Petty Officer was marching towards the car as they got out. 'Thank you Mr Brockett,' Finlay said. 'And please Auntie Niney! Don't kiss me in front of this chap coming.'

'AIB cadet?' the warrant officer asked.

'Yes Chief,' Finlay answered.

'Right! Name please.'

'Finlay, Keith, Chief.'

He looked at his list. 'Right. Go to that chap on the main door. He'll take you where you have to go. Good afternoon Madam. If you can be back here in a couple of hours, that should be time enough.' For once, Niney's smile had no effect. 'Right! Off you go Finlay,' the warrant said sharply.

He was pleased to see Andy Bretton sitting with some other youngsters. 'Hello again,' Finlay said, shaking his hand. 'You got past scruffy Doctor Williams then?'

Bretton sprang to his feet and introduced him to the others, most of whom had elected to go into the Royal Marines. A door opened. 'Adams!' someone shouted. They all wished him luck. As the other candidates waited, they chatted together easily. They were a fairly disparate group. One wanted to be a doctor within the service, another a lawyer. It seemed only Finlay and Bretton had a yen to take on The Queen's enemies.

Another candidate was called. 'They're sending them out another way, so we can't speak to them. That's a bit sneaky!' Andy observed.

'Finlay!' someone shouted. He walked into a magnificent room. Huge windows looked out on to the Thames, with high ceilings. The walls were decorated with a bright-ivory paint. The reflected light made the room look homely. He walked up to a long table where the interviewers were sitting. There were two marine officers, five naval officers and one civilian.

'Good afternoon Finlay,' a captain said.

'Good afternoon, Captain,' Finlay answered. 'Good afternoon gentlemen,' he said to the others.

'Well, you're an interesting one. Why should I want you in my Navy when you were flung out of school, do you think?'

'I wasn't flung out Sir. I elected to leave. The teachers were far too shallow for me and had very few principles,' Finlay said.

The Marine Colonel covered his amusement. 'You refused to accept an award for saving a girl's life. Why was that?'

'I didn't save her for an award, Sir. I knew I could, so I did.'

'Supposing you thought you might only have been able to save her?'

'She was a classmate Sir. I wouldn't have watched her float away down to the Solent. Anyway, I knew I could save her... Sir.' He almost forgot the last word.

'How are things down on the farm Finlay?' an Admiral asked.

'Busy Sir. It's harvest time.'

'Wouldn't you be better suited staying at home, helping to produce food for the nation?' the Admiral asked.

'I love my home Sir, but if everyone sat at home, there would be no Navy and nothing to protect what we love. I don't want to see the Hammer and Sickle flying over the Abbey in Romsey, Sir!' Finlay said, with passion.

The Admiral handed him a wooden pointer. 'Go to that map and point out the places I call for. Try Murmansk.' Finlay pointed it out. 'That was easy. Your father was there. Try Manilla.' Finlay pointed it out. 'Halifax,' the Admiral ordered. 'Nova Scotia or Yorkshire?' Finlay asked. 'Both,' the Admiral smiled. For the next ten minutes, Finlay answered questions on world affairs, the type of ships needed for the future and how to recruit the best personnel.

'Your sponsors speak very highly of you,' the Captain said.

'Sponsors, Sir?' Finlay asked.

'We don't ask for references from you. We find them ourselves,' he said.

'Oh I see,' Finlay said, wondering who they were.

'You probably don't. Finlay, you were fishing with my elder brother a couple of weeks ago. Lord Keith spoke very highly of you.' He closed the file in front of him. 'You'll be called to spend time at Brittannia around next Easter. I'll see you a year this Christmas, at the end of your first term.'

'Do you mean I'm in, Sir?' Finlay asked, astounded.

'Well, it certainly seems like it. Carry on with your studies. I know you'll not let this Board down. Carry on then. Out through that door,' the Captain ordered, smiling at him.

As he went to walk out, the Captain called him. 'Finlay, we'll signal your father and let him know.'

'Thank you, Sir,' Finlay answered.

Outside the door in the corridor, the leading hand was waiting for him. 'First happy face I've seen today!' he said.

'I'm in!' Finlay said. 'I'm going to be an officer in the Navy!'

'Have to call you Sir then, sprog. Well done, come on,' he said, leading him away.

Walking towards the car park, he was stopped by the Chief Petty Officer they had seen earlier. 'Well, you look happy. Are you in?' he asked Finlay.

'Yes Chief. I go down to Dartmouth next Easter and start next autumn,' Finlay said, elated.

'I'll see you there then. Glad to see you carrying on the tradition. I served with your father, a proper bastard but a good fighting officer. Look forward to teaching you,' the warrant officer said.

Though delighted, Niney seemed more concerned to get home and was unusually quiet as they threaded their way through London.

'Did you get your shopping done?' he asked.

She ignored the question, but pressed the button which raised the glass panel in front of them. 'Sorry Mr Brockett. Family stuff,' she said. Turning to Finlay, she spoke intently. 'You must treat Jenny with kid gloves over this one Kee.'

'Janey you mean?' he said.

'No, Jenny, you fool! She'll move heaven and earth to keep you. She doesn't want you to go. I worry if you were not there, at home, I think she'd leave.'

'But what about Grandfather?' Finlay asked.

'At best, she's your grandfather's companion, my dear. Not what everyone thinks she is. Do you understand? When your mother comes home, I think she'll go her separate way.'

'I'm going to have to choose between Jenny and Mama? Well! I can tell you now. It won't be my mother.' Finlay was certain.

'Be careful. Don't burn any of your boats or bridges,' Niney warned.

'Why's life bloody complicated?' Finlay began. 'I thought Jenny just popped along the corridor at night or something like that!'

'It isn't complicated, if you think about it. James lost his wife, then he lost his favourite daughter. Jenny filled the gap. She looks after him, directs his life. James is too lazy to do that. Actually, Jenny's almost the same dilly day-dream that Bibby was, and she needed a father. She stayed because of habit and then you came along and gave her a reason.'

'You don't want Jenny to leave?' Finlay said.

'Of course not. But Jenny and your mother won't mix long term, if at all. Just be careful with Jen,' Niney said.

'I always am. She's my soul-mate. My big sister.'

'I don't think she sees it like that,' Niney said softly, pushing the button to open the partition again. 'Sorry, family wranglings.'

Mr Brockett smiled gently. Niney settled back into the leather seats and closed her eyes. 'You do that when you don't want to talk Auntie. Pretend to be asleep.'

'I need to think.' She smiled, without opening her eyes.

Finlay was determined his aunt would not ignore him. 'If you tell me you're plotting that vicar's downfall, I'll stay quiet.' Niney ignored him. He picked up her hand and kissed it. She tried to suppress a smile. 'Can we go to the beach hut before summer ends?' he asked.

'Is there a suitable tea shop on this road, Mr Brockett?'

'Yes Miss. Alresford has one.'

'Good! You and I can have tea and this creature can go without,' she said, entwining her long fingers through Finlay's. 'You can go after the barley is cut, as arranged. Now, let me sleep.'

As they passed over the Hog's Back, Finlay felt Niney's hand relax into his. As they came into Hampshire and the chalk downs, Finlay could see the cereal harvest was in full swing. He badly wanted to be home. There were several fields being cut with binders and the fields were coloured by the people standing the stooks of cut cereal. Sitting in the small tea shop, they watched as the grain trailers were being hauled through the small town by the inevitable Fergies. The solidity and comfort of the eternal continuity of the farming cycle.

He got out of the car in the top lane to open Niney's newly installed gate to allow the Armstrong through. He could hear the buzz of machinery all around him. It sounded louder than usual and the air was hung heavy with the smell of TVO and diesel exhaust fumes. 'Let's hope James doesn't go soft on the idea when the Council come out. The gate's stopped that rat-run out to Totton. It's become dangerous to anybody walking it. Back me up on it darling,' Niney said.

'Of course I will Auntie. Keep the buggers out! When are you dealing with the vicar?' Finlay asked.

'Shortly my dear!'

As they pulled into the yard, Jenny and Janey came out to meet
them. 'Congratulations, buggerlugs!' Jenny said happily, and hugged
him. Janey seemed a little more restrained. 'Well done! England now
expects!' They both had a dusting of flour on them, evidence of cooking, their faces flushed red. The kitchen smelt deliciously and the
large table was covered in pasties and sandwiches.

'What have you been up to? What's all this food for?' Niney asked,
looking for somewhere to put her parcels.

'The contractor had a combine spare for a couple of days so he
brought it here. James thinks to get all the oats cut in one go. They are
going on until they finish. We have to feed everyone at six o'clock in
the top fields,' Jenny said.

'Wonderful!' Niney said. 'You seem to have everything under control. I shan't interfere. How did you know about Kee?'

'A telegram came,' Jenny said. 'It was just addressed here so I opened
it. It's there, on the side.'

Finlay picked it up and read, 'Congratulations. Do well. Mama.'
Finlay handed it to Niney. 'They said at Greenwich they would let my
father know. Jolly fast, the Navy. Do you know what Grandfather
wants me to do, Jen?'

'Yes. Go to the picnic and then be on dryer duty at ten until they finish. You ought to get some rest. You'll be on right through the night
probably.'

The picnic, if such an occasion could be so lightly named, was an occasion to remember. Everyone on the estate was there. Even the dairymen and their families, who held themselves aloof from such things,
arrived. They considered themselves the aristocrats of the workforce,
highly paid and standoffish, but they would help with stacking and
loading straw bales. At six, the combines drew in close to the blankets
and tablecloths strewn out, covered with food. Untold, the tractors
came in and parked in a circle around the area. Last to arrive was Carl
in his Jeep and with him was a young lady whom Finlay recognized as
one of the girls who worked in the local tomato nursery. The welcome
she got must have surprised her. Carl was now much respected by the
estate staff, whom Finlay counted as being thirty-five. He studied

them. These people, so closely bound together by their love of the countryside, seemed to him unknowing saints. They always looked after each other at all times, lived almost on top of each other and knew each other's joys and sadness.

When at last Finlay's grandfather arrived, they cheered him. Their faces burnt brown from the sun, they showed their love and respect. He, in turn, glowed with pleasure and bade them eat and rest. He came and sat in the stubble with Finlay, who was sharing a rug with Jack and Niney. 'The girls have done us proud! Congratulations Kee! A Queen's Commission is a very great honour!'

'I haven't got there yet, Grandfather!' Finlay said.

'You will,' he said.

When Ron came to join them, he gave his congratulations. He was covered in dust and dirt from the combines and smelt heavily of diesel oil. 'We'll finish this even if we have to leave trailers full up overnight. The balers will be down as soon as we've finished with the food, so we'll see if you did a good job on that engine, nipper.'

'Oh yes, the bloody engine!' Niney said, smiling at Finlay. 'You've no idea how boring Kee can be on the subject of cam-followers and collets, Ron. And I do object to bits of engine on the kitchen table.'

'It was only a couple of valves Auntie,' Finlay objected.

'A couple of valves that should have stayed in the workshop!' She laughed.

The meal over, the combines began their steady march up and down the standing oats, the plump ripe grain cascading into the trailers running alongside them. All was as it should be. Finlay spent till ten stacking the straw bales in heaps ready for the loading tractor and then hitched a lift on one of the tractors back to the dryer. As they left the field, the combines, now flooded with lights, were surrounded by clouds of dust and insects shining in the artificial brightness. He worked alone in the dryer, checking the cleaned grain as it was elevated to the storage bins, making sure that bearings were not running hot anywhere and moving the heavy bags of rubbish from the cleaner.

Jenny came to see him at around midnight and left the pick-up outside for his return when he had finished. Outside, away from the noise of the barn machinery, she said goodnight and hugged him tightly. 'I've left a towel in your pick-up, in case you want to get clean in the river before you come home.'

At three, one of the tractor drivers came and told him no more grain would be coming in. The oats were finished. Finlay ran the couple of tons remaining over the dryer and then shut it down. A soft silence suddenly surrounded him. He checked nothing was running hot anywhere and carefully left everything ready for the morning and went outside into the awakening world. There was almost a chill in the air as the strengthening light gradually changed the trees from the black of night into the green of daylight. The oak leaves were already looking tired and worn; the summer had been almost continually hot. Only the conifers stayed dark green and bright. The birches were already turning the yellow and gold of autumn. Skeins of ducks came sweeping up from the estuary, bickering and quacking softly as they plummeted down on to the stubble to feast and fatten on the gleanings.

Finlay stood and watched the beauty of the day unfold before him. A long skein of Canada geese passed over, honking mournfully and suddenly dropping at huge speed on to the stubble.

He drove to the hatch pool and stripped off his clothing, walked on to the lip of the pool, and for once soaped himself energetically with the bar of soap Jenny had left him. He knew his grandfather disapproved of soap in the river, but on this occasion the dust was so thick upon him, the chalky water had a job to reach his skin. Once clean, he towelled himself dry, dressed and drove back to the house, coasting the last hundred yards with the engine switched off, to arrive as quietly as possible.

He lay in bed listening to the moorhens on the garden feeder stream. For once the martins were up early and wheeling around the yard, taking the insects and flies from above the stable yard muck heap. The swallows were probably feeding above the stubble further away. He heard the whistling rhythm of swans flying over before he slept.

He slept dreamlessly until he was woken by Jenny's voice, gently cajoling him. 'Hey buggerlugs! Are you going to sleep all day?'

'Hiya you,' he said, reaching up and pulling her face down to kiss it. 'God I was tired. What time is it?'

'Eight o'clock.' Her breath smelt sweet in his face. 'Breakfast in half an hour. We want to know about yesterday, so get up, you tired sod.' Her hair was over his face and smelled as only her hair could. Her face was beside his and he suddenly wanted badly to kiss her. He kissed her mouth, tasting the minty taste. 'I love you Jen,' he said.

'I know you do,' she said softly. 'Now get up!' She pulled away from him gently. 'There's a cup of tea there, drink that and get up or I shall pour some cold water over you! There are your clean clothes,' she said, going to the door. She turned and watched him get out of bed. 'You smell and taste of Lifebuoy soap and the river!' she laughed.

The oat harvest had been heavy. It was more than apparent there would not be enough storage space for the barley and wheat yet to come in. Something had to be sold to clear the space for the wheat, the most important crop. The annual ritual of getting samples to the buyers had to begin. Some firms sent buyers to the farm to take the samples and make offers, but this year his grandfather told Finlay to go to the Corn Exchange in Salisbury and give them around to potential purchasers. 'Get your face known, for the future. In case the Navy doesn't suit you,' he said.

The following Tuesday, Jenny ferried him to Salisbury and dropped him at the Corn Exchange. 'I'll buy a couple of cheeses from the market for the harvest supper and come straight back,' she had said. Finlay walked up the stairs to where the Corn Exchange was held, clutching one of Niney's large shopping baskets filled with the samples. The room seemed full of large men in tweed suits and shiny brown brogue shoes. As he entered there was a sudden silence. The buyers, now not used to farmers coming in, viewed him suspiciously. Finlay consulted his list. 'I'm looking for Mr Lennox, Mr Wright and anyone who wants to buy some racehorse oats. My name's Finlay and I'm from Lee Park.'

There was a rush towards him. Finlay put the basket on a table and stood in front of it.

'I'm Lennox, young man. Have you got some malting barley for me?'

Finlay handed him the packet. 'There you are Mr Lennox. Write a spot price on your card and give it me.'

Another pushed forward. 'Wright's the name and right's the price. Mine will be an oat sample.' He opened it immediately. 'How much like this have you got?' he asked, liking what he was looking at.

'About two hundred and fifty tons. All like that. We can load a twenty-ton lorry in three or four minutes, so bear that in mind when you make an offer,' Finlay said.

A younger man approached him. 'Could I have a sample of the race-horse oats, young man?' he asked. He spread some in his hand, then into his mouth and began chewing them. 'Beautiful! Are they just in bulk? I wonder if you could bag me off twenty tons?'

'I don't see why not, but at the moment we're too busy. After harvest no doubt. Give us a call and make an offer. You want them for now or later?' Finlay asked. He liked this chap.

'November time probably.'

He spoke to several other dealers and merchants and was asked how long before the wheat was cut and whether they had enough storage space for all their crop. 'Oh yes, we've plenty of space,' he lied easily.

'So why are you wanting to sell early?' a merchant asked.

'Who said we were? We may sell some feed barley early, about a thousand tons, because that never really pays for keeping. We have to keep enough back for our own use,' Finlay said. He sounded more knowledgeable than he actually was.

'Any milling wheat?' another merchant asked.

'Yes. That's what we grow most of, but you'll have to compete directly with the flour mill for that.' Finlay smiled.

He looked around the room and saw the one man he was looking for. He walked across to him, a large fat man, dressed in beautifully cut tweeds. A large gold watchchain was strung across his huge stomach. 'Ah, Mr Blundell, you are to present yourself at the house a little after nine tomorrow to talk straw with my grandfather.' He affected Niney's autocratic manner, which brooked no argument, and watched Mr Blundell's face.

'There's plenty of good straw about this year, you know,' the man said, tetchily.

'Shall I tell my grandfather you're not interested then?' Finlay said. He didn't wait for an answer but turned on his heel and with as much dignity as he could ever muster, carrying a woman's shopping basket, left the Exchange.

'Who was that shitbag?' Blundell's companion asked.

'That's the grandson. I'm not going to enjoy dealing with that little snot-nose in the future!' Blundell said venomously.

'Who are they?' his friend asked.

'Old gentry! Fucking bastards! Still think they rule the world! Nasty bastards as well. They've cut the power to a friend of mine's house. They want them out of the village.' Blundell spat.

'Tell the whole story, Percy,' Lennox said, joining them. 'They're wonderful farmers. Have some of the best stock in the country and they don't like church people. You were just walked over by a boy Percy. By a boy!' Lennox laughed. 'You'll be there in the morning. Touching your forelock!'

'Will I buggery!' he said.

In the car, Finlay laughed. 'Grandfather said I should leave the Corn Exchange with the buyers wanting more. Think I've done that. I ordered that Blundell chap to be at the house in the morning. I did it in the best Auntie Niney manner.'

'But he's one of those Bible bashers. A friend of that bloody awful Phillips woman!' Jenny said.

'I know. Fun, ain't it?' Finlay laughed.

Chapter Three

•

Harvest was over by the third week of August. The hoped-for break that usually happened between the barley and wheat harvest did not come. The wheat ripened early so the combines never stopped. By the finish, everyone was tired and when the last sweep of the cutting heads was completed there was a collective sigh of relief. It was a Wednesday evening when the barn doors were ceremonially shut and everyone was given till the following Monday off. Only the stock men had to work. The ceremony of harvest bonuses came next, when more than a little whisky was drunk and wives, suddenly, could revert to normal meals and mealtimes.

Harvest supper was fixed for the following week. It would combine the end of harvest and wish Janey well before the start of her university life. Though invited by Finlay's grandfather, Janey's parents refused to attend, claiming they no longer had a daughter. Niney told Janey her parents were too busy arranging their relocation. There was a sadness for Janey, but anger from Niney. The estate church would be shut forthwith. Naomi Phillips had given up the unequal struggle and her house was bought by the estate, rather cheaper than it should have been. There seemed to be difficulty in getting mains electricity. Owners of the other houses supplied by the estate turbine reflected on how fortunate they were.

Niney's next move, high on a flight of autocracy, was to invite the vicar to tea. A sumptuous meal of scones and honey followed by a wonderful Dundee cake with a chunk of Stilton to complement its taste and texture. After tea, Niney gave him the outstanding account going back some eight years. The total was just over ten thousand pounds. 'I seem to remember having this conversation three years ago, Vicar.' Niney smiled at him sweetly.

'I shall certainly speak to Winchester about it Mrs Terry,' the vicar answered.

'While you are speaking to them, you must inform them the church will have to close immediately for repairs. As owners of the church, we would be responsible if anything fell and injured your flock. If the insurance company thought we had been dilatory about repairs, they would never pay. You do see our position, don't you?' Niney said, sweetly.

'But… how long would the church have to close for? It's fairly sound in its structure, Mrs Terry.' The vicar suddenly looked uncomfortable.

'Well, as you say, Vicar, only fairly. We must stop any further deterioration, so I should think probably some years. No more than five or six. You see, we're very much on short commons here. With the church continuing to refuse to abide by agreed terms, we cannot make it a priority. You can live on in your house for six months, or until you get another parish. Whichever is the sooner,' Niney said.

'We have a harvest festival planned,' the vicar objected.

'Completely out of the question, I'm afraid. We'd be grateful if you would remove anything from the church that doesn't belong to the estate, and give me the key in seven days. The formalities involved can be dealt with by our land agent. He'll deal direct with Winchester no doubt. He'll also deal with the outstanding account,' Niney said, getting up and intimating the meeting was now over.

'It's preposterous!' the vicar said.

'Yes. Outstanding accounts always seem that way Vicar, but we don't hold you responsible,' she said, aiming him towards the front door. 'We'll look after the graveyard and the headstones as usual. They pertain mainly to our own people anyway.'

His impulsion towards the front door was firm and swift and the vicar found himself standing outside in the sunshine before he could formulate any sort of defence.

On the estate the closure of the church was met with a degree of satisfaction. It was the new incomers into Romsey who seemed the only people who now used it. When a letter was delivered to everyone in the village notifying them the Post Office was to close, to be replaced with a mobile service to arrive at nine-thirty on Thursdays, all began to see the hand of Niney behind it. 'I'll not have that bastard Jenks parading himself around the village in his wheelchair. It upsets Janey and if we get the bloody Chapel people gone, there'll be no excuse for him being here. A good dose of persecution will do them all good. They may begin to see what fanaticism can cost them,' Niney had said.

Finlay was delighted by Niney's high-handedness. 'The more we do for them, the more they take advantage, it seems to me.'

The arrival of a telegram threw already made plans for a short holiday into confusion. 'Angus has invited Jack and me to shoot grouse,' Finlay's grandfather announced.

'You must go!' Niney exclaimed. 'The way things are going with the bloody do-gooders you must surely make the most of it. We'll borrow the new keeper from next door and have the BROCKetts move in here. We can still go down to the beach hut. Kee needs a break and Janey can have a holiday before university.'

'You don't mind me taking Jack away?' he asked.

'Oh James honestly! What do you think he'd rather do? Sit twiddling his thumbs on a beach, or shoot grouse? Are you taking the car or one of the Land-Rovers?'

'The car, I think,' Finlay's grandfather replied.

When Finlay came up from the workshop, helping Carl get ready for the autumn sowing, his first question was whether his aunt had decided on Hengistbury.

'In the morning first thing and this time we'll stay longer.' Niney explained about his grandfather's invitation. All the arrangements had been made, so now it was just a case of going.

Elated, Finlay began packing what he needed immediately. 'Are we taking the Land-Rover?' he shouted downstairs to anyone who might have been listening.

'Of course!' he heard Niney shout back.

Downstairs he dumped his bag in the passage by the kitchen. 'I'm ready!' he announced.

'So am I,' his grandfather said. 'Look after the womenfolk, my boy!'

Uncle Jack and Finlay's grandfather almost ran to the already loaded car. 'See you when we see you,' Jack said as the car, with indecent haste, pulled out of the yard.

Niney stood watching the car flying along the top lane, her hands on her hips. 'Not even a bloody kiss goodbye. Marvellous!'

As the Land-Rover breasted the rise above the spit, one of the most beautiful vistas in England lay spread beneath them. The Solent, green with just a few mare's-tails chasing each other shorewards, the Isle of Wight with its patchwork of fields in the distance, some showing green, others the striped yellow of cut cereal fields and the chalk cliffs of the Needles, white now in the morning sun. 'Is there anywhere more beautiful than this in the whole world?' Niney said, to no one in particular.

'Only the hatch pool,' Finlay answered.

'You're as bad as Jack,' she laughed. 'OK! The second most beautiful place. Take either one of you away from your beloved river and you both start to wilt.'

'There'll be no wilting. I won't allow it. It's almost Janey's last week at home and we shan't be back here until next summer,' Jenny said, easing the Land-Rover into the steep drop.

The beach itself seemed deserted, its popularity lost after the thunderstorms and the deaths that had occurred. With the Land-Rover unloaded, they settled down to making tea and cooking breakfast. Finlay sat alone on the verandah drinking in the smell of the sea, listening to the bird life and was happy.

'Breakfast, buggerlugs,' Jenny called.

'I love this place,' he said, coming back inside. 'Why do we never come here in the winter?'

'You'll be here on your own!' Niney said. 'Far too cold for me.'

Jenny and Janey elected to go and find driftwood for a fire that evening while Finlay and Niney did nothing but lie on a car rug on the sand and read until the sun was warmer and they could swim.

'I think Janey is feeling it now, about her parents. I think she misses her home.'

'She feels awkward about living with us,' Finlay suggested.

'We must give her a special going-away present,' Niney said.

'What about we give her a new bicycle? All the students ride them. That old thing she rides must be older than you.' He said it with all-seeming innocence.

'An inspirational idea! That's what we'll do. I'm not forty yet. That bike must be fifty. I'll show you how old when I get changed!' she said sharply.

The next five days passed quickly. They spent the last day as they had spent the others. Jenny collected strangely shaped pieces of driftwood and unusual shells, while Niney and Janey lay about reading. In the evening they sat together talking, watching the strangely coloured and beautiful flames of the fire. They left around ten the next morning.

As they approached Romsey, without any bidding, Jenny turned down left and went along the track to Saddlers Mill. 'Get out then, buggerlugs. Pay your homage while I turn round. If I can't keep you here, maybe the river will for me.'

Finlay walked on to the bridge above the fish pass. He watched and smelt the river crashing through, the foaming current pushed into the middle of the pool. As it eddied around right-handed, several large grayling hovered on the edge of the main flow, picking invisible food particles from the current. Downstream, the raft of starwort which always grew every year looked tired from its constant movement of the summer and was dying back with the cooler nights. The river was lower than normal because of the long dry summer, but as clear as tap water. The gravel bottom showed clear and clean with myriads of fry and minnows chasing across it.

'Hello you,' Finlay said softly.

'Come on!' Jenny shouted. 'You can have a long love-in at home!' She revved the engine impatiently.

The yard was empty of cars when they arrived back. Finlay helped unload and then went to see that his horse was looked after.

Indoors, when Janey had gone upstairs, Niney said to Jenny, 'I'll go up to the Grieveses' place in a moment. Have another go at getting them to at least see Janey before she goes off. I'll say I'm going up to see Granny.'

Jenny nodded her agreement, but didn't look hopeful.

When Finlay came down the next morning, the day of the Harvest Supper, he found his grandfather and Uncle Jack asleep on the sofa and chair. The air was thick with whisky fumes, an empty bottle on the floor and the remains of their scratch meal scattered everywhere. He put the kettle on to the hotplate. 'They must have had a good time,' he thought. 'But if Niney comes down, there'll be Hell to pay.'

As the dawn chased the shadows from the yard and stables, Finlay could see the Armstrong with both rear wheels clear of the ground, its long, elegant bonnet buried deep in the muck heap and both front doors open.

Thinking that discretion was the better part of valour, Finlay decided that he should flee. An hour and a half later he was back at the workshop, studying the damaged Armstrong.

'Vat everyone zink I am? De parts not possible fer de two veeks!' Carl was cross.

'If you can't get the parts Carl, then you can't mend it. I'll deal with Grandfather,' Finlay offered.

Niney was alone in the kitchen. 'Morning Auntie! Bit of a shambles in here this morning. How are we getting Janey to Oxford with no car?'

'All dealt with darling. As George was involved, Janey will be going up in his new car. Your grandfather has gone into Totton to buy the bicycle with Janey and Jen is upstairs.' She gave him a gentle hug and kiss.

'You're taking all this lightly. I thought you'd be madder than Hell,' Finlay said.

'Oh I haven't started yet. I just don't want Janey upset. Her parents have disowned her. They were very articulate and absolutely immovable. Never mind.'

The day passed slowly with everyone waiting for the storm to break. Janey was delighted and surprised with her new bicycle. The hall was laid out ready for the Harvest Supper. Fortnum & Mason's arrived to deliver the food and still Niney was calm and sweet to all around. Finlay spent the day in the workshop. At last it was evening. He walked back to the house. The swallows and martins were in long lines on the electricity cables, looking like a huge necklace, gathering for their long flight to Africa. They had had a wonderful breeding year. They sat hunched in their hundreds. Finlay was always sad to see them go. The swifts that flew over the town in screaming lines had gone already. The end of the year was upon them.

Harvest Supper was a less formal affair than Christmas. Everyone arrived in casual clothes, the check shirts of the countryside, the tweed or cord trousers but always the highly polished shoes. The food laid out upon the long table in the hall looked inviting and wholesome. When Niney added the legs of lamb and huge joint of beef to the whole, everything was ready. The yard gradually filled with what cars were coming and by 6.45 everyone had arrived. The visitors were shy about helping themselves but the waiters from London were instructed to get things going. Gradually, everyone began to relax and wait about in groups for the start of the supper.

Niney banged a serving spoon on the table. 'Before we start there are one or two things to say. I'll begin with the church. How many of you want it kept open, just for our own people?' There was a fair showing of hands. 'Good! Then it'll stay open for you. The current vicar is on his way. If there's need of one, we can get a proper sporting parson in for any marriages or deaths. I did what I did because I was sick of the newcomers. The churchyard is your responsibility. Take what men of your team you may need to do it.' She paused. 'I hope you all approve of the new Post Office.' There was a long cheer. 'The Phillipses' house now belongs to the estate. Anyone who fancies living there, come and see me. I hope you all approve.' There was a longer cheer. 'Now, we have to look at trespass. The only riders allowed over the estate are the Ward family. Anyone else is trespassing. As far as walkers go, move them on. If you see them more than once, let Ron know. We want no more people wandering about. Disease precautions.

'Now to something closer to your hearts. There are lots of pike in the river since the flood, which have to come out. There'll be a whole week's wages for the person who catches the biggest over the salmon close season, and another week's wages for the chap who catches the biggest number. Live and dead bait only. No spinning, so as to protect the late salmon coming in.

'Lastly! Thank you all for what you do. Here we are at another year's end. We haven't had anybody leave to go elsewhere, so we hope you're content. If you aren't, talk to Ron and we'll always see what we can do. That's all I have to say, but as you know Janey is off to university tomorrow. She's the first person on the estate to ever do this, and I want you all to wish her well.'

There was prolonged cheering. Janey looked very embarrassed.

An hour into the celebrations, Ron was forced to his feet. He banged on the table and called for silence: 'All of us agree with you, Miss Niney. The village will be better off without them and it'll be good not to have the townies pushing our people out the church. I'll make sure the churchyard is the best in the county and we wish Janey the very best. I know she'll make us proud. Thanks Boss, Miss Niney and Miss Jenny. You put yourselves out for us. As for the pike, you might as well give me the money now. I'll win both them prizes!' The ribaldry that followed was long and loud, till Niney stood and spoke.

'Well Ronnie Drew, I'll give you the money now, but if you don't win, you'll work a fortnight for nothing. How about that?'

'Is the nipper fishing?' Ron asked.

'No point! He doesn't get paid, and shooting them wouldn't be fair!' Niney laughed.

'Then you're on Miss Niney,' Ron said.

By midnight all was finished, the people from Fortnums packed and gone and only the family was left.

'OK Niney, let's get it over with,' Finlay's grandfather said.

'I am truly ashamed of you both. That's all,' Niney answered. It could not have been more crushing.

Janey was packed and ready to leave at nine the next morning. Sir George's Bentley whispered into the yard with Brockett driving, packed with the new bicycle safely in the cavernous boot. Finlay had dreaded the moment, but she said her goodbyes and thanks with the greatest composure. As the Bentley pulled away she flashed a smile at Finlay through the first of her tears and then she was gone.

'Poor girl!' Niney said. 'She doesn't know what she's getting into, nor yet what she will come back to. How can anyone treat their child like that?'

'I'm away to the workshop,' Finlay said to no one but the few remaining martins swooping around the yard, fighting the lump in his throat.

Finlay buried himself in work. He missed Janey dreadfully and thought he should go to Oxford. She had telephoned and written. Told him about the college and where she lived. How hard she was having to work and that she would come home shortly and for him to be at the station to meet her.

Finlay had a message from Ron. The spare parts for the Armstrong had finally arrived. Finlay went to the workshop, glad at last to be able to get the repairs finished. He was unpacking them when the telephone rang. 'Yah, at vonce Miss Niney,' Carl had answered. 'Com, Miss Niney crying. You hev to go to de house.'

Finlay swore.

'Com now in de Jeep!' Carl ordered.

He could see Niney had been crying, something he had hardly seen before. 'What's happened Auntie? Where's Jenny?'

'Jenny's all right, darling. You'd better sit down. There's no easy way to tell you this,' she gulped. 'My love… Janey's dead.'

Finlay's stomach turned to ice. 'How?' he whispered.

'Meningitis. There was an outbreak at her college.'

'Why weren't we told she was ill? She must have been ill? Why weren't we told?'

'The college telephoned her parents. They said she was nothing to do with them. It was only after she died that they went through her belongings and found a letter from you… I'm so very sorry, Kee,' Niney said, staring out of the window.

'Those bastards denied her when she was dying. They let her die alone?' Finlay felt rage boiling inside him. 'That bastard Jenks! I'll see him dead. I'll wring the life out of him!'

'No darling. You'll end up with your life ruined. Janey wouldn't want that…' Niney began.

'No Niney. He has to die for this. I'll find a way, I promise you. I'll see him dead!' Finlay was shaking with cold rage.

'Never say such things out aloud Kee. If anything happened to Jenks, the police would be after you. I hate the man for what he has done... Here, drink this and don't argue. It'll help you calm down.' Niney handed him a large drink of brandy. The liquid burnt its way down his throat and made him shudder. He sat numb at the table, not knowing what to do. 'Where's Grandfather, Auntie?' he slurred.

'Ron's gone to find him,' Niney said, coming and sitting beside him. She enfolded him in her arms. 'It's all right to cry my darling. Somebody has to cry for Janey.'

Finlay wanted to cry but every emotion he had within him seemed locked up. He remained cold and motionless.

A gloom, usually so foreign to it, descended over the house. The Grieveses were adamant Janey was not theirs. It was decided she would be buried in the churchyard, without any religious ceremony and just her friends present. The day came and went. An aunt of Janey's turned up for the funeral, revolted by the way Janey's parents were behaving, but left once the burial was over. There seemed little point in recriminations. The disease had taken her and she had died alone. For Finlay there was just cold hate.

He withdrew into himself over the next few weeks. He worked and slept and tried not to think too much. He started to come out of his gloomy despondency somewhat when the Grieveses moved away. When Jenny saw his spirits lift a little, she walked with him to the churchyard. 'Next spring this will be a picture. Filled with flowers and birds. Come home when you're ready,' Jenny said. For the first time since Janey died, Finlay wept.

Chapter Four

•

Autumn arrived with wind and rain. The earth, parched by the long hot summer, greedily drank of its softness and despite the chilly nights, a dusting of tender green shoots covered the barley and wheat fields. The valley trees changed from their greens into yellow, reds and copper. The now colder light of coming winter showed their glory against the grey rain clouds that daily swept in from the west. The trees, forced into acknowledgement of winter's arrival with the first frost, dropped their leaves in showers. They blocked the drains and culverts, spun in whirling circles on the village street and mischievously jammed themselves into every inconvenient nook and cranny they could find. The river, swollen slightly by the rains, had lost some of its clarity. The surface became coated with leaves moving in lines to the sea. The eddies on the bends became choked with leaves moving in lazy circles until perhaps a capricious wind blew them with the ripples into the current and, the decision made for them, they drifted towards the Solent.

Finlay didn't shoot much that season and, with such a rapid leaf drop, the river was for a while soured. Fishing was only fitful. He spent his time studying and helping in the workshop. When time allowed, Jenny and Finlay went to the cinema in the evenings. Such times were a great pleasure to them both, sitting together eating treats in the dark and talking about the film on the way home in the little pick-up. Finlay's birthday arrived with presents and cards in some number. There was one from Janet Ward, hoping to meet him at the Boxing Day Meet and expressing sadness about Janey. His grandfather gave him some binoculars from Germany. Niney and Jenny, clothes. There was a telegram from his mother wishing him a good day.

The Christmas Day celebrations were, if anything, better than the previous year. The hall was once again decked out with winter greenery in the Saxon manner and the food was tastier, coming from their own kitchen. Carl attended with the young lady first seen at the cricket match and an announcement of their spring marriage made the day a double celebration. The new gardener and his wife were formally welcomed, especially by Niney who was looking forward to a 'proper kitchen garden' again. Dinner for the family in the evening was a long and easy affair. For the first time, Sir George and Lady Goulding attended. Sir George kept everyone laughing with his veterinary stories and Auntie Niney kept him sober by removing the brandy decanter to the kitchen. Granny's conversation sparkled like her diamonds.

Before being ushered to bed Finlay put a rod up for the morning, to catch the grayling for the Boxing Day breakfast. He woke at the usual time the next morning. Though the room was dark, he was aware he was not alone. He raised his head and saw the darker silhouette of Jenny standing, looking out of the window. 'What are you doing?' His speech was thick with sleep, his mouth dry from the coldness of the air. 'Just came to see you were all right. You looked dreadfully tired last night. I thought you might be sickening for something,' she answered. 'Would you like some tea?'

'Oh Jen, honestly! I worked for sixteen hours yesterday. Course I was tired. You mustn't worry about me so, but thanks and I would like some tea. Plenty of sugar though. None of your healthy ideas,' he said.

She left the room, her bare feet squeaking against the polished floor, her long dressing gown rustling against her legs. He had almost drifted back to sleep by the time she returned, leaving the bedroom door open and the passage light on. The room was softly lit in a golden coloured light. She handed him a cup.

'Move over and let me sit on your bed. I want to talk to you,' she ordered. They sat side by side drinking the hot tea. 'Enough sugar, buggerlugs?' she asked.

'Yes thanks.'

She stood, wrapped her dressing gown around her and retied its belt. 'Push your pillow over my side a bit,' she said. They lay facing each other, their faces almost touching. Finlay could smell the sweetness of the tea on her breath. 'You don't really want to go to the Meet today do you?' she asked.

'Not really Jen. I'd much sooner stay at home and fish all morning.'

'It's a bit close to Janey I know, but if you want to avoid the Ward girls, I can head them off for you. I don't want to interfere unless you want me to. Your grandfather would be disappointed if you didn't show the hunt support,' she said, resting her hand on his face.

'You sometimes see what's in my head, Jen. I still miss Janey and they just remind me,' he said.

'I know. Janey will fade. Just remember how happy she was to be here. How she enjoyed being free of those dreadful people. You did that Kee. You have an ability to make people happy, even though you're a sod.' She laughed. 'Now let's cuddle and go back to sleep for an hour.'

'Why don't you get in bed properly? You'll freeze out there,' Finlay said.

'You were a child then. It just wouldn't do now,' she said softly.

'I suppose not, but please don't get cold Jen,' he said, trying to get as close to her as the blankets allowed. He did sleep, with the smell of her breath and her hair in his face, her arm around his bare shoulders. They slept, their breathing in unison, content.

The beginnings of dawn and her hair tickling his nose woke him. Jenny's head was on his shoulder, her breath was like the stroking of a feather on his skin. She had covered herself with an eiderdown. She woke and looked up at him. 'Hello buggerlugs. Wasn't that lovely?'

Finlay kissed the top of her head. 'It was, like a long time ago.'

She shuffled up to his pillow. 'Are you going to get breakfast, mighty hunter?' She laughed. 'Put your tongue out.'

They touched the tips of their tongues.

'Come on Kee, get up,' she said, gazing into his face.

He kissed her long and gently. When it was over she whispered, 'That's not the way you kiss your sister. Now get up and go. I'll redo your bed.'

'Did you ever mind about these other females?'

'Darling, I'm the wellingtonia on the lawn. They're but crocuses beneath me. This year, I want you to study hard and get these A levels. Forget about girls for a bit. I'm here for you all the time. Now get gone!' she ordered.

He kissed her again. 'My Jen,' he whispered.

'Yes, your Jen,' she said.

When he came back from fishing, Finlay was surprised to see all three cars of the Goulding family. There was a considerable noise coming from the kitchen window. 'I hope you don't all want fish for breakfast,' he said, walking into the kitchen. 'I've only brought five back.' He placed the bass bag on the draining board. 'Will that be enough Auntie?'

'Good Lord, yes darling! Can you get them ready?' Niney said.

Breakfast was very noisy. Jenny, still in her dressing gown, her hair loosely tied back, smelt of her bath and toothpaste. 'Well done buggerlugs...'

'Yes, well done Keith. Excellent start! Who can we rely on when you go to Dartmouth?' Sir George boomed.

'Uncle Jack and Grandfather, of course,' Finlay replied.

'When do you go off to the Navy?'

'I've an assessment at Easter. And then start next September,' Finlay answered.

'Well, I think you'd be better placed here,' Sir George said firmly.

'No use bleating when you wake up and find half a dozen Russian cruisers tied up at Ocean Terminal...' Finlay began.

'You think the Russians would come across the Channel?' Sir George asked, amused by Finlay's admonishment.

'Not on my watch they won't!' Finlay said.

'Well said Keith! We shall all sleep sounder in our beds knowing your generation is more ready than we were!' Lady Goulding said.

'Put in your place again, George!' Niney said. 'Let's get this lot put away again and then we can get gone. Are you staying out James?'

'Depends which way they go my love. If they go into Pondhead, they'll rattle about in there all day, and we shan't see a thing. If they head across Matley we can stay and watch,' Finlay's grandfather said.

'Well, I'll take the pick-up and get back here and do a late lunch, around half-past two if that suits. I've some reading to do,' Jenny said, getting up.

'Look at these people!' Jenny exclaimed, as they approached the Grand Hotel in Lyndhurst. 'There must be over two hundred!'

'Wonderful! The country's getting back to normal,' Finlay said. 'They should have some good scent today. Let's hope they find a fox.'

Jenny parked the pick-up and they started walking towards the crowd. 'Don't look Kee, but over on your right are the Ward sisters and the Keighley girl. They've seen you.' She took his arm. 'Now look at me.' Finlay looked. Jenny gave him a huge wide smile and momentarily rested her head on his shoulder.

'What did that say in female speak? Keep off the grass?' Finlay asked.

'No my darling. It said keep off of my grass, or you might find yourself beneath it!'

Finlay laughed out loud. 'And will that work?'

'Well, it will for today! Let's see them move off in whatever direction they go,' Jenny said, hauling him up towards the yew trees at the top. She stood in front of him and leant back into his chest, her face level with his own. 'Put your arms around me Kee. Shelter me from the wind,' she ordered.

A hundred yards away, Cassy Ward eased her horse over nearer to her sister's. 'Well Jan! You've lost that one. Five thousand acres and a big house down the tubes! She won't let him out of her sight again.'

Janet Ward glanced across at Jenny and Finlay, their backs towards them and the coming drizzle. 'We'll see about that!'

'Jan, her estate's been settled. Didn't you see in the paper? She's not just one of the best-looking females in the area, she's one of the richest. She gets the biggest part of her father's firm. Forget it Jan. You had your chance and you blew it,' Cassy scoffed.

'Well I didn't see it, did I?' Janet answered petulantly.

'In the business section dear! A little above your pretty head I think!'

Janet pulled her horse's head around. 'Come on! They're ready to move off.'

The huntsman blew his hounds together and took them towards Matley Wood. With the field well behind, he cast them forward into the gorse. Hounds cast back and forth into the wind-blown drizzle. The few remaining flowers in the gorse breaks showed brilliant yellow and clashed in beauty with the dying blue of the heather and the golden brown of the dead bracken. Hounds were about half a mile away when they found, and they ran away towards Beaulieu Road with the huntsman beside them. Finlay and Jenny heard the urgent twang of the horn from their vantage point and saw them disappear into the gully on the far side of the heath. Jenny and Finlay ran back down the hill, laughing in amazement at the figure of Sir George, leaning backwards to counter the weight of his large middle, charging down the track towards his car. 'Come on slow coaches!' he yelled.

Niney arrived back with them panting heavily, her face alive and laughing. 'Are you still going home?' she gasped, bending over trying to get her breath.

'Yes. There'll be a line of cars two miles long Niney. What a beautiful sight! To see them go away like that!' Jenny answered.

'Well, we'll see you when we see you.' Niney gave Finlay a wet and breathless kiss and started trotting to where the Armstrong had been left.

The two walked back to the pick-up and drove down to the main road. 'Cadnam or Totton?' Jenny asked.

'Cadnam Jen. Let's go the pretty way.' The New Forest dripped mournfully in the drizzle as they passed by Moneyhills. The tiny tyres of the pick-up splashed along the wet surface of the road. There was very little other traffic as Jenny slowed down, passing Paultons.

'I often wonder what happened there Kee. It used to be such a lively place, lots of shoots and the gardens were beautiful,' Jenny mused.

'Just another casualty of both wars probably. No male heir to keep it going. The soil has as much life as Bournemouth beach. It's not a place I'd like to try and farm,' Finlay said.

As they pulled into the top lane they could hear the shooting from next door, almost a continuous barrage of gunfire. 'Too much time spent worrying about the bloody pheasants and not enough time spent spreading cowshit. That's their trouble, not farmers at all really!' Jenny scoffed, half-joking.

'Not like us!' Finlay said as they reached their own land. 'Look at that wheat up against theirs. Looks wonderful doesn't it?'

Jenny laughed. 'God, your self-assurance and smugness is going to smother you one day!'

'Well, I like to see things done properly.'

'And when you're not here, will you worry that it's done properly?' she asked softly.

'Of course I will. Jenny, that was bloody sneaky!' he said, looking at the smile hovering at the sides of her mouth.

'I know it was, but if you don't want to speak about it ...' Her mouth was still smiling.

'Look Jen. I shan't stay in the Navy for long.'

'Well, that's a step forward. Six months ago you were going in for good!'

They had pulled up into the yard.

'I'll very subtly fight you to the last on this. Keep dissolving into great big sobs. Make you feel guilty about leaving me. I shall be totally pathetic and cry into the washing-up.'

'Oh Jen, you know I have to do this,' Finlay said, exasperated.

'I'll pine. Refuse to eat. My skin will go saggy. My tits go flat and hang like spaniel's ears. My bum will collapse around the back of my knees and finally, I'll become incontinent and smell awful. All because of getting mixed up with an uncaring brute like you. So you'd better give me a proper kiss while you can still stand the sight of me.'

For the second time that day they kissed as lovers do. She pushed him away and sprang out of the pick-up. 'Get the fires built up in the hall and switch the Aga up full. I'm going to change.' She walked away, exaggerating the swing of her hips. At the door she turned and faced him. 'You won't be away for long. Not if there was any truth in that kiss!'

He was stacking logs on the fires when she came back downstairs. She was wearing her old breeches and a thick pullover, her hair back in its normal long plait. She came and knelt beside him. 'Sorry darling. That was cruel of me. I know you're torn about what to do.' She smiled into his eyes. 'Do you want a suck of my sweet?' She passed a boiled sweet from her mouth to his. 'Don't crunch it buggerlugs. I said suck!'

'Why are you dressed like that Jen?' he asked, sucking the sweet hard.

'Aren't you shooting ducks later? I'll come out, stand with you and mark your birds down.' She took the sweet back into her mouth.

'I thought you didn't like to see the ducks shot,' he said, surprised.

'I don't. But I like to see you shoot. Come on! We must get lunch started, then we can sit by the fire.'

In half an hour the table was laid. Baked potatoes washed and in the oven, the potatoes for mash danced about in the saucepan on the Aga's hot side. Jenny moved them to the warm side to finish. 'There's something I have to tell you Kee,' Jenny started. 'From the fifth of January, I'm a woman of very independent means. My father's estate is finally settled. I'd like to get you something special, you know, something personal. From me to you.'

'You don't have to do that Jen.'

'I know I don't. I just want to. How about a good watch?'

'I'd only break it.' He thought for a moment. 'I'd like a Parker 51 please. A grey one.'

'You've already got a Parker.'

'But you didn't give it me Jen. There's a difference. I want you to use it so the end gets chewed. As you always do. When I get it out, I can see the chewed end and know you did it.'

She dried her hands from the sink and walked over to where he was sitting. 'That's a lovely thing to say, darling.' She held his head to her middle and hugged it. He stroked and held her bottom in his hands. Standing, he kissed her.

'What will happen to us Jen?' he said.

'The world will condemn at first. Your mother will hate me, but the world can do as it wishes. For the moment, we must be careful. This morning I wanted to be with you, but if we were caught, there'd be no commission for you or silk for me. When you're sixteen, you can please yourself. And if I still please you, I'll be there.'

The potatoes were mashed, left-over sprouts from the day before were cut up and mixed in. A cup of flour and two eggs were added and the whole spread spooned into a large skillet and put on to the warm side of the Aga to cook gently.

'Darling, you should know I was raped the night I left Southampton. Several women were. My attacker was not entirely successful though, thank God. When James found me I was pretty hysterical.'

'I see now why the sirens upset you so. My poor Jen.' Finlay held her close.

'If I'd have had you there I would be more grown-up than I am, maybe.'

The afternoon wore on. They sat together talking in the large armchair by the fire. Everything was ready for lunch, but there was no one to eat it. 'They must have had a good day to be so late. It's too dark to shoot now,' Finlay observed.

'You don't sound too disappointed,' Jenny said, absently brushing his hair from his forehead.

'Not ducks. I don't mind shooting pheasants. I'd shoot them all day, but ducks are different,' Finlay said.

Eventually everyone arrived home, animated and happy. The hunt had hunted hard and long, chased two foxes. Both of whom bettered the hounds and everyone agreed that for a Boxing Day hunt, it had been a classic. Enormous amounts of food soon disappeared. The cold meats, pickles and Niney's chutney made a wonderful end-of-day meal, after which they sat around the fire and talked. Finlay was soon nodding off, the sound of the voices fading in his consciousness. 'Come on, buggerlugs,' Jenny said, giving him a gentle shove with her foot. 'Time for bed, I think.'

It had been a wonderful Christmas, Finlay thought. Everything as it should have been.

Chapter Five

•

With the holiday over, normal routine fell into place. Finlay worked out a timetable for his study and the work he could do outside, mainly in the workshop. A letter from the Admiralty, telling him the dates and times he was expected at Dartmouth and a travel warrant telling him to be on a specific train stopping at Southampton, arrived. There was also a letter from his mother informing him the two-year posting was to extended to four, and that she wanted him to come to New Zealand. Even if it was 'just for a couple of weeks' to meet his father and brother and look at the country.

Much more importantly, there was an invitation to shoot next door, cocks only, two Saturdays away, and to furnish his own loader. He handed the letter from his mother to Niney and the embossed card from next door to Jenny. 'You can come and load for me,' he said. Niney bit her bottom lip as she progressed through the letter and handed it to Jenny, then busied herself noisily in the sink.

Jenny looked at him sadly over the top of the letter.

'What are you going to do Kee? You could take some time off and go, just two weeks. You might enjoy it. I know Kath would love to see you,' Niney said.

'Why on earth go to the farthest ends of the earth to meet a complete stranger?' he said. 'Anyway, there's no time and it'll cost the earth. They want to settle out there and expect me to. I won't go. Not for two weeks, not even two days!'

'Perhaps you should telephone, darling. Speak to your mother,' Niney suggested.

'What on earth for?' Finlay answered sharply.

'Because she's your mother, that's why!' Niney retorted.

Finlay stood and went to Niney, handing her a towel. 'Please dry your hands, Auntie, and come and sit. Please!'

Finlay took both her hands in his. 'My beloved. I consider you my mother. I may not have sprung from your womb, but it's you who's guided me, fed me, washed my clothes, clouted me when I was wrong and praised me when I was right. Cuddled me when I was hurt, laughed and cried with me. I'm not going to argue about this, not even get cross. I'll not even discuss it further. I will however write and tell her "No". Can that be an end to it please?'

'It will be as you wish then, Kee,' she said sadly. Niney remained looking at him. 'I may have given you the odd clout, but I never gave you a hiding, did I?'

'The odd clout? One word out of place and bang. What about the time I climbed the wellingtonia? Sweet-talked me down with lies about a choc-ice and then you beat me with a leather dog lead. I wonder I ever trusted you again!' He pulled her face to him and kissed her.

'Sod!' she said. 'I cried when I saw what I'd done, and that madam wouldn't speak to me for a week,' she said, alluding to Jenny. They were still laughing when Finlay's grandfather came in for breakfast. Niney showed him the letter.

'Are you going out there?' he asked Finlay.

'Of course not Grandfather!' Finlay said firmly.

'I should think not! I spoilt that girl. A good dose of leather rein about her arse would have done her good when she was younger!'

'You're probably right there Grandfather! Did me the world of good didn't it, Auntie Niney?' Finlay laughed.

Jenny handed the old man the shoot invitation. 'And who do you think has been invited to shoot next door, a week on Saturday?'

Finlay's grandfather studied the card. 'Bloody Hell! Didn't I get one as well?'

''Fraid not James! And I'm going as the young master's loader!' Jenny said, proudly teasing.

Finlay's grandfather grunted. 'I haven't shot there for four seasons!'

'Only because you shot so well the last time. I mean, four dead in the air is a bit showing-off,' said Niney.

'I'll have my breakfast in the market café another time!' Finlay's grandfather muttered.

'So that Heather can brush the back of your head in passing with her huge chest!' Niney was laughing.

'She does a turn for thirty bob, James!' Jenny said. 'Breakfast with a bang, thirty-five shillings. Thank you very much!'

Finlay's grandfather started to laugh, and into this walked Alan Goulding.

'May I come in?' Goulding asked from the kitchen door.

'Niney, put my breakfast on a tray and bring it into the hall,' Finlay's grandfather ordered. He glanced at the young vet. 'I'll deal with you in a minute... Niney, my breakfast!'

She put his breakfast in the slow oven. 'Alan! What lovely flowers,' Niney smiled.

He handed them a bouquet each. 'For yesterday,' he said simply. 'Didn't you ought to take Sir James's breakfast to him?'

Niney glanced at her watch. 'In less than two minutes, he'll be sitting here eating it. He hates eating from a tray.' She laughed.

Jenny wiped the table clean. 'Would you like some breakfast Alan?'

'Yes please! I've brought the schedules for the TT tests over. I did rather want to get Sir James to look at them.'

'Well! Eat some food and we can look at them. You look tired young man,' Finlay's grandfather said, sitting in his normal place.

Niney put his breakfast in front of him. 'There you are Mr Grumpy. Sorry to have kept you waiting.' She smiled at him sweetly.

'You're not too big to have your arse smacked young lady!' he grumbled.

'Well, you couldn't miss hitting it!' Jenny giggled.

'Women are tricky things young man. I lost one daughter to the Japs and now I look like losing another to New Zealand. Along with another grandson I've never seen, and all these two can do is fool around!' Finlay's grandfather said.

'James, I'm sorry. We didn't think,' Niney said. 'The way you spoke to Kee I didn't think you minded.'

'Of course I mind. I'm not getting any younger and, of course, Keith can't go over there. He has his studies at Dartmouth. I'd just like us to be together a bit more. Is that too much to ask?'

Finlay studied in the music room, away from the normal hubbub of the house. Outside, the bulk of the work on the farm was concerned with the stock, moving food and bedding to them and maintaining the level of resultant muck under some sort of control. Work on the new trout stream was started and the first stage had to be completed by February, when the salmon fishing started. The alders along the banks were taken down, trimmed and anything at all useful for bank support was snedded down and made ready.

In between work and study Finlay wrote to his mother. He explained that time did not allow him the chance to come to New Zealand. He took some trouble over the letter, filling it with newsy paragraphs of what was happening on the farm, and how he hoped to get some A levels that year. How much he was looking forward to one day meeting his brother. He pondered long and hard on how to finish it, but eventually just signed his name.

At last, the day of the shoot arrived. Jenny and Finlay were packed off in Ron's Land-Rover with instructions, advice and exhortations to shoot safely and the proper way to tip the head keeper. It was, for Finlay, a rite of passage. The first time he would stand in the gun line on a formal driven shoot. This was what Finlay would be judged on. Making a mistake or exhibiting any degree of bad manners would brand him for years to come as perhaps 'not suitable'. A name to be passed over and ignored.

As they pulled in around the back of the house, Finlay was glad to see a familiar face among the other guns already there. Hodinott came over to greet them, doffing his cap to Jenny and shaking Finlay's hand. 'We're just waiting on three to come. We're pleasantly early. I hear you're more of an angler than a shot, young man. I'm afraid the drives they are putting on today are the hardest. Just relax and do your best,' he advised.

Another Land-Rover arrived, driven by a liveried chauffeur. It was Angus Keith and his brother, the friendly captain who had been one of his inquisitors at his AIB. 'Miss Jennifer, Finlay! How lovely to see you.' He introduced Jenny to his brother, Robert. 'You two have already met, I know. Are you going to show me how to shoot as well as fish, young Finlay?' he beamed.

'No shop you two!' Jenny said. 'Honestly, if you put two fishy people together, they become very boring!'

They all laughed politely.

'Ah, here's our hostess,' Lord Keith said.

'Good morning, good morning! Jennifer, how lovely to see you. And look at you Kee, haven't you grown into a fine young man. Come with me. I want you to meet someone.' Lady Edwina led him away, arm in arm.

'Well, young Finlay has a fan there I'm thinking!' Angus said.

'I spend my time fending women off him. Excuse me please, I'd better go and rescue him,' Jenny said, somewhat dolefully, walking after Finlay.

'What a beautiful woman, Angus! Who is she?' Robert Keith asked.

'That, my dear Bob, is the heiress Jennifer Vaughne. And you couldn't afford the stone in her right ear. Never mind the pair!' Angus laughed at his brother's obvious chagrin.

'And I suppose the young chap is a brilliant shot!' Robert moaned.

They watched as Jenny and Finlay returned with Bill, the young keeper.

'I have to stand with you first drive Keith. Sorry. I know you're safe, but it's the form. Harry's worried somebody might shoot the Foreign Secretary,' Bill said, getting in the back of the Land-Rover.

'I won't, Bill. He's a Conservative!' Finlay laughed.

'I swear I'll kick that bloody Edwina in the teeth,' Jenny seethed, as she started the Land-Rover and followed the others out of the yard.

'I didn't know you didn't rate her Ladyship, Miss Jennifer,' Bill volunteered.

'If you call me Miss Jennifer once more, Bill Webb, I'll kick you in the teeth as well. It's Miss Jenny to you in company and Jen or Jenny any other time,' Jenny said, sharply.

'It's all right Bill. Edwina gets up Jen's nose!' Finlay laughed.

'You just outshoot all of them, Kee. What number peg have you got?' she asked.

'Harry fiddled that, I'm afraid. You should be four, Keith. In the middle, on Ressi Drive. We're starting at Sandpits. You'll get a load of shooting. Hope you've brought plenty of cartridges,' Bill said.

'Six hundred, or thereabouts. That do?' Finlay asked.

'Should be,' Bill said, evenly.

The first drive began. Finlay missed the first bird over by 'three fields'.

Jenny sucked in her breath. 'Concentrate buggerlugs!' she hissed.

'Only joking, Jen!' He laughed.

The next thirty-two that came his way, he downed. Only one wanted a second barrel. Bill was marking down and Jenny concentrated on keeping him loaded. When the finish whistle blew, Bill ushered them away. 'They want the guns over Ressi quickly. There's another team of beaters there waiting. I'll be there before you start.'

Again, lined out, Finlay was out in the open, on number six peg, for all to see. They had been standing for about five minutes when Bill arrived. The whistle was blown and the legendary Reservoir Drive began. 'Just pretend they are sparrowhawks Keith. Coming to eat your corncrakes,' Bill said.

Jenny just kept him loaded. The pheasants came screaming over the guns. The whole place sounded like a war zone. At one point, Finlay's gun got too hot to hold properly until Bill gave him a glove. When the finish whistle went, Finlay had lost count of his numbers.

'Fifty-bloody-two! Without a miss, Keith! I ain't ever seen shooting like that, for Christ's sake!' he said, excited.

'Well done buggerlugs,' Jenny said softly.

'I'm exhausted!'

'We have a break now, Miss Jenny. Soup and things. You can have a blow and receive congratulations for a job well done. Harry'll be pleased. The cocks have to be killed else there's too many in the spring. Let me carry your gun, Keith,' Bill said.

They went and sat on the front bumper of the Land-Rover and waited to be served up with some food. The winter sun showed a pallid yellow through some wispy cloud, watery and weak, but with a little warmth none the less.

'Look out! Here comes Atcost Grade. Thinks he's a real lady-killer. I'd better leave you to it. Circulate with the other guns,' Bill said.

'Why Atcost, Bill?' Jenny asked, smiling.

'They make barns Miss Jenny, and this prat couldn't hit one flying!' He moved away, leaving Jenny and Finlay giggling.

'Good morning. We haven't been introduced. I'm Captain Jeremy Grade.' He shook Finlay's hand briefly and turned his attention to Jenny. Finlay introduced her.

'I must say, you seem very young to have four rings, Captain Grade,' Jenny said, giving him the benefit of her widest smile.

'I'm an army captain, Miss Vaughne. Blues and Royals.' He stumbled out the words.

'Oh I see,' Jenny said dismissively. 'Could you move that way a little. You're blocking the sun.'

Finlay thought he heard some stifled laughter from the back of their vehicle.

The unfortunate Captain ploughed on. 'Yes, I'm an equerry at the palace now.'

'Excuse me,' Jenny said. 'Darling, can you get the glasses. I think I can see a roebuck under the wood opposite.' Finlay handed Jenny the glasses. 'Yes it is. Do look Kee. It's good they're spreading this far over from the New Forest!'

Finlay took the glasses, but could see nothing. 'It's got the makings of a good head Jen!' He handed the glasses back as the disconsolate Captain moved away.

Hodinott joined them, laughing quietly. 'That, Miss Jenny, was the finest dismissal I've ever seen. Show me the roebuck.'

'There isn't one!' Jenny laughed. 'Your dogs, Mr Hodinott, are an absolute inspiration! They really have quite made the morning for us all!' Jenny was standing, shaking his hand.

'Thank you, Miss Jenny. I am rather proud of them. And that was some good shooting, young Finlay.'

Finlay thanked him for the compliment.

They got the order to move again. Bill waved them on. The next drive was a shortish one. This time, at number eight peg, Finlay was on the far outside and had only three shots. He added two partridges and a woodcock to the bag, and then it was lunch. It was sumptuous but brief. There was another drive to do, in time for the birds to go to roost before it got too dark. Harried out by the head keeper and into the vehicles, the guns were transported to Toot Hill. Bill found Finlay and gave him some cartridges.

'Alphamax fours. Harry wants you to kill them right out in front, for some reason. These'll give you a fair bit more range. I shan't see you again before you go. As soon as the drive's over I've to go and find any dead birds not picked. It's been great! Don't forget. They're sparrowhawks after your corncrakes.' Then he was gone.

When the drive started, the birds came from the wood, climbed over the massive pylon wires and flew straight at them. There was a short but intense barrage, the whistle went and the day was over. 'How many Jen?' Finlay asked.

'You missed one, so if we count the cartridges, you'll know! Looks like twenty-nine. Well done, buggerlugs! You shot better than any of them,' Jenny said, animated and obviously thrilled.

They watched the dogs bringing the dead birds back to their handler, who laid them in a row alongside the shooting peg, ready for the game cart. The head keeper marched past, without even a glance, calling for the beaters to get their transport back to the estate yard. He turned and came back towards them, harrying the beaters to hurry up. Without looking in their direction, he said, 'Bad form to single out a gun for praise. But that was impressive.' He continued harrying the beaters. The other guns wandered back towards the field entrance chattering and laughing.

'Well young man! What do you think about driven pheasants?' Lord Keith asked.

'I've had a lovely day,' Finlay answered.

The Foreign Secretary joined them, smiling and gentle. 'Thank you, young lady, for your charming company and sparkling conversation over luncheon.' He turned to Finlay. 'Angus tells me one has to buy some pigs to be able to fish on your beautiful river!'

'Not really Sir. If you'd like a day, I'm certain we could arrange it without pigs being involved,' Finlay laughed.

'I would like that, young man. Fishing is a much better way to judge a man's character than shooting. I'll be in touch.' He shook hands and went to his vehicle.

The convoy made its way back to the house. The final ritual of the day was to be completed. The handing out of a brace of birds, thanking the keepers and beaters for their work and handing over the tip to the head keeper. As the head keeper handed over a brace to Finlay, he tried to avoid taking his tip. 'Nay lad,' he said quietly, pushing his hand aside gently.

'Grandfather will be cross if I don't, Mr Grass. He even made me practise,' Finlay said quietly. They shook hands again and the money changed hands.

'I'll come and see your grandfather tomorrow,' he murmured.

Then it was all over. Last goodbyes said and they were on their way home. Jenny turned to him. 'An important milestone in your life, and you passed it well. Even I was a little bit proud of you.'

Finlay smiled. He removed her hand from the gearstick where it was resting and kissed it. 'I was a bit sorry about shooting the woodcock you know. They're so beautiful.'

'Everybody was watching. You could hardly have said that you didn't see it. Never mind. You killed it dead,' Jenny said.

At home everybody seemed to be waiting to see how the day had gone. Even Granny had been brought up for tea.

'Well?' his grandfather asked.

'We both enjoyed it Grandfather. A splendid day and I don't think I let the side down,' Finlay said. He found it was very difficult to describe his feelings.

'He shot wonderfully well. Missed four all day and was the absolute epitome of good manners. They'll all have something to talk about. You would have been so proud of him, James!' Jenny said, gushing.

'Course he shot properly. He's like his great grandad, ain't he? Even though he's got some of the wrong blood. But his is strong enough to let that pass!' Granny said.

'Granny!' Niney snapped. 'Don't say things like that!'

'I'll say what I bloody well like Miss. His father, if he was his father, is about as much use as tits on a boar. 'E don't hunt, shoot or fish and looks like a ballet dancer with hob-nails on. Useless bastard!' she snorted.

Finlay started to laugh. 'Are you saying my father ain't my father, Granny?'

'I wish I could my cock-bird, but...'

'Granny! Will you please stop!' Niney hissed.

Granny ignored her. 'No, he's your Dad all right. We cannot gainsay that, more's the bloody pity of it, though. I'd have sooner seen it Ronnie Drew, but Kathy's so much up her own arse that would never happen!'

Finlay's grandfather sat staring, waiting for the next pronouncement.

'Granny, I'm warning you!' Niney snapped.

'Shut up, and listen!' Granny ordered. 'Keith's the male heir and James ain't getting any younger. The boy's going off within the next year to God knows what. Niney and you, Jenny, could have this place cut from under you if anything happened to James before the boy's eighteen. Kathy would have it sold before you could say knife! She don't think anything of the place, or the boy. Else she'd be here with him. Make the place into a company with shares each, but Kathy can only let hers go to Niney or the boy. Jenny, give they diamonds in your ears to Niney and get the ring that I gave you that goes with them. Now girl!'

Jenny sprang up and left the room quickly, looking a little pale.

'Where on earth did these come from Granny?' Niney asked, studying the jewels. 'I thought they were imitations Jenny had on for the day.'

'Well, they ain't. They was made by that Russian bloke, Faber something. I don't have false things!' Granny said.

'Fabergé for Christ's sake. They're worth a king's ransom!' Niney said, handing them to Finlay's grandfather.

'They are! Thank you girl,' she said to Jenny, taking a small box from her. 'Why didn't you wear it today?' she asked, rather sharply.

'I was frightened of it slipping off,' Jenny said quietly, sitting back down next to Finlay, still not sure of what was happening.

Niney began to giggle. 'Jenny! You've been tripping about a pheasant shoot with about five thousand pounds in each ear!'

'Lumme! I wouldn't have worn them had I known,' Jenny breathed.

'They're for wearing. Put 'em back on girl!' Granny ordered.

'But Granny, I don't think I should,' Jenny objected, studying the jewels herself.

'Put them on!' Granny ordered, sharply. She waited until Jenny had screwed them into place. 'I was going to give them to you when I died, but I wants you to have 'em now.'

'But Granny, surely they should go to Niney,' Jenny objected.

'I'll second that!' Niney said.

'Shut up the pair of you. Get your stupid heads out of the clouds! I'm being serious here, trying to show you the way to go. Are you listening James? Are you still blind to what's happening or could happen?' She turned to Finlay. 'This is yours cock-bird.' She handed him the ring. 'This ring and those earrings belong together. A proper set. When you're eighteen, make certain they do. Now get this trust set up. I want to go to my grave knowing that this bugger, who I love more than you know how to, together, is safe along with this place.'

There was a long silence. 'But why today Granny?' Finlay asked.

'Because, my cherub, today you became a young man in the eyes of men. You must live up to that. Now, Niney, Jenny, this boy's been in for the better part of an hour and is not fed, no more than I've been. Have I got to do everything around this place?'

Finlay went to Granny and gave her a kiss. 'You don't think much to my mama, then Granny?' he smiled.

'No I bloody don't! She should've married her own sort. You're Niney's child more than hers. I don't suppose I'll see her again. I shan't lose sleep over that. And you, James, should have knocked some sense into her. But for her, Bibby would still be with us and I'll never forgive her for that.' Granny folded her arms smartly.

'Charity, I don't think that's fair!' Finlay's grandfather said quietly.

'She wouldn't have been in harm's way if bloody Kath hadn't sent for her. She should have had the boy here, upstairs in the proper manner. Specially if she was going to dump him here for Niney to rear!'

'You're right about the company, Granny. Mr Lunn and Jenny can get it done. I've never wanted to face it. Seemed disloyal somehow. As to the rest, that's for the future. Now tell me about the woodcock Kee,' Finlay's grandfather said.

'What about the other diamonds, Granny? What's going to happen?' Niney asked, with just a hint of a wheedling tone in the question.

'Gimme my 'andbag, cock-bird,' Granny ordered. She drew out a tattered brown envelope. 'There's the insurance list, madam. You'd better read it and we'll make some decisions.'

Niney took the two sheets of unusually heavily laid paper. She gasped as she read and sat down heavily, her hand flying to her mouth. 'For Christ's sake Granny! Where did this lot come from? You haven't got it at home, have you?' She handed the paper to Finlay's grandfather and waited for his reaction.

'My father gave you this?' he asked.

'Where the Hell do you think it came from?' Granny snapped. 'I didn't go on the game, Jamie.'

'You would have been busy at thirty bob a go!' Niney shrieked.

'Did my mother know about this? How did the old bugger get away with it?' Finlay's grandfather asked.

'I was his wife as much as Niney is the boy's mother. I'm sorry James, but your mother had ice between her legs and I didn't. And, but for what people said, he would've married me. She knew what was going on. But not about what he gave me!' She chuckled quietly. 'He was some man, but if he'd have married me, he'd have lost this lot. The farm, the river and what goes with it. I put up with it, but it didn't stop us.'

'You carried on together after you were both married?' Finlay's grandfather asked.

'Bless you Jamie, course we did! All the time. Your mother would've had me gone, except he said he would go with me. And think of that scandal!' She laughed.

'It's something in the local water. Must be!' Niney said.

'Is there anything to eat?' Finlay asked. 'I wonder anyone can keep up. You ain't my cousin as well, Auntie Niney?'

'Where did the money come from to buy this?' Finlay's grandfather said, still not certain about what he was hearing.

'The Civil War of course,' Granny said.

'What Civil War for God's sake?' Finlay's grandfather exploded.

'American of course! Your grandfather and some of his friends financed blockade running to the Confederates...'

'Oh wow!' Finlay shouted with glee. 'I come from a long line of smugglers! Do you want to get mixed up with this lot, Jen?'

'This family and its bloody secrets!' Niney sighed. 'Now tell me we were into the slave trade.'

'Of course not! What kind of people do you think you came from?' Granny said, quite shocked.

Finlay and Jenny were laughing so loudly that his grandfather called for quiet. 'Can we eat? This has been something of a day.'

Granny, triumphant, cackled loudly. 'Makes Kathy's up your arse respectability look a bit thin, don't it?'

'Jenny. Want to hand over those earrings? Now you know they're paid for with blood money?' Niney asked brightly.

'Niney, I'm just going to live with my conscience. Couldn't give them to you for you to worry so. Best I keep them I think.' She smiled sweetly at Niney.

Later in bed, his hands behind his head, Finlay lay listening to the rain on his bedroom windows. There was something infinitely comfortable in this. As the small scuddy showers came blowing in from the Solent, lying beneath blankets and hearing the raindrops hitting the windows like spent shot, and the silence until the next shower arrived. It had been a strange sort of day.

The year had turned and the evenings drew out slowly. The arable fields had earlier shown a dusting of pale green shoots and now became covered in green. The promise of good things to come. The rooks argued in the rookery and floated about the sky carrying twigs. The first ducklings were seen on the feeder streams and gradually the air warmed. Finlay worked on his studies in the music room. Jenny did the same, fretting over law books which Finlay could not even understand. They would sit working away silently, the only noise perhaps the rustle of paper and the scratch of pens. He would look up suddenly and see her watching him. She would wrinkle her nose at him and chew her pen. Occasionally they could hear Niney singing to herself, or listening to the wireless, or something that would make her swear.

On Sundays they would go off together in the pick-up. They went to Stonehenge and wondered, like others, how it was created. Another Sunday, they climbed the hill to look at the White Horse of Uffington and walked part of the Ridgeway in a screaming gale. One Sunday they had lunch at the Bustard Inn on Salisbury Plain and walked the tank ranges, an area where the hand of whoever or whatever made the world was still visible.

The first fledged blackbirds were calling for food in the hedgerows when it was suddenly time to leave for Dartmouth. The list of things he was told he would need were gathered and packed, one large suitcase sent as instructed in advance, the small one in his hand as he waited on Southampton's Central Station for the designated train. They had driven there in the Armstrong, Niney and his grandfather in the front chatting easily about the spring sowing. Jenny, sitting in the back, was brittle but cheerful and pale, gripping Finlay's hand tightly.

When the train pulled into the station and stopped, from a rear carriage a Chief Petty Officer descended and waited with a clipboard.

'Off you go then,' Niney said. 'See you in a couple of weeks.' She kissed him briefly.

He shook hands with his grandfather and walked towards the officer. Jenny kissed him and her tongue flicked into his mouth briefly. Her eyes were brimming with tears. 'Bye, buggerlugs,' she choked.

'Shouldn't make too much of a meal of it, Miss. The others will only give him stick all the way to Exeter,' the officer said brusquely. 'Get aboard Finlay. Jump to it!'

Finlay found a compartment and sat down near the window. He was upset by Jenny's tears. As the train began to move, he waved to her and then she was gone. Niney and Finlay's grandfather waited for Jenny, who watched the train out of sight, but still remained watching in that direction. 'Oh shit James! He didn't look big enough, did he?' Niney gulped. 'And look at her for Christ's sake! Has she turned into a pillar of salt?' Niney walked across and led Jenny by the arm. 'He'll be all right Jenny. You know he will be. Come on, we have to go home,' she ordered.

The journey home was quiet, except for the occasional sniff from the back of the car. 'Do shut up Jenny!' Niney said crossly. 'It's only ten days.' This only occasioned more sobs. 'Stop the car James!' Niney ordered. Transferring herself to the back seat, she held Jenny to her shoulder. 'Come on love. He had to grow up at some stage.'

For the first time since he met her, Finlay's grandfather heard Jenny begin to cry the anguished wailing of real sadness. 'Oh come on Jenny! It's not that bad surely?' he said quietly.

'Just shut up James and drive home,' Niney snapped, tears now falling freely down her own face. 'How would you understand? You're only a man!' She handed her a handkerchief. 'Come on Jen. Dry your eyes. You don't want to let anyone see you in this state.'

When the car stopped at the front door, Jenny jumped out quickly and ran up the steps and through the door.

'The girl's gone hysterical,' Finlay's grandfather grumbled.

'Just be careful James. Give her plenty to do and mind what you say,' Niney said firmly.

'I'm not going to spend the next ten days walking on eggs! It's time she did some growing up. The sooner the better,' he answered.

'Well just watch what you say!' Niney said, sharply.

'Look, don't start snapping at me...' he began.

'I'll snap at who I want to and when I want to!' Niney had reached the front door. She turned, thoroughly upset. 'And if you want any lunch today, you can get it at the pub. There won't be any here!' She walked through the front door and slammed it hard.

Chapter Six

•

The Keith Finlay who joined the train at Southampton that day was five feet seven inches tall, weighed just above ten stone and had a shock of ash-blond hair. He spoke generally correct English with the soft burr of the Test Valley. His speech was on occasion peppered with swear words, some of them of Anglo-Saxon origin and he used 'ain't' as freely as it was used by good company in the nineteenth century. Niney had done her best to correct any lacking manners, and set out ground rules which were not to be broken. Rearing a boy, she stated, was much the same thing as rearing a gundog puppy, a mixture of firmness and love. In other ways, she had indulged his every whim. The family ate what Finlay liked to eat. The best of the joint was put on his plate. There was always his favourite Dundee cake in the cake tin. At fifteen he had the strength of a man. The constant heavy lifting of farm work had broadened his shoulders, thickened his arms and legs. His hands were wide and flat, each capable of holding a one-hundred-pound struggling porker by the back leg for loading on a lorry, or threading a tiny fly on the finest of casts.

As the train steamed westwards, at each station stop more cadets boarded. The first of Finlay's travelling companions was named Norman Hill, seventeen and very nervous. About the same height as Finlay, but slightly built and having black curls and a snub nose with freckles, he seemed desperately shy. He sat opposite Finlay and told him he wanted to be a lawyer and to that end he was hoping for the Supply and Secretariat Branch. Finlay told him he loved the sea and couldn't wait to get on it, preferably in a destroyer.

At Exeter, cocoa and sandwiches were brought on to the train and a table set up at the carriage's end. The Chief Petty Officer called to Finlay, 'Hey sprog, give me a hand to get this doled out. I'll do the grub,' he said. Finally, the queue diminished.

'Would you like to share this last cup, Chief?' Finlay asked.

'No. Get on sprog. Got a drink here,' he said, patting his breast pocket. He looked on, amused, as Finlay removed some of the corned beef from the uneaten sandwiches and constructed one with more meat than bread. Finlay saw the look. 'Well, they're starving in India, Chief,' he said.

'They ain't going to want that are they? They're Hindus!' he said, laughing at Finlay's mouthful. 'Buggered if you ain't an oldfashioned sort! Come from a Navy family?'

'My father's serving with the New Zealand Navy at the moment. Don't know what he's doing exactly.'

'Regular?' the Chief asked, looking at him hard.

'Very. I'm fifteen and I've never met him. Can't get more regular than that!' Finlay said.

'He ever serve on the *Rodney*?' the Chief asked.

'Yes, he was a mid on her. Don't tell me you knew him! I've been told he was a proper bastard!' Finlay sighed.

'Let's just say he liked things right. But he had a good war.' He looked at his clipboard. 'You was named after the *Keith* then?'

'Yes Chief. She was lost at Dunkirk,' Finlay said.

'Don't that beat all. Christ! I was on her when she went down! Bloody Hell. Let me shake your hand. She still had her oerlikons going when she hit the bottom. He wasn't afraid your daddy. He marched about keeping the guns firing,' the CPO said, pumping Finlay's hand. 'And now I'll be teaching his nipper. Well, well. Don't that beat all!'

They talked for the rest of the journey. He warned Finlay he would be watched and assessed the whole of the time, even when off duty. He was told not to bugger about, be positive about everything he did, ask the right questions and be seen to help other cadets. His final warning was not to be flash about anything. The Navy didn't like flash.

Several lorries were waiting at the station to transport the cadets to the college. As another train was to arrive, they waited until another thirty youngsters, all looking apprehensive, were on the same platform. Finlay saw a familiar face. 'Bretton!' he called, leaning from the back of the lorry. 'Andy Bretton! Over here!'

Bretton pushed his way through the other cadets. 'Finlay, you made it through then?'

'Get up in this one,' Finlay ordered, holding down his hand to give Andy a pull up. 'I wondered whether you had got through. You were pretty fed-up at Greenwich.'

'Scraped it matey, scraped it!'

They were unloaded on the parade ground and sorted into their designated houses, shown where they were sleeping, told to unpack and get cleaned up. Senior cadets guided them through what they had to do. They freshened up after the journey and gathered in the main mess-hall. There was a brief welcome from Captain Keith, a very large mug of cocoa each and the assessment started. They were given a timetable for the ten days and a severe lecture on the dos and don'ts. To Finlay the whole time was a whirl of activity. Breakfast lasted ten minutes, lunch was cocoa and a huge wedge of fresh bread coated thickly with butter, usually eaten on the move or during a lecture. Anywhere they happened to be. There was a morning spent in an engineering shop away from the college. Finlay drooled over a large Rolls-Royce Merlin engine. They sailed in the estuary, where Finlay fell overboard, plummeting beneath the surface in fine style and having to be rescued by the following whaler. They spent one night on Dartmoor, without tents, and froze. Practised dealing with casualties and fell exhausted into their cots at night. Some cadets fell by the wayside each day, not wanting to continue or being told they should not. Finlay and Andy met up at dinner each night and as the days passed, theirs was the only dinner table where there was constant chatter. Finlay acquired the nickname 'Farmer' because of his accent, strength and appetite and Andy was nicknamed 'Frenchie' for obvious reasons.

'Do you get the feeling, Finlay, that we are among the few enjoying this?' Andy had said. As the days passed the dining hall seemed to coalesce into those who were enjoying the experience and those who were not. Towards the end of the course there was a meal that was particularly rumbustious and noisy to the point where Captain Keith banged his table with a spoon loudly and called them to order. 'Cadet Finlay!' he said sharply. 'Could you and the bunch of cut-throats around you make a little less noise!' Finlay jumped to his feet and apologized.

Bretton was worried, 'That'll be a black mark, matey!' he said softly.

'Not really, I'm the only name he knows, cos I shot with him last season,' Finlay said, hanging his head.

On the last day, each cadet was called up in front of Captain Keith. When Finlay's turn came he was a little apprehensive.

'Ah Finlay!' the Captain said. 'Have you enjoyed your stay?'

'Immensely, Sir!' Finlay answered, truthfully.

'What was the most interesting part of the course?' He was watching Finlay intently.

'Difficult to say, it's all passed so quickly,' Finlay answered.

Keith looked at some papers. 'Well. There are two things for certain Finlay. You are the youngest here and also the noisiest. You've been good for morale. I'll look forward to seeing you in September. I take it there's no difficulty over the financing of the kit you'll need?'

'Shouldn't think so, Sir,' Finlay answered.

'Good. You'll be hearing from us next week. What you will need and things like insurance. Good day to you Finlay.' He stood up and shook hands. As Finlay reached the door, Keith called him back. 'You haven't asked me how you've done, Finlay.'

'Sorry Sir, I didn't.' Finlay felt abashed.

Captain Keith smiled for the first time. 'Go home Keith. You've done OK.'

Jenny walked into the kitchen, threw her gloves and riding crop on the table and sighed. 'It's bloody quiet. Boring even, without the little turd! I'm not going to let it get to me though.'

'No I shouldn't, dear. How was your ride?' Niney asked.

'I did all the young stock and the dry cows. The river's wonderfully clear this morning. Do you want a hand to finish the breakfast?' She sat down and glanced at the newspaper.

'No, but I'll tell you what you can do…' She turned and held out her hand. 'Look at the post!' she laughed.

'Why haven't you opened it?' Jenny said, grabbing the letter with Finlay's writing on the envelope. 'As it isn't addressed to anyone specific.'

'I thought we should leave it to James,' Niney said, taking the letter from her.

'He'll be ages yet. You open it Niney,' Jenny said urgently.

'No! I really think we should leave it for James. He's been going through the post looking for it each day. We'll wait.'

When Finlay's grandfather eventually arrived, both women pounced on him. 'There's a letter there from Kee, James,' Niney said, handing it to him.

'Oh yes. Breakfast ready yet?' he asked absently.

'Open the letter James. Please,' Jenny said.

'When I've had my breakfast,' he said, pretending impatience.

'Stop teasing, James!' Niney wheedled.

He smiled at them both. 'Go on one of you. Open it for me.'

Niney opened it and began to read. '"You cannot believe what fun we've all had"… he's been shooting with a bren gun… spent a night on Dartmoor…'

'Read it properly, Niney!' Jenny snapped. Niney handed her the top page and read silently herself, laughing at what she read. The letter was passed around sheet by sheet. 'He doesn't say anything about missing us. Bloody toad!' Jenny said.

Niney, triumphant, read aloud. '"I would like you to know how much I miss you all"… "and having a proper breakfast"… "Can we have roast lamb this weekend?"'

Jenny tried to trump her. '"My darling Jenny, please be certain to watch Misty's shoe"…"I can hardly wait to see her"… Bloody Hell! He thinks more of that sodding mare than you or I, Niney!'

'And get this… "Please give Granny a kiss from me"… No "thanks, Niney. I send you my love,"' Niney said.

'He says the winter wheat down there is more forward than here, but has a lot of mildew on it,' Finlay's grandfather noted. 'And he'll be home on Wednesday! So where's my breakfast?'

The large green Southern Railway's Pacific came to a gliding halt on platform two. She heard her name being called and Jenny began walking down the platform following its sound. There were wolf whistles and comments from the windows. She was dressed in summer jodhpurs, a check shirt and her hair was tied back with a green ribbon. As she grabbed Finlay in a fierce hug, one of the cadets yelled, 'I'm in love with your sister Finlay. Let me come and stay at your house.'

The CPO got down and marched down to where the three cadets from Southampton were joining their parents. 'Sign here, please Miss. To say we gave him back to you,' and handed her his clipboard. He shook hands with Finlay.

'Thanks Chief,' Finlay said. 'See you in September.'

'Indeed you will, sprog.' He reboarded the train.

As it began to move, Finlay waved the train out of sight, laughing.

'You look different. They've cut your hair too short and you smell different,' Jenny said, holding him at arm's length.

'I've had thirty-two showers! I wonder there's anything left of me,' Finlay said.

She laughed at his disgust. 'Come on. Let's get you home. Did you miss me at all?'

Finlay stopped walking. 'Of course I missed you.'

'Well! You might at least kiss me!' she said. He did. When he let her go, she breathed, 'That's what I needed most.'

They left the station arm in arm. 'Niney's getting tea ready and waiting on the telephone. Everybody wants to come and fish. James is tied up with some machinery firm, demonstrating a new drill and there are about one hundred other farmers going to have tea in the barn afterwards.'

'Niney ain't feeding that lot, surely?' Finlay asked.

'No, the Fergie people have laid that on,' she said. 'The blacksmith came and put new shoes on Misty and the new Armstrong is coming tomorrow. Carl has the new welder he wanted. Starwort's litter has been weaned and the price of wheat has dropped through the floor. I took my last exam last week.' She paused for breath.

'Whoa, what's with the litany?' he laughed.

They had reached the pick-up truck. 'Because I don't want to talk now, any more. I want to be kissed and molested for the next ten minutes. When we get home, Niney will commandeer you, then your bloody mare will want to lick you all over, so I'm getting in first!'

Fifteen minutes later, they wiped the mist from the windscreen and drove out of the car park. Jenny, her face flushed, took his hand and rested it on the top of her thigh. 'Better wind the windows down,' she said. Her voice was husky and deep in her throat.

At home, Niney's welcome was effusive. She put a cup of tea down in front of him when they had finished hugging and kissing. 'When you've drunk your tea, get changed and go see that bloody witch of a horse. Another female pining away for you!' She looked at Jenny.

When Finlay went to see the horse, she seemed pleased to see him, but spent the better part of the time he was with her with her ears cocked towards the kitchen. The sound of Jenny's laughter drifted down across the yard to them. When Jenny came to the stable yard, the mare left him abruptly and went to her at a fast trot. 'Shouldn't have left her should you? It's only cupboard love,' Jenny said.

They walked back to the house, hand in hand, chatting and laughing. She laid her head on his shoulder. 'I did miss you, you know buggerlugs.'

'I did you, I promise. Even when we were flying about from pillar to post, I wondered what you were doing.' He kissed her on the cheek.

Niney was looking from the kitchen window. She watched them walk across the yard, so close, and thought about what Jill MacFarlane had said. Only a brave or foolhardy woman would try to come between them. 'For my part, Jill MacFarlane, I shouldn't ever try,' Niney said, aloud to herself. 'But I can't think that his mother won't have a good stab at it.'

Finlay's grandfather came back to the house at around seven. He looked tired and worn, but pleased to see Finlay. He made much of him. Told him the food had gone badly backwards in his absence and 'the bloody females' had been scratchy all week.

'What about this new drill?' Finlay thought he would try to cheer his grandparent up.

'Machines like that, my boy, are going to change the face of England. To make best use of such a thing, fields will have to be made bigger. Hedgerows will go. Even our diesel Fergies can't pull the damn thing empty. It'll mean new and bigger tractors tearing the land to shreds!' he said. There seemed a sadness in his voice. 'We have to point the way, Kee. For the good of the industry. It's our duty to do such things.' Finlay thought his grandfather did not believe what he was saying.

'What's the matter Grandfather?' Finlay asked. 'There's something sticking in your throat.'

'I don't want to be party to turning Hampshire into some kind of howling wilderness. Just one big prairie.'

'We'll be forced into it by the government, Grandfather. They've no feeling for the countryside. As long as they control prices, they control us,' Finlay sighed.

'Farming used to be fun,' was his grandfather's answer.

The following week the letter and instructions from the Admiralty arrived. Finlay handed the letter to Niney. 'September the seventh,' he said, with some finality.

'Oh,' Niney's face clouded over. 'That doesn't seem long.'

'It's not far away, Auntie. I'll be home all the time. As soon as I can drive, it'll be home every weekend.' He knew she wasn't fooled.

'Well, we've always known it was going to happen. Do you want me to break it to Jenny?' she asked, watching his face.

'No.' He said it airily. 'Where is she anyway?'

'In the office, catching up. She didn't do much when you were away.' She sounded cross.

'She said she'd be perfectly all right,' Finlay laughed, remembering what Jenny had said. 'Anyway, she said she might well buy a house down there,' he said artlessly.

'Oh,' Niney said. 'Well that's OK, then.'

She walked around the table and sat close to him on the bench. Taking one of his hands in her own, she pressed it to her lips. 'I hope you know how proud of you I am.' She took his eyes with her own. They were cornflower blue in the light, huge and deep. 'You were a lovely chap to bring this far...' Niney seemed to want to say more. She kissed his hand again. 'Go tell Jen your news, but do it gently...'

Finlay wandered through the hall and into the office. 'Hello Rat Fink! What've you been up to?' Jenny asked, without looking up from her work.

'Looking for mildew on the barley,' he said, kissing the top of her head.

'Find any?' she said, lifting her face for him to kiss.

'Yes. We'll have to spray the whole lot. I don't know why that should be a surprise, it happens every year. What are you doing?' he asked, looking over her shoulder.

'Lime subsidy forms. Marrying them to the quarry invoices. Shall we go somewhere after tea tonight?' she asked.

'What, the cinema or something?'

'It's spring!' Jenny scoffed. 'No, I was thinking more along the lines of looking at the river further up. Or walking the old drove tracks over Chilbolton. What do you think?'

'Miss Vaughne, I'd be delighted to accompany you for a field trip on the Downs.' He bowed theatrically.

'What did you want when you came to find me?' she asked, laughing at him.

'I've got my start date at Dartmouth. First week of September,' he said.

'In that case we'll find lots to do this summer. Make it one to really remember. Spend as much time as possible at the beach hut. Now off you go and let me get on. Else I shan't be finished by tea time.' She held her face up to him and he kissed the tip of her nose gently.

He was late for tea. Finlay had wanted to finish the Armstrong that day. 'Sorry everyone,' he said, coming into the kitchen. 'I've finished the car Grandfather. I think she'll pass muster.' He went to the sink and washed his hands. 'It's suddenly gone very quiet. What were you talking about before I walked in?'

'Not you!' Niney answered. 'Jenny says she wants to buy a car, but doesn't know which. You might as well have your say.'

Finlay thought for a moment. 'What do you want the car for, Jen? You'll have the pick-up when I go in September.'

'So it'll be all right for me to turn up at your new school in a truck. Me and Niney in all our finery, posh long frocks and high heels. That'll really make everyone think we were Hampshire Hogs,' Jenny snorted, dismissively. 'Anyway, it would take a week to get there.'

'Are you both coming down to see me then? I mean, as a regular thing?' Finlay seemed surprised.

'There are lots of social things parents are meant to attend Kee,' Niney said. 'You do want us to come, don't you?'

'That's it Niney... he doesn't. He wants to be free of the witches of Nursling. What a vile child you turned out to be,' Jenny scoffed.

'I don't think you should head down this track,' Jack suddenly said. 'The boy's a bit upset already. So leave it!' he ordered.

'Thanks Jack,' Finlay's grandfather said, from behind the newspaper. 'You two have all the sensitivity of a Sherman tank. When are you and Kee coming back from the nature ramble?' He looked at Jenny, folding his paper.

'Come on, Kee,' Jenny said getting up. 'The older family members want to talk.' She giggled.

'If you are going out, bugger off! Dinner'll be at seven-thirty and don't be late,' Niney said sharply.

'What was that about?' Finlay asked, as the pick-up left the yard.

'Jack and Niney giving up their home and moving in permanently,' Jenny said seriously. 'Then renting their place out to boost Jack's pension.'

'It's more than that, Jen. Niney was bristling. She lives with us mostly anyway.' Finlay needed to know.

'If I tell you Kee, you mustn't know. You promise me?'

'OK,' Finlay answered.

'It's about you being sixteen and replacing the pig buildings with industrial units. There's a big electrical station being built, whether we like it or not. Another sixty acres will be compulsorily purchased, if we don't agree.' Jenny sighed. 'The way things are shaping up darling, you're better off in the Navy.'

They were past Motisfont before Finlay spoke. 'We mustn't let them have it without a fight. We'll have the industrial estate, then sell the land above the top lane for development. It'll make millions. We may as well get out before they destroy everything.'

'Would you leave?' she asked quietly.

'In ten year's time Jen, Southampton will be on the back lawn. Would you still want to be in the house then? Look at what they have done at Millbrook. That's their plan for the valley. We can't hold the slavering hordes back. That's why Testwood House could never be rebuilt and they stuck that bloody awful pub at the lodge entrance. That's their marker. Look out posh people, you've had your day.'

Jenny gave a small brittle laugh. 'Socialists are sneaky sods. Keep watching Kee.'

The Downs looked stunning. The spring barley gave them a mossy green covering, the wheat, by contrast, much darker. They listened to the click of the cooling exhaust and the songs of the myriads of sky-larks.

'What will happen to us Jen?' Finlay asked.

She didn't answer, but stuck the notice in the pick-up's windscreen on estate paper, 'It's us. Looking at birds.'

Finlay followed her out on to the chalk track and they leant togeth-er, out of the wind, on the side of the vehicle. She remained silent, deep in thought, her chin almost on her chest, her long hair shielding most of her face from him. 'Come,' she ordered, taking his hand in hers. They walked for about half a mile, stopping sometimes to watch the peewits and looking at hares through the field glasses.

They stopped and sat together, their legs swinging from an old load-ing ramp.

'What will happen with us?' Jenny repeated the question. 'I wish I knew. When I'm Niney's age, you'll be twenty-eight. I couldn't bear for you to look at me and wonder how you came to be stuck with some old bag.' She turned away and swung her legs over the opposite side, with her back to him. 'I used to love you as maybe an older sister. Now, I think I love you as a woman loves a man. It's not something I chose. At first, I shielded you from Niney when you got buggering about with the girls. Then I didn't like it. I laughed about Jill. I was a bit miffed about Janet always hanging around, but Janey was different. She replaced me and no woman can stand that. Come,' Jenny said, getting down on to the track. 'We can walk on a little. My love, I know I've a nice bum and lovely tits, and now, oodles of money to spend keeping myself young for you. But the fact remains, if your mother or Niney knew what I really felt, I'd be out on my ear in very short order.'

'I wouldn't stay without you,' Finlay said simply.

'Oh, I know that my love, but do you honestly think you could turn your back on Niney? Come on. Tell me the answer,' Jenny demanded.

'No. I couldn't.'

'There you are then. I don't know what will happen to us...' She stopped and held up her hand. 'Put your arm around me.'

They walked on for another ten minutes and then turned to go back towards the pick-up, stopping by a gateway. They counted the hares in one of the fields. 'Seventeen,' Finlay laughed.

He turned to give her the glasses. She was crying. He held her and she snuggled close and for the first time, pushed herself into him. 'I love you Kee. You made that bit easy at least.'

'I don't think Niney would have you gone,' Finlay said. 'She loves you too much for that. I even think she'd understand.' Jenny was not convinced.

Chapter Seven

•

The question of Finlay's relationship with Jenny came to a head when Young John had a puncture in one of the balers the following harvest time. Not realizing what had happened, he had continued to pull it up the main Southampton road. The tyre shredded and the steel wheel collapsed. The tractor slewed into a ditch and the large red baler blocked the main road. Young John, thrown from the tractor, sat rubbing his leg on the far side of the ditch, ruefully studying the wreckage in front of him.

The police telephoned Niney. Niney telephoned Carl. Jenny walked into the kitchen. 'Trouble?' she asked.

'Yes. Go find Ron and tell him to get the winch tractor over to Toothill. A machine's crashed and the main road's blocked,' Niney said.

'Where will I find Ron?' Jenny asked.

'Up on the top somewhere. Come on Jen. Do buck up a bit,' Niney chided.

'I am bucked up,' Jenny protested.

'Jenny, sit down please,' Niney ordered. 'My love... I'm getting a little fed up with you wafting about like a lovesick heifer. If you haven't found a way to get what you want from him, you don't bloody well deserve him! Now get your pretty arse in gear. Get it in the pick-up and find Ron. If it was Kee you had to look for, you would have gone by now!'

They looked at each other for some seconds. Niney was smiling. 'Will you go please, Jenny.'

They both started to giggle. Niney would have continued the conversation when the crisis was over, but the long-awaited delivery of the new Riley Pathfinder happened while Jenny was out and this rather precluded the subject. All Niney said was, 'A Riley Pathfinder in British Racing Green, that's what he wanted wasn't it? You ain't kidding me, Jenny.' Niney and Jenny abandoned the farm and whisked the new car up to Stoney Cross Aerodrome, an ideal place to put the car through its paces.

With the haymaking over, there would be a wait of a few weeks, weather provided, before the winter barley harvest. It was the fourth year in the farm's cycle. Hundreds of acres of grass were ploughed up.

The ground would go into undersown wheat and barley, undersown with grass, after being covered with tons of muck, still yet to be hauled from the cattle's winter yards. It was the natural order of things. Finlay's grandfather and Uncle Jack were going to fish on the Spey. Niney was undecided whether to go with them or not. There was, she felt, nothing she could do that would stop Jenny and Finlay rushing down the road of seeming inevitability. She could have sent one of them away for awhile, or insisted that Finlay accompany her, but she knew he disliked Scotland with its variable fishing and midges. The decision, however, was taken from her. Finlay was to stay to look after the paying rods and make certain that the dairies were cleaned and sorted first thing in the mornings, when the running of the farm was most vulnerable to sickness or breakdown.

They left for Scotland after dinner on the Saturday. Niney had hugged Finlay and said when they got back they would go straight to Hengistbury for his time off. 'Look after him Jenny,' she had said, and the car was gone. They watched it over the hump-backed bridge and then turned and went indoors. There was a certain tension, neither one really knowing how to deal with the situation. Finally Jenny said, 'I'll have the first bath and leave my water in for you. Go settle your horse, then lock up.' She got up and left the room without looking back at him.

Outside, the evening was golden and cooling. The martins were swinging around the chimneys almost ready to settle for the night. A blackbird was pinking in protest over something Finlay could tell was not that important and he glimpsed the white shape of a barn owl scouting the edges of the barley field nearest the house. There was a quiet over the meadows and houses. The men, who had worked so hard for weeks, were now resting or gone on their own holidays. The tempo had slowed, for tonight there was not a sound of a tractor or machine working. When he turned back to the house, after leaving his mare, a slight breeze from the south brought the smell of the sea to the yard.

Indoors, he climbed the stairs to his room. The bathroom opposite was empty and the pillows had been removed from his bed. He bathed carefully and when he had towelled himself dry, he walked along the corridor to Jenny's bedroom. She was lying on her front, facing away from him. Without looking, she flicked the sheet back on the vacant side of her bed. Her hair lay on her bare shoulders and across the pillow. Finlay could hear her breathing almost staccato. Climbing in beside her, he saw the whole of her. Beautiful and golden. She turned to face him. He could see she had been crying.

He woke with a start, seeing the dawn flickering below the horizon through a window strange to him. Jenny lay beside him breathing easily, tiny beads of perspiration mingled with the pale golden freckles that splashed across the bridge of her nose. Her lips, looking full and damp, parted easily as he gently pushed his tongue into her mouth. She moaned her agreement and Finlay remembered sinking through the deep green water of the pool at Hengistbury. It was her foot pushing him that woke him next time. 'Out buggerlugs,' she laughed. 'Go and get some work done and if you're very lucky, I might get you some breakfast.'

Finlay went to the bathroom, splashed cold water on his face, dressed and went downstairs. The world outside was coming awake. Blackbirds seemed to be everywhere singing, and there was a feeling of rain in the breeze. Away to the north, he could hear the yap of the dairyman's collies as Frank, no doubt as sleep-befuddled as he was, went to collect his charges from the water meadows. Close to a couple of hours later, having checked the young stock and dry cows, Finlay stopped at Granny's house. The back door was open.

'Come in, my cock-bird,' he heard her shout.

'You OK Granny?' he said, finding her in the tiny kitchen.

'Of course. Why shouldn't I be? There's your tea.' She kissed him, loud and wet. 'Hah, you bugger! You might wash the smell of the previous female off your face before you come calling on another!' she cackled. She pushed him out of the door as he swallowed the last of his tea. 'Get on back to her. You've only got a week to give her memories.'

It passed very quickly for them. They ate out one evening in Southampton, the others they stayed home. Finlay was flattered his grandfather had only telephoned once to find out how things were going. It was a good week for salmon and the paying rods seemed happy in his company. More importantly, they all caught fish. He had the excuse of being too young to go drinking with them afterwards, so he was back home by six. On the Thursday, Jenny received notification that she could join her father's old firm in September. 'That's useful, I think,' she said. 'It'll take my mind off of you.'

Finlay congratulated her. 'Do you remember telling me you were going to be a lawyer?' he asked.

'The same time you said I had amazing tits.' She put her arms around him. 'Well, now you've had the chance to make free with them...'

Finlay walked into the kitchen to catch the tail end of a conversation Jenny was having on the telephone. Replacing the receiver, she said, 'We'll pack my car ready to go to Hengistbury when they get home, Kee. You were promised some time down there, and I'm going to see that you get it. I have to come back Thursday, to see about my new job. I'll come and get you on the following Saturday. How does that sound?'

'We're staying down there on our own till Thursday?' he gasped.

'As I just said to Niney, there's no difference between staying here together and staying down there.' She was laughing.

They even had the Riley pointing towards the road when the rest of the family arrived home.

Finlay's grandfather laughed uproariously. 'Done without us, just back and you still prefer life without us!'

'Something like that!' Jenny said. 'You've had your holiday and now Kee will have his. Lunch is ready indoors and we're going before something happens that stops us.'

Niney climbed slowly out of the Armstrong. 'I've walked the length and breadth of Scotland, caught two fish and been chewed and spat out by sodding midges! Jenny, you look fantastic! My darling boy! You look all in. Take him Jen and when are you back?'

'On Thursday, but I'll leave buggerlugs there and pick him up Saturday when you go down. Everything's done. John's looking after Misty, there's a stack of cash to go in the bank.' She climbed into her car. 'Hello Jack, hello James, we're gone.'

Finlay went and hugged Niney tightly. 'Love you Auntie! See you Auntie!'

'Come on Kee! Else you'll be stuck here for another year,' Jenny said impatiently.

As the car pulled away, Finlay's grandfather looked at Niney. 'Are you sure that is entirely proper, my dear?'

'What on earth do you mean, James?' Niney said, shocked. 'You surely can't think... James! Honestly!'

'No, my dear. Of course not. Let's get the car unloaded, shall we?' he said, admonished.

—

The summer flowed through their lives with the gentle harmony of nature. The barley harvest began at the start of the third week of July. Back from Hengistbury, by various turns they were all seemingly rested and content. When the combine harvesters began their stolid, dusty marches through the smoking ripeness of the cereals, all went as planned. The years of good husbandry gave the land a richness that others envied. The proper way of doing things. The persuasion of the fecund earth into giving.

The start of the grouse season was given scant regard by the family. The wheat was pretty well ready, certainly too near ready to chance leaving. August faded gently into September in warm and golden glory. Finlay's kit had been packed and unpacked, checked and rechecked. Niney needed him to be the best turned out, and fussed. Jenny seemed like the summer's end, by turns bright and cool, giving and loving. The harvest finished two days before he left for Dartmouth. There was sadness, but not much. Jenny was going to be a lawyer and Finlay a sailor. All had been planned and executed in the proper manner.

Niney had driven him to his new life. Jenny, with the excuse of starting her new life on the same day, avoided the sadness of formal parting. She had come to his bed on his last night and made brittle lightness of the next day. His grandfather had been gruffly nonchalant, shook his hand and left quickly in his Land-Rover. There was something to do at the hatch pool. Niney delivered him to the college, bidding him, 'Make me even more proud.' She removed some imaginary dirt from his face with a spit-moistened lace handkerchief, stuffed it in his pocket and left. He stayed, watching the direction of where the Armstrong had gone.

A voice behind him made him start. 'Who are you?' The tone was menacing.

'Finlay Sir,' Finlay answered, turning to face a commander.

'What are you doing here, Finlay?' he asked. 'Just seeing off my aunt, Sir.'

'Why aren't you properly dressed? Get into a uniform. The only aunt you need worry about is Auntie Elizabeth in the big house at the end of the Mall. She owns you, body and soul. So go and put her uniform on!' The order was made in a crescendo of malice.

'Yes Sir,' Finlay said, and hurried away.

It was six weeks before Finlay saw the outside world. He had just about time and energy to write short notes home and was allowed one call per week. Niney wrote a weekly missive with relayed comments from his grandfather and Uncle Jack. Jenny wrote when she had the time and was seemingly cheerful and happy. She told him about her new job, the river and warned him she had had her hair cut, to accommodate a wig. It was now shoulder length and she thought it made her look more sophisticated.

His short weekend began at Friday noon and ended at 'twenty-two hundred', the following Sunday. The journey home seemed interminable, the train stopping at every station until at last it slowed into Southampton Central. At first, he couldn't see her, but he was looking for the wrong person. This new one wore a tailored black skirt and white blouse, black stockings and hair, just barely shoulder length. When Jenny saw him, she started to run and he caught her. They spun around on the dusty platform.

'You look so grown up!' she laughed.

'I was going to say that to you. I love your hair,' Finlay said.

The crowd of passengers swept around them.

'Let's go somewhere where we can stop for a few minutes,' he suggested.

'This will have to do,' Jenny said, parking by the bridge at Ridge. 'Everybody knows the car anyway.'

It had taken some time to clear the rush-hour traffic.

'Come here,' Finlay said, and held her. He smelt her perfume and touched the softness of her face. 'I missed you so much.'

She breathed his breath. He looked at the love in her eyes and was happy again.

They went in the back way to the yard. Niney saw them arrive and watched them walking up towards the house together from the kitchen window. 'James,' she ordered. 'Come and look, quickly.' They watched as Jenny and Finlay walked together, laughing, arm in arm. 'Well, James. Are you proud of them? The two orphans we raised?' she asked, tears smarting in her eyes.

'Yes of course! And we should be!' Finlay's grandfather answered.

Niney wrested Finlay from Jenny, on the steps to the front door. 'Hello sailor.' She smiled and hugged him. 'I bet you had a job to recognize Jenny. She's gone grown up on us.'

Finlay turned and looked at Jenny. 'She's very beautiful,' he said. Niney looked. 'Is she?' she said, dismissively. 'Can't see it myself. Her arse is too small and her legs are too thin!' She took each of them by the arm and walked them inside.

'I didn't mean she was as beautiful as you, Auntie,' Finlay wheedled.

'Thank you, my dear. But we know that, don't we?'

They all laughed, happy to be back as one.

Contrary to what Finlay had expected, he did not get home again until Christmas and then only for ten days. The following session he would only be due 'short, short weekends'. Saturday noon till Sunday, eighteen hundred. Jenny bought a small house near to the college and they were together, at least sometimes, but barely had this been discreetly achieved when Finlay was transferred to Portland and drafted to a frigate. The Fates seemed against them. For the next two years they were together infrequently.

The Christmas of his eighteenth birthday, however, he had been granted two month's leave. When he got home, Jenny was somehow different, even moody. If he enquired why, it was to be told that it was his imagination. At night, she still held and kissed the same and loved him frantically.

'Jenny,' Finlay said quietly, one night in the dark of his bedroom. 'I think we should get married. I'll leave the Navy and come home.'

She didn't answer. She stiffened, turned away from him and began to cry. 'We can't. I'm too old. We talked about this before you went. It cannot be, Kee. Not because I don't love you. Good God…' She started to sob again.

'But Jen… We have to be together. I can't be without you,' Finlay began.

'We'll sort it on your next leave, Kee. Not this one,' she said, pulling into him.

Finlay returned from Gibraltar a week early and was on his way home within an hour of his ship docking. He was driving the Wolseley he had purchased at Christmas and he was pushing it hard. Two hours later, he was coming over the hill into Romsey. Five minutes later he pulled into the yard. 'Hello, beautiful Auntie, I'm early.' He kissed Niney. She went pale. 'What is it?' he asked. 'Where's everyone? Where's Jenny?'

'James has gone to the airport. To bring her home, my love. She's been to Canada,' said Niney. For once, she avoided his eyes.

'What's happening? Why has she been to Canada?' He knew something was wrong.

'Best she tells you, Kee. It has to come from her. Not me.' Niney choked it out.

'Please Auntie! What on earth has happened? Is Jenny leaving?' He felt cold saying it.

'My darling, she loves you. She cannot marry you...' Niney started to cry.

'If she loved me like I love her, she would never go...'

'Kee! She has to go. To save you both. You must see that she cannot be your wife.' Niney got up and banged her fists on the table. 'I knew it would come to this... all those years ago. God damn it! Jill MacFarlane, you saw it.'

'She doesn't want me then?' Finlay said, angry. He picked up his case. 'I'm going back to my ship, Auntie.' Finlay kissed her and looked at her tenderly. 'I'll see you later my love.'

'When will you be back, Kee? Don't you want some tea at least? You can't just go,' she pleaded.

Finlay drove back to Portland just as quickly as he had driven up to Romsey. He didn't know what he was going to do. He just wanted to be back. The policeman on the dock gate smiled. 'Forget something?'

'Hello, Fred. Yes I did.' He searched in his pocket and sorted twenty pounds. 'Can you do the usual and get my car back home for me please?'

'Yes, Sir. Be a pleasure.' He took the keys from Finlay. 'Always a good feed at your place.'

He was surprised to see the frigate still had her boilers fired up as he walked up the brow. 'Evening Hatch,' he said to the AB at the top. 'We got some problem with the engines?'

'No Sir. Didn't think you'd make it back. We were leaving without you.'

'Leaving?' Finlay asked.

'Best see the Jimmy, Sir. He'll be pleased to see you,' Hatch replied.

'Find somebody to get that to my cabin please, Hatch. I must find out what's going on.' Finlay made for the bridge, dropping his case at the top of the brow.

'Evening, Sir,' Finlay said, coming on to the bridge.

'That must have been low flying, Finlay. How did you know to come back? Mid Brooks told me there was some confusion where you were. He telephoned your home. Anyway, you're here now. Get something to eat and come on at midnight. We'll be casting off in about ten minutes,' the Captain said.

'Where are we going, Sir?' Finlay laughed. 'I'm here because of something that happened at home. In something of a bate I might add.'

'Biscay. We have to intercept some Libyan ship. The powers that be think she's running arms to Ireland.' He picked up the bridge telephone. 'Engine room, how much longer? Go get some food, Finlay. We're short of watch officers. You'll probably be eating on the run.'

'Yes Sir,' Finlay said, easily. 'Suits me,' he thought to himself.

Niney's heart lifted for a moment when she saw Finlay's car coming up the front drive, but only for a moment. She could see he wasn't driving it. 'Hello Fred,' she said, meeting him at the front door. 'Time for some tea and something to eat?' She was ushering him indoors whether he had time or not. 'Did you see my nephew last night?' she asked lightly.

'Yes Ma'am,' Fred said, sitting down heavily at the table. 'Coincidence wasn't it? The mid had only just telephoned from the dock office when up he drives. Telepathy I shouldn't wonder. He had time enough to go on board. Ten minutes later she slipped and was away down the Channel.'

Niney handed him the mug of tea. 'I know you're not supposed to, but I need to have notice of the ship coming back. It's a personal matter, with a young lady involved. She's going away and wants to see him before she goes.'

'Well, I will try for you Ma'am. She won't be gone long, only a couple of weeks probably. I'll call, but don't let on please. He asked me to give you this... came running down the brow as she was already slipping.' He handed her an envelope just as Jenny walked in. 'Sorry Miss. *Nubian* will be in the Atlantic by now. I just bought the young gentleman's car back. As he asked.'

It was obvious they were both upset.

'I'll get Mr Brockett to get you back to the station, Fred. There's been something of a drama here,' Niney said sadly. 'This is to me Jen, but perhaps you had better get it straight from the horse's mouth.' She handed her the envelope and telephoned for Brockett.

Jenny walked out into the hall, opening the letter as she went and Niney heard her sob.

'Brockett will be here in a moment, Fred. I'd better go to Jenny.'

Finlay had written instructing Niney to get Carl to store his car and sell Misty. If Jenny wasn't going to be there, it would be just another job for somebody else to do and the mare would be wasting, anyway. He wrote he was giving up on the opposite sex and, with that in mind, would not be home for some months. He hoped she would understand. Jenny was to be the last female in his life and now, he would stay in the Navy. He sent his love.

It was more than some months. It was well over a year, and even then it was only Granny's death that brought him back. It had been sudden. No time to warn him that it was near. Granny died in her sleep just as spring had arrived. With no more than minutes to spare, Finlay had made it to the crematorium at Stoneham, having bent all the Navy's rules coming back from Gibraltar. He stood at the back of the chapel. Niney and his grandfather knew nothing of his presence. He could see the back of his mother's head from where he was standing, but nothing of Jenny. Ron Drew turned and saw him. He smiled broadly and poked the person in front of him. Soon, the news that he was there reached Niney, who turned and walked to him. She pulled him outside and hugged him. 'Thanks for getting here darling, and for the flowers and letters… Everything.' She was crying.

They walked to the far corner of the garden, 'How are you, Auntie? You look beautiful. How's the farm? And the river?'

'Are you coming home?' she asked.

'No… I can't. I have to go back. I suppose Grandfather knows about Jenny now. Does he forgive me?' Finlay asked.

'Don't be stupid. He doesn't blame you or Jenny. Darling, come back, for just an hour even. Your mother's here, and your brother.'

'Niney, my love. I can't come home yet, not even if Jen is not there and certainly not if my mother's there. I'll say hello to Grandfather and leave. But I'll come home soon, my love. I promise.' He was holding her hands in his as the doors opened from the chapel. People began spilling out.

'Oh Jesus Christ, Auntie! I wish I hadn't come. I'll go and see Grandfather and Jack and come back to you. Then I'm gone,' Finlay said.

His grandfather saw him and looked shocked. 'My boy! You've come home,' he said.

'Only briefly, Grandfather,' Finlay said. 'Hello, Uncle Jack. Look after my river please. I'll make it back to fish soon. I can't stay...' he began.

'Are you my brother then?' a young voice said beside him.

Finlay looked and saw a younger version of himself. 'By the look of you, I suppose I must be. Got any brains?' Finlay laughed at him.

'Some,' his brother answered.

'Then I must be your brother.' Finlay laughed again.

'Your mother wants to speak with you, Kee,' his grandfather said.

'Next time Grandad. Maybe. Are they home in England now?' he asked, turning and walking with him back to Niney.

'Next year...' his granfather began.

'Maybe then. Not now. I must spend what time I have with Niney,' he said firmly.

'But Kee! You must speak with your mother. I insist.'

'Insist on Grandfather. I want no part of her, or my father. Now leave me with my auntie please. I'll see you in about a year.' Finlay turned and went to Niney.

'Walk me to my car, darling love,' he said. 'Let me get out of this. Give my best to Ron and say sorry. There's only you now.' He looked at her, smiling. 'I'll write soon.'

From then on, he changed. He became somehow detached from the ache that Jenny's decision had caused his heart. He went to the little wars and upsets, especially in the Middle East, and became known for his coolness under fire. Finlay knew it to be something else. An indifference to staying alive, which eventually became habitual. He wrote long letters to Niney, saying when he could where he was and what he was up to. He even admitted to 'loving a good scrap', knowing he was good at what he did.

It was the second Christmas after Granny had died that he eventually went home. He docked at Portsmouth, caught the harbour train up to Romsey and took a taxi to the house. He walked into the empty kitchen, which smelt of fresh baking and the same smell of milk and butter he had yearned to smell again. He could hear someone moving about upstairs, so he moved the kettle on to the hot side of the Aga and went to look. He met Niney in the hall. They fell into each other's arms. She had been upstairs making his bed, ever hopeful he was coming home. Her welcome covered him with joyous tears and kisses.

They took their tea into the hall by the large open fire.

Taking his hands in her own she said, 'Can you talk about Jenny yet?'

'I think so. Have you heard from her?' he replied, the familiar crashing feeling in his stomach returning.

'Yes, of course. She's fine, doing well. She did the right thing, darling. It sounds silly, but it was only because of the way she loved you. You promise you won't go after her. Will you do that for me?' Niney said, her eyes filling with tears.

'Yes, Auntie Niney, I shan't go after her. Now, I know why she went.'

'Good boy. Let it rest. And let's have a little less of this covering yourself in glory. I know what's making you do it,' she said, softly.

'You always know everything Auntie.' He laughed. He paused. 'Has Jenny found another chap?'

'No. There won't be,' Niney said. 'That type of love leaves room for no other.'

Chapter Eight

•

Finlay was sitting at the wardroom table trying his best with the *Telegraph* crossword. He had been off watch for about an hour but there was no real case for sleep. The violence of the storm they were passing through precluded that. The frigate rolled and pitched her way through the weather, heading for the South West Approaches. He glanced at the young midshipman who fell through the doorway, soaked through and looking green. 'Never mind, Mid. We'll be in the Channel in an hour. It'll calm down then.'

'I'm sure it will, Sir. The Captain wants you on the bridge, Sir... can I go, Sir?' He needed badly to be out in the air, away from the smell of vomit and the ship's sludge tanks, stirred up by the storm and their noxious odour pervading the ship.

'Away you go, Mid. I'll get dressed.' Finlay smiled.

Outside, the air was full of spray and wind. The dawn was breaking in the east and the ship seemed to be taking on the full fury of the storm, alone. Despite his oilskins, by the time Finlay had reached the bridge he was soaked. 'Morning, Sir,' he said. 'You wanted me?'

'Ah yes. Rather looks, Finlay, as though you'll be leaving us. Signal came in.' He handed Finlay the flimsy.

'Any idea why, Sir?' Finlay said, reading the signal, which directed him to Horse Guards the next day.

'None at all, old chap. Bloody nuisance though. Probably promotion. I gave you too good a ticket on your last assessment.' He smiled. 'Hope we're not going to lose you entirely. Certainly not to a desk.'

The ship lurched and buried her bows into the sea, sending tons of water over the upper works, soaking everyone not under cover. The next wave seemed to fire them forward. The frigate landed suddenly in a trough, with the seas around towering above the ship. Tons of water came crashing down. Suddenly, for the briefest of moments, they were waist deep, before the ship rose again, shaking herself free of the wave. Finlay started to laugh. 'Who in their right mind would swap all of this? Nature's glory, the smell of the sea, the wind blowing through one's salt-encrusted hair, for a desk. Being served tea by a pretty WREN. Not some hoary matelot!'

'You wouldn't, Finlay,' the Captain answered. 'You've never been in your right mind from day one!'

'Probably not, Sir,' Finlay answered. 'Torquay coming up on the port side.' The rain momentarily cleared, allowing the town to be viewed through glasses.

'We should perhaps wake them up with a round or two of starshell. Give their day a wonderfully bright start,' Finlay suggested.

'Make that H.E., Finlay. My mother-in-law lives in Torquay.' The Captain smiled grimly.

Finlay brought the hire car to a shuddering stop in front of Admiralty Arch. It had been a hellish drive up from Portland and he was feeling distinctly peevish. He got out of the car, locked and kicked it, muttering, 'Heap of crap!' as he walked away.

'You can't leave that there, Sir,' a policeman said, approaching him quickly.

'Constable, I can promise you, I'm not driving it another inch!' Finlay replied.

'It'll be towed away!' the policeman threatened.

'Good, Constable! Promise me it'll be burnt at the end of its journey and there's a drink in it for you. Now, I'm going in there and you do as you wish… it's a hire car, a death trap and there it stays!' Finlay said firmly.

'Can I see your ID, Sir,' the policeman said, sensing the battle lost.

'Certainly…' Finlay showed his card and went into the building.

'Name of Finlay. Here to see Admiral Winter,' he said to the man on reception, proffering his ID.

'Through that door there. Up three landings and the door is right in front of you, Sir,' he said brightly. 'Sir, I should put that fag out. The old bat in the office up there don't like it.' He pushed an ashtray towards Finlay.

'One should always defer to old bats on first acquaintance,' Finlay said, stabbing out his cigarette. 'Thereafter, it should always depend on how old they are and how bat-like they have become with age.'

'Believe me, Sir, this one sleeps upside down in a cave!' the receptionist said, glumly.

'In that case, thanks for the warning,' Finlay said, walking to the doorway.

As he mounted the stairs, he wondered what sort of person could have ordered the interior of such a beautiful building to be painted in a sick green and pallid cream paint. The place was dirty and smelt distinctly of mice. He knocked on the door and walked straight in. Five young females were busy and a woman, the wrong side of fifty, advanced rapidly towards him. 'You can't just walk in here!' she snapped, taking his arm firmly, trying to guide him back through the door.

Finlay remained standing, unmoved by her tugging. 'Name of Finlay. Here to see Admiral Winter.'

He looked with distaste at this tiny creature pulling at him. She was dressed in a pink cardigan, over something else pink, with a grey skirt and stockings of a deeper grey. Her eyes were small and dark and Finlay's first thought was that she looked like a female bullfinch. She went to a door at the far end of the office and said to someone within, 'Finlay is here, Sir.' She returned towards him, moving a little like a crab. 'You must wait outside in the corridor!' she said, pulling again at his sleeve.

Finlay winked at a good-looking girl, working on some papers. The crab-like woman's efforts to remove him became more urgent.

Finlay stood outside. The steel and canvas chairs were too filthy to sit upon and he reflected on the female civil servant he had just encountered. Menopausal women should not be put in charge of anything more lethal than a tea-tray. He stared glumly out of the window until his eye was caught by a pile of mouse droppings on the window-sill. An orange-yellow stain among thick grey dust, where it had obviously urinated. 'Oh, for fuck's sake!' he muttered, lighting a cigarette. The Navy had imbued in Finlay that godliness was nothing, cleanliness everything.

The door swung open and the crab woman stared at him. 'We don't allow smoking in here!' she snapped.

'Nor buckets and swabs, by the look of it,' Finlay answered equably. 'Ever think of picking up a cleaning rag?'

She made an explosive noise through her nose, and slammed the door. He lit another cigarette. The door opened again. 'I've told you already. No smoking!'

Finlay curled his lip. 'You tell me nothing. Sling your hook!'

Inside, the office was clean and airy. It smelt of pipe tobacco and coffee. The Admiral was in civilian clothes, stockily built with white hair and half-moon glasses, over which he stared at Finlay, his elbows on the desk, his fingertips together under his chin. 'It might be as well, Finlay, if you tried to get on with Miss Grant. Do you not like women?' he asked coldly.

'Good morning, Sir,' Finlay began. 'Yes Sir. I do like women.'

The Admiral tried to stop the flicker of amusement his lips betrayed. 'Miss Grant is a very senior civil servant,' he observed.

'She doesn't wear our uniform, Sir,' Finlay answered.

'I've brought you up here, Finlay, because I wanted to speak to you. You may sit, stand, walk about, smoke and relax, pretend for the moment I'm not an Admiral. I need to know what makes you what you are. Something of an uncompromising bugger on first meeting, I'd say.' He started filling his pipe.

'Not really, Sir. I don't like civil servants or politicians. They bugger up our lives and are usually a waste of space!' Finlay said.

'Explain!' the Admiral ordered.

'It was probably somebody like your Miss Grant who made us return from Iceland at half-speed to save fuel, without knowing that the men were overdue for leave and there was a socking great storm due. We could have avoided it, if we'd been allowed to crack on.'

'Yes, I heard the trip back was fairly bumpy. Any damage?' the Admiral asked.

'Yes Sir. One of the leading hands had his arm broken when the whaler was lost over the side,' Finlay said. 'As I say Sir, it could have been avoided.'

'What do you think civil servants do, Finlay?'

'Get underfoot mostly, Sir. I know they have to deal with pay, supply, welfare and the rest. But they're lazy sods, most of them, with an inflated idea of what they're actually worth.'

'Why did you join the Navy, Finlay? Tell me honestly,' the Admiral asked.

'I joined the Navy, Sir, to protect this country from its enemies. That may sound trite Sir, but that's the truth of it. I didn't join to be anything else. To land a good job later in life, become a lawyer or a doctor on the cheap. I don't want to see the Hammer and Sickle flying above us, and though this may also sound glib, I'd lay down my life to prevent that happening,' Finlay said.

'Do you have a young lady in your life, Finlay?' he asked, watching him closely for his reaction.

'No Sir.'

'Are you a homosexual?'

'Certainly not, Sir!' Finlay answered, emphatically.

The Admiral thumbed through some papers. 'You are over Miss Vaughne then?'

'How do you know about her?' Finlay asked, somewhat aggressively.

The Admiral looked up sharply. 'I know everything there is to know about you. Did you think we did not know about Jennifer Vaughne and spending all the spare time you had at *Britannia* with her?' He held up his hand to stop Finlay. 'Nobody condemns you for that, Finlay. I just need to know your take on it.'

'It hurt like Hell, Sir,' Finlay said.

'I can only imagine Finlay... but relationships like that cannot...'

'No, Sir. I see that now,' Finlay interrupted, wishing to move away from the subject.

'Have you been keeping up with this Profumo thing?' Winter allowed his interruption.

'Not really, Sir. Only reading about who was banging whom. Things are sure to happen when you put shallow people in positions of responsibility,' Finlay said.

'You're something of a prig, Finlay,' the Admiral said.

'I've been called that before, Sir. But you would have thought that any War Minister might have thought to ask MI5 to check her background. Miss Keeler, I mean. At least find out who else was blessed with her favours.'

'And then?' the Admiral asked, his eyes twinkling.

'Get her to find out what she could from the Russian chap. Make the whole thing worthwhile, I would have thought,' Finlay smiled.

'I understand you're a very good shot, Finlay,' the Admiral offered.

'Thank you, Sir,' Finlay answered.

'I don't mean shooting pheasants, Finlay!' the Admiral said testily. 'I mean with the weapons you are issued with in the service.'

'I keep myself up to the mark, Sir. Always allowing for the restrictions that are put on us,' Finlay said.

'I want you to see a Doctor Williams at Haslar tomorrow. Have a more in-depth analysis done, than has been done,' the Admiral said.

'Really Sir? I saw him not long ago. He wanted to know how killing Arabs had effected me. He was a wanker!' Finlay said, wondering suddenly if the epithet was entirely suitable.

'It wasn't about the people killed in the air strike. The report said you shot a man with a sniper rifle before the air strike came in. We just wondered why,' the Admiral said. 'It was me who had you sent there.'

'He was browning a small boy, Sir. The marine was not certain he could hit him. I was. So I shot him. The air strike may not have killed him. The boy was in agony, Sir. Anyway, I'm not going through, justifying that,' Finlay said, impatiently.

The Admiral looked at his notes again. '"Yes, I shot him… Took his head straight off and I don't give a flying fuck what you think, Doc." That's what you said.'

'Probably did, Sir. Is that why I'm here? Yes, I shot him. He was one of the leaders, so I would have shot him anyway. The bullet, a point five, sent his head spinning up in the air. Should I justify the others I shot that morning? There were ten or twelve more, Admiral!' Finlay said.

'That's not why you're here, Finlay,' the Admiral said, in a placatory manner.

They talked on for another two hours about Finlay's career to date and some of his personal life. The Admiral organized another hire car, sending him on his way and telling him to be back in two day's time.

The interview the following day with Williams was not easy. The conversation was opened by the doctor. 'So you think I'm a complete ass head, Finlay?'

'Nothing personal, Doctor. Some people are born that way.' The day following this interview, he was again in front of Admiral Winter.

'Same rules as before, Finlay. I'm not an Admiral,' he said.

'Yes Sir,' Finlay replied.

'Doctor Williams says he really doesn't understand you…'

Finlay began to laugh. 'I thought that was his job!' he said.

Winter dropped his notes. 'I think I understand you Finlay. You're an arrogant young pup, but I think you might be made of the right stuff.' He paused and looked at Finlay, long and hard. 'I've been charged by the PM to set up a small, but effective, intelligence-gathering unit. Not the usual sort of thing, pen pushers, but thinking service people, capable of working under orders. Flexible, tough but, above all, thinking people. I think you're such a person Finlay.'

'I don't want to leave the Navy, Sir,' Finlay said quickly. 'If I like what you are offering, I'll have a go. But leave the Navy? No! Not ever!'

'You won't have to. You keep your rank and your progression upwards would be quicker in terms of seniority. When you've finished training for this unit, should you complete it, you'll get a half-ring, with consequent increase in pay and pension. There would be other benefits. Increased leave, almost limitless expenses, that would be accountable, and a very great deal of trust. Interested?' The Admiral smiled at him.

'Joint Services, Sir?' Finlay asked.

'No, Navy. Though three of the group would be from the Army,' Winter said. He never stopped looking at Finlay's face.

'Which regiment, Sir?' Finlay asked.

'Two from the Green Jackets. One from the Inniskillens.'

'That's all right, then. So how many in total?' Finlay asked.

'Glad you approve!' the Admiral smiled. 'Five Navy, five Royal Marines and the three from the Army. There'll also be two helicopter pilots on attachment. They're also Navy.'

'Do we have a name yet?' Finlay asked.

'Not really. At the moment it's just called the Recce Group.'

'Based where?'

'Here. After it's been cleaned up. We only moved in last week… hence the dirt that offends you. Now Finlay. I cannot emphasize this enough. This is an experiment and very secret. I ask again. Are you interested?' the Admiral asked, leaning forward, studying Finlay's face, ever more closely.

'So… I stay as a naval officer. I can go back to that if this doesn't work. I have a lavish expense account. There must be a downside to this,' Finlay said.

'There is. You cannot tell your family what you're doing, and you'll probably be killed,' Winter said, equably.

'Well. I suppose I can live with that!' Finlay laughed. 'OK Sir, I'm in. What now?'

The Admiral went to a cupboard and removed a large attaché case. 'In here is what it's all about. Go home and study it. Don't leave it about. There's the key. Go and enjoy some of…' He looked at Finlay's record on his desk. 'Yes, go home and enjoy some of Mrs Terry's cooking. You'll receive a letter from me, detailing your next move. In the meantime, you've been allocated a Wolseley.' He pointed at it on the parade ground, below. 'Which you have to sign for please, and this…' He handed Finlay a brown envelope. 'Five hundred pounds in cash,' the Admiral said, smiling. 'When in England, you'll have to keep account of it. When abroad, you'll be given more in the relevant currency. Don't be stupid enough to abuse any trust, Finlay. You'll find your personal gear from your ship in the boot of the car. Study what you've been given. Ground rules, etc. You'll be signed up next time we meet.'

'So my kit is in the boot, Sir. You were confident I was going to agree?' Finlay smiled.

'I would have been mortified if you hadn't. I've watched your career since Angus Keith told me about you. Now, off you go, Finlay. I've others to see.' The Admiral shook hands and saw him to the door.

Finlay drove home. As he pulled into the yard he smiled to see Niney hanging out some washing. She glanced at the car and, not seeing who it was, ignored it and went back to her task. The muck heap, with its still frozen covering of snow over the dark rich detritus, looked like a large, iced Christmas cake. He wound down the car window. 'I was told this was a good berth. Specially for young sailors!' he yelled.

Niney spun around. 'What are you doing here?' She came running towards him and covered his face with kisses. 'Why didn't you tell me you were coming... and what are you doing in your best uniform?' she carried on, hugging and kissing him.

'Let me look at you,' Finlay said, easing her away to arm's length. 'You really are a bloody gorgeous creature, Auntie Niney.'

'Nonsense! I found a grey hair this morning!' She laughed. 'What's this?' she asked, looking at the car. 'That's a bit rich.'

'Been offered a new job and this goes with it. Don't ask any questions because I don't know too much myself yet. Anyway, I'll probably get a half-ring out of it shortly,' Finlay said.

'Well done! Come on in and I'll get you some food. How long have you got?' She led him towards the house.

'Week or more, probably. I don't know. It's all up in the air at the moment. I've been hob-nobbing with an admiral since first thing, in London. Anyway, enough time to have a rest.'

The warmth and familiar smell of the kitchen caught him unawares. Niney saw his look. 'Stop it Kee!' she said quietly.

'It's not that, Auntie. I'm just glad to be here.'

He could hear somebody moving about, working a vacuum cleaner. 'Who's that upstairs?' he asked.

'Judy. One of the tractor drivers' wives. She comes in to clean. There's so much paper to deal with about the farm these days, it seems to take all of my time. I even have a bloody secretary twice a week now. Would be some sense to the job if we made any more money,' she sighed.

'Is it bad then?' Finlay asked.

'Not that bad, really. The pigs barely break even, now there's no swill. But for the breeding sales, they'd lose money. The dairies and fishing keep it all going. The feed wheat actually loses money. Thank

Christ we still get top whack for the milling wheat. Anyway, it all goes around and comes back again, to be all right,' Niney said, not even convincing herself.

'Maybe I should jack in the Navy and come home, Auntie. I feel guilty being away all the time,' Finlay suggested.

'And do what, my love? The prices won't alter for what we produce, because you're here. As the men retire, we replace them with bigger machines. The wages we save are spent on bloody great tractors. They bully the land into submission. No, my love. You're better off where you are, with a career. Away from it. Maybe when you're older and have had enough of fighting the Queen's enemies, farming may be back in fashion again.'

For the next ten days, Finlay looked at everything, fished and studied what was in the briefcase. His horse had been sold back to her breeder and the little pick-up had discreetly disappeared. There was nothing of Jenny left. The photographs had been put away and the room across the passageway from his was empty and locked. The sparrows still fought out their family squabbles in the bedroom chimney, but the house was, to him, unnaturally quiet.

On the third day, driving down towards the wood yard he saw Janet Ward riding one horse and leading another. He got out of the Land-Rover and waited for her to come up to him.

'Finlay!' she yelled, happily. 'Well! You ain't a little boy any more!'

'Hello Jan. You look good. How have you been?' he said, taking the lead horse and helping her down.

She hugged him and kissed his cheek. 'I've been good. How long have you got at home?' she asked.

'Couple of weeks at the most. Are you still at home? Still got your horsey business?'

'Yes. Goes from strength to strength. Doesn't make much money, but I'm happy. What about you? Cassy came home one day and told us you'd been decorated for being brave. She's in television now, so she knows everything,' Janet gushed, yet looked the same beauty that had always been promised.

'What about Jo? What's she doing?' Finlay asked.

'Still changing the world. Bit of a balls-up really. Got in with the Ban the Bomb lot. Become a bit of a drop-out.'

'And your mother?' Finlay asked.

'All sweats and sobs,' Janet smiled. 'Look, why don't you come over in an hour? I'll get these exercised and come on back. We can talk then.'

'OK. Do you want me to get you up?' he said, offering his hand for her foot.

She swung up into the saddle and looked back down at him. 'You're still a fucking bastard, Finlay!' she said softly, and taking him by the shirtfront hauled him closer, demanding a kiss. She tasted as he remembered.

Chapter Nine

•

He was almost glad when the letter arrived from the Admiralty. His leave had been a mixture of extremes. He was sad he could see some of the changes that would have to come, yet glad because at least Niney seemed to have everything in order and was still the same lovely woman. He had taken Janet out for dinner, enjoyed her company and wonderful green eyes, promising to do the same next time he came home. When they said goodbye and kissed, they both felt the strange magnetism that had been there before. 'Bugger off, Finlay!' she had said. 'You were the last one to get my pants off and so it will remain. Stay safe and come back and marry me when you're thirty. With lots of money and terribly famous.'

He said his goodbyes at home, having left a telephone number where a message could be passed to him; his BFPO remained the same.

He had been told, and supplied with a map, to go to an unnamed training camp in Warwickshire. The map instructions were detailed, letting him know it was going to be difficult to recognize. When he reached the end of his journey he was convinced he had gone wrong. In front of him was a muddy track that led off between rhododendron bushes, hung low enough to obscure the windscreen of the Wolseley. He eased the car through gently. At one point, the exhaust scraped along the track's surface. After at least one hundred and fifty yards of this he was suddenly in the open, confronted with an ordinary wooden farm gate with a simple private sign on it. Behind the gate the track improved, made up with what looked like ash from some industrial process. When he opened the gate, he knew he was in the right place. He saw he had broken an alarm circuit attached to the gate's upright. As he drove on, he noted the fences either side of him were getting closer and more substantial. No chance now to turn around. The only way out would be in reverse. He rounded a tight left-hand bend and came to a sliding halt. In front of him was a high metal gate and four men with machine pistols, who quickly surrounded the car.

Finlay wound down the window. 'Morning,' he said, smiling.

'Leave the keys in the ignition. Get out and put your hands on the roof,' a man, with sergeant's chevrons on his sleeve, said.

Finlay did as bidden. The sergeant patted him down. 'Turn around,' he ordered. He compared Finlay's face with a photograph. Leaning forward, he removed the keys from the ignition. 'Open the boot please,' he asked. As he went to do so, the soldiers moved right back but kept him covered with the machine pistols. The boot came open with a hiss from the air struts.

The Sergeant looked in briefly. Standing back again, he ordered Finlay to open the suitcase within and then stand back. Again, Finlay did as bidden. Inside, Niney's beautiful packing was evident. One of the soldiers moved forward to search it. 'Don't put your dirty hands on my white shirts, soldier, or you might find yourself eating one of them!' Finlay said. The soldier ignored him and gave the suitcase a very professional search.

'OK you! Move forward and close the case. Now the boot, then stand away from the car,' the Sergeant ordered.

One of the soldiers looked underneath with a large mirror on a pole, opened the bonnet and studied the engine compartment. The Sergeant gave him back the ignition keys. 'Right Sir. You may proceed. Someone will meet you at the main building.' Then, into his wireless. 'Another Rupert on his way up, John. Black Wolseley. K1 out!'

As he drove down the track, Finlay saw the property around him had once been a fairly substantial farm, but now the fields were neglected. Once in what had been the farm yard, he could see new buildings among some very dilapidated barns and disused stables. A soldier was waiting for him. 'Morning Sir,' he said evenly, to Finlay. 'If you would like to follow me, please, I'll get someone to deal with your luggage.'

Finlay followed, as the soldier knocked on the door and ushered him in. 'Good morning, Keith. I'm Andrew. It's first names from now on. You'll have read what's expected. It doesn't matter about rank or which service you come from. The less you know about each other the better. If you transgress any of the rules here, you'll be out. No exceptions, no arguments. In a moment, you'll be taken to your room. You'll wait till someone comes for you. There's food and drink there waiting for you. Stay in your room, which I hope will be comfortable, and don't start wandering about please.'

The door opened behind Finlay. Another soldier said, 'Follow me please Sir,' and led Finlay up a flight of steps, handing him a single key. 'Your room, Sir,' he said, and walked away.

Unlike most rooms dreamt up by civil servants, this one was surprisingly comfortable and exhibited none of the sparseness that usually is the case. The corned beef sandwich with a small glass dish of pickled onions, an apple and a large wedge of Dundee cake, told Finlay 'they' knew quite a lot about him. His clothes had been unpacked, his suitcase had gone. Even his toothbrush stood like a sentinel in a small glass. A large, sealed cardboard box, marked DO NOT OPEN, was on the floor. He tipped it about and judged it to be books. He made some tea and began to eat. Even the pickled onions rested on an absorbent wedge of paper, to soak up any spare vinegar. The more he looked, the more suspicious he became. On the most formal nights on board, such attention to detail was not seen. If there was one thing the Navy had taught him thus far, it was that if there was an opportunity to sleep, you took it. He flopped down on the bed.

He was woken by a knock on the door. 'Outside, please Keith. Two minutes. No talking.'

He swung off the bed, into his shoes and went to the shower room. He splashed his face with cold water, swallowed a couple of mouthfuls and went out into the corridor. There stood a row of men. He quickly counted fifteen.

'Bear with me gentlemen, please. I'd sooner you didn't speak with each other for reasons that will become apparent. If you could follow me, all will be revealed.' It was Andrew.

They followed him into another building and were shown into what looked like the dining room. 'Please sit and remain silent please,' Andrew ordered. They sat and waited. They were joined by three men, who walked up on to a small stage area and sat down.

The first to speak was a tall, gaunt man, close to sixty. He stood and cleared his throat. 'My name's Louis. That's probably all you need to know. We're not trying to turn you into a bunch of trappist monks. We just want to emphasize how important your personal security needs to be. You will not give out your surnames. You will not give out where you come from, nor any of your service background. We want, and shall want, you all to muck in together. Have fun together, work together and spend time together but the less you know about each other, the better. What you do not know you cannot repeat. Initially, this will be difficult for you. Things will be let slip. Forget them. I can promise you, you'll be so busy here your conversations will be about what you're doing, before falling into bed exhausted. Your initial period will be ten weeks. During that time, you'll not leave the base. Everything you need is here and all will be done for you. Any mail will be read, first by me, and anything we judge urgent, you'll be told about. You will not try to telephone or communicate in any way to the outside world. This must be clear to you.' He sat down.

The next to speak was Admiral Winter. 'You're here because you are different. I could flatter you by saying we have scooped up some of the best brains available, but I won't do that because you have brains enough to know that already. You're here because you exhibit traits that make you different. Some of you have extraordinary skills. What you all have is resilience, composure and a sense of honour. Over the next ten weeks, we're going to teach you skills you may wonder that you're ever going to need. Certainly, some of those skills are ones your mothers would not approve of. Some skills will, hopefully, keep you alive until you draw your pensions. We have chosen carefully enough to hope, with some confidence, that you'll all get through. With injuries, which will happen I assure you, there's a medical facility here that can cope with anything. Other facilities are open to you. There's a sports hall, swimming pool, games room and everything for your creature comforts, except the opposite sex. This, you'll have to forgo for the moment. You're the first group to be trained here. Make the most of it. Help each other and listen to the people training you in each particular skill. Some of them are civilians and may seem strange to you. One of your driving-skills trainers was the best getaway driver the civil police ever ran up against. Lastly, you are all very much part of an experiment. We hope you'll be able to help prevent the cold war turning hot. Now, go away and change into your tracksuits. Meet up together in the sports hall and get to know one another. Dinner here, at eight. Casual dress. Thank you gentlemen.' He sat down. There was silence. The third man on the platform just watched.

Admiral Winter said loudly, 'Go on then. Bugger off and play! It'll be your last chance for ten weeks.'

They filed out of the hall quickly. Finlay was walking beside a tall burly man. 'You've got to be the one from the Skins,' he said.

'How d'ya make that out then?' he said, and began to laugh. His soft Ulster accent showed Finlay was correct.

'You look like an Ulsterman and you were the only one who smiled over the getaway driver.' My name's Keith.' They shook hands.

'Would you believe, Pat?' The Ulsterman laughed. 'I don't know what the fuck we've got ourselves into here. What sort of age are you, for Christ's sake. You've only just left school, I know!'

'Older than I look, Pat. Comes from clean living and a clear conscience,' Finlay said.

'Be fucked for sure, I've never seen such a bunch of hoods in me entire life!' Pat said.

Back in his room, the debris of his meal had been removed, the counterpane respread and another pillow added to his bedding.

The sports hall was a misnomer. It was an indoor arena measuring, Finlay judged, at least three hundred feet each way. There was a whole gymnasium complex with every conceivable piece of equipment needed to train an Olympic team. Finlay was glad to see a netted section, laid out with a proper wicket. It was quickly apparent to them all who was who and which service they came from. They did not, however, coalesce into their service groupings. The bland tracksuits made all men the same.

Winter and his two confederates watched the men on television monitors. 'Pleased with your brood, John?' one asked.

'Interesting bunch. Any bets on the outcome?' he asked the other two.

'I rather fancy the young Green Jacket. Looked at his profile. Quiet, thoughtful chap. Maybe a little lacking in practical skills, but bright enough to learn them quickly,' one said.

'How about you, John? You know them best,' the other asked.

'The young one, Finlay...' Winter began.

The man who had not spoken in the mess hall seemed surprised. 'The farmer chap! Had an odd sort of upbringing. Doctor Williams was almost dismissive. Comes of letting a child run wild, I would have thought.'

'Unconventional, maybe. Finlay's an adventurer and God help him, something of a crusader. As for the farmer tag, that makes him practical. A field-sports devotee and a survivor,' Winter said.

'We shall see,' the other man said, unconvinced.

'He also thinks sideways. Did you see what he said about the War Minister,' Winter continued, determined to press his view.

'Too clever by half! But I could be wrong,' the man said.

Their training began the following day and was something of a shock. The day began at five. Split into three groups, they spent half an hour on circuit training, half an hour running, then half an hour in the swimming pool. The circuit training in the gym was so severe only a few of them were able to complete it. There was little sympathy from the trainers for those who fell by the wayside.

Breakfast followed. Finlay was amazed some of the men, already with an inkling of their training regime, choose to eat only bread rolls and drink coffee. Finlay wolfed down cereal followed by bacon, eggs and sweet tea, in ever increasing amounts as the days passed.

'Ah, my friend,' Pat said. 'You've already found out. You can't fuck on bread and jam.'

'Have you noticed?' Finlay observed. 'They're watching us. Some kind of monitors.'

'I wouldn't want your mind.' Pat laughed. 'So don't play with yourself in the shower!'

Finlay's group was designated as 'C'. They spent the week learning how to open doors and windows that were nominally locked against them. The more complex locks had them baffled for hours. Dismantling alarm systems became nothing to them, even the most sophisticated, and the week ended in the delicate and fine art of blowing safes with tiny amounts of plastic explosive. 'That was the finest apprenticeship a man could ever want,' Pat had observed. 'I need never work again.'

Group A had spent their week learning to drive. They learnt things the constabulary would certainly not approve of and they sustained the first casualty of the course, a broken arm. The injured trainee, James, was eventually patched up the evening of his accident and was, apart from rope climbing during circuit training, given no respite. Group B were told to not discuss their training with the others. They all looked haggard and nervous at the beginning, but as the week progressed, became more confident, even cocky. They intimated the job was something special, something to be achieved, but it was going to be painful.

When C group started their second week, they were taken to the sports hall and each was issued with a strange-looking pistol, powered by air, single shot, calibre .22 and recoilless. They shot at man-sized cut-outs. It was fun to begin with, but got boring as they became proficient. Next, they were shown a model of one of the buildings in the whole complex, showing every detail in miniature.

'Imagine this house is in Moscow, say, or Prague. Go in and bring a hostage out – it's a dummy, by the way. In and out fast. There are five of you and there'll be three guards. You'll not know which room the dummy is in. For the purposes of the exercise, on this first attempt, we'll say the hostage wants to leave. You have a week to achieve this. The guards know you're coming, but not when. They will be protected against your pistols and will play dead, if you hit them. They have the same pistols as you. Apart from your eyes and balls, you'll have no protection. The guards will try to avoid hitting you in the head. They're very good shots. So don't worry.'

'Hang on! I've just watched these pistols punching holes in hardboard at thirty yards. If they hit us, it's going to be serious,' Giles, one of the group, objected.

'The object is not to get hit, Giles,' the trainer said easily. 'Some of you will be. It'll be painful. There has to be realism.'

'And who are these guards?' Pat asked.

'SAS troopers from Hereford…' the trainers began.

'Ex-paras, I expect. Thick as planks… no problem!' Bill said, with venom.

'Where are they now?' Pat asked.

'Waiting for you. Then they go into the house. Work out what you're going to do, and I'll buzz them,' the trainer said.

C group went into a huddle for five minutes. 'OK! Buzz them now,' Pat said.

They went outside and watched the three guards walk towards the house. They looked smug. 'Hello, wankers!' one of them said. 'Hope you do better than the last lot!'

They all laughed dismissively.

'We're going to smack your little bottoms,' Pat said evenly.

'Oh, a fucking Paddy… This'll be easy!' another of the guards laughed.

They reached the door and unlocked it. The second one was about to enter when Pat called, 'This Paddy used to shag you mother, Lofty!'

He turned to answer back. The third one in line cannoned into him and C group struck. There was a brief struggle as the weight of five fit men hit them. The door smashed one of them to the floor immediately. 'Kick the shit out of them!' Pat shouted, and they did. 'OK Keith! Go get the dummy. This job's done!'

'Well, that's one way of doing it,' the trainer said, a little non-plussed. 'Not really what we had in mind though!'

'We were nowhere near ready!' one of the guards objected, his mouth bleeding.

'Oh diddums!' Bill laughed.

The trainer threw the dummy at one of the guards. 'We'll start again.

You three get cleaned up, and somewhere between now and Friday, these chaps will try again.'

'We'll fucking banjo the lot of you next time,' the one whom Pat had christened Lofty, snarled. 'And I'm saving my best for you, Paddy gobshite.'

'We've just seen your best. It ain't that good,' Pat answered. C group went back to plan and study their best approach.

'I fear you may have made it more difficult for yourselves, C group,' the trainer observed.

'Not really. They're going to be keyed up for the next couple of days. They'll get tired, so I think we hit them Wednesday night,' Finlay suggested. 'Now let's study how I can get in there. I need to be in the roofspace before the rest of you come in.'

'And who said you were running the show? You've still got the marks of the cradle on your arse,' Pat said, smiling at him.

'I did. Because I don't want the cradle marks on my ass added to with an air-gun pellet. Having watched you all in the gym, I'm the best climber. With some sort of distraction, I need to get on to the roof and through the skylight window. Once I'm in, we'll have won.'

'Ah, the confidence of youth, Pat,' Giles said. 'Come on then, sprog. Let's hear it.'

'There are five of us and three of them. I suggest a feint tomorrow night during which you remove the lock from the cellar door. They'll see it's gone and assume we're going to go in that way. Or some of us are. Before dark tomorrow, two of you get seen around the back of the house, out of range of their guns. Wednesday, just after dark, another distraction and I'm up on the roof. I can get on to this outhouse here, then the roof and into the roofspace. Then through this hatchway, on to this landing.'

'And how do we get in?' Bill asked.

'You may not need to,' Finlay said. 'A split attack. One'll go to the hostage, probably. I'll have him first. If you make sufficient song and dance, they won't even know I'm there until I shoot them. Get them separated. That's the key.'

'What makes you think you can pull this off?' Giles said.

'I'm a sneaky bastard, and I know I can. Look, like most farm houses it has the big front door and a little back door. Bash the front door in, but don't enter. They'll have to protect it.'

'And how do you reckon to bash in the door, sprog?' Bill asked. 'Looked pretty good and strong to me.'

'I saw a stack of sleepers outside, probably from an old silage pit. Run one of those into it at high speed, that'll probably break it down. Doesn't really matter if it doesn't. The guards will still have to protect the doorway. The back door'll be simple. Just kick it in. Doesn't matter about storming the place. I'm already inside. Just keep them occupied and I'll have them,' Finlay said confidently.

'OK,' Pat announced. 'The boy and I will get the timings down on his plan. You three come up with another.'

'Yes, we have to have another. If it rains, that roof will be as slippery as anything, and it's a long way to fall,' Finlay said.

At the end of the day, C group came together again.

'It's a bit like a crossword clue. Once you have it in mind, what the answer is, you can't get it out of your head,' Giles said.

'No plan B then?' Pat asked.

'Not as good as Keith's, I'm afraid. It looks like shit or bust on his.' Giles laughed.

'If it works, we'll have two days off. Think about that!' Pat said.

'Don't bank on that. We might gain two days for more work. You can get driving earlier.' The trainer answered the implied question.

'In that case, we'll leave it till Thursday,' Pat suggested. 'No sense in looking for work.'

'No!' Finlay said. 'Keep the window wide. The less time we have, the more they're going to be ready. That's why we had them first time. They weren't expecting it. Anyway, driving's the easy bit.'

'Your confidence, Keith, borders on the arrogant,' Giles said, with some feeling.

'The kind of child only his mother could love…' Bill began.

'My mother abandoned me!' Finlay said, sharply.

'A woman of great sensibility!' Pat laughed. 'You realize if you get shot first, the whole thing goes out of the window?'

'I know, but I won't be,' Finlay said firmly.

In the event the hostage was rescued. Only Bill got shot at, and the pellet left an angry score mark across the front of his thigh. 'Only a scratch!' Finlay said, laughing at their success.

'Well done C group!' the trainer told them. 'Bloody good team effort, executed with élan and confidence.'

The driving instructor got out of the car. With exaggerated despair, he flung his clipboard on to the back seat and stood with his head resting on his hands on the car's roof. 'I have to say, Keith, in all my years, I have never met anybody with such lack of feeling in what a car is actually doing. You've not the least feel for impending disaster. You're hopeless. Did you learn to drive on a bloody tractor? You're trying to drive the car without being, in any way, connected to it!' he sighed deeply.

'I did!' Finlay said. He was not affronted and felt stupid. 'Doesn't everybody start on a tractor?'

'For Christ's sake! Did you ever get beyond a tractor?' he asked.

'I was driving a Land-Rover by the time I was thirteen, and I don't think there's any need to be quite so rude,' Finlay said.

'So I can look forward to you doing the cross-country course. That's something I suppose,' the instructor said.

'A Land-Rover does as it's told. This heap of shit has a mind of its own. Let's put some weight in the boot, to stop the arse catching up with the front all of the time!' Finlay said loftily.

'No. Let's have a break. I've an idea that might work, because something has to. You're ten seconds slower than the slowest person so far!' There was real despair in his voice.

They walked back into the hut. The rest of C group were working on driving theory exercises. 'Here he is,' said Pat. 'Driver of the year! "Oh yes. The driving'll be easy." That's what you said boy!'

'Last week you balanced across a roof in your bare feet and this week you're behaving like a complete tart, Keith,' Giles said.

The driving instructor interrupted. 'Come on lads. It's encouragement he needs, not a lot of piss-taking. Everybody has different talents. Driving just isn't one of Keith's.'

'I'll get it right. I'm just sorry I'm letting the group down,' Finlay said, embarrassed at his failing.

They sat around together drinking tea and smoking. Outside, the day held the promise of spring. The sparrows were quarrelling around the eaves and Finlay thought of home. A Land-Rover pulled up outside, and the driving instructor went out to speak to the soldier driving it.

'Right Keith!' the driving instructor said, coming back in. 'Let's see what you can do in this.' He was surprised when they all started laughing.

'This I've got to see,' Bill shouted, as they trooped outside.

'Would you like to familiarize yourself with the vehicle, Keith?' the instructor asked. Even he seemed amused.

'Sure. He probably cut his teeth on one!' Pat joked.

Finlay got in, started it and tried the clutch and brakes.

'You want to get in?' he asked the instructor. As he did, Finlay said, 'You don't mind about the engine?'

'I'd be flattered if you blew the big-ends out. It'll show me you've at least been listening,' the instructor said.

Finlay was angry with himself. He felt foolish that special provision had been made. The rest of C group were singing a ragged version of 'To be a Farmer's Boy' as he shot the vehicle forward.

'I'll show you bastards!' he said aloud to himself, and to the car. 'Come on girlie girl. Lift your skirts. We are going to the beach!' He had no inhibitions. 'Driving a Land-Rover, Mr Instructor, can't be taught. It's a gift! Away girlie!' he yelled. 'Whee!' He shot around the tightest bend and floored the throttle. Without even the slightest sideways motion the vehicle screamed forward. Never out of third gear, the engine up to its peak, Finlay hurtled the car around the course.

'When we get in, straight into the other heap of rubbish and I'll have it cracked!' he said. The driving instructor nodded and held on tightly. As they passed the finish line, the rest of C group was cheering loudly.

Finlay got down, laughing. 'Right then. Now let's do it in this tin can.'

'Let's leave it at that, Keith,' the instructor said. 'You've done the time.'

'Oh no matey!' Finlay said. 'I insist. I'll give you country bumpkin!' He opened the passenger door for the instructor.

'In you get!'

The instructor shook his head vigorously. 'You've passed. No need for more. It was just a matter of putting you into the right vehicle.'

Afterwards Pat said, 'Well done boy! Isn't it amazing what two or three swallows of Bushmills can achieve for a chap?'

'Certainly wonderful stuff Pat,' Finlay agreed, laughing. 'How did you smuggle it in here?'

'That, as they say, would be telling. But there's a pretty little thing in the village will do anything for me, provided I do the right thing to her!' he said quietly.

'Christ! Have you been out of here?' Finlay asked, amazed at the Irishman's daring and energy.

'Sure. But keep it to yourself. Ten weeks in here without the softness of a woman on the odd occasion, would be more than flesh and blood could stand,' he said softly.

The rest of the training course passed quickly. They were worked hard mentally and harder physically. The subjects covered were as diverse as medical emergencies, bullet wounds, blast wounds, stab wounds yet also covered the recognition of disabling diseases and how best to cheat at cards. A poker school where everyone cheated was hilarious. Delving about in a dead body to remove a bullet was not. One week they spent on the Brecon Beacons, living off what they could get. C group fared well out of this while Finlay had more cause to thank his country upbringing.

There was the occasional letter from Niney, newsy and happy, detailing the fishing and the price of milk, everything important that was happening at home. Janet Ward had taken the stables, she wrote, so the whole place was filled with young ladies in tight trousers looking after their charges. A new loo had been put outside to cope with them and there was now 'oodles of wonderful warm horse muck' for the kitchen garden. Finlay read and reread her letters. They were written in the same manner as she spoke.

They learnt escape and evasion techniques and the difficulties involved with tracking dogs. In the countryside, Finlay understood where and why things happened. An escape into the town of Cheltenham proved far more difficult, and it brought home to Finlay the difficulty he might one day encounter hiding in a town in a hostile environment.

The ten days of weapons training were the hardest for them all. With no let-up on the physical fitness regime, eighteen hours a day were spent using and maintaining a variety of weapons. Learning how to make bombs, the best way to blow somebody into the next world or the delicate art of opening a window with tiny amounts of plastic explosive. With just two days to go, they were all brought together again to be given instruction on the actual administration of how and where they were going to live. They were told that they would never stop learning. They would study terrorist groups, past and present, spend time on something called 'forward strategic scenarios', trying to see into the future and taking steps to guide it. 'There would be no more Koreas.' Above all, the cold war with the Soviets and their acolytes, willing or unwilling, would be waged with no let-up and no quarter given. It seemed quite a task for fifteen men.

The group broke up on a Saturday morning. There had been the last breakfast together, when Winter had given a short speech telling them how pleased he was. Afterwards, he had interviewed each one of them briefly, telling them where they were initially to report.

When Finlay went in, the Admiral smiled at him warmly. 'You've done well Finlay. We've given you new skills and developed the ones you already had. You'll be based at Horseguards, so go home now and have some leave. I'll see you a fortnight on Monday. If you leave home, let us know where you can be reached. Please don't leave the country. When your leave is over, we can work out how best to use you.'

Driving home, his thoughts were entirely his own for the first time in nearly three months. He thought about what Winter had said. 'Only a fool would leave England in the spring without good reason,' he said aloud to himself, and at that moment there was no reason, good or otherwise. Passing around Oxford there was nothing of the dreaming spires. Just car factories and the rows of identical houses accommodating the factory workers. The hedgerows were showing the first green leaves and the grass on the verges was beginning to cover the litter thrown there. It was not until he was through Newbury, heading for Winchester, that the countryside seemed in any way familiar. He stopped and bought two massive bouquets of flowers from a roadside stall near Freefolk.

He drove into Winchester and out on to the Romsey road. Through Pitt, he slowed almost to a crawl and his nose tingled with joy to see the chalky fields and the emerging spring barley. Peewits wheeled over, protesting at a tractor harrowing an island of grass. Suddenly he wanted to be home. He flicked the car into third and floored the throttle, half-way up through the revs, then switched on the blower and felt the familiar surge forward; black smoke swirled in a vortex behind the car. Only slowing through Hursley, he hurtled the car along the Ampfield straight and swept down the hill into Romsey. He fiddled his way through the town and down the gravel lane to Saddlers Mill. Parking the car, he walked on to the bridge above the fish pass and drank in the smell of the river as the water crashed through beneath him. Downstream fifty yards, a long ribbon of new-growing starwort swayed in the current, not flowering yet, but the fresh green gave him a catch in his throat. He stayed watching the river for ten minutes or so. The grayling flashed in and out of the current, the cockfish brilliant in their spawning colours, chasing each other and the henfish they desired. Content, Finlay drove home.

The stable muck heap was a neat stack of quietly steaming manure.

Four hunters were tied up outside the stable block, attended by three young females he had never seen before. One of them came walking over. 'Can I help you?' she asked.

'Not really,' he smiled.

'There's no one at home. Mrs Terry's gone to Southampton shopping. Perhaps you should come back later,' she suggested.

'I live here.' He smiled, and began taking his two cases from the car's boot. 'Are you part of Miss Ward's establishment?'

She looked embarrassed. Finlay took his cases up the front steps, put them down and walked round to the back door. He quickly had it open, walked through the house and picked up his cases, after sliding the bolt on the front door.

'How do I know you live here?' the girl asked. She seemed genuinely concerned.

'Come with me,' he ordered. On top of the refrigerator was a picture of himself with Niney. 'Who do you think that is?' He smiled. He moved the kettle on to the Aga. 'Tea?' he asked.

'I must go and finish my work,' she said suddenly and left quickly.

Finlay was reading the newspaper when he heard horses in the yard. He went to the window and saw Janet throw the reins of her mount to one of the girls, turn and start heading for the house. He met her halfway across the yard, where she flung herself at him and kissed him.

'From whence comes this sudden and unwarranted affection,' he mumbled into her copper curls. 'Jesus, you smell good.'

'Make a big show of it Finlay! I don't want my pupils distracted by you. I've already let them know that you're off limits!' She laughed, stinging him again with her green eyes.

He kissed her again, and ran his hand down over her bottom. 'That wasn't for show!' he gasped. She did feel good. He held her close and felt her trembling slightly and they were back in time to when they were younger, enclosed almost in a bubble of their own world.

'You've lost a lot of weight, Finlay,' she said softly. 'What have you been doing?'

'Working extremely hard, Jan. I'm pretty well exhausted,' he answered.

Her hips were pushed hard against him. 'Not totally!' she giggled.

'Come indoors,' he said.

'No. Niney will be back and I don't want another false start. How long are you home for?' she asked.

'Couple of weeks I shouldn't wonder. Enough to get to know each other again, perhaps?' he suggested.

'You can take me to some posh hotel, with a big bath and a double bed. Look, Niney'll be home soon, and I've work to do. I'll see you before I go.'

He watched from his bedroom window as Janet helped Niney unload the Armstrong and walk towards the house. He met them in the kitchen, dressed now in his country clothes.

'Why didn't you write, you little shit?' Niney said, as they hugged and kissed. 'What on earth have you been doing for God's sake! Have they stopped feeding you? You're as poor as a crow. I can feel every one of your ribs!'

Janet, standing back watching, began to laugh.

'Well, where've you been?' Niney asked severely. 'Is this the only country in the world with a postal service?'

'Thanks Auntie. I really treasure your letters, but I wasn't anywhere where I could write back,' Finlay answered.

'Well, Janet Ward. You can bugger off now and leave me with this creature. The first twenty-four hours are mine. You can come and see him tomorrow.' Niney began showing her out of the kitchen.

'Till coffee time then,' Janet said. 'He may be yours, but you can't keep him all to yourself.'

After she'd gone, Niney turned to him. 'You're being evasive and I know when you're lying to me!' Niney still spoke to him as though he were a child.

'Put your boots on, Auntie. Come and walk with me down to the bridge. We can talk there,' Finlay said, in a way that brooked no argument.

They walked arm in arm along the lane to the bridge. Niney told him about the farm and his grandfather, who had been in Scotland with Sir George for practically the whole summer. Prices were not too bad, milk the mainstay and looked to be the best bet for keeping the place paying its way. They leant on the bridge together, looking upstream as the river rolled silently beneath them. There was a huge shoal of dace cruising past and running into the mill stream.

'Auntie Niney, I want to tell you what I'm doing, but I'm forbidden. I'll tell you if you want, but if you know what it is, believe me, my darling, it will be a burden to you. You'll find yourself being evasive. Wouldn't it be better if you just said it's a staff job and you don't know much about it?' Finlay said.

'Is it dangerous Kee? I wouldn't want to live if anything happened to you,' Niney said, staring at the river.

'I don't know. It's a new thing and I've only just finished the training. I'll be based at Horseguards, so when I'm not out doing something, I can come home most nights. I'll have loads of leave.'

'How long are you home for this time? Extra pay, extra leave. That only means what you're doing is difficult or dangerous.' Niney looked at him, looking for the truth of it.

'Until the telephone rings. I have to let them know if I leave here and where I can be reached. It's all up in the air at the moment. If they want me, I expect Admiral Winter will telephone and I have to be packed and ready always. More than that I don't know,' he answered truthfully.

'Not the sort of job if you get married,' she observed.

'If that happens, I'll have to leave and go back to the Navy proper. But I shan't be doing that. I'll not ever get involved again,' he said emphatically.

'Darling, you have to move on. At the same time, you mustn't string Janet along. It wouldn't be fair to her. Please be careful.' Niney was staring into the water.

Finlay started to laugh. 'Auntie Niney, I've come so close to bedding Janet many times and been foiled, I'm sure it's not meant to happen.' He paused. 'Do you remember finding her bra in the drawer of the television table? We were very close to it then!' He laughed.

'You sod! You can't believe how worried I was, about you getting one of them pregnant.' She smiled. 'Come on darling. Jack will be back soon, wanting his dinner. We'll just have to play it by ear. Wing it.'

Finlay's first week passed easily. He spent his time fishing and caught salmon every evening. The new trout stream was fully booked all the hours of daylight, which brought seemingly enormous sums of money to the estate. He spent long hours in the music room studying what were termed his Rules of Engagement. What was legal and what was not. He made some notes of matters he felt needed to be clarified.

He took Janet to dinner in Lyndhurst on his second night home. It was fun to be with her. She seemed to blossom and become ever more beautiful. On the Thursday, she had gently insisted that they ride out together. It was the first time in some years that Finlay had been on a horse. He missed Misty. 'Where are we going?' Finlay asked, as they left the yard.

'You'll see!' she answered quickly. She rode away quickly ahead of him and headed for her home. 'My mother is away, Finlay, in London. Don't you think this has gone on long enough?'

She rode into the yard and threw the reins of the two horses to a slightly built blonde girl. 'Box these, rub them down and then go to lunch. I'm going to be busy for the next few hours and if you dare disturb me, you're sacked!'

The blonde girl understood. 'Good for you. I'll not say a word.'

'Say what you like, Jane. I'm not bothered any more. Come on Finlay. Bedtime I think!' she said firmly.

Janet showered with his help, squealing and laughing at what he did to her. When eventually they entered the bedroom she seemed suddenly afraid. 'I don't think it'll work Finlay. That'll never go in!'

She relaxed enough to let it happen on their third attempt. She was noisy while it was happening, and afterwards lay quietly on top of him. 'Beats the hell out of eating,' she giggled. 'Now you can go away and do that to me every time you come home.' The final time was so right, they drifted to sleep afterwards, exhausted, and woke only when the stable girl called up at the window.

Later, back at the house, Niney said, 'That couldn't have been a very comfortable ride for you, Janet.' Janet blushed. 'Your Admiral telephoned, Kee darling. Wants you up to the office by eight in the morning. So much for your fortnight's leave. Sounds quite a nice chap. Would like to come and fish. Did you know he was a friend of Angus?'

'Yes. Angus's brother is part of our department,' Finlay answered.

After Janet had gone, Niney said evenly, 'I thought you said you were not getting involved again, but if it moves you on from where you were, well and good.' Then she dropped the subject.

Chapter Ten

•

Finlay arrived at Horseguards early the next morning. There were no office staff around as Finlay knocked on the Admiral's door.

'What's this, Finlay?' Winter said, poking an obvious rod case, on his desk.

'A case for a Sharpe's rod, Sir,' Finlay answered.

'Belongs to a very senior civil servant. He left it in a hotel in the Orkney Islands.' The Admiral lit his pipe.

'Obviously paid too much, Sir,' Finlay volunteered, but the Admiral ignored his comment.

'The thing is, it had a fingerprint we know. From a chap who was working for the Russians during the war. I want you to go and see what he's up to now.' Winter puffed heavily on his pipe.

'Any photograph, Sir?' Finlay asked.

'If there was, we would know who it was, wouldn't we? Go up to Kirkwall, to the hotel, and find him. Should be a milk run for you,' Winter said testily.

'And then?' Finlay asked.

'I don't know! See what he's about. Maybe let him know that we know where he is. We know he's not active now,' Winter said.

'I take it you mean now, Sir?' Finlay asked.

'Of course I mean now! When did you think I meant?' Admiral Winter snapped. 'But discreetly Finlay, discreetly!'

'Yes Sir,' Finlay said, picking up a brown file, pushed towards him.

Twelve hours later, in Aberdeen, he found a bed in a commercial hotel. By ten the following morning he was on a ferry to Stromness, having hired a car, his own left at the small airport. Throughout the passage, he read about what was known of the civil servant's movements. He had stayed at the Standing Stones Hotel, the file read, close to the Loch of Stenness, and Finlay cursed to himself that he had not brought any fishing gear in the car. The hotel wasn't full, but was busy. He booked himself in for a fortnight and was accommodated in great comfort with good plain food and the company of anglers, mainly English. He had to pretend that he wasn't interested in fishing, only the bird life on the island, hoping that the waders would yield a rarity. He watched who handled the rods, who packed them in the cars and fetched them from the rod room in the mornings. It came down to two people, a barman named Ian and the hotel owner, who after one or two whisky-soaked sessions, informed Finlay that his five years owning the hotel had been wonderful.

One evening, he asked Ian to pour him a last whisky to take to his room. It had been a good day. He had seen lots of waders he could not identify and in the evening, joined the other guests singing local songs and listening to the mournful tunes of Scotland.

Once in his room, he emptied the whisky from the glass and coated it with graphite dust for the fingerprint. It was not that distinct, but clear enough to tell him the barman was the person he was looking for. He lay down on the bed and decided his next move. Ian seemed an ordinary family man. He had seen him with his wife and two children, the young son helping him in the daytime, while he pottered about the hotel gardens. It all seemed, suddenly, very sad.

The next morning he waited until he saw Ian in the gardens and followed him into a large shed, where he found him tinkering with a mower.

'You've come for me then. I knew somebody would one day.' Ian opened the conversation.

'Yes, I'm afraid I have. Maybe not come for you exactly. We need to speak at some length. Will the hotel let me hire you for the day, to show me the islands?' Finlay smiled.

'Are you police?' Ian asked. He was starting to sweat.

'Good Lord, no! I just need to know some things about you... take any old radio gear you have and get as much information about you and your contacts, then and now, as I can. And also warn you not to try and leave here without the say so of my people in London. If you try, you will either be arrested or killed.' Finlay said the last sentence as nonchalantly as he could.

'Would you kill me?' the man asked.

'If you give me cause to, certainly. But nobody wants that. You have a lovely family and a dead spy is no use to anyone. Just tell me what I need to know. I'll go back to London, tell them and that will probably be the end of it. Do you have any contact at all with the Russian trawler crews who come for shelter when the weather is rough? And remember we know practically everything about you, so please don't lie.'

'No! There's never been any contact from them!' Ian choked.

'What about the sailor who had his appendix out in Kirkwall two years ago? Did you or your wife visit him?' Finlay asked.

'No! My wife knows nothing of this!'

'Ian, my friend, that'll do for now. If you don't want to spend the rest of your life in Parkhurst, just get it off your chest. I'll speak to your boss. Just pretend today never happened.'

The next day, arrangements made, Finlay left the hotel with the barman and drove out to a deserted headland. Finlay questioned him, going over his background and reasoning. Ian answered quickly and, Finlay judged, truthfully. He didn't seem to know his grandmother's maiden name, nor where she had come from. Originally from Glasgow, he had been recruited by the local Communist Party. When war had broken out he was judged unfit for active service, having had rickets when young. His communist contact got him a farm job on Orkney and provided the communications equipment. His job was to report on ship movements and any defensive measures taken. When the Russians had signed the non-aggression pact, his continued support was insisted on by blackmail or death for his non-compliance. He spoke to Finlay of his joy when the blackmailer had been arrested, quietly tried and executed. Since then he'd had no contact and had 'put a hammer through' his wireless.

Finlay closed his notebook. 'I can't promise anything Ian, but I'll do my level best for you. Let us check what you've said about yourself and that should be the end of it. However, I do want you to report to this telephone number every time a Russian trawler arrives here and any contact at all with the locals, note and let us know. You'll, of course, be paid for this. We've already someone doing this, but a cross-check will do no harm. If your information does not check out, you'll be hauled off to Edinburgh to explain. I'll leave in the morning. Play it right and you'll be able to live on here until you die.'

The barman seemed very relieved, even happy. 'I knew you'd come for me when I first saw you. The way you took in a room full of people, at a glance. Hope I never see you again. You may be quite a bastard to cross.'

'Believe it, Ian. Go home and look after your wife and children,' Finlay said quietly.

He left the next day and, once on the mainland, picked up his Wolseley and drove as far as Harrogate. He found the best hotel available, dined alone and in style that evening and left early the next morning, arriving just as the office staff were coming back from lunch. Miss Grant displayed her usual acidity, the dark-haired girl displayed just a little too much of her chest for it not to be deliberate.

Winter saw him almost immediately and ordered tea and biscuits,

'Back so soon Finlay?' He studied the file that Finlay had written in the hotel on the previous night.

'Do you know, Finlay, I like the way you think. Leave them in place working for me. Just one thing: could you not find a less expensive hotel in Harrogate? It's more expensive than London!'

'It was a very good hotel, Sir,' Finlay said easily. 'Reward for a job well done. It only took a couple of days.'

'Go home Finlay,' Winter said severely. 'We must have a chat about your sense of humour another day.'

He was home later that afternoon. The yard seemed full of horses and intense young ladies, busying themselves. Finlay grabbed up the flowers he had bought near Basingstoke and walked indoors. 'Hello beautiful Auntie, how are you?'

Niney was baking. The air smelt beautifully of fresh bread. She looked startled by his return, but overjoyed. 'I think I like your new job. Can I ask what you've been doing?'

'We can go for a walk later and I'll tell you all about it… the Admiral was pleased with the result and I'm home again… I don't know how long for… but I'm home,' Finlay said happily.

'Push the kettle over darling and I'll get you something to eat,' she said, smiling, and touching him in passing.

'The yard's as busy as Bond Street. How many has Janet got in?' he asked, looking out of the window.

'Yes, it's lovely having all these youngsters around, laughing and chattering, and have you seen the lovely muck heap? The gardener's over the moon.'

They sat together drinking tea and chattering easily about the farm. True to Finlay's prediction, the Russians needed wheat and the price had gone up. Niney had sold the feed wheat from the next harvest for October delivery.

'I hope I've done the right thing, Kee. James was not available to ask and it looked too good a price to miss,' Niney said.

'I'm glad Auntie. You should have the say so for selling it. I would have urged Grandfather to do the same.'

Later, they walked down to the river. The starwort was in flower, great fronds of it swaying in the shallows, the martins and swallows swooping and dipping into the surface of the water snatching flies. Two bends up from the bridge, three of the Shorthorns were grazing the weed in the river, up to their bellies in swirling water, while others looked on jealously, not having learnt the trick yet. Finlay told Niney about his trip and what it had accomplished.

'The poor man. Fancy having that hanging over him for years, and with a wife and children. I can't pretend to understand how people can betray their own country, but it must have been awful for the poor chap,' Niney said.

They walked back towards the house, arm in arm, and discovered the first of the early purple orchids under the hedge by the mill. There were myriads of primroses on the banks and the milkmaids looked almost like a low delicately coloured mist across the waterside meadows.

As they walked back into the yard, Janet came walking towards them. 'Hello Finlay!' she said, and gave him a very proper and maidenly kiss on the cheek. 'Coming out for a drink tonight?'

'No he's not. But you can come and eat with us tonight at around eight. Only in the kitchen, so there's no need to get glammed up. And think yourself lucky at that, Madam. The first day of his leave is for me and he'll be sleeping in his own bed tonight,' Niney said, pretending severity.

'Oh Niney I thought maybe...' she began.

'Well, think again. You have work to do! Now go and get on with it, else the invite for tonight will be withdrawn.' She turned away, saying, 'Kee has better things to do than rolling you in the hay as soon as he gets home.'

'Have I?' Finlay said wistfully, watching the retreating Janet and noting her tight jodhpurs.

'Honestly, these horsey girls are never satisfied! A horse between their legs all day and a bloke all night. Look at them, all watching, like a bitch pack watching a fox!' Niney laughed. 'Come on you, get unpacked. I'll sort your laundry. I can't see any of them making such an offer.'

Uncle Jack came in at around six, happy that he had had a good day on the river and to see Finlay. 'Thirty-two-pounder today Kee,' he enthused. 'Seven in total, one hundred and twenty-eight pounds, and the trout stream is booked all the time.'

'We ought to teach Janet to fish, Uncle Jack. It was her design in the first place, the trout stream I mean,' Finlay suggested.

'Couldn't get her interested. I asked her earlier this year,' Jack answered, pouring another whisky.

'Well, I didn't hear about that!' Niney said. 'If you think for one moment, Jack Terry, you're doing an evening rise or two with her, you can bloody well think again.'

Jack and Finlay began to laugh. 'Take half an hour to get her out of her tight trousers my dear,' Jack said. 'By then the moment would have passed!'

'She's coming to eat with us tonight, so I'll be watching you like a hawk. Any hanky panky from you, Jack Terry, and you'll find the shutters up.'

The men were not sure how serious she was. 'Don't be stupid, Niney. She's a nice little thing, but not my sort. Anyway, whose idea was it to fill the place with horses and girls?' Jack said, trying to recover some ground.

'She pays two hundred pounds a month and buys all her hay and straw from us. I want it to continue, not least for the horse muck we get from it,' Niney said, seriously. 'Janet has become an asset and I like having the girls about. They keep an eye on the house when it's empty.'

'Where do they all live, Auntie?' Finlay asked.

'Four of them live with Janet. The others lodge with the chap who lives at the vicarage now,' Niney said, in between making gravy and swigging down best brandy.

'Well, he's got it made.' Finlay laughed.

'My dear, he's a pretty boy! They're perfectly safe there, I can assure you.' Niney laughed.

'How do you know that, Auntie? What does he do for a living?' Finlay asked.

'My dear boy, he wears pink shirts and red trousers and always has a beautiful pink scarf around his neck. I believe he's a surgeon from South Hants hospital. As long as he keeps paying the exorbitant rent, I don't mind what he does. Are you ready to carve, Jack, as soon as that pretty little minx gets here?' Niney was on a brandy-driven roll.

Jack got up and started sharpening the carving knife on a steel. 'Here she is. Good God! What is the girl wearing?'

Janet arrived in the kitchen. She was wearing a gingham dress, her hair controlled by a green ribbon. 'Please don't laugh. My mother has become impossible. When I said I was eating here, she insisted I wear a dress on pain of her throwing one of her sulks, so here I am, looking like a schoolgirl. I haven't any dresses. I last wore this in the sixth form!'

Jack and Finlay were stunned into silence. Niney looked at Janet, smiling fondly. 'Darling you look… you look absolutely feminine. You're a real beauty! Isn't she, Jack?'

'If I answer that, up go the shutters. Janet, you look no different now than when you first arrived on the scene. You should wear a dress more often,' he said.

'Finlay?' Janet asked looking at him imploringly.

'Jan… I've never seen you in a dress… you really are a girl!' was all he could manage.

'Finlay, you stupid… you know I'm a girl better than anyone,' she said, laughing at him.

'I'll get on and carve, Niney,' Jack said, turning away.

They began their meal. 'The vegetables are all from the new garden, Janet. Thanks to your horses, the gardener thinks he's in Heaven.'

'The text for today is: Is Heaven Horse Shit?' Janet laughed.

The conversation strayed over the relative merits of the benefits of the different sorts of dung, as applied to a garden. Finlay remembered townies' dinner-table talk – the price of property, increasing traffic problems and the latest London plays – here it was dung. The thought made him smile.

'Auntie Niney tells me the chap renting the vicarage is of the lavender persuasion, Jan,' Finlay said.

'You'd better believe it, Finlay. He was asking who the young sailor was, last time you were home. He's some kind of psycho doctor, weird bugger,' Janet said.

'Let me have any old dresses you have, Janet. I'll alter them for you,' Niney said.

'I'd love that, but would you have the time?' Janet asked.

'Evenings drag these days, with the house empty,' Niney said.

'I saw that bastard Jenks in the town the other day. It was as much as I could do to stop myself running him over,' Jack remarked quietly.

'One day,' Finlay said, firmly.

Suddenly, it was eleven o'clock and Niney got up. 'Come along Janet. You have to be up and about early in the morning. Kee and I can do the dishes. We'll see you tomorrow. Walk her to the car, Kee, and not too much canoodling or I'll switch the outside lights on.' Niney smiled.

Outside, Finlay and Janet kissed.

'You look good in a dress Jan…'

'Shut up, and make the most of it,' she mumbled into his chest as he pressed his hands around her waist.

The kitchen window opened. 'Ten seconds to lighting-up time, you two!' Niney shouted.

'She's a real love, you know, your precious, bloody Niney. She doesn't miss a trick. Get out of my knickers and go and help her with the washing-up,' Janet said, starting her car. 'See you tomorrow.'

The yard lights flared on, chasing the darkness into the far corners. The muck heap was shrouded in steam and one of the horses whickered quietly. Finlay watched Janet's tail lights disappear down the back drive and he then went indoors.

A blackbird, singing to the dawn, woke Finlay the next morning. It was sitting in the ivy just outside the open bedroom window. Finlay watched the bird from his bed and wondered at the beauty of its fluting song. Somewhere across the yard, another started in song, then another, from, he judged, the roof of the old dairy building. Gradually, as the light increased, other birds joined in this worship of the rising sun until the air was filled with birdsong. Only in England was the dawn chorus so full and complete. As the light became full and the sun came above the ash trees, the chorus died away as the birds went about their search for food. Only the moorhens on the feeder stream, above the garden, clucked their fussy way around the new weed beds.

He rose and went downstairs in his dressing gown. Uncle Jack was in the kitchen drinking his morning tea. 'You should take the chance to lay abed and rest, nipper. Ron has everything sown up outside. If you intends to keep that little maid happy while you'm here, you're gonna need to rest.' He smiled.

'I'll just have some tea, have a bath and have a wander about. Go and look at the river. Those rivers up in Scotland, Uncle Jack, ain't worth a candle. No character at all.' Finlay sugared his tea heavily.

'Know what you mean. Can't think why James goes up there. Well, I can I suppose. He and the mad vet can drink what they want, without Niney seeing,' he said.

'It's a bloody good job Auntie's here. Without her, we'd all sink. Even with help in the house, she still does too much. I don't think she needs the worry of the farm and the house,' Finlay observed.

'Try and tell her that, Kee,' Jack said. 'Took us all our time to get her to have one person doing the housework. Was different when Jenny was here.'

'Do you mind if I suggest it?' Finlay asked.

'Go ahead nipper. She might well take it from you. If me or James said anything, she'd tell us to mind our own selves.' He thought for a moment. 'Then again, she might well give you a clout across the ear.' He laughed.

'Where does that Jenks live now, Uncle Jack?' Finlay asked.

'Right next door to his chapel. But don't you do anything, nipper. The matter, as they say, is in hand. I'll leave the subject there, if you please.' He got up and slipped on his jacket. 'Tell Niney I'll be back a bit late, about nine,' Jack said, and left.

Later, bathed and refreshed, Finlay walked down through the newly refurbished kitchen garden, to the hatch pool. He lay on one of the fishing platforms and gazed into the deep water, clear and smelling of chalk and water celery. He scooped up some in his hand and drank it, savouring the chalky taste. Below, a huge shoal of dace circled lazily in the current. Slim and lithe like small herrings, they seemed unconcerned by his presence. He wandered down to the big bridge, the birds now singing again fitfully. He watched the current eddy where the mill stream ran in, tiny whirls of shining water spinning downstream, playing with the bankside vegetation. He spotted two salmon in the pool, head and tailing at the end of the starwort fronds, fresh from the salt and adjusting themselves to the lesser density of the clear fresh water. Away to his left, he saw the flash of a fishing rod on the trout stream and walked closer to see who it was, fishing this early. The angler looked old and frail, but had that look of contentment anglers recognize in their brothers. He gave Finlay a small wave by way of 'Good morning' when Finlay was fifty yards from him. He waved back and left the old man to his labours. There was barely any sound in the valley, save the distant quiet hum of the milking parlours and the birds. This was surely the most wonderful place on earth, he thought.

When he walked back into the kitchen, Niney was getting breakfast. The smell of frying bacon and mushrooms filled the large room and made his stomach rumble. 'Hello darling. Been down to the hatchpool?' Niney said, kissing him. She ruffled his hair, destroying the brushed symmetry. 'Don't slick your hair down like that. Makes you look like the Duke of Windsor!'

Finlay laughed.

'Well, it does.' Niney smiled.

'Uncle Jack said he would be back before nine, Auntie,' Finlay said, pouring some tea. He sipped at it quietly.

'Spit it out then. What is it you want to say?' Niney asked, hovering over the Aga with her back to him.

'How do you do that?' Finlay asked. 'How do you know what I'm thinking?'

She turned and faced him. 'By your breathing. When you're working out what to say, you breathe differently. That's why you could never fool me.' She laughed.

'I want you to have more help, Auntie. I don't want you wearing yourself out. You should be doing things that you want to do…' he started.

'I can cope, darling,' she answered.

'I don't want you to have to cope. Take money from my side of things and get more help. Please… for me,' Finlay begged her.

'Well… we'll see…'

'No. I want you to promise me,' Finlay said, getting up and holding her. 'I want you to stay young and beautiful. Promise me.'

'Look…' she began.

'Auntie Niney, you must promise me,' he wheedled.

'I promise,' she relented. 'I can never say "no" when you insist.'

'Thank you Auntie. I really don't want to see you having to wash the floors. I want you to be Queen Bee again. All beautiful and organising,' Finlay said.

She came and put her arms around him. 'You can be the most delightful little sod sometimes, darling. Queen Bee indeed!'

The days of Finlay's leave passed easily. He spent time with Ron and Carl, looking at the machinery required for the new progressive agriculture. Though he knew it had to happen, it didn't make him happy. It made sense to have a tractor which had one driver and did the work of six of the old Fergies. It made sense to have sprayers which seemed to spray a forty-acre field in a few passes, but the yards were empty of people and characters. And the accounts books only showed they were running to stand still. The same as ever.

Finlay spent his time fishing and riding out with Janet, as she exercised her charges. She had managed one day off and he had taken her into Bournemouth, shopping and to the theatre. They were relaxed together. There was never seemingly time for bedroom exercises, but it didn't seem to matter. There wasn't the driving intensity between them, as there had between himself and Janey and Jenny.

'Plenty of time for that in the summer, Finlay,' she had said. 'I'm pleased though, that you do not seem to treat my girls as your very own harem. I think Jenny's still in the background somewhere.'

Finlay had not answered this observation, but he knew it to be true.

On Friday the inevitable telephone call had come. This time, it was Miss Grant who informed him that from the following Monday, he would be required in the office daily. She had told him no more, other than that an office had been made available for him and it had been cleaned. Niney was overjoyed. He would be home each evening and suggested that she drive him to the railway station each morning. So it was that Finlay joined the ranks of commuters doing the daily journey to London.

'I've made you Head of Section, Finlay, for the moment. That means a fairly substantial increase in pay and a fairly substantial increase in responsibility. You'll study the reports of the rest of your section and comment on them. This is an ongoing task. In a couple of weeks, I want you to go to Finland. Something may be coming off in a year or eighteen months and I want you to get to know the border area. You can stay in the embassy's summer house. There's the file and very detailed maps. And buy yourself a city suit, Finlay. You look like a bloody farm boy,' Winter said.

'I am a bloody farm boy, Sir,' Finlay replied.

'Well, you stand out like a sore thumb. Do something about it lunch time,' Winter ordered.

'Aye, aye, Sir,' Finlay replied, trying not to smile. Winter looked at him hard.

Finlay found the work interesting, but the commuting tedious. Having to travel with people who all seemed so pleased with themselves and their routine. One day, a man told him, 'You're in my seat!' when there were plenty empty in the compartment.

'Be brave. Try that one.' Finlay pointed to an empty seat.

'I want this one!' the man said, with an air of petulant aggressiveness. He was tall, slim with perfectly manicured hands and smelt heavily of after-shave. He stood over Finlay, expecting him to move.

To his own surprise, Finlay rose. 'If it's that important to you, you must surely have it.'

The training had sunk home. 'Don't get noticed' the rules said. From that day on, Finlay travelled first class.

The two weeks passed quickly and then he left for Helsinki, attached to the Naval Attaché's staff there. He soon found that the embassy people, as a whole, viewed him as an intruder to their world. They treated him with studied indifference and were obstructive. Even the Naval Attaché, a Captain, seemed to view him with distaste. He decided there was nothing to be gained by staying and left for Sotkamo in a hire car, loaded with supplies. He found the summer house easily, on the shore of a lake, and moved himself in. Over the next two weeks he acted the tourist, driving as far north as Tana, stopping nights in various hotels in various towns along the way. The further north he went, the more accommodating he found the people. On his journeys south as far as Kotka, they were more urban and distant. The country was, to him, beautiful and the fishing, which he spent lots of time at, was extremely good, especially the grayling. At the summer house, he spent time on the nearby lake, fishing from the small dinghy that was provided.

The last Saturday of his stay, he decided to write his reports, list out the films he had taken and make ready for leaving on the Monday. The Sunday he had earmarked for a day's fishing. At around eleven, he was surprised to hear a car pull up in front of the house and two women, one of whom he recognized from the embassy, came into the house, surprised to find it unlocked and Finlay in residence. He said a polite 'Good morning' and asked them if they wanted some coffee.

'Oh yes, you're the illegal chap. We were told you would be gone. Please pack up now and go today,' the dark one ordered. She seemed a very confident person, about thirty Finlay judged, and quite good-looking. She also seemed sure of her position. The other one, small and blonde, hung back, happy to let the older one do the talking.

'Show me some identification!' Finlay ordered, curtly.

'Certainly not!' the dark one snapped.

He snatched her handbag from her hand and emptied it on a table. She tried to stop him, but he shoved her away and picked up her passport and studied it. 'Give me yours,' he ordered the blonde.

She handed it over quickly and he noted their names down on part of his report.

'What's your position in the embassy?' he asked the dark one, whose name seemed to be Caroline Stewart. 'I'm a second secretary and I'm reporting this to the ambassador.'

Finlay ignored her.

'What do you do, Miss Butler?' he asked the blonde.

'I'm on the cultural staff,' she said meekly.

'I'm going to call the embassy!' Stewart said.

'Coffee, Butler?' Finlay asked.

'Yes please, Sir,' she answered.

Caroline Stewart returned. 'It seems I owe you an apology. I'm sorry... may we stay?'

'Accepted,' Finlay said. 'I have the single bedroom on the right. I also have my work spread out in the drawing room. Don't go into either or I'll have you shipped out so fast your feet won't touch the ground. I shall, of course, be reporting on the way I was treated. We may be a nuisance, but we allow people like you to sleep safe. You're here to help, not hinder... do you want coffee?'

'I'm really very sorry,' Stewart repeated.

'Forget it,' Finlay said, easily. 'I've work to do. There's plenty of food here. Help yourselves to anything.'

Finlay was back at the embassy by midday on Monday and reported his departure to the Naval Attaché, who seemed not to be interested. 'By the way,' he said. 'You have to go to Oslo on your way home. There are your flight tickets. Goodbye!'

Smarting, Finlay left for Oslo where he found the attitudes somewhat different. The Naval Attaché there, Duckworth, couldn't have been more accommodating and arranged dinner with an old friend of Finlay's. Lars Husoysund was a Norwegian marine major. Finlay had spent time with him on the Mountain Warfare Cadre. Their common bond, apart from fighting, was fishing. The dinner was noisy and fun. Finlay had spent a long time alone and was glad of conversation and company.

Finlay walked into the office at Horseguards the next day, at lunch time. 'Is the Admiral here, Miss Grant?' he asked.

'No Finlay, he's at lunch. Should be back by three,' Grant said, in her clipped icy manner.

He handed her his reports and files. 'I'll cut across to Farlow's then. Perhaps you could give him these, Miss Grant?'

'I hope you're not thinking of going before he gets back, Finlay.' It sounded like a suggestion.

'No. Of course not, Miss Grant. Shouldn't dream of it,' he said. 'I'll have some lunch, perhaps.'

He had been trying to treat Miss Grant with a little more friendliness, but it was very difficult. He returned to the office at four, laden with parcels from Farlow's for himself and a small one, from Asprey, for Niney.

'We can look at your reports on Friday, Finlay. Now though, in your own words, tell me about the embassy, please,' Winter had said.

When he had finished, Winter snorted heavily through his nose. 'You'd stand by this in an enquiry, Finlay?' Winter asked, obviously angry.

'Yes Sir. They were obstructive,' Finlay answered.

'Right. Off home with you Finlay. Have a few days off. Come in Friday. Good night then,' he said, by way of dismissal.

Later, Niney met him at Southampton. 'Hello you,' she said. 'Good trip?'

They kissed and he smelt her familiar scent. 'Easy one, Auntie. Finland's beautiful, but I think the diplomatic service is bloody useless. Bunch of upper-middle-class idiots.'

'Soon be home darling. There's an Irish stew in the oven and the fish are coming in droves. We'll have to see if you can break the thirty-pound mark this leave. Janet's running herself ragged and James is staying in Scotland till after the Twelfth. Told us to get on with the barley harvest even without him being here.'

'Sort of backhanded compliment I suppose, but it's the first time he's been away for more than a few days since I came home to England. He deserves the time away,' Finlay observed.

The telephone was ringing as they walked into the kitchen. Niney answered it impatiently: 'He's just walked in the door, Admiral!' she said shortly. 'Can I at least feed him...? Well, that's your fishing out the window, Admiral!' Niney snapped. She handed the phone to Finlay.

'Yes Sir. I'll come at once... yes Sir... couple of hours.' Finlay replaced the phone. 'Bugger that! Can't be helped. I'll only be gone a week, Auntie. I'll get my other case. Sorry, darling Auntie... the downside of the job, I suppose.' He ran upstairs to his bedroom and collected his suitcase.

Niney's disappointment was profound.

'Did you get the extra help in the house?' he asked, climbing into his car.

'Yes. I promised, didn't I?' She was crying. 'Then a Dundee cake in the tin, in a week, my love.'

He kissed her again and was gone.

In point of fact, it was five days later when Finlay and two others of his section landed at RAF Lyneham, happy and elated, having shown those in the know that Winter's new group was more than effective. An explosives factory on the coast of Albania lay in ruins, and the supply of the new plastic compound going to rogue Arab states, and thence to Ireland, was cut off. Winter was effusive with his praise and amused by the speed and effectiveness of Finlay's plan. Finlay had telephoned home and asked Niney not to lock up. He would be home by midnight and she was to leave the cake tin out. Winter had said, 'Your aunt seems a very forthright lady, Finlay!'

'Comes from having hundreds of years of deference from the peasantry, Sir!' Finlay had answered.

Finlay wrote his report on the group's latest escapade, in easy, clipped English, only describing in detail the spectacular show of the factory blowing up from where the group were watching, six miles offshore. As the long rumbling noise of the explosion reached them, Giles had remarked, 'That fucked their batting average.'

Finlay arrived home just after midnight. The yard lights were on, as were those in the kitchen. He wandered in, dropping his suitcase in the passageway and pushing the kettle on to the hot hob of the Aga. Sitting down, he realized, suddenly, how tired he was. On the table, the cake tin sat in solitary majesty. Inside, smelling fresh and fruity, was a perfect Dundee cake.

As he began to cut into it, Niney arrived, sleep-befuddled in her dressing gown. 'Hello sod,' she said, kissing him and smiling. 'Are you staying this time?'

'Yes, unless something happens abroad our lot don't agree with.'

They sat together, drinking tea and talking about the farm and the river. To Finlay's delight, the sudden lightening of Niney's workload with the new help, seemed fine. 'What joy it is,' she said. 'Just to pack up the dinner things and not have to do the bloody washing-up.'

'Well, if you don't have to do anything but supervise, perhaps we can have Ron and Wyn in for dinner? How does that sound?' Finlay asked.

'Yes darling. Time to to sit down and enjoy again. Just enjoy being people again,' she said.

Two days later, Admiral Winter had lunch with one Rupert Smith, an urbane intelligence officer, desk-bound in London and a great theorist and planner. 'John,' Smith said, over the pâté. 'I can only congratulate you on the success of your Recce group. It's wonderful to see some proper action being enacted without the interference of the FCO. Wonderful, indeed, to see a decision taken and acted apon without the formation of endless committees to discuss the matter.'

'What's the position with your asset in Russia, Rupert? Do we need to move on him yet? I suppose he's better in place while he's safe?' Winter asked.

'Be as well to get the teams up together ready. In case we have to lift him in a hurry. That'll be your pigeon, John. Albania's one thing, the Soviet Union quite another. Your chap Finlay would seem best suited to lead the teams,' Smith said.

Winter laughed loudly. 'The one you were so set against in the first place. Really Rupert, you bend with the wind.'

Smith laughed in turn. 'OK. I was wrong. Maybe I should meet him?'

'Not a good idea, Rupert. He'd see through you in seconds, as not being his sort of person. You don't hunt, shoot or fish and your name would be wholly against you. Smith hardly conjures up the field sport set, does it? Finlay despises townies and you, Rupert, are the archetypal,' Winter said, amused.

'Well, we shall have to meet at some stage,' Smith said, just a little affronted.

'Don't say I didn't warn you then. He'll probably view you in the same way as he does Miss Grant. Something he inadvertently stepped in.' Winter smiled.

Finlay's leave this time was uninterrupted. After ten days, he motored up to London early and went into the office. There were only the communications staff in the outer offices. The constant clatter of the telex machines seemed louder than usual in the quiet building. He gingerly knocked on Winter's door.

'Come in!' Winter called, testily.

'Morning Sir,' Finlay ventured.

Winter smiled. 'What are you doing here Finlay?' He almost beamed. 'You're meant to be on leave.'

'Just wondered what was happening, Sir,' Finlay said. 'Like to keep up with events.'

'That's appreciated Finlay! I think I'm ready for breakfast. Would you like to join me?'

'Yes please, Sir. Skipped mine this morning. Not a good idea.' Finlay laughed.

Winter rang down for his car and, locking some documents in his safe, they left for the Dorchester.

'This is a hell of a place, Sir,' Finlay observed. 'Grub any good?'

'Probably not up to the standard you're used to. I understand your aunt is something special in the kitchen. Angus Keith was extolling her virtues only the other day.' Winter smiled.

'He's good company Sir, and knows his pigs pretty well,' Finlay said, artlessly.

Winter laughed. 'I'll pass that one on, Finlay.'

They chatted over breakfast about things happening in the world, the best way to improve lawns and the best pubs in Hampshire.

When they finished, Winter dismissed him at the office entrance. 'Go home boy,' he had said fondly. 'You cannot save the world on your own. As far as the new suit is concerned, you stand out more than ever. Perhaps you'd better go back to the clothes you were wearing. Let people think you're eccentric.'

Finlay found himself looking forward to the coming harvest. There was a new, huge combine harvester, the dryer upgraded and no more sacks. All was 'bulk'. Enormous bins had been installed and everything was ready. Throughout the weeks of the summer he had been commuting once more to the office, by car mostly, and his hours were not regular enough to make anything of a routine of his life. He went over reports and briefings submitted by the rest of the group and railed at their doing things out in the field, while he was stuck behind a desk. It did have its compensations. He was home most nights and, as the evenings became ever more light, he could generally do some fishing. He had to spend one week at the Warwickshire training base honing fitness, but saw none of his original group there.

With her horses mainly out to grass, Janet had more time and energy. She seemed to want to dissipate these as often as possible in bed with Finlay, when her mother was away. It worked well. It could have been almost described as convenient.

Finlay, sitting at his desk, studying a report on the Lebanon, was surprised by the arrival of Winter into his office. 'Put your mind to this for me, Finlay,' he ordered. 'Operation Lordswood. I want you and a couple of your section to disrupt it. Show the top Army brass and NATO that such set-piece exercises are of little use, if they're not realistic. You'll have SBS and SAS to draw on for bodies. More than you'll actually need. Select a team to achieve this.' He handed Finlay the inevitable brown file. 'Not to be removed from this building for any reason. It concerns an important job you'll be involved in. We want you to extract a KGB colonel from Russia, by way of Finland. Probably in the next few months.'

'Does he want to be extracted, Sir?' Finlay asked.

'Oh yes. He's staying one jump ahead at the moment. They do not, in any way, suspect him. But I would like him here, so we shall make his position untenable in Russia. He'll want to come all right.'

When the Admiral left him, Finlay swore to himself. He had been hoping to join part of the section on an up-and-coming job in Sweden. It looked interesting and there was the spin-off of some very good fishing.

For the next six weeks, Finlay worked on the theoretical operation and when fully satisfied, he handed it to Winter. 'I think that should do it, Sir,' Finlay said, matter-of-factly. 'I think that covers all angles. Except, perhaps, the uselessness of the embassy staff in Helsinki.'

The Admiral smiled. 'Don't worry about that Finlay. Moves have been made.'

Chapter Eleven

•

August

The general buzz of conversation stopped as the Major walked into the room. The dozen men remained seated, but prepared to listen. 'OK, you lot! You've been chosen for this job because of your general thoughtfulness. By that, I don't mean you take your boots off before you start banging the ladies.' The Major had made a joke, but nobody laughed. He coughed uncomfortably and went on. 'This job will not come off until next year, if at all. And all your officers will be from the Navy.'

There were howls of derision and a general air of ribald protest.

'Laugh that one off!' The Major smirked. 'You'll be leaving for Poole in Dorset at eleven hundred today. You'll be gone on this training exercise for a minimum of six weeks and your initial embarkation will be for Germany.'

There were more howls of protest as one wag shouted, 'Will the Navy be able to find Germany, Sir?'

Forced to smile, the Major went on, 'I hope I've no need to tell you that I expect the very best reports from the senior naval staff...'

'Bollocks!' someone shouted.

'Because,' the Major continued, 'I believe the end game of this job is vitally important to national security.' And will shorten the war by a year...'

'You're beginning to sound like a bad film, Sir. What's this job?' Sergeant Proudfoot asked.

'I don't know!' replied the Major. 'Only the three going will know that. I don't even know what you'll be doing in Germany. Nobody tells me nuffin!' The officer had made another joke.

This time, the men as one laughed, but only just. 'Are we flying up to Poole, Sir?' asked a trooper.

'No, coach. Any other questions?' asked the Major.

'Have I time to get the wife up the duff, before we leave, Sir?' another trooper asked from the back of the room. There was more general laughter.

The major looked at his watch in a theatrical gesture. 'Well, one of the girls in Ops said you were quick, so I imagine you have.'

This time, the laughter was loud, long and genuine. The trooper in question was subject to a barrage of missiles, ranging from coins to rolled-up paper.

The Major coughed to achieve silence. 'OK! Get your personal kit ready. That's all you'll be taking, the Navy will supply the rest. Have a good trip.'

The briefing broke up noisily, with lots of speculation about what they were going to be doing.

Just before fifteen hundred, the coach pulled up at the security barrier at the Special Boat Squadron's base. As the coach door opened with a hiss of compressed air, a Royal Marine Corporal jumped on board. He grimaced in an exaggerated way and held his nose, looking over the soldiers seated in the coach. 'Are you lot the Royal Ballet or the Special Air Service?' He looked at the clipboard he was holding, 'Sorry. You must be the Special Air Service. Only soldiers could smell like you lot.' The Corporal ducked out of the coach, avoiding the bits of the soldiers' kit being hurled at him. As the fusillade ended, he jumped back on and shouted, 'Visitors' delousing block on the right.'

He would have come to harm were it not for the intervention of a Marine Major arriving. He eyed the Corporal icily. 'Hop it, Wilson!' he snapped and, clearing foot space among the debris of kit around his feet, said to the driver, 'Right! Straight ahead and turn left at the end.'

'He means port, driver,' one of the troopers shouted. 'Bloody Bootnecks don't know left from right.'

'Silence!' the Major snapped. He looked at Sergeant Proudfoot. 'I want that man's name, Sergeant.'

There was an immediate chorus of 'oohs and ahs' and howls of derisive laughter. 'Get him!' the mouthy trooper shouted amid the laughter. 'Little bastard's only five feet high.'

By the time order had been restored, the coach had arrived at a number of portacabin-like structures and the soldiers began to file off. As they passed the Marine Major, he checked their names and identities until he came to the trooper who had made the comment about his height. 'You stand there,' he ordered the trooper to his left, and then checked the others from the coach.

He turned to the trooper standing beside him. 'Name?'

'Pitt, Guv,' the trooper answered.

'Right Pitt, nineteen hundred in the gym, PT order. And I'm Sir, not Guv. Got it?'

Again, there were hoots of derision from the trooper's companions. A shout of, 'He fancies you, Jonty!' made the Marine glower.

The soldiers were quartered and shown the mess hall. Inevitably they complained bitterly about the food served up to them by two naval ratings. One of them, particularly stung by a remark from one of the troopers, poured a large spoonful of custard over the trooper's corned beef salad.

'What the fuck you doing?' exploded the trooper.

'Eat it, or go home to mummy, you bloody toss pot! Wait till our Marines get hold of you lot!'

The trooper could hardly believe what he was hearing. 'Do you know who we are?' he snarled.

'Bunch of fairies from Hereford. That's who you are. Now, go over there, sit down and eat your tea,' the young sailor ordered.

It was the timely intervention of a leading hand that prevented blood from being spilt. 'Leave it trooper!' he ordered, marching across to the serving area. 'Over there and pipe down,' he ordered the SAS trooper, 'or you'll feel the weight of my hand.'

This time Proudfoot intervened. 'Jonty, over here, and keep stumm.' Proudfoot acknowledged the leading hand with a wave. 'He won't be any trouble, Sergeant.' The sailor gasped at the insult and marched out of the mess hall, muttering dark threats about the Marines having a field day with these uncouth bastards.

At nineteen hundred, Pitt presented himself in the gym. He was surprised to find a dozen Marines lounging about the walls and a large rubber mat the only visible piece of equipment. The other SAS men followed, inquisitive as to Pitt's punishment. They loitered in the doorway, unsure of what was happening. The Marine Major arrived, followed by a Petty Officer carrying two towels. 'Come in all of you. Gather round the mat.' He looked at Pitt and smiled. 'Right Pitt, choose yourself a second.'

Proudfoot suddenly knew what was happening and stepped forward, taking one of the towels offered. 'Pitt, when PO White blows the whistle, you have two minutes to kick the shit out of me and then we will be friends. The seconds can throw in the towel if they think their man has had enough. Got the picture?'

Jonty Pitt smiled. 'Kick the shit out of a Rupert! I'm going to love this place, Simon,' he said to Proudfoot. Ominously, the Marines were silent. The SAS troopers began to make loud comments. 'Don't hurt him Jonty. He's only a little bugger,' was one.

Pitt, over six feet and possessing a rangy power, stared at the man in front of him and suddenly became uneasy.

'Take your tracksuit top, Sir?' PO White asked the Marine Major.

'No, this will only take a minute. Blow the whistle. I've got a stack of paperwork to do,' he said, easily.

The whistle blew and Jonty Pitt advanced on the Marine with evil in his heart. He grabbed the Major by the hair and tried to spin him over his leg. However the Marine was under his guard already, and Pitt gasped in pain and surprise as the Marine's elbow drove into his kidney. Another surprise was his left leg, which suddenly didn't seem to have any feeling. It refused to take any of his weight and two jabbing fingers deprived him of his vision. He didn't need to see. The mat beneath him seemed to slam into the side of his head. Pitt didn't move. There seemed to be a percussion band playing in his head.

A Marine sidled up to Proudfoot. 'I should chuck the towel in, matey,' he offered quietly. 'He won't get up from that.' The voice was very quiet and positive.

Proudfoot looked at him scornfully. 'Fuck off! Jonty'll kill him!'

'Not from where I'm standing, he won't. He's out with the fairies.'

Proudfoot threw the towel on to the mat and turned away in disgust. The Major picked up the towel and fastidiously wiped some of Pitt's blood from his left hand. He walked across to Pitt and helped him up. Pitt's eyes were streaming salt tears, his nose bubbled bright red blood. The Major took Pitt's right hand in his own and shook it warmly. 'No hard feelings. Well done!'

'No feelings at all, Sir,' Pitt mumbled, through split lips. He staggered across to Proudfoot. 'Like trying to fight a jet-propelled Dinkum digger.'

The Marine Major brought them to attention. 'This is the last fight between Marines and the Army on this deployment. Any soldier guilty of brawling will be RTUed back to his original regiment. Any marine so doing will spend two years with the Naval Party at Moody Brook. Got it?'

'Where's Moody Brook?' Pitt asked Proudfoot.

'Fuck knows,' said Proudfoot. 'But I don't think the Marines like the sound of it.'

'Falklands, mate,' the softly spoken Marine standing next to Proudfoot said. 'He was sent there,' he said, nodding towards the Major. 'But he enjoyed it. Let's get your mate to the sick berth shall we?'

'Permission to take the soldier to the sick berth?' the Marine asked the Major.

'Yes, get him cleaned up. He'll be all right in the morning.'

The next morning, the SAS team were led to a different mess hall and found themselves sitting with about a dozen Marines and a scattering of white-shirted, black-tied naval officers. Food was quickly distributed on plates too hot to touch. Proudfoot made to pick up his knife and fork to attack the bacon, eggs and black pudding. 'Not yet, mate,' a Marine sitting opposite said, 'Grace!'

A tall thin Navy officer stood and the room was suddenly silent. 'For what we are about to receive, may the Lord make us truly thankful.' He then sat again.

'Who was the kid?' asked Proudfoot, amazed at his obvious youth.

'Senior Snotty, Midshipman,' the Marine answered. 'Seventeen, and currently in charge of this lot.'

'Bit posh, even for a Rupert!' Proudfoot remarked.

'Eton. Going back to do his A levels. Bloody nice nipper, he'll be a lifer.' Before he could finish, a small group of naval officers arrived through a door at the head of the mess hall.

'Christ! Is that who I think it is?' Proudfoot exclaimed. His Marine companion did not answer, but as with the others, rose quickly to his feet and remained at attention.

'Silence!' snapped the seventeen-year-old.

'Jesus,' whispered Proudfoot.

'Carry on,' a Captain, at the head of the hall, ordered.

'We allowed to speak now?' whispered Proudfoot.

'Quietly,' suggested the Marine.

'Top brass, eh? Is that Admiral Winter? Who are the others?' asked Proudfoot.

'Commodore James, Captain Kicker, the other two young ones I don't know by name. They're the ones in charge of you.'

'The Lieutenant Commander's only a kid, for Christ's sake. In charge!' Proudfoot scoffed.

'Product of Dartmouth, mate. They turn them out quiet, clever and hard. He's probably a secret squirrel as well, but don't say I said so. That'll get you in a rattle,' the Marine said, warily.

'What the hell have I got into here?'

'Don't worry about it mate. It's a lot of fun here. Always doing different things, charging about in the raiders, learning how to steal cars, blowing up buildings, language courses. You name it, we do it. Best grub in the fleet as well.' The Marine eagerly attacked the black pudding.

'Can't argue with that,' responded Proudfoot.

Later that day, the SAS men met with Admiral Winter. They were led to another part of the base, ushered into a room and ordered to make themselves comfortable. There was more food available and what seemed to be an unlimited supply of beer. 'Easy on the beer, lads. This looks like a test of how we behave,' Proudfoot warned. They ate, drank and relaxed for about half an hour before Winter arrived. With him were two younger officers. Knowing the form, the men stood in silence and waited.

'Relax everyone. Someone pour me a pint,' Winter began. 'You may smoke.' He looked over the men in front of him and generally liked what he saw. Proudfoot handed him a glass of foaming bitter.

'To begin then.' He paused. 'As you will be aware, the NATO exercise in Germany at the end of the month is the biggest in ten years. Designed to see what would happen if the Soviets decided to have a go.' He paused again, and began filling his pipe. 'In my opinion, it's a waste of time. It always works out that blue forces win. Any other way, and it's bad for morale. You will be attached to orange forces and I expect not just mayhem from you lot, I want the whole exercise thrown into complete confusion. You see, no one in charge knows you are going to be there. And gentlemen, I want realism. I will give you some ground rules. One, no damage to civilians... and that's about it, short of actually killing blue forces. There will, of course, be structure to this mayhem which my colleagues here will detail you about. As to these two officers, they'll be in charge. You will be split into two groups. You, Sergeant Proudfoot, will organize that. Not by mates, but by skills. This is very much a shakedown cruise, gentlemen. Three of you will be going with one of these officers on rather a special job next year. If you volunteer, that is. More of that if, and when, the time comes. If you have any doubts about a sailor on land, forget them. Any questions?'

'What if we get arrested by the monkeys, Sir?' asked Proudfoot.

'You have my word you will be out as soon as I know. My two officers here will deal with any nonsense from the Redcaps. Any other questions? Doesn't anybody want to know about increased pay on this one?'

No one answered.

'Right! This chap here is Pat and this one, Keith. You don't need surnames. To you, they're "Sir" until they say otherwise. Learn to work with them. You'll learn a lot from each other. I'll say goodbye and leave you to it.'

Admiral Winter got up to leave. The whole room jumped to their feet.

Keith Finlay began formally. 'First of all, I'd like to welcome you all on behalf of the Royal Marines and Royal Navy. At first, you may find our ways strange to you and some of our terminology, a little obscure. You also may find our formality a little irksome to what you have been used to. It's the thing, these days, for the media to portray what they term dramatically as Special Forces as a section of men who treat their officers with scant regard. Refer to them as "Ruperts", in general, and respond in answering them by "Guv". This, I'm informed, has become the norm in your regiment.'

There was some uncomfortable coughing and mumbles from around the room. Ignoring the obvious disquiet, Finlay continued. 'When I was told that for next year's Op, we were going to be stuck with SAS personnel, I was not at all keen on the idea. In short, I did not want you.' Finlay paused for effect and watched the men in front of him. He could see jaws tightening and was aware of several hard stares. 'It's my belief,' Finlay continued, 'that your regiment has been drawing to itself too many men from the Parachute Regiment, which has changed the ethos of the Special Air Service. You will have noted, I'm sure by now, that none of you have that background.'

'Well, I'm fucked!' Proudfoot said, in a loud stage whisper.

'You will be Sergeant, if you speak out of turn again!' Finlay said, quietly. The relaxed attitude of the meeting evaporated.

'If I had wanted tough fighting soldiers for this operation, I would have gone to Aldershot and drawn them from the Parachute Regiment. What I want is tough fighting soldiers with stoicism and patience. Who can go three or four days without food and without sleep and still have a sense of the ridiculous. Anyone who thinks they cannot be that person may as well leave now.'

Proudfoot rose to his feet.

'Sit down, Sergeant,' ordered Finlay. 'You've already been selected.'

'Can I object, Sir?' asked Proudfoot, with a look something akin to smugness on his face.

'Yes of course you can, Sergeant Proudfoot,' Finlay answered with studied brightness. 'Object all you want, but the fact is Admiral Winter chose you, and since admirals consider themselves, and generally are, somewhat above God, archbishops and prime ministers, you will be going and I shall not trouble to note your objection. I do not believe your objection to be serious anyway. Please sit down.'

Proudfoot sat, with a now definite smugness, while Finlay looked around the gathered group for any more movement. There was none.

'To continue. The Admiral said he wanted mayhem during the upcoming exercise. Mayhem, begging the Admiral's leave, is not the correct word. What we are going to produce is confusion. Confusion that has senior officers being sent home in disgrace and causes an ongoing enquiry at NATO headquarters that will have heads removed. The point of our operation is to force the staffers to realize that exercises which cost millions, must be realistic. If the Russians ever do choose to come and take the wheat they need, instead of waiting for the West to sell it, there will be confusion. Despite what the top brass and planners think, their initial thrust could not be stopped. Their specialist units would go for NATO's communications. To hamper build-up and re-enforcement.

'I can tell you now. In the Ural mountains, the Russians have built a town modelled on Redhill, where they train their people to become English. No doubt they have other places imitating an American town, a German town. My point is, because a chap wears a Barbour jacket, green wellies and says "hise", doesn't mean he's a British officer. By the same token, a staff car with a general in the back and a Fortnum's hamper beside him, may not be what it seems.' Finlay paused once more, for effect, and was glad to see smiles of anticipation on some of the faces in front of him.

'Sergeant Proudfoot. I understand, because of the likeness in build and features between yourself and your CO, General Allard, and in your cups, so to speak, you're given to carry off a very good impression.'

Proudfoot looked a little abashed, but said, 'Yes Sir. How did you know that, Sir?'

'Doesn't matter Sergeant, but perhaps you would be so good as to come forward and show us just how good you are.'

'Now, Sir?' asked Proudfoot.

'Right now, Sergeant,' answered Finlay. 'Let's see whether you can ape your betters when you're not drunk.'

Proudfoot seemed unwilling to move. 'I don't know whether I can, Sir. Just like that. I mean, without the beer.'

'I'm sure you could, Sergeant. Are your stripes important to you?' Finlay asked. With some alacrity, Proudfoot went to the front.

'Now. I want you to come through that door in a moment, transformed,' Finlay ordered. The sergeant eyed the younger man coldly for a moment and left the room. There was total silence and not a few looks from the men to Finlay. They thought their Sergeant ill-used.

Without warning, the door burst open with a crash that shook the room. Stiff-backed, and fairly bristling with rage, Sergeant Simon Proudfoot marched into the room. Kicking an innocent loose chair from his path, he marched up to the table where Finlay was sitting and slammed his fist down on the surface so hard that a packet of cigarettes lying on the table, leapt on to the floor. 'Just what exactly are you about, Commander?' began Proudfoot. 'Do you treat your own NCOs like shit? I've not had much to do with the Navy in my time and having you to judge from, I can only be very glad. I shall speak to your CO about this morning's nonsense and make damn certain there is no repetition of it!' The other officer sitting next to Finlay started to laugh. 'And just what are you laughing about, you bloody nincompoop?' Proudfoot roared. The room erupted into gales of laughter.

'That was brilliant,' Pat McHaffey said, through tears of laughter. 'Tony Allard, to a T.'

Proudfoot relaxed and began laughing himself. 'I've been stitched up.'

'Perhaps we'll break there,' said Finlay. 'Sergeant Proudfoot, I think you can keep your stripes. For the moment, anyway.'

Chapter Twelve

•

September

'No Captain. That's that wood. Your HQ is just over there,' Finlay said to a young Blues and Royals Captain, with feigned patience. Operation Lordswood was in full swing in northern Germany. Finlay smoothed out the Captain's map again. 'You see the high ground there?' he said, pointing to a small rise in the east. 'That's that bit.' He stabbed his finger on the map.

The young Captain looked perplexed. 'I'm sorry, Major, to be so silly. I do appreciate your help. Lucky we ran into you.'

Finlay patted his arm gently. 'No matter. That's what we're here for. Would you like some tea, perhaps?' Finlay was playing for time. 'I believe one of my chaps has some on the go. Get your Scorpions under cover. Stop and have a rest.'

'What splendid chaps your Marines are, Sir. Always ready to muck in and help. I'd love some tea and I've some food in my vehicles. It's almost like a picnic, isn't it?' The Captain seemed delighted to have such accommodating men, helping to move his tanks under the trees. As the Scorpions were guided into the clearing under Jonty Pitt's direction, Proudfoot jumped up on each one in turn and offered a brew. Suspicious at first, the tank crews were slow to dismount. As they saw their own officer enjoying tea and fruit cakes with the Marine officer, they relaxed and joined in.

Finlay extended charm and helpfulness, cracking the odd joke, until one of the team signalled by an eyebrow twitch that all was ready. As gently as possible, Finlay wound up the impromptu party, and offered up Proudfoot as the guide. Just to get them on the correct route. This was refused and, in a line the young Captain knew his CO would be proud of, the nine Scorpions headed for the headquarters they would be protecting that evening.

Finlay and the three SAS troopers waved them goodbye and watched their dusty progress towards the wood he had directed them to. When they were about a mile away, and all that could be seen of them was dust and blue exhaust smoke, Proudfoot said in his best Peter Lorre voice, 'Shall I kill them now, Sir?'

Finlay nodded. In the distance, the blue exhaust fumes became tinged with scarlet as the electrically detonated smoke grenades that Proudfoot had rigged on to each Scorpion, exploded. 'Nine, us. Blues and Royals, nil!' Proudfoot said proudly. 'And one poor little Rupert with egg on his face and red dye all over his tanks.'

'That cake was good, Simon,' Finlay remarked.

'Fortnum and Mason. He had a whole hamper in his Scorpion. Don't know they're living, these boy soldiers. I'll give him, "Thank you dear chap."' Proudfoot scoffed scornfully.

Simon Gandy handed Finlay a notebook. 'Identity codes of their staffers, Sir. Copied them out while you were all having tea and cakes.'

'Looks like you've got to give a performance then, Simon. Well done, Stewart. Did you save him some cake, Jonty?' Finlay laughed.

'Pinched the whole hamper, Sir,' responded Pitt. 'We can all eat well tonight. Does anyone like walnuts pickled in sherry?'

They continued in the same vein for about another week. The confusion Finlay's group sowed, across the German plain, caused headaches all the way back to NATO headquarters in Brussels. Eventually, the Orange and Blue Staffers had to liaise with each other over what was going wrong. It took them some three days to work out that a rogue group were systematically destroying any co-ordination between each other, and the word went out to find and arrest the group. To send them back to Colchester. Blue Force's Chief of Staff was an Italian Major General, one Alfonso Spinnelli. He was based, mainly, behind a desk in Brussels. Finlay's group, by way of a finale, decided they should capture him.

'I'm really not enjoying this hat,' remarked Pitt, adjusting the maroon beret on his head. 'People might think I'm a psycho.'

'Thought you didn't like paras, Sir, or didn't rate them at least,' moaned Gandy.

Finlay, brushing imaginary dirt from Proudfoot's resplendent uniform, ignored them. 'There you are General Allard, Sir. How does it feel?'

'I could get used to it. Do I get a general's pay while I'm wearing it?' asked Proudfoot.

'If we can bring this one off and grab this macaroni General, I'm sure my admiral will stand you the biggest piss-up you've ever seen,' Finlay answered, setting about brushing down his own uniform, that of a Parachute Regiment private soldier. 'Are we ready?'

It was all too easy, Finlay reflected afterwards. Disturbingly easy. They had driven up to Blue Force HQ, as Finlay had ordered, 'as dramatically as possible'. The guards did not question a Land-Rover containing General Tony Allard was in any way out of the ordinary. Proudfoot had marched in, asked General Spinnelli if he would like to watch an air-drop and then be entertained for lunch. The Italian was only too happy. He was being blamed in Brussels for the disorganization of the exercise and felt he needed some relief.

They were two miles from Blue Force HQ when Finlay said, 'You going to tell him Simon, or shall I?'

Proudfoot removed his officer's cap. 'General Spinnelli, let me make some introductions to you. Simon Proudfoot, Special Air Service, Stewart Gandy and Jonty Pitt, of the same. The little chap behind you, I don't even know. Fact is, mate, you're our prisoner.'

The Italian seemed not to be able to take it in at first, then the awkwardness of his position became clear. 'What do you do with me now?' he asked.

'Well, we're going to deliver you to some waiting top brass. Then we're going home,' said Finlay.

Two days later in London, Admiral Winter studied Finlay's report on Operation Lordswood. Occasionally he would glance, over the top of the report at Finlay. A smile meant, 'Well done,' a hard stare and sigh was disapproval. Eventually, he laid the report on his desk and took up his pipe. 'Well, it's as I thought. Thanks Finlay. Now, tell me about your team.'

'They were a bit hesitant at first, Sir. But once they'd crossed what I'm certain they thought of as a point of no return, they gelled together nicely,' Finlay said.

'Suitable for next year's job?' Winter asked.

'Perhaps, if I knew what the job was, I might be able to answer that Sir,' Finlay answered, seriously.

'You'll be extracting that KGB colonel, by way of Finland,' Winter said simply.

'Is he still willing, Sir?'

'Very willing. You OK with that?' Winter looked hard at him.

'Yes Sir,' answered Finlay.

Chapter Thirteen

•

December

'I don't want another fare, for God's sake!' the Moscow taxi driver shouted into his two-way radio. 'I have one to pick up by the bridge at eleven, and then I'm going off duty till the second of the month. It might even be until spring.'

The controller receiving the message looked at his microphone. 'What the fuck are you talking about, Rocki?' he asked. 'Are you cracking up?'

'Sorry Petre,' the driver answered, in a resigned way. 'Thinking aloud.'

'You're not paid to think, you're paid to drive…'

'Capitalist!' shouted the driver. He rammed the car in gear and fired it towards his home. The brief conversation was monitored in England and was the last move in a game of chance that had been played out over the last year and a half. The conversation was typed out verbatim, the exact translation added, then pushed into an envelope marked Admiral Sir John Winter and handed to a uniformed Chief Petty Officer. 'That's what he's been waiting for, Chief,' the radio operator said. 'Have a good trip.'

The CPO left the building and walked briskly to a waiting car and said to the driver, 'Right, let's go. This place gives me the creeps!' It was GCHQ, part of Britain's overt spy system.

Three hours later, the car pulled into the car park allocated to Admiralty Arch and the envelope was delivered into the hands of Admiral Winter, who had been waiting for the message with some impatience. The man sitting in the office with Winter was a more patient man, Rupert Smith. He looked enquiringly at Winter as the latter opened the envelope carefully.

'Oleg is coming out on the second of February. We have to do it then or leave it till the eleventh of May.' Without waiting for any opinion from Smith, Winter said, 'Second of February. Not so much daylight. OK?'

The other man nodded his assent. 'Have we picked the back-up team?'

'Yes. Finlay to lead and three from Hereford, a sergeant and two troopers.' Winter replaced the message in the envelope. 'If we can bring this off, Rupert, it'll be something of a coup. A full colonel of the KGB!'

'I would be happier if Finlay was going in. Oleg knows of him and Finlay wouldn't stand any of his prima donna nonsense.'

'No, I'll not risk Finlay. He knows too much and he needs a milk run. In fact, he needs a good long rest. He can have this one easy, though Finland in February can never be said to be that easy.'

'Don't you go spoiling him, John,' laughed Smith. 'He'll only take advantage. I'll get a message back to Rocki, that the second of Feb is the day. We'll have plenty of time to filter the teams in through Helsinki. Duckworth has done his part with the embassy summer house. They can go any time they want. Get them acclimatized.'

Over the next three weeks, five British nationals entered Finland under various guises, disappeared into the interior of the country, all to rendezvous at the embassy's summer house. Everything was set to bring out a willing enough defector, who promised to shed some light on Soviet espionage activity in the West.

Janet Williams was sitting in front of a radar screen. It was mid-morning break and she was standing in for one of her juniors. Her sandwiches were dry, her coffee lukewarm and she was bored. The track of the Russian satellite curved across the screen in a series of red dots, overlaying the previous series, the one before and the one before that. She moved to another screen to check another, glancing at the large time digits on the wall.

'Ten minutes,' she thought. She gathered up her handbag and headed for the lavatory. She fell to chatting with a colleague. It seemed only the briefest of conversations, but it was enough to make certain of missing the track of the satellite she should have been watching. Had she been at her screen, she would have seen that the new track of this particular craft was different from the last. She settled herself back in her seat and looked at the screen. Across it ran two dotted red lines, diverging.

'Oh Lord,' she breathed and reached for the desk phone, pressing in a single digit on the keypad. 'One of the Comstocks is moving off course, Sir. Looks like they are retasking it.' She waited. 'I'm sorry,

Sir. I was in the loo at the time. It's Comstock 13.' She waited again, said, 'Yes Sir,' and put the phone down.

By the time David Allen had arrived in the main tracking room, Janet Williams had plotted the wayward satellite's course, speed and height. The speed and height display came up on the digital counters under the screen.

'So where does that put it now, Janet?' asked Allen.

'Just cleared Iran, Sir. Height is constant, but if you look, it has shifted another point 001 of a degree already.'

Allen glanced at the time. 'OK Janet, I'll be back in time for the next pass. Keep your eye on it.'

Janet Williams watched until the satellite went below the Earth's curvature, and then relaxed. When the rest of the staff arrived back from their break, she began moves to get Comstock 13's track up on to the big screen. There was a buzz of interest in the room as Comstock 13 appeared above the horizon over the South Atlantic. Janet Williams called David Allen. 'It's up, Sir, Comstock 13.' Up was a way of saying it was now above the horizon. 'A lot lower, Sir.'

David Allen arrived in seconds. He quickly grasped the situation. 'This pass will take it over Chad, Egypt, Israel and Syria, before their own territory. Wonder what they're looking for?'

Nobody ventured an opinion.

Allen came to a decision. 'Right Janet, the whole team on to this one. Call me in good time for the next pass. If there is one, that is. At its present rate of descent, it's going to have a job clearing the Arctic.' There was a hum of excitement.

David Allen was back in the tracking room some twenty minutes before Comstock 13 was due to reappear. Most of the staff stood in a tight group around the big screen, waiting. As the first contact was made, the height and speed indicators began their crazy, clicking whirring. 'They're trying to bring it down, and they've lost it!' said the excited Allen. 'Right you lot, and quick about it! Is it going to make it through the atmosphere? If so, where's it coming down?' There was a certain competitive rush back to desks, as everyone tried to be the first with the answers.

First up was the youngest of the team, so young she raised her hand like a keen schoolgirl. 'Sir! If it doesn't burn up it will land in the northern Baltic. The angle's too steep to allow for a bounce off the atmosphere.'

'Verify that someone!' Allen said impatiently. 'Well done, Carol.'

'That's it, Sir,' said Janet Williams, smiling her approval. Without anyone saying anything, the staff drifted back to the big screen, watching the red dotted trace.

One of the scientists said, 'Will the people in Stockholm please duck.' There was a ripple of laughter around the room.

'Ought we to tell someone, Sir?' asked Janet Williams.

Without moving his eyes from the screen, David Allen answered simply, 'Already done.'

The red dots came to an abrupt halt. 'Co-ordinates somebody please… quick as you can,' ordered Allen.

Again, it was the youngster who handed Allen a pad with a grid reference on it. Without looking at her he said, 'Thank you.' Then he left the room quickly.

Just south of Ivalo, in Finnish Lapland, a small group of ptarmigan hens pecked and fed avidly at the moss and lichen uncovered from beneath the snow by the satellite's impact.

Admiral Winter was packing up to go home. It had been a long day. He looked out of the window at the gridlocked traffic around the Mall. He debated whether to call for his car and decided not to. 'Let the traffic clear a little first,' he thought.

There was a light tap on the door, and Miss Grant's small bespectacled face appeared around the door. 'Mr Smith is on his way around, Sir. Asked that you should hang on for him.'

'Thank you. I was going to stay till the traffic thinned out a little. You can stand down though. No point in us both being late home.'

'Sir,' she answered simply.

Winter began to fill his pipe. He picked up a file in his in tray, glanced at it then threw it back into the tray. 'If I'd have left at four,' he thought. 'I would be almost home by now. Bugger it!'

Rupert Smith found him dozing in an armchair when he arrived. 'Sorry to hold you up John,' he began. 'Bit of a flap on up in Finland.'

'They're not due out for a couple of days yet, Rupert. What the Hell's gone wrong?'

'No, not that John. Fylingdales informed us a Soviet satellite has come down in Finnish Lapland, and everyone's getting worked up about it.'

'Everyone?' queried Winter. 'Why everyone?'

'Well, the Finns have been told by the Russians that they want any bits back immediately, and for some reason the Americans and the Jews have been buzzing back and forth to each other's embassies for the past hour and a half. Bruce Winchester is with the Man from Marks, as we speak.' Bruce Winchester was the CIA Chief of Staff in London. The Man from Marks was his opposite number in Mossad, with a predilection for dressing in women's clothes.

'Where did this thing come down, Rupert?' asked Winter, moving to a large wall map.

'Around this area,' said Smith, tracing a circle around Ivalo. 'It may of course have hit this mountain, somewhat south, or come down in this lake, somewhat north.'

'The lake would be frozen, surely. How big is this thing, anyway?' The Admiral was losing interest.

'It's about seven metres long' said Smith.

'What's that in English!' snapped Winter, more testily than he meant. He immediately drew back. 'Sorry John, I can't visualize things in these damn Froggie measurements.'

'About as long as one and a half Range-Rovers...'

At which point, Winter's telephone chirped into life. With the instrument to his ear, he nodded, 'Yes, bring him up.'

He looked at Smith and smiled. 'Bruce Winchester is on his way up, Rupert.' They moved away from the wall map, almost like guilty schoolboys, and took up rather theatrical positions close to Winter's desk. When Winchester entered, Winter met him effusively. 'Bruce! To what do I, or rather we, owe the pleasure?'

'Admiral, Mr Smith, glad you could see me at such short notice. Are you both keeping well?' Bruce Winchester was a product of Harvard, tall, tanned and beautifully suited. 'I'll come straight to the point. About the Soviet satellite just down in Finland, we could do with your help. If, that is, you have anyone in Finland?' He waited, coughed, and waited. 'Have you anyone in Finland? At the moment, I mean, on the ground?'

'Sorry, Bruce, we don't. But tell me how we can help you?' Winter answered. 'Can I offer you a drink? You look a little bothered.'

'Admiral, this satellite may have the potential to cause my government a great deal of embarrassment.'

'Tell me how,' Winter said softly. 'If it's a concern to Washington, it must concern London.'

'It passed over a sensitive area in Israel, just at the wrong moment it seems. It may have been filming at the time and the film may have survived re-entry and a fairly hard landing. We believe it deployed parachutes.'

'What do you want us to do, Bruce? Always supposing we could get some of our people there before you or the Russians, or indeed the Finns. I do not suppose the Finns are going to be slow off the mark.' Winter toyed with the American.

'Just, if you had somebody in the area, destroy what is left of it. I mean at this stage, we don't know what is left of it, if anything. I mean it might have been destroyed. Nothing much left at all.'

'Well, let's hope, shall we Bruce?' Winter paused. 'Of course we know the machine is down. It might have survived, it might not have. It may have come down in a lake in the area. It might indeed have practically burnt up.' He paused. 'But Bruce, that's an awful lot of mays and mights. It may be sitting in a snow drift, bleeping away, flashing lights, etc., etc. So what did it photograph, Bruce?'

The American looked uncomfortable. 'That might be a little difficult to explain...'

'I imagined it might be.' There was just a hint of a smile on Winter's lips. 'But Bruce, let's not get into detail. You want me to get somebody up there and take stock. I'm sure we can help. Now! About that drink.'

'I ought not to stop, Admiral. Time's very much of the essence. Can I take a rain check on that? You'll let me know what you decide?' He moved to the door. 'It might well be a storm in a tea cup, Admiral.' He had reached the door. 'I'll call you in a couple of hours, if you don't mind. You see, it could all be nothing.' He left.

Rupert Smith walked to the door and checked the corridor. He turned to Admiral Winter. 'Have you got anyone up there, John? Anyone spare that is?'

Winter smiled broadly. 'They are in something of a flap, Rupert. I think we should give them a hand. I think we might well help our American cousins and, perhaps, ourselves. Let's get moving! As Winchester said, time is of the essence.'

Chapter Fourteen

•

January

About a mile short of the tree line in Finnish Lapland, four men lay in snow holes, taking what shelter they could. It was not actually snowing, but a fierce easterly wind picked up crystals of snow and drove them horizontally into the scrubby birch and willow trees. Two of the men were sleeping fitfully, the other two were keeping stag, as best the weather would allow. Finlay rolled on to his side and the frozen snow cracked beneath him. He undid the wrist band on his mittens and looked at the luminous dial of his watch. 'Nearly time to call in. Let them know we're still alive. Wouldn't want to spoil your mummy's weekend,' he said, digging his companion in the ribs. There was a mumbled curse in answer.

Finlay took from the top of his Bergen something that looked much the same as a calculator and a small pencil torch. Removing his right mitten and holding the torch in his mouth, he got below the edge of his snow hole and began typing into the machine. A tiny plastic tape began to edge out of its top. It came free when he touched the perforation button. Placing the tape into a slot in the bottom of the machine, he again consulted his watch. As the minutes ticked away to twenty hundred hours, he waited and watched. As the sweep second hand reached the end of the sixtieth minute, Finlay pushed the send button.

The machine uttered a tiny squeal as the tape shot through it. About to put the machine back, Finlay was more than startled when it squealed again, and produced another tape. 'Oh balls!' Finlay breathed.

His companion edged closer. 'Trouble?' he asked.

'Christ knows,' answered Finlay. 'Just got a message back, which means decoding.' He again went to his Bergen and produced a small acetape pad and scribbler. Readjusting the machine, he pressed in a series of numbers. The tiny screen lit up and began passing a series of numbers. Finlay waited, almost ignoring what was happening, until the machine went dead again. He keyed in 22101805. The screen lit again and slowly unfolded the briefest of statements: 'Go to the following grid ref: Bear satt. down. Film container like flat six-inch rugby ball. Get it and return. Immediate.'

Finlay sighed, deeply. 'Jesus Christ! I just wonder whether Winter is on the same planet as the rest of us. Get a brew going, Simon. We're moving out.'

The figure on the ground sat up. 'Where we going?' he said, with feigned disinterest.

'North. About eighty or ninety miles... or more.'

'Who have the extraction team got navigating? A bloody RAF wallah? Nobody could be that far adrift!' Simon Proudfoot assumed something had gone wrong with their current task.

'Sorry Simon. It's not this job. A Ruskie spacecraft has come down. We have to go and get something from it. Wake the others. Really make their day.' Finlay got the small jelly stove lit and began getting a drink under way. Waiting for the water to boil, he got the plastic maps from his Bergen and began matching the co-ordinates given to a specific point on the plastic surface. Proudfoot joined him. 'About there Simon, just short of Ivalo. Ever been there?' Finlay asked.

Proudfoot swore lustily. 'I've been all over this bloody country. It's either covered in snow, or covered in midges, depending on the time of year. It's little wonder the Finns are such miserable bastards.'

Two others, Jonty and Stewart, joined them. 'Fuck-up?' asked Jonty Pitt, conversationally.

'Change of plan. We've got to go north about one hundred miles. Get some bits from a Russian spacecraft that's come down,' Finlay answered. He motioned to the map. 'It's about here. What we're looking for is apparently like a flattened, small rugby ball. So we'll have a drink and push off. The message said "Immediate".'

'What does that mean, in Royal Navy parlance?' asked Pitt.

Finlay laughed. 'It means we have time for a drink. "Most immediate" means move now.'

'Lovely way with words, your lot,' Proudfoot remarked.

'What? Do they say please and thank you in the SAS, these days? Here, take your drinks and get packed up. We're out of here in three minutes,' Finlay ordered, impatient now to move.

In something less than an hour, the four men were above the tree line and taking the full force of the wind. Proudfoot led the group through knee-high scrub willow, over the rock-hard ground, leaning sideways, as the wind, now gusting to gale force, tried to buffet the men off their feet. By keeping to the scree areas, avoiding the pockets of blown snow, the group made another two miles before they paused to rest. They gathered together and, as one, came down on their haunches without removing their Bergens.

Proudfoot pushed his face close to Finlay. 'I'll stay on point till it gets light, then we'll swap. We should make better time in the daylight.' Daylight, such as it was so far north, was perhaps an exaggeration and was not due until about ten the next morning. Even then, the darkness just became a little less opaque with the sun.

'What a shit place,' Stewart Gandy said to no one and everyone.

'The food's fucking rubbish, as well,' answered Jonty Pitt, laughing.

Finlay knew, by their laconic humour, that spirits were high, despite the prospect of marching something around one hundred miles in appalling weather.

As they moved off again, determined to show its perversity, the weather worsened. The wind picked up and raged itself into a full gale, blowing the ground snow into an almost solid wall of tiny stinging particles. After another two hours of marching, they stopped again. They had travelled a mere two and a half miles. As they huddled down, Finlay said, 'This is bloody hopeless. We must find something to shelter behind. We're using up energy too quickly and for no result.' There was no cover, no shelter whatever, so the group lay down behind their lined-out Bergens, and waited. They managed to doze fitfully, despite the intense cold, until the Arctic dawn glimmered on the northern horizon. The wind had dropped a couple of notches to a gusty force six. There seemed less snow in the air. 'Everybody alive!' asked Finlay. There was no answer. 'Anybody want a brew?'

This time, they all answered. The tiny jelly stove was lit and tea made with melted snow. They ate reconstituted beef stew and wheaten biscuits and suddenly the weather didn't matter. They were full and warm again. They moved off, making better time in the gloomy half light, marching towards the flickering northern horizon. As the storm began to abate, they were surprised by a propeller-driven aircraft roaring overhead. They stopped.

'That sounded like a Herc, Keith,' Proudfoot announced. 'Do the Finns have Hercules?'

'Not that I'm aware. He wasn't that high either, below a thousand feet. The weather must be clearer further south. He must have a job flying in this weather, though.'

'Come to drop something to us, perhaps,' Pitt ventured. 'Them not knowing where we are wouldn't stop the RAF. Anywhere with ten miles, is near enough for those dopey sods!'

'Maybe they dropped another team in to help us out, or cover our backs,' offered Gandy.

'That'll be the day,' Finlay said, in a troubled way. 'I'm beginning to think that maybe we aren't alone. Someone was watching the weather up here pretty closely, to get here as soon as the wind began to drop.'

They debated no further, but as one, began the march north again with more urgency. It was around midday when Finlay, marching at the head of the small column, suddenly stopped and signalled with his hand for the others to get down. Jonty Pitt joined him. 'I hear it too,' he said. 'There's someone ahead of us.' The others of the group joined them.

'Problem?' asked Proudfoot.

'Someone up ahead,' said Finlay. 'Heard some kind of shout.' He removed his radio from a breast pocket. 'OK. Channel E, two bleeps we've made contact, three bleeps we're coming back, one long bleep, come up to us quietly. Got that? Jonty, ditch your Bergen and come with me.'

Pitt and Finlay went forward. Without the weight of the Bergens, they moved easily and quickly. Four hundred yards into their forward move, voices came to them clearly, and they could see the glow of some sort of artificial light. As they crept in closer, Finlay and Pitt struggled hard to control their laughter. In front of them, in a small depression, a group of four men were sitting in various angles, resting around a small jelly stove, guttering into the wind and blowing small yellow flames. One of the group picked quietly at a guitar. The sound of American-accented English reached them. Finlay took his radio and pressed one long bleep. As Pitt and Finlay lay waiting for the others, snatches of conversation reached them, too unconnected to make anything coherent of, but enough to let them know the group were Americans.

'What have we got?' asked Proudfoot quietly. He was breathing heavily.

'America's finest,' Finlay answered. 'Don't know what exactly they are, but they're servicemen.'

'I'll get a bit closer in,' volunteered Pitt. 'Listen to the music.'

Pitt crawled away as the rest strained their ears, trying to make something of the scraps of conversation. Pitt was gone for more than half an hour, before he reappeared, snaking along on his stomach. 'Yankee Seals, armed to the teeth and looking for the same thing as us. They're in uniform for Christ's sake!' he reported. 'That either means the Finns have given them permission to be here, or they just don't give a fuck. Either way, they're fresher than us and better fed, so let's get around them and get some distance between us. I didn't go through last night to have that bunch of wankers beat us. Let's move,' Proudfoot ordered, shoving Finlay's Bergen towards him.

'Mercy sakes! Looks like we got ourselves a race,' whispered Gandy in an arch southern American accent. 'And yo' damn Yankees about to find out what crap yo' is.'

The others sniggered and moved towards the west, to effect the overtaking of their rivals. They marched till six that evening before stopping to rest and fed themselves on their remaining corned beef, wheaten biscuits and soup. They only stopped for little short of an hour and marched on in the dark, until midnight, before resting again.

'Get a fix Simon,' ordered Finlay. 'We'll sleep for four and move out again. We can take a proper rest when it's daylight again. We shall need to keep an eye on our erstwhile cousins. I just keep wondering what's so important about this bloody satellite, that the Yanks would drop a team of blokes on to this terrain to get at it. There's probably nothing left of the thing anyway, or it's down in a lake. As soon as the weather allows, the Finns will chopper up to it and beat the lot of us.'

'Whatever,' said Proudfoot. 'Your boss pulls you away from an important job, sends us away after it, the Yanks drop a team after it, so it's important, yeah? And we ain't letting a team of idiots like the one behind us beat us, are we?'

'Simon, I'm tired, knackered. I've been up here for two months, don't forget. I brought the in team up. The bloke we were bringing out of Russia was important. If the in team mess up and we don't get the Russian, and this lot now proves to be a wild goose chase, I'm going to be fairly pissed off. We ain't even half-way.'

'Oh, for Christ's sake, stop dripping! Where would you be now if you weren't in Finland?' Proudfoot laughed, trying to lighten Finlay's fatalism.

'England. Beginning of spring. Daffodils, new season's lamb with fresh mint sauce and Jersey Royals. Girls stepping out, starting to wear skimpy knickers. Horse coats smelling nice in the sun. That's where I'd be now.'

'And you'd sooner that, than all of this? You must be fucking certifiable,' Proudfoot scoffed, waving his arm at the darkness. 'What girl in skimpy knickers is going to look at you for Christ's sake! You smell like a public lavatory!'

'You'd know about public lavatories then, Simon?' Finlay laughed.

'Fuck off!' snorted Proudfoot. 'You're the lot who live with sodomy and the lash!'

—

Winter walked into Whites to find Rupert Smith already ensconced in the morning room. As though by some unwritten rule, those other members already there moved away, leaving them to discuss the country's secrets.

'Any news yet, John?' asked Smith, knowing it most unlikely.

'None, I'm afraid. Early days yet and the weather's pretty bad up there.' He glanced at his watch. 'Should be getting light up there by now. Well, dimpsy.'

'Dimpsy?' queried Smith.

'It's a word I've heard Finlay use. It beautifully describes the sort of half-light they should be getting now.'

'Well, our American cousins have dropped a team of Navy Seals into the dimpsy, so they must be fairly frantic. I just wonder what they're getting so bothered about.' Smith poured himself another coffee. 'Do you think we should let Finlay know to get a move on?'

'No point Rupert.' Winter waved his hand dismissively. 'My message to Finlay said, get it and return. I know him well enough to know he wants to be in England at this time of year. He'll make the best speed he can.'

Proudfoot was the first awake. He gave Finlay an unceremonious kick. 'Time to wake, sailor. Show a leg or something!'

Finlay groaned, 'Another glorious spring day?'

Pitt and Gandy rose from what little cover their Bergens had given them, variously groaning and complaining of the cold.

'Right! Someone get a brew on. I'll just pop back, and see if the Yanks are on the move.' Proudfoot glanced at his watch. 'No more than three parts of an hour. If I can't find them by then, we've no need to worry.' He walked away into the darkness.

The jelly stove didn't want to function properly, and the tiny kettle wouldn't boil. It looked like being a bad day.

By the time Proudfoot returned, the tea was only just made. He took his tin cupful eagerly. 'You lot go back to bed or something? This is fresh made.'

'Stove played up, Guv,' Pitt volunteered. 'Doesn't like working this far north. Bit like me.'

'We should be there tomorrow, Simon, with a bit of good going,'

Finlay said, looking at his map with his pen torch. 'What were the Yanks doing?'

'Couldn't find them, so they're more than two miles back. Unless, of course, they've got themselves lost, which is always on the cards with that lot!'

They began to pack up ready to move out, when they heard the sound of a rifle. 'How far?' asked Finlay.

'Must be the Yanks,' offered Pitt. 'If you think how far sound carries up here, not too far. Perhaps a couple of miles.'

'I could have missed them,' followed Proudfoot. 'Anyway, they're too close. Let's get on. We need some distance between us.'

They quickly shouldered their Bergens.

'I'll go point, Simon,' Finlay said. 'We'll stop when it gets light. Right, heads down, arses up, away we go.'

The thought of another team making the area of the downed spacecraft before them was enough to put more of a spring in their step, despite their overall fatigue. They marched on until the first glimmer of light appeared under the glowering clouds on the horizon.

'OK,' gasped Finlay. 'Let's have a blow and some quick grub.' The group dropped their Bergens off and began rummaging for food. 'Anyone want a Mars bar?' Finlay offered.

The first bullet passed between him and Pitt. They dropped and scattered almost before the boom of the rifle reached them. 'Can you see anything, Keith?' Proudfoot shouted. There was no immediate answer. 'Keith?'

'North-east Simon, about twelve hundred yards,' Finlay began.

The second bullet threw up flint and ice, about ten yards short.

'About twenty of them, and if they can all shoot like this one, we're in the shit.' Another bullet smashed into the ground about five yards in front of them.

'He's a bit good, Keith,' laughed Proudfoot, clinging to the ground. 'How the fuck is he seeing us? Is there someone closer spotting for the bastard?'

Another bullet passed a foot over them, shredding some willow stems in its path.

'Spread out more,' shouted Finlay. 'Keep your heads down,' he added needlessly, as all four men tried to force themselves further into the frozen ground. Finlay struggled to remove his binoculars from beneath his Arctic clothing. Another bullet slammed into the ground beside him. There followed the boom of the rifle. Finlay rolled sideways and raised his binoculars. As they came into focus he shouted, 'They're Russians!'

'No,' shouted Proudfoot. 'They're pissed-off Russians.' He rolled over on his back, as far as his Bergen would allow, cupped his hands to his mouth and yelled, 'OK you bear shaggers! We ain't gonna pinch your fucking spaceship. We're just helping you to find it!'

A bullet hit the stem of a stunted birch tree, which slowly bent and fell, leaving a large white splintered stump.

'Scatter,' yelled Finlay. 'His spotter will mark that white!'

A bullet hit the ground about three feet in front of Jonty Pitt, driving a shard of flint into his face. Finlay saw the back of his parka hood explode into a shower of blood and kapok. Gandy reached him first and began dragging him from the spot where the last bullet strike had been.

'Bring the medi-kit. He's alive, it's only his face that was hit,' Gandy shouted, but ominously finished his sentence by breathing quietly, 'Oh Jesus!'

When Finlay reached Pitt, he pushed Gandy to one side and removed the remains of Pitt's parka hood. Pitt's face was bleeding heavily from a deep wound running from the left corner of his mouth, across his cheek, almost to his ear.

Finlay could see Pitt's teeth through the wound. 'Hang on Jonty! It's not too bad,' he lied, and began cleaning the wound with part of a field dressing. Pitt gritted his teeth and gasped with the pain. 'It'll sting a bit tomorrow, when it comes round,' joked Finlay. He was amazed to see Pitt's eyes smiling. 'I'll pack it out and clip it together.'

The bullet that tore into Finlay's Bergen almost lifted him from his leaning position over Pitt. 'Simon,' he yelled. 'What are they doing? Are they coming closer? Speak to me!'

'No. One shooting and one spotting from bino's on a tripod. The others are having a smoke,' Proudfoot answered.

'Having a smoke? They're a bit bloody confident. I'm patching Jonty up. He'll be able to move in a bit.'

Another bullet whistled its path just above the crouching Finlay. 'I'm going to be very cross in a minute, Simon. I'll speak very severely to that bastard with the rifle. He's ruined Mummy's photo in my Bergen.'

'I should Keith, I should. You'll be able to tell him face-to-face in about ten minutes. A group of them's broken away and are coming in to see us,' Proudfoot said easily. 'Any suggestions?'

'I need a bit more time, Simon. I've nearly finished. Start shooting at them with your sidearm. Might make them think we're better armed than we are.'

Proudfoot removed his pistol from his parka and fired five shots towards the Russians. The pistol sounded puny after the boom of the rifle. 'Yes! That's really frightened them, Keith! They've stopped, but only because they're paralysed, laughing.' Proudfoot fired another four shots.

'OK! I'm ready with Jonty. Here, Stewart, help me get him up. Simon, come to me. Get Jonty back, lead the Russians on to the Yanks, but don't get involved. Get back to the embassy's summer house and get on to Duckworth. He'll get you a medic up and get you out.'

'And you?' asked Proudfoot.

'I'm going on, alone. Don't argue! Get Jonty back, he's lost a fair amount of blood. But lead this lot on to the Yanks. Give me time to get some distance between us. Now get off quick, before that bastard ranges us again.'

An almost enquiring shot from the Russians whistled over them.

'How do you read the situation, John? We're shooting in the dark, but give me your ideas.' Rupert Smith look troubled.

'Let's invite Bruce Winchester to lunch, Rupert. Pump him gently, offer to help now that we know his lot have run into trouble. We don't have to admit we've someone on the spot,' was all Admiral Winter suggested.

'We don't really know we do have someone on the spot. I must say the Finns have behaved like absolute bricks over this.'

'Did you say bricks?' queried Winter. 'More like the other thing, honestly. They always give in instantly to the Russians. Not the stuff they used to be made of.'

'Perhaps not, John, but if you had an aggressive lot of bastards living next door, you'd try and keep the peace.'

Winter cut Smith off with his laughter. 'Don't forget Rupert, I have an aggressive lot of bastards as neighbours. I do have an inkling of what the Finns feel. They had me up in court for allowing silage effluent to get into the river...'

'I'm quite sure feuding between the landed gentry has its fascinations, but we have one of the worst diplomatic crises on our hands at the moment. Not in Wiltshire, but in Finland!'

'My point is those neighbours still sit next to me at the Riparian owners' meetings. Russia, America and ourselves will sit down with each other, next month, as though none of this ever happened. America's not going to war over two of its citizens being shot by the Russians, any more than we would. The politicians have to make the right noises for home consumption, the same as we would. It's a storm in a tea cup, and a very small tea cup at that. Don't let's make more of it than we have to.' Winter was getting bored with the affair. For him, the extraction of the KGB Colonel was the issue of most importance.

'So why did the Russians think it was our forces they clashed with?' Rupert Smith persisted. 'They also said the British opened fire on them. Would Finlay open fire on foreign nationals, while he himself was on foreign soil?'

'Finlay would defend himself better than most, but he would sooner slope away and keep his head down. Don't worry about Finlay. He's probably close to the area now with the SAS troop, and nobody knows they are there. When in doubt, Rupert, it's generally best to do nothing. Let's see if Winchester would like to dine with us, shall we?'

Winter picked up the internal telephone on his desk. 'Miss Grant. See if you can track down Bruce Winchester and ask him to lunch at thirteen hundred today. If he's free, ask him to present himself at White's as my guest.' He smiled at Smith. 'That'll bring him. Such a class-ridden race, the Americans. Not like us at all.'

He was correct. Promptly at one, Bruce Winchester was ushered into one of the inner sanctums of the British establishment. Winter met him with as much effusiveness as the club's atmosphere allowed. Winchester's American accent caused some sniffs from a few of the older members present. Winter thought there may well be a note from the club's chairman, about bringing colonial types for lunch, but he was after information. Any means justified the end. 'My dear Bruce! How lovely to see you,' began Winter. 'Would you like a drink?' He took Winchester by the elbow and guided him to an opulent leather armchair. Smith watched the charade with inward amusement. A little like watching a cat stalk a mouse.

Winchester asked for a bourbon and branch. The club steward walked away with eyebrows raised. 'A little unpleasantness in Finland Bruce I hear, from our Russian friends. Two dead they tell me.'

Winchester always seemed to wear a puzzled expression. At this moment he looked positively perplexed. 'They had rifles...' he began.

'Ah, they've always had rifles, Mr Winchester,' Smith interjected. 'They've just never shot at Americans before. Any details of what exactly happened?'

'I want to be quite up front with this,' said Winchester. 'They came upon a team of our Navy Seals and started shooting. We didn't have a chance. They even accused us of beginning the shooting, half an hour previously. I mean, our men didn't even know they were there.'

'All seems very odd, Bruce. Not like the Russians. How did your lot get there?' asked Winter.

'We dropped them in, as the weather began to clear...'

'It would have been nice to know, Bruce. You might have told us you didn't need our help, after all.' Winter sounded wounded. 'I was about to send a young officer of mine. I find I have one up there at the moment on holiday. Should I not bother?'

'One?' asked an amazed Winchester. 'You could send one? I sent four and two are dead! Would he be armed?'

'Sidearm perhaps...' Winter looked at Smith. 'Could that be arranged, Rupert?'

'Certainly Admiral. The Finns might prove a little tricky about it. Foreign nationals gallivanting about their country, armed.'

'A sidearm, Admiral!' said Winchester. 'He's going to be a little under-gunned, don't you think?'

'The Royal Navy has a history of being under-gunned, Bruce. It's never stopped them doing their duty and winning though,' Winter said softly. 'If you want my man to help, just say, and he'll be yours. But first you must tell me what he's looking for and why.'

Winchester looked slightly exasperated. 'Admiral Winter, where is this man of yours and what experience has he had?'

'Well Bruce, he's currently waiting my instructions in Ivalo, which as you know is on the spot. As far as experience goes, we choose our officers very carefully. I'm sure our chap will prove up to the task.'

Smith could see that cat had mouse in its claws.

'You said you wanted to be... how did you put it... up front about this. What don't you want the Russians to know? Why the rush to get to the satellite before them? If I'm to help, you must at least tell me that,' Winter cooed. 'Ah, here's lunch at last. We're having the lamb, Bruce. I ordered the same for you.'

'To the slaughter!' thought Smith, passing potatoes to Winchester. 'These are Jersey Royals, Mr Winchester. New season, wonderful taste!'

'It's very difficult, Admiral,' said Winchester, taking the dish of potatoes. 'You see, Washington has made something of a faux pas...'

'Oh really Bruce, do tell. You haven't been giving the Jews something you shouldn't have?'

Winchester looked up sharply. 'You know then, Admiral?'

'Of course we know, Bruce. We've been at this game much longer than you, and we're much better at it. When did you deliver the system?' Winter was guessing, but only Smith knew.

'About a month ago,' Winchester sighed. 'How long have you known?'

'So the Americans have broken the Non-Proliferation Treaty, as we thought you would, and upset the balance in the area. Why, for God's sake Bruce, does the CIA not see any further than the ends of their noses? And now we have a situation which will allow Russia to give the same to Egypt and Syria.'

'They'll have to prove it though,' objected Winchester, almost truculently.

'Not really Bruce,' Winter said. 'If we knew, the Russians knew. The merest whiff of this is going to blow the treaty out of the water.' Winter sighed deeply. 'I don't think this can be kept from our government, Bruce.'

Smith had taken no part yet. 'Let's see if we can keep the lid on a little longer, John. We may yet be able to salvage the situation. After all, we are on the same side.' He gave Winter a look that told him to agree.

'There may well be no film salvageable from the satellite. As I said at the outset, this could all be for nothing.' Winchester had not even convinced himself.

'Could we have your word, Bruce? That you'll leave this to us?' Winter smiled benignly.

'I could not give you such an assurance, Admiral. That goes a long way beyond my remit. We have to make certain the film, if there is one, is destroyed or goes to Washington. I mean, if you lay hands on it, will you hand it over?' Winchester squirmed uncomfortably.

'Oh, surely Bruce.' Winter smiled. He cut some lamb and savoured its flavour. 'With certain provisos. Of course, we should. We have to be certain of the Little King's continued support in the area, for example. Looking at it from a purely British perspective, we get oranges from Israel. The Hashemite Court, however, buys our arms and keeps us informed of Arab intentions. The one makes the other seem somewhat insignificant, wouldn't you say?'

The mouse looked at the cat, knowing the game was up. The cat offered its silken paw. 'I hope you enjoyed lunch, Bruce. We must do it again and soon. Meantime, I'll contact you this evening for your decision about my chap in Ivalo.'

Winter and Smith watched Winchester leave in the direction of Grosvenor Square. 'Contact time for Finlay, I think, Rupert. Now we know, we must have the film, if it exists. I think we must back up Finlay somehow. Perhaps another troop from Hereford.'

Winter's car pulled into the kerb. 'Let's get back to the office Rupert.' He glanced at his watch. 'I wonder where Finlay is right now.'

Finlay was moving faster now. The weather had cleared and there was little wind. A sharp clear night was in prospect. He had cut his load down to the barest minimum. There had been little enough food before the group had split up. Finlay had taken four chocolate bars and some biscuits, preferring that the others, moving more slowly, had enough to eat. Finlay thought he could find enough food, even in this barren place, to get him through the five days he estimated it would take to complete his task.

Though fully aware of the terrain around him, Finlay was day-dreaming as he marched forward. His radio began to vibrate in his breast pocket. He snapped back to reality. Glad enough to stop for a rest, he began the job of extracting the incoming message. It said simply: 'Most immediate. Imperative you get there first and retrieve that which we require. Any way you can. You will be opposed. Respond.'

Finlay sent back: 'Am going as fast as conditions allow. Stop getting in a fuss and holding me up by sending inane messages.'

When Winter was given the message from the communications desk, he was angered by Finlay's tone, but soon began to smile. Only Finlay would take such a liberty, but at least he was sharp and still going forward. The news of the wounded Jonty Pitt and the withdrawal to the embassy's summer house did cause Winter some consternation. The naval attaché in Helsinki had got them over to Oslo and into the Norwegian Military Hospital, their authorities more willing to help than any of their neighbours. Proudfoot and Gandy were just exhausted. Pitt's face was a mess, but nothing the hospital couldn't mend. A Royal Marine Colonel arrived more or less at the same time as them and insisted on a preliminary debrief.

It was his news that was concerning Admiral Winter, as he spoke on the telephone to Rupert Smith. 'Finlay has gone on alone, Rupert.

With barely any food and he has not responded to the daily contact message.'

'It wouldn't be the first time he's refused to stay in touch, John. Is the wireless room confident the messages are reaching him?' asked Smith.

'No way of telling for absolute certain. The transmissions are going out and the wireless room's fairly certain Finlay's receiving them. There's no way of knowing whether somebody else has his kit and is receiving what we're sending.'

'His past record on staying in contact is pretty poor but let's not worry yet. He must be fairly close to the crash site by now. As far as his food supply is concerned, that's not something I'd worry about. Finlay could live where a fox might starve. I think perhaps we should contact his chum, Husoysund, in Bergen. Tell him Finlay may be in touch, looking for help. What do you think?' Smith asked.

'I'll get someone round from the embassy to have a word with him. Good idea, Rupert!'

It was almost light the next morning when Finlay arrived in what was supposed to be the satellite's crash area. He was cold, bone-weary and hungry. He decided, after some sleep, he would lighten down even further and anything he couldn't carry on his actual person, he would ditch, Bergen included. He cast about in his immediate area to find the largest patch of scree available to him. He reasoned if he was going to be opposed, he needed to stay aware of his opponents, but he still needed sleep. Sleeping on what loose scree was available, he would have warning of anyone's approach. He looked about in the lightening gloom and thought, only by accident would anyone stumble over him.

Before settling down, he ate one of his remaining Mars bars, carefully replacing the wrapper in what he termed his rubbish bag and putting it in his Bergen. Next, he checked that a round was chambered in his pistol. The holding band on his knife, strapped to his calf, was loose and using his Bergen as a makeshift pillow, he tried for some sleep.

It was wholly instinct that saved him. His eyes flicked open in time to see the figure above him descending and the downward sweep of the knife. It bit heavily into Finlay's forearm and a huge strong hand tightened around his throat with the downward pressure of his assailant's weight. He felt his left arm being tugged and pulled, before his instinct for self-preservation took over and he struggled to lift his leg to get his own knife from its sheath. Suddenly, it was there in his hand and sweeping sideways into his assailant's ribs. He felt his attacker tremble as with the second sweep, Finlay's knife buried itself in the neck above him. A spray of warm blood blinded Finlay before he fainted.

When his consciousness returned, he could hardly breathe. His attacker lay on top of him, his dead weight on Finlay's chest. It took some time before he could wriggle out from beneath the body. His left arm was refusing to work and lay numb at his side. When eventually he could sit up, he saw the haft of his attacker's knife proud of his forearm, the point protruding from the other side just below his elbow. He could feel his blood running from his fingers, his own knife embedded in his attacker's neck. Finlay started to shake. Somewhere, in his mind, he knew this to be shock. He became unclear about what to do. He knew the heavy knife in his arm had to be removed, but the medical training he had received told him deep puncture wounds had to be treated with utmost respect. Removing the knife might cause irreparable damage. He studied it closely. His fogged-up mind registered his attacker had lost his life, because the serrations in his knife blade, near its haft, had caught in the tough wax cotton threads of Finlay's parka. It still looked hopelessly caught. Finlay pondered how to remove it. He absently touched the knife's handle. This was enough to make him vomit with pain. The remains of the chocolate bar lay in a sticky mess on the scree. His mind jerked back to reality. The knife had to come out, no matter what the risk. He struggled with his teeth to remove the mitten on his right hand. Once free of it, he leant across the body beside him to remove his own knife. It came out easily, sticky with coagulated blood, which Finlay wiped away on his dead attacker's neck scrim. It was only then that Finlay's assaulted mind saw that he was Russian. But Finlay was not clear enough to make anything significant of this.

With his own knife, he began picking the cotton threads away from the knife in his arm, until he judged it free. He studied the angle closely, trying to remember where arteries, veins and tendons would be. Then he decided. He pushed the blunt side of the knife's blade towards his hand, jerked it free, and flung it from him. His head spun briefly before he passed out.

The sound of helicopter blades, chopping the clear Arctic air, woke him with a start.

'What now?' his mind questioned him. He lay where he was and listened. The aircraft was landing somewhere to the east of him. He turned over on his stomach and gasped at the pain in his left arm. The fog of unconsciousness left him instantly. Raising himself up slightly, he looked across the barely sloping tundra and saw a helicopter with Finnish markings, landed about four hundred yards away. He watched the crew descend from the aircraft and make obviously to prepare a meal. Finlay relaxed a little and decided to check on his wounded arm. It was, he knew, deeply hurt. His left hand felt numb, which worried him. He tried to flex his fingers, but they refused to work, and the attempt made fresh blood flow.

With some difficulty, he removed his parka and the various layers of wool, until the only covering of his torso was his heavy silk underwear. He gently pulled this back from his wrist, groaning, until the wound was exposed. The cold freezing air attacked the deep tissue and renewed the intense pain.

It had stopped bleeding at least. He reached for the medi-kit in his Bergen and began the process of repair. With only his teeth and right hand in use, he managed awkwardly to clean, dust with antibiotic powder and bandage the area. Finlay knew his left arm was badly disabled. He hoped it wasn't permanent. He dressed again and thought about his next move. Common sense told him to approach the Finns, get himself back and take the flak from Winter for putting his government in the embarrassing position of having to admit using Finnish territory for an espionage mission, without permission.

The thought was tempting. The aircrew from the helicopter seemed to be enjoying their meal, and seemed in no particular hurry to win the race for the downed satellite. 'Sod it all!' Finlay thought. 'I'm going to be out of food. I've probably lost the use of my arm...'

But Finlay did not have to decide. From across the tundra he heard the high-pitched whine of an aero engine start. He crawled off the scree and into the scrub to hide. Soon he heard the blades begin to churn, then the dull roar as the aircraft became airborne, and to Finlay's surprise, it rose, turned south to fly back towards civilization.

Finlay rose and went to the dead Russian. He began going through the man's pockets, until he found what he was looking for. Cigarettes. He had smelt tobacco on the Russian's breath. He lit one, and almost gagged on the strong harsh taste of the tobacco. His brain began to swim pleasantly as the nicotine entered his system. He patted the dead Russian on the arm. 'It's an ill wind, Ivan. Now where did you leave your Bergen, old chum, before you thought you'd top me?'

Finlay rose and studied the ground, eventually finding it. He rifled through it, taking chocolate, another packet of cigarettes, and a pre-packed dehydrated meal. A rifle lay on the ground next to the Bergen. He emptied it of ammunition and bent it over a protruding rock with a series of sharp blows. His left arm ached intolerably as he tried to lift his Bergen over his shoulders. Failing, he slung it on his right shoulder and began his search.

For two days Finlay quartered the area slowly, finding nothing. He studied it closely through his binoculars, but could see nothing that led him to think he was even in the right place. Several times he had to hide quickly from helicopters criss-crossing the area, which told him that the missing satellite had still not been found. It was only after re-dressing the wound in his arm and finding the area inflamed, he decided that enough was enough. He would abandon his search and make his way out of Finland.

That night, taking a bearing from the stars, he elected to make his way to Narvik in Norway, by way of Ivalo, hoping to steal a car there and get out quickly. Once in Norway, he thought the home run would be easy. He had friends in Norway, many friends, and England would be the next stop.

He emptied his Bergen in preparation for travelling light and quickly, taking only what scant food he had, his gun, knife and money. A small tobacco tin in which he kept what he thought of as his survival kit – matches, nylon fishing line, a couple of small fly spoons, ordinary fish hooks and a small pack of sealed glucose tablets he also pocketed. His communications equipment he smashed between two rocks until it was unrecognizable and placed the maps under a flat rock. He was ready to move, but decided first to sleep for a couple of hours, to arrive, he hoped, in Ivalo at about four in the morning, when he judged all good Finns would be asleep. It was therefore with much disappointment that Finlay found he had slept for about ten hours when he awoke. He had lost another day and he knew he did not have enough margin of food for this. His arm was now badly swollen, and looked very inflamed despite the re-dressings and antibiotics the wound had received. The last time he had changed the dressing, it had begun to smell unhealthily and there was nothing left in the medi-kit of any help. He removed the soiled dressing to see if there was any deterioration and did not like what he saw. He knew within forty-eight hours at most, septicaemia would set in, and that would be the end.

'I'll get across to Ivalo, and present myself to the local police, and bugger the consequences,' Finlay thought. The decision made, he rose and began what he judged to be a fifteen-mile trek. He crossed a small ridge and began to walk down a long slope. On his right, he could see much higher ground as a black shape. Confident now of his position, he quickened his pace. As the light grew steadily, he changed his line of march once, before the stars disappeared, and was about to halt for a rest and a smoke, when a ptarmigan exploded from under his feet. Momentarily Finlay was startled. His heart knocked quickly. 'Christ!' he swore. 'Getting jumpy.' It was then he saw further forward of him the disturbed soil and broken scrub, and knew he'd found the satellite.

The news that Finlay's communicator was no longer receiving was not what Winter wanted to hear. They were, he knew, utterly reliable anywhere in the same hemisphere as the transmitting station. So he judged Finlay to be in trouble.

'He'll still be all right, John,' Smith said confidently. 'Every machine fails at some stage.'

'Why does he do this? Every time Finlay is out on a job, we lose contact with him. Every bloody time!' Winter banged his hand on the desk.

'That's why I'm not worried, John. It's just the way he is. His way of thumbing his nose at authority. Always has been. I wonder he bothers to take any sort of communication with him.'

'Well, if he comes back from this one, I'm going to ground the arrogant bugger...' Winter began pacing the room, rubbing his forehead with the flat of his hand. 'If he ever gets back, I'll see the bastard never leaves England again!'

'That would seem like a reward, John!' laughed Smith. 'Post the bugger down to the Falklands.' He thought for a moment. 'That wouldn't do either. He'd think he was in Heaven. Spend his time fishing. Did you get in touch with Husoysund?'

'Yes. Claimed he'd heard nothing from Finlay in a year. Bloody liar!' Winter snorted.

'Goes with the job, John. Might pay to keep an eye on Husoysund. Do the Americans know he's Finlay's chum?' asked Smith.

'Doubtful. The Americans barely recognize that Norway exists, except as a holding place to counter any move by the Russians.'

'It's not a lot of good worrying, John. I'll perhaps get someone to keep an eye on Hosoysund's home,' Smith said.

'How do you do that, Rupert? Everyone knows everyone else in Norway. Any stranger stands out like a sore thumb. I think we might send a frigate up on a courtesy visit though. It was ever a good run ashore, and if Finlay makes it back there, he'll have immediate passage home.'

'He's in Finland, John. Not Norway. Aren't we jumping the gun a little? Who says he's heading for Norway, anyway?' Smith questioned.

Winter moved to the wall map. 'This was where he was, last time we sent a message.' Winter's finger traced a circle south of Ivalo. 'We know he received the communication. Granted, he didn't respond. Where else could he go? My own feeling is he'll head for Narvik.'

'Send a frigate to Narvik then, John,' suggested Smith. 'You can show the flag in Narvik, just as well as in Bergen.'

'Hardly Rupert! That would upset the FCO. Would look like triumphalism. Rubbing the Jerries' noses in it. And for goodness' sake, we mustn't upset them. They're our new partners in Europe,' Winter said, with heavy sarcasm. 'We can't have one of the Leanders passing wrecked German destroyers from the last lot. Might bring out the worst in some of our matelots.'

Smith laughed. 'Sod the FCO! Bunch of spineless bastards. Go on John, order a ship up there.'

'We'll see,' mused Winter.

Finlay began quartering the crash site, not really knowing what he was seeing or even looking for. The satellite had hit the top of the slope, bounced on the frozen earth, smashing itself to pieces, before the larger parts rolled downwards. Starting at the top, Finlay began examining the pieces as he moved down the slope. Another ptarmigan flew away from Finlay's feet. He smiled as he realized why they were there, after the food. It was with some triumph that Finlay found the flattened rugby ball. He studied it carefully. Badly knocked about, what electrical connections there had been were either burnt or torn out. He tried to open it with his knife, but couldn't. He threw it into the air, caught it and stuffed it into the poacher's pocket of his parka. 'Right Keith,' he said, out loud to himself. 'Let's get home.'

There was a definite spring in Finlay's step now. He was pleased and just hoped the flattened rugby ball had been worth all the trouble. He marched as briskly as the terrain would allow and, breasting another rise, could see the outline of the hills that sheltered Ivalo forward of his position. What light there had been that day would soon be fading, and Finlay decided to make the best speed his throbbing arm would allow. He almost jog-trotted down the side of the valley, until his now coursing blood made his arm just too uncomfortable. He stopped and lit one of the cigarettes he had taken from the dead Russian.

It was like a blow from a sledgehammer that swept Finlay's feet from under him. He heard the boom of a rifle before he hit the ground and rolled twice, so he knew he was alive. He lay still and watched the blood bubbling from a hole in the instep of his boot. His heart was pounding and the pain in his arm seemed intolerable. Just below the rise he had so recently come over, he saw a figure start coming towards him. Quickly, he cupped a handful of the bubbling blood and dropped it on his own temple. Finlay's anger was livid.

As the figure approached, through his lightly closed eyes and lashes, he watched as the figure came within five yards. Seeing the blood on Finlay's head, the figure shouldered the rifle and approached, confident Finlay was dead. Bending over him, Finlay smelt the other human's fear, before he swept his only good arm into a savage arc, his clenched fist making a satisfying crunch as it made contact with a now broken cheekbone. Savagely, Finlay struck the face again, and dragging his knife from its sheath, made to stab the now lying figure. He dragged back the hood of his attacker's parka to make certain of stabbing the right place. He was suddenly aware that his attacker was a woman. The girl lay unconscious, a large greenish bruise forming on her damaged face. Finlay rose heavily and kicked the inert figure hard in the ribs.

'You stupid bitch!' he raged. He kicked her again. 'Wake up you dopey cow!'

The girl slept on. Finlay removed her rifle, emptied the ammunition, removed the bolt and threw it away in disgust. He thrashed the frozen ground with the rifle, until its stock shattered. He threw the barrel and action away from him. He roughly searched the girl for more weapons, and removed a small Beretta pistol from a rear holster. Again, he unloaded it and threw the magazine one way and the rest the other. His anger dissipated slowly as he searched the girl's backpack. There was nothing to show him who or what she was. He leant across her and gathered a handful of snow and let it trickle over her face. Her eyes flickered open briefly and she lapsed back into unconsciousness again. Her mouth fell open and her breathing rattled in her throat. Finlay gathered more powdery snow and filtered it into her mouth. 'You'll either choke or wake, girlie!' he said easily.

The girl half rose, choking and coughing.

'Nice try, girlie. Thought you were playing possum. Now who the fuck are you?' snarled Finlay.

The girl eyed him coldly and said nothing.

He picked up his knife and stroked the point across her face, leaving a deep scratch. She flinched but did not cry out. 'Toughie, are you?' asked Finlay. He hit her with the flat of the blade across her nose. The blood spurted from her nostrils, but still she remained mute.

He pushed her back roughly and held her down with his wounded arm, while he sliced the belt holding up her trousers. He cut the clip holding them together and pulled them down. Gasping with the pain in his arm, he rose and roughly kicked her over on to her stomach. Leaning forward, he roughly pulled her trousers down to the back of her knees, exposing a rather shapely bottom. The girl began to struggle until Finlay struck her again with the flat of the knife. 'Lie still,' he ordered and pulled her knickers around so as to read the label. In the half light he read the name of the maker and the town where they were based, Haifa and Jerusalem. Finlay kicked her over on her back. 'OK! Ruth, Esther or whatever your name is. Why are you trying to kill me?'

The girl eyed him coldly and tried to cover herself.

Finlay knocked her hand away roughly with his knife. 'You've got nothing I want.' He glanced down to see that her pubic hair had been shaved off cleanly. 'You ought to take more time washing the bloody thing. You stink like a whore!' Finlay said. 'You half-French or something?'

She tried again to cover herself and Finlay knocked her hands away. 'You lie there, until your arse freezes to the ground. Then we'll see if you can talk. Why did you try and kill me?' he asked again.

Still she said nothing. Finlay began to admire this tough scrap of humanity. He began talking to her normally, as he went through her possessions, 'Look Esther, normally I would just kill you, but I really need to know what's happening. Everyone I meet lately wants to see me dead, and I don't know why. So why not tell me and we'll see if we can't have a deal.' He produced the rugby ball from his jacket. 'Is this what everybody wants?' he asked lightly. 'What's it worth to Mossad? I could be willing to sell it.'

She eyed the thing in Finlay's hand. He felt she knew what it was. 'Now, I'm going to take my boot off, to see what damage you've done, and you're going to sit very still, or I'll damage you some more.' Finlay removed his boot and sock, now soaked with blood. He turned his foot up and saw a large burnt and scored cut across his instep. 'Glad you underestimated the range so badly, Esther,' Finlay said, glancing up to look at her. 'How's your bum? Frozen yet?' She remained looking straight ahead.

From the pile of her belongings, he extracted a small pack of sanitary towels and proceeded to use one to cover the wound in his foot. He rewrapped the others and put them in a pocket. He sorted and pocketed what food she was carrying. There seemed to be little else of any use. 'You weren't expecting to be up here by the look of your supplies, or have you got someone coming to pick you up?' Finlay wasn't really expecting an answer. 'I suppose your bum is well stuck down by now, so I'll take your boots if you please.'

She couldn't shift her frozen buttocks from the ground. He moved to her feet. 'Just try kicking me once, and I'll slice your nose off.' She lay very still as Finlay cut up through her bootlaces. He removed her boots, all the pieces of the laces and cut through each one in turn. 'Now, Ivalo's over that way, about five miles.' He shoved her roughly over and she yelled loudly as the skin on her buttocks remained on the frozen earth. 'With a very sore bum and boots which can't be done up, you should make it, in, say, three or four hours.'

Finlay got up to leave. The girl lay on the ground sobbing, her backside weeping spots of blood.

'Nothing to say?' he asked, conversationally.

'Cunt!' she spat.

Finlay laughed to himself as he limped away.

Chapter Fifteen

•

February

There was but one thought – Norway – in Finlay's mind as he reached the surrounds of Ivalo. To get there, he needed a car, with fuel. He knew Narvik was some two hundred and fifty miles due west of him, but there was no direct route overland. It would mean something of a trek. North to Tana, south, south-west towards Tromso and thence to Narvik.

He decided to try the small internal airport recently built at Ivalo. Even this early in the year, he reasoned, someone will have left a car, before flying. He wasn't disappointed and chose the inevitable Volvo, easy to break into, but harder to start. The engine turned over slowly; the sump oil, thickened by the cold, seemed unwilling to let the engine turn freely. Eventually it caught and fired into life. The fuel gauge indicated three-quarters full. This was enough to get him into Norway, but barely enough to get him to Tromso, where the next petrol station would be. With his left arm in such a bad way, he did not want to get stuck anywhere in Norway's mountains.

The road sign said Hammerfest three hundred and two kilometres as Finlay left Ivalo. He knew it was roughly half that distance to the main road between Tana and Tromso. It was going to be a long drive. Some eighteen hours later, Finlay drove into Tromso, tired, sick and out of fuel. The journey had been made slow by his arm, which was now very swollen.

The whole town was seemingly closed for winter. Eventually he found a petrol station. It was firmly shut. He waited and slept in the car, the cold biting into him. The garage proprietor arrived and filled the Volvo with fuel. As there was nothing else open, in the way of food shops, Finlay carried on to Narvik. At least Narvik was awake when he eventually drove into the town, such a town as it was. He left the car parked near the harbour front, and walked back. Some of the local people stopped and stared, and it wasn't until Finlay caught sight of himself in one of the tiny shop windows that he understood why. He was, in his own words, 'in shit state'.

A small guest house, just off the town centre, a place where he had stayed before, was where he headed and he was relieved to see the windows ablaze with light. The house belonged to Mrs Inger Daniellsönn, GC, something of a legend in the Royal Navy. A whisker short of six feet tall and now close on her pension, she had been a classic Nordic beauty in her time. Her hair, once a dark rich auburn, was now heavily streaked with grey, her voice a deep contralto when she sang sad Norwegian folk songs. In her thirties she was every sailor's fancy.

When the Germans invaded Norway, Inger and her husband joined the Resistance and Eric Daniellsönn had paid with his life. During and after the two Narvik battles, Inger Daniellsönn had helped with the British wounded. After they left, she had sheltered, at risk to her own life, five English sailors left behind in the rush to leave. Before helping to get them all to neutral Sweden, she had bedded them; in her own clipped English: 'Food was rationed, but love wasn't.' She was pleased to find she was pregnant, after the British left, by which sailor she couldn't know, so she called her son Eric Pompey Daniellsönn. And when in 1947 she was called to Buckingham Palace for the investiture of her George Cross, she had told The King her story and presented her son as 'a gift from grateful allies'. Finlay adored her and when she had glanced up, on a previous visit, and caught him admiring her, she said, 'Such a look some years ago would have made me cream my knickers, but now I'm too old for ship-wrecked sailors to rest between my legs.'

Inger did not recognize him at first, but after expressing some hor-ror at the way he looked, almost dragged him inside. After kisses and many 'tut, tut's he asked to use the telephone. As the connection was made and Lars Husoysund answered, Finlay felt he was home and dry.

'Where the goodness are you, Keith?' his friend asked. There was relief in his voice.

'Narvik Lars, at Mrs Daniellsönn's. I'm ill, I've been stuck through the arm and it's gone septic.'

'Winter has already been on to me. For Christ's sake, Keith! Do you know what you've got?'

'Yes, like I said Lars, a very badly damaged arm,' Finlay replied, a little impatient that his friend didn't seem to be listening.

'The thing you picked up in the mountains is red-hot, Keith. They'll kill you to get it, I'm going to fly up now. I've had an aircraft on stand-by since your Admiral telephoned. If you are badly hurt get Mrs Daniellsönn to get the doctor. Pay him to keep his mouth shut. Just stay where you are. I'll be there in three hours.' He rang off.

For the first time in three months Finlay bathed. He looked at his various wounds and winced. His foot seemed to be healing well enough, but his left arm looked as though hospital was going to be its only saviour. When he was clean and shaved, he presented himself to Mrs Daniellsönn in the borrowed dressing gown she had left him. 'I wonder if you could get the doctor to call,' he asked. 'I've had something of an accident with my arm. It needs some professional help.'

The lady made her usual clicking noises with her tongue. 'You forget young man, I came through the last war, when the accursed Germans overran this place. I'll get the doctor, but you'll need to pay him. I'll call him now.'

'Of course. Lars is coming up to collect me. You remember Lars, of course, from Bergen. Is there any chance of something to eat, Mrs Daniellsönn?' Finlay realized he was hungry.

'Another five minutes and your dinner will be ready, young man. I know what you English are like. Bath, food and then sex if you can get it!' She laughed at her own joke and smiled fondly at the memory. She rose lightly from her chair. 'I've kept some old clothes stored from all those years ago. I'll take yours and wash them. You can wear some of the others. I don't suppose they're coming back for them now.' Her face, lined but still beautiful, took on a wistful look. 'The damned Germans shot my husband, along with nineteen other men of the town, and now they come on holiday in the summer. We took in their starving children, fed them and looked after them. Some of those same children took part in the invasion. Horrible people.' She went to prepare Finlay's food, and left him wondering at the resilience of the Norwegians, thanking God he was English with the North Sea and English Channel to separate his country from the curse of Europe.

He followed her into the warm kitchen, which smelled of burning paraffin and hot food. Mrs Daniellsönn bade him sit and pushed a plate of stew with dumplings to him. 'Who are you running from young man?'

Finlay wolfed down his food, as Mrs Daniellsönn hovered over him with another helping ready. After he had finished, she shoved him into her best room overlooking the town and handed him a packet of English cigarettes.

'Please smoke. I like the smell in the house and it reminds me of my husband.' Such philosophical sadness tore at Finlay's heart.

He was sound asleep when the doctor arrived, who took one look at his arm and sonorously declared, 'Young Englishman, you need to go to hospital. What I can do with your arm is very little.'

'I can't do that. You must do what you can to make it comfortable and stop the infection. I must leave for England today. Just stop it getting worse for twenty-four hours.'

'If this is your wish,' the doctor said to Finlay. 'Come into the other room.'

The doctor opened up the wound without too much ceremony, bathed it, redried it and re-dressed it. The wound in Finlay's foot was painful but clean and apart from re-dressing it, the doctor seemed satisfied.

When Finlay offered to pay for the treatment, the older man seemed almost offended. 'We owe the English, young man, and always will. So what will you do now? I have a car if you need to go anywhere.'

'Someone is coming for me, Doctor,' Finlay assured him. 'I'll just rest up for a while, until he arrives.'

'He will need to come soon, Finlay,' Mrs Daniellsönn said, going to the window. 'It's snowing again.'

Lars Husoysund arrived in a flurry of snow and noise; even without his great bulk he would have filled the room. 'Ho, you mad English bastard!' he swore, shaking Finlay's hand. He grabbed Mrs Daniellsönn, pulling her to him, kissing her fully on the mouth, his hand wandering to her bottom. 'Still beautiful Inger!' he announced, now shifting his attention to her left breast.

Inger Daniellsönn swore at him in Norwegian, but didn't shift his hand. 'You boys are all the same. I had your father three times in a night, pushing his great beard between my legs, and now I have to have the son. Get your hands away from my chest. There's nothing there for you.' But she pushed her hips hard into him.

'You had my father, Inger? The old bugger. It's a good job my mother didn't know!'

Inger Daniellsönn laughed in her deep-throated way. 'She was in the next room, sleeping like the babe she was. I had a job to walk the next day.'

Without releasing Mrs Daniellsönn, Husoysund turned to Finlay. 'You look better than I expected, Keith, so it's thanks to Inger again. You might think you've saved the world, but it's women like Inger who make it worth saving.'

Inger Daniellsönn protested that she had only done what any other person would have done.

Ignoring the protests, Finlay left five hundred dollars under the clock on the mantelpiece. 'It was given to me to use, so you must take it. Anyway the dumplings were worth that much at least,' he told her.

'We must go, Keith,' Husoysund insisted. 'I've brought some gear up for you to wear. Dress now. I'll go and hire a car somewhere, or even steal one. There'll be no flying back in this weather.'

An hour later, they were heading south in a car Husoysund had seen for sale in the local garage forecourt. 'A bit precipitous Lars, buying the bloody thing...' started Finlay.

'That bloody camera you've got, Keith, means we have to stay on the move. Have you any idea what this is about?' He emphasized 'any'.

'Not a bloody clue, Lars! I only know that everybody seems to want it, or is it they want me dead? Do you know?' Finlay asked.

'The Americans have given the Israelis a delivery system for their atom bomb, broken the spirit of the non-proliferation treaty, and the Russians want the proof you've got in your pocket. But the Americans are our biggest problem at the moment. They'll stop at nothing to get it.'

Finlay recounted the various attempts on his life in the past five days, expanding only on his brush with the Israeli girl.

Husoysund couldn't stop laughing. 'You let her bum get frozen Keith? That's properly making use of local conditions, as our training manuals tell us!'

Finlay laughed. 'I was getting pissed off with the whole bloody thing. I don't mind somebody taking a crack at me, but I do like to know why. What did Winter have to say for himself?'

'Didn't speak to him. He got the information to me by way of Ewan, the attaché in Oslo. The Russians killed two of the Seals, before reason prevailed. The SAS trooper's face was a bit of a mess and the Finns found a dead Russian who'd been stabbed twice. They put that down to the Americans, and have lodged a pretty strong protest. Whether the Israeli girl got back, I don't know, but don't worry about that...'

Finlay snorted. 'I shan't Lars. If she didn't make it back, she shouldn't have gone there in the first place.'

Later that day they stopped for the night in Mosjöen. The little Saab that Husoysund had purchased easily ploughed its way through the snow that covered the old coastal road. 'Better going in the morning, Keith,' announced Husoysund. 'The snow will be gone by then.'

Finlay grunted non-committally, but knew better than to question a native's knowledge of the weather.

They dined and slept well, in a small hotel which Husoysund persuaded the owner to open to them, even though it wasn't the season. And true to Husoysund's prediction, the next morning dawned bright and sunny. The small town's streets were awash with slush and melting snow.

'How did you know?' asked Finlay over breakfast, alluding with his eyes towards the morning sun.

'Listened to the weather forecast on the way up,' Husoysund smirked. 'And of course, we're further south. Lunch in Trondheim, this evening Bergen. I know a lovely fish restaurant in Trondheim, Keith...'

Finlay cut him short. 'Meat, Lars, meat! I need beef. The only thing I like that comes from water is boiled eggs!'

'That's what makes you English so savage, my friend. Too much meat... wasn't it what the Beadle said in *Oliver Twist?*'

They both laughed. Old friends, they were easy in each other's company. The trust between them was complete.

The road from Mosjöen towards Trondheim was almost what Finlay termed a main road and travelled alongside the railway which ran north to south in Norway. The green of the spruce trees, losing their cloaks of snow, was almost startling and the tarmac road began to dry in smoky wisps.

'Don't you just love Norway, Lars?' exclaimed Finlay. 'Christ, it really is so bloody beautiful. I could live here you know.'

'Leave your precious England!' Husoysund shook his head vigorously. 'Anyway, you have to be tough to live up here. We eat fish as well.'

They travelled on in silence for a few miles.

'Look!' exclaimed Husoysund. 'A fish eagle.' They were both craning their necks to keep the bird in sight as the car swept around a tight right-hand bend, and the first bullets slammed into the Saab. Husoysund swore in Norwegian as the car slewed off the road and slammed into the roadside bank. Finlay had his door open instantly and instinctively dived out, pulling Husoysund with him.

'This side, Lars. For Christ's sake, get down behind a wheel!'

More bullets slammed into the car.

'I'm pissed off! Who the fuck are these bastards? Can you make it to those logs?'

Finlay was struggling to chamber a round into his gun. Husoysund backed away from the car on his stomach and, with one quick roll, made the corner of some spruce boles left from the previous year's cutting. His movement occasioned another fusillade of shots. Finlay started to back away from the car until he, too, was level with the tree trunks.

'Distract them, Lars,' he hissed.

'How?' Husoysund said, almost normally.

'I don't know. Shout to them. Throw something at them, but do something.'

'You are rotten bloody shots!' shouted Husoysund.

Bullets began burying themselves in the spruce, throwing large splinters into the air, allowing Finlay the moment to roll behind the logs.

'"You're rotten bloody shots!"' mimicked Finlay, in Husoysund's sing-song English. 'They think you're taking the piss!'

'You're here are you not?' Husoysund sounded peeved. 'Don't be so bloody pedantic Keith.' They both started to laugh.

'OK,' shouted Finlay. 'Who d'you think you are? Dick-fucking-Turpin?' He whispered to Husoysund. 'How many did you see?'

'I think it was three,' Husoysund said easily.

'Haven't you got a gun for Christ's sake, Lars?' asked Finlay, looking at his friend brushing spruce needles from his trousers.

'No, of course not. I'm at home. But I'm still getting very angry!' He shouted towards the other car. 'Listen you fucking gringos! This is your last chance. Fuck off now and we shan't say anything!'

Finlay couldn't stifle his laughter.

A voice from where the bullets were coming from shouted back. 'OK Brit! Give us what we want and you and the troll can walk away.' He emphasized his point with more bullets.

'That's it!' shouted Husoysund. 'Nobody calls me a troll and lives. You got that, you cocksucking Yank!'

He was answered by another stream of bullets.

'OK! OK!' shouted Finlay. 'You've made your point. You can have it.' He removed his jacket and threw it, half-way between the spruce logs and the American's car. He nodded to Husoysund. 'It's in the jacket, Yank,' he yelled.

Husoysund crawled towards the Americans, keeping well down behind the logs. They both listened.

'Stay down Brit. We're coming to get the jacket. If it ain't there, you're both dead men.'

'Come and get it, we not even armed, for Christ's sake,' Finlay yelled.

Finlay and Husoysund waited, listening. They heard footsteps on the tarmac surface. Finlay nodded to Husoysund who briefly showed his head from behind the logs and shouted, 'Trick or treat prats!'

Finlay rose above the logs and shot a very surprised American between the eyes. The answering fusillade of bullets was immense.

Husoysund came crawling back. 'Get him?' he asked.

Finlay put on his most theatrical look of surprise. 'I fired didn't I?'

They could hear mumbled conversation, and then a shout. 'You're dead! Do you know that? We know who you are, Finlay. We can get the troll any time.'

'You bastards just won't learn, will you?' yelled Husoysund. 'You think a couple of machine pistols frighten us? They would perhaps if you fucking Yanks knew what to do with them.'

Another batch of bullets slammed into the logs, achieving nothing.

'Where's the tank on a Ford, Lars?' asked Finlay.

'Strung between the back springs generally,' Husoysund said, catching up with Finlay's idea.

Finlay crawled along beneath the logs towards the American car and snapped three bullets into where he thought the fuel tank would be. Nothing happened. Husoysund motioned to him with his hand, urging him to shoot again. Finlay shook his head and pointed to the pistol's magazine and put up three fingers.

'You haven't any bullets left!' yelled Husoysund in mock disbelief.

'You won't catch us that way, Troll. We ain't that bloody stupid!' an American yelled.

'Fucking near though, you dumb bastards,' Finlay answered, scuttling back to his companion.

'You got any matches, Lars?' he asked. He grinned evilly. 'There's petrol running down the road towards us.'

Husoysund patted his pockets and produced some matches. 'What kind of bloke runs out of bullets?' He crept away to his right and took a quick look around the ends of logs. His temerity was answered by another stream of bullets. He nodded to Finlay, struck a match and threw it. He looked at Finlay and shook his head. He threw another match and again shook his head. He tried again. This time, he ducked quickly behind the logs. There was a yell of warning from the American and a satisfying boom of exploding petrol.

Finlay rose from behind the logs and took in the situation at once. He snapped a shot at the one man standing and saw him spin away. The other man was screaming horribly, a pillar of flame. Finlay sprinted across the road. The man on fire stumbled towards him, arms outstretched. Finlay shot and killed him. The other man was slumped against the roadside bank, blood oozing from his left shoulder and trying, with his right hand, to reach the machine pistol lying on the grass. His eyes met Finlay's as Finlay shot again. The hand clawing for the machine pistol stopped moving and relaxed.

Husoysund walked up beside the dead man and said, 'Told you not to call me a troll. You had your chance and you blew it.' He looked at the dead man burning, and threw up noisily. They surveyed the scene around them. 'A short sharp action was fought...' said Husoysund.

They got the Saab going again, drove around the burning Ford, and under Husoysund's guidance, Finlay let it drop back on to the burning car. As the Saab's rear end crashed into the flames, Finlay jumped clear. 'Bloody hoofing it again,' he swore.

'Have you got that pack of Ruskie cigarettes Keith?'

Finlay nodded, and handed it to the Norwegian, who dropped them near one of the bodies, pushing it into the roadside mud with his foot. 'Give me your gun,' he ordered. Taking it, he wiped it clean and then bent the dead fingers of the last man to die around it. Then he threw it down, near the body. 'It won't fool anybody for long,' he remarked. 'Enough to confuse the issue, until I can get it cleared up. You ready to move?'

There was, thought Finlay, something painfully wasteful about killing another human being. During any engagement, the adrenalin rush was tremendous. He often said it was the biggest high possible. Afterwards, it was different. Sometimes friends were killed or horribly maimed. All enemies look insignificant when they're dead.

'You ready, Keith?' Husoysund repeated. 'We ought to move. The midday train will come past soon and this lot will be reported when it stops at Trondheim.'

They walked into the spruce until they found a ride between the trees that allowed them to continue towards the south. 'How the hell did they know where we were, Lars? They were waiting, for Christ's sake,' Finlay said.

'Deduction, anticipation, luck or they have some way of tracking,' Husoysund mused. 'Have you looked properly at that part you've got?'

'No, not at all, really. I tried briefly to open it. Let's have another go at the bloody thing.'

Finlay produced the camera. It looked malignant in his hand. Husoysund took it from him and studied it closely. He turned it over again and studied it from every angle. 'No, we should want a drill and cutting gear...'

'Or a big rock, Lars. Give the bloody thing here!' Finlay said, taking it back. He looked around himself and walked to an outcrop of rock. Selecting one he could manage with one hand and using another as his anvil, he struck it sharply on its edge. 'It might have some kind of booby trap. Had you thought of that, Keith? What if you damage the film?' Husoysund asked.

Finlay ignored him and struck at the elongated sphere more sharply.

'Come out of the way, you stubborn bloody Englishman,' Husoysund said wearily. He pushed Finlay to one side and wedged the sphere between two rocks on its edge. He looked around until he found a large lump of rock he could hardly lift. Struggling with it manfully, he brought it above his head and pounded it down on to the Russian equipment. The elongated sphere split down a seam.

'Now get your knife in there, Keith, see if you can lever it apart,' Husoysund said triumphantly.

'Hit the bloody thing again Lars. I'm not snapping my knife blade in that. It's the only weapon we've got between us. If it goes ratshit, so be it.'

Husoysund struggled and lifted the rock again, smashing it down. The sphere gave up its contents. It popped apart to show the terminal ends of connecting wires, something that looked to Finlay like a capacitor, and a smaller version of the sphere itself.

'OK. Lars! Which is the important bit?' asked Finlay.

'The two main parts are not connected,' reasoned the Norwegian. He picked up the smaller sphere, studied it, shook it and placed it against his ear. 'Nothing,' he announced. 'Look, this thing that looks like a capacitor. That's the bit that's powered. The bit you've got is totally separate. No power to or from. Just sort of brazed on to the inside of the shell. My best estimate would be this is the thing everybody wants.' Finlay weighed the cylinder in his hand. 'And this is the tracker, if in fact there is one. If I'm wrong, then we will get waylaid again. If I'm right we're home free. This other bit we can float down a stream, or chuck it on the midday train. What do you think?'

'Sounds good to me, Keith. We make a little raft and let it float down to Trondheim. That's the way the streams and rivers run this far south. Meanwhile, we fuck off in a different direction. What about your arm?'

'Well it ain't any worse, but it ain't any better. And I don't see any choice. We haven't anything to defend ourselves with if somebody comes after us again, and this place is going to be buzzing with police when our last little effort gets discovered.'

They walked on for about four miles before they found a fairly substantial stream which Husoysund was sure ended in Trondheim. Together, they constructed a small raft of dead spruce branches snapped from the lower trunks of the growing trees. It looked more like a floating nest of some huge waterfowl, as they pushed it into the swift current of rapidly rising snow-melted water. 'A bit like a Viking funeral, Lars,' Finlay laughed.

'Let us hope it isn't ours, my friend.'

They watched the raft spin away downstream until it disappeared around a bend.

'It's heading in the direction they seem to think we're going,' said Husoysund. 'They'll be on to it fairly quickly, so let's head east. Maybe we can pick up some kind of transport.'

Winter strode through the outside office and into his own, slamming the door heavily behind him. His staff were silent, heads down, giving the impression of committed industry. 'Fetch a dustpan, brush and mop, Sarah,' whispered Miss Grant.

The young girl tiptoed away, to do as she was bidden, as the rest of Winter's staff waited for the inevitable explosion of his temper, which the pacing of his footsteps in his office presaged. Miss Grant began to count under her breath. 'One, two, three, four...'

The sound of cursing and of broken crockery came from Winter's office. Miss Grant began walking towards Winter's door. She was three paces away as it swung open, and Winter yelled, 'Miss Grant, get in here!'

Grant went in and closed the door quietly behind her, went to her usual chair and sat down without being bidden. 'Admiral, there is more tea on its way, with enough sugar, and I do wish you wouldn't let them upset you so.'

'Don't you bloody start!' Winter snapped. He looked at his secretary sitting coolly in front of him, realized he was making a fool of himself and started to smile. 'Amelia, what would life be without you?' he said with genuine affection.

'A series of heart attacks, no doubt, Dick,' she answered demurely.

They allowed each other these small familiarities, which years of working together had brought about, but neither let it interfere with the essential working of the organization.

There was a light tap on the door and a young girl brought in a freshly laid tea-tray and another followed with equipment to clean up the mess.

'Finlay?' she asked, when they were alone again. She said the name with more impatience than distaste.

'Yes, Miss Grant,' Winter answered, formality returning. 'Still no contact and the Foreign Secretary is pushing me for answers.'

Miss Grant sighed heavily.

'I know you two don't get on, but he is generally speaking good at his job. It's just the mayhem that always seems to follow him when he's doing it.' Winter said as he reached for his pipe.

'There are people like that, Admiral. Dunderdale was another of the same ilk. Treated the female office staff at Naval Intelligence as his own and broke hearts and heads everywhere he went.' There was a touch of warmth in her voice.

'Yours, Miss Grant, I mean Dunderdale?' Winter smiled.

'That was all a very long time ago, Admiral. There has been a war and a string of Finlays through Storey's Gate since then. The trouble with this one is that he's never grown up and doubtless will never have the chance to.' She brushed something invisible from her skirt. 'Was there anything specific you wanted me to do, Sir?'

Winter smiled at her warmly. 'See if you can track down Rupert, and get him over here. I think somebody is going to have to go to Finland and find Finlay.'

'No news then, John?' Smith said, as he settled in an easy chair. 'The ructions in Scandinavia have at least allowed us to get Oleg out easily. Wonderful diversion. We've lodged him in Hatfield. Give him a couple of days to settle and then we can see what he has for us.'

'Well, at least that side has gone smoothly. I'm assuming Finlay has the film. I'm also fairly sure that it was Finlay who took out the Americans. The Norwegians have been fairly philosophical about the whole thing, reporting the affair was drugs-related. It would just be nice to know where Finlay is! Then we could send him some help perhaps. It has, after all, been five days since the incident near Trondheim. The only thing that causes me some concern is the fact that one of the Americans apparently had Finlay's gun in his hand. Or rather what I take to be Finlay's gun. Thirty-two-calibre...'

'Who was it registered to?' asked Smith.

'A Frenchman living in Bordeaux,' Winter said.

'Left to sow some confusion. Helps with the drugs story though. Sometimes one gets the distinct impression that Finlay is lifting our legs, John.'

'Oh, he's sharp enough. Too bloody sharp on occasions, but don't think he's trying to save the politicians any embarrassment. He covers his tracks to avoid any flak from me.'

'We are both assuming that he's alive, despite losing his sidearm, and Husoysund is with him perhaps. So I don't think there's anything too much to worry about. What's Bruce Winchester doing? Has he given up on the job?'

'Absolutely convinced the Russians have the film. Very despondent about the whole thing. No doubt, when we produce Oleg, he'll be called back to Washington to explain.' Winter smiled at the thought.

Husoysund was waiting with another Saab when Finlay was discharged from Stockholm's most exclusive private clinic.

'Now that's the way to live, Lars,' he announced, as he walked down the steps. 'Beautiful nurses, good food and pampering like you just would not believe. Beats the hell out of Haslar.'

Husoysund laughed. 'Had a good rest? Arm better now? You great booby! What a fuss you make about a little stab wound.'

'What's the news, anyway?' asked Finlay, ignoring the insult. 'Any fuss about the Americans? I do feel a bit bad about them.'

'They were trying to kill us, for God's sake! No, my boss smoothed it over. I asked him to say nothing about our whereabouts, so we can have a few days R and R if you like.'

They both climbed into the car.

'This stolen, hired or yours, Lars?'

'Hired, Keith. Registered to Avis in Copenhagen. I know it's a little early, but what do you say about trying for a salmon or two?'

'Or even three, Lars,' Finlay said. 'Where's the thingy?'

Husoysund leant over to the back seat and dragged a canvas bag into the front and dropped it on Finlay's lap. 'I've put all this stuff on my American Express. You can pay me back in dollars. The fishing gear, the thingy as you call it, I've wrapped in your spare leaders.'

Four governments' intelligence agencies, perplexed, anxious and impatient, waited for news of the evidence the crashed satellite might or might not have carried, as Husoysund and Finlay discussed suitable flies for their trip.

Chapter Sixteen

•

March

Ten days later, Husoysund and Finlay sat drinking tea in the departure lounge of Oslo Airport, waiting for the BA flight to take Finlay back to London.

'You should be due for some leave after this trip, Keith,' said Husoysund. 'Let's meet in Ireland and catch some fish there. Make use of your new rod, courtesy of the taxpayers.'

'I'll ask,' replied Finlay. 'Winter gets a bit stirred up about going on leave suddenly, at short notice.'

The airport address system announced the last call for Finlay's flight and they walked to the relevant check-in.

'Let me know the outcome, Keith,' Husoysund said, as they shook hands. 'Get back here soon. You're rotten company on the job, but I'd sooner fish with you than anyone.'

Three hours later Finlay paid off the taxi that had taken him to St James's and it was with some trepidation that he asked the receptionist to call Winter to let him know he had arrived.

'You're to go straight up, Lieutenant Commander. The Admiral will see you straight away,' the receptionist said blandly.

As he walked into the outer office, Miss Grant rose and came to meet him. She seemed pleased to see him. 'Sir John will be happy you're back, Finlay. I hope you had a good trip. Can I bring you a drink?'

Finlay was suspicious. 'Tea and a couple of biscuits perhaps, Miss Grant.'

She opened Winter's door and announced, 'Finlay, Sir.'

'Where the bloody hell have you been, Finlay?' Winter roared. 'I am going to have your guts this time boy…'

Miss Grant closed the door to Winter's office and raised her eyes to Heaven. 'He's for it this time!' she announced, to the five other ladies in the outer office. 'Leave it for a while and then take some tea in, Sarah. I think, by the sound of it, Finlay's going to need something to re-wet his throat.'

The staff in the outside office listened with genuine dismay at the roasting Finlay seemed to be having to endure. 'You might as well know, Finlay, I'm kicking you out! You'll be getting a drafting back to sea as soon as it can be arranged. I am sick and tired of you not keeping in touch as you should. I should dismiss you from the Service...Where the hell have you just come from?'

'Oslo, Sir. And I think you're being just a bit unreasonable, Sir...' Finlay wanted to defend himself.

'Unreasonable, for Christ's sake! You're supplied with communication gear that costs thousands and you don't use it and I've got to stand here with my dick blowing in the wind, informing the Foreign Secretary I don't know what's happening.'

'It's sometimes very difficult in the field, Sir, so to say, to keep in touch. It's not always possible... can I ask how Jonty Pitt is, before you go on?' Finlay asked.

'He's OK,' Winter barked and, as an afterthought almost, said, 'Are you OK? Are you hurt in any way, I mean?'

'Well, I was shot and stabbed. Spent some time in a Stockholm hospital, but that's by the way, Sir. I didn't keep in touch because my wireless packed in,' Finlay lied. 'But apart from that everything went swimmingly...'

'Don't get bloody smart with me, Finlay. Did you get what you went for?' Winter was quieter now.

Finlay produced what looked now like a spool of fishing line from his pocket. 'That, I believe, is what the fuss is about... and yes Sir, my arm is mending and the bullet wound in my foot will doubtless mend, once I'm back at sea, which by the way can't be soon enough, and I pray to God I get a more reasonable, even-tempered Admiral than I've got now!'

Winter ignored him. Picking up the telephone, he waited for a connection. 'He's back, Rupert. Here in my office ... Yes, I have it in my hand... No, I've no idea where he's been.' He listened to the voice from the other end and then looked closely at Finlay. 'Yes, he looks in good fettle... Yes, I am relieved.'

Finlay knew what had just passed between them was over. There was a knock on the office door and Sarah Burt brought in a tea-tray. She almost curtsied to Winter, but smiled warmly at Finlay. 'I popped out and got some Jaffa cakes for you, Sir,' she said softly to Finlay. 'We're really pleased to see you back.'

Finlay swallowed a mouthful of tea, which tasted like tea should, for the first time in months. 'Now Sir. Are we going to debrief?'

'Yes, we may as well.' Winter came around the desk to Finlay and put his hand on Finlay's shoulder. 'Glad to see you back, Keith. When the Norwegians found your gun, I did begin to wonder if you were all right.'

Finlay made the most of the moment. 'Any chance of some leave, Sir? I am pretty worn.'

'Take as much as you like, Keith. After you've debriefed, you'd better pop down to Haslar and get checked over… just for insurance purposes. I'll get Miss Grant to make the arrangements.' Winter glanced at his watch. 'Come along Rupert, we'd all like to get home tonight.'

'I wonder if I could get the mechanic chap to get my car going, Sir?' Finlay asked. 'She's been standing for months.'

Winter picked up the telephone. 'Miss Grant, can you get whoever is responsible to get Finlay's car started and fuelled up, thank you.' The Admiral went behind his desk and looked out from the window.

They both waited in silence until Smith arrived. He turned to face Finlay. 'Brought off the impossible again then, Keith? Bit rough at times.'

'Cold,' Finlay answered. 'Next time war's declared, perhaps you'd let me know.'

Winter laughed. 'I rather think our allies fared worse than our enemies. Nice touch, the Russian cigarettes. The CIA are convinced it was them who took out their chaps.'

'Yes, nice touch, as long as somebody else is pressing the button. That sort of thing ain't easy, Sir,' Finlay said, quietly.

'Better cold war than hot, Keith. That's what your job is all about, remember, and you do it well. I'll get the film along to the boffins as soon as possible today.'

Finlay's debrief took about two hours as he recounted the details of his trip. Miss Grant sat in and took notes, ready for typing and making up the official report. Several cups of tea and sidetracks later, they were finished and ready to call it a day.

'I've booked you into Haslar tomorrow, Keith, and your car's ready. Send your medical clearance to me as soon as you get it, and have a good leave.'

Finlay found the new Miss Grant quite novel.

It took him the usual couple of hours to drive home. The sun had long since sunk below the horizon, leaving a suffused pink glow as an afterthought. As his car entered the top lane he noticed two things: tractors working, with their lights ablaze, on the spring drilling fields and his hand on the gearstick shaking badly. As he brought the car to a sliding stop on the gravel of the yard, normality hit him. A layer of ammonia-laced steam hung above the muck heap, opaque and surreal in the yard lights. A horse whickered from the stables. There were tears suddenly coursing down his cheeks. His hand locked tightly on the steering wheel, his whole body shook violently.

Niney's voice brought him back. 'Whatever is the matter darling? Are you ill?' She helped him from the car.

'No Auntie, but I do feel distinctly odd.'

Niney shepherded him into the kitchen. 'Good Christ, look at the state of you! What on earth have you been up to? You're as pale as snow!'

'It's just reaction to being back, Auntie. It's been a pretty rough couple of months, one way and another. I'll be all right after some sleep in my own bed,' Finlay said. He looked at his aunt, dressed in dark blue trousers and a white blouse. He stood up, took her in his arms and hugged her. The smell of baking and shampoo made his head spin. She felt soft and smelt wonderful. 'I'll tell you all about it tomorrow, my love,' he said.

'Well, I hope whatever you've been up to has been worth it. If that bloody Admiral wants you back before summer, he can bloody whistle. You won't be going!' Niney said firmly. 'Come on, let's get you to bed. I'll bring you up a drink to help you settle.'

Later, with half a pint of rum-laced cocoa inside him, Finlay thought, 'Always a problem, coming home. Being normal.' Then he slept.

'I'm afraid it's nothing more than a capacitor, Mr Smith. Interesting design, but that's all it is.' The white-coated scientist handed Smith the satellite part.

'Are you absolutely sure?' Smith asked. 'Absolutely certain?'

The scientist looked affronted and turned away. 'Take it to the corner electric shop. They'll tell you exactly the same thing.'

'I'm sorry. We thought it may have been something else,' Smith apologized. 'Thank you anyway.'

He picked up the capacitor and left, deciding to go straight to Winter's office to give him the bad news. Smith placed it on Winter's desk. 'It's a capacitor John, nothing more than that. So where do we go from here?'

Winter thought for a moment. 'You know it's a capacitor, Rupert. So do I, but nobody else does.' He picked up the capacitor and weighed it in his hand. 'It can still be worth something. Leave it with me. Best use will be made of it.'

'Will you tell Finlay? Where is he now, anyway?'

'On leave. Stupidly, I said he could take as long as he wished.' Winter could not hide his annoyance at the thought.

They remained together, talking over the debriefing of the Russian defector until Winter decided he had had enough of London for one day and called for his car.

'I'll play it by ear as far as Finlay is concerned. I don't really think there is anything to be gained from telling him.'

Chapter Seventeen

•

April

'Well, Bruce,' Winter said, 'what do we do now?' Between them, on Winter's desk, lay the piece of satellite Finlay had returned with.

Winchester shuffled uncomfortably and then needlessly blew his nose. 'Have you looked at its content, Admiral Winter?' he asked.

'Yes, of course we have. We had to know what it was and what it was worth to you and the Jews. I really don't know what to think.' There was admonishment in his voice and just a touch of resignation. 'Did you honestly think that we would not find out?' he continued. 'Your government must really start to see who their real allies are.'

'What's this going to cost us, Admiral?' Winchester asked, positively enough.

'You make it sound like blackmail, Bruce. At the moment this is just between ourselves ...'

'And the Norwegians!' interrupted Winchester. 'What do they want... to stay quiet?'

'Oh yes, the Norwegians. Without whose unstinting help, we could not have got this for you. Well, I can't speak for them, but they will no doubt follow our lead. What I think would be a good start, would be the removal of the delivery system from the Israelis, and for your President to insist on talks between themselves and the Palestinians. Must be worth trying for. After all, with your country's backing, they are ignoring more than a few UN Resolutions.'

Winchester was given no chance to argue the point.

Winter pressed on. 'The Jews claim Palestine as their homeland, and call it Israel... They got it with your backing, against all our protests. Saying that claim goes back a couple of thousand years is fatuous. What we call the American Indians would have entirely the same claim, by those lights, and the whole of the United States would have to be given back to them. You see my point?'

Bruce Winchester did not seem to want to see the point.

The Admiral continued, 'It's now the Palestinians who need a home. Time enough to re-dress the balance.'

'But the Israelis will never agree...'

'Make them!' snapped Winter. 'They're your pigeon now. It's only because of your support that they feel they can run roughshod. At the moment, the Little King keeps us and yourselves au fait with Arab thinking. Upset Jordan and the pot boils over again. There are people still in camps from 1948. Don't you think they deserve help? Do you not see that people must have hope? What do we get from Israel? Oranges and grief. The Arabs have the oil.'

Winter rose to signify the meeting was over. 'You can have this,' he said, pushing the satellite part with his pipe stem. 'When such things are set in motion.'

First published in Great Britain by:

Elliott & Thompson Ltd
27 John Street
London WC1N 2BX

© Rod Brammer 2007

ISBN 978 1 904027 55 3

First edition

Book design by Brad Thompson

Printed and bound in England by Biddles Ltd